Let the Torrent Dance Thee Down

Books in the Sartorias-Deles Timeline

HISTORICAL ARC

"Lily and Crown"
Inda
The Fox
King's Shield
Treason's Shore
Time of Daughters (two volumes)
Banner of the Damned

MODERN ARC

The Young Allies as Kids Series:
The CJ Notebooks
Senrid
Spy Princess
Sartor
Fleeing Peace
A Stranger to Command
Crown Duel
The Trouble with Kings

The Rise of the Alliance Series:
A Sword Named Truth
The Blood Mage Texts
The Hunters and the Hunted
Nightside of the Sun
Sasharia En Garde
The Wicked Skill
Ship Without Sails
Marend of Marloven Hess
Seek to Hold the Wind
All Things Betray
A Chain of Braided Silver

Let the Torrent Dance Thee Down

SHERWOOD SMITH

BOOK VIEW CAFE

Published by Book View Café
304 S. Jones Blvd., Suite #2906
Las Vegas, NV 89107
www.bookviewcafe.com

ISBN: 978-1-63632-149-3

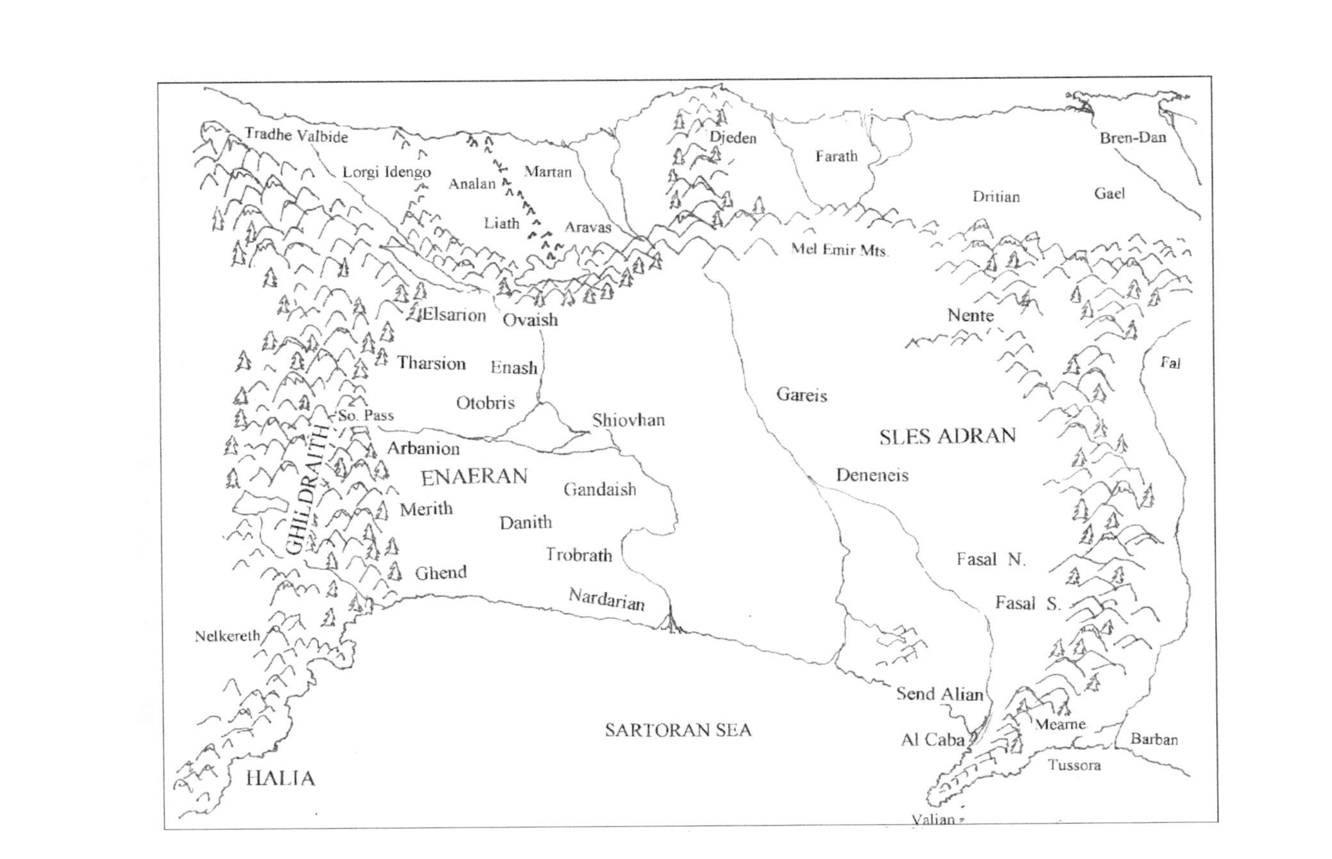

HALIA
Nelkereth
GHILDRAITH
Tradhe Valbide
Lorgi Idengo
Analan
Liath
Martan
Aravas
Dieden
Farath
Bren-Dan
Dritian
Gael
Elsarion
Ovaish
Mel Emir Mts.
Nente
Fal
Tharsion
Enash
So. Pass
Otobris
Shiovhan
Gareis
SLES ADRAN
Arbanion
ENAERAN
Gandaish
Deneneis
Merith
Danith
Trobrath
Fasal N.
Ghend
Nardarian
Fasal S.
Send Alian
SARTORAN SEA
Al Caba
Mearne
Barban
Tussora
Valian

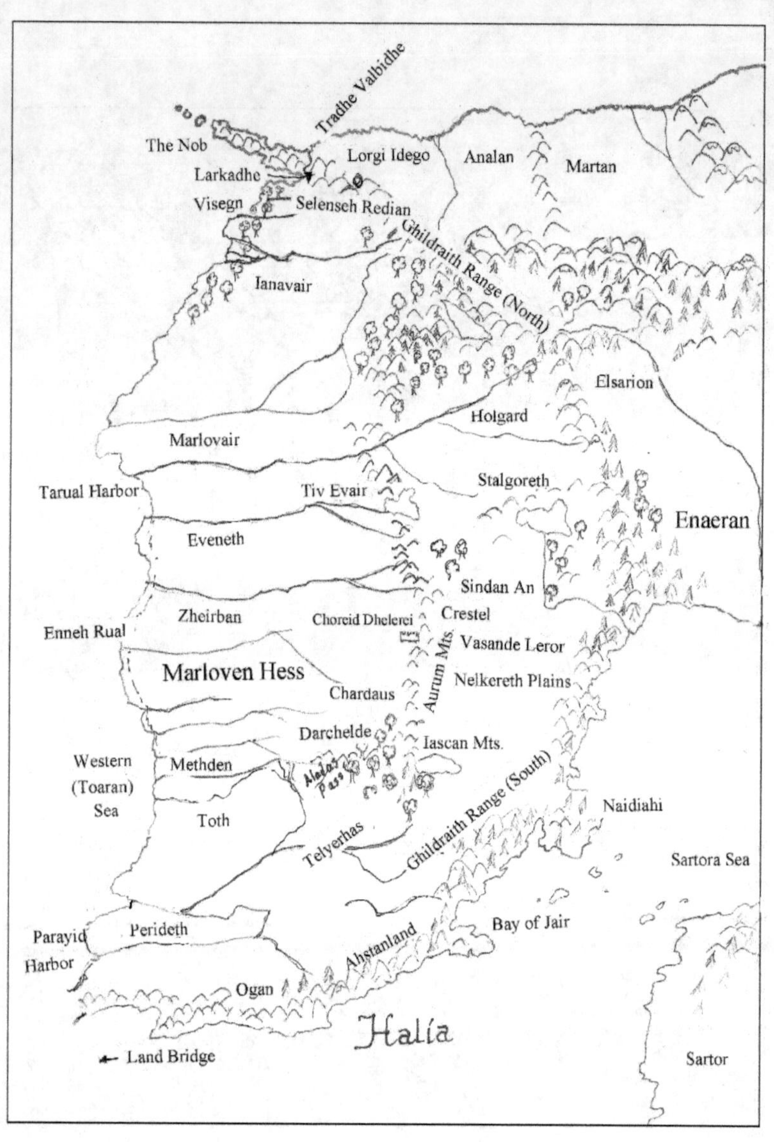

Tradhe Valbidhe
The Nob
Larkadhe
Lorgi Idego
Analan
Martan
Visegn
Selenseh Redian
Ianavair
Ghildraith Range (North)
Elsarion
Holgard
Marlovair
Stalgoreth
Enaeran
Tarual Harbor
Tiv Evair
Eveneth
Sindan An
Zheirban
Choreid Dhelerei
Crestel
Enneh Rual
Vasande Leror
Aurum Mts.
Marloven Hess
Nelkereth Plains
Chardaus
Darchelde
Iascan Mts.
Western
(Toaran)
Sea
Methden
Alalar Pass
Naidiahi
Toth
Ghildraith Range (South)
Sartora Sea
Telyerhas
Parayid
Harbor
Perideth
Bay of Jair
Ahstanland
Ogan
Halia
Land Bridge
Sartor

Dramatis Personae

NOTE: Name most frequently used comes first, so sometimes first name, sometimes last, sometimes nickname.

Erai-Yanya Vithyavadnais: One of a long line of mages dwelling in the ruined city of Roth Drael. Trained partly by the northern Mage School at Bereth Ferian, and partly by Tsauderei, she works independently, her specialty magical wards. She has one son, ARTHUR (see BERETH FERIAN). Erai-Yanya's student mage is the Marloven exile Hibern Askan.

Evend: [deceased] One-time colleague of Tsauderei, King of Bereth Ferian (a courtesy title only) and head of the mage school there, he surrendered his life to bind rift magic from being used in Sartorias-deles by Norsunder. His place as titular king was taken by ARTHUR.

Igkai: Hermit mage living on the peninsula on the Sartoran Sea. An oddball all his life, he is a friend to birds and animals—and tolerates humans who do well by animals.

Lilith the Guardian: She was a lower ranking mage and what might be called an officer of rites and rituals in Ancient Sartor, which was as close to a government as they got. She had one daughter, Erdrael, who was killed along with most of the rest of the population when Norsunder tried to wrest control of the world, for reasons explored in a volume to come. Her name is a modern adaptation, and she found herself trying to combat Norsunder on this and other worlds around the sun Erhal; has chosen Hibern as her replacement

Mondros "Rosey": Big, bluff, and bearded, he began life as an exiled son of the disgraced Glenereth family, warlords of Ralanor Veleth. He studied magic, aided by Gwasan Sonscarna,

Princess of the Chwahir, whom he married and had a son, REL (see SARTOR). When Mondros made it his life's goal to defeat Wan-Edhe of Chwahirsland, he stashed Rel with a trusted friend, where Rel grew up a part of the family, until the urge to travel caused him to take to the road. Father and son found one another relatively recently. Puts in great effort guarding and guiding Jilo of Chwahirsland.

Murial of Mearsies Heili: Recluse mage, living hidden in the western wilds of Mearsies Heili. Born a princess, she supported the transfer of the throne to her niece CLAIR (see MEARSIES HEILI) on the death of her sister. Protecting the kingdom from a distance, she has seen to it that Clair got magical training.

Oalthoreh: [deceased] Head of the northern mage school in Bereth Ferian

Randon Amdrelya: Originally from Vandary, Randon is an accomplished mage who did the Child Spell when around thirteen, to avoid limiting expectations of his culture. Travels around looking for kids to rescue.

Tarael of Drael: A morvende mage of a Drael geliath, captured by the Host.

Tsauderei: [deceased] Oldest of the senior mages, independent of the two leading mage schools, living in a historic mage retreat located in the mountains bordering Sarendan and Sartor in the Valley of Delfina. Worked until the end, aiding Mondros against Wan-Edhe of the Chwahir. Having lived more than a century, he was ready to die, taken by Detlev to a Selenseh Redian.

FROM OFF-WORLD

Caris-Merian Rhoderan of Geth-deles: "Rhoderan" is a name adopted by her father, the disinherited and disgraced Harold Dei, who tried to take the throne of Everon a couple of times before he was booted off-world. He had three children, the middle one being Caris-Merian. She came to Sartorias-deles's northern mage school to study magic right before the invasion. An accomplished singer and a scholar, when she was not seeking revenge for her brother's death—nearly killed David of Detlev's gang, after which she was caught up with by Cath, another victim of Norsunder.

Les (Leskander) Rhoderan of Geth-deles: [deceased] elder brother to Caris-Merian, and a problematical figure in his home archipelago. He discovered vagabond magic, and tried to weaponize it, in order to win freedom for the underaged and poor. Very charismatic. Laban's brother.

Mildred of Geth-deles: a martial artist.

Zairna Raadi from Sri Fortnu: A worldgate traveler and beginning mage, born a prince in a very problematic kingdom; a dragonflower inked into his neck and curling up over one ear testifies to serious rituals. Ditto the diamond earrings he never removes. Ended up at the Northern School of Magic, and then went back to his home world.

June from Earth: From a parallel of Earth in even worse shape, who got caught in someone else's conflict. Has been traveling through worldgates since, and become a sort of magical lightning rod without knowing. No matter how far or fast she goes, she cannot outrun her own shadow; she too left through a worldgate after the war.

THE YOUNG ALLIES AND OTHERS, LISTED BY KINGDOM

ALCANDAMER

Charlana, Queen of Alcandamer: A mage of sorts, possessor of the double crown, which distinguishes between lies and truth.

AMA HAZANTH

Crow (Prince Marseth Ghandorjien): Crown prince, keeper of the Fire Ruby (which wards storms from the island)

BARBAN

Dara, Leela, Yovres, Honey-blossom: vagabonds, present day

Ancient Tower that once had a window to the past, and to residents from the world Elesh Orom-alsh, guardians of the Fifth Protection of Alsheya (the cup Ethe)

BERETH FERIAN

Arthur (Yrtur) Vithyavadnais: He adopted the nickname Arthur after his rescue by young world-gate crossing friends. Son of mage Erai-Yanya, he early showed great ability in learning and magic, but he was unhappy living in isolation. He was adopted as heir by Evend, the former head mage of the Bereth Ferian Mage School, and presiding King of the loose federation headquartered at Bereth Ferian. After Evend's death, Arthur shared this courtesy title with Liere Fer Eider in her persona as Sartora, the Girl Who Saved the World. Became an archivist.

Evend: (see Light Mages)

Liere Fer Eider: Also known as the Girl Who Saved the World, she was the first of her generation to be born with *Dena Yeresbeth*. At ten years old she left her small town to escape being captured by Siamis, who had extended an enchantment over the world, which Liere later broke. The enchantment is generally known as The Lost Year, as most lived in a dream world while it lasted. She was lauded by all, and given the courtesy title of Queen in Bereth Ferian, a title with no powers or responsibilities whatsoever—but which still chafed her unbearably. Liere was the poster child for Imposter Syndrome until she went to Geth-deles for five years to study magic; on her return she aided Andri Elsarion, king of Enaeran, in regaining his kingdom from a cousin several times removed, Adon Marsael. During the Norsunder War, Liere and Andri married, and she became queen of Enaeran.

CHWAHIRSLAN (AKA LAND OF THE CHWAHIR)

Dassler Anjit, Company Scribe, Crimson Army of Chwahirsland: One of the "Sunrise Generation"—so named after Jilo removed enough of Wan-Edhe's toxic magic for awareness to return. A leader of the resistance to Wan-Edhe.

Dirk Sonscarna: Son of the problematical Kessler (see below), on the verge of adolescence. Has Dena Yeresbeth and considerable martial arts as well as magical knowledge. Assassinated Wan-Edhe, after which he left the world to study for a time.

Crimson General Furo: Chwahir general on Jilo's side. Worked a silent truce of sorts with Shontande Lirendi, without Norsunder realizing.

Gwasan Sonscarna: [deceased] Princess and mage, married a disinherited swordsman from Ralanor Veleth who later became the mage Mondros (SEE Mages). Their son is Rel the Traveler (SEE Sartor)

Kirech, Gold Army General: Utterly loyal to Chwahirsland, which for most of his life was embodied in Wan-Edhe. So loyal that to call his work into question—his loyalty—was a blow worse than mere sword wounds.

Jilo: Son of a lowly one-syllable sergeant, heir to elderly *Prince Kwenz Sonscarna,* he finds himself acting king of Chwahirsland, after Norsunder's removal of the previous king, who had ruled for more than a century. What that means is, he was slowly poisoning himself in trying to remove the toxic accretion of dark magic enchantments over Chwahirsland, and especially its capital. At the end of the war, was a king in all but name.

Prince Kessler Sonscarna: [deceased] (SEE also Ex-Norsundrians) The single living descendant of the ruling Sonscarnas, who were systematically killed off by Wan-Edhe, blood relations notwithstanding. Prince Kessler escaped at a young age, made his way to a martial arts group where he mastered military arts. He allied with a Norsundrian mage, Dejain, and began to assemble followers for his plan to remove all the hereditary rulers of the world, and replace them with his followers, chosen solely on merit. When defeated, he was forced into Norsunder by Dejain, who betrayed him. He learned magic, his secret goal to take Norsunder-Beyond for himself, so that he could once again implement his plan to reorder the world according to merit. Killed by Efael, leaves a son, DIRK.

Gold Admiral Opun: current naval commander, after several purges of his predecessors for mad reasons, or no reason at all. Like Furo, a two-syllable Chwahir, meaning not the lowest background, but low enough—no Nanijo, or warlord background—that Wan-Edhe did not think it necessary to hold his entire family hostage or slaughter them outright in case any of them thought of conspiracy.

Wan-Edhe (born Shnit Sonscarna), King of the Chwahir: [deceased] Descendant of the ruling Sonscarna family, has ruled for close to a century. A powerful dark magic mage, he has managed to create a powerful citadel in the heart of his kingdom, where time itself is distorted in his effort to ensure that he will live, and rule, forever. He killed off his family and descendants, including his brilliant heir, Princess Gwasan; only his grandson Kessler escaped, but years of abuse told on Kessler's emotional landscape. Known as The Hate to most of Chwahirsland, at the end of the Norsunder War, he was killed by Dirk Sonscarna, after Jilo confronted him, and tried to get him to reconsider his rule.

COLEND

"Bee" (Aural) Keperi: Chief scribe to Shontande Lirendi. Being blind, he does all his work by memorization.

King Carlael Lirendi: [deceased] Regarded generally as Mad King Carlael before he was assassinated by Efael of Norsunder. He was as beautiful as he was strange. He mostly existed in a world of dreams imposed by magic, from which he emerged now and then, very alert and very aware. There was a regency council made up of the chief nobles who oversaw the kingdom when he was unable to respond to the world around him, and they ruled until very recently, refusing to relinquish power, though Carlael's son Shontande had come of age.

Prince Shontande Lirendi: Son of Carlael, King of Colend, and new king. During the war, ran a resistance group while disguised as a woman. Very close to Jilo of Chwahirsland.

Karhin Keperi: [deceased] She was a teenage scribe student in a small town in the west of Colend, who volunteered to function as the center of the young allies' communication network. An indefatigable letter writer, she first met Puddlenose of the Mearsieans, and gradually got drawn into the Alliance; she was murdered by one of Detlev's boys, and she is still missed.

Lisbet Keperi: Younger sister of Thad and Karhin.

Thad Keperi: Red-haired brother of Karhin, also a scribe student, but much less passionate about the scribe life. Very social, and friend to all the Alliance; he and his brother Bee are very close to Shontande Lirendi.

ENAERAN

Adon Marsael: [deceased] Distantly related to the royal Elsarion family, tried to take throne. Allied with Norsunder in order to keep the throne. Killed by angry dock workers at the end of the Norsunder War, after extremely repressive rule.

Andri Malcolin Elsarion: Inherited his throne very recently, after years of civil war.

Gared Inmael: Close friend and adoptive brother of Andri Elsarion: it was Gared's father, the Elsarion Master of Horse, who took in Andri when he was disinherited. The boys grew up together.

Marten (Martande) Eldias: Lifelong friend to Andri Elsarion.

Baras Parael Otobris: [deceased] The new king's Commander of the King's Guard.

Thadara Otobris, Duchas of Merith: The new king's Chief Minister and treasurer, who had her eye on marrying Andri and sharing his throne.

Trevor Macael Elsarion: third cousin to Andri, from what had been the main branch of the family. Holds the rank of duchas in Elsarion, a very old province. At the end of the Norsunder War, he married Chantala Shagal, heir to Sles Adran, and was crowned king when Chantala took over after her uncle's death.

EVERON

King Berthold and Queen Mersedes Carinna Delieth: [deceased] Former king and queen, survivors of rough earlier years. Mersedes, daughter of a con man, became one of the Knights of Dei, dedicated to protecting the kingdom. They were both killed (at different times) by Henerek of Norsunder, who had come from Everon, and had been booted out of the elite Knights of Dei for countless crimes.

Prince Glenn Delieth: [deceased] Heir to the throne of Everon, and convinced that a strong army solves all questions, especially the threat of Norsunder attacking; he died in a duel with David, one of Detlev's boys, after forcing the fight on him.

Hatahra Delieth (Tahra), Queen of Everon: Younger sister of Glenn, passionate about numbers and in her unrelenting hatred of Detlev and his boys. When the war begins, has twins, Jessan and "Carl" (Berthold Jessan, and Mersedes Carinna), and four younger children: Madelon, FJ, twins Sedron and Glenn, and the youngest, Gwenlin.Glenn, and Gwenlin.

Roderic Dei: Commander of the Knights of Dei, once defenders and protectors of the realm. The Knights were decimated in the war Henerek brought, and Kessler Sonscarna finished. Roderic Dei survived to serve as regent for Tahra Delieth until she reached the age of majority.

IMAR

Fer Eider family: Liere's mother, Elen; one of Liere's five brothers, who owns a pastry shop. Has two sons and a daughter: Lesim, Milnat, and Marga.

Marga Fer Eider: cousin to Lyren-Sartora, niece to Liere Fer Eider: sirei-atanrial

Tolia: baker, Marga Fer Eider's best friend. ERAS, harborworker, Marga's male best friend. Both regarded Marga as their beloveds.

KHANERENTH

Jehan Merindar Zhavalieshin: Adopted into the ruling family on his marriage to Sasharia. Became king not long before the war began. Attended the Marlovan academy as a teen and spent many years afterward at sea, fighting pirates and dodging his father's forces until the former king, Math, was restored.

Sasha (Sasharia) Zhavalieshin: Daughter of former king Math, married Jehan Merindar, who adopted into her family. She and Jehan became co-rulers when her father retired from the throne not long before the war began. Sasha studied some magic before she and her mother, Sun, lived for a number of years on Earth as fugitives.

MARLOVEN HESS

Baudan, Anderle: One of Senrid's inner circle of desk jockeys.

Crystal Ingrid Montredaun-An: [deceased] Daughter and heir to Senrid, the king. Did not make it to five years old, killed by Imry Llyenthur. Her chief passion was dogs.

Daltan: Cobbler, middle aged. She was a resistance leader.

Forthan, Retren*:* [deceased] A young man from a farm background, the best of the leaders to come out of the military academy. He became Harskiald, a resurrected title that means trusted commander in chief of Marloven Hess's standing army; before then, commanders in chief were appointed per mission. Struck his banner at Aladas Pass before the defeat of Marloven Hess. Married to Fenis Senelac (see her entry for their children)

Hibern Askan*:* Light magic student, tutored by Erai-Yanya of Roth Drael, who learned in the northern mage school. Hibern was disinherited by her family; during the war she was imprisoned in Norsunder-Beyond by Ilerian before the world was closed off. Too bad, so sad, Ilerian—Hibern was the wrong person to leave loose in the Beyond. She figured out the time-bindings and lattice understructure and gutted the place. After the war, Lilith made Hibern her heir as Guardian.

Indevan-Harvaldar Montredaun-An, previous king of Marloven Hess: [deceased] Second son of Kethadrend, and raised to be a scholar. Indevan was, like his elder brother, skilled in martial arts but was never competitive. His leadership was entirely through a likable, easy-going nature and intelligence. He traveled to the neighboring lands where he conducted himself so well and so knowledgeably that he did a great deal to lessen the negative Marloven reputation. Married the King of Telyerhas's daughter, Lesra. Had one son, SENRID, [see below] before he was killed by his younger brother Tdanerend, who was appalled at his ideas about limiting royal power and disbanding the army in favor of a militia defense.

Kendred Montredaun-An, Prince of Marloven Hess: [deceased] Eldest son of Kethadrend, son of the grim Senrid who caused the various treaties to be made limiting Marloven Hess. Trained in martial arts at a very young age, sent to the academy too young. He had too much of his grandfather's angry drive, and when his father failed in various forays against those treaties, Kendred tried to rally the young Marloven heirs around him to take the throne. He ended of escaping over the border at the gallop with a company hot on his heels. Had two sons, IMRY and DAVID both of whom he sold to Detlev after unsuccessful plots. Changed his name, became a pirate, before joining Norsunder, dead by age thirty.

Keriam, Janec: Career military man, Commander of the Marloven military academy, also titular head of the Palace Guard. Acted as guardian and foster-father to Senrid, protecting him from the regent as much as possible.

Marec, Evred: Academy instructor, now interim Senior Instructor.

Mordan Nauldra: formerly the royal desk jockey for the Jarl of Methden. Interim military commander for Methden.

Senelac, Fenis: Wife to Retren Forthan and head of horse training for the military academy, equal rank to the Master of Horse in the city guard. She also was a chief figure in the resistance, communicating with her brother Janred. Has four children, three boys and a girl, Mardran "Hatch" [more below], Evred "Yip", Senrid "Stinker", and Maddar "Fuzzy."

Senelac, Janred, "Jan": Cavalry Captain in the army, now chief of Senrid's coverts. Youngest of elder generation of Senelacs, brother Jardan, eldest, is a cavalry captain (skirmishers) who defended the northern border of Marloven Hess in the war.

Senelac, Mardran "Hatch": Eldest son of Retren Forthan and Fenis Senelac. Served in the war as a runner. At the academy, along with Blackeye Ventdor, led the seniors; the pair hunted down and caught the first Norsundrian commander, which led to a ritual trial and execution. Senrid reacted by giving the pair scutwork for two years, after which Hatch was appointed Garrison Commander at Methden.

Senrid Montredaun-An: Young king of Marloven Hess, a

mage studying both dark and light magic. First friend to Liere Fer Eider, and second to make his unity in *Dena Yeresbeth*. The Marloven army is one of the most formidable in the world.

Stad, Indevan (Van): Second in command, Marloven army, at the start of the Norsunder War, promoted to commander in chief on the death of Retren Forthan.

Tdanerend Montredaun-An, Prince of Marloven Hess: [deceased] Third son of Kethadrend, raised to be "shield arm" to his brother Indevan. Tdanerend was short-tempered as well as short-sighted and uncoordinated. He tried to learn magic but where that came easy to Indevan, as well as everything else, he had trouble, and eventually surrounded himself by toadies and the traditionalists who were uneasy at the changes Indevan contemplated. He married Caras, the second princess of Telyer-has, and there, too, he was unfortunate: she was ambitious, despised him as much as he came to despise her after she tried to scorn the Marlovens into setting up a court. He killed her first before he took out Indevan and Lesra. His daughter NDAND was Senrid's chief companion. Tdanerend tried control spells on her meant for Senrid, which motivated Senrid to master magic at a young age so he could fix her. Tdanerend went over to Norsunder before losing the kingdom and then his life. NDAND left the kingdom to become a musician.

MEARSIES HEILI

Aurora of Mearsies Heili: Clair's small daughter, already showing signs of being a wanderer, like her Uncle Puddlenose.

Clair of Mearsies Heili: Young queen of Mearsies Heili, a small agrarian polity on the northeast corner of the continent Toar. Niece of the hermit-mage *Murial*, and cousin to the wandering boy known only as *Puddlenose*, she has adopted a group of girls, most of them runaways. Her right-hand and designated 'heir' is *C.J.*

C.J. (Cherenneh Jenet): Found by Clair, who traveled through the World-gate, C.J. is from Earth, adopted into Clair's gang of runaways and rejects. She learns magic fitfully, and is generally regarded as the leader of Clair's gang of girls.

CJ's Gang of Girls: Falinneh and Dhana currently wear human form but are not actually human; Seshe has a mysterious past, suspected of being a runaway princess (which is actually correct); Irenne thought the world was a stage and she was the heroine of the play, which got her killed by accident by one of Detlev's boys, but she is still very much a presence among the girls; Diana, killed by Efael during the war, was a martial artist and forester, also very much missed; Sherry and Gwen (a scrappy street kid from Australia) are followers. They are a very tight found family.

Mearsieanne: [deceased] Once Queen of Mearsies Heili, on her return to the present time, she stepped in and in the nicest way possible, shouldered aside Clair, her great-granddaughter, in order to show her how ruling ought to be done. After the invasion, she bound Mearsies Heili in a protective lattice-ward that was tied to herself, then she walked into a Selenseh_Redian and surrendered her life, binding the enchantment onto her. The key is Clair.

Murial: *(see Light Mages)*

Puddlenose of Mearsies Heili: Bereft of family at a very young age, thus no one knows what his actual name was. He was abducted and used by The King of the Chwahir in his complicated plots, he was rescued several times by Rosey (Mondros, see LIGHT MAGES). He wanders the world, determined to have fun. His chief companion is a world-gate wanderer from Earth named CHRISTOPH but sometimes he's joined by Rel (see SARTOR). Gradually he traveled on land less and on the sea more, until he was made second in command by Captain Heraford of the *Tzasilia*, former privateer. During the Norsunder war, Puddlenose was promoted to captain of the

Lheit, Christoph to be his first mate.

REMALNA

Bran (Branaric) Astiar, Count of Tlanth: brother to Meliara, wife NEE

Meliara Astiar, Queen of Remalna: children Alaraec, Elestra, and Oria (born during the war, and submerged while in utero in a magical pool in the goldenwoods, which may have influenced her development of Dena Yeresbeth)

Nadav Savona: Vidanric's oldest friend and chief aid, son Nadav

Vidanric Renselaeus, King of Remalna: children Alaraec and Elestra

RALANOR VELETH

Flian Elandersi, Queen of Ralanor Veleth: was a princess from Lygiera, distant cousin to Garian Herlester of Drath.

Jaim Szinzar: Brother to the king, and nominal leader of the army, though Jason commands in action.

Jaimas Szinzar: Younger child of king and queen

Jason Szinzar, King of Ralanor Veleth: [deceased] military background, inherited the throne, and the care of his siblings, at a young age. His chief rival is Prince Garian Herlester of Drath.

Jewel Szinzar: married to the King of Lygiera, Maxl Elandersi, has several children

Liara Viana Szinzar: Eldest child of king and queen

Markham Glenereth: disinherited, technically denied the Glenereth name, though the king intended that to be temporary. Liege to the king, a martial artist of superlative skill.

Lexan Glenereth: son of Markham Glenereth; runs for help to Sartor, becomes a guerilla fighter under his father; later runs to Sartor for help, is rescued by Detlev's boys.

SARENDAN

Darian Irad: [deceased] After his defeat in a vicious civil war, Darian Irad stepped down from the throne and ended up as a military consultant on the sister-world Geth-deles. On his nephew Peitar's assassination, Darian Irad insisted that he was a regent for Peitar's son Darian, and not a king: he had gone to Geth, where he married and had a family.

Darian Selenna: son of Peitar Selenna, and heir to the throne. Has Dena Yeresbeth. After the war, Rel acted as regent for him.

Derek Diamagan: [deceased] Charismatic leader of the revolution, a commoner who wished to overthrow all the nobles, and institute common rule. He was a far better speech maker than he was an organizer; his revolution was a disaster. Close friend of Peitar Selenna until his assassination by Siamis, at that time nominally of Norsunder.

Lilah Selenna, Princess of Sarendan: [deceased] Younger Sister to Peitar. She, with friends *Bren* (artist), *Innon* (a noble-born accountant at heart) and *Deon* were deeply involved in the revolution.

Peitar Selenna, King of Sarendan: [deceased] Reluctant king who would rather study magic, he came to the throne after an especially vicious civil war. He, nephew to the former king, Darian Irad, was one of the leaders of the revolution, but advocated non-violent means. His accession was a compromise between the commoners, who adore him, and the nobles, who recognized that at least he is nominally one of their own; on his assassination, he was, at his own order, replaced by his uncle.

SARTOR

Atan, (Queen Yustnesveas Landis V): New young queen of Sartor, after the oldest kingdom in the world was removed from time by nearly a century. She was found as an infant on the border by Tsauderei the mage, and raised by him before the enchantment was broken. She began her queenship as a mage student with little training in statecraft but well-read in history. Married Rel at the end of the war, and now they are co-equal rulers.

Gehlei: Former guard in the days before Sartor was enchanted for a century, escaped with the infant Atan. Raised Atan to age fifteen along with Tsauderei the mage.

Hinder and Sinder: Morvende (cave dwellers), friends of Atan; Hinder chose self-imposed exile, with a band of other morvende, in order to aid the counterattack.

Julian Landis: born Julian Dei, she is Atan's cousin who wore the Child Spell for a considerable time. She relinquished it on Atan's promise that she would not be considered an heir, nor a princess. She is a wanderer by nature, and was happiest when staying with Dtheldevor of Wnelder Vee's gang.

Mistress Veltos Jhaer: [deceased] Former chief of the prestigious Sartoran mage guild, until the enchantment the foremost mage school in the world. Now a century behind. She was further burdened by guilt for having lost the kingdom to enchantment, she left the guild woefully behind as they struggled to recover their old prestige. Assassinated by Efael of Norsunder, she was replaced for a time by Tsauderei the mage.

Old Helas: One of Rel's city guards, left from before Sartor's 100-year enchantment. Along with BEAK, a young guard.

Rel: Known as Rel the shepherd's son, and more widely as Rel the Traveler, he was happily raised by a guardian in Tser Mearsies until wanderlust caused him to leave home. Met

Puddlenose of the Mearsieans and consequently became tangled in some of the Mearsieans' adventures. Friends with Atan, and one of the Rescuers. He was the only outsider ever invited to join the Knights of Dei in Everon; in the previous volume he discovered his parentage (SEE Mondros the mage), which he is still trying to process. He is very proud of being the son of Princess Gwasan Sonscarna of Chwahirsland and of Mondros Glenereth, formerly of Ralanor Veleth. At the end of the war married Atan, adopted into the Landis family, and is now King of Sartor.

Rescuers: The name given to a band of children who had lived in a magic-protected forest during the enchantment. They sheltered Atan before the enchantment was broken. Ostensibly highly regarded as heroes by the Sartorans, there are the aristocratic Rescuers, and the non-aristocratic, Rel among them.

SLES ADRAN

Bartal na Shagal, King of Sles Adran: [deceased] Allied with Adon Marsael of Enaeran, and Norsunder; killed by his Norsundrian commander in chief toward the end of the war. After which TREVOR MACAEL ELSARION took over as king.

Chantala Shagal: Niece and heir to Bartal, daughter of Chantal, Bartal's sister. Cared for by her elderly nanny MARIANA, who was Chantal's devoted nanny. Married Trevor Macael Elsarion at the end of the war, and is nominally co-ruler with him.

Haries: Last name of the pair of artists who shelter Chantala na Shagal during the war.

Kinarde, Arandos: [deceased] Sarendan-born Norsundrian, placed as watchdog and then commander over Bartal by Norsunder. Assassinated, along with his minions, by an action backed by Macael, soon-to-be king.

Navor Mandracar: [deceased] army commander and close

friend of the king.

Master Orthal: runs an art school along the river. Other artists in training: LEMETH, LISI.

TELYERHAS

Havlan Casarod, King: Family the most direct descendant of the Cassadas, who were regarded as visionaries (or mad). Son of a queen known for her lack of skill at ruling but her genius for music, he had two sisters, LESRA and CARAS, who married Marloven princes and ended up dead. A scholar, he has a consort, who is also a scholar but he handles a lot of minor ruling issues. Has a son and a daughter.

VASANDE LEROR

Kyale Marlonen: Adoptive sister to Leander, relished being a princess, and was jealous of Leander's attention. Discovered her family in northern Goerael, and has become a stage magician and player.

Leander Tlennen-Hess: Like Senrid, a young king, though of a tiny polity that historically belonged to the Marlovens, then broke away four centuries previous. Leander prefers scholarship, and before the second year of the war began, formally ceded Vasande Leror back to Senrid.

Llhei: [deceased] Sarendan-trained nanny (sister to Lizana, nurse to the royal children of *Sarendan*), governess to Kyale, remained after evil Queen Mara Jinia defeated.

Alaxandar: Captain of royal guard, quit under evil queen Mara Jinia, protected Leander. Became a ranger after the war.

LAND OF THE VENN

Erenlara Sofar: Barely into her teens, princess of the Venn until her brother's death in the invasion. Has Dena Yeresbeth.

Kerendal Sofar: [deceased] Was king of the Venn, until the invasion. He committed suicide rather than submit to a blood-binding forcing him to act according to Norsunder's will. Met Rel the Traveler [see SARTOR] the one time he was able to escape Venn and his duties, as a young boy.

WNELDER VEE

Dtheldevor: [deceased] Daughter of a privateer (some say pirate) who was killed when Dtheldevor was small, but not before she was taught martial arts. She became the champion for the young prince Murgeh Troiad, sailing against pirates infesting the shores, and helping to fight off an enterprising Norsundrian.

She established a hideout called Dthel Rendm, on one of the hundreds of islands off Wnelder Vee's coast. She did the Child Spell decades ago; in lived time she is in her late seventies. She accepted kids on the Wander on her ship and her island, but her most loyal shipmates were: Sarmonwilda, born a dawn-singer; Sharly, a centaur from the northern reaches, and Sidres, another centaur; Gloriel and Peridot Warren (twins, from Earth, born with mundane names) and Joey and Ellen Warren. All died with Dtheldevor in the war except Gloriel, who became a mer and now lives near the island.

Troy, King Murgeh Troiad: [deceased] was regarded as king in Wnelder Vee. Though kingship was little more than a title — the guilds do what little governing is required in small, very rural Wnelder Vee — he resisted even that much, preferring to wander the world and master music, and kept the Child Spell in order to avoid royal duties. Was considerably skilled as a bard.

NORSUNDER

Aldon: [deceased] Military leader with a thirst for warfare, the bloodier the better. Wants to command the invasion in order to foster eternal war, his goal to take over Marloven Hess, where he was born, to make it an empire again. Killed by Siamis.

Alsaes: [deceased] First came to notice as Kessler Sonscarna's companion in Kessler's plan to take over the world. Given a mortal wound, surrendered self in exchange for bloodknife spell to preserve his life. Extremely vain. Dyes hair blond to hide Chwahir origins.

Benin: [deceased] Ambitious mage, his specialty the soul-bound (people caught at the point of death, their wills bound to the command of whoever holds the soul-bound magic). Benin tends to not wait until potential soul-bound are dead in order to experiment.

Bergan: [deceased] one of Imry Llyenthur's staff, along with Colleron, and Duin [see below] These are all typical flunkies, though Bergan sells info to whoever will buy it, most of all to Aldon and Efael, the latter of whom tortured him to death in order to elicit a confession that he was secretly conspiring with Imry Llyenthur — the only one Bergan wasn't conspiring with.

Bostian: [deceased] Ambitious Norsundrian military captain, obsessed with making himself king of Sartor.

Connanre of the Host of Lords: [deceased] A charismatic musician. It's still unknown if he was turned or born without a vestige of conscience. He was the one who precipitated the Fall of Old Sartor by turning one of the rituals into a bloodbath, it is said to win the attention of Yeres. He is the Host's master spy.

Dejain: [deceased] Mage specializing in dark magic, one of a succession of Norsunder Base commanders, who tended to be summarily replaced by violence. Now deceased

Duin, Fassler: (Duin his chosen name) Imry Llyenthur's chief aide-de-camp. Born in Chwahirsland. Began life as a cull under the Bi name; at end of war went to Chwahirsland.

Efael: [deceased] Considered himself one of the Host of Lords, the authors of Norsunder. Had a penchant for cruelty. He was the Host of Lords' chief assassin, bloodhound, interrogator, and errand boy; he and his sister Yeres considered Detlev their rival for a seat among the Host of Lords, until the war, when Efael was forced to share command with Imry Llyenthur, after which he spent a great deal of his time plotting against Llyenthur. And Aldon, another rival commander.

Elzhier: One of Connanre of the Host's best spies. She joined Norsunder as a young, angry teen.

Henerek: [deceased] Ambitious low-ranking young Norsunder military captain, originated in Everon. Wanted to be one of the Knights of Dei, but was cashiered due to excess cruelty, drunkenness, and inability to follow orders. Led a brutal war in Everon, now deceased.

Host of Lords: [deceased] Authors of Norsunder, existing beyond time, readying for a second try at taking the world. Or worlds. Why and who they are will become clearer in the succeeding volumes.

Hyath: Very young, ambitious, and cruel mage studying under Yeres.

Ilerian of the Host of Lords: [deceased] Currently wears the shape of a beautiful and promising morvende, though morvende did not come out of their caves until a couple thousand years after the Fall of Old Sartor. The story put around is that his turning was Detlev's first act on emerging from Norsunder-Beyond. Ilerian is not the architect of Norsunder; he founded Norsunder-Beyond using the life of the architect, Sfenaraec. Destroyed by Detlev with a circle of Dena Yeresbeth youth at the end of the war.

Imry Llyenthur: Shared field command of invasion with Efael of the Host. A mage and a martial artist, he has Dena Yeresbeth.

He's essentially a strategist. Now at large.

Lesca: Apparently lazy steward in charge of Norsunder Base. Overlook her at your peril.

Svirle Treloar of the Host of Lords: [deceased] He was heir to Yssel, and still uses that title, though Yssel is long gone. His underlings address him as "Lord Svir", the word 'lord' being an ancient title. He was the organizer of the Fall of Old Sartor, recruiting and forming plans. He is the ultimate in assumed privilege: nothing he does could be wrong because he deserves the world. It was he who lured Ilerian to the world, then discovered that he could not control that entity, so he exerted himself to function as go-between between Ilerian and everyone else—until Ilerian turned on him at the very end of the war. He lived just long enough to see the Beyond destroyed, his pet project.

Theronezhe of the Host of Lords: [deceased] Their military chief.

Yeres: [deceased] She and Efael, her brother, were born off-world, and so thoroughly and spectacularly corrupted that they caught the attention of Svirle of Yssel, one of the authors of Norsunder. Yeres was a powerful mage. She and Efael gladly executed the errands that the Host of Lords, steeped in evil, consider too distasteful, but her true desire was to live forever young, and win the worship of all men. Killed by Imry Llyenthur.

Ex-Norsundrians

Detlev Reverael ne Hindraeldrei: Chief visible mage and sometime military leader, answerable to Norsunder's Host of Lords. Born four thousand years ago, has lived in and outside time ever since. Like his nephew Siamis, has Dena Yeresbeth. Left Norsunder in 4753: much speculation on both sides as to why.

Kessler Sonscarna: [deceased] Renegade Chwahir prince with considerable military abilities, forced into Norsunder as a result of treachery by the mage Dejain. Hates Norsunder. (See *Chwahirsland* below)

Siamis Reverael: Nephew to Detlev. Formidable mage, and like Detlev, has Dena Yeresbeth. Left Norsunder previous to Detlev, after furnishing the means to free the Venn from an eight-century-year-old binding of their magic. Adopted Yanli, the last descendant of someone Siamis was close to on his first visit to Sartorias-deles. He has reason to believe that the woman, Isa Cassadas, was pregnant with his child before he was forced to return to Norsunder. They were both teenagers.

Sveneric Reverael Hindraeldrei: Detlev's son, trained with the boys.

DETLEV'S BOYS

Adam: Artist, formidable talents in Dena Yeresbeth, artist until his hands were ruined by Efael

Alaki (Ferret): Acutely observant, aware of overlapping worlds, spy

Curtas: [deceased] Strongly responsive to line and harmony, especially in building

David: Captain of the group, best in most areas

Erol: Chwahir born, plucked off a battlefield. Excellent at stealth

Edde (Noser): [deceased] Taken from another world, at best a mascot

Laban: Volatile and longing for what he cannot have, a Dei descendant

Leefan: Quiet, strong martial artist, cousin to Rolfin

MV (Mal Venn): Martial artist, studying magic, excellent sailor

Rolfin: Cousin to Leefan, superlative martial artist

Roy: Strong Dena Yeresbeth, mage and scholar

Silvanas: Martial artist and horse master

FOR MORE INFORMATION. . .

Visit the Sartorias-deles wiki here: https://reqfd.net/s-d/

Author's note

Written with F. and B. and B. very much in mind.

With grateful thanks to the daily readers at Patreon for their observant comments, discussions, and enthusiasm.

Extra gratitude to Rachel Neumeier, who was a champ for setting aside her own work to provide a fast beta read.

The title is taken from THE PRINCESS: COME DOWN, O MAID by Alfred Tennyson (1809-1892)

What pleasure lives in height (the shepherd sang),
In height and cold, the splendour of the hills?
But cease to move so near the Heavens, and cease
To glide a sunbeam by the blasted Pine,
To sit a star upon the sparkling spire;
And come, for Love is of the valley, come,
For Love is of the valley, come thou down
And find him; by the happy threshold, he,
Or hand in hand with Plenty in the maize,
Or red with spirted purple of the vats,
Or foxlike in the vine; nor cares to walk
With Death and Morning on the silver horns,
Nor wilt thou snare him in the white ravine,
Nor find him dropt upon the firths of ice,
That huddling slant in furrow-cloven falls
To roll the torrent out of dusky doors:
But follow; let the torrent dance thee down
To find him in the valley; let the wild
Lean-headed Eagles yelp alone, and leave
The monstrous ledges there to slope, and spill
Their thousand wreaths of dangling water-smoke
That like a broken purpose waste in air:
So waste not thou; but come; for all the vales
Await thee; azure pillars of the hearth
Arise to thee; the children call, and I
Thy shepherd pipe, and sweet is every sound,

Sweeter thy voice, but every sound is sweet;
Myriads of rivulets hurrying thro' the lawn,
The moan of doves in immemorial elms,
And murmuring of innumerable bees

About the only testimony to be made in favor of war is that threatened people will band together—petty conflicts forgotten, or at least forwent—to strive against the greater threat.

It also conveys coherence to chronicles.

When I turn my attention to the aftermath of Norsunder's war, I am aware that the coherence still ought to exist, at least symbolically. Everyone concerned, while perhaps not speaking of alliances and greater causes, is absorbed in a similar task: rebuilding, bridging past to future.

A world-wide striving can achieve an equal outcome, but daily life seldom remains at that elevated effort. It is entirely human nature to turn one's attention away from what occurs beyond the horizon to the neglected garden and the scattered rubble before one's eyes. There are vegetables to weed, a task all the more urgent when the larder is empty after a rough winter, following a very rough year.

This all is to say that the daily tasks of recovery, while vital, are not always interesting to record or to read, except if one is enamored of numbers. My concern is with individuals: Jilo, who faces what some consider the insurmountable task of rescuing Chwahirsland from itself; the establishment of the new dyranarya school, the disparate challenges of recovery for the young allies, especially the two I have been following since childhood, with whom I began and ended the chronicle of the Norsunder War: Liere Fer Eider, and Senrid Montredaun-An.

Part One

Bridges

4760-4765

It was generally understood in Marloven Hess that the counterattack truly began when the old king Ivandred rode back out of Norsunder at the head of his First Lancers, and charged the enemy at the northern border. It was equally understood that the war ended the day the bloody-handed Norsundrian captain Aldon died in the middle of Choreid Dhelerei's main square.

That next day, very early, Fenis Senelac was shaken awake by a delegation of two graying women and one man: the women had run the resistance in the royal city, and the man, stumping on one leg, was a veteran light skirmisher from what had been East Army.

"Wha…" Fenis said stupidly, for she felt she had shut her eyes heartbeats before. (And she was not far wrong. She'd been asleep for a little over an hour.)

"You have to be the one," Daltan said, her voice gritty. "The king just left my basement, where he spent the night. He hasn't been upstairs yet. You know that's got to be where he's going."

"No!" Fenis expelled a breath as if she had been punched. "Not me. Not me." She was still struggling to accept the death of her husband, Retren Forthan, but she could see in all three faces that they knew that.

"It has to be you," Daltan said, the other two opening their hands in agreement. "You're the only one among the handful of people he trusts whose loss is as bad."

"Almost as bad," Fenis forced herself to say. "The worst is losing a child."

No one argued.

There was no perfect person to speak about what everyone knew would stir up grief. But there were degrees, from the least painful to the worst possible. Fenis believed that the Little Girl would have been the least painful, except she had not turned up but once in the past few years, that day right before the invasion.

Oh yes, Liere was not the Little Girl anymore. She, like the king, had grown up. And apparently she had grown away, despite their years of friendship. Once, she had been the only person the king laughed with, and even played with, what seemed a lifetime ago. When Ret was young, new to the academy, and Fenis herself had been young.

Ah, Retren.

She waited for the spasm of pain to ease enough for her to say, "The best would be Keriam."

"He had another syncope last night, this one bad," the old cavalryman rumbled, eyes down. "He can't hide them from the king anymore. I don't think he'll last out the week."

"But he understood what happened? That we won our freedom back?"

"I think so," Daltan said. "But I really think what was more important was finding out that that never-to-be-cursed-enough Aldren Rodac was dead. Scragged by their own company. Along with Tdanerend Sindan. Who everyone knows put him up to it."

"Rodac," Fenis repeated, then had it. "You mean Aldren Keriam."

Daltan crossed her arms. "The Commander accepted Aldren into the family, but after he tried to sell the king to the Norsundrians, and claim he was heir to the kingdom, no one wants to acknowledge him being a Keriam, legal paper or no legal paper. And Dannor says, she kicked him out when she found out about the plot, and threw his clothes out into the snow. Ripped his name out of the family register." She dusted her hands together. "Gone."

Fenis had slept in her clothes, as they all had, these days; as Daltan spoke, she pulled on her boots and then her gloves, giving in to the inevitable. Like it or not, the demands of the world were rising with the winter sun over there behind the castle.

Seeing that she would not deny a duty absolutely no one

wanted, the others slipped away to their own tasks, leaving Fenis uncertain what to do first. See to the horses, or go straight away to face the king? How did the animals understand what had happened to them? All very well to tell each other that the First Lancers had ridden out of the Night Gate of Norsunder to their rescue, but in fact, it seemed that they had been imprisoned in timelessness, released once early in the war — many of them had had half-healed cuts from that experience — forced into captivity again, then released once more on home ground. Home ground, she amended, after four hundred years. With orders to fight their own people, and when they refused, some evil mage had poisoned the riders' blood. But they fought anyway, more than half of them dying of wounds that wouldn't heal.

How do you explain that to horses? She yanked on gloves and cap, then went around to make sure the horses' water barrels had no ice filming the top. These might be the same stables — not a lot had changed in the royal castle, the First Lancers had said — but surely it must smell different.

The horses were fine, she knew. She scolded herself out of being a coward and leaving Senrid to face those rooms alone.

By now he would have crossed most of the city from Daltan's shop. The sun had not yet paled the northeastern sky as Fenis crunched from the garrison stable yard toward the castle. It seemed strange to walk in the open like this. Her body wasn't even sure it was safe yet; the back of her neck tightened until she reached the harskialdna tower, with a few chunks missing, otherwise intact. The brutes who'd gone around trying to destroy things had given up on that tower. It was just too thick, and probably laced with magical protections, however that worked.

Fenis ducked her head as a gust of sleety wind howled around the corner. She shouldered the heavy door open, noting that hard-working hands had already swept up the broken crockery and other litter left by the Norsundrian occupiers. Someone had even wanded the area, which had smelled like pee, probably from Norsundrians too drunk, or too brutish, to bother with the Waste Spell. Who would live like that if they didn't have to? But she didn't have to understand them. They were gone.

Think out your words, she told herself as she started up the spiral staircase. Plan it carefully—

She halted when she heard footsteps one turn above her. Habit brought out the knife she'd learned to carry everywhere as she walked on her tiptoes—to find the king himself on the first landing, waiting for her.

"I thought I heard the door," he said.

"I was coming to find you." She ran up the rest of the way, then put the knife back into the wrist sheath that Retren had made for her himself. Her fingers lingered there on the leddas that he had touched, then she dropped her hand, remembering that the king could hear thoughts if he tried. He looked too tired to try.

"For?"

Here it was. Her stomach clenched. "I—none of us— wanted you to see the little princess's room alone. We sneaked up here three days ago, when the news came that the First Lancers were riding to free the royal city, and that Aldon and his band tried to go to ground." Fenis made a spitting motion. "Someone had been living in her rooms. Her things had been flung into a corner, along with broken dishes."

Fenis sneaked a look at Senrid's profile, his utterly still profile, then away, fast. A hissing breath, and she made an attempt to ease the atmosphere. "I don't know what they had against dirty dishes. Judging by the mess, they broke everything after every meal."

Senrid remained still. Fenis waited for him to say something. Anything. An order concerning Crystal Ingrid's clothes—her heartbreakingly small clothes—but when the pause racked itself into a painful silence, she threw words out, as fast as she could speak them, "We scoured out all the rooms in the residence wing. We also have the throne room banners. When you want them rehung along with the First Lancers' banner, just say the word. Lnar-Steward has all the things we saved." *Including the princess's things.*

"Thank you," Senrid said—and that was when she understood he was still because he was waiting for her to leave. He wanted to be alone.

She slapped her fist to her chest and withdrew, every word of that painful, clumsy attempt at conversation echoing in her ears the entire way to the stables, where she went to find Clove, the sweet, grandmotherly mare on whom Fenis had taught the Little Girl to ride. She put her forehead against Clove's warm neck and wept, hard, until her eyes stung. Then she splashed her face with the shockingly cold water, grabbed a wand, and moved along the stalls: the only anodyne to grief was work.

Over the following weeks, as Firstmonth folded into Secondmonth, the horses from four hundred years ago settled in. It seemed to help when the weather thawed enough now and then for some of the few surviving First Lancers to be brought out into the training yard to sit in the sun, where their animals could see and sniff them. The stable people learned the horses' signals, which helped, and so the talk turned to how to integrate these horses with the academy animals. Then there were the Norsundrians' riderless horses. Some of those would be turned out to pasture, but the rest were sound, if skittish.

Fenis was grateful for the unending stream of tasks, until there was enough of a thaw to ride out to Nelkereth, to discover how many of the animals left there for the entirety of the war would return.

Most did. And there were a number of yearlings and pregnant mares, plus a few wild horses curious enough to follow the herd.

At the beginning of Thirdmonth, two days after Fenis and the others returned with strings of horses, she found the academy almost restored. Only the roofs remained to be tiled, and the smaller constructions such as target posts and sentry towers. There were a few small changes, much debated; everyone had wanted the academy to look exactly as it had, as if nothing had ever happened.

She hadn't seen the king. If he wanted to see her, he knew where she was.

Fenis finished packing their belongings into a cart, and hitched longe lines to the back, connected to the halters of the three older animals being retired. She'd let them live peacefully in the meadows out beyond the apple orchard that Retren had inherited on the death of his great-grandmother.

Fenis's children joined her, three mumpish, reluctant to leave their friends, except for Hatch, the eldest, who would drive the cart back after helping his mother get the others home. He couldn't hide his glee at the prospect of starting at the academy again.

Clove whinnied, calling to the others in the stable as the cart bumped through the gate. I wonder, Fenis thought as she ran absent fingers through Clove's coarse mane, if the Little Girl ever thinks of the king? Or remembers those summer days and her riding lessons?

This latest thaw seemed likely to last, but despite the relatively benign weather, Fenis felt as mumpish as her children; the previous day had been the memorial for Commander Janec Keriam. The entire city had turned out yet again, the mood subdued, for everyone knew that they were not done with memorials yet. But so far, at least, the city seemed determined to do things right, no matter how many times they dropped tools to gather on the streets, drums in hand. No matter how grim the weather.

At least, everyone had reassured each other, the commander lived to see the end of the war. And he had been so very old. And he had not suffered. One moment he was wheezing with laughter at dinner with the invalids, then he set down his cup with his one functioning hand, blinked, slurred something unintelligible, and slumped gently against Captain Marec, his favorite instructor.

I hope, Fenis thought, when my turn comes, I go as fast, surrounded by everyone I cherish.

Fenis cast her eye over her brood: her two youngest, Senrid and Maddar, sharing a frisky young mare; her second son, Evred, driving the cart; and her eldest riding beside her. As the early spring sun began to burn off the chill of the morning, glistening in the stubble of green grass shoots at either side of the road, their moods began to lift and they chattered back and forth.

Fenis was grateful for the resilience of children, as she was grateful for the mild sky overhead, and for the prospect of a peaceful journey. If they saw riders on the horizon, her heart might speed up, but then she could smile and remind herself that there were no enemies left so close to Choreid Dhelerei.

I don't want them growing up thinking that savagery is normal, the king had said when he first brought the news of the Aladas Pass slaughter, more than a year ago. Fenis flinched as she recollected her own response. Her furious response. But the king had understood her rage.

"… but Yip, you *can't* go, until next year," Mardran—who had become Hatch sometime in the last year—was saying. "This year, it's only *us,* who were at the academy before. Next year, the king promised, everything will be back to how it's supposed to be. You'll both get to go."

"But that's not *fair,*" Yip yowled.

"That's not *faaaaaair,*" echoed Senrid in a squeaky voice, making fun of Yip's treble.

"Shut up, Stinker," Hatch and Yip said at the same time.

Fenis did not know how Hatch had gotten his nickname, only that it had happened while he was running messages in the teeth of enemy scouts, and that a now-dead captain had given it to him, which cemented it.

Stinker grinned. "All I know is, I'll be ten, which means I'll get to go!"

"He should have to wait a year," Yip grumbled.

Those two had stuck to their babyhood pet names because their brother had a nickname. Fenis tried to hide how much she disliked these. She and Retren had lain side by side talking through many night watches, choosing names for their children, but she knew he would have shrugged off their choosing names of their own. Which might change sooner than later.

She knew why she hated it, because it was a reminder, far before she was ready, that they would all have lives of their own one day, maybe settling in different parts of the kingdom.

"I have to wait two years," Fuzzy piped up—she being eight, and out of all her infant pet names, Fuzzy, which Yip had given her after feeling the top of her infant head the day of her birth, had stuck.

"But we'll make sure you're the best," Yip called back. "See if we don't!"

"Yeah," Stinker echoed. "The best."

Fuzzy accepted that with her usual tranquility. She was the only one to inherit Retren's easy-going calm. The boys were all summer-storm Senelacs. But Fuzzy also had inherited Retren's steel-spined tenacity, which enabled her to cope with three older brothers. It made her stubborn at the oddest times, like when Fenis tried to coax her back into accepting Maddar as her name, given in honor of Fenis's oldest and best friend. *I'm Fuzzy*, the child insisted, lower lip out.

Parenthood is an expanding perimeter, Fenis remembered Retren saying, and she'd smiled at the military analogy. Fenis reflected, as the children began chattering about what to eat, that her own mother had probably bitten down on regrets when Fenis and Retren had been given their little house between the flax farming and the saddle-making branches of the Forthans, away from the royal city. But the Senelacs, though a very old service family, had no land of their own. For generations they'd made their home wherever the clan eldest was posted.

They camped at sunset, seeing that it was clouding up. A thin, chilly rain started up around midnight, but they'd put up a kind of tent in the cart, and squished together for warmth, the children falling into the deep, uncomplicated sleep of childhood.

The rest of the journey was uneventful.

When they crested a low hill and spotted the dark line of Darchelde on the southern horizon, the children stopped squabbling over whether a distant dot in the sky was a hawk or a falcon and began shrieking about what they would tell the cousins they had not seen for a year and a half. The sun was sinking when they passed the first farms, then the tiny village; Fenis, whose mood had stayed fairly buoyant, saw startled, then solemn faces as they passed. Not good. Not good.

The village wall was in the process of being rebuilt with the old stone, added to considerably with new ones, she noticed. The stonemasons, finishing their day, looked up as the cart approached; Camrid, one of Retren's third cousins, put down his trowel and headed their way. But before he could say anything, Stinker leaped down, leaving the horse to Fuzzy, and pelted off beyond the east end of the square, to where their house lay — and then halted.

Fenis lifted her head.

"Cousin Fenis," Camrid called. "Come by for supper."

"Yes, do that," echoed some others.

Really apprehensive now, Fenis guided the cart around the last house, to find blackened ground, mostly thawed, almost unrecognizable. "What?" she said to the air.

"Ma, it's gone," Stinker shrieked.

"It's burned down! You said it was fine," Hatch shouted, tears in his eyes.

"It was, when I stopped here last summer," Fenis said numbly.

"It was that shit Aldon," Camrid said, spitting to the side. "Sent a party to burn it down New Year's Week, along with the houses of all the South Army captains, we heard. Said that Aldon's new law was to eradicate everything belonging to losers, as the first step to making Marloven Hess as mighty as it once was." His voice snarled on the word *mighty*. "We knew it for a lie. As if we'd forget. We will *never* forget," he finished savagely.

Fenis cleared her throat, but before she could voice her next question, Camrid forestalled it. "We sent a runner to the royal city to tell you, but he came back saying you'd gone into the Nelkereth, so we knew there was no finding you until you returned with the horses."

Fenis tried to swallow past the boulder lodged in her throat. She turned to see her three younger children looking at her anxiously, Hatch mutinous.

"You can stay with us," Camrid said. "We've cleared the attic. That is, they took most everything, so that loft is bare. We swept it out. And we all agreed, when you returned, we'd pool together for meals. And rebuilding, we'll all pitch in."

Fenis closed her eyes, then opened them again, glad that they remained dry. She'd cried herself out at last. And it had done nothing for her. "I thank you, Cousin Camrid," she said clearly, as several villagers had come to their doors and windows on the square. "Thank you for hosting us tonight, but tomorrow, I think we'll return to the royal city. There's enough to be done here, without the added burden of rebuilding that house. My mother is getting on in years. She could use the help."

Fenis heard a hiss of excitement behind her, and sent a glare that shut her children up. "But not before I leave the stores we brought down. The king gave us plenty, retaken from the enemy when we recaptured the royal city. Since I'm going to go back, we might as well leave these with you." She indicated the bags of rye flour, the three baskets of olives for making pan biscuits, the rather withered but still fairly sound cabbages, the wrapped bag of raisin, nut, and honey-studded travelers' cakes, and the two huge cheeses.

These precious items were lovingly unloaded by willing hands, as other willing hands helped with the horses. What to do about Clove and the other two retirees? It was one thing to turn them loose on one's own land, and another to expect people who had tightened their belts and endured for a year to support three retired horses.

These and other small questions could wait; when these immediate tasks were settled, she walked over the square that had been their house. Now rubble.

She had seen herself living out her life in that house, but in truth, she thought as she paced the perimeter, they had scarcely lived there. She had few memories looking out the windows, except one: viewing the apple orchard, now burned away, and the dogwoods that had guarded it. Most of their married life had been divided between East Army, where Ret had been a captain, and South Army, once he'd been promoted to commander. He had also traveled a good deal to foreign parts for the king, as well as riding the country on the tasks expected of a commander.

The sun had gone down, and savory smells drifted from the house where everyone was gathering, when Hatch came running to find her. "Cousin Nad says, the Norsunder turds wanted to make sure there was nothing left of Da."

"Not that he ever had much," Fenis said, trying for an even tone.

To her surprise, Hatch said, "There's this."

He slowly, carefully, removed something from his inner pocket. It was a strip of cloth, originally green, but faded over the years.

Even in the gathering gloom, she recognized it at once. It was Retren's headband, the one he'd worn as commander at his last academy summer game. He'd kept it to commemorate his academy days, but he'd worn it from time to time, mostly in summer, to keep sweat from his eyes.

Fennis Senelac reached to take it. She pressed it between her palms, eyes shut, then held it out. "You should have it," she said. "He gave it to you."

"He didn't. I stole it. Before he left for the border." Hatch's teenage voice cracked. "I know I won't be able to keep it. I know the academy rules. No one brings anything extra. I decided I'm going to change my family name. To Forthan."

She locked her jaw on the urge to shout *NO!* Instead, she regarded her son's steady gaze, and the desperation tightening his young forehead. "Why would you do that?" she asked, carefully.

"Because I'm *proud* of him. Because I want *everyone* to remember his name." His voice broke on the last word.

"Mardran," she said. "Hatch. Do you really think any person in this kingdom is ever going to forget your father?"

His breath caught on a ragged sob, and she was glad she had spoken carefully. His grief was as strong as hers, she reminded herself. It might come out differently. How he expressed it was not wrong.

She said, even more carefully, "Your father loved his family, but he adopted into the Senelacs because we're an army family. Have been for a long time. The Forthans are land folk, and justifiably proud of that."

"I know that," Hatch said sullenly.

"So," she continued, in that even tone, "there are no other Forthans at the academy. Which means, were you to use your father's name, it would carry a heavy cavalry charge of moral weight, and not through your own merit. Do you see?"

"But they gave their lives. Everybody honors them," Hatch muttered.

"Yes. But I know your father better than anyone. And I know how *very* much he would have hated anyone using what happened at Aladas Pass to gain merit." She considered that, then added, "He would not have liked it had he won victory, either."

Hatch was silent. He understood each of the words, but sensed he was missing the meaning. Like … like seeing all the elements of the landscape, but missing the right way to defend it, a game his da had played with him when they were out riding.

His mind flashed back to the night he and two friends sneaked into the castle to see the First Lancers for themselves, and discovered Captain Marlovair holding his ancestor Haldren while his bandages were changed. The boys overheard some low talk about how the wounds would not stop bleeding, but what Hatch had noticed was how Haldren Marlovair was covered with old scars.

The air smelled of kinthus when the bandaging was done, and Haldren settled comfortably. The two boys wanted to return, but Hatch made them wait until the servants carried the old bandages and the medicine dishes away. Haldren had closed his eyes, but in the next bed over, Ivandred, the king from long ago, sat awake, the single candle reflecting in his eyes.

Hatch gathered all his courage, and crept in. "When you're better, will you teach us?"

Ivandred didn't seem to hear at first, then he turned his gaze to Hatch, and said, "No."

"No?" Hatch repeated. "We're not good enough? But we want to be the best! Like you!"

Ivandred was silent. The boys heard footsteps coming back, and they had been told not to disturb the invalids.

Then Ivandred spoke, his accent funny. "You'll learn better." Then he shut his eyes, and the boys slunk away.

Hatch did not understand that, either. They were the best. Everyone said so. Maybe if Da had learned from them, he would still be here.

Fenis said, "When you come of age, of course you may do what you wish. But you are signed in at the academy as Senelac. And, son, remember, your father was the one who wanted you children to be Senelacs. It wasn't that he didn't love his family. He was proud to join a family that had a long tradition of service to the kingdom. Until you come of age, and make your own decisions, you will continue that, as he wished."

Hatch jerked a finger to his chest, turned about and ran. Fenis followed more slowly. Give him time to recover. As for her, she was glad of the gathering darkness, for it enabled her to brace her shoulders back, to even her voice, and to enter the house of her family-by-marriage with a smile.

On a crisp morning in early spring, the sun rose on the reassuring sight of the king riding back and forth in the practice fields beyond the academy wall, shooting at targets.

Such a sight had not been seen for nearly two years. It heartened the sentries, who gossiped in the guardhouse when the watch bell rang, gossip that carried into the city.

Up in what had been Commander Keriam's tower, Marec, a tall, slat-thin, somber-faced man with dark red hair, now senior instructor; black-haired, wire-tough Van Stad, the new army commander; and tall, husky, pale-blond Baudan, one of Senrid's inner ring of desk jockeys, were still finalizing the list of instructors and support staff for the academy, which would hold its first callover in two days. The rebuilt buildings—looking skewbald with new stone patching the old—were nearly full of boys and girls, more arriving daily.

But none of the three glanced at the barracks buildings, where most of the young people were still asleep, after staying up far too late the night before, gossiping, bragging, and eyeing the very few newcomers.

"It's good to see the king riding again," Baudan said during a pause, as all three tried to reform their arguments for or against a new instructor.

Marec said, "Agreed. You can almost pretend that life is back to normal."

Van Stad was thinking: That's why he's doing it. Out loud, he said only, "Listen. The king will probably want to try Cama Sindan for a year. It's not like we have a lot of candidates, and all the Sindans under the age of fifty feel the shame, though they had nothing to do with what Hotears did."

Baudan sighed. "I've hated the Sindans for so long, I can't see any merit there."

Marec, ever the peacemaker, said, "Let's put a mark next to his name. Let the king decide."

They moved on.

By the time Senrid's brisk step was heard on the stairs below the round tower room, the three had a list with a dozen marks next to certain names. Senrid appeared, patches of red along the sharp edges of his cheekbones from his ride in the chilly air.

He glanced at the list. "No. No. Yes. Yes. The rest of these, try them for a year. Nothing wrong with them, but their wounds might be too severe." Camerend Sindan topped that group of names.

Stad looked out the window, to avoid any appearance of *told you*. Both Marec and Baudan, who had been barracks-mates with Stad all through the academy, knew exactly what he was thinking, but nobody said anything, except for Baudan's, "I'll go over to guard-side and let them know."

Senrid had also been looking out the window, his attention drawn to two black-haired figures among the others roaming around the practice court, one already with his father's shoulders, though he was just beginning to get his height, the other figure diminutive. Senrid could feel the crackle of rivalry from here.

He caught a glance of inquiry from Marec and Stad, decided against marking those two out—yet—and commented, "The new roof tiles look older than the previous ones."

They all glanced at the grayish-brown tiles, Marec remembering clambering over the old ones that had been much the same. These new ones had been made entirely on faith by a potter the king had met near the southern border, and hidden buried in various places against Norsunder's defeat. The king, in turn, had given this potter the order for replacing the royal castle crockery, most of which had not survived the war. Marec believed that it was this kind of exchange—the first made on trust, the other in gratitude—that was weaving the kingdom back together at least as well as the high spirits down there in the academy.

Senrid said, "Anything else?"

Marec and Baudan flattened their hands in denial. Senrid got up to leave. Senrid ran back down the stairs, reflecting — as the other three had earlier — on how very much Keriam's presence still lingered in that tower room.

Keriam had been the one sure fixture in his life since he was small. Now gone. But he was not the only one in the kingdom with rooms, benches, tables, bridles, trunks, and pathways empty of a person who had usually occupied them, leaving only a presence. An actual ghost, he thought wryly would be welcome. But Senrid didn't believe ghosts existed. Whatever ghosts seers saw had to be illusion of some sort.

He took a look at his desk, noted that all the most pressing emergencies had been dealt with, and so it was time to keep a promise he'd made to himself. He calculated the time difference between Marloven Hess and Mearsies Heili: morning there, and he remembered that Clair rose early.

He transferred.

The Destination outside the white palace was empty. No refugees lounging around. He went inside, spotted the duty servant, and said, "Are they in the back?"

The young woman, who recognized him, said cheerfully, "Kitchens."

Senrid found himself glad that life seemed to have return-ed to normal here, though last year this palace, and the king-dom, had been packed with refugees.

No noise from the throne room. The refugees were all gone, apparently. Senrid headed down the side passage to the kitchens at the west end of the palace, hearing high voices before he arrived. They were all there.

No, not all.

"Boneribs," CJ cried, leaping up. "We haven't seen you for a million years!"

Senrid turned her way, but saw no accusation, or even question in her face. And with CJ, though she was loud and opinionated whether you wanted to hear it or not, you always got a straightforward response.

"Got caught up in the defense," he said.

CJ bobbed her head, her long, straight black hair swing-ing. "Yep. We were lucky that way. No fighting all over the country. But rotten luck that Clair got turkeyed by Norsunder all by herself."

Senrid didn't bother asking what "luck" was. He knew CJ spewed idioms from her birth world all the time. "Where is Clair?"

"Still at that place where Siamis took her."

Clair? Gone? After all these weeks? Things were different even here, then. He'd thought at least Mearsies Heili and the always-young circle of girls around Clair would remain unchanged.

As usual, CJ hadn't bothered with a mind-shield, and he caught a vivid glimpse of Clair on the surface of CJ's thoughts, amid a wash of unspoken worry. On the surface Clair looked the same, though thinner. Still a girl of thirteen or fourteen, with long blue-white hair, and a square, unremarkable face. Her thinness was the case with a lot of people, including himself, he'd discovered when he put on some of his clothes from the winter before the war. Getting flesh back would come; what he couldn't square was the lingering traces of anguish in Clair's countenance, relentlessly clear in CJ's memory.

He met CJ's stark blue gaze, and saw a little of his own shock in her stillness. What did she see in him? He didn't want to hear it.

"Have you breakfasted?" CJ asked, looking away.

Senrid also looked away. "I'm sorry about Diana," he said. Because one must; it was the decent thing to do, and he'd liked Diana almost as much as he liked the quieter Mearsiean girls, but he hated saying it because they, in turn, would have to be decent.

CJ blundered on, her transparent emotions like a battering ram, "We still really miss Crystal Ingrid." And there it was.

"So do I," Senrid said.

Before he could change the subject, Clair's young daughter ran in, white curls bouncing. She held out a ragged, almost shapeless stuffed dog that Senrid recognized instantly. It had been stitched together by one of the household in his castle, one of many toys his daughter had had.

"Would you like to have it back?" Aurora asked, her greeny-brown eyes shaped like Clair's round and earnest. "I liked to sleep with it when I was little, but I will be *eight* in summer, and I don't have to sleep with pretend animals."

Senrid had known this visit would hurt, but the blows were going to come anyway, if not here, then from other well-meaning friends. Either you weathered it, and maybe that would inure you, or you avoided all your friends. Which had been his first idea. It hadn't worked. "No," he said. "She gave it to you. That means she wanted you to have it."

Aurora dipped her chin in a nod, then crushed the stuffed dog to her chest. "Sometimes I still sleep with it." Her gaze strayed toward CJ. "Until Clair comes back. And I talk to Crystal Ingrid. Uncle Puddlenose said I should, that we never should ignore our friends, even if they happen to be not alive. But I don't know if she hears me, since she doesn't talk back."

CJ's wide blue gaze flitted from Aurora's earnest expression to Senrid's tight mouth, and she tried to think of a subject-change wouldn't be as obvious as *Look, the Winged Victory of Samothrace!* "Aurora, aren't you keeping your tutor waiting? You know Clair's gunna ask about your studies soon's she gets back."

Aurora's eyes rounded, and she flitted off, the toy dog still clutched to her.

CJ said awkwardly, "We have freshly scalded coffee. Aurora's tutor likes it."

Senrid found Janil, Clair's grandmotherly steward, at his elbow, holding a tray with coffee on it, her manner reassuring. Senrid perceived then that there was a mild sort of conspiracy among the servants, who seemed to have decided that his visit was to be encouraged.

Senrid said, "When I left, this was the only safe place in the world. What happened?"

"Ilerian." CJ tapped her forehead. "He got at Clair through dreams. She finally lost. But you—all of you in that circle, and that person who looks like a silver comet in the realm of the spirit … Marga, she said her name is. She, and your circle, saved Clair, when we couldn't. Though we tried. We all went to Imar to try."

Senrid whistled softly, amazed at their loyalty. And their stupidity.

CJ scowled down at her hands, flexed them, then laid them loosely on the table. "She's not dead only because that scunje-bucket Ilerian had shelved her for later, then your circle went after him, and you won. But Sveneric told us each day was killing Siamis by degrees. As Ilerian sucked life out of the world."

Her tone was flat. Senrid had had a taste of what Ilerian was like at the end. "I'm really sorry," he said. "I didn't know about any of it."

"Everybody said that you had your own battles," CJ responded, jerking a shoulder up by her ear. "And you couldn't have done anything even if you had come here. No one could. Though the girls tried. Clair kept me in Land of the Venn, because she couldn't bear me knowing what was happening to her. Until Dhana called me at the end, and we went to Imar to rescue her."

Senrid couldn't help the thought that that was exactly why Clair hadn't told CJ what was going on.

". . . the one who was able to help most was Siamis. At the cost of ... everything." The bleak expression that narrowed her eyes made it clear enough that the "everything" had been harrowing.

Her tone shifted slightly, to a higher register. "Did you know that this palace was his original home?"

"This? The white palace?" Senrid asked, astonished. "Never would have guessed. Didn't think it could be that old. It doesn't look old, the way Atan's does. I guess that has to do with whatever this stuff is made of?" He leaned out to pat the slightly iridescent wall. "And I thought nothing they built back then survived, except a tower or two here and there."

"It was a healing center back then, Sveneric told us, and Siamis agreed. An important one. The Host couldn't quite destroy it, so they did the next best thing: destroyed the people here. Then it got hid by enchantment. It was frozen in time for centuries and centuries. Ilerian forgot about it, which is how it made it intact until the magic wore out eight centuries ago. Sveneric told us it was Detlev who laid another enchantment over it, so that everyone who came here went away thinking that it was another ordinary palace. Made of marble, or some light stone."

"But not Wan-Edhe, I'm guessing," Senrid said. "Jilo told me once that Wan-Edhe was obsessed with taking it as his own, and did his best to conquer this country, but came up against indigenous magic. So he tried to destroy Clair's family."

"He did destroy them, kinda," CJ stated. "Clair says she didn't understand that until recently. Wan Edhe lured her uncle into evil by promising he'd be king here. He got two of Clair's aunts fighting each other, after which Clair's mom started chugging wine, all three aunts gone batso over mush. Blech."

"Mush?"

"Kissy slurpy stuff, yech. The only smart one was Aunt Murial, who ran off to study magic, then became a hermit. When Clair was little she thought disaster was what always happened to adults, and that only children could be safe and happy. I *totally* agreed, when she found me."

Senrid thought about their years under the Child Spell, which didn't actually protect you from much except the physical changes of puberty.

CJ shrugged again. "Anyhoo, you couldn't have done anything if you'd been here last year. Siamis knew what to do, and did it."

"Where is he? With Clair?"

"No, he left her at some mysterious place of Detlev's. No one knows where Siamis is."

Senrid understood then that Siamis was blocked on the mental realm. There was no one alive as good at being undetectable than Siamis and Detlev when they wanted to be.

Senrid drank off his coffee, and set the mug down. "About this palace. That would actually be an interesting question for the archivists and heralds, I guess: would ownership from four thousand years ago still hold now?"

"Oh, they resolved that question in Sartor, after it came back into the world. Atan told us when she was here." CJ waved off the subject. It was clear she didn't care who owned what. "Atan told Clair it wouldn't apply here. And Siamis said that Ancient Sartor didn't have the view of ownership that we do. Or, some did, and it was frowned on. But even though Siamis was our age, twelve, when he was captured, he knew that they regarded houses and land as a kind of custodianship. Especially this place, with the Selenseh Redian, and the lake right below, with Dhana's people in it. Some of whom were around then. Can you imagine? But Dhana says that their view of time is so different, she doesn't have the words."

Twelve-year-old bodies housing minds of what age? Senrid thought. When did that widening gap begin to distort a person into Dtheldevor? Or Mearsieanne?

He was not going to share that thought. He knew CJ clung to the Child Spell as though the alternative was death. "I've always known those like Dhana's people were here among us, but since we never see them, they were easy to forget. Until I saw them in the mental realm, when we were fighting Ilerian," he said. "Saw in some sense. Turns out we all perceived them differently."

They talked about perceptions on that plane until Janil came in to say that two representatives of the Stringers' Guild had arrived for an audience, and Seshe was heading to the throne room.

"I better go," CJ said. "It looks good, even though half the time I don't know what they're blabbing about. Luckily Seshe does."

"Weights and measures," Senrid said, snapping his fingers. "A guild no one keeps waiting if they're smart. I'm on my way."

"Thank you for visiting," CJ said, remembering her manners, as Senrid transferred out.

Back at his desk, Senrid reflected that that had been as bad as he'd expected it to be, but he'd survived it.

The rest of the day was spent in work. The next morning he was, as usual, awake well before sunup, and finished morning drill with his new swordmaster before heading up to Keriam's dark, empty tower to watch the academy.

A lone figure, barely visible in the light of the sinking moon, tramped out to one of the corrals, which was completely empty. Senrid immediately recognized newly-arrived Marend Ndarga, who looked around a time or two, clearly expecting to be alone.

She also clearly did not expect to be followed by someone as well-trained in covert movement as she was. Hatch Senelac slipped along from wall to building, on her trail. Not even making an attempt to speak to her. Senrid frowned, then opened his field glass. In the darkness the two teens were grainy, mostly silhouette, but he didn't need to see their faces.

These were the two he'd expected the most trouble from, and sure enough, they had managed to find one another before the academy season even began.

No, more correctly, Hatch had spotted her.

Senrid wondered if those two were already creating factions before the academy season even began. Marend was so very much her father's daughter, sure that the old ways were the best. Whereas Hatch was very much like Retren Forthan, sprung from the commons, and proud of it.

To make matters even more complex, both were experienced beyond their years in resistance thinking.

Neither was aware of having been observed by the king over the past couple of days, since their arrival. Of the two, Marend had dreaded it the most. Conscious of all her past mistakes, she had been very circumspect ever since her arrival. She had been prepared to be ignored; she had not been prepared to get looked at as though she was a bug that had crawled into someone's food.

What had she done wrong? It couldn't be her being a girl. There were a bunch of girls here already, and further, two were only a finger's breadth taller than she was, though one was solid, built like a barrel. Marend half-admired, half-envied her effortless lifting of a bundle of heavy spears when the group of them were put to work helping to organize one of the practice yards.

Hatch was the least concerned about being observed. Why would he? He'd been top of the class of third-years before the war. Forced to return home instead of being permitted to help, as the seniors had been, he'd gone from hot resentment to stunned grief when not only was his father killed, but the Marlovens lost the war. And then had come the call he'd waited for: they needed runners, because there weren't any left. Either they were fighting, or dead. And he'd done well.

So Hatch, two years older, had come prepared to be king of the seniors.

Except... things had changed. It was Hatch who'd first spotted the newcomers. "We were supposed to be just us, the last ones at the academy," he protested to Blackeye, his best friend.

"The scrubs are all invites from the king." "Scrubs" was

the usual term for ten-year-old newcomers, but it had been repurposed to cover those who were coming for the first time — even if they were eighteen. Like the small, pretty one with the blue-black curls, who cat-footed like a warrior.

"Why?"

"Ah," Blackeye retorted sarcastically, "the king forgot to summon me up to explain his thinking. How should *I* know? All I've been able to pick up so far is that the pretty one's Methden's daughter."

"A spoiled jarl's brat?" Hatch said, his upper lip curling in a sneer. "I thought the king didn't favor jarls' brats just because of their famous names."

"Maybe because he died at the outset of the fighting?"

Hatch shrugged a shoulder. "He's not the only one."

Over those next couple of days, Hatch had glared at all the newbies, longing to show them what real training was. So far, most of them didn't seem like much. The only one who didn't do any showing off was that jarl's daughter.

And that morning, as Senrid watched from Keriam's tower, Hatch heard footsteps passing their barracks. There she was. Carrying a sword, yet. He vaulted out of bed, thrashed impatiently into his clothes, tiptoed out, holding his boots, and then shoved his feet into them when he reached the small courtyard outside the door.

Then he shadowed her, all the way to the longe-line corral. There, he faded back between stacks of water barrels, as the Methden heir walked out to the middle of the corral and stood there, sword in one hand, her head down.

She began swinging the sword lightly, back and forth, right hand then left. He was tempted to call an insult when she abruptly went into a drill pattern.

All right, it wasn't bad. The pattern was similar to one they were taught their first year in the academy, the focus to get the stances correct, and to bring power from the back leg up through the hips.

When she'd finished both hands, he shifted, ready to leave. Then she stamped, and began the pattern from another angle, her moves faster. Sharper. This was defense against a rider, much like an upper-level exercise.

Her form, he had to admit, was excellent. But anyone

could be good at drill. Once again, he was ready to leave when she stamped a second time, and began moving even faster. He forgot himself as she whirled through defense against mounted and foot, each move crisp, clean, strong.

And when she'd done all four directions, she stamped a third time, and moved even faster, so fast that the sword voomed and rang in the cold air. And when she'd done all four directions, she stopped—looked down, and let out a single curse: "Damn." She'd finished two steps off to the left; she was drifting to her defense side, still.

So she started over, this time very slow, each movement precise, executed so sharply that her clothes snapped as she lunged and whirled and changed direction.

She didn't speed up this time, but kept the same steady beat, as Hatch watched, fascinated. He tried to memorize the last two patterns, but they were far too complicated. He only got a couple of sequences here and there.

When she finished, she looked down, and this time the corners of her mouth lifted a little. Then she turned and walked out. The sun had come up, and he hadn't noticed.

He pressed back behind the barrels, not even sure why he did that. Neither of them had done anything wrong. But every instinct clamored not to let her know he'd watched. That he was interested.

Not in a rich jarl brat, who of course would have had private tutors. We'll see who wins.

3

As Liere Fer Eider settled into her new life as queen of Enaeran, she left the question of another, more official, wedding up to Andri Elsarion. Aside from her dislike of being the center of attention, where lay her duty? What did royals usually do in situations like theirs? Was she queen, or consort? She didn't care what she was called, but she did need to contact her family in Imar, which she had been intending to do the day war broke out, and she'd gone to Sartor instead. She decided that her duty as Andri's wife meant she shared his burdens, and if his burdens had to do with ruling the insolvent ruin that was Enaeran, she would learn how to do it.

But as their first week home turned into two weeks, and then two weeks became a month, she began to suspect it wasn't going to happen after all. She was secretly glad. Not solely for her own sake—she was willing to do her duty—but because of the question that nagged her night and day: who would pay for it?

She finally made herself broach the subject with Andri when they sat together at a table, trying to compound with the impossible, once again. "I take it we do not need to host a huge wedding?"

"Host," Andri said, the dimples beside his mouth deepening. "Interesting, how you put that."

"I think of it that way because it seems to me a royal wedding means feeding half the city as well as all the other things that go with a wedding—decorations and music and beautiful clothes and the like. All of which are costly."

Andri chuckled. "Aren't we already feeding half the city?"

"If not half, it seems to be close enough," she remarked, looking at the pile of papers that constituted their attempts to make a nearly empty treasury somehow stretch fifteen different ways.

"No need for another wedding." Andri leaned over to kiss her. "You won't hear the gossip because it's about you, and people know you don't like flattery, but I hear plenty."

"Gossip?" She flinched in readiness.

He saw the flinch in spite of her attempt to hide it, and covered her hands with her own. She discovered she had tightened her fingers into fists, and consciously relaxed as he said, "Nothing bad. The opposite. Everyone seems to accept us as married. You are Sartora, Queen of Enaeran, and of course you married me in a faraway land, officiated by the Queen of Sartor herself, with kings and queens as guests, in a place so full of magic that the war couldn't touch it. Then the great Sartora did not stay there, oh no, she came to Enaeran to lead the resistance."

Liere clapped her hands over her face. "I had to ask. I'm never getting rid of that stupid Sartora twaddle, am I?"

"Liere, see it this way, it boosted spirits," Andri said. "In a way I never could. I'm popular with the city, and most of those my age or younger, but a lot of the oldsters don't trust me. Some outright hate me. But everyone admires you."

She sighed. "That will change fast if we don't somehow make sense of this mess."

They eyed the scraps of paper in the biggest pile, many waterlogged and wrinkled, scrawled in several varieties of ink, each containing a promise of some sort. Andri suppressed the urge to tell her not to worry about it, that no mobs were going to come with torches to burn down Brydon, but he had learned that from her earliest childhood her father had hounded his children to be responsible for every copperpiece that came through their shop. Carelessness, profligacy, and debt were moral failings, and being thrown out to starve would be no more than deserved.

Just as he thought, she was tensing up as she said, "I'm so sorry."

Andri hugged her up against his side. "That was not a stab at you, not at all. Aside from the fact that I adore you" —a smacking kiss here—"it would be stupid as well as useless to take a swing at the one who'd had boots on the ground here while I was off learning how to fight on the brain plain." He smacked the side of his head. "You did your best at the time, and further, you didn't know about these." He tapped a small pile of three papers, set aside from the other welter. "And didn't they know it, every one of 'em."

She straightened her back. "Still, it was I who made contradictory promises, so it is I who must figure out a way to honor them both."

He hugged her again. "If anyone can figure it out, it's the mighty Sartora."

She looked away. "No, please, I really, *really* hate that Sartora nonsense. Even as a joke."

He laughed, and they bent to the task. Liere strove to get the material evidence of wartime debt into some kind of order as Andri tried to make sense of a string of numbers. They had to comprehend the recent mess before they could look at the debt that Adon Marsael had not even attempted to ameliorate when he returned to the throne with Norsunder's backing. To Adon Marsael, the specter of debt dissolved before force. Simple.

At the end of a fruitless watch, they were both hungry, and tired, and aware that most of their ideas had already made the rounds three times, the objections to each *But if we…* unchanging.

"Let's break for supper," Andri said when the bell rang for the watch change. Already the savory smells of slow-cooked onion with lots of garlic and a dash of white wine had drifted along the passages. Those aromas were not new: the scant remains of their stores were being rationed carefully, while the meals consisted more and more of pan-friend river fish in onion, garlic, and wine left from Adon Marsael's considerable cellar.

After they ate, Liere made a motion to return to the table. Andri said, "I was thinking. Maybe there would be less pressure if I took the worst of the hot-heads and invited a couple of the loudest troublemakers along for a perimeter ride? Make sure there are no pockets of enemies. Do some games masked as drills, or drills masked as games. Talk about readiness, and the renewing the King's Guard, while they're still full of martial ardor after the successful counterattack."

Liere could see he thought it was a great idea, and she knew that it would be a popular one. She glanced toward those piles in the other room, and said slowly, "Is it a crown exercise? By that I mean, the crown has to pay for it, don't we?"

"Yes—and no. It's customary for the duchas we visit to host. I'll make sure our route takes us only to those who can afford it. Or who might need a reminder."

"Such as Trobiath? Right there on the river," she said appreciatively. "But Danith isn't."

Andri grinned. "I'll make Danith part of a perimeter anyway. Serve him out for flanking you so deliberately, right in your teeth."

"While telling me how wonderful we are." She tapped the paper signed with her name so self-consciously, forgiving Danith from paying taxes for ten years in trade for horses and fodder for the counterattack, while all along the duchas had known perfectly well that Andri, before he met Liere, had promised that when he came to the throne, the commons' yearly house tax would be absorbed by the duchas for five years.

"It's winter," Andri said. "The weather is terrible. It would be understandable if we were driven off the road into Danith during a storm, and forced to remain there until the weather cleared, wouldn't it?"

They laughed over it, and fell into bed with happy ardor.

He rode out the next day, in spite of a white sky and drifting flakes. And she chose a day to transfer to Belann, and walked into her brother Milnat's bakery. She reunited with her family in a very quiet way, beginning with commiserating over the death of her second brother, who had always been rather a brute. Then she listened to accounts, and complaints, about the success of her eldest brother, who was so like their father that she got the impression the entire family had moved to get distance from him. She'd forgotten how quiet Milnat was. Rather like she'd been. Now she had gained enough maturity to recognize his kindness, both his and his son's. In her turn, she told them she was married, leaving out the horrible Sartora nonsense.

She had—as usual—formed quite a knot of guilt for neglecting her mother for the five years she had been away, but one look at Elenzeh Fer Eider's face, and Liere knew her mother was just happy to see her again. "The kingdom is a ruin, or I'd bring you to visit," Liere said finally, her throat aching.

"It can wait," Grandma Elenzeh said, her sincerity shining as unshed tears in her eyes. "Just send for me when your first baby comes along. I'll help, just as I did with little Lyren."

Liere transferred back to Enaeran, feeling a lot better about her family, and ready to tackle learning how to be a queen.

A month later, Andri still wasn't back. There had already been two thaws. They were brief, but surely he could have made it back? Shiovhan was midway between the northern and southern borders. Oh, but the roads were so terrible.

She could, and did, scan on the mental plane. Of course he was fine. After living on the run for most of his life, he landed like a cat. In the meantime, she did what she could to paper over the mounting debt with promissory notes; the guilds at least were still cooperating, but she began to go to her solitary bed at night dreaming about chasing butterflies that slipped past her fingers, or skimming her little boat from her Geth days toward an island that always receded toward the sinking sun, as her boat turned to paper and dissolved around her.

Then one day, a servant came up to announce, "Her grace of Merith requests an audience."

Her grace of … "Thadara?"

"It is I."

Liere looked up, assuming an interview smile. Thadara, she remembered from the summer she first came to Enaeran, had been a complex, one might say difficult, person; enamored of Andri (which Liere completely sympathized with) but unable to take no for an answer. Not because of her personal qualities, but because royal birth ought to match with noble birth, and hers was noble.

Thadara had worked hard for Andri to prove she was a match for a king, but though he'd genuinely appreciated her brains and abilities, he'd never seen her as a queen. Liere had begun to learn how hard Thadara had worked when she excavated the ledgers and records left from the revolution years, before Adon Marsael wrested control of the kingdom to himself. Not all Thadara's records had survived, but Liere had seen enough of them to feel a small sense of relief each time she recognized Thadara's meticulous handwriting. Thadara's ledgers always made sense.

"Welcome! Were you hiding in the kingdom?"

Thadara's brows rose. "I take it Senrid Montredaun-An did not describe our encounter early in the war?"

A pang squeezed Liere at the mention of Senrid. "Not to me."

Thadara blushed, then shrugged. "In truth, I did not come off well. Nor did he. Nevertheless, rude as he was, he did save me, and gave me the perfect disguise. I traveled as a young man, until they began rounding up able-bodied men and boys to serve as lackeys at the outposts and garrisons. Where is Andri?"

"He is making a perimeter ride with what he hopes will eventually become the King's Guard."

Thadara uttered a "Huh," then said, "I gather he still refuses to get a notecase, now that those are working again?" In other words, he had not tried to write to Thadara to see if she was even alive.

Liere blushed; she didn't have one, either. Yet. She hadn't had one earlier in her life, and so the habit never formed. She tried to think of some mitigating excuse, but Thadara was no longer interested. "I came," she enunciated, "to discuss renouncing my title."

Liere's eyes rounded. "I hope for a good reason?"

Thadara said composedly, "I am marrying a Hanbrian prince. We met during the war. I have been given complete control of the exchequer, which is a ruin, thanks to an avaricious Norsundrian in charge and her pirate friends. Probably as bad as Enaeran's exchequer. I gather there is no improvement here?"

Liere hesitated, then shook her head. "Worse."

Thadara cast aside her cloak, sat down uninvited, and said, "Tell me."

Remembering those ledgers, Liere did. Thadara listened

all the way through. At the end, she said, "That smiling snake Danith. Ten years?"

Liere blushed. "The Duchas of Danith asked for lifetime, and I thought I was doing well to get him to compromise at ten years. I guess it's the sort of mistake a beginner would make."

Thadara had sifted quickly through the piles still sitting on the desk. She looked up. "It's a beginner's error, yes, but it seems to me that you have been tasked with an almost insuperable quandary. The same one I faced, in the two weeks we had before Norsunder invaded and Bartal of Sles Adran declared an alliance with the enemy. And I knew what I was doing."

She shook her head; Liere noticed that Thadara kept her hair short now, and had dyed its dull, ash-blond shade to a warm auburn that suited her complexion. Thadara had a very nicely shaped head, emphasized by the little wisps of curl on her neck, and the pretty pearl and lace headband threaded through the auburn locks.

She turned her gaze to Liere. "What is Andri's solution for this debt? Has he offered to use this new King's Guard to suppress unrest over the unpaid royal debt?"

"No. First, there really is no King's Guard yet, and secondly, no one among his followers has been paid. Nor would I agree to using what is meant to be border patrollers against fellow Enaeraneth even were he to suggest it. That road lies tyranny. I think … I think he believes that good will on the part of the commons, who do love him, will smooth the way."

"It'll smooth the way until the city falls apart even more than it has, and people go hungry for another winter, for which Norsunder can't be blamed. But I'm glad of what you say. The prospect of keeping order by suppressing dissent is what sparked the final uprising against Andri's father," Thadara said. "And once the populace got going, they didn't stop burning and looting whenever they didn't like new laws. Especially in Shiovhan."

"I'm beginning to learn that," Liere said.

Thadara said, "I did offer to teach Andri what I've learned about royal treasuries. He resisted, saying that there would be time if he actually survived long enough to be king. I thought that so, hmmm, romantic when I was younger. Well, we all did. And we certainly understood why he thought that way, having lost so much. And so many."

Thadara looked away, frowning into the distance. Then she said, "I've changed my mind about seeing Andri. I think I will give the formal papers to you. And with the title reverting to the crown, though I'm taking my own treasury, if you put someone wise in, and not one of Andri's roisterers, Merith will help bolster the sagging exchequer over time. Before that happens, you'll need funding, and I'll give you my father's. There's no one left to inherit Otobris, and I think he would have wanted that. If you will promise to pension off the servants, I'll sign all over to the crown. This will maybe buy you five years. If you are very, very frugal."

Liere's eyes strayed to the promissory notes. "What about these?"

"I brought with me my suggestions for Enaeran's future, which I was endeavoring to get Andri to adopt before Norsunder invaded. I still have them. Andri had given me an open hand, which I thought flattering at first, but of late I wondered if it was simply because he couldn't be bothered. He said not to trouble him with details, as he was overwhelmed with immediate problems." Thadara looked away, tapping her long fingers on the table, then she looked back. "You know that he is utterly ignorant in state affairs, much less treasury matters."

"He admitted that to me himself at the outset. Having been disinherited at ten, and after that surviving on the streets, he learned nothing whatsoever of royal affairs."

"I *tried* to get him to learn about token-coinage, which is the only method besides beating it out of the guilds, the towns, or the populace, but he mumbled about sticking himself with more debt, or worse, his children—should he have any," Thadara said acidly. Then she caught herself up, adding quickly, "Of course. He'd just been badly hurt. He'd only had those two weeks to begin to learn, and he was spending a lot of that asleep because of blood loss … But you know that. Listen, Liere. I'll leave the treasury suggestions with you." She laid down a scroll on top of her sealed papers. "I need to wrap up my life here before I move to Hanbria, and become my highness." Thadara rose.

Liere thanked her, feeling somewhat overwhelmed by this conversation, especially those pauses, during which Thadara clearly debated inwardly. But, remembering Thadara's emotional history with Andri, Liere had scrupulously kept her mind-shield firm. "I will speak to him about notecases," she added as Thadara went to the door.

Thadara cast a twisted smile back, saying under her breath, "Too little, too late." Then shut the door behind her, leaving Liere to look at the scroll Thadara had laid down, containing her ideas on rescuing the treasury.

But Liere's mind was not on that so much as on notecases. And Senrid. If she was honest, she knew why she didn't want a notecase. She didn't want it to lie empty day after day. Lyren-Sartora wouldn't think to write; it was faster to reach for one another mind to mind. Of course Liere could write to Senrid first, just a friendly note to ask how he was, except she knew how he was: he was grieving. And surely he was working from before dawn to well into the night. Because that was what he'd always done at difficult times. He'd never had any patience for chit-chat, and a letter full of it would be even worse.

No, she would never do anything so ... so false. If he didn't have time for her, he didn't have time. Life moved on. *She* had moved on.

She shut her eyes, searching on the mental plane for Andri. There he was, his emotions absorbed. Of course he was fine, and outside in the fresh air with friends around him and open road ahead. That was what had made him happiest, in her experience. And if he was happy, his followers would be happy.

Leaving her time to study. She picked up the scroll, and went in to eat her solitary meal.

By week's end, Thadara had left the country, but true to her word, she arranged her affairs so that a banking agent arrived at the palace to teach Liere about bank seals, credit, and sveds.

Enaeran had the beginnings of a treasury once more.

$$\text{4}$$

The only warning Marga had that she was no longer alone was the coolness of shadow moving between the sun and her eyelids.

She'd flung off her clothes and stretched out to nap on the beach under the warm sun, toes pointed skyward in the cool spring air, arms outflung, palms up. When a shadow interposed itself between Marga and the sun, she looked up, and blinked, trying to bring the silhouette into focus. As if obliging her, the head moved, long hair wind-tangled.

She knew who it was before she recognized the side-lit features of Imry Llyenthur. Her gaze traveled up a muscled, scarred forearm, to the sleeves rolled back to the elbow, to the rumpled, half-laced tunic, and to the green eyes smiling directly down into her face.

"I have a few questions for you," he said.

"Ask them!" She smiled back.

"Circumstances conspired against my seeing the very end. I understand that the new lake in Imar was your inspiration."

She nodded once, as the breeze ruffled across her flesh.

"How?"

"I've been told that the proper name for me is sirei-atanrial. Find that in your training memories," she added, in mirthful challenge.

He was silent for a few long breaths, while she considered the intense physical awareness between them, so much like the charge of lightning in towering summer clouds.

She said, "In your turn—" And waited.

His brows slanted up. "Ask."

"Why did you lay dark magic wards onto Brother David's sword, and then give it back?"

"A whim."

"A long-labored whim."

His smile turned sardonic. "What do you wish to hear, that I wanted to make amends?"

"I want to hear the truth, of course."

"There is no truth."

"There is truth."

"Then it changes from hour to hour. Right now, the truth is that I did it for amusement."

She smiled again, her sky-colored eyes like jewels in the direct sunlight. "What other questions have you?" She chuckled, again in challenge. "Ask me, Imry. I always tell the truth."

"No Brother Imry?" he asked mockingly.

"You are not my brother," she responded in exactly the same tone.

The challenge was not the least angry, or pettish, or even afraid, though she lay there naked on the sand, as he stood there, knives in his boot tops and at his back. But though most social forms had become, if not quite meaningless, more like symbols to be adopted or discarded when interacting with other humans, so too had modesty or nakedness ceased to concern her. And so she lay there robed in the peace of early spring.

To Imry, her proximity was almost dizzying in its intensity. Just so had Laban smiled in the bad old days, even after Imry had beaten him nearly senseless. Yet there had never been any hint of surrender in Laban either, despite Imry's always having had the advantage of strength, speed, force.

Nor had Laban's challenging smile ever struck him with the lightning of desire.

"You are related to the Deis," Imry said finally.

Laughter quirked her eyes.

"We are." The smile like Laban's deepened at the corners.

The ambiguousness of her response did not escape him, and once again he considered her words, as in the sky birds cried one to another, and nearby the breakers mumbled and hissed.

Marga said, "I will converse further with you whenever you like, but you must first abandon the habit of sneaking up on a person."

As he stared down at her, one of her palms turned slightly. He perceived the subtle shift of her muscles, smooth as a cat's. The gesture she made surprised him, because it seemed deliberate, yet had no meaning. He became aware of the hiss of the sea, a persistent, proximate hiss — and looked up just as a huge green wave crashed down on them both.

He meant to catch her, as much to keep her from drowning as anything, but the cold, roiling currents tore him away, and when the water receded, he was left sitting, sodden, on the beach some thirty paces farther up, blinking brine from his eyes.

He looked out at the now peaceful ocean, saw only little ripples, and then the sparkle of a silver fish leaping from one wave to another, its airborne form somehow expressive of joy and laughter, before it disappeared into the deeps.

And though he watched for a while longer, the fish did not reappear.

A little later, Marga swam upward through cool green water. Occasional shafts of sunlight shot downward, the luminous blues and greens of stained glass. As she neared the surface the colors brightened in slanting rays of gold, molten yellow, melding to pale blue.

She broke surface, changed to human between one step and another, and ran up the sand to catch up and don the clothes she had left lying there. Then she stood in the sunshine, watching the sea until she sensed presence. She ran up the beach, laughing in greeting. "Here you are!"

Detlev smiled as he patted her cheek. Most people who thought they knew him would not have thought him capable of affection or tenderness; nor would they have recognized his beaming smile of paternal pride.

Marga laughed. "How have you been, Benefactor Detlev?"

"You would know if you came to the plateau to visit."

"A place of great beauty," she said. "And so I shall come when you finish building." Then, "Imry was here not long ago, interrupting me while I was contemplating which of the world's wounds to dress next."

"Show me the encounter with Imry?"

She shared the memory.

Detlev considered in silence for a time. It was probably inevitable that the brothers would both, without being aware of the other's interest, be attracted to the same girl. And given her nature, it was equally inevitable that she would be—however briefly—responsive to the one who needed healing.

None of this was permanent. For David a first crush, though intense; Detlev was very sure that most of the attraction was for the shimmer of Marga's innate power. As for Marga, she was mated to the world, and likely incapable of a long-term relationship with another human being, at least for the foreseeable.

As for Imry? Detlev had known the boy well, but the young man was far more elusive.

"It will work out for the best," Marga promised. "Don't be sad."

He was not surprised she had guessed the general direction of his thoughts. "Shall I assure you comfortingly that sadness is a luxury I gave up long ago?"

She gave him a lopsided grin, both wicked and a little wistful. "Great-grandpa!"

"Senility is the luxury I've earned."

She laughed. "You called to me. Is there a need?"

His smile faded. "I know you have urgent tasks."

"Chwahirsland needs me, oh, so very, very badly," she said. "But I've had to wait while the binding spells are undone. They are all so wicked, and so specialized. They are like the kind of web that sticks to you if you try to break it, and poisons you the while. I tried to go there, and had to go away again. But I have been working out what I will do when I can get in."

He inclined his head. "Had you planned to do anything about the blasted region of Norsunder Base? I ask because Siamis has been spending time there undoing the same sorts of wards that Jilo is dissolving in Chwahirsland. But he has recently discovered that the last of the inner ring of saboteurs has been turning up. The last and worst of them is on the road in southern Sartor right now. Siamis means to resolve the matter."

"Saboteurs." Her smile vanished. "These are the ones who poison ground, water, blood, and flesh, yes?"

"They were not commanders or army leaders, but every one of them has bloody hands. A few of them left damage trails behind them as they retreated, for no reason beyond general retaliation, and perhaps entertainment. I was going to go deal with them, but Siamis insists on expiation."

"For?" Marga said. "I understand that the enemy coerced him into wickedness, but that was so very long ago, yes? And he left them."

"Your learning has progressed exponentially," Detlev observed. "Your sight reaches the entire world. But you are still very young, and perhaps might contemplate time?"

Marga's countenance clouded. "Time?"

"I think you are forgetting that when people were prisoned in the Beyond, centuries could pass. But it felt like hours, or a few days, at most, when they emerged into time's stream again."

Marga dipped her head, accepting that.

"Siamis is not a lot older than you are in physical time. You're right in that he left them long ago by the way the world measures time, and once he left, I did what I could to help him separate himself from what they did to him. What they made him do. But all that was stirred up again, in the worst possible way, while Ilerian tried to break Clair. Every day, Siamis was forced to see his past actions through the eyes of an innocent, and he was helpless to halt it. We all were."

Marga's eyes filled. "I see! I see. If only I had learned faster, I could have freed him from that burden, and helped Clair, so that he could aid you." The sheen in her eyes formed into tears, and slipped down her face to fall.

Before the drops could land, a bright red shape swooped out from the trees, and caught both tears in its beak. A brief glimpse of pearlescent shapes—bound into spheres by the intensity of the magic in Marga—and the bird flitted away, to bring the healing liquid to its nest.

So like the Sunchild, now escaped beyond Ilerian. Detlev said to Marga, "Siamis chose to endure Ilerian's torment of Clair, since no one could ward it. He said that he already knew the extent of those memories. He wanted no one else to have to

endure them. And he aided me as well. It was two persons'
work. More. That work gave him purpose, if not surcease.
Now..."

"Now he secures to himself the grim tasks that no one
wants?" Marga put her hands together. "I see. And so,
Norsunder Base, which is not empty, then? I have not looked
that way, as no life was there when I looked last. There is no
need for Siamis to hurt himself further. I think I know a way."

She flung her hands skyward. A flicker of light, and a lark
arrowed toward the sun, singing.

Elzhier made it all the way from Yaldar to the southern reaches
of Sartor before she suspected that she was being followed.
Having been trained in covert action by Connanre of the Host,
she prided herself on there being none better, excepting her
fellow spies and saboteurs among Connanre's elite.

The understanding among them had always been to go to
ground whenever there was a possible threat. If they could,
plant evidence to point another way, or even (if there was time)
cause a disaster of sufficient scale to keep nosers busy elsewhere.

She had always liked causing disasters—fire was the
best—and then sitting at a table with something hot to drink,
and watching the mad scramble to put it out. Extra fun if there
was wailing and commotion when someone was caught inside.

She considered her shadow. It had only been half a day.
When she stopped, they stopped. When she ran, they ran. She
abruptly took a side-path when surrounded by rock and trees,
so that no one could possibly have seen her. She grunted her
way into a tree and came down on rock, cursing at the sap on
her hands and the needles all over her clothes. She was still in
enemy territory, so circumspection was paramount; she decided to see who it was before attacking in the open.

She looked down from the little bluff to discover a girl
who couldn't be over twenty, if that much. No weapons. No
one else in view, and the borderland visible beyond a couple of
hills.

Making a noise of disgust at how much trouble she'd been
put to, she dropped onto the path to confront the girl, who

smiled.

"Where do you think you're going?" Elzhier demanded, to establish hierarchy.

"To Norsunder Base," the girl replied.

Elzhier shrugged mentally. She was not averse to company on what had been an extremely tedious journey. "Where were you posted?"

"Oh, all over," the girl responded brightly.

So brightly that Elzhier frowned. She was always suspicious, tempered by what she considered a sensible outlook. Such as, no lighter, all alone, with no weapons, would ever go to Norsunder Base, even now. "You're another covert?" Elzhier asked.

"Oh, very," was the reply.

Elzhier nodded. Of course she was. No one would suspect a stupid-looking teenage girl. But in Elzhier's experience, they were the most vicious in underhanded tactics. Well, she had been living proof, heh! "Under whose command?"

"Right now, no one's," the girl replied cheerfully. "The last commander I saw was Imry Llyenthur."

"So he's not dead," Elzhier said, disappointed, then a thought occurred, "When was that?"

"This morning," was the surprising answer.

"What did he say?"

"Little. He asked questions. I deflected him, and left."

"Too bad you had no weapons on you," Elzhier said. Because it was clear that the girl didn't—though the sun was beginning to gain spring warmth, the shadows were chilly, and the girl only wore a loose cotton tunic-shirt, and knee pants. Her feet were even bare.

"Where were you posted?" the girl asked.

"Yaldar. I was queen," Elzhier added. "I will say this for Imry the Shit, he did keep his promises. Though I wouldn't have trusted for how long, if Efael hadn't booted him out of Larkadhe."

"What happened in Yaldar?"

"Nothing. Until I made it happen," Elzhier said with a laugh. "When the rumors started flying that Yeres was dead—Efael was dead—Svir was down—I got out ahead. Though I hated leaving."

"Why?"

Elzhier gave her a scornful glance. "Didn't you hear me? I was queen. Luxury! And I'd just gotten them obedient, too. Populace and our defense. I was so angry at losing it all I torched the palace. It was too beautiful to share with some lighter," she finished. "And the fire thoroughly covered my exit." Elzhier usually didn't say as much, but she discovered in herself a wish to impress this girl, who, young as she was, had (supposedly) deflected Llyenthur.

Also, the journey was boring, and once they crossed into the deadlands, it would be even duller, unless a miracle happened and someone at the old sentry tower had transfer tokens.

Elzhier turned to the girl, a sudden thought occurring. "Where did you encounter Imry Llyenthur? Is he around here?"

"Our encounter was on a beach, on an island where the gardenia is in bloom."

"Then—do *you* have transfer tokens?"

"We can transfer," the girl said, stopping.

"You could have mentioned that before!"

"I wanted to talk to you," the girl replied. "To understand, a little?"

"To understand what?"

"You."

Elzhier sighed. "Are you mad?"

The girl tipped her head. "Some might think so. Here. Transferring another person takes a bit of concentration—"

Midway through the last word, Elzhier sustained a slight tremor. She blinked, finding herself in the familiar gloom of Norsunder Base's commander center, which smelled of stone and mildew and male sweat. She sneezed. So did the girl.

Four men whirled around, their expressions startled, suspicious, wary.

"Elzhier," her fellow spy Red exclaimed. "I haven't heard about any conflagrations of late. Didn't know if you were still alive!"

"Just the Yaldar palace, my abdication gift," she answered.

Red laughed, then turned his gaze to Elzhier's companion. "And you?"

"One of Imry's mutts," Elzhier said. "She had a token on her. Whose? Why didn't it hurt?" she added. "We weren't that far, but even from the border it's usually a kick in the head."

"Ambient magic, I think it is called," said the newcomer.

Red stroked his chin. "I've heard of that."

"We all have. But it was restricted to Them," Elzhier said. "I guess they can't complain if anyone uses it now."

The Norsundrians laughed at the fate of their former masters.

"So. What did we walk in on?" Elzhier asked. "New plans?"

"Always," said one of the other men, someone she didn't know. She began to scrutinize these others for signs of a leader, someone who might need to be extirpated quickly. Strike when unexpected, and make it fast—

"I think I understand you all a little now," came a comment from the girl.

"Who are you?" one the men asked.

"My name is Marga," said Marga. "I came to begin the process of restoring this land. It's going to take a hundred years, but now I know how to begin."

"What?"

"Restore? Is Theronezhe coming with reinforcements?"

"You're talking about carting soil down here?"

Elzhier's suspicions had died at that first blithe smile, but now were back. "What exactly do you mean?"

"Marga?" That was a new voice—and the Norsundrians whirled around to discover Siamis there.

The five Norsundrians stilled in a moment of shock, into which Marga said, gently, "There is no need for blood. Let us give our companions here a chance to consider the world, and their place in it. Yes?"

The men all began to bark orders at each other. Two pulled weapons and advanced on Siamis.

Elzhier operated on the assumption that one struck first as soon as doubt appeared. She turned on Marga, a thin blade in her hand. As she brought it down, Marga grasped Elzhier's wrist. Elzhier began to fight, as Red leaped to her aid. He and Elzhier suddenly found themselves entwined with a huge snake with green back scales and a yellow belly. "Yagh!" Red shouted.

"Get away," Elzhier shrilled.

But everywhere the snake touched their flesh, a numbness began to spread, as their skin roughened to bark.

The snake vanished, leaving the two struggling, Elzhier to grip her knife, which fell from fingers that suddenly shot five twigs toward the ceiling. These rapidly branched, as Marga reappeared between Siamis and the ring of men spreading out in a half-circle, ready to attack him. She was there for a heartbeat, then a hummingbird flitted to each man in turn, touching each with the flick of a wing, sending them to different points in the vast stone complex that formed Norsunder Base.

Marga reappeared. Siamis gazed at Red and Elzhier, whose arms had tangled together. Their limbs pushed up and out, seeking sunlight, as their boots dissolved around their feet, which ramified downward, causing the stonework to crack.

The building trembled. Marga touched Siamis's hand. *You are loved*, she said, and her voice was not that of a young girl, but resonant as the winds and the thunderous cataracts of pure water from mountain to sea. *Seek no more pain.*

The ceiling cracked then, a massive chunk of stone falling to crash where the two had stood.

As the fortress creaked, cracked, and crumbled into rubble, five great trees reached skyward, roots seeking deep to the hidden waters below. Three golden Colorwoods grew in the center of three of the main wings, and two intertwined took root in the main building. Their growth began to slow as branches formed twigs, and twigs began to bud; gradually, the trees stabilized into the season's natural rhythm, where they would be left to leaf, and seed, forming new trees, and when their leaves and seeds dropped, it would happen again and again, breaking stone into rubble. In time — in great time — there would be a rich forest floor, as once again life returned to the region.

Overhead, clouds, unimpeded at last by the layers of wards that Siamis had finished dissolving, formed and condensed, then began to rain. Siamis found himself standing outside, gazing up at those trees caught fast in the deluge.

5

J ilo woke early, aware that if today's task was successful, tonight, for the first time in uncounted years, there would be starlight over Chwahirsland.

There was only set of wards, and one task, left.

What would happen to the climate? Perhaps it had been a mistake to remove all of Wan-Edhe's old wards right away, for if there was no rain, the kingdom was in for a horrific summer. The Chwahir would suffer in their grayish-black woolen clothing—unthinkable to wear anything else—and their heavy stone houses, built to withstand those cold, scouring winds that even Wan-Edhe's spells had not been able to ward for all those long years. Would the rivers flowing down from the border mountains be enough water? Or would those dry up in the unblocked sunlight?

Jilo rubbed his temples, then sighed. Worry about that later. Today he had to face the task he'd worked steadily toward for … however long it had been: Mondros said it had been weeks, and spring was nigh, but here in Narad, it had felt at first like a day or two, as Jilo broke the mirror ward apart that had used the lives of the city folk to bind time. Once Mondros was able to come to help, the sense of day and night had slipped back like a thief in the night.

Jilo stepped through his cleaning frame and left his room, making a mental note (as he had pretty much every day) that he ought to change it and make it less like a prison cell. Except he left each morning thinking that, but by the time he returned at night it was all he could do to fall into bed.

He paused, extending his senses. No assassins lay in wait.

His spirits sank at the thought of the most recent one, still waiting down in the cells, the guards under strict orders not to harm him, and to see that his meals were the same as theirs.

He crossed over to the wing that had been closed off during the past seven or eight decades. Once it had been the family residence. The bricked-in windows still formed grimy scars in the stone of the walls, but so far, the workers had chipped out six of them, letting in what light and air existed.

He heard the low rumble of Mondros's voice, and Retren Ndarga's treble. From the cadences, they were reviewing magic fundamentals.

He knocked.

The heavy door of near-petrified wood opened so promptly that Retren must have flown across the chamber. Like an escapee. Jilo didn't say anything, but he suspected that magic studies was not in Retren's future after all.

"Ready?" Jilo asked.

"Jilo, have you breakfasted?" Mondros replied.

"Ah, no. I usually don't."

"Yes, I discovered that when I asked the kitchen. I ordered one for you." Mondros pointed a huge finger at a plate. "Nothing to be done about the taste, but at least it's nourishing."

Jilo looked down at the shallow dish of thin rice slurry, seasoned with turnip and cabbage. He looked up at two pairs of waiting eyes, and sat down to ply his spoon. Hunger woke at the first bite; he recognized that it did not have the flavor of Colendi food, but the familiar tastes brought memories of childhood, and he finished the bowl with more enthusiasm than he'd expected.

"Now we'll go," Mondros said, and to Retren, "except for you. We're dealing with the old king's things today. It will no doubt be sordid. You may finish practicing your firestick renewal."

Retren laid his hand to his chest, and went to retrieve his books in his room, which, like Mondros's, contained only a bed and a trunk. Furnishings, Jilo reminded himself for the tenth time. But first, the breaking of the last wards.

"How is Retren progressing?" Jilo asked. "I see him studying diligently."

"That's because he was raised to discipline," Mondros

said. "But he hasn't the joy of discovery anymore, now that he's heading into what can be seen as the tedious stretch of practicing the fundamentals. I think he misses the company of others, which might make it more bearable."

Jilo considered that as he and Mondros climbed to Wan-Edhe's chambers, which Jilo had kept locked. Stale air wafted out, bringing that stench of old laundry and mildew. Sourness pulled Jilo's mouth awry. How he hated that stink! It brought back all the bad old memories of fear and humiliation and impotent anger.

Deep breath. Already sweating! Damn.

"One step at a time," Mondros murmured, his deep-set eyes under their fierce wooly caterpillar brows sympathetic.

The two of them moved cautiously, sensing and breaking wards as they progressed into the work chamber. Here was a ward above the table. There was another, over the open book on the table, far more lethal than the first.

That one they had to work at together, but between them at last they attained the inward snap of release, and it too was gone, its supplying magic — yet another binding pulling life from the land — irretrievably gone as well.

They ventured deeper inside, the air a compound of dust, the faint metallic bitterness of a chamber bound by far too many dark magic wards, and a lingering stale-food aroma mixed with the ubiquitous stink of unwashed laundry, the kind of old fug you got in rooms that were never aired out.

"Go ahead," Jilo invited. "Do the first layer of release."

Wan-Edhe had become so arrogant about his invincibility, here in his citadel. Mondros and Jilo had worked long hours on a lattice that would unravel the webwork of lethal spells in the room, for here, where Wan-Edhe spent the most time, was the center of the time-binding. Mondros performed his share with a piratical grin and a flourishing gesture, following which Jilo spoke his part of the spell, feeling. The room glowed greenish with the building of magic, then released with a visceral *snap!*

Gone.

Leaving a square, high-ceilinged room surrounded by moldering books, and on the table, Wan-Edhe's recent projects. Before it, an old cushioned chair with a divot the size of the evil old king's skinny butt.

Jilo advanced toward the table, aware of the sound of his boots scraping on the stone floor. He examined it, reluctant to touch anything that had been last touched by Wan-Edhe. Hah. A map of Colend, and a thin book that was written in Kifelian, Colend's language: a closer look revealed a description of the leading families of Colend, from right before the war.

Jilo turned his attention to the remaining two books. Those were both in Wan-Edhe's hand. Magic books. A quick glance revealed one that seemed to be yet another foray into developing mind-controlling spells.

Jilo tossed the first magic book into the fireplace, raised a vagabond fire, and watched in satisfaction as it burned. No one would be tempted to read, or use, what didn't exist.

The second book was enchantments of chain-locked, lethal perimeter spells, which Wan-Edhe must have used before he discovered the complexities of lattice wards. That, too, went into the dying fire, which flared up again, hot and red and hungry. Jilo folded the map, slid it into the spy report on Colend's elites, and tucked it under his arm, with the idea of maybe sending it to Shontande Lirendi, then he looked down at the now bare table. A barren table, like Wan-Edhe's life.

"What could have made him choose such a life, when he could have anything he wanted?"

"The answer is obvious." Mondros retorted, his voice an abyssal rumble in his barrel of a chest. "If he'd had everything he wanted, then he would not have trod this road. I use that metaphor because I'm certain it was no single decision, but a series of them. Like walking a new path, this way or that way? This one looks like it will get me where I am going." Mondros grunted, pointing. "That room must be the bedroom. I'll deal with it."

"Thank you. Burn or bury everything in it," Jilo said. "Let the components turn into soil."

"Done." Mondros went into that room and performed the spells.

Jilo looked around, and as an afterthought, he sent the old wooden table into the ground as well. Wan-Edhe had worked at it all his life; perhaps objects did not really become imbued with evil, but one could imagine that they did. Jilo would never sit at that table by choice, nor would he like to see anyone use it, either. Let the wood be rendered down into dust, and then reformed again, a new tree, with a new possibility of life in sun and rain and wind.

The rooms were now bare of furnishings.

"All right, then. Back to the library question." Mondros lifted his hand toward the room of books. "The decision is yours."

"I sent a note to Clair," Jilo said. "It seems she's somewhere else, but CJ answered for her. She and Seshe both thought we ought to seal them all away. We might need them someday, to undo something some villain does, the way I used that blood mage text of Kessler's."

We. Jilo had liked that, how Clair's gang always unthinkingly included him as an ally, despite the ancient enmity, an enmity so old that both the Chwahir and the Mearsieans — according to Clair — had forgotten that it arose initially over the Mearsieans' ability to shape-change, brought when they first came to this world.

"Uhn," Mondros grunted in agreement. "Tsauderei had suggested the same, though my own thought had been to get rid of the whole. Then one never has to think about the wrong person unsealing them."

Jilo pressed his hands to his face. Yet another much-worried-at dilemma. "I think … I think, if someone is determined, they'll invent all that anyway, yes, if they can't find it? If so, to counter it by unsealing that putrid set of books would save labor? And I could store the key to the seal elsewhere. Clair would keep it."

"So would the Sartoran Mage Guild. Or your friend Arthur."

"Arthur! Yes. He is not part of any government. I'm thinking of the future. He's solely an archivist first, and a mage second. Yes, I will ask him about a way to store it, where I hope future villains won't find it."

"Sounds like you've made your decision, then. I'll talk to my banker friend in Everon, who knows how to create vaults and seals."

"Thank you," Jilo said. He turned around, looking high and low. "I sense no more wards."

"How does it feel?" Mondros asked, his beard bristling as

he smiled.

"How does it feel for you? You fought him longer than I."

Mondros propped mighty fists on his hips, and tipped his head back. "It feels … poignant. I wish Gwasan could see it. I'd like to think that somehow, she can."

Jilo was not certain what to say to that. Mondros didn't give him time to consider his words. "Eh, I might as well return to my cottage, and clear out my notes on Wan-Edhe. And I promised Tsauderei I would catalogue his library, if he never got around to it." He led the way out, and back to the guest wing. "I also promised Rel I'd come to Sartor to visit when we finished here. Looks like I'll need to keep that promise."

Jilo said, tentatively, "It sounds as if you don't want to."

"Oh, I want to see Rel. Make no mistake about that. Especially now that he's going to become a father."

"What?" Jilo managed. Somehow fatherhood seemed a greater change of state than kingship.

"Early days. Very," Mondros said, grinning with satisfaction as he shouldered open the heavy door. "I guess I'm overwhelmed at the idea of city living again. I've gotten used to my hermitage. Ah, that's enough from me." He clapped Jilo on the shoulder, and Jilo tried not to stagger. "Retren, we're off to Eidervaen. That means, if you like, you may test at the Mage Guild, or whatever you decide."

Retren had time to give Jilo a flickering smile before both were gone.

Jilo ran back to the other wing, and out onto the balcony to see what the sky looked like now.

He stumbled to a stop when the air scintillated, and a girl appeared on the balcony beside him. She had dark hair, but she wasn't Chwahir, as her skin was too brown. And despite the chill in the shadows, she wore summer clothing, her feet bare. She smiled at him and said, "You have broken the last of the bindings."

"Who are you?" Her face reminded Jilo a little of Lyren-Sartora, though this girl's was rounder, her nose a blob, and her brows straight, rather than winged.

"My name is Marga." She spoke Chwahir, though her accent was Imaran. "This kingdom has been like a bruise on the world. A worsening bruise over far too many years. The land will not heal overnight, or even in a year. Not with so much sustained damage."

"If it can heal at all, this would be better news than I'd feared," Jilo said.

Marga smiled. "Come."

She did not go down, but up. Unerringly up, using a secret passage, which she found by shutting her eyes and holding out her fingers, and then the door sprang open, and Jilo caught a brief sniff of new wood.

He clambered behind her dusty bare feet. She seemed tireless. He was glad he'd kept vigilant with those exercises David had showed him, for he puffed no more than she did, quick breaths, as they reached the highest tower.

She faced east. The sun rimmed eastern border mountains. Ruddy light washed Marga's profile. She lifted her face, her eyes closed, and stood motionless. Jilo watched, puzzled, for he still did not know where she came from, or why she was here. But he waited in patience. He sensed she was no threat.

Presently he became aware of a change. At first he couldn't identify it, but then the backs of his arms twinged as if from cold. The air had changed. It was cooler, but not just that. It smelled different, like, like what? Like water was nearby.

He frowned and looked up at a peaceful blue sky. Blue sky! Over Chwahirsland! He glanced down, to see people going about their affairs, but here and there a pale face furtively lifted, then quickly lowered, old habit being strong. He sensed amazement, bemusement, and of course fear, ringing outward.

Marga said, "You will have a long, wet spring, and a short, hot summer. In fact, that will be the pattern here for…" She closed her eyes. "Oh, ten or twenty years. That might change. I am still learning." She opened her eyes, and gazed at Jilo with unblinking intensity. "But mark this. You must tell your people not to plough or plant in the plains or the mountains. Only along the rivers, as before. This is for the next five years. And they are not to touch any of the trees that sprout up, no matter who wants to own what land. Do you understand me?"

"Yes. Ah, I understand your words, but not why." Or how I'm to turn all that hoarded gold of Wan-Edhe's into food for the people, he thought, but habit kept that from coming out. It was his next task, one he was completely unprepared for, as he had not expected to discover Wan-Edhe's hoard. Though he ought to have, probably. It was so very characteristic of Wan-Edhe.

"I think you will find that with seasons returning, your rice harvest along the rivers will improve," Marga said, unsettling him, for he was quite certain he had not spoken aloud, and his mind was habitually shielded. "I do know the world. None better, now. And I say the forests must come back, or you will indeed have a desert here, and I won't be able to heal it, because the clouds will diminish more each year. And if you plant beyond the rivers too soon, the soil will never recover."

Jilo sighed. "I hear you. Do I thank you?"

Marga waved her hands as though dispersing cobwebs. "Gratitude is fine, but heeding is better. Oh! I think you have another arrival."

She vanished, and a heartbeat after he blinked at the spot where she'd been standing, a familiar contact pulsed at his mind-shield: *I'm here.* It was Shontande Lirendi, the king of Colend, who, despite their very different characters and background, had become Jilo's friend. He'd used the courtyard Destination that had been laid down in tile centuries ago, was warded by Wan-Edhe, and now was clear.

Jilo provided a wordless image of his location and used the time it took for Shontande to make his way through the castle and climb the tower steps to consider what he'd just learned.

This Marga, who looked like one of the Fer Eiders, except with blue eyes instead of brown, seemed to have some version of what David had called the old magic. Jilo had no doubt that Marga had somehow niffed Shontande's presence. He was quite used to those with Dena Yeresbeth being much better at mental conversations, or contacts, or sensings, than he was, just as he was used to others being better at every other more ordinary skill. Fact of life.

Shontande topped the last stairs as the noon watch bell rang. He looked around swiftly, saying, "There's a rumor that a method of magic transfer that doesn't hurt is possible now. If true, I need to learn that."

Jilo was fairly certain he knew how, but a person also had to be very sure where to go. He kept meaning to experiment;

until he felt confident, better to say nothing, so he shrugged, glad to see his friend. The climb had merely heightened Shontande's spectacular good looks. Of course. Whatever he did looked good. That cool, clean smelling breeze that had kicked up toyed with his long auburn hair and rippled through the plain but finely woven linen shirt he wore.

"Spring has arrived in Colend," Shontande said. "This breeze of yours is brisk. If I were home, I'd say it means rain on the way. Heavy rain."

"Funny you should say that," Jilo responded. "Let's go on downstairs, then. I wanted to watch the rain come, but if my recent and mysterious visitor is right I'll have plenty of opportunities soon enough." And then, conscientiously remembering Mondros's admonition, "Have you eaten the midday meal?"

Shontande opened his empty hand in a gesture of negation. "Late night." He looked apologetic.

Jilo grinned. "Still courting the older nobles?"

Shontande's smile flashed. "Now, it appears, they are courting me."

Jilo told him about Marga and her words about the climate as they descended to the next level. Shontande said nothing in response, which meant he was thinking.

They walked in silence to Jilo's rooms. An orderly stationed there straightened up, and Jilo said, "Meal, please. Whatever the garrison is having is fine," he added, as usual.

The orderly glanced past Jilo at Shontande, stared, then turned away. Jilo turned, frowning up at Shontande. The contrast between his appearance — gold-touched auburn hair, embroidered tunic-shirt of fine linen, flowing trousers of eggshell blue — and the grim, unrelieved stone was startling.

Shontande, however, was looking sardonic, and so Jilo forbore commenting.

"No planting," Shontande repeated as they sat down in the padded armchairs that Jilo had recently bought in Danara. The chairs were plain but well-made; they would not have been deemed fine enough for the servants in Shontande's palace, but here they seemed so luxurious as to be out of place. Wan-Edhe had not permitted any padded chairs. Except in his own rooms.

Shontande's mind flitted from the no planting exhortation to Jilo's emergence as king, and he said, "How many attempts against your life have there been?"

Jilo looked up, his light brown eyes round with surprise. "Three. How did you know? Have you heard gossip?"

"I guessed."

Jilo held up a finger. "Second day after Wan-Edhe was gone, one of his ferrets showed up and tried to knife me when I went to bed." He winced. "That was close."

"But he didn't succeed."

"No, I flailed about, trying to use some of those poopsie tricks David taught me. Managed to knock the knife out of his hand long enough to drop him with a stone spell. His surprise at my resistance, I suspect, was more effective than my skill," Jilo added.

Shontande shook his head. "You're going to have to alter that inner mirror, Jilo."

Jilo sighed again. "I know. I keep thinking: I can't really be as bad as I think I am. As I used to be. Or how could I still be alive?" He shrugged. "Mondros says that habits can alter and become new habits."

"I salute his wisdom."

Jilo hunched a shoulder, his expression sober. "I know. It's that way with the people, too. For the older generations it's as if the last half century has been one long nightmare, and the habits of fear are still keeping them alive."

Shontande said, "Those habits made what sense could be had out of Wan-Edhe's madness."

"Heh. Reminds me." Jilo brought forth the book that he'd had tucked under his arm, and tossed it onto the table, along with a rolled map. "That map is Colend," he said. "It and this book were lying on Wan-Edhe's table."

Jilo watched him take up the objects. Shontande's fine long hands were expressive of his unspoken distaste as he unrolled the map, scanned it, and then glanced through the book. "It appears," he said, "that my kingdom was to be his next project. Not just your people but mine have you to thank for your timely intervention." He cast book down and then pulled from his trouser pocket a beautifully made handkerchief, with which he wiped his fingers.

"Timely." Jilo snorted. "Timely would have been years ago."

The orderly arrived then, with two plates on a tray. Shontande eyed the boiled oats-and-barley, which was, for Chwahir, a great delicacy. So too was the honey to put on it. They each also got a gut ball, a round rye biscuit, standard fare for Chwahir soldiers. Fresh baked, yet heavy as a shoe. Shontande broke it in half.

Jilo smeared honey on his, and bit in. Shontande did as well, and further he evidenced enjoyment, knowing his skills at dissimilation were better than Jilo's at discernment. Shontande took care, when their meetings were in Alsais, to serve very plain food to limit the contrast.

Jilo watched him eat, his brows canted at an anxious line. Shontande appeared not to notice, and Jilo returned to his own meal. Presently he said, "I have to tell you about the other two attempts, because they relate to what I wanted to talk to you about before that Marga person came."

Shontande waved a bread piece for him to continue.

"The ferret believed Wan-Edhe was still alive, and my being here was only the latest ruse on the part of Arech and Wan-Edhe to catch out traitors. Once the stone spell wore off, I had three of the many witnesses tell him about seeing his body. The other two were different. See, I've heard all my life the grumbling about the enforced conscription. I thought they all hated army life as much as I did. But I was wrong. It was the hardships of army life that they hate."

"Ah. Rumor got about that you might disband the largest army in the world, eh?"

Jilo gave a sour smile. "That it did. An old vet tried first. Since there was no retirement under Wan-Edhe—if you got too old to march, you worked in the stables repairing gear, or in the barracks sharpening swords and repairing gear, or in the cookhouse. At least you had food and a rack the rest of your days, until you were purged when deemed useless. A good death was when you dropped in the middle of work. So, this old fellow thought he and his mates would be purged outright, at best turned out as beggars. And the young fellow thought he and his mates were going to be forced to become slaves to the land. Both times it was David's poopsie tricks that saved me. Just barely. Now I scan ahead everywhere I go."

"A wise idea." Shontande sat back, studying Jilo. "Don't

tell me that you had them shot in a fit of probably justifiable temper?"

"No! Just stuck in the garrison prison, until I can figure out what to do." He looked up, his eyes bleak. "The old one was killed during the night by his secret twi. See, he was expecting one of Arech's long-drawn public entertainments, I guess. A swift and painless death was something they had promised one another. I let them all go, and promised that no one would be beggared."

"Ah-ye." Shontande winced, his hands swooping in the gesture for regret.

"The ferret was so twisted that I knew I could never trust him. Mondros said it would be a mercy to put the stone spell back on him for a century, and let him listen to the changes, so that when it wore off again, he might be ready for another life, in a far different Chwahirsland. Lacking other ideas, I did that. The young one is still sitting in the west garrison. I had a talk with him a few days ago, and I promised no torture. He's my age, not a bad sort. Not at all. But he really believes that every calling is shameful—women's work—except fighting. That's the way they've been raised."

Shontande sighed. "I don't envy you the task ahead."

"I still don't know if I'll succeed. At first they were so stunned I thought it would be easy. The ferret was my first jolt. I'm sure there's more to come. But I expected no less. This is why I wanted to talk to you. If you are finished, come with me."

"Thank you, I'm full," Shontande said, having forced down as much as he could.

Jilo led the way into the lower prison wing, where Arech had had his torture rooms and special dungeons. No one liked to go there; the guards believed those chambers were full of ghosts thirsting for vengeance. Back of that area was a narrow door, now visible with all the wards removed. Jilo pulled a key from his inside pocket, unlocked the door, touched a new glowglobe to light, and led the way down mossy, narrow steps.

He clapped, and a vast, low-ceilinged chamber lit, its contents glistening richly. Shontande gasped, and nearly stumbled down the remainder of the stairs. "How much gold is *in* there?" he whispered.

"Five more rooms like these, below. They dug down so

deep I'm surprised it isn't under water. It's the treasury, plus all that Wan-Edhe has grasped from his various exploits. Hoarded. I wonder what he thought he would do with it?"

"Buy Norsunder?" Shontande said, half-joking as he looked around in amazement. "Jilo, between this and the fact that your leddas is still the best in the world, I'm beginning to think that your Chwahirsland might be wealthier than Colend, at this juncture."

"Not Chwahirsland," Jilo said soberly. "If there are any poorer people in the world, I'd be surprised. How to turn this wealth over to them without causing disaster? Mondros took one look and walked straight out. He said that greed and gold and the power they buy got him into trouble as a youth—that was the way *he* was raised—and he knows utterly nothing about governing, an ignorance he cultivated carefully. I don't dare tell any locals, because I know that the sight of this much gold can have a wicked effect."

"Truly," Shontande murmured.

"I wrote to Senrid, and he reminded me that the army and navy will be more likely to fall right in line if I arrange for supplies for those still at sea, at the Nob and Jaro at the other end of the strait. I've got to learn how to do that, in addition to everything else, though at least I have another month; Furo told me that they sailed with six months' stores when they left the blockade and stocked at the Nob. But the goods came from what Norsunder forced from the people in northern Halia. I need to learn how to buy what we need."

Shontande half-heard all this, overwhelmed not only by the sight of that much gold, but by the implied trust. "My first thought is, now you have the means to ensure that that Marga person's command is heeded. You arrange trade with a kingdom that is right now planting everywhere it can, in hopes of recouping their own losses."

"But *how?* I am so ignorant of such things."

Shontande considered the complexities of Colend's barter system, which was age-old, its mutual agreements based on melende. Then he remembered a mild rebuke he'd been given almost a year ago. "I know who you ought to talk to: Rel."

"Rel?"

"He's a king now, but he's also half-Chwahir. The king

part I believe will benefit you because Sartor is also having to arrange trade. Apparently the conquerors there left it pretty much a ruin, and it was Sartor's stored grains and so forth that the worst of Norsunder's forces were helping themselves to before going out marauding. At least Atan had, like us, shifted their treasury into hiding for the duration. Norsunder never cared, as they had a world full of slave labor."

Jilo nodded slowly, shrugging off Norsunder. They were gone. "That's a very good idea. Rel has to be learning about trade, and such things, from Atan."

"Your second problem, as I see it, is getting your people to learn about trade as well as you. Remember Crimson Army's covert market?"

"But we don't want a secret market. Do we?"

"Ah-ye! You might have people willing to work for wages, as well as for trade. Rebuilding is going on everywhere now that winter is over. Wages have gone high because the demand for labor is so high. There is also friction between those who wish to hire farm labor and those who wish to hire those same people for rebuilding."

Jilo led the way back upstairs, and relocked the door.

They returned to the area that Jilo had adopted for his work room, with two new windows letting in light. "Right now, I have Gold Army and Gold Navy scouring the seas above and below the strait for the pirates Norsunder had loosed in the world. Silver in the Eastern Waters. Purple is still holding the garrisons along the strait, and cruising those waters for pirates. That was Senrid's suggestion, and it is working. That ought to keep them busy for a year or two. Green Army is still here, protecting Narad. Maybe I could begin with Crimson Army? They brought back tales of wonderful goods, of foods, of clothes, of fine things for homes. Or are they not welcome in Colend? They did invade."

"Largely because of Furo, the Chwahir army was not nearly as hated as the Norsundrians in gray, who had no discipline. I would say, we could try it with a small number. They must come without weapons. It might be tense at first, but I will have my heralds be vigilant."

"That is no problem. You have to remember that for generations, all Chwahir life was in support of the army.

They're used to having their weapons strictly controlled, thanks to Wan-Edhe's fears. But If I call them laborers, they will think themselves demoted."

"Then say it's an army exercise. My suggestion is, talk to General Furo. Or better, to Scribe Anjit. They will know what to say, and you can emphasize that they will be paid wages."

"Wages for the first time in memory for most. That would mean many of them bringing those goods home. Families and neighbors would see the goods. More of the goods. Many had hidden things they traded for, during the occupation, and smuggled back. I can monitor the flow of good things coming back to Chwahirsland, as they spend their wages over in Colend. I'm afraid to proclaim this as a solution. There are sure to be problems I don't see yet. But I want to try it."

"Excellent, because Colend really needs labor," Shontande said, hands clasped in the peace. "While we cannot compare our damage to Sartor's — we have very little in the south, where the Adranis were — there is much to be done."

He left soon after, and Jilo vaulted up to the tower again, in time to see the beginning of the rain. He breathed in the clean smell of wet stone, with only a hint of the oily, acrid stench of the grime on the walls.

As he stood there, feeling the rain on his face and hands, and loving the soft pats on his clothes, he saw people emerging tentatively from doorways, peeping upward. Some dared to put a hand out, then scurried back inside, as if Wan-Edhe lurked about waiting to smite them for what anywhere else in the world would be so normal a gesture, it would go unremarked. But Chwahir had been so long forbidden to raise their eyes or their heads, or even their arms, that Jilo could feel the alarm from where he stood.

"Give them time," Shontande had said.

"Give them something else to expect besides executions and punishment," Seshe of the Mearsieans had said quietly, the last time Jilo had seen her.

Seshe! He'd been wondering how to make use of this rain. For example, how did one go about establishing things like gardens?

Seshe would know.

❧ 6 ❧

Jilo was confident that nothing would be different in Mearsies Heili. Everyone who knew the place felt the same, if they thought about it at all. After a horrible war, and then facing the resultant damage as winter slowly warmed toward spring, it was comforting to think that there would be one place in the world untouched.

But nothing human remains untouched. We all know that, even if it's knowledge buried so deep it shapes muscle and bone before reaching conscious thought.

CJ knew that change was inevitable, though she fought hard against the idea. Every time she vowed she'd redo her ill-written records of her adventures with Clair's gang of girls, she'd argue that change, if *she* initiated it, was improvement. But change imposed from outside usually reeked. Like the entire war. Which she didn't want to write about, mostly because of the terrible cost to Clair.

As far as CJ was concerned, the worst was far from over. Nothing would be right until Clair came back well and herself again. Yet it had been kind of a relief there, at the very end of the war, when Siamis took Clair away, because that meant he knew how to fix her, didn't it? Neither CJ nor the other girls knew what to do for Clair, who physically was completely untouched, but emotionally so damaged that, at the last, she lost cognizance of what was real and what was nightmare. Everything had become nightmare.

Clair was also relieved when Siamis took her to the place Detlev had once so briefly shown her. Though there was no building to protect her from the icy winds of winter, the sense of balm in the realm of the spirit was so soothing, for a while all she could do was sit in a tent, surrounded by a moat of blankets, and permit the vast benevolence to ease her frayed soul, as outside the tent cheerful voices called back and forth.

When human needs such as thirst and hunger forced her awareness to the surface again, she discovered that Siamis had left soon after bringing her. She'd expected that. She already felt badly enough that he'd had to tie himself down by minding her instead of helping run the counterattack, and all the other urgent tasks relating to the end of the war.

Clair walked endless loops around the campsite with Adam, talking and thinking, until one day she looked at the brown slush of her trail, and exclaimed, "I'm trying to do the Purrad."

"It's a good pattern," Adam said peaceably.

Clair looked into his kind, patient eyes, having no idea how the grief etched in her once-childish face hurt him, then she said, "I think I have to go home. I think I need the true Purrad."

Adam began to assemble arguments against it, though his instinct was to avoid arguing with Clair. Then came Detlev's thought: *That palace retains all its disirad. Let her go. Make it clear she is always welcome back whenever she needs it.*

Clair transferred back to Mearsies Heili.

Within a very short time, bang! Aurora, her seven-year-old daughter, impacted her with her small, solid weight. Others arrived from various directions at a run, their faces expressive of worry and hope and gladness.

It was all Clair could do to shield Aurora from her own emotions. She had no words, but she hugged Aurora tight. And it seemed to be enough. Aurora walked next to her as Clair, relieved to be at home again, wandered from room to room, trailed by anxious friends and servants alike, everybody trying to think of things she might need. Food? Drink? Blankets? Was it warm enough?

For Clair it was both profoundly sweet and emotionally excruciating, because she had no answer except no, no, no. Especially before Aurora's wide, questioning gaze.

Finally she was able to say, "I truly don't need anything. Except all of you just being yourselves. I'm so glad to be home. Has Siamis been back at all?"

The girls all looked at one another, and CJ said, "Nope.

And Gwen is at Dthel Rendm."

"Ah, to be expected, I suppose," Clair murmured, as if to herself. As if she'd been talking to herself so much it had become habit.

Sherry's eyes gleamed with unshed tears, because Clair didn't look or sound glad to be back. She looked exactly as unhappy as she had that last terrible day when they were all in Imar. CJ thought so, too, her gaze sliding away from Clair's attempt at a smile.

Seshe said, "Let's all go back to what we were doing, and give Clair a chance to make up a list of things she'd like to do."

"Okay," Sherry said cheerfully, certain that that would be all that was needed.

"Okay," Falinneh said, sure that what Clair required was something to laugh at. Laughter always made things better. She decided to go down to the Junky, and work up a new play. One with all the old, silly villains. She was pretty certain that mentioning the Host wouldn't get any laughs, especially that nasty Efael who had killed Diana. And Ilerian. What joke could she possibly make about him, when he wasn't even remotely human?

Dhana closed her eyes, disturbed by the shadows swirling around Clair, but then she sensed a familiar, benevolent human mind aware and watching from far off. She dipped her head in a nod and flitted

CJ was going to argue, but looked from Seshe to Clair — who hadn't said anything like *No, stay,* in the half a minute or so since Seshe's suggestion. Once again she tried to read Clair's face. CJ had thought she knew all the range of Clair's expressions, but this one, she did not recognize, except it hurt somewhere right behind her ribs to see it.

She forced a grin. "Sure! I was in the middle of a letter to Erenlara. I'll just hop to it. She'll be glad you're back, Clair. Unless you'd like a drawing lesson, Aurora?"

Seshe said, "First the tough subjects. Get those out of the way, and then you can draw."

Aurora looked from one to the other, reassured by this return to routine. "Okay!"

CJ and Seshe walked off together toward the library, Aurora hopping between them.

Gratitude for their understanding — their lack of questions she could not answer — hit Clair so hard her throat closed and her eyes stung. She leaned against the glistening wall, trying to get hold of herself. Her emotions were so close to the surface these days. Anything could set her off, like the sight of the first bee of the season, buzzing about the tiny nubs of flowers on that plateau above the circle of tents.

She straightened up, a new thought shooting fear along her nerves. Would the Purrad still have its effect? Had Ilerian's poison tainted everything, not just her?

The Purrad still worked, easing her spirit until she floated, her toes barely touching the ground. A sense of well-being banished that shadow-cold impulse to throw her polluted self from the highest spire.

She knew that urge would be back. Adam had warned her. "It's Ilerian's last strike against you," he'd said. "Don't let him win."

Out of sheer habit, she looked around for Siamis, but of course he was not there. He could not lead her life for her. When she saw him next, it must be as a friend, and not as a victim. But surely she was now ready to be a friend?

She walked the Purrad, then walked it again, and when she came down at last, and smelled grilled cheese on toasted bread — her favorite meal — she was ready to eat it.

Once she had eaten, and every bite was so savory that again she teared up, struggling to hide it lest she upset the others, she found herself so overwhelmingly exhausted that she went straight to her own bedroom, untouched since that other, earlier lifetime, the one she would never get back.

Unknown to her, Adam watched over her dreams that night, and the night after. Every time an image appeared that he recognized as a residual distortion of Ilerian's torture, he introduced a means for Clair's dream-self to defeat it. Once the distortion was big, devouring sunflowers, but he gave Clair enormous bees with glowing eyes. He knew she liked bees, and she sent them to sting the flowers into dust. Another time it was slimy rope-like tendrils slithering to hold her fast, but he gave her fire, and she burned away the tendrils, which withered to ash.

At the end of the week, the dreams still came, and when

she looked in her closet one morning, and found the same shoes she had worn ten years ago, she knew what she had to do to begin to truly heal.

The next day, as a sleety rain roared over the white palace, Clair put her plan into execution, then summoned the girls, who had carefully gone on with their routines while orbiting her like satellites in an effort to be within calling distance. "Let's go down to the Junky to talk. I just sent Aurora to Everon, offering a visit with Madelon as her reward for doing good work while I was gone. She won't hear us."

CJ said, "Okay," as cheerfully as she knew how, but her guts squeezed up. What would they talk about that Aurora couldn't hear? She wasn't sure she wanted to hear it.

Maybe it was a *shouldn't* rather than a *couldn't*. That was slightly less threatening. Holding to that thought, CJ transferred to the Junky, breathing in its reassuring amalgam of dirt, roots, dust, and ancient meals.

They sat in a circle on the multicolored rug in the central room. Every one of them noted the empty spots where Irenneh and Diana once sat. But no one spoke. Clair had something to say. She very rarely had something to say. Clair had usually been the listener. She liked it when they came up with ideas, or worked out arguments. But that look was still in her face, and once again, CJ's gaze slid away.

Clair said, "I think I need to let go of the Child Spell. Um, I know I have to." She swept her gaze over the circle of faces, but she was really watching, and listening, to CJ.

"Okay," Sherry said cheerfully. To her, all that mattered was everyone being happy together.

"Not me," Falinneh said just as cheerfully. She wasn't quite human anyway, Xubarecs being shape-changers. With adulthood came powers that too often had been used for ill purpose, and Falinneh didn't want the temptation. But she could adapt her form to fit the company.

Dhana shrugged. Human forms of any kind were merely a mask anyway. She could as easily assume a boy's form, an adult, or an animal. Though she liked her present body because it danced well, and the best part of the human world was music and dance.

Seshe said quietly, "I'm ready."

The others studiously avoided looking at CJ. She turned desolate eyes to Clair. "Why?" she whimpered. "Maybe it's just leftover nasties from Ilerian? You'll be yourself again, won't you, if you get some rest here?"

Clair said, "CJ, this has been coming on for some time now. Before the war. Before Aurora was born, even. I've resisted it, and I was fine for that time. But I cannot be even a semblance of a child anymore. Ilerian took that away from me, leaving me feeling as if I've been crammed into a tiny box."

"But we're perfect as we are," CJ wailed, the protest wrung all the way from the inside of her toes.

Clair's eyes filled, and CJ's heart shredded to see it.

"We were perfect as we were," Clair said slowly, wistfully. But certain. "What gives me hope is that there can be another sort of perfect. Can you take some time to consider it? And if you can't bear it, don't fret. We'll adapt. Just, know that I have to relinquish that spell because it no longer fits me."

"How long?" CJ muttered, hating herself for resisting. But all her old fears and humiliations and angers whooshed up in crackling flames inside her.

"However long you need." Clair turned to the others. "I know we've done things as a group, but this time, I would like to ask you all to relinquish the Child Spell on your own, if you so choose. When you choose. And you needn't say anything. The change will be gradual, just as it was when you grew to the physical age you are now. That will give us all plenty of time to adapt."

CJ knew that Gwen—if she returned at all—would do whatever Sherry did. This suggestion of Clair's was entirely for her own sake. Her throat closed up and she gritted her teeth, holding onto a mask of nonchalance for Clair's sake, until they dispersed to their various pursuits.

CJ ran to her room in the Junky and stood breathing hard as she reassured herself with the sight of all her things exactly as they had been. Her battered chest of drawers. Her drawings affixed to the smoothed dirt wall. Her small desk at which she'd written out their adventures, always looking toward the next one, and drew her pictures. Her trunk, with all her souvenirs and odd-sized things. Her fuzzy forest-green bedspread with the tufts that looked like pine needles, only soft.

Her eyes strayed back to the drawings, which she had swapped out on her birthday each fourth-month. Okay, strictly speaking, those were changes.

She turned in a circle. Would she suddenly hate all the things she loved, if she—ugh—grew up? She couldn't imagine being grown up. Growing boobs. Getting periods. At least they had the Waste Spell for that, but why even bother? Worst of all, getting soppy over boys. Ugh, ugh, ugh, adults were so *disgusting*. Well, some. All the villains she knew were adults. Of course, she'd met some pretty nasty kids. But none of that predicted what would happen to her as an adult.

She prowled around her room, longing to find someone to complain to, but who? She couldn't say anything to the girls in case some part of her rant strayed to Clair. Even worse, she couldn't talk to Clair. Bitterly, she reflected that for the first time, they couldn't talk, and it was *adultery* that got between them.

Well, except that Clair had kept Ilerian's torture from CJ. But that was different. Wasn't it?

Suddenly she knew whom to complain to.

She flung herself down at her desk, crumpled up her half-finished letter, and poured everything out in a fast scrawl to Erenlara of the Venn. Who sometimes took a couple of days to answer, for CJ had begun to suspect that Eren went out adventuring in secret sometimes. Who could blame her, when she was surrounded by guards in that glittering palace underground?

Once CJ got it all out, she felt slightly better. She transferred up to the white palace, intending to act as if nothing was wrong. She knew none of this mess was Clair's fault. You only had to look at her face to see that. But why should CJ have to suffer, too?

She heard the sound of voices—a new, familiar one, only deeper than she remembered. Jilo had come himself, for the first time since the war ended!

"Chwahirsland has a long way to go," he said to the girls' questions. "But already it's better. Mondros helped me break the time binding. There is blue sky over Narad, for the first time in years."

"Wow! I almost want to go see," CJ exclaimed earnestly.

Jilo smothered a laugh at this typical CJ attempt at a compliment. "Just give me some time," he said. "And you might actually want to come." *If I survive*. His gaze strayed to Clair — and away. Wherever she'd been, the traces of anguish were still in her face. "How are things here?"

"We're great, now that the supreme stenches are gone," Falinneh declared.

"We've been trying to figure out how to de-cootie-ize the world, now that Norsunder has been squelched," CJ added.

"That's right," Sherry fluted earnestly.

"Is Retren still with you?" Seshe asked.

"He's gone off with Mondros, I think to study magic."

The chatter went on for a while, then Falinneh offered to get some props for the new play she was putting together, with Wan-Edhe as the villain, and Dhana flitted off to dance in the rain. Jilo looked at the rest of them, his gaze turning most often to Seshe, who had showed the most interest in Jilo's work on breaking the lattice wards. He said, "Now that I have blue sky again. One of the things I want to do is start a garden. But I don't know anything about gardens."

"You gotta have dirt," CJ said. "I don't remember anything but stone in that city. Where would you put a garden? Outside the city?"

"I want one right there. By the castle. So it can be seen. Once all the bricked-up windows get restored," he added.

"Stone can be removed," Clair said.

Seshe nodded. "Exactly. And it depends on the type of soil. If you like, I can come with you to inspect, once you choose your spot, and get the flagstones removed. I also can recommend some hardly plants to begin with."

That was what Jilo had been hoping to hear, and his sudden smile revealed it. There was a little talk establishing the best time for Seshe to transfer to Chwahirsland in order to take advantage of sunlight, then Jilo said he'd make her a token for returning whenever she wanted.

After he returned to Chwahirsland, CJ went down to see if there was any chance of a letter — and to her surprise, found that Erenlara had responded. At length.

CJ: Have you forgotten that I, too, will soon leave
childhood behind? For my own part, I can scarcely

wait, for many reasons. One of them is my determination to grow into my beloved brother's shoes, as our saying is. I fear I will never be even a part as wise and as generous as he was, but I must try.

But you are not living my life, with my goals and my goads. I want to ask first, what are you truly afraid of? I remember well what you told me about how children were treated in the world you came from. And we discussed that we still have a ways to go here, Norsunder being proof, but in others our customs are far superior to the horrors you described. And yet in both worlds, the context was the relative powerlessness of the young. As an adult you would not be in that position.

Another advantage: you would be able to talk to Clair, instead of in a sense being another child for her to watch over. I know that that is an exaggeration, and yet I am minded of many things Clair's Aunt Murial told me about Mearsieanne. It seems that should you live a long life—and I hope you will—is there not a very great danger of becoming much like her?

You honored me with your true thoughts, and so I offer you mine. Eren

CJ dropped the letter as if it had bitten her. Mearsieanne! There was no chance she'd *ever* be the *least* like Mearsieanne, who wanted to be a ruler, and flounced about in fancy clothes, and tried to bring back bowing and scraping. Ugh!

CJ jammed her pen into the inkwell, ready to refute every point with at least a hundred examples, but she paused, remembering that Mearsieanne had set up the ward that had, in effect, made Clair a target. Oh, she'd meant well. Everyone said so. That is, the key to the enchantment she'd spent years putting together was Clair permitting Norsunder to enter Mearsies Heili, which of course she would never do. The question was, had Mearsieanne deliberately set up the magic so that Ilerian could get at Clair sideways, in the realm of dreams? Or had it been Mearsieanne's ignorance of magic … or maybe some flaw in her thinking, because she never released the Child Spell?

Except CJ could name a zillion adults who didn't seem to be all that smart despite their size and age. And there were zillions of smart kids. No, that argument was boring, because it meant futzing around with hypotheticals and dragging in other people and defining who was smart and who wasn't.

Her gaze strayed to Eren's other questions. Being able to talk to Clair was important. That is, if CJ became the sort of adult Clair would want to talk to.

No, the really important question was, what was she afraid of? She poked at that, until she saw that her fears were mostly of some unnamed "they" — like the mass of adulthood she'd left behind on Earth — somehow ripping out her entire personality and all her likes and dislikes, and stuffing her with new, boring, proper ones, Just Because.

When she looked at that, even she could see that that was ridiculous. Well, what *was* she afraid of? That she'd suddenly become a mush mind, that is, obsessed with boys, or girls, in a romantic sense? But there were even people like Clair's aunt, who seemed to be perfectly happy being on their own, with no slobbering over each other and moaning and groaning about *luuurve*. She liked not having any of those feelings. Was it possible to stay that way?

She wrote these thoughts down and sent them, to receive a reminder that no one outside her was going to make her think one way or another.

> As for mush [Eren wrote], it seems to me that by twelve, which was the age you did the Child Spell, if you'd never had a crush or anything like it, is it not likely you will continue that way? If not, it will be your own feelings changing, yes? Not someone stealing into your mind and planting these unwanted sensations?
>
> But mostly, it appears to me from so far away, that you could have faith that your future self will be the best CJ that she can be, even if she chooses adulthood.

Oh.

For an entire day, CJ wandered around the cloud top, wrestling with that idea. She even tried walking the Purrad, but got impatient on the second spire, and transferred down to take a long run in the forest, her favorite way of clearing her head.

When she returned, it was with a resolution: to be the best she could be, even if that meant aging up until she was an old granny, as long as her best friend was there to share life with.

The following day early, Clair rose from breakfast and headed toward the spire for her morning Purrad walk, when CJ sidled up, looking every which way, and muttered, "I know you said to keep it to yourself, but I just wanted you to know. I took off the Child Spell last night."

Clair wrapped her in a wordless hug.

Yeah, I can do this, CJ thought.

7

Jessan and Carl Delieth woke up early.

They could smell spring on the breeze that no longer nipped noses and ears, bringing lovely scents of growing green things. Flower Day was nigh, so full of promise, and today was their birthday!

These were Carl's thoughts on waking. She sat up in bed, smiling around her familiar suite. Oh, it was good to be home again. She'd liked Mearsies Heili, of course, and she did miss her friends there, but it wasn't home, it wasn't Everon, and though two months had gone by, that didn't seem to be enough days to take away that snuggly feeling of waking up in her own bed, and no danger.

She ran to her window, opened it, and looked out at the balmy sky. In the garden trees, birds chirped and chattered.

Sending a joyful zap of wordless thought at her twin, she wrestled into one of her new pretty robes. She'd grown taller during the war, and her babyish clothes were too short. And Tahra-Mama didn't want her wearing old riding pants and scruffy tunics like Aurora, but since Carl liked pretty dresses, her mother's command to present herself like a princess ought to make her happy.

Jessan appeared, black hair uncombed, and his tunic wrinkly from having been slept in again. She pushed him through her cleaning frame since he hadn't bothered with his, singing out, "Happy birthday!"

"And to you, Carl!" He grinned.

The grin would have been the happy grin to anyone else in the old palace, but not to Carl. Her smile faded, until it matched what she saw in his face: sympathy, a wish to please one's twin, but beneath it apprehension.

"That dream again?" she asked.

"One like," he said, standing at the window and looking out, his fingers running back and forth over the sill. Then he turned around. "Now I'm old enough to actually go."

"You're not thinking of leaving today?"

He saw her thin little fingers clasp anxiously before her.

"And spoil the birthday?" He scowled: *You must think I'm as selfish as —*

: Don't.

Jessan's shoulders hunched. "You see? If I keep having those thoughts about Tahra-Mama, it means I've got to leave."

"I'll go with you," she said. It wasn't quite an offer. They had been near each other since birth. Before.

He hesitated, his expression a mingling of several emotions. "No—" he started. Then he wavered, and frowned. "No." He shoved his hands into his pockets. "You love Everon, and you didn't feel a prisoner in Mearsies Heili."

"I just missed home," she said.

"I didn't." He shrugged. "I thought I did, but I've been thinking, and I know I didn't miss home. What I hated was her forcing me not to act, to learn, to talk to the people she doesn't like." He sighed. "I felt like a prisoner there. I feel like one here. Not a prince, but a prisoner." His voice soured on the word *prince*. "What is a prince anyway? It's all pretense. I want to do something interesting with my life, and being forced to ride around with the Knights isn't, but *she* says I must because one of us has to be a Knight."

"I will do it if you would rather —"

"There you go, always taking the drearier chore so I won't have to. It's *all* dreary, Carl. I don't want it. And I really don't want to be forced to hate this person or that because I'm told to, or to study numbers and ledgers because a monarch has to study numbers and ledgers, though I *loathe* numbers, especially when they turn backwards on me. I can't get her to understand that 37 and 73 look the same to me, especially when I'm tired. *She* says I'm being lazy, or sloppy, or inattentive, and makes me copy out the multiplication tables fifty times, *again*."

Carl could feel his conviction. "Then you're not leaving

merely to hurt her:" *I've felt that intention beneath some of your words.*

: *It's there. It's a part. But I think it's an effect, not a cause.*

"Will you talk to her before you go?"

"No." *Each time I try to plan what I have to say I hear what she'll say in return, that I have to do what I'm told because she's the adult and I'm not, so what I think and feel doesn't matter.*

Carl's vision blurred and she ducked her head quickly.

"I'm sorry." Both spoke at the same time, and then he gave a mirthless laugh and she did her best to smile. "Shall we have a ride before breakfast?" he suggested.

The rest of the day Carl's emotions veered between pleasure and anxiety. She felt Jessan's emotions doing the same, though she did not delve below the surface of his thoughts. They'd learned long ago to give one another mental space; as babies, they'd had difficulty perceiving that they weren't one person, and they both remembered the inner vertigo they'd endured while trying to find and establish identity limits.

But now, the urge to cling nagged at her like a sore muscle.

She noticed that he made certain each of the sibs got his whole attention for a time. That included Aurora from Mearsies Heili, there for her week's visit. Nobody else seemed to notice how he made time for each person, or the way he looked around as though impressing things onto his memory. The entire day he spent saying good-bye, though the actual words never came out.

He was pleasant and smiling with their mother, artificially so. Carl knew it was to please her, not Tahra-Mama. But she sensed how their troubled mother appreciated that he was less distant than usual.

Right before dinner Carl felt the warning pangs in her temples that always came if she'd been open to too many people for too long, while squashing down her own feelings.

It was then that Lyren-Sartora arrived.

"I'm not too late," she cried, dancing into the dining room. "Please say I'm not too late?"

"Lyren-Sartora!" Maddy yelled, bouncing up, Aurora at her side.

The youngest ones crowed; even Tahra-Mama smiled,

and beckoned for Lyren-Sartora to join them.

Late, hem splashed with mud from a long ride in the spring rains, hair wind-blown, still Lyren-Sartora was beautiful. It was more than just her face and her graceful way of moving. Even the air she stirred was somehow brighter. Carl's pain faded before longing. She remembered Lyren-Sartora saying on her last visit, *The pretty smell is easy. When you rinse your clothes, you put a drop of perfume in the water, and then put them out to dry in the sun. If you only use cleaning frames, then store them with fresh blossoms.*

"... and you should see the flowers blooming! The rains have been wonderful," Lyren-Sartora exclaimed, after having answered some question from Tahra-Mama. Then she turned to the twin boys. "So, Sed, how's the new colt?"

She had something to say to everyone, swooping down to do pinchies-and-nuzzles with five-year-old Gwenlin. Carl didn't hear what she said so much as she watched the effect. More properly, she drank it in, with a thirst of spirit impossible to explain, or to deny. Instead, when it was her turn at last—for Lyren-Sartora saved the birthday twins until the end—she said, "This is the best birthday ever."

They were stupid words, but how could one express how she felt? Lyren-Sartora's sudden appearance was like a roomful of single candles had been transformed into a great chandelier. She absorbed all the light—all the attention—and threw it back out again not just brighter, but warmer. Oh, to *be* her!

With Lyren-Sartora among them there was talk and laughter now, where before there was just politeness. Music burst out next. Lyren-Sartora somehow always brought music: the Sandrial stable boy who played the flute appeared, followed by two of his cousins, one with a drum and the other with a steel-stringed tiranthe, and everyone danced about, Tahra-Mama watching with her rare smile.

Yet somehow, while the younger twins and Maddy and FJ and Gwenlin danced in a circle Lyren-Sartora turned to Carl, and it was as if they were alone.

"Here," Lyren-Sartora said, bringing a tiny package from a pocket in her riding clothes. "It's what they call in Sartor a romantic conceit, whatever that really means," she whispered, making a comical grimace as Carl slowly unwrapped it, and discovered a tiny carved box. "They got it from Colend, which everyone says is even more confusing. It's popular in Eidervaen right now. They're making them for Flower Day," she went on. "It's a memory box. Never mind the sappy or mushy reasons the grownups give 'em to one another. The idea is nice, especially with people all getting over the horrible war. See, you save the box for a special day, one you want to remember, and at the end of that day you gather some flowers, or a piece of ribbon, or something you wish to keep, and put 'em in the box. And then some day in the future when you want to really remember the day, you take the things out and look, and smell them, and there's your day again! There's a spell on it to keep them the way your put them in."

Carl opened and closed the tight lid, sniffing the sweet smell of the wood, and fingering the wrapping silk, which she would cherish secretly along with the box.

Lyren-Sartora's golden eyes crinkled, and she didn't wait, forcing Carl to have to think of something to say. "Go ahead, put it into your pocket." And when Carl had, Lyren-Sartora took her thin, cold fingers into her warm ones. "Let's dance!"

Across the room, Jessan watched. He saw his twin's face go from quiet tension to a kind of wondering bloom, and realized that he'd been tormenting her all day without either of them knowing it. That made him understand that she wouldn't be able to bear a week of knowing he was leaving. He kept himself thoroughly blocked as he watched Lyren-Sartora change yet another dreary evening in the Delieth palace into a party.

Next morning he woke Carl up, and before she could speak gave her a hug. How skinny she was! He faltered, aware that he wanted to never come back, but for Carl. And the other sibs.

"I have to go," he murmured. "Now." His eyes blurred, and a sob caught in his chest when he heard her gulp.

"Not off-world?" she whispered.

"No. I'd never reach you then."

"You'll contact me?"

"Of course, silly!"

"Where—?" He could feel how fearful she was to intrude. He sighed. He'd known all along that a secret not shared would be hard on her, but not as bad as having to hide the destination from the family. From Tahra-Mama.

"I'll tell you later," he said. "Not now. It's where I want to go." And at the anguish in her face that she tried so hard to fight, he muttered, "Bye."

They looked at one another for a long moment, and then he slipped out, and ran. She did not follow with her mind. Instead she looked down at her hands, willing herself not to reach on the mental plane, to cry for him to wait, not leave. She had to give him time, if he was riding away; as soon as Tahra-Mama found out, she would be angry, and would order the Knights to search and force him to come back.

Therefore her task this day was to be normal. If Tahra-Mama saw nothing, she would not question. Jessan had spent every day as far from her as he could, so she was used to not seeing him for long periods.

Control, then. Control. She could do it, for his sake.

Jessan kept running, though he felt at every step he took away from Carl as though he'd have to stop and spew.

Instead he steeled himself inwardly with anger, which was a lot more bearable than grief. Anger at Tahra-Mama's determination to force them all to be just like her. Anger at her having forced him and Carl to give up seeing their first and and strongest friends while in Mearsies Heili, especially Sveneric. It was Sveneric who had showed him the best books to read in Clair's library, and who had convinced him that the numbers that betrayed him were not the only truth. Sveneric had showed Jessan that there were so many other things to learn, and finally, had given him the magical signal.

When he reached a secluded part of the garden, near the old swing, he closed his eyes and used Sveneric's signal. And disappeared.

Carl felt like a doll, and moved like one, through the day.

At sunset she went out into the garden and gathered flowers, and put them with a little silly drawing Jessan had made, into Lyren-Sartora's box.

When she blew out her candle that night she permitted herself, at last, to listen on the mental plane, and when she heard nothing, she reached farther, and farther yet.

Nothing.

Liere was deep in ledgers, reflecting that she'd never thought to be grateful for the lessons she had endured under her father's withering, sarcastic, stressful teaching in the shop. The balmy spring air stirred, bringing in the refreshing scent of jasmine and bergamot, and to her utter surprise in bounced Lyren-Sartora.

"Lyren-Sartora? Are you all right?"

Lyren-Sartora saw the anxious look, and — having reached fifteen — misinterpreted it. "Nothing wrong with *me*," she stated. "In case you haven't figured it out over these past two years, I am *quite* adept at taking care of myself."

She saw the impact of that in Liere, and remorse cooled her hot temper. "I'm sorry," she said far less heatedly. "What did I interrupt? Your fingers are inky, and you look tired. Writing letters? Ugh! No, those are ledgers. "

"Compounding with money matters," Liere said, after a small hesitation. "Credit-tokens. Those are actually fairly straightforward: the stonemasons' guild gives us an amount, and we give them a token. In ten years, we pay that back, with extra for each year. But twigs are not straightforward, especially on the kingdom scale."

"Twigs?" Lyren-Sartora repeated. Not that she cared, but she had interrupted Liere late in the evening, just to snap at her, when Liere had done nothing wrong — and was in the middle of some sort of tedious work.

"You know," Liere said, and made a gesture as if breaking a twig. "Sartoran twig-treaties."

"Oh!" Lyren-Sartora exclaimed. "I know what that is. You

owe something to someone, you both write your names on either end of a twig, and when it gets returned, or paid back, then you both burn the twigs together. But how do you do that for a kingdom? No, don't tell me. I won't remember anything if it has to do with money, or numbers, which are more tiresome than anything in the *world*."

"Not when you remember that behind every number is a human, with passions and expectations, and implied trust and honor. And on the kingdom scale, to break it might end with more than one hungry family, it might end with civil war. The reality is an empty treasury, when the whole point of a government is to ensure that nobody goes hungry, or afraid."

Lyren-Sartora's lips parted, her gaze arrested. "I … never thought of it that way before. I think because Tahra seems to regard numbers as wonderful for their own sake? But why are you doing that? Isn't there a staff? You can't be like Tahra, insisting on doing it all yourself,"

"No, but it falls to me to oversee everything that the guilds are turning in, because I know how. We can blame King Alored for gutting the Scribe Guild twenty years ago, and civil war and Adon Marsael made things worse. There are few trained ledger-keepers left in this kingdom, but that is not your problem. Do you have a problem? It's very late for a visit, not that you aren't welcome!"

"Oh, I do have a problem. Or, the Delieths do. Everything was fine, except Jessan left, and Carl got quiet, then Flower Day came, her favorite day, but instead of celebrating it, she took to her bed with a cold. The others had pestered me, so since Carl wasn't doing anything, and Tahra hates parties, I told Madelon I'd take her Flower Day gift to Aurora, before I went to Sartor. You surely must have heard that Atan had invited everyone, the allies, that is. I didn't see you there!"

"No," Liere said. She began to feel her way toward her possible news, uncertain how Lyren-Sartora would react. "I was a bit queasy…"

But Lyren-Sartora had a mission, and swept on. "Carl had been looking forward to it, then said she had a cold, and I really wanted to see Sartor have its first Flower Day since the bad days."

Liere accepted that with a smile, and Lyren-Sartora

perched on the end of the table, and began talking fast, her hands swooping and fluttering. "I went to Mearsies Heili first. The Mearsieans do celebrate Flower Day, but not in a big way. You wouldn't even know it in the white palace, except for all the windows being open to the garden. Clair didn't go to Sartor, either. She's still really quiet. The others are fiercely protective of her. Senrid—he was there—is much the same, sort of."

"He was there? For Flower Day?"

Lyren-Sartora chuckled at the idea. "No! I don't think they have it in Marloven Hess, or at least I don't remember. He was there with Jilo, something about the architecture of the white palace. Seshe was making drawings with them. She's the one with a good eye."

"Did Senrid seem recovered?" *Did he ask about me?*

"He didn't say much of anything while I was there. You know Senrid. I asked how things are in Marloven Hess and he said fine. He was pleasant, like … oh, like a long row of rooms whose doors and windows are open, you know, airy and completely empty. Do I make sense?"

The back of Liere's neck prickled. *Message received, Senrid.* "Yes."

"Anyway, Aurora got her gift, gave me one to take back, and I went to Sartor. The parties were wonderful! Better than I expected. So many fun games, and flowers everywhere, and colorful tents and bunting, especially covering building still going on. From what I saw, Rel has taken to kinging—is that a word?—as if he practiced all his life. Though he told me in private he still keeps his 'real' clothes in a cedar chest." Lyren-Sartora smothered a snicker. "Julian was not there. It seems that when the scribes over in Valian, across the Sartoran Sea, finally got a desk, some old fellow sent a piece of paper with blood on it, that seems to be Dtheldevor's will, ceding Dthel Rendm to Julian. She was going there to see if anything is left of it."

Lyren-Sartora's eyes rounded. "But I didn't *tell* you. Trevor Macael Elsarion, the new king of Sles-Adran, showed up, along with his ambassador. He *and* the new queen. Despite Sles Adran having sided with Norsunder. He said something about being in the resistance."

"He was. He smuggled weapons to us."

"I don't know anything about that. All I can tell you is,

he's got … *presence.*" Lyren-Sartora threw her arms wide.

"That he does," Liere said.

"You met him? Not that summer when I was with you, surely. I'd have remembered. I thought all Andri's relations were goons and loons, like that Adon Marsael, and what we heard about the old king, and the queen, who was worse. And Andri's sister, who'd been mean to him when he was small."

"I met Trevor Macael in Sles Adran. You liked him?"

Lyren-Sartora wrinkled her brow. "Well, 'liked' isn't quite the word. Impressed by. Intimidated by, except he is so very, very polite. So much so that you can't read a thing, really, and so you end up chatting about summer-steep and finger-cakes. At least I did. Maybe I have to be ten years older, for that kind of person."

"I've only met him three times," Liere admitted. "But you're right, he's probably the most polite person I have ever met."

"Queen Chantala was odd. Sweet, but odd, and clearly as harmless as a bunny. People gave him wary looks, but not her. I felt like I was talking to someone Carl's age, even though her face was that of a grownup, but so pale and sickly! Anyway, though the Adranis were the enemy in the war, that Trevor Macael faced them all down in that polite way of his, and — well, I said he showed up, but he has to have sent someone over first to hire that fine house off Chandos Way, and furbish it, and hire locals. And at first there was some muttering about throwing gold around that had been looted by the Adranis, and resentment about being the enemy."

"What did Atan do?"

"She didn't do anything. That I saw. But I didn't see their meeting, of course. Just, after it, somehow, the resentment that some didn't even try to hide changed, especially when he and that sweet Chantala hosted a concert. Music every day at their hired house, and they gave little gifts like memory boxes and lockets made of gold to everyone who called, and by their third day, before they left, everybody was full of peace talk and allies and trade with Sles Adran, and Atan gave them a farewell party on the canal, with colored lanterns everywhere. That was fun! And the new Adrani ambassador not only was accepted into the first circle, but granted that house as an establishment. I thought only Colend and Khanerenth got that distinction."

"Sles Adran is as large as Colend. Larger, actually."

Andri appeared then, hair damp, shirt open and sleeves rolled, smelling strongly of stable. A pair of men-at-arms followed him.

"Phew!" Lyren-Sartora held her nose. "I know who's been riding. Or did you carry the horse?"

"Move downwind," Andri said, dropping into a chair and stretching out his long legs. At a casual sign from him, his guards also sat, and helped themselves to the waiting jug. "No cleaning frames on this floor, and it's too hot to sweat upstairs just for you."

"Well!" Lyren-Sartora huffed. "I shall get Tahra *and* Laban to declare war, see if I don't."

"Have 'em wait until winter," Andri said. "Too damn hot now, especially for spring."

As they bantered back and forth, Liere reflected sadly on how well the two got along when she herself was not the focus of their attention. From the beginning, Andri had treated Lyren-Sartora like one of his gang of street urchins, and she'd adored it—until she discovered Liere's interest in him.

"… so you'd better stay until late supper," Andri was saying. "I need some target practice."

"Hah," Lyren-Sartora said, and snorted. "You don't scare me."

Liere bit her underlip, and again debated revealing to Lyren-Sartora that she was fairly certain that she was pregnant. No, it was better not, she decided. It was far too early. "Lyren-Sartora, you began telling me about a problem?"

Lyren-Sartora looked a little guilty. "I really sidetracked myself. Look, I got back from Sartor, to find out that Carl hadn't woke up for two days. I think there might be something wrong."

Liere blinked, perplexed. "Carl? You mean little Carl Delieth?"

"She and Jessan are eleven now," Lyren-Sartora said. "Not so little. Jessan vanished right after their birthday, and Tahra went off into a rage and ordered out the Knights, and though everyone whispered and worried and wondered, no one dared make a peep. They all tiptoed around, and Carl walked around like a ghost before she took to her bed. One of the main reasons I told Maddy I would take her gift was an excuse to get away! I thought it would all be over when I got back. I even arranged for a surprise, which will vastly improve Tahra's mood, at the least," Lyren-Sartora added with the confident assurance of fifteen.

"The Tahra I know hates surprises," Liere interjected dubiously. And so do you, unless you like the person or the context.

"She didn't hate it when Atan organized the refurbishing of Ferdrian's royal castle," Lyren-Sartora stated. "I barely remember it, but one of my clearest memories is how happy Tahra was. She likes *good* surprises, and this one is good, because it'll make Merry happy, and Tahra likes making Merry happy. But right now, things are *worse*. Carl didn't get up at all, like I said, and when I tried contact, I couldn't hear anything. It's horrible! But you're good at farsense, even though I'm not. That's why I came. Can you call her back?" Lyren-Sartora asked.

"Maybe. Perhaps I had better see Tahra first, and make certain of the atmosphere Carl comes back to."

Lyren-Sartora smacked her hands together, her intense golden gaze grateful. "Please. Do that. Tonight! Carl hasn't eaten for two days. Tahra won't listen to anyone else anymore, not anyone. Except maybe you."

Liere decided that she would reveal the coming child when Lyren-Sartora contacted her next by mind. That way, if there was an explosion, at least it wouldn't be in person. She murmured a few words to Andri, kissed him, and then mother and daughter transferred to Everon's royal palace in Ferdrian.

As rain drummed against the windows, Lyren-Sartora slipped away, and Liere went downstairs, noting as she walked that the palace had not altered in any way from the time that Atan had organized Tahra's friends into refurbishing it. How long ago was that? Over ten years at least!

Liere found Tahra in her study. This tall, gaunt, tight-faced woman was such a contrast to the teenage Tahra of years ago. Rain tapped at the dark windows as Tahra worked. No one was about.

Tahra glanced up in surprise and concern, and then her

expression shuttered. "Permit me a moment to finish here, Liere, for I take it this is not a social call." She indicated the darkness outside.

Liere wandered to the window, glad of the respite, her insides roiling with stress that she sensed from Tahra. Calm, calm.

When Tahra laid down her pen, Liere turned, her face and voice under control as she said, "Tahra, if Lyren-Sartora hadn't noticed something was wrong with Carl, you would soon have had one missing twin and one dead. For someone so protective as you, such ignorance is astonishing."

Just like that. No anger, but no forewarning, no social niceties, and how have you been doing since the war ended?

Tahra frowned, the frown of perplexity, of worry, not of rage. "I am not the only—"

Liere heard the hedging tone and cut in, "You *are* the only. A couple of the others noticed, for Carl is not sick and merely sleeping off a cold, she's gone, lost in farsense. Yet everyone seems to be afraid to approach you. Why have you turned into such a tyrant?"

Tahra looked at Liere in silence. Looked at *Sartora*, the girl she admired most in the world when she was young. Now grown up, a queen in her own right, and a distant relation.

What could she say? She had turned away from seeking Liere's company when it had become obvious that she was on good terms with Detlev's murderers, she and that yellow-haired husband of hers. Men. Ugh. So loud, so bullying without even being aware of it. Their natural state. They smelled, even when stepping fresh from a cleaning frame.

And yet. And yet. Sartora had obviously made some unexplainable choices, but she was who she was.

"Call off the hunt," Liere said, still quietly. "Jessan is not in Everon. If I had to guess, I'd say he's on the road, maybe at Dtheldevor's island, where youth on the wander are drawn. That is a guess. The important thing here is that your daughter is slowly killing herself listening for him in farsense. Beyond her strength, and she's not aware of it, for she's had no training. And meanwhile everyone is talking, except before you."

Tahra's face tightened in anger. But then came an echo, *one dead* and the anger congealed into terror.

Tahra's lips parted, but Liere waved a tired hand. "I've never interfered in your government affairs before. Not in anyone's, and I don't intend to start. I have enough to learn where I am. But I do want to say some things about raising children. First: I took to the road at age ten, because I felt I had to. And I did all right, despite Norsunder and all the rest of that mess. What mistakes I made thereafter would probably have been worse if I'd stayed in South End."

She paused. Tahra nodded; she vividly remembered the raggedy Sartora of those days, her cuticles chewed raw.

"And two. Tightening your grip on children, without a reason they understand, will drive them to escape."

"You mean run away from responsibility —"

"I mean escape. I *escaped*, at ten. Never mind Siamis and the enchantment. I escaped from my family. Siamis's spells if anything made my father less tyrannical."

"I am a tyrant?"

"I speak only of what the children might perceive. Wrong or right."

"You suggest I turn them loose?" Tahra demanded, incredulous.

"Within limits, of course. Though Norsunder is gone. If they're free to go out, after they do their daily tasks, whatever those are, then they'll feel free to come back. Third..." She hesitated.

"Well?" Tahra gave a wintry smile. "Why stop now?"

"Because it concerns me," Liere said with disarming honesty. "It's Lyren-Sartora. Your Carl seems to have formed an attachment to her, going all the way back to when they were all small and busy learning farsense, and I think the attachment intensified while they were in Mearsies Heili. It's brought out good qualities in them both. I know you invited Lyren-Sartora to come and go, being a companion for Carl. You might consider *hiring* her. It would give her a home, and a focus. And I think it would be good for Carl, at least for a time, until she adjusts to Jessan being gone."

Tahra pressed her lips together. Inside, emotions whipsawed through her, anger, of course, foremost. "You said." She stopped, gripped her hands in her lap. "You said Norsunder is gone, but we both know there are still renegades, and you as much as said my son is outside my borders. Do you mean he is in danger?"

Liere spread her hands. "I don't know. How could I? All I know is this: if he were close by, then Carl would have found him by now, and I wouldn't be here, and we wouldn't be having this conversation."

Tahra drew in a steadying breath. "All right. Go on."

"I suspect, given the twins' bond, he will contact Carl before too much time passes, and in turn, if she can do it safely, she will find some way to let you know his status. But if you demand that she break her trust with her twin by interrogation and threat, she will never again repeat the mistake."

Liere took a deep breath, a shaky one—they both heard it—and smiled ruefully. "Well, this has been a nice, chatty visit, eh?"

"I will give thought to everything you have said."

"A person can ask no fairer. The thing is, Tahra, I made dreadful mistakes with Lyren-Sartora. Different, but dreadful just the same. I'm so relieved to see her exerting herself on someone else's behalf."

"Lyren-Sartora has courage as well as compassion," Tahra observed, her expression unreadable.

Liere did not pursue that, for she sensed dangerous territory. Instead, she grinned. "Lyren-Sartora has moods. But she'd give that child the very best of herself, of that I'm convinced."

"I will consider it."

"Good. I'll go to Carl's room and see what I can do."

She did not return, and Tahra forced herself to resume her work, rather than go hover over Liere's shoulder.

When Tahra took up a candle and entered her daughter's room at last, it was to find Liere had gone, and Carl was asleep. Tahra stood silently, looking at the little narrow-featured face on the bed. Even though she knew nothing of Dena Yeresbeth, she could see that this sleep was more natural than that previous. Guilt smote her for not having noticed something amiss, but she dismissed it. She could not be expected to understand the strangeness of Dena Yeresbeth—it was the same as expecting someone who had never heard music to take up an instrument and play it—and she had a hard enough time not resenting something to which she had no access.

As she turned away, the gathering shadows in the room flickered, flowing over the folds of a skirt, and Tahra turned back. She stared into another pair of golden eyes. These ones were dark-fringed and enigmatic where Liere's were cool and straightforward.

Lyren-Sartora sometimes seemed far older than fifteen. And sometimes younger. Now was an old time. She smiled over her shoulder and whispered, "This is a good sleep. As it happens, just after Liere brought her back into focus, Jessan contacted her. He was worried because he couldn't find her. He gave her pepper!"

Brought her back into focus. What did that mean?

Tahra's lips burned to shape the words, but she pressed them into silence. As she stared into Lyren-Sartora's face, she became aware at last that Liere's daughter was standing ready to defend Tahra's own daughter.

"He is well?" Tahra asked, rather flatly.

The intensity left Lyren-Sartora's expression. "Very. Apparently. And, no, he didn't give a location."

"I was not going to ask," Tahra said, and turned away, leaving Lyren-Sartora biting her lip. She almost burst out with the surprise she had arranged, but then it wouldn't be a proper surprise, would it? Surely by tomorrow!

Unaware that Lyren-Sartora had been maneuvering in Wnelder Vee, Tahra went off to her room at last to sleep off the remaining few hours of the night. She arose early, as always, placed her feet to the floor at the same time, and methodically readied for the day.

One of the Sandrials was waiting outside her room to let her know that Carl had woken, and was at that moment eating breakfast. Heartened, Tahra broke routine long enough to fetch coffee herself. She walked past her workroom to the old parlor, which had been given over to her fourth-cousin Mercedes Dei, now working quietly on a tapestry stretched out on a tapestry-rack.

"Good morning, Merry," Tahra said, her heart easing as always when she saw her cousin. "Do I disturb you?"

Merry smiled. "Not at all! This is your home, not mine, remember." It was a joking reference to the war, and the fact that Merry's little house, inherited from her grandmother, had served as Tahra's HQ and communications relay. Often—too often—Tahra had stopped herself and said, *This is your home, not mine*, but she'd still taken it over, until at the very end the Norsundrians discovered it at last, and fired it. And there had never been any hint of resentment from Merry, only support, friendship, and serenity.

"This is your home too, until the house is rebuilt," Tahra said, meaning it. *You could live here forever*, she wanted to say, but it was—somehow—not the right thing to say, for dear Merry, dearest and kindest soul who walked the world, had kindness but no ardor in her eyes. And Tahra was not certain that even if she were to find a woman who loved her back, this other woman would love the way she loved, fiercely, but without the smothering sense of flesh to flesh. Tahra had never in her life been able to bear being touched.

And so silence prevailed as Tahra sipped and watched Merry's hands work thread and needle with an easy rhythm that was oddly soothing. This was utterly out of routine, but who was there to enforce the routine besides Tahra herself?

Presently she put words to her thoughts. "Sartora maintains that I am a tyrant to my children. Do you perceive me that way?"

Merry said, "Her idea of a tyrant must differ from mine."

"She implied that others besides her feel that way."

Merry shook her head, her hands not pausing.

"She said that I oppress my children. She really meant the twins, for the others are so small. There somehow was never a chance to point out that all I've done is minimize contact with Detlev's criminals, but that's to protect them until they can reach an age of discernment."

Merry's smile faded, her gaze pensive. "I have never heard before," she murmured, hating any kind of contention, "that Sartora could be malicious."

"She wasn't." Tahra flushed, hearing a very gentle rebuke in Merry's soft words. "Perhaps I repeated her words in a harsher tone than she used, because I'm worried. She used to agree with me that Detlev was the cause of the world's evil. Ah, if not the cause, certainly the willing executioner, whatever his poses to the contrary."

Merry looked up, query puckering her high, smooth brow. "Are you worried?"

"Some. I'm afraid that no one is telling me that Jessan went straight to them. But there is all the rest of the world to explore. Far more likely he went to Dtheldevor's island, which was Liere's first thought. The children have talked about it so often, and I did promise they could visit once they turned twelve. Though with Dtheldevor dead, I think —"

The door opened then, and a steward said, "Pardon me, Your Majesty —"

Tahra never heard the following words. Merry either, for they were both too shocked by the figures who came in, streaming wet from the rain.

Lyren-Sartora lurked in the hallway, full of glee, for she was the one who had insisted that Laban send them on to Ferdrian, so that Merry and Caris-Merian could meet. Surely that would make Tahra happy, and a happy Tahra might turn into a reasonable Tahra...

Tahra and Merry stared from a tall, blond young man (Merry's eyes lingered on that comely countenance) to a young woman who had Merry's heart-shaped face.

Tahra had never glimpsed the reclusive Caris-Merian Rhoderan during the latter's brief stay in Mearsies Heili. Caris-Merian's dark hair was now slicked back over her wide Dei brow, her bones emphasized by cold-weather redness on cheeks and nose. The wide-set gray eyes dominated her face, just as did Merry's.

A ghost Dei?

The young man spoke, in Geth-accented Fer Sartoran: "Tahra, have we permission to enter?" At her silent, mazed nod, he went on, "Do you remember us? Cath and Caris-Merian? We met when you came to Geth. We are going to return to Geth, now that we can, but Caris-Merian wished to meet her relations first."

Caris-Merian sagged down onto the edge of a hassock, rubbing rain from her eyes, all her attention on Merry, who dropped her sewing and knelt down beside Caris-Merian, and the two exchanged a few low-voiced remarks.

Tahra stared as she realized that Harold Dei really did have a daughter. This, right here, was the solution to the problem of that evil Laban infesting Wnelder Vee, directly over the northern border! "Surely you will stay and do your duty in Wnelder Vee, yes?" Tahra addressed Caris-Merian.

"Duty?" Caris-Merian repeated, looking up. "I don't see any duty."

"You are queen of Wnelder Vee!"

"That, I am not. All I see in that regard, me, is an accident of birth that I had not even known about."

Tahra began to protest, and Caris-Merian raised her hand. "I still have trouble thinking of Laban as a brother, not through any fault of his own. I could blame Detlev. I did." She glanced tiredly up at Cath, who gazed somberly back, hands clasped behind him. "But I have an obsessive personality that would make the very worst sort of queen, even if I wanted to stay. Even if I knew the slightest thing about Wnelder Vee. Or its language. And I could see, in the two days we were there, that he is very good at what he does. Better than I would be. I merely came to meet family."

I have an obsessive personality... "Take your time. You are welcome," Tahra said in a wooden voice, and stalked out to get to work.

In the background, Lyren-Sartora flinched, aware that she had somehow made a horrible mistake.

❧ *9* ❧

DETLEV'S HOUSE

F ar to the southeast, on a plateau at the western border of Sartor, David had just emerged from a pool filled with snowmelt from the higher altitudes. Hot and tired after a hard morning of labor, he had transferred down, kicked off his shoes, and fallen in.

When he stood up, his clothes sodden, he found Detlev sitting on a large flat rock that the boys had dragged there for summer sun-drying purposes.

"Detlev. How was Songre Silde?"

"Misty."

"Isn't it misty four seasons of the year?"

"Yes. If you call their climate seasonal. They accepted Hibern for study. Lilith intends to remain there for a time."

David tried to unpack these simple sentences, figuring the most important was the one not spoken, but implied: Detlev had been exonerated by the Norss, most likely spoken for by Lilith, or he would not know that much. Though he wouldn't say, it had to mean something to him.

"Here?" Detlev said.

"In general, the things I'm tasked to watch are quiet enough, and I finished my reading."

"Senrid?"

"Same. I haven't been there for weeks, as he's busy with his academy, acting as headmaster for the interim, so he can keep an eye on them. Marend Ndarga is a model student, but that can't be said for some of the others."

"It's to be expected they would act out," Detlev said with a total lack of surprise, and David remembered how wild his own group got during their mid-teens. A memory that did not reward examining too closely. "We've finished excavating the white stone. It really isn't rock, is it?"

"For our purposes, we can think of it as stone. I still do not know how it was…"

"Extruded?"

"Formed, if it was formed differently than other varieties of stone. That it contains disirad is clear, but little else is. We don't need to know at this juncture. There is enough now to construct Curtas's House."

The sun of early summer was drying David's clothing fast. They began the walk up to the house, buffeted by a breeze carrying the scents of new grass, pine, and wildflowers. Snow still lay higher.

Detlev said, "I wanted to give you your first task while the laborers commence building."

David grinned. "Now that the grunt labor is done?"

All winter, he, Adam (after Clair returned home), and the others whenever they turned up, plus hired labor, had worked hard at excavating the shattered remains of white stone buried for four thousand years. Each day had begun with sweeping off the latest accumulation of snow, which worked bodies, and then thawing the iron-frozen ground, which worked their focus in mastering the old magic. Then digging, more muscle work. After that, stacking. Still more muscle work!

"You are finished up there for now. Unless you want to observe the stonemasons?"

Curtas would have liked nothing better. In fact, he probably would have been the one to hire them. Ah, when was memory of Curtas not going to hurt?

Detlev looked toward the sea before stepping onto the terrace from the pathway, and David knew he felt exactly the same, though there was no sign of it. When did his many griefs go numb? Or did they ever?

Detlev said, "Siamis reports that the last of the Fhlerians set sail from Goerael this week. Markham Glenereth is flushing out Efael's mercenaries. When he returns to Lathandra, he ought to find his son there, as promised. While you're collecting Lexan Glenereth, I want you to evaluate him as a possible candidate for dyranarya training."

"Me!"

They went inside, and Detlev steered them to the broad room that overlooked the terrace. Here Adam sat, translating one of the ancient texts that had been housed in the dyranaryas' sanctuary, hidden from Norsunder for those four thousand years, and sealed in time. He looked up, blinking.

Detlev dropped into one of the comfortable chairs, saying, "What sort of person do you think we ought to look for?"

"I don't know." David shrugged, hands out; he sat in the open window to finish drying out. "I thought you'd pick them. Someone who wants to learn how to use a dyr might be the first requirement."

"It might," Detlev agreed. "Except that beyond your group, who knows what a dyr is, and what its purpose was?"

Adam reached over to tap one of his piles of neatly written paper, waiting to be bound. "I have two texts that appear to discuss that question," he said. "Their thinking back then was so very different. There are whole passages I translated, but don't really comprehend."

"Did you do what I asked?" Detlev inquired.

"I didn't forget," Adam said. "All such passages are writ in green ink. Passages I understand as guiding principles are in black, and queries, questions, discussions, and opinions, are in blue. Their annotations are in brown, in their own column, and I left space for our annotations at the outer column.

"Excellent," Detlev said. "To my question. What sort of person do you think we ought to look for?"

"Curiosity," Adam said. "A desire to improve."

"Improve what?" Detlev looked David's way.

"Others. Self. Situations."

Somewhat to the surprise of both, Detlev said, "That's a good enough start. As you progress, be on the watch for people you might want to work with. I've marked out a few, but you'll save a say. Lexan Glenereth is one. Retren Ndarga. There's a girl named Hlareas, who works in her mother's establishment on Blossom Street in Eidervaen. She's a bit young, but time fixes that. There's another girl named Candra, working off restitution for theft up in Everon. One of the many orphans left after the war years. Sveneric's friend Jessan Delieth, of course. Liere, perhaps, one day, though it might occur later in life.

Yanli, certainly. She won't make a dyranarya, most likely, but she will be a better healer mage for some training. Where is Jessan?"

Adam said, "He's in Sarendan, buried in tutoring with Darian Selenna. They seem to have accepted Rel as an overseeing regent. I thought the people of Sarendan would be afraid of Sartoran annexation, but I'm glad to be wrong."

"Sarendan knew and liked Rel before he became a king in Sartor," Detlev said.

David looked askance. "What about Dirk?"

"Very much include Dirk. If he shows up and show an interest. At this juncture I don't foresee him becoming a dyranarya any more than Yanli will, but training can only benefit him." He clapped his hands on his knees. "I'll go to the plateau and oversee the next stage." Detlev vanished, leaving the two alone.

David eyed the bright-dyed kerchief tied around Adam's high brow, which kept his curly mass of brown hair from falling into his face. "Why don't you just cut that hair off?"

"Beginning of summer," Adam said tranquilly. "That way I only have to think of it once a year. What did you get assigned?"

"Evaluating Lexan Glenereth before taking him back home."

"Mmmm." Adam's gaze had already gone absent, his pen scratching rapidly over his paper.

David downed a courage-bolstering meal, then transferred to northern Goerael.

He found himself in the early evening outside a huge house with a golden glow of many candles all along the third story. The door was not locked. The air inside was warm, with the lingering traces of a long-consumed dinner whose main components had apparently been garlic and cabbage.

Midway up the second flight of stairs he heard voices. A few more steps, and the chatter resolved into a distinguishable, and impassioned, exchange, ranging from a high woman's voice to a man's raspy rumble.

"And we need an independent message transport. No more of this determining the importance of letters by the rank of the sender!"

"Then who's going to house the carriers?"

"Huh? Oh, well, we'd keep the same buildings. Everyone knows 'em."

"But who pays the upkeep? Who's going to pay the messengers, and feed their horses? The nobles got priority because they paid for the posting-houses in their areas of governance. In case you've forgotten."

"You don't need to get sniffy. It's obvious. The funding will be the same as for healers, or hiring mages for fire and natural disaster, of course. Everyone contributes, according to ability."

A new woman's voice struck in, cool and emotionless. "I've counted four separate items, now, that our towns will be responsible for on their own. Unless you are willing to delineate just how the towns are to 'contribute', and whether or not the farmers do the same, you're going to have chaos right from the start."

"It sounds to me," an older male voice stated, "like your 'contributions' are another name for taxes. Why bother with ridding ourselves of taxes if we're still going to have to pay them even if we call them another name?"

David topped the last stair, and moved silently to stand beyond the reach of the light so he could look in the open door. He saw the tired, messy, forward-leaning group of conspirators. From their appearance (and from the piles of dirty crockery around them) they'd been at it for some time.

And there, far corner, listening intently, was a teenage boy. Tall, broad-shouldered already, overlong dark hair, intense gray eyes in a bony face the color of bronze.

David took a step into the pool of light, and was immediately seen by a tall, bearded bear of a man who had been sitting in the opposite corner from Lexan. His voice David had not yet heard. He uncrossed brawny arms and stood up, interrupting the others with just his presence.

"David!" Salvec the Bear boomed. "'bout time, eh? But what timing!" A laugh like boulders in an avalanche followed this witticism.

David entered the room, smiling around at the gathering of disheveled folk, and saw a mixture of expressions, from wariness and suspicion to curiosity.

He turned back to the bear. "You're drunk," he observed.

"Not so!" Sal threw wide his huge hands. "We been at it here two days. Whoever thought inventing a government would be work? All we ever saw were the parties!" Again the booming laugh, ignoring how the others in the room had stiffened at the word "government."

"Who's he?" a thin tenor voice asked suspiciously.

David turned to the spare, long-nosed man. "A friend of Sal's. A foreign friend, not here to interfere. I'll soon be gone."

David felt the gaze of those gray eyes on him.

"Back in shortly," Salvec announced, turning to the door.

No one argued.

They walked all the way downstairs, the wood creaking under Sal's step. When they reached the lower hall Salvec lit a candle, and turned a mighty brow ridge, expressive of relief and exasperation, toward David. "Thought you'd be here right after the graybacks ran."

"Detlev must have thought Lexan needed to finish out the winter here."

Salvec grunted, a sound not unlike the start of a continent-shifting earthquake. "Lexan ain't been any trouble. In many ways, a help. I'll be sorry to see him go."

"How are your plans progressing?"

A rumble of disgust. "Lettin' 'em talk it out. Now they're gettin' back to another monarchy, with different names. Damn-ation!" The windows rattled. "How is it going to be if every-body votes? I still think the guilds should form a council. People can be trusted to vote for their own guild, people they presumably know and work with. They all seem to think there has to be one person at the top, but that person has to be wiser than the First Sartora, but tougher than Nyal Bloodriver of the Venn, just to start their list. Which gets longer and longer by day. Why not stick Peddlar Antivad on a throne? Bah! Maybe they'll come around to my council idea after they get tired of arguing against each other."

"No wide swathes of fallen heroes, I trust?"

Salvec grinned, showing strong white teeth. Hundreds of them, it seemed. "I promised Detlev my irregulars would go home. They have. I stick to my word."

"Then I'll grab Lexan and be on my way."

A banana-sized forefinger touched David's shoulder. "Tell Detlev to come see us maybe end of summer. If we're not any farther along by then, maybe we need some more ideas."

"I'll tell him."

Back upstairs. Conversation halted as the big man pointed at the boy in the corner and then jerked his thumb toward the door.

Lexan sloped out. As he passed Salvec, one of the giant hands came down in a rough caress on the top of his head. "Yer a good little sod," Sal said. "You worked hard. Come back anytime. You'd be welcome."

"Thanks, Sal," Lexan said.

David walked him out, and then said, "Sounds like you've been their runner, eh?"

Lexan's smile was brief, and a little shy. "Runner, cook, laundry, with a few fights here and there during winter."

"How about a good night of sleep? It's night in Ralanor Veleth, too. A good meal in the morning, and then back to Lathandra?"

Lexan agreed, and they made their way to an inn in silence. David got Lexan a room, where the teenager dropped into sleep as if he'd been knocked out, and David retreated to read until he, too, after a long, tiring day, retired.

Over a substantial breakfast the next day, as if his tongue was loosened, Lexan began talking, his body vibrating like a knife in a tabletop. Once started, he couldn't seem to stop, a nearly incoherent flood of words not only about his failed quest to find Sartora, whose legend in landlocked, magicless Ralanor Veleth testified to supernatural powers, but about his desire not to see his father waste his life serving as steward to the otherwise blameless queen. He reverted back to his father's disgrace, and the subsequent loss of land and title.

David recognized instantly the brief but characteristic Detlev-interferences. Two visits, maybe three, perhaps an hour's time in total, and all these lives permanently altered.

David could see why in the individual sense, but as yet he couldn't explain why these particular people, and how they all fit together. Oh, some was clear enough: cutting the Glenereths free of the Norsundrian interloper who chose power over honor, truth, kin, and everything else. Detlev hadn't explained at the time, but David had assumed he'd find out after the war. Well, here they were, and he still didn't have the entire map, only a corner.

David forced his attention back on the fast flow of words. "… and for diversion, Sal sketched for me the different types of ocean-going ships, and talked about sails, and rigging, and how warships are built for the archers in the shrouds shooting flame-arrows. I learnt them over winter. Had you known that Salvec was a pirate in his youth?"

"I know a little about his past," David said, and seeing the empty plate around which Lexan was chasing a last bit of grape jam with a crust of bread, held out his hand. "Ready to return to your father? But before you do, there's a possible opportunity I invite you to consider…"

MV breezed into the terrace room, bringing a whiff of brine. "He's back?"

"He is."

"Uhn." MV scratched his chin. "Mentioned Imry at all?"

"Not today. Nor before he left, either speculations or allusions to the future."

MV tapped a finger on the table. "Sure sign he's got plans. Huh."

Adam's increasingly distracted look cleared. "You're avoiding Detlev, aren't you? I just realized. And all your questions—"

"Damn you, shitbird, why do you keep doing that?" MV exclaimed without heat. "Wanted to get my guesses confirmed and get back to serious lazing on my boat!"

"Isn't Mildred with you?"

"Yup."

"Lazing, and other things, is my guess." Adam laughed. "So now you're yanking on your shackles, are you? How futile!" He laughed again.

"My suspicions weren't roused until recently. He's been damn sneaky. I thought challenging Tsauderei was my idea, way back when. Didn't notice until later that the geez and the gray became tight before he died." MV took out one of his ever-present knives, sent it spinning into the air, caught it, then jammed it back into its hidden sheath. "I know what he wants, he wants me out there villain-hunting, and I ain't finished with my long overdue laze."

Adam hadn't stopped chuckling. Shaking his head, he said, "Futile, MV. Futile."

"Ah, he knows where to find me." He vanished back to his boat, where Mildred was waiting.

Adam kept working steadily at his translations, the remains of an hours-long forgotten meal at his elbow, until Sveneric turned up, having also sensed Detlev back in the world.

Sveneric waved and the dirty dishes vanished below to the cleaning tub—a spell he'd set up himself, and exactly for this reason. Adam looked up, blinked as though he'd never seen dishes before, then laughed softly, pushing back a lock of curly hair that had worked free of his bandana.

"Where is Detlev?" Sveneric asked.

"I was to ask first if you had rested well."

Sveneric snorted a laugh. "A whole night and half of a day logged and accounted for."

"I was then to say—" Adam paused, his light brown eyes focusing on a point somewhere just beyond Sveneric's shoulder. "—Having experienced a taste of leisure, perhaps you will find time to remember some of your obligations. There. Was that a fair representation of his tone, or did I just sound pompous?"

"Sinister is more like it." Sveneric rolled his eyes. "What can I have forgotten?"

Adam scratched his head, expressive of a vague sort of sympathy. "That's all he said to me. But he's up at the plateau if you want to find him." His gaze drifted work-ward, and he picked up his pen again.

Sveneric wandered outside into the garden's blossom-scented promise. He stood, breathing slowly, but his eyes did not see the wildflowers around him. Instead, his mind ran through an astonishing number of people and places, as he searched for obligations. Immediate ones first: Detlev's group were either busy or else gone. Jessan Delieth was with Darian, and Darian was busy. Yanli back studying magic with Erai-Yanya. Lyren-Sartora was Carl's new governess. Marloven

Hess had become David's concern. Everyone agreed tacitly to keep hands off.

Others? So many others!

Inside, Adam watched him as he pulled off the kerchief and retied it. Then he saw Sveneric stiffen and look upward, his posture a mute expression of *Oh! How could I forget!*

Sveneric appeared a heartbeat later. "What time is it in Land of the Venn?"

Adam briefly closed his eyes. "Actually, some four or five hours earlier, but remember, they mostly live underground."

"Right." Sveneric vanished, to keep his casually made promise to visit Erenlara. He was surprised his father thought it important enough for a reminder, but then keeping promises was important.

Adam sat back and fingered his collarbones in the open neck of his shirt as he meditated upon the messages given and received, and how they had been conveyed. When Detlev had formed their defensive circle for the last stage of preparation before the final attack, he'd told Adam to wear Nevraeth's dyr day and night. When he'd taken it back, Adam had secretly wept at the sudden blindness within.

But on coming to this place he'd felt his inner eye opening once again. Only clearer, stronger. Much stronger, in some ways. Did Detlev know? Adam could find out, if he really wanted; he'd discovered that in this place he, like the unknown Nevraeth four thousand years before, became exceedingly powerful in the realm of the spirit.

In the meantime, what of all the things his formidably shielded companions could no longer hide from him while they slept? He had decided to stay silent about much of what he observed. Expectation blurred clear perception; his first internal goal must be to learn to descry the difference between that and possibility.

Adam once more picked up his pen.

10

Summer waxed and waned as Curtas's vision for the dyranarya school began to take shape. The plan was to get the foundations excavated and laid before the winter snows came. Then winter would interfere very little with building. David became involved in the process, as he had when Curtas translated his designs into actual form. Evenings, he transferred back down to Detlev's house, where he worked on translations in the library.

But a part of his mind marked the passage of time. He'd told Senrid that he would turn up again when it came time for the academy games, the first since before Norsunder's invasion.

When he'd promised, that day seemed far in the future. But the sun was dropping more each day. Summer was ending. It was time to keep that promise, and David presented himself in Choreid Dhelerei, dressed in Marloven summer uniform, ready for his first week away from the mountain.

As before, Senrid welcomed him casually, as if he'd been gone a day or two, and not months since his last visit. David was glad he'd come a day early, for he needed a little time to mentally set aside Curtas's House, and wrap his thoughts in Marloven concerns.

They rode out early the next morning, to a place Senrid had chosen on the plains beyond Choreid Dhelerei. Midmorning, Senrid called a halt, and opened his hand toward the campsite alongside a stream.

As the combatants went about setting up the camp, Senrid beckoned David to ride a little ways away with him. David followed, his hands light on the reins. His silk-mouthed filly came obediently to a halt, nosing Senrid's mount beside her.

They stopped on a gentle rise above the forming camp, as cool summer winds blew unhindered from the far west horizon, teasing his hindbrain with the familiar smell of summer grasses, the astringent scent of sage, and—distant, who knew how distant, in these unobstructed winds—the aroma of ripening barley.

Was there such a thing as inherited memory? It was easy enough to imagine his Montredaun-An forebears associating these plains winds and scents with impending action. What did it mean to Senrid? David shifted his attention to the orderly lines of forming tents and horse-pickets, and back to Senrid, whose profile was toward him as he watched the camp, eyes narrowed against the ends of his wind-whipped hair. No expression there. Surprise.

Then Senrid glanced his way, shifting his balance as his mare leaned down to crop at the tough prairie grass. "I want you to take the academy, while I run the new city guard against them. I warn you, I mean for them to lose hard."

David lifted a shoulder. He'd figured as much. Senrid would lead the city guard, as none of the seniors were ready yet.

David said, "You haven't told them I'll be their commander?"

"No. Wanted to talk to you first, without ears. Soon's as they know for sure, the older ones'll probably try to test you."

David shrugged. He knew the minds of war-trained teenagers. This news was no surprise.

Senrid said, "I hope you haven't been lying in bed reading all summer."

"Not quite," David said genially. "Because…?"

"I want them busy. Run 'em till their heads rattle. And for those who find excess effort to challenge you—and they will—I want the shit thrashed out of 'em."

Right. David had no difficulty translating that. The new academy, it seemed, was probably twice as warlike as their dead seniors had ever been, for how else could one compete with the memory of those who fell in Marloven Hess's defeat? In typical Marloven thinking, it meant one had to earn back lost honor at any price, including against one another if there happened to be no enemies handy.

"Six duels since the first callover. One death. That was more deserved than not. He probably would have gone over to Aldon before the year was out, if Norsunder hadn't lost. But I still don't like them taking matters into their own hands, because it's getting worse. Three almost died. Officially I don't know about any of 'em, because I'd have to flog them at the post, and I hate that. But it's time for consequences."

The punishments would have to be profoundly unpleasant, was his implication. You'd think, David thought sourly, that the prospect of a week of war-gaming with wickedly cut ash swords that left horrible welts underneath the summer tunic-shirts — for no one was permitted to wear quilted padding, much less chain mail — plus the tired muscles after the extra drills, and camp duties, would satisfy the most warlike. Oh, no. No chance. He'd listened to the bragging chat in line between a few of those first and second year seniors, and a rough gang they looked. And after a spring and summer of daily drill in six or eight forms of lethal contact, they were going to be tough.

"I'm here to provide a handy substitute for their urge to let one another's blood, eh?" David asked.

Senrid looked sardonic. "It will be a busy week." And, clucking to his horse, "Let's get 'em going."

Under a weeping gray sky exactly a week later, Senrid's chosen company from his city guard lined up facing the academy. Rain splashed down on close-rooted grasses growing there for a thousand years or more, on the high-bred Nelkereth plains horses, and on bared human heads and already sodden uniforms, but no one moved as David looked right and left at his erstwhile command and then stepped across the five or six paces, saluted fist to chest, and offered his ash sword to Senrid in surrender.

No one breathed. Would Senrid keep it, thereby signifying his disapproval of their conduct, and their disgrace? Or would he give it back, acknowledging that the loss was honorable?

The loss had been honorable. They all knew that. They'd acquitted themselves quite well. Had even managed to take their elders by surprise a couple times, though they couldn't take them in battle. But there were some of Hatch Senelac's and Blackeye Ventdor's followers who knew that their conduct outside of the fighting would not bear close examination, and how much did the king know? Nobody could get clues from his face. Worry, worry.

Senrid took the worn ash hilt, nodded, then reversed it and handed it back. David tapped his fist against his chest again, everything according to form, and pretended not to hear the deflating lungs behind him, audible over the drumming rain.

He gestured with his ash sword, and the academy ran (or in a few cases, hobbled) to mount up. Senrid dismissed his company, who rode back to the city. David and Senrid rode side by side back to the academy. The ritual wasn't over yet. The tension, so briefly relaxed at the surrender, intensified.

Good. Let 'em sweat, David thought, bracing himself so he could dismount without his knees buckling. What hurt worst? He could count up and compare all his aches and pains later. Not long now, and he'd be far away, relaxing in a hot-stream somewhere near the disirad mountain. Far, far from Marloven Hess.

But first. He straightened his dripping tunic, pulled the wooden sword from the saddle sheath, and handed the reins over to the waiting fourteen-year-old "colt".

Senrid stood at the stable doors.

"Change into dry clothes. Line up in the senior barracks," he said.

Covert gestures of help to four of the biggest, including Hatch and Blackeye, all of whom shrugged off would-be aid in characteristic manner; David noticed the big, brawny one with the lemon-yellow hair. What was his name? Hamet something. Hamet snarled a low curse at the boy who offered him an arm, and won a flush and a resentful glare.

David, of course, had nothing here to change into, but a cleaning frame waited in the instructors' outbuilding. He stepped through it, wishing that the magic that zapped away dirt, sweat-salt, grass, and the rest of the detritus of a taxing week would also zap away bruises, welts, cuts, and what felt like a strained shoulder, damn damn damn.

He took his place beside Senrid in the senior classroom, and watched as the seniors scrambled in, amazingly fast despite the fact that—as David knew quite well—some of them were a lot worse off than he was.

The whole school crammed in, sitting shoulder to shoulder on the floor, and the big ones on the tables around the perimeter.

"You held yourselves well," Senrid said. "Your sortie across the river on Day Five was neatly carried out." He gave them a breath or two for whispers and murmurs, then said, "You and your instructors will go over the skirmishes in detail next week. In the meantime, I see some casualties that were not reported on the skirmish lists. Senelac? Your arm is in a sling. When?"

David waited—as did all the rest—to see what the dark-eyed, dark-haired, spectacularly bruised mauler would say. Interesting that Senrid began with that one.

"Fell off my horse, Senrid-Harvalder."

"I see. Ventdor? What's that, your knee is out? Why?"

Blackeye Ventdor rose, wincing in pain. "Fell off my horse, Senrid-Harvalder."

"Ah. Hamet? Collarbone broken? I don't remember seeing that on the casualty listings."

Hamet the bully stood up, his purple-and-rose decorated jaw corded. "Fell off my horse. Senrid-Harvalder."

"Farendaun? Another broken arm?"

"Fell off my horse, Senrid-Harvalder."

"It appears we have a rather clumsy group ostensibly leading the school. Can't have that, can we? What will the enemy think if they come back?" Senrid looked around, unsmiling. "I tell you what. We'll give you some thinking time, because you four are going to take the city guard's stable duties until Academy Games Day. You are also going to sweep the parade ground every morning before callover."

Pause. Silence.

Senrid added with wry cheer, "Anyone who also fell off his or her horse can feel free to help them out. Dismissed."

When they were gone, Senrid and David retreated to Senrid's study. David collapsed with a sigh.

"Did they hit you with more than four challenges, then?"

he asked.

"Five. Those were fairly routine. Though that Senelac is hot enough with his hands, especially backed up by Hamet. That one took a little effort."

"Then? What, last night?"

David nodded. "Our loss appears to have served as the excuse. At any rate one of them seems to have inspired the others to do a group drop on me. It was either break bones or else get my head kicked in."

Senrid frowned.

David offered: "Senelac called it off after I dislocated his shoulder."

"After. As in fair's fair?"

"I think that was the idea. At least, there were more of 'em waiting; they could have gotten me down." David half-lifted his left arm, and felt the strain in his shoulder. "I was running fresh out of bright ideas."

"Was it an ambush?"

David hesitated. "I think … let's say one of them might have wanted it to be, but a couple of his friends made sure I heard 'em coming. Since I didn't actually see who was speaking, and they sound a lot alike when whispering, I don't want to guess at names."

"Ah." Senrid sat back. "Is there any hope for them?"

David had been considering that very question the entire day. "For most of 'em, yes. But this wasn't the crisis. I don't know what that will be. Or if it'll be that easy. But this wasn't it."

"Thanks," Senrid said.

David waved a hand. "Until next time!" He transferred out.

The disirad mountain was, of course, dark, for in Sartor the night was midway over. The only light glowed in Adam's tent. David sat on his bedroll and—wincing and cursing—eased off his boots.

A tap at the tent frame.

"Yeah."

It was not exactly an invitation, but Adam and Sveneric entered anyway, Sveneric carrying a knapsack. Drawing paper stuck out at one corner, and a couple of paintbrushes protruded from a side-pocket.

"Ah," Adam said. "You are back, I see. Good. We're off."

"What?"

Sveneric grinned. Adam mimed surprise. "You had a week's vacation from the onerous chore of building Curtas's House, and I believe that you'll agree fair is fair, and now it's my turn. Leander has a translation project, and the River Eth is reputed to be the most beautiful in the world for wildflowers at this time of year."

Sveneric said, as Adam seemed to think that enough explanation, "We're going on a drawing expedition, and we hope to wind up the trip in Alsais to catch the tail end of the music festival, if the new king doesn't have us arrested on sight. We're counting on Leander to give us credence."

"Wait." David winced. "Wait. You're not serious."

"Yes," Adam said tranquilly. "As for your busy week: reflect upon the maxim that virtue is its own reward."

And they were gone.

❧ 11 ❧

David walked out the morning after they declared the house done. He paced a circle around the marked-out paths in the dirt, which was their nascent garden, admiring what Curtas had envisioned, though he had not lived to see it.

"Detlev's on his way," Adam commented, an easel with a chalk drawing set up before him.

"He contact you?"

"No," Adam replied serenely.

It was the disirad, David thought, looking over the riot of flowers spreading uphill toward the far plateau. They were all sensitive to it, but Adam seemed to be especially so. No wonder Detlev hadn't gone about organizing his dyranarya training in a formal sense yet. He probably wanted the two of them—and Lexan Glenereth and Jessan Delieth, who were rambling somewhere about—to get accustomed to the presence of the disirad, and what it did to thoughts and dreams

The new school was vaguely chevron-shaped, its windows angled to take advantage of the sun in all seasons. The evening before, David had seen the sun set over the distant western sea, throwing reddish reflections in the winter-sun west windows (so named because the north sun would be direct—the summer-sun windows would not get direct light, only reflected).

David finished his circle, wishing he could summon Curtas to see through his eyes as he looked in at the wide, shallow stair. He appreciated how the morning light flooded the open, airy central hall. "We did do a good job."

"But?" Adam murmured.

David decided he ought to resign himself to the fact that he was never going to block Adam completely.

"Missing Curtas," he admitted. "Now what?"

A familiar hoarse snicker caught their attention. MV? Coming from the big salle just off the entrance hall. That sound only escaped MV when he was fighting.

They went back inside and into the salle, where they found Detlev and MV involved in a fast game of what the boys used to call Touchie, a fight technique that required speed and control. Lexan Glenereth had come in through the other door, and froze, watching.

Both glanced at the doorway, then, in a blur of movement impossible to follow, Detlev backed away, smiling, and MV lay on the floor in defeat, laughing and cursing with characteristic fluency.

"What purpose is using fingertips and the sides of the hands so lightly?" Lexan asked, watching MV roll to his feet.

"You don't need to be punched to feel a touch, do you?" David answered, joining him. "The idea is to maintain fast speed, but limit the impact. It requires concentration and control. MV," he called. "Signing up for the student life?"

"*Shit* no," MV returned cordially as he wiped his hair out of his face and lounged against a long side-table bearing an impressive array of weaponry.

"MV stopped in briefly after his visit with Laban and Van before he resumes his travels," Detlev said in a bland voice.

"Yanked me in," MV stated. And, as he sent one of the knives flying across the room to slam dead center on a target. "Nice balance. Where'd ya get these?"

"They were a gift," Detlev said, with his usual amount of specific and copious detail. He turned to Adam and David. "The house here is complete, and so is your first group. Though, of course, you might eventually want to make additions or changes. The rest are down on the terrace at my house, waiting for you. I suggest you round everyone up and get them settled before they commence their studies."

David glanced at Lexan's stunned expression and closed his mouth firmly. Detlev's really enjoying himself, he noticed.

Don't give him the satisfaction—

Adam blinked once or twice, staring into the middle distance, and them looked up. "Second floor, with Jessan and Sveneric?"

Detlev gave a nod of assent, his face still deceptively blank, except for a suspicious narrowing of the eyes. "I do have one request to make. Not that I wish to interfere—what was that, David?"

"My teeth. Grinding. Do go on."

"Thank you. If they want to share a room, let them, otherwise there's space for everyone to have their own."

"That's it! Too much interference," David exclaimed, throwing up his hands. "I quit!"

Adam, however, was still gazing intently at something beyond the vision of those in the room. He blinked and glanced up. "What shall we teach them?"

"Whatever you like," Detlev said. Then turned away, beckoning. "MV?"

David met Adam's eyes: *Us? We're the teachers?*

: So it seems.

: Us. What kind of game is he playing? I know damn-all about dyra! I expected to be sitting with quill in hand listening to some formidable Old Sartoran academy master he'd spring on us, having been squirreled away somewhere all these centuries.

: I confess I did as well. But you know what he always said, that you learn most by teaching.

The exchange was rapid; the sound of the retreating footsteps hadn't died away before David broke off the contact, shook his head, and motioned to Adam, who closed in next to Lexan. Everyone shifted to Detlev's house, where very soon thirteen pairs of eyes waited expectantly in the big salon overlooking the terrace.

David stared in blank amazement. Adam slid his hand over his face—smearing chalk over his forehead—and gave himself up to silent laughter.

Behind them, Lexan leaned against a wall, and he too laughed inwardly. For against all his expectations, he now found himself among people who were very much like him, and he perhaps had a place in the world after all.

If the very first day of the new dyranarya school ever makes it into general records, David thought later, it will be a cause for universal mirth.

They did the round of names each wished to be called, then transferred their thirteen students up to the academy building

Three of the students, of course, had already been there, but for the sake of the other ten—actually for his own sake—David suggested a tour. He left most of the explaining to Adam as he struggling with inner question. Why would Detlev pull so cruel a joke on fifteen people, most of whom were total strangers? And why didn't David just leave, rather than fumble through so obvious a farce?

He wouldn't leave, he was too well trained for that, he thought with some bitterness. He'd wait, and stumble along, looking and feeling stupid, until Detlev returned and took over his rightful place as leader.

Damn. They were already back in the main hall, and the group still was mostly a clump of tight shoulders and sidelong glances, some clutching parcels of belongings to their chests, others empty-handed. A pang of sympathy unsettled David's annoyance, forcing his self-involved focus outward.

"… and we will trade off doing kitchen work." Adam gesture to David, handing them off.

"Go upstairs and choose your rooms," he said. Then, quoting Detlev, he added with inward irony, "You can have your own room or share. You can also trade the furnishings, which we brought in from all over the south here, and there are several baskets of clothing of various sizes, for various seasons. We can make straw shoes when the weather is nice. You'll see which room is mine by the cloak on the hook, and a pair of forest mocs—" He glanced down at his bare feet, and all thirteen pairs of eyes lowered, too. "—beside the bed. You'll know Adam's room by the papers all over."

He waved a hand, releasing them, and there was the muted thunder of feet trampling upstairs in a rush.

Adam pointed to the library, and as soon as they got there, he watched David shut the door and set his back to it. "I hate being set up," David admitted. "Maybe I ought to take off, before they feel it. Sveneric already feels it. I caught that much."

"Never mind Sveneric," Adam said. "Did you look at them?"

"Of course I did."

"What did you see?"

David gave a rueful snort. "A bunch of scared brats, mostly. Even Jessan was, a little, though he's been up here off and on since we began the building."

"And?" Adam asked.

David's eyes narrowed. "Of them, maybe two know how to move — ah." He snorted again. "Ah. Huh."

Adam saw the shift of paradigm, and rejoiced, though he did not betray it.

And David felt the shift as he muttered absently, "We two did spend a great deal of time up here during the war, did we not? And camping here before we began excavating the white stone?" But his thoughts raced beyond the fact that it would take time for their charges to get accustomed to the resonance of the disirad.

Instead, he looked back down his own life. He knew what training they needed before they could even begin thinking about dyra, much less how to use them. He knew what kind of training because he'd lived it. The best kind, and the worst, so he knew what mistakes to avoid.

As for Adam's and his own training as teachers, would that begin with interacting with people while in the presence of disirad? Yes, so it seemed. He said to Adam, "History, analysis, and rhetoric to begin with? Self-defense to get them moving?"

"I think so. Why don't you get them settled in? Outline a schedule?"

"Which will be — ?"

Adam shrugged. "Why not our old one? It's a schedule we're comfortable with. With a few emendations," he added wryly, and vanished on David's laugh.

David emerged from the library, and heard sounds from upstairs. He liked that sound, though he'd liked the peaceful silence before. He shut his eyes, reached — and felt Sveneric's quiet enjoyment. He'd taken charge of most of the furniture buying, sometimes alone, but mostly with Jessan along, to give Jessan a chance to see places that he'd never seen. Sveneric liked shifting from capital to capital, visiting artisans and buying handsome pieces in varying styles. Nothing absurdly ostentatious, though there was no limit on money; the boys had learned, after they'd switched sides, that Detlev had made investments centuries ago under his various personas that benefited various guilds, kingdoms, and other enterprises, and he had amassed a fortune. Several fortunes, actually.

And all of it, or a good portion, had been designated for this vision: his dyranarya school. No outside government or person controlled it. Anyone could join, background unimportant. The school would be completely self-supporting, like the Eriveidian House of Knowledge, which was nominally overseen by the Sartoran rulers, but hadn't been interfered with for over a thousand years or more. Their entire purpose was to find and copy records exactly as written —

Was that something of Detlev's as well?

David shook his head, trying to free it of centuries of typical Detlev Long Vision. He had enough to think about right here and now.

Sveneric's thought came: *They are done. Ready?*

: Bring 'em down.

Sveneric was probably going to be as much of a teacher as Adam or David, though he wouldn't pose as one. But of course they were all students, weren't they? Roles could be defined later. Thinking back over how their lives had evolved during his childhood, David decided that the fewer rules the better. At least at the beginning.

They didn't trample back down, but came more slowly, some alone, others in whispering couples. Learning one another's names. And — this time he really watched them — asking, or avoiding, questions.

"In here," he said, pointing. "This is where we eat, and for now it will do for general meetings."

As soon as they sat down, he said, "There won't be many rules as yet, because you've probably surmised that we're learning, too. For now, we'll begin with just this one: no questions about people's backgrounds. If they want to offer that information, it's up to them."

He saw four pairs of shoulders drop, and heard on the mental plane one great internal sigh of relief. Who was that? The girl over there in the corner. Ah, yes, Candra the Everoneth street thief.

He let his gaze drift on as he said, "Schedule will also start out simple enough. Mornings, we'll work on studies. Afternoons, on handling yourselves adequately. When the weather gets warm, we'll reverse those."

Jessan frowned slightly. "You're not gonna make us into poopsies, are you?"

"No," David said. "Some of the same training, yes. You need to know how to handle yourself so you can stay out of trouble, not cause it. The idea is to use your dyr, not knives, to solve problems, but if someone comes at you with steel, you can't just stand there gawking, right?"

A titter, still nervous.

Sveneric said, "Detlev hasn't told us much about the early dyranarya training, outside of the fact that people were dedicated to peace, so much so that when the Host came hunting them, they had no idea how to defend themselves. Many were taken, and used against others."

That hit home. They all seemed to know who Sveneric was. Of course he wouldn't exploit his identity, but neither would he hide it.

A girl said slowly, "But Detlev is the chief here, because he's a real dyranarya. Am I right?"

Sveneric smiled a little. "You'll see him up here from time to time, and he may even do some teaching. He might talk about the past, but seldom his part in it, unless it directly applies."

"And if we ask?" a boy ventured.

"You can ask him anything, but he has a habit of responding with a question, usually something that reflects on your motivation for asking."

David watched the group consider that. They were all smart, and curious, and probably subtle, of course, or they wouldn't be here. Most were Detlev's picks, but not all. David knew that Adam had chosen one or two, and a couple had been put forward by people Detlev knew. Nor were these all; others had been ... what would you call it? Invited? Designated? David thought of Retren Ndarga, and Yanli, and even Liere Fer Eider, all three of whom Detlev had mentioned as likely candidates. But they had to want to come, to be ready to come.

For them, and others, it might very well be years.

Well. That for later contemplation.

"So, if you have questions for me, how about we get to them over a meal?" David said, when the silence had gone on too long. "Tomorrow we can divide up the chores, for there won't be any servants up here. We'll cook and clean for ourselves, though we do have the usual magic aids. Cleaning buckets and the like. You'll learn how to renew the spell."

As he went on to demonstrate the various spells they'd designed, he assessed the candidates as much as he could. Interviews tomorrow, he decided. One at a time, because he had to get to know their names. Casual, no standing before desks, but while they walked, or cooked, or did other things.

The atmosphere eased as they ate, the laughs more genuine and less self-conscious or nervous. What next? He'd decide that when the time came.

It was going to work, it seemed. Amazing.

And best of all, he hadn't thought about Marga for an entire day.

✦ **12** ✦

On the surface, the second year of the Marloven Academy Games went better as far as David was concerned.

Though the seniors had not seen him since the previous year, they remembered him well enough to snap to his orders, even his suggestions, and no one dared disturb his tent in the night. In fact, they seemed to be somewhere else altogether, but there was no rule that David was aware of keeping the seniors tied to their tents. If they wanted to run off to drink, or carouse, he mentally shrugged: they would learn the cost before dawn the next day.

As each day of the wargame progressed, his awareness of the seething river of anger and grief and bloodlust intensified. It still ran hot. He braced for trouble when the anniversary of the invasion approached. Everyone was aware of it. But except for an added vigor in the skirmishes, the day passed without further incident.

If he discounted a whiff of intent, of teenage gloating. Of anticipation.

At least the Games would be over before the anniversary of Marloven Hess's surrender occurred. If Senrid asked him to return, he would, but as the blazing, dry days wore on, he longed the more to get back to Curtas's House. Adam seemed to understand that the Marloven youths were stirring up memories David would rather not revisit, and used farsense each evening to share the minutiae of the day. Each cool, quiet, day.

The wargame ended without untoward incident, though by now David sensed something amiss. But Senrid, who had been more preoccupied by the day, dismissed them to prepare for the competitions portion of the Games, which the city always came out to watch, and as he didn't ask David to stay, David transferred back to Curtas's House, relieved to have that over.

Adam eyed him late the night of his return. "You seem a little too relieved."

"I hate that," David retorted. "Stop it!"

"Guilt?" Adam asked, as if David hadn't spoken.

"I probably ought to have stayed. Something is going on. But it's Senrid's kingdom. I'm as fake an heir as it's possible to be with a king's collusion. And he didn't ask me to stay. Whatever it is, he'll handle it."

Two mornings after that, Erol appeared for the first time, looking very out of place in his black Chwahir uniform. "This is nice," he said. "I know it was impossible, but I wish we'd had it."

"We never would have appreciated it," David groused.

No one argued. Though they were all thinking of Curtas, and of course Adam was right there. They knew that both Curtas and Adam would have been happy there, so happy no one would have been able to get them to go anywhere else.

It was Adam who said, "You are welcome anytime, but it seems you're here because of trouble?"

"Yes. No," Erol said. "Not with Jilo. He's taking it slow. He's managed to ward a few who want the old ways back, and I've warded more of them. Winters are tough, but the Chwahir are used to that. It's Retren Ndarga," he admitted.

"I know the Sartoran Mage Guild made it clear he was very much on probation," David said.

Erol's expression soured. "Atan apologized for that. Blamed the war. You can guess the rest. The fact is, they still are wary of Marlovens, so Mondros brought him back, though he's going to go sailing with Puddlenose. He'll probably be ready for you two after that, is my guess. He wants to have it all."

"Why not?" Adam said. "He'll come when he comes. Getting in a couple of years is all to the good. But...?"

Erol's sallow skin flushed dark. "This is nothing more than snooping, but he had a nightmare. I heard him, and, well, listened in. You know I'm no good at sorting the sensory jumble…" He closed his eyes, and shared what he'd seen.

Adam flinched. "I'll leave you to it," he said to David, his gaze bleak. "The weather is excellent. I'll take them down to do the trail ride today, to spot and identify different types of rootstalk."

Erol said to David, "I don't know any of the people in that nightmare. I don't even know how much is real. I hope it's not real," he added under his breath.

"It's real," David said heavily. "I'm fairly certain that the dream is a memory from his sister. Let me think." He walked out, angry, disturbed, and furious with himself for having ducked out of an unpleasant duty when he ought to have stuck it out.

Presently he went to Leander, who was staying with Adam at Curtas's House while they worked on a translation of one of the precious sanctuary texts, and asked, "When was Senrid's little daughter's birthday? Wasn't it around the same time as the Marloven surrender?"

Leander's smile vanished. "Yes, day before. Twelfth of this month. She was killed just short of turning five."

"Tomorrow," David said.

After a restless night, David rose before dawn, and made himself eat something. When it was about four in the morning in Marloven Hess, David started toward his room to put on his Marloven clothes, then halted. If he was about to end this farce, why bother changing?

He transferred, and ran up to the residence wing of Senrid's castle, which was off-limits to everybody but Senrid and service staff. He topped the stairs, wondering if he'd be stopped. The guards let him pass; his mood was so bleak he found he was sorry.

He ran soundlessly down the hall, to what had been Crystal Ingrid's room. Light spilled out. There, sure enough, he found Senrid, and David understood just how much Senrid hated his appearance by his total lack of reaction. "Laying ghosts?" he asked.

Still no reaction. "The sunlight is good through those windows. I was thinking that this end of the wing might serve as classrooms for the academy."

David was very certain that Senrid only came here once a year. Today would have been Crystal Ingrid's eighth birthday. He also knew that on the anniversary of Crystal Ingrid's death, the previous year, Senrid had been nowhere to be found. Probably holed up somewhere, alone, getting skunked. He'd probably done the same this year as well—and the next day, he'd presided over that travesty of justice...

"The problem," David said, moving farther into the room, his steps causing dust motes to spiral up in a cloud of fiery pin-points, "is neglectful housekeeping."

He leaned against the still-dark window, arms crossed. "Senrid, I understand why those flags are in the throne room. The problem with a bare room as a memorial is that it tends to commemorate only the worst moment of the person's life."

Senrid stood there unmoving except for a muscle twitching in his jaw.

David tried again. "I wonder if Imry ever came in here?"

Senrid shot him a fast glance, which told David he'd nearly succeeded in breaking that wall of ice. Then Senrid said, in that blandly indifferent tone, "There must be some reason why you're trying to provoke me."

"I'm trying to be helpful. If you want to pound Imry—which I completely understand—I'm here to offer you the next best thing."

"Is that an invitation?" Senrid said, the edges of his teeth showing in a semblance of a smile. "You didn't get enough of that on the Games? What do you do on your mountaintop?"

He walked out on the last word, leaving the candles burning and the door wide. David sauntered after him. "Whom? I? Peaceful book-studies, translating. Discussing—we get in a lot of that. Then there's weeding the vegetable garden, for excitement."

Senrid slanted a sardonic glance his way. "And no contact-fighting in the two-hour watch before dawn?"

That was Senrid's daily routine. "Oh, not before dawn," David said. "We're civilized on our mountain-top." Coward, he thought. Using humor gives him an out. Get to it. "Unlike the recent ritual dismemberment of that miserable sod Imry first put in charge here after the city's surrender. Neglected to tell me about that?"

They reached Senrid's study. Senrid sat down behind his desk before observing, "I wondered when some self-righteous ass would come around to howl about that. I didn't think it would be you."

"Pardon my hypocrisy," David retorted in exactly the same tone.

Senrid's sharp cheekbones betrayed a hint of color. "I didn't know," he said flatly. "Until it happened. They maneuvered covertly, using all their skills to set it all up. And when Senelac, Ventdor, and their two conspirators proudly presented me with their prisoner, witnesses ready to speak, and spectators gathered to judge, I probably could have contacted you, but I didn't know what would happen."

David was so surprised at his wrong guess that the meaning beneath that simple admission at the end passed right by.

Senrid said, still in that flat, detached tone, "They conducted the trial, and the hours that took were because of the number of first-hand witnesses who demanded their right to be heard. The sentence was also theirs, also according to law. A foregone conclusion. I merely presided. I did not speak."

David lounged in the other chair. "Isn't that odd! How dense I am not to realize you were constrained to inaction according to some centuries-old edict, no doubt passed by one of your worst kings!"

"Get to your point."

"My point is that nobody within a week's ride scratches their ass without first inquiring your policy on itches." As Senrid began to say something scathing, David flung up a lazy hand to cut him off. "That four-hour execution went on because you allowed it. You could have stopped that legal lynching any time by lifting a finger. But you didn't."

Senrid let out a short sigh. "Who was your witness?"

"Retren Ndarga lifted the memory from his sister. In the form of a nightmare. I don't know if it was hers or his. Erol alerted me."

"I said." Senrid's voice was so devoid of tone it was like someone else speaking. "I did not know what would happen. Once I understood the whole, I let it go to the end to kill their bloodlust. I knew what it would be like. As a young boy I was forced to witness far too many such scenes, staged by my uncle when he was regent. By the third hour those boys'd had a bellyful. So had most of the spectators, and I watched to see who was enjoying it. There were six. I know who they are."

David grimaced.

"At the end, I still did not speak, but let them contemplate the fact that all that effort had brought them absolutely nothing, save that bloody mess in the parade ground."

David opened his hand. He was beginning to perceive how wrong he'd been. First, he needed to listen.

Senrid said, "Senelac and Ventdor were still expecting me to hail their prowess in the track and hunt. I walked out. Nothing happened, except that the crowd dispersed. I waited a night. So did they. In the morning I sent them off to spend the winter boat scraping and night sentry duty at the outpost on Tarual Harbor, under the eye of the Iascans."

"Who won't be impressed with them."

"Not in the least. As for the two clever would-be desk jockeys, they are as we speak translating the entire archive of old laws, so that I can go through and rescind the worst of it. If they comply, I will assign them to recopy the new laws. And if that transpires, I'm evolving a new plan."

David ventured a remark at last. "Imry might find that execution an irresistible challenge."

"Already happened," Senrid said, not saying how or where. "I handed the matter over to Jan Senelac, to chase or not as he and his coverts wish. I expect Imry finds them boring. He ought to know by now that he's warded against entering this city. I'm not going to stir five steps to chase him no matter how much he might want the attention, until I know I can slit his throat." Senrid sat back. "Inquest over?"

"Your evolving plan?" David asked. "The last plan you told me about was the eventual dismantling of the army. You said last year that plan was set back a generation, at least."

"Maybe not. Since I still seem to be here, why not move things up a few years." Senrid's hands had reappeared, one drumming on the desk. "As I said, they got nothing. Certainly no praise from me. Though I absolutely understand wanting a physical sign of our victory over Norsunder."

David accepted that. Human nature being what it is.

"I've spent two years putting the army back together. Learning who they are. What they can do, for a good number of them have infirmities. Everyone rebuilt the academy — everyone, from old instructors down to the city urchins. Even old Keriam was seen sweeping rubble, till felled by another syncope. They were proud that we were able to begin that spring, in spite of Norsunder's attempt to obliterate the academy."

David exclaimed, "So your plan is rebuilding?"

"Exactly. We're still in for lean winters and tough springs, as the treasury pretty much went to feeding us all that first winter. But I don't see that as an effective way to rebuild the kingdom, popular as the crown providing all might be. Better to rebuild in ways that last, and if I'm right, the treasury, and the kingdom, will regain balance the faster."

"That's strategic. No argument. Tactically? You have a kingdom full of warriors still hot to ride against the enemy."

"We're going to triumph by eradicating every sign of the enemy, as if they were never here. I saw it in the rebuilding of the academy. I need to make that attitude kingdom-wide. I'll hand rebuilding out as orders. My test will be nearby, a locale everyone knows. Like the academy was. Everyone — army, merchants, all between — complains bitterly about the North Road bridge. No one wants a fine gallop interrupted by a meandering and wet crossing by raft."

David grunted, then gave Senrid a look. "Except I remember Jan Senelac telling me that his company destroyed that bridge to slow down the invasion from the north, which means Norsunder actually didn't destroy it. And I also remember you going about lifting the wards on at least a dozen other bridges, which your people then sabotaged."

Senrid's lip curled. "We got pretty good at it, too. And I think it helped us, at the end, because we knew the safest crossings, and they didn't. Mostly. Anyway, whoever flooded roads and took down bridges, it was still a part of the war. I'm going to try it with the first-level seniors next year. Which will include Senelac, Ventdor, and Marend Ndarga, among others." He paused, then said, "Retren Ndarga. I take it he's back in Chwahirsland?"

"Only until Puddlenose gets to the strait. He wants to try

his hand at sailing, then I expect he'll turn up on my mountaintop."

"How is Jilo? We haven't spoken since last winter."

"He got labor flowing over the mountains into Colend.
There were problems at first, but workers, especially skilled
ones, are so sought that those being exploited simply downed
tools and walked…"

"… and as he could have written to Jilo any time," David
finished later, when he was alone with Detlev and Adam, "I
took that question as a sign that I wasn't about to be turfed out
of my heirship. I don't know if I'm to be glad or not. The only
thing I'm sure of was that I completely misread the situation,
drawing from Marend's memory of that execution. I could
blame the distortion of nightmare, except I know how to see
past dream symbols."

Adam and Detlev sat amidst a moat of old manuscripts
from the sanctuary under the Ghost Lakes, but they both gave
David their whole attention as he repeated the rest of the
conversation. "I thought he was hiding it from me because he
knew I'd argue."

Adam looked down at the books as Detlev said, "You see
you were wrong, but I suspect you still don't see how much."

"What?" David sighed. "I wish I'd slept last night. What
am I missing now?"

"What does every king fear most? No, don't say war,
though recent events might bring it to mind first. There remain
enough kings who use war to bolster their own esteem, to hide
their problems, to refill an empty treasury. Think again."

"Oh. Right. They fear an overthrow."

"Exactly. You were seeing that incident as a step toward
tyranny. It was a legitimate fear, if a wrong supposition. I
suspect Senrid, in retrospect, would even find your reaction
reassuring."

"Somehow I doubt that, judging by *his* reaction."

Detlev turned his palm up. "Oh, he did not like being
accused of lying to you any more than he liked the imputation
of bloody-mindedness. But there's, ah, call it a corollary that I
think you need to consider, which is related to your equally
logical attempt to break past what you call his ice wall."

Adam looked up. "He said, twice, *I didn't know what would happen.*"

"None of us know what will happen—ah." David winced. "Ugh."

Detlev got up and left, as David muttered, "Stupid, stupid. 'I waited a night. So did they.' And, 'If that happened.' He didn't know if they were going to assassinate him and put in some bloodsucker who would lead the Marlovens in a revenge ride all the way up to Larkadhe, eh?"

"And he was going to face it alone," Adam said.

"In other words, let them kill him. It would be the last betrayal, wouldn't it, if the Marlovens turned against him? Suicide by rebellion. That's what he thought he was seeing, when they only wanted to surprise him. I really blundered, didn't I? For my reward all I came away with was Senrid's headache." David thumbed his eye sockets, then dropped his hands. "Detlev just as much as told me I lost the long view, didn't he."

Adam blinked, his gaze diffuse. Then he murmured, slowly, "I don't want to say anything, because I was not at your encounter, and I haven't seen Senrid for a long time."

"You don't have to. I'll say it for you: Yes, David, that really was a double-bladed Detlev doomer, and you grassed yourself badly. Not just the wrong guess about that damned parade ground spectacle, but the attack on the ice wall when I found him rubbing salt in the still-bleeding wounds, there in Crystal Ingrid's room."

"The Senrid I used to know loathed pity," Adam said, looking back down at his moat of ancient records that people long ago had written in faith that someone among their children's children would seek their hard-won wisdom.

"Still does."

"I'm sure the Senrid of today wouldn't tolerate sympathy any better," Adam said. "But every living thing can use a little kindness."

David said nothing. Inwardly he resolved that from now on, he would keep his mouth shut on that anniversary, and make himself available in as unobtrusive a way as possible.

"Now, about the schedule for the first field run…"

While they were talking, Detlev slid between Curtas's House and his house. He felt no sense of ownership, though he and Curtas had planned it together, discussing every detail so that Curtas could write it all up to submit for his mastery sved. He welcomed the intensity of this liminal awareness of Curtas's benevolent presence, though it came, always, with the knife of regret.

He'd begun reading a report from Ferret when Sveneric walked in. A glance, and Detlev laid aside the paper with a serious air.

Sveneric flushed, his smile twisted. "How do you gauge us? I know I'm not projecting."

"Habit. What's amiss?"

Sveneric migrated to the window seat where David habitually perched. "I went to see Erenlara. She'd invited me to one of their events, where they perform special music that only is done when the lights dance over the Venn sky. Soon as I saw her, I knew something was wrong."

"Is she ill?" Detlev asked.

"No, but if she persists doing whatever it is she's doing, I think she will be. If she doesn't kill herself first. I wish you'd go talk to her."

"Why can't you talk to her?"

"Because she won't tell me what's wrong! She would only say she practices magic at night. That's after finishing a day schedule that would kill one of *us*. I think it's not merely magic practice. I think she's going off somewhere at night, but after I tried to question her, and got walled, I picked up thoughts from one of her attendants. Very worried. Eren supposedly goes to sleep at night, and in the morning when they prepare her bath, she turns up with bruises, once a knife wound!"

"It sounds as if she puts herself through some sort of rough training run."

"Or worse," Sveneric said. "I did ask her, and when I said that even queens benefit from sleep, she said in a voice I barely heard, *When I am worthy.* Where did she get that? I never met the brother, of course, but from everything I've learned he was excellent, but not driven. Same with the old queen."

"It doesn't matter where she got it. That attitude has to end."

"Yes! I was hoping you might go talk to her."

Detlev frowned outside the window. "No. I'm not an authority in her life, and ought not to become one. She has a sufficiency of guides up there." He smiled a little. "She doesn't need more authorities, she needs someone to argue with. I think you ought to handle it; this will be an excellent learning experience for you. Recruit CJ of the Mearsieans, maybe?"

"I hadn't thought of her at all. Eren really liked CJ, who made her laugh. Made her play."

Detlev said, "CJ is still grieving over releasing the Child Spell. Why don't you invite her to go north with you, and bring her particular perspective. Eren might be able to do her some good as well."

"Perspective," Sveneric repeated, his tone warming. "Yes, I'll do that. Erenlara really, really needs to laugh. And perhaps CJ's cock-eyed opinions will get her to see how ridiculous is her sense of unworthiness."

"Do that." Detlev's nod conveyed, unspoken, his trust in Sveneric's ability to surmount this difficulty. Sveneric felt it, and left grinning.

In the doorway he almost rammed into Adam, who looked thoughtfully at that proud grin, then passed inside the study. "Did you know before David mentioned it that Imry is back in the world?"

"Is he?"

"You knew, then." Adam did not look surprised. "Are you doing anything about it?"

"Leave him be for now."

"But you're not doing anything."

"That doesn't mean nothing is being done. I'm not saying more because if Imry does contact you, it would be better if you knew nothing of his doings."

Adam stared at his paint-stained, misshapen thumbnail for a few heartbeats—he had taken off his gloves to make tiny comments in the margins of a translation—then looked up. "Yes, I see, he'd hate the sense that we're hovering. Very well. Back to work."

"Adam."

Adam paused in the doorway.

"Go ahead and begin wearing it. Listening with it. Your

handling of Clair's start toward recovery was excellent. Nevreath would have chosen you to pass her dyr to. It's yours."

Adam flushed, his eyes stinging. Somehow he'd thought if he ever became a dyranarya, there would be trumpets and heralds and banners and singing. It would be a pinnacle, beyond with was the empyrean of wisdom. He saw now that such things were milestones on the upward path of learning.

He walked away, beaming with joy.

✦ 13 ✦

Not long after dawn in early autumn, and already the sky curved overhead, a polished sapphire bowl. Hannla Thasis looked out her window onto Blossom Street. The orange trees were in full bloom now, their fragrance delicious. She walked through the house, opening windows and doors. Though she felt no breeze, the stuffy air, stale with the previous night's aromas of candles, wine, food, and overheated humans, began to dissipate before fresh morning air.

She leaned in the front door. It felt good to breathe while reviewing the morning tasks, a formidable list that vanished when she saw a familiar figure appear directly before her, blinking as though dazed.

"Hlareas?"

Her daughter: small, round, a cloud of curling light brown hair, honey-brown eyes wide set, her ears sticking out, her nose just a button. Hannla smiled, adoring her daughter all over again, for she had not seen her for three months.

Hlareas blinked rapidly, then drew in a shuddering breath. "Oh, Mama!" Hlareas exclaimed joyfully, cheeks and chin dimpling. "It's so good to be home! Though it's boiling here."

"Is it balmy on that mountaintop?" Hannla asked.

"Very. That is, it gets hot at noon, but then the breeze comes straight down the waterfall and through the halls, and brings with it all the fragrances of the flowers on the plateau."

"What an exquisite image!"

Hlareas clasped her tiny hands. Hannla noticed new muscle contour in her round upper arms. "It is exquisite. But I have been so homesick!"

"And you couldn't come home because…"

"Because I was too silly to ask," Hlareas stated, looking rueful, and Hannla's catalogue of worries eased somewhat.

"Come inside. Have you breakfasted?"

"Oh, yes. Just now."

"Keep me company while I eat, then, and tell me all about your mysterious mountaintop school."

Most of the house was still abed, especially those who had retired at dawn, their work ended. But Hannla had relinquished that part of the profession. She was now administrator, mediator, and sympathetic ear.

She and her daughter walked quietly through the house to the kitchens, where the pastry-cook was already done with the day's bread; from the looks of his tired face and the warmth in the room, he'd finished the baking well before dawn, so as not to further heat the house after the sun rose.

"It's wonderful," Hlareas whispered as Hannla snagged a cooling roll, and some fruit compote to put on it.

"Not a military camp, then."

"No. But I heard Adam promise you it wouldn't be."

"I had my doubts. The queen insisted that Detlev doesn't lie, but I thought that his idea of 'not a military camp' and mine might vastly differ."

Hlareas stared at her mother in surprise. "I did not know you had so much doubt. If you did, why did you let me go?"

"Because…" Hannla spread her hands, trying to find the right answer. Because Atan thought it would provide insight into the workings of Detlev's mind, to see what and how he taught? Because you are something special, have been from birth, and I must give you every opportunity to find your future self? "Oh, I don't know. Because that Adam can be very convincing, especially with Detlev standing there behind him."

Hlareas sensed her mother's ambivalence. Underneath it lay more ambivalences, and a kind of inner sorrow. But it was private, briefly glimpsed, and so Hlareas resolutely closed herself off from probing. Before she went away, she'd prided herself on being the youngest one in the house, yet the only one who could see through everyone's shields. She'd learned in her three months away that "seeing" was not always understanding. Which sometimes caused harm.

They stepped through the kitchens to the little room beyond, where the household could take quiet meals when they did not want to interact with patrons.

"Tell me about it," Hannla said, spreading compote on her bread.

"Oh, there is so much to tell! Where to begin? When I got there I found out I was the youngest, but all the girls treated me like a little sister. I liked them all!"

"How many of you are there?"

"Thirteen. Eight of us are girls," Hlareas said proudly. "When we finally went up from Detlev's house to Curtas's House, I chose a room that faces east, because Eidervaen is just over the mountains from me, and I feel closer to home that way.

"Detlev's house. Curtas's House. Now, what is the difference?"

"Just that. Curtas's House is the name of our school. Detlev's house is where he stays, though he says it belongs to them all. People come and go there, many of whom I don't know. It's upland from the coast below the mountains where the academy is located. We travel between the two by a kind of magic sign that they set up, that makes it slightly easier for transfers. Otherwise it would take at least a couple weeks to travel back and forth. Probably longer. I know nothing about how you travel in mountains."

"No more do I," Hannla said, smiling. "Detlev has mysterious guests, does he?"

"In the sense that no one asks who they are. Just as David told us we were not to ask one another's backgrounds in our academy unless the information was offered."

"Was that a delicacy provided for your protection, do you think?" Hannla's brows quirked in irony.

Hlareas shook her head.

Hannla said, "You have grown up learning some of the outward etiquette of pleasure houses. Perhaps you are old enough to understand why."

"Oh, I've been thinking about it," Hlareas declared. "How odd grownups are! I know it's quite all right for people to talk about going to pleasure houses to friends, or family, or even make up a party to do so, but I haven't lived here all my life

without figuring out that the people who work here can't talk
socially about their own profession or they cross some kind
of—" She waved her hands.

"The invisible boundary of privacy," Hannla said.

Hlareas chuckled. "Like clothes! Everyone is naked under
them, but we agree not to say so. I do know that a gabby person
who works upstairs would get no more custom. But that rule at
Curtas's House wasn't made for me. It was for some that I think
might have been outlaws of some sort. No one looked at me
when he first said it. Or even away, like people do. But I saw
several were relieved when David told us that, almost first
thing."

"Ah. Hadn't thought of outlaws." Hannla frowned, apprehensive at the idea of her daughter living with outlaws. It
might depend on what made an outlaw an outlaw. That
required further thought. Anyway, her child was right here,
obviously unharmed. "Tell me about your day."

"We begin quite early. Adam and David are up even
earlier," she added, and looked rather conscious.

"Go on."

"We begin class with history studies, and linguistics. They
both insist that seeing how language has shaped and reshaped
itself gives insight into the forming of cultures, though I confess
I don't see it yet. We read literature, talking about the minds of
the writers, and the people in the poems or stories or histories.
I like that best. We do maths, which I hate because it's so easy
it's tedious, after helping you with accounts since I was small.
We do self-defense classes afternoons, though some do it in the
morning, too. And we study the world. You know, geography,
and weather patterns, and different kinds of plants and why
they grow here and not there, and so forth. I am not very good
in that. I sometimes daydream."

"Do they remonstrate with you?"

"No. But there are certain things you must know before
you get to go on the field excursions, like canoeing, or sailing,
or things like that."

"Interesting. What does Detlev teach?"

"He doesn't."

"What?"

"It's Adam and David who teach most, though not all.

Sveneric teaches a lot of the history classes, only he doesn't think of it as teaching. He thinks of it as a kind of discussion group, where we share our reading. But he's read the most. Let's see... Everyone has to mend their own clothes, and they asked me to teach that, and embroidery to those who want to learn it. Demac teaches tiranthe to those who like music. Jessan Delieth and Lexan Glenereth do the horse lessons. Ascol shows us cooking. And so on."

"Why do you mend your own clothes?"

"We're to be self-sufficient when we leave. Adam was going to have us make our own clothes, too, and you should have seen everyone stare! But then David said *Wait. Wait. WE don't know how to make clothes!* And Adam looked around, and blinked, like he does sometimes, as if he just woke up, and said, *Ought we to learn?* And David said, *I can't teach anyone how to make trousers that I'd trust on a long hike.* Then Adam got the idea that we ought to barter with one another for some of the things we can't easily do for ourselves. It's funny, sometimes, being the very first group in over four thousand years! We also have to take turns cooking and cleaning, though there are magic aids."

"Why must you be self-sufficient, if you are to learn a skill that presumably will earn you good money?"

"But we won't go out as dyranarya. We'll earn our way some other way, as we're to never take pay for using the dyra."

"Never take pay?" Hannla repeated.

"It's like the healers' guild in many lands. They can't take pay, so that the poor will get exactly as much care as the wealthy. The guilds subscribe, or the crown supports them. Only no crown will support *us*. I might go out as a seamstress, because I don't know that I'd want to work in any pleasure house but ours."

"And maybe not ours," Hannla reminded her. "You have plenty of time to decide that."

"Oh, I might," Hlareas said, considering, as she so often did, the haze that seemed to obscure her future path. "What I like is the way people feel, afterward." She tapped the middle of her forehead.

"Tell me more," Hannla said, busying herself with another piece of bread so that her daughter would not descry how closely she was being watched and listened to.

But Hlareas wasn't fooled. Even though here at sea level there seemed to be a soft cotton blanket over her inner senses — she'd been told to expect that, after getting used to the Singing Mountain sensitivity — she'd still learned, even in three short months, some of the subtle clues of body that gave hints to what went on in minds.

She admitted, her face warming, "I, um, really like looking at Adam. Is that a crush? You told me about crushes once, but I wasn't really listening."

"Ah. Do you really know him?"

"Uh uh. That is, only as a teacher."

"Do you want kisses and hugs?"

"Eew! No! I want him to notice me. To … to find me interesting and wonderful the way I find him. But," she sighed, "he and David said almost the first day that we students could be with each other that way if we want, but not with them. Not until after we graduate."

Hannla pursed her lips. "I am relieved about that rule, I confess."

Hlareas chuckled. "Why, did you think there was going to be more flirting than learning? Ha, ha! That first week, we saw that we had no mirrors. At first we all assumed that it was to a purpose, but one girl had come with gowns that laced up the back, and she had an awful time with neither servants nor mirror, and one day she got mad at David and said she had to have one or the other."

"And?"

Hlareas laughed. "He and Adam looked so foolish! It hadn't been to a purpose, it had been oversight. We not only got mirrors in our rooms, if we wanted, but David decided that we needed them in the practice salle, so we could see our mistakes."

"Interesting. And Detlev lets them make their own way?"

"Yes. He comes to visit sometimes, but as yet he only talks to a few people — not me, yet — and then goes away again."

"Hummm."

"Anyway, not long after we got the mirrors, Adam was out on his balcony in the morning, and the sun was quite bright. And I saw him take this knife in one hand, and his ponytail in the other hand, and he sawed it all off, like this—" Hlareas demonstrated sawing behind her head. "Then he disappeared the hair, and never even looked in a mirror, or felt the edges to see if they're even. Not that you could tell, for it's all over curls on his head." She gave a little sigh. "I would like to embroider all his scruffy old shirts, and tidy the stitching. But I don't think he'd even notice."

Hannla smothered a laugh. She herself had begun to have crushes at about age eight, though she hadn't done anything about them for another ten years.

"Go on," she said. "I confess I am intrigued. They are not teaching you to be assassins or fierce warriors, then?"

"No, and some of the group are very disappointed." Hlareas pronounced these words with some satisfaction.

"Oh?"

"When we first arrived—very first—there were all kinds of nasty-looking weapons in the room they call the salle, which is where we do our practicing. But by the next day they'd vanished, and a couple of the boys and this one girl even went hunting for them. And David told us—very firmly—that we were only going to learn self-defense. No weapons, even, until we can disarm someone with our hands."

Hannla frowned. "But that sounds more dangerous than a duel."

"You'd think so, wouldn't you?" Hlareas said. "But it works, if you know what to do. How to move, when to fall. Not that any of us can, yet, but we've seen them do it. In fact, the third day, David brought out those knives and things and invited anyone who wished to come at him with one, and they did, and he took 'em all away again. Even from Lexan, though that was quite a fight, and David ended up getting this cut. Eugh, it was quite disgusting. Though they didn't get mad or anything. Not even David."

Hannla shuddered, frowning.

Hlareas hesitated, saying tentatively, "They don't want to teach anyone the bad stuff, but some of the others really want to learn it. I don't," Hlareas said in a rush, "I hate it. That MV comes around, and he's a real assassin, you can just tell. When he teaches us, everyone gets slammed around. It's horrid. I much prefer Mildred, who has come twice with MV. She's just as fast—she can dump MV—but she's kind with us. There's something in the way they move their bodies—"

She paused, her head canted. "Well, let me begin at the beginning. See, few get up really early. I do, because I always have. But I discovered a few weeks ago, when the weather was nice, and I went walking up above the waterfall so I could look down and see it in the morning light. I looked back at the house, and there was Adam on the balcony outside his room, doing this … this kind of a sword dance, sort of." She swept a hand in defensive blocks high, and then low, but in a sustained movement that did resemble dance even to her mother's critical eye.

"And?"

"And it's not warlike, though they do it with a sword. How can I explain? It's … when Adam does it, at least, it's grace. Sveneric as well. Some days it's the three of them together. But most times David seems to go up on the plateau with Sveneric, and only Adam is on his balcony."

"And?"

"And that's it. I love watching Adam. He's so graceful. It's like watching a hawk soaring on the wind, just moving the outer feathers…" Hlareas closed her eyes, her arms outflung, her fingertips arced. Then she opened her eyes. "And it's not the same with David. He's graceful too, but he can change, quite suddenly, and be warlike, and he enjoys it. He grins, and he dashes and flashes like that MV, if they practice together."

"But Adam doesn't."

Hlareas shook her head so vehemently her curls bounced over her shoulders. "No. Though he can. There was a time when that MV was here, and at the end of one of our lessons, he set out all these sharp knives, instead of us using the dull wooden ones, or our hands. Adam said to put them away—and MV said he was going soft, and threw knives *right at* Adam. We all froze, like a bunch of stones, and David was over at the window laughing so hard he wheezed."

Hannla frowned. "And?"

Hlareas lifted her hands. "And so Adam caught them. Right out of the air! And then he tossed the knives up high, and then juggled them! MV just kept throwing them, until he had all eight."

"Eight! Eight knives, with sharp sides?"

"Yes. Both sides! I was so terrified, I couldn't help counting. Adam juggled them, and then he said, *Target, MV.* And MV went over—even when he moves it's like he wants to start a fight—and stood flat against the big target, and then, quite suddenly, Adam threw the knives right at MV."

"You did not tell me anyone had gotten killed, or hurt."

"That's because no one did. Those knives all went like this—" Hlareas made a fist and thumped the table several times. "Right around MV into the target. And when I say around, I mean close. So close that his shirt was pinned, here and here and here, and his trousers down both sides. David had to free him. The two were laughing fit to fall over, and after he was free, with holes all over his clothes, MV said, *Mildred was right.* And he went away by magic, and David was still laughing when he fisted Adam on the shoulder and said that he was going to be laughing over that for the next ten years."

"Then?" Hannla asked.

"Then nothing. Though everyone was whispering at dinner, Adam started the lesson about translation as if nothing happened. And when when MV taught us this week, it was back to our wooden knives."

Hannla frowned. "Well. I must admit I have had severe doubts about the wisdom of handing you over to them, though the idea of the dyra, of mind-healing, is so very important. But since you've been gone, I've wondered what they mean when they say heal."

Hlareas said, "You can always ask when they come to get me."

Hannla's brows rose. "They are coming here?"

Hlareas shrugged, looking a question. "When I asked Adam if I could have a day home, he said, after a wait—he is so very absent minded, sometimes it takes him a long time to answer the simplest question—*Of course you can. We will see you this evening, how's that?* It sounds like they'll come for me, doesn't it?"

"It does indeed," Hannla said, intensely curious now, and mentally rearranged her schedule. "Come along," she said, rising. "I hear people astir. You can help me by silk-stitching fresh lace onto the winter curtains. I took them out of the storage chest where I'd put them when the attack first came, and there wasn't time last year, you remember..."

Nightfall on the mountain. Adam stood in the doorway of the refectory and watched the group around the far table.

"I don't care how bad you say you are," Jessan Delieth declared. "Anyone can tap a drum, or a tambourine."

"The idea is to listen to one another, and try to harmonize," Tcherys added reasonably. But Tcherys was always reasonable.

From behind Adam, David said, "They're busy. We'd better fetch Number Thirteen before we forget about her. You, or I?"

Adam's mind winged out in a spiral of connections. David — time — Hlareas — Detlev saying, on his second visit, *Teaching is sometimes likened to marriage, for you not only cleave to another, you take on the person's family.* There was a reason Detlev had insisted on Hlareas being one of the group, Adam knew that, though in some ways she was very young, and could have waited another year.

"Adam." That was David, sounding exasperated.

"Sorry." Adam ducked his head in apology, an automatic movement, while inward he wondered when he would ever develop Detlev's speed in considering the myriad ramifications of the simplest questions? "Both of us," he said.

"What?"

"I said, both of us."

"Why? If I want to get laid, I shift up to Siamis's place, where no one knows us, or is ever likely to." *Siamis's place* being an otherwise quite ordinary pleasure house far in the north that Siamis had discovered in the course of his wanderings, and had introduced the boys to after they left Norsunder.

"Diplomacy. Learning." Adam grinned. "We said we're giving lessons in various aspects of life, but do you know how to behave in a ballroom?"

David knew quite well that Adam remembered Siamis offering to teach them Colendi court dance and etiquette, saying that if they knew Colendi ways, they could go to most courts, especially on the Sartoran continent, and adapt quickly.

In those days David had sneered at anything that wasn't related to magic or weapons, though he'd learned the basics. MV had as well. "Ah. That," David said, hanging his head. "Yep. You're right."

"Blossom Street has music, so of course they'll offer such lessons. We learn, our students learn."

"Dance it is, then."

Adam fetched a purse they kept against marketing exigencies, and then transferred them to Eidervaen's Blossom Street.

The air was considerably warmer here, and quite still. David followed Adam inside the open doors, where mellow lighting spilled out in a welcoming golden glow. Four wind instruments braided a romantic ballad, a melody that dove in and out of minor and major keys. Music that somehow sparked expectation, David thought as they walked in.

The frisson of auditory anticipation fired the other senses. Adam looked about with mild interest. And there was plenty worth observing. Someone had broken sprigs of cedar from the rows of trees outside and decorated the light blue curtain sashes, and candle sconces, and each of the little tables in the great parlor had them as well.

The room was filled with people, of all ages. A huge group of journey youths were half drunk over in the far corner, celebrating one of their number, for there in the center was a crimson-faced young woman, laughing. Others talked and flirted, some carried food and drink back and forth, a few danced to the music of those four up in the gallery. David's eyes lingered on a circle of young women his own age, their arms intertwined, performing a slow dance, dip, turn, clap hands over their heads in counterpoint. Two cast laughing looks over their shoulders at their audience, before they twined their arms again.

A man approached David and Adam, smiling in welcome. David said, "Here to learn to dance in a ballroom, if you offer that sort of lesson?"

"We do indeed."

They went off, leaving Adam contemplating various perceptions of time. How the unhappiest people lived always just into the future, rushing through their current task against what they might get, or find, or enjoy (or dread) later. Then there was Detlev, who thought across the span of centuries.

Sometimes Adam stood on the upper plateau, the soundless harmonics of the disirad resonating through body, mind, and spirit, and he felt the reach of his own mind running limitless to the horizons, not just geographical but those of time, and beyond.

He felt Hannla's mental inquiry, unshielded, and turned his head. "Welcome back," she said. "Here to fetch Hlareas?"

"I'm in no hurry." He nodded to where a couple charming young women had taken David over, and were demonstrating steps.

Adam said, "Tell me: what did Detlev do here? Sit and watch?"

She hesitated, then gestured him through into a small office. Good furniture, the desk piled with accounts. An open window, through which came the distant sounds of laughter, and the steady music.

"We do not ordinarily talk about customers," she said. "But in this situation, I think it would be absurd since, as you surmised, he did come here from time to time during the war, but nothing happened in the usual sense. He seemed content to eat as good a dinner as we could contrive when supplies were scarce, drink a glass of wine, and listen to the music. Hlareas told me once that he was spying on what was going on in the palace, at a distance, by his mind."

"You do not believe that?" His voice was low — lower than you'd expect from someone so slender — and pleasant to listen to.

"No, I do." Hannla wiped her damp forehead, then made a self-deprecating gesture. "I just don't understand how. But that he could, I make no doubt." She hesitated, studying this young man who had talked her into sending her only daughter into his care. In some ways, he reminded her of Detlev: ageless, in a way she couldn't define.

She could see how her daughter would find him fascinating. There was a restful affect to his manner, a neutrality that transcended the frenzied focus of seduction. Just so had Detlev been, though in him Hannla had sensed the intensity of a banked fire. No, a sun, its light hidden from physical view. She was as glad that he had never asked for any of her people, because she suspected that that magnitude of intensity emotionally consumed a partner who could not match it.

She met the eyes of her visitor, to find that they were no longer vague, but direct. Direct—the dense golden brown of morning sunlight on new bark. Steady, unblinking.

"I spent the early part of my life learning the skills, and the mindset, of war," he said. "And when we left Norsunder, I wanted to explore its opposite. So I went off world, and I came to a place very much like this." He smiled. "I worked there for a couple of years."

How did he do that? Moments ago his aspect had been as neutral, as sexless and serenely sunny as a child, but now she was very aware of the male form under those blanketing clothes, the trained cat-muscles, the long, sensitive hands. Some were born with ardent natures, attracting without effort— sometimes without knowing—everyone around them. Others had to work hard to learn the tricks of charm, of enticement. Here was a rarity indeed, someone who could cloak passion behind a calm detachment, and then lift that cloak when he chose.

"And so?" she asked.

"And so I've a partner now. I hope for the foreseeable. I was attempting by sharing my past experience to set you at ease, a little, about our mountaintop school?"

She laughed. "My daughter did that. She is very happy there." Hannla smiled with parental joy, and while David mastered the intricacies of ballroom etiquette, they chatted about teaching, and parenthood, and a range of subjects that had nothing to do with war.

14

This time Lyren-Sartora appeared directly in Liere's own sitting room, while outside the windows, the last spurts of rain from a departing storm rustled the last leaves in the garden below.

Liere smiled a welcome; she had given her daughter permission to transfer directly to her, but this was the first time Lyren-Sartora had done so.

As she had feared, Lyren-Sartora had not welcomed the news that Liere was going to have Andri's child. But she'd had half a year to get used to it, and then a year to accustom herself to the idea of a brother; her excuse for not visiting in person had been her task as Carl's governess.

Liere exclaimed, "I'm so glad to see you!"

"Thanks." Sixteen-year-old Lyren-Sartora breathed a not-quite-laugh; she couldn't quite bring herself to say *I'm glad to see you, too,* when she wasn't glad to see Liere still here, stuck in Enaeran. Even more stuck, having had that baby. That somehow made Liere's presence here seem permanent, as if she'd willingly entered a cage. She knew no one wanted her opinion, least of all Liere. "Is Grandma still here?"

"No, she went back."

Though Liere's mother was in her sixties, she'd still come to spend a few days after the baby was born, and again to see his first birthday.

Lyren-Sartora swooped to the floor in a welter of ice-blue silken panels and fresh herbal scent, kneeling next to the bright-haired one-year-old who sat in Liere's lap, a prism clutched in his chubby fingers. Shards of light painted rainbow sparkles over the walls and floor.

"Happy birthday, little brother," Lyren-Sartora said, and won a fleeting smile. "Watch!" Lyren-Sartora moved his crystal into a square of sunlight that had just appeared on the floor. With a flick of her finger, she sent it spinning.

The little prince gasped in delight as light sparkled round and round the room.

"Ya!" he shouted. "Mo!"

Lyren-Sartora moved more slowly the second time. On the third try he bent and gave the crystal a hefty smack with stiff fingers. The stone bounced away instead of spinning. His brow puckered as he stared, perplexed.

Rising to fetch it, Lyren-Sartora smiled up at Liere. "Do you ever think about how far you've come from that shop in South End? Prince Trevor Andiran Malcolin Elsarion! Where did all those names come from? They aren't Fer Eider names."

"I do, but I always have reflected on that, ever since I left home the first time. Diplomatic choices both, Trevor being common on both sides of the Elsarion family tree, and Andiran, Macael's grandfather. Malcolin is Andri's second name. As for Fer Eider names, the only brother I'd name a child after would be Milnat, who was named after the only uncle I ever liked. That will be our second son's name. If we have one."

Lyren-Sartora determinedly said nothing to this reminder of Liere's chosen cage. She smiled at the baby. In his round face she could see the beginnings of Andri's chin. His eyes were large, and golden, but with hints of green around the pupil. Lyren-Sartora played with him for a few minutes more, deft hands juggling the crystals, then she set them all spinning, and rose.

After one considering look, Trevor did not call her back.

"Already has a block of sorts, I see," Lyren-Sartora remarked.

"I had it young as well," Liere said, holding hard on the instinct to blather details. She would only if Lyren-Sartora asked. But mostly she hoped that Lyren-Sartora would show him the affection she offered every small creature she met. "How are things in Everon?"

"Going well, for the most part. The siblings are growing like weeds, and Madelon is showing signs of wanting to wander, much the same way Jessan did. Only for her, it's Dtheldevor's Island. Tahra blames Aurora for that, and wants to forbid it, because Dtheldevor's Island is so close to Wnelder Vee, which is polluted by the Evil Laban, but that opinion nearly caused a riot. She said that if a suitable ship stops at the island, Madelon might go after she turns eleven, so there is peace in the house. Tahra thinks a few night watches tending sail in the rain might cure Madelon of the wanderlust. I'm not so sure."

"And Carl?"

"She's more romantic than a ... what's the most romantic thing you can think of? A bard who only sings love songs? Anyway, I told her I'd take her to Eidervaen. Atan has invited all the allies, surely you know that, for New Year's Week, and Tahra gave her permission, since it seems Detlev's evil people never pollute the place."

"She checks?"

"Oh, she checks," Lyren-Sartora said. "Tahra is so..."

"Tahra is so Tahra," Liere said, gently.

"I was going to say stubborn, but if you don't want to gossip, I won't."

"There is no point in it. We both know what Tahra is like," Liere said.

"Anyway, I repeat, I know you've been invited. I asked. Atan wants to see you. Rel wants to see you. Does Banana-Brain have you locked up here?"

"Nobody has locked anyone up. I can't leave him," Liere said, smiling at Trevor Andiran. "This is not a good age for travel. I learned the hard way with you. He's happiest with his routine, everything the same every day. And there is so much to do."

"Are you *still* stuck with all the ledger-drudge?" Lyren-Sartora asked, chin in hand. "Andri doing his share yet?"

"We divide tasks," Liere replied evenly, wishing that Lyren-Sartora would grow out of her resentment. "It is easier for me to deal with treasury matters, and those related to it. I do have a staff, but whenever there is a problem, people ask for me. I like being useful. It makes me feel ... useful." Liere smiled ruefully. "I've learned so much, too. Andri handles the parts I would find an onerous duty, such as watching the border, inspecting the mines, and training the Guard."

"Is there already trouble with Sles Adran?"

Liere rubbed her thumb across her lip, then consciously lowered her hand, still feeling a faint pulse of guilt left from chewing her cuticles, even though she hadn't done it for years. But the psychic scars from her father's excoriating sarcasm still lingered. "N-no. Not really. Though there is grumbling now and then, about the fact that so much of Enaeran is open land unsuitable for much beyond riding across, and of course the heavy woods. The rich farmland is the Riverland, between the rivers, and until Andri's father lost it, it had belonged to Enaeran."

"I'm not very good in local history," Lyren-Sartora said, "but wasn't this all one kingdom for a long time?"

"It was, much longer ago. There are many who consider Enaeran unfairly truncated still, then there are the Riverland farms that belong to people on both sides of the border. We, and Macael over in Nente, have agreed to leave them alone, for they have a delicately balanced net of obligations going both ways over the borders. Andri and I don't want to touch it, lest there be problems, and we're still recovering from the war. The treasury seems to empty as fast as it fills." *Faster.*

Lyren-Sartora shrugged, having reached the limit of her interest. She could see that all Liere's brains and talent had been firmly squeezed into this beggarly little cage called Enaeran. And of course she was wrapped up with her baby, which at least was understandable, unlike Liere's hermit existence here in rundown, boring Shiovhan. Lyren-Sartora would not resent this new little brother for his mother's attention, not, not, not. She knew her childhood had been unusual, and Liere had not known how to be a mother, but Lyren-Sartora had come to see that she'd had more family than most children got to have, and most of it lived in palaces.

Lyren-Sartora watched Trevor Andiran's attempts at crystal-spinning as she asked about various members of Andri's old street gang, though she half-heard the expected, and rather dull, answers; the only one she found interesting was Marten, who was the Enaeraneth ambassador to Sartor's court. She reminded herself to seek him out to say hello.

At the end, she said, "I'd hoped to see you in Eidervaen,

but I guess it's not to be. I'd better get back, for we've still much to do to get ready."

And she was gone, leaving Liere to reflect with a sigh that Lyren-Sartora had not touched Trevor-Andiran.

NENTE, CAPITAL OF SLES ADRAN

"Oh, do let us go visit," Chantala exclaimed, waving her latest letter from Liere. "Liere said that they are hosting their court again now, over New Year's Week, and she said we would be welcome."

"We?" Macael smiled. "Or is that an invitation to you?"

"She said both of us," Chantala replied seriously. "She says that peace is so very important, and people need to see the alliance between our kingdoms, after all the troubles. Don't you agree?"

"I do."

"Their child, who is named for you, has already turned one. I would so like to celebrate the new year with Liere, and see their baby while he is a baby. I do like babies." She looked up at Macael, who sat down beside her.

Winter had settled in firmly the month before in Nente, which had been built up against the mountains. Chantala never seemed able to get warm. She looked anxiously into his face, saying, "Are we truly settled now? I know you hide troublesome affairs from me so that I will not be vexed."

"Would you like to go visit Liere over New Year's Week?" His verb was in the singular.

Her thin fingers touched the lace over his wrist, and she gave him a frightened look. "Please come. Or can you not? Is there hidden danger?"

"Not at all," he said in a soothing voice. "We are at peace. The harvest was excellent, and I have no reason to believe that next year's won't be even better. Though it's true I don't like to be away long so early in our reign. Would you rather I come with you for the first day or two, then return once you're comfortable? You can then stay as long as you wish."

"Please stay with me," she implored. "Liere says she made a Destination, and I remember you hired mages last year to fix ours so that we could go comfortably to Sartor. That was so very nice."

"If you want to accept Liere's invitation, we'll go together." He touched the top of her hand. "I'll make the arrangements."

She smiled, then gave him another anxious look. "I cannot define your expression. Are you wishing there would be an heir for us?" Her thin shoulders hunched closer to her ears as she spoke. She once had taken his hand without thought, but that had been before some helpful courtier had told Chantala that the Birth Spell came if you took hands with your partner or partners.

"I am in no hurry," Macael said. "I believe Andri and Liere decided to get their heir right away because life has been so uncertain for Andri. We haven't that problem. We can wait."

Chantala sighed with relief. "I do like babies. But they scare me when they wail. I like to hold them when they are small and asleep. But they are fun if they belong to someone else, who knows what to do if they get noisy."

"I'm certain that Liere will have nannies on hand."

People familiar with Enaeran and Sles Adran attested that the Adrani Debt Day was significantly different from that in Enaeran. The Adranis considered their ancient court too elegant for brangling and bartering in the middle of a festival, and so, traditionally, crown, guild, and nobles settled their affairs well before the end of the year, and then made sure that there were no outstanding disputes among individuals in their lands that might reach the royal ear. Thus Debt Day was usually celebrated at night by a sumptuous ball, hosted by the crown. That freed up the king and queen to confine their appearances that day to an hour or so at their royal affair.

Unfamiliar with magic, Macael and Chantala had learned that the now-restored Destinations were still limited to one person at a time, with rather longer wait periods between than previously, as Norsunder had abused them, especially in the last days of the war. Some were reliable for very short periods, and many were unusable, their tiles destroyed so that no one would try to shift to a pattern that might kill them.

Macael sent an Elsarion steward ahead to see to arrangements at the Enaeraneth end; being from that side of the river, the steward was able to move about freely. Also spend freely, which won a great deal of good will from the local merchants.

The steward was also able to advise his king about the best way to please the volatile Enaeraneth, and so, when a contingent of finely dressed Adrani guards accompanied the king and queen over the river—Macael and Chantala having transferred to the outpost on the Adrani side—they knew to toss a rain of silver pieces out as New Year's gifts to those lining the road up to Brydon Palace, and not a few gold pieces, which would have been deemed pompous. Even though there were those who scrambled hard to pick up rather more silvers than one golder was worth.

Watching from their proclamation balcony, Andri murmured to Liere, "I have to say, Macael does know how to make an entrance." Neither assumed that Chantala had had anything to do with the planning. Andri grinned, adding, "Better than me."

The cavalcade clattered up to the broad parade ground beneath the balcony, where the citizens gathered to hear proclamations (or to start riots, back in the bad old days). Andri and Liere went down to welcome them in proper state, after which the hired carriage was quietly returned to its owner, and the outriders to trot back to their outpost.

Macael had already sent over well-trained guards in the livery of servants, who had prepared the magnificent guest suite, which had all new furnishings that had been left by Adon Marsael. They had also set up a protective perimeter for their king; all this was understood by Andri's new guard, who were cooperative, so all went smoothly.

It was Liere's thoughtfulness that assigned Macael and Chantala a suite of rooms that included two bedrooms as well as dressing rooms and a salon; Chantala chose the smaller room, saying that it was sure to be warmer, and her servants quietly set about making it as familiar as possible with all Chantala's things.

Macael and Chantala left the servants to it and went down to join the company. Macael had never seen Brydon as an adult, and looked around with interest. It was in better shape than the city, probably due to Adon Marsael's love of luxury; Andri later confirmed that with a laugh over dinner, which was served in a dining room decorated in white and gold, the company including all the nobles above the rank of baras.

"I hope you like the place," Andri said, leaning back in his chair, a wine goblet in one hand. "If you do, we've Adon Marsael to thank. Everything he wrested from the people he put into refurbishing the royal wing, after my father's troubles left the place a shambles."

Liere noted Chantala's eyes rounding, and sent a quick look Andri's way. He recollected Chantala's sensitivity to any kind of discord, even suggestions of past problems, and shifted the conversation to the weather, then made some mild jokes about the local youngsters constantly testing the river all the previous month in hopes it would freeze solid enough for ice sports.

The court took their cue, with many a covert glance between Macael and Chantala, and the conversation remained determinedly stilted for the remainder of the dinner. Liere labored to bridge that, talking far more than she ordinarily did. It was a relief for all except Chantala when it ended, Chantala thanking Andri and Liere sincerely for a delightful meal.

After dinner there was a musical concert, which Liere knew Chantala would like, and things ended early for a court occasion—which meant the Enaeraneth were free to go on to affairs more in keeping with their interests, as the royal Adrani visitors retired.

As soon as Macael and Chantala were bowed off to the guest suite, Andri gusted a loud sigh of relief. "I think that went all right. Don't you?"

"Chantala was happy," Liere said. "And though I still can't read Macael, from his frequent looks her way, my guess is that he's content if she's happy—"

Right then she felt Trevor Andiran wail. "Mama call," she said, as she and Andri walked hand in hand upstairs toward the royal suite, spread along both sides of the main wing.

The door to the king's side opened at their approach, and a lively face peeked out, a tangle of curls swinging. "Is it over already?" Althora asked, eyes round; she looked good in a palace guard uniform.

"They retired early," Liere said.

Althora laughed invitingly. "I just got off-duty, and Gared got us a good game of Cards'n'Shards going."

Nobody there thought it amiss that this impromptu party was taking place in the king's suite. All they knew was, Gared was still holding out against a noble title, which meant he didn't have to attend court except as Captain of the King's Guard, which was what he'd wanted to be since he and Andri first met. Andri clapped his hands and rubbed them. "Perfect."

"I might come over. The small one is fretful," Liere said.

"Does he want me?" Andri asked.

"I'll call if he does." Liere tapped her forehead.

Andri slung his arm around Althora, who gave him a smacking kiss, and they went in to join the party, as Liere trod across the hall into the queen's suite. It was quiet, except for Trevor Andiran's tearful little voice, and the nanny's soothing tones.

"I'm here," Liere called, and Trevor Andiran waddled out, arms up to be lifted. "It's bedtime," she said.

"Mama."

"Yes, sweet one?"

Instead of speaking, he projected an image of a cup of warm milk with honey; it was the honey in it that was inspiring him to want to drink out of a cup. She had decided to let him dictate when he'd be ready for weaning, as no two women had given her similar advice.

"Use your words," she said.

"Mok," Trevor Andiran replied obediently. "Nee."

"Milk and honey it is."

The nanny, hovering in the background, gave a quick nod and noiselessly departed to fetch it, leaving Liere to sit with the baby on the floor with an illustrated book. She read the simple poems inside, as Trevor Andiran liked the rhythms as much as he liked the animals the poems were about. She traced her finger over the letters, sounding them out for him, especially the animal noises. Trevor Andiran wiggled with delight when they reached the "Ssssss," for snake, and "Glup! Glup!" for fish. But the birds were his favorite, and as usual, he struggled to get his tongue and lips to cooperate in a whistle. Then he laughed riotously at the fart noise he got instead.

The milk appeared, and he drank it down.

"All right, into bed, young rover," Liere said.

Trevor Andiran padded to his bed and crawled obediently in. She sat down beside it and read the story through a couple more times, keeping the noises soft. He was soon asleep, but she stayed by his side, loving his small breathings as she considered the long day.

It was so strange, having Macael Elsarion in Brydon, which was still shabby in so many places. Adon Marsael had only put work into the portions he used, and repairs on the rest kept getting postponed in favor of fixing other disasters. Liere remembered Macael's exquisite taste, first encountered in the remote valley where the artists had their colony. Macael had dressed like a courtier even though there was no one to see him but Chantala and the artist couple who hosted her.

Such a difficult person to define. He was utterly shielded, yet she could sense him in the other wing. That is, she sensed his presence, but not an iota of what he thought.

A shout of laughter from across the hall caught her attention, and she smiled. Andri's venture into monogamy hadn't lasted past Trevor Andiran's birth, when she had lost all interest in sex for the month after she recovered.

Althora had made it clear she was available, right from the start. Liere admired her for her ability to go, single-minded, for what she wanted, but without trampling others in the process. Andri and Althora were still hot for each other, but she always deferred to Liere and Andri if they wanted to retire together; as she told Liere mid-summer, "His interest won't last, everyone tells me. But he always stays friends, and he's generous."

Already Liere had observed Althora's roving eye on Gared. Again, not a surprise. Andri and Gared had shared lovers ever since they were teens.

What a tumble of puppies we all are, Liere thought sleepily, for she'd risen early to see all was ready for the arrival of Macael and Chantala. Though it was Macael's winter-blue gaze she had imagined when inspecting everything.

✦ **15** ✦

The morning of Debt Day, the weather changed dramatically, and Chantala retired to their private salon to read, since she did not have to preside over what might be a stressful time. Macael dressed soberly, and chose an unobtrusive place from which to observe the Debt Day traditions in his kingdom of birth.

Liere and Andri sat together on twin thrones, but that was the extent of their formality. The Elsarion liveried servants kept the multitude of petitioners and supplicants in more or less of an order. Andri lounged back, booted feet stretched out before him, spiced wine at hand to warm him from the chill that the four braziers set around the throne could not banish. For once he did not have a chest cold. He insisted it was the spiced wine with citrus shavings in it that kept the colds at bay.

Liere, dressed in celestial blue and white, drew the greater portion of attention, for she seemed to know most petitioners by name, after two years of overseeing the kingdom exchequer.

Neither of them, it was plain to all, made a decision without the other, even if their discussion was confined to a look, or the nod of a chin or the turn of a hand as if handing something off. Few understood that the two communicated by mind. Not that they had to do a lot of it; Andri could see in Liere's expression when she knew she was being lied to by someone hoping to exploit the queen's legendary sympathy with the plight of those civil war and Norsundrian attack had left poor. Her expression was never a sneer, or an eyebrow lift of disbelief, it was invariably sad, as though being lied to hurt her. That appeared to discommode those who still had a modicum of conscience, and many a falter and backtrack ensued.

Otherwise the atmosphere was one of mercy. Small debts—large to individuals—were postponed, their form altered to restitution, or were outright forgiven, disputes settled, and the day ended at last, with whispers going out about how the queen really was as beautiful as it was said, and even kinder than that. Not one speculation about how the exchequer was going to accommodate this munificence.

When the evening bells rang, it was time for ready for the masquerade.

Andri scarcely bothered with a costume; he pulled out a favorite embroidered shirt, hung a gaudy baldric over it, put gaudier earrings into his ears instead of his usual diamonds, and tied a bandana around his hair to go as a pirate. No mask, as he couldn't stand anything covering his face, which might obscure his view. He took over as host, leading his rowdier courtiers (many of whom were friends from the days of his street gang) in all the fastest dances, hot spiced wine flowing freely.

Between one dance and another, an imposing figure robed in shades of white to contrast with his dark hair approached Andri, a wraith on his arm robed in floating green. They both wore fine masks of silver and blue. "Liere is not present, Cousin?"

That was Macael's voice. "Who are you supposed to be?" Andri asked.

"Martande Lirendi," Macael said with a smile. "Not exactly imaginative, but suitable for these affairs."

Andri had to dig in childhood memory of history lessons to recover Martande Lirendi, and all he came up with was some old king in Colend. "True," he said, figuring that was diplomatic. "Liere went off to sleep off a headache, after sorting surface thoughts, as she puts it, all through the day." Andri tapped his head significantly. "She figured no one would know she wasn't here, it being a masquerade."

Macael turned to Chantala, murmuring, "I'm sorry you won't be able to sit with her, then. Would you like to retire?"

"Only to sit," was Chantala's faint reply. "The music is too fine to leave entirely. I'll enjoy listening, if you wish to dance."

"I'll sit with you," Macael said, and they went off, after a courteous nod to Andri, who never saw Chantala without being grateful still that he had not been inveigled into marrying her. Macael seemed to be content, though. And there was no gossip about him enjoying himself otherwhere while Chantala was holed up in their suite, which might be reasonably expected. Eh, it takes all kinds to make a world.

The rest of the week passed without untoward incident. Chantala attended every concert, Macael invariably at her side; people did not know what to make of Chantala, whose conversation seemed at times childlike, and at others as erudite as that of a poet. She seemed oblivious to innuendo, and as for Macael, courtiers of both sexes who thought he might venture outside of what had to be a bloodless marriage found him as cold and remote as an ice castle on a cliff.

Liere saw a great deal of Chantala, and almost nothing of Macael except in company, until the last day, before the Adrani royal couple was to depart for Nente.

Liere had finally finished going over all the decisions of Debt Day, which had been scrupulously recorded by the new ledger keepers she had been training. She would be glad one day soon to relinquish that duty entirely, and yet it had been instructive, realizing she knew so many of the individuals who had petitioned that day.

She gratefully laid down her pen and went out into the secluded garden beyond the royal wing to get some exercise under the yew trees, which she had discovered were beautiful in every season. No wonder Andri invariably took that route in the mornings, on his way to the guards' court for a brisk workout.

She strode briskly, coming to an abrupt halt when she spotted a tall, well-built, dark-haired man coming the other way, his attention upward, hands clasped behind him. Macael looked like someone enjoying a solitary, contemplative walk, and Liere would have whisked herself along another path, so he could pretend not to have seen her, but his politesse prevailed. "Good morning, Liere."

"Good morning," she said. "I beg pardon for intruding on your solitude."

"Not at all. My grandfather wrote about this yew walk.

He claimed that Shiovhan was built around it some ten centuries ago, before the city spread below, and Brydon replaced the original trade town."

"There are some very old drawings of that town that survived the various ructions of recent years, over in the library. It seems neither Adon Marsael nor his Norsundrian friends ventured much into libraries."

Macael smiled absently, then said, "I meant to ask. Since you are reputed to possess considerable magic knowledge, would that not obviate the need for Andri having to fund border patrols and the like?"

Liere returned his smile. "The answer should be obvious: how much magic was I able to use during the war?"

"None, from my very limited perspective."

"Your perspective would do for the whole. Magic is largely useless for war, unless you speak of the levels the Host were willing to employ, that destroy kingdom-wide areas, denuding them of life. If one mage comes up with a clever way to kill people in a battle, another mage will surely ward it very quickly. In the meantime, the residue is dangerous to both sides."

"So Adon Marsael's fears that mages could take his throne were absurd?"

"Yes. And no. There are wards and tracers and stone spells and the like, though it takes years to learn to master such things—and there are ways to guard against them. I remember speaking to him, and I got the impression that he did not like the idea of anyone having access to a kind of power, however it was used, that he did not have."

"I see."

"It's a common attitude among rulers. There are kingdoms where law and custom require that the monarch have no magic knowledge, to keep a balance, and to prevent, oh, the likes of Wan-Edhe of the Chwahir."

"Yes, I've seen references in my reading. Now I'm beginning to understand why—"

Macael broke off as a pair of figures became visible among the hanging green branches of the yew trees.

The two pairs met at an intersection in the path, and here was Andri—with MV! Liere stared in surprise, then remembered that MV and Andri had become fast friends during their war experiences.

"Look who dropped in," Andri said, grinning broadly. He quickly performed introductions, paying no attention to the niceties of etiquette, after which Macael said, "Are you one of Detlev's associates?"

MV's strange eyes widened. "Is this fame, or has someone been doing a lot of yakking?" He punched Andri in the arm.

"Not me!" Andri protested.

"Your name was featured on the capital lists found in the headquarters of the Norsundrians in charge of Sles Adran," Macael said urbanely.

"Shall we go in? Perhaps Chantala will want to join us," Liere suggested, hoping to deflect any discussions of Detlev, in case Macael numbered among the haters. But Macael was too polite to offer unasked opinions.

Trust MV for that, Liere realized belatedly, when he asked, "Chantala. She the one who was nearly poisoned?"

"Yes," Liere answered.

MV squinted at Macael. "Catch the murderer?"

"Murderer?" Macael repeated.

"Did for the mother, right?"

Andri put in, "Didn't you say you found out who it was?"

Macael brought his chin down in a nod, but he refrained from adding anything, his gaze lifting. Liere turned, and there was Chantala at the door, muffled in a yeath cloak. Macael said softly, "The problem was solved before she left the Harieses' house in the valley, as I'd promised." He raised his voice to greet her, and Liere performed the introductions.

She was surprised when MV showed no inclination to depart, in spite of the tame conversation in Chantala's company. Perhaps even more surprising, MV said nothing to alarm Chantala. Liere was used to thinking he had no manners. Of course he'd had the same training as the rest of Detlev's boys.

At the end of the afternoon, they all gathered to say farewell to the Adrani visitors, who departed the way they had come.

Once they were gone, the other three retreated to a small salon on the second floor. MV flung himself into one of the big, comfortable chairs, and began to pick his teeth with a knife. He cocked an eye at Andri, and said, "You're right. Can't read him."

Andri poured out spiced wine for everyone. "They love him in Sles Adran. And he's helped us out."

"You asked for my opinion." MV wiped his blade, then slammed it into its wrist sheath. "Which is this: find out who that poisoner was, and how Cousin Macael solved the problem. It might tell you what you want to know."

"Macael's given me no reason to distrust him," Andri said. "Quite the opposite."

MV shrugged, unconcerned. "I'm suspicious of everybody. And think of what blood ties have done for Laban and Senrid! Pass that mulled wine! These little cups are for doll houses."

16

"*I* don't feel we've changed," Atan said to Rel, looking out over the great ballroom, which had finally been refurbished after almost two years of labor. Pale marble between blue marble pilasters crowned by stylized acanthus in gold, a ceiling of stars set against deep blue, golden sconces holding crystal candle holders. It actually looked better than it had before the Norsundrians destroyed it.

Atan turned her attention to Rel, who looked handsomer than ever. Time had sharpened his features. He looked like a king.

He turned to her, his brows quirked. "Atan, you sound as if we've suddenly leaped into old age. Most of the people here look on us as youngsters with milk still drying on our lips."

That was not at all true. For one thing, more than half the guests leaping, clapping, and twirling in ever-changing patterns in the ballroom were young people. But she smiled, accepting the thought behind the statement. "What I was really referring to was Lyren-Sartora. She is not a baby anymore."

The two turned their attention to the slim, shapely figure in floating rose and gold, dancing in the middle of the room with one of the most notorious flirts in Atan's court.

"She did draw Chandos's interest with commendable speed," Rel observed.

"All three of them."

There were twelve duchas holdings in Sartor. The number of counts and barases had waxed and waned over the centuries, but tradition had established twelve duchases, and twelve there remained. Though Chandos was in name only, the land having been taken by Norsunder Base centuries ago, Korendemar was another in name only for more obscure political reasons that were even older. These two duchas families owned no land, but they were exceedingly wealthy as well as influential.

As a fifteen-year-old queen, Atan had inherited a First Circle full of older folk who had endured the terrible war more than a century ago, before Sartor was taken from the world. Between the time it reappeared after that century passed, and Norsunder's war, most of those stern old figures who had regarded her as a figurehead requiring their firm guidance had retired or died, replaced by young people — some younger than she.

Focus of today's court were three young men whose wealth, rank, and looks had been weaponized for the so-called tender field of romance, mowing down the young and passionate. At least, so it was until Lyren-Sartora entered, wearing no jewels, her accessories fresh flowers. Instead of the latest fashions, which were pleated and tailored, she wore a layered robe of her own design that made her appear to float as she moved. Atan suspected there would be versions of it appearing in court for the rest of winter.

"She dances with whoever asks her," Atan says. "And then bestows the kind ones on sweet little Carl."

Rel turned to observe the thin, narrow-faced little figure in the far corner, where the underage guests congregated. They were performing a dance of their own, a simple ring dance, unlike the complicated figures of the adults in the center of the room. Noble parents deemed it good practice for the future.

"I thought I was asleep and dreaming when Tahra, of all people, wrote to me to request permission to send Carl along with Lyren-Sartora," Atan commented. "But it's clear she's loving every moment."

"Mmmm," Rel said. "I know you haven't had the time, but I talked to her yesterday. She's nearly as opposite from Tahra as possible, yet with the same ardency. But hers is all romantic, I guess you'd call it."

"I know what you mean. Not flirting, so much as the beautiful setting, with everyone looking and acting their best, and all set to music. And yet I sense that there is a purpose here.

Could it be Lyren-Sartora's, luring that child after her? She definitely seems to have reached the age of flirtation," Atan added, noting the new Duchas of Chandos cutting a swathe through admirers to claim another dance.

Rel said, "I think you're seeing what isn't there. Lyren-Sartora may have reached the age of interest, but that's barely. She's closer to Carl's age than to she is to most of these others, except perhaps Ryados. He's not yet twenty."

Atan was quick to say, "I'm not accusing her of anything! You know I really like her. Always have. It just seems to me there's … intent in the two of them wanting to come to Eidervaen. I think it's completely normal for Lyren-Sartora to want to try her powers to attract and be attracted, but Carl is far too young, and too anxious for that, however much she might admire ballrooms and great orchestras."

Maddeningly, Rel's only reply was an uncommunicative "Mmm." Then a quick intake of breath caused her to turn to see what caught his eye—and there was Mondros, almost unrecognizable with his beard neatly trimmed, and wearing a blue mage robe of finest merino, embroidered with stylized oak leaves in gold, and beneath the robe another in a deep crimson.

He caught their eyes, and had time to think what a handsome couple they made before they arrived. He began to make the court bow of half a century ago, but Rel quickly put out his hand. "Please don't. Not you. Not ever."

Mondros rumbled a laugh.

"I'm so glad you are here," Atan said. "Welcome! Stay as long as you wish." At that, she left father and son together, aware that they had not seen one another but briefly after the war was over, long enough to ascertain that the other was alive. Then Mondros went to aid Jilo, and after that to catalogue Tsauderei's library for the unaffiliated mages. Rel of course remained in Sartor.

"Are you finished in Narad?" Rel asked. "Is Iog well-established?"

"She was my first concern. She won't move, or take any extra aid, I think mostly out of residual fear. This is true of most of the elders, alas. Only time will cure that, I expect. But Jilo and I both saw to it that her entire neighborhood, plus the outpost, got their share of the improvements Jilo is bringing in by degrees. You'll have to come to see her."

"I will," Rel promised. "When Jilo is ready."

Mondros nodded. "Not yet. But he's doing admirably. And that boy of Detlev's, Erol, shadows him when he can."

Rel said, "Have you gone back to Ralanor Veleth?"

Mondros had been rubbing his hands as he approached the refreshments table in a side chamber, but at this, his smile vanished. "I've considered it. Word is, things are still unsettled over there. They don't need another distraction."

"How can family be distraction?" Rel asked.

"Will they see it that way?" Mondros countered. "I left in disgrace. Exile. Promised never to pollute Velethi soil, blah, blah, you know the sort of thing I mean. I'll go when I'm ready. In the meantime, I'm keeping my promise to Tsauderei. Sartor! Who would have ever placed any of us here?" He chuckled again, and as he began sampling delicacies, he said, "How are my grandchildren? Will I meet them?"

"Tomorrow," Rel said, aware that Atan had scrupulously sent images of Kaslan-Dei and more recently of infant Meridanaria to Mondros.

They chatted about the doings of very small people as Mondros tasted his way through the offerings, then Mondros said, "What about here? Anything I should know about?"

"Mostly recovery and rebuilding. Sartor is so old they have plans for every eventuality, including this one, and the mandate is that rebuilding comes first. I've been busy with that."

"Seen anything of Detlev?"

"Briefly. You know what he's like."

"I don't know what the post-Norsunder Detlev is like. Tell me."

"He came, he looked around with an air of approval, he asked if there was any more trouble from the direction of Norsunder Base. I said there wasn't, and according to Hinder, who went down there via tunnel to look around, it's aged a hundred years overnight. Buildings crumbled. Trees growing in the rubble. Very eerie."

"That won't be Detlev's doing," Mondros said.

"Atan thinks so as well. I'm not willing to make a guess either way," Rel admitted. "I'm too ignorant about magical things, and that reeks of magic. But on his way out, he mentioned that a fleet whose purpose is to oversee the waters of the Sartoran Sea might be something to consider. Then he was gone."

Mondros's brows shot up, corrugating his forehead. "Was that a suggestion or a warning?"

"Neither? Both? Whatever impulse lies behind it, Atan and I agree that it's an excellent idea. Norsunder was far too effective in taking Mardgar and Al Caba, which tied down all ship travel for the duration. I've spoken with Vidanric Renselaeus of Remalna, who keeps in touch with our old escape route alliance, and he agrees fervently. Remalna has a stake in safe waters, too."

At that moment, a servant approached, and whispered that the head nanny needed a parent. "It's my turn to be on call," Rel said. "Want to meet the rugbugs now?"

Father and grandfather went off, and Atan was left to serve as host. She divided her time between surveying the whole and watching for Lyren-Sartora in specific. She did not want to see Liere's daughter get hurt by Chandos, who had a reputation for flirting desperately for an hour or two, and then suddenly not recognizing a person he'd been dancing with two dances previous, leaving them looking hurt as he paraded away on the arm of another aspirant for languishing glances from his pretty eyes.

Atan watched Lyren-Sartora dancing with Chandos, her lips curved in a dimpled smile. Her eyes shone golden in the scintillating candlelight. Atan wished she had Dena Yeresbeth, if only to hear what they were saying, then she was distracted by a pair of diplomats with a question about tariffs.

She finished that conversation after the dance ended, and she looked around, in time to catch a glimpse of what she was fairly certain was Lyren-Sartora's long, floating sleeves vanishing through a side arch toward what Atan knew was a private side chamber.

No, no, no, it was far too early for that.

Atan knew better than to stalk in a bee's straight line after her. Regretting the necessity for every pause to bow and smile, she made a languid circle, and then slipped through the arch, and sped toward that far room.

From which rose a masculine voice in laughter. She hastened her step, then caught several treble voices, and slowed before she reached the door. Which was partly ajar.

She peeked through, and froze in complete surprise. Atan had momentarily forgotten little Carl, so worried was she about Lyren-Sartora. But here were Carl and Lyren-Sartora both, Carl dancing happily with her twin Jessan, and of all people, David of Detlev's gang. They were stamping and clapping in one of the court hops, as Lyren-Sartora stood by, clapping in counterpoint.

So that was why Rel had in essence cut her off. He probably knew about this meeting. And he didn't tell Atan so that if Tahra contacted her to check up on her daughter's behavior — and she would — Atan would be able to say truthfully that Carl had not met anyone on Tahra's list of potential execution victims, a list that began with Detlev and included all his followers. Tahra would be doubly furious if she found out that Carl had met Jessan there in David's company.

Atan backed away slowly, glad no one had seen her. *I was not here*, she decided, slipping back into the ballroom.

And she was unnoticed. Lyren-Sartora, usually so very aware of everyone in her proximity, had not caught her, for all her attention was focused on the sight of tall, curly-haired David dancing with the freedom of one who cared nothing for what others thought.

He danced just to be dancing, with an abandon that Lyren-Sartora found far more compelling than the well-practiced, slack-lidded blandishments of that Chandos, so very full of himself. Refused to even dance once with Carl, because "how would it look?"

The dance ended, and Lyren-Sartora smiled, and approached, saying, "I didn't want to interrupt. Now it's my turn?" She held out a hand in invitation to David.

He glanced her way. "Ah, I promised the princess a taltan, and a taltan she must have." And he bowed absurdly to Carl, who giggled, flushing bright red.

Lyren-Sartora, finding herself acutely sensitive in a new and utterly beguiling way, blinked, not quite sure how to respond. But she didn't have to respond, for David and Carl swept into the intricate steps of the taltan. Leaving her pondering the little hitch of breath, and this fascinating sensation, almost as if her skin hurt, except it was more of a tingle, as her eyes appreciated David's back, the molding of his shirt over his shoulders, and the curves of musculature beneath the loose fabric all the way down his body.

This had to be attraction, sneaking up on her like a thief in the night. But *he* obviously wasn't feeling it! She forced her gaze away, chagrined, for until now she had firmly believed that these things were a matter of self-control. But here it was, after she'd been wondering about it so long. It had ambushed her, yet she was the only one sensing it.

Time to get herself away, and let it die. But she had to remain with Carl, as she'd promised. She sat there with a determined smile, utterly unaware of the heightened simmer of her proximity, until at last David said to Jessan that it was time to transfer back. Jessan wished his sister and Lyren-Sartora a good year. David raised a casual hand, without looking at anyone. Did that mean he'd noticed after all, and was pretending not to, the way people pretended not to notice if you had a bit of spinach between your teeth? Ouch.

Lyren-Sartora resolutely laughed at herself for all her wrong expectations, as she superficially listened to Carl's happy chatter on the way back to the ballroom — and David got himself out of there, feeling as if he'd sidestepped a bolt of lightning. One moment Lyren-Sartora had been laughing and clapping, the next she had pinned him with those wide golden eyes, her lips parted, her cheeks flushed. His nerves flashed — mostly warning.

At least, he strongly suspected, that sudden sizzle of awareness had taken Lyren-Sartora by surprise as much as it had him. She was too young, too volatile, and she was blooming into one of those rare people who entrance everyone in proximity just by their presence. Better to avoid her until she got enough experience, or emotional awareness, to bank that fire. Or settled on some poor soul her own age who would cheerfully burn with her.

Atan breathed in relief when she observed Lyren-Sartora's and Carl's reentry. She looked for them from time to time as Lyren-Sartora once again appeared on the ballroom floor, though her smile seemed less joyful than fixed.

Once, they spoke. "If you're tired, you can always retire," Atan said. "Carl probably ought to be in bed soon. Though I noticed the others her age are being permitted to stay up. But don't feel obliged."

"No, no, it's fun. I'm fine," Lyren-Sartora said, her voice a little breathless, and those great golden eyes glittering in the brilliant light of twelve chandeliers. "Just, sometimes I get reminders that I'm young. And stupid. And too much like the worthless Deis, ha ha."

She whirled away before Atan could say anything, and next was seen dancing with Chandos again.

But when Carl yawned one time too many, and Lyren-Sartora began to take her away, Atan observed that it was Chandos left gazing after her straight back and the long gold-touched, rippling dark hair, as Lyren-Sartora exited in a cloud of draperies.

17

*T*ok-tak! Z-i-n-n-n-g!
"Point to red, disengage."
Marend Ndarga lifted her swordpoint, though her opponent hadn't. He was enraged at having lost, and sure enough, as Hamet brought up his point ostensibly to salute, the sharp end flashed within a finger's breadth from her right eye. She felt the breeze, but neither blinked nor moved her head: his control was excellent, and he wouldn't dare touch an out-of-bounds portion of her body, especially after the call to disengage. Hamet the bully wanted to ease his loss by making her flinch.

The others caught the move, and jeered at Hamet, who ought to have foreseen that reaction even if she had flinched.

"Point against green, feint after disengage. Green retires from the list," came the dispassionate voice of the referee, muffled because of his face mask. That meant Hamet would not get another bout, though he'd won his first two.

Marend ignored Hamet and sat down on the bench. The next match had begun, but she didn't see it. She was mentally reviewing her bout with Hamet, and savoring her win.

The first point happened quickly. Marend flexed her fingers on her thighs, and breathed deeply. She hoped this match would go longer, so she could rest her arm. She knew she wasn't the best. You had to be fast and strong. She was only fast. At least she was fast enough to make it to the finals in the sword competition, which was up there with archery and riding as most popular academy contests.

Hamet had given her trouble from her first week, and all through the following three years, but she'd discovered early on that she was not his only target. For two years she'd longed to get skilled enough to challenge him to a blood duel outside the academy, until she found out that the king disapproved of duels. She then decided that victory would be sweeter if carried out right there in the academy, within the regs. It would also not risk her main goal, which she had never lost sight of: to earn enough credit to be chosen as her father's replacement, and become the Jarlan of Methden.

"Point to red," declared the emotionless voice of the referee.

Marend wondered who the ref was today. He was good. Not a hesitation. But then they were always good, it's just that this one was not gray-haired, as usual. He was tall and blond, which meant he could be pretty much anyone.

"You'll fight Keth, I think," a voice murmured in Marend's ear.

She glanced at the long nose and gray eyes of Tem, one of her barracks mates. "And you?"

He squinted at the other students. "Hatch, I think. Or Blackeye. Either way, I'm dead."

"Ndarga, red. Hardaun green," the list-keeper called. And, "Temerec red, Ventdor green."

Tem sighed and headed for the green rack. Marend went over to pick up a blade from the rack of swords with a thin strip of red painted around the guard.

"Stance."

Marend fell into position, facing tall, weedy Kethadrend Hardaun. He was a lot like Marend, great with a bow, uneven with a blade. Her one advantage was speed and precision; hard as she'd worked, she was never going to have commensurate strength. She was just too small and light, which she had hated until the last year or so, when she'd become resigned. It helped that she was not the only one. Seret, a barracks mate, was actually scrawnier than Marend, and only a finger taller, but she was like a stooping hawk on the back of a horse, and her shots always hit the center of the close target, even in rain and wind. If Seret didn't end up a captain of light skirmishers in the cavalry, then Marend would eat that sword.

Keth finally made his move after shifting from foot to foot, and she let him blow by, tapping him over the heart. And again. And again.

"Point to red, disengage. Green retires."

Keth flashed her a quick grin as they saluted one another. He was no grudge-holder. And he'd beaten the entire school at long-range target, where strength prevailed over precision.

Marend sat down on the combatant bench, which was now thin of bodies. The spectator benches were now full. Nearly the entire academy was there to see the final matches.

"Ndarga, red. Senelac, green."

Marend got up. Her arm was tired. She flexed it unobtrusively as she walked to the rack, and tightened her gut. She wouldn't mind losing to Blackeye or Tem, but Hatch Senelac was a smartmouth flash who'd galled her her first two years by calling her by the title she did not have, even though she'd twice said her name was Ndarga, not Methden.

He hadn't done so this year, but she'd put some effort into avoiding him. She took up her stance, raking her eyes down his tall form. She was going to lose, but she wouldn't let him have it easily.

She breathed the way Sveneric had taught her, and when the ref called out, "Stance," she was half-aware of her spine straightening, and strength flowing through arms and legs to hands and feet.

Hatch charged off the mark. She beat off his initial attack, aware, as he was, of each of them assessing the other. She saw three death-wound openings, and knew them for traps. Once, she pulled back from an outer-edge scoring spot. A clean point in senior training was a tap over the heart.

There was his throat again. This time she briefly met his eyes. Why was he baiting her? She struck low, smacking his leg hard enough to sting: stop that.

His grin flashed as he beat her blade back and then renewed the attack. Back and forth, each trading the offensive twice, then she turned her right shoulder a hair too far to ease a hard riposte, and whump. There was the tap straight over her heart.

"Point to green, disengage. Red retires."

That was three, she realized belatedly. She saluted and

turned away without looking at her opponent. If she saw him sneering, she'd stew in impotent rage. Who needs it?

"Ventdor, red. Resanen, green."

Marend reached the red rack and dropped her blade in, then turned away to climb up into among the spectators. A thump on her shoulder stopped her.

"Close one, Methden," Hatch said.

She sifted his words and his face for sarcasm, and even if she didn't see or hear it, she knew it was there, because he'd called her Methden once again. She turned away without speaking—and Hatch, who had had a very rough year, took in that cold expression, wondering why she was such a snot to him, but to no one else. Especially when *everyone* knew the king was training her to take Methden over.

Marend climbed to the benches to sit with her barracks mates. One of their number was among the last three, then he, too, joined them, and they sat forward to watch the final bout, between Hatch and Blackeye. Those two were very evenly matched. It was a pass so fast it was difficult to follow that netted Hatch his win.

After the final salutes, all gazes turned to the ref. If he saluted them with his referee's blade, it would signal general approbation for them all. If he pulled off his mask with no salute, it would signify disapprobation, which was as bad as an outright accusation of cowardice or loss of honor in some other way.

That was to the seniors in general. In specific, if the king himself came down to award the shoulder flash of a first place, it meant his approval. But if he didn't...

Up flashed the sword, and down. The room erupted in cheers. The ref laid down his sword, then pulled off the mask. Sweaty blond curls stuck to a familiar face, flushed from the heat in mask and padding—David of Detlev's gang, who turned up occasionally, only seen from a distance, as when he commanded one side during the first two Academy Games.

David awarded the first place patch to Senelac, and they were dismissed.

Seret, who could do anything on horses, fell in step beside Marend. On her other side Tem fell in. Rom hailed them from across the parade ground, and they soon found themselves at the alehouse where the academy congregated. Rom, who Marend thought of as Rom-Red in order to distinguish him from her friend at Methden, always had plenty of money, and bought them all a round.

"The king didn't come down," Seret said.

Marend made sure her face didn't show her inward gloat.

"I'd say we've not done too badly, at least," Tem began.

Seret grunted. "I won't say anything until I know what our first assignment is."

"Oh, it'll be scut-work, no doubt," Rom predicted. "That's traditional. But it's only a year. Then … North Army for me, I hope. Close to home."

"Desk-jockeys," Tem said, raising his mug. "No more rising before dawn and running around the academy."

They all knew Seret would end up in North or South Army, as those were where the light cavalry were posted, unless she was sent to the rangers, who roamed from Sindan-An to the Nelkereth. They debated those in a cheery way, everyone refraining from commenting about Marend's future, which she appreciated.

They moved on to speculate about the rangers' duties as Marend surveyed the room. There was Hatch's curly dark head in the middle of a rowdy group. Judging by his flushed cheeks, he was already drunk. Why? He'd won first place in most of the Games, and he and Blackeye were so obnoxious they surely didn't care who awarded their firsts, as long as they got firsts.

A shift of movement as someone in their group brought a fresh tray. In the general grabbing, a space opened up. Hatch happened to turn, and their gazes met. She let hers go diffuse and turned back to Seret, pretending she'd not seen. Ugh.

As soon as she could, she excused herself, and made her way back to the barracks. Bragging parties were dull, and she had no head for drink. One was enough to put her to sleep. Her eyelids were already heavy, as she hadn't slept much the previous evening.

Before she reached the building, a shadow flickered in the side archway, directly under a torch, and David stepped out. She jumped, then hissed out a breath. "Don't … do that. I thought you were Imry, about to gut me."

David laughed. "I don't know why he would slink around

here just to knife you, but I'm sorry I startled you."

They went inside the empty barracks building, and Marend sat on her bed, eyeing David in question.

He raised both hands. "I'm not here to rake up old mistakes. Have you heard my list?"

"I thought you never made mistakes."

"Wrong. We'd be here all night. Senrid told me to pass on his compliments on your handling of the Hamet situation."

"He saw?"

"Yes. He was in the back. Slipped in while all of you were watching the last rounds."

Marend was still wearing her black jacket. She found it stifling suddenly, and unfastened it to fold away in her trunk, then straightened out her wrinkled shirt as she said, "I haven't spoken to him in the three years I've been here."

"Did you think you were in disgrace?"

"Yes. No. I know he doesn't chat with students, unless there's trouble, and I worked hard not to break even the tiniest rule. But I can't help remembering all the stupid things I did. Thought he hated me, and I can't blame him."

"No, no. It's just that he really dislikes ..." David hesitated before saying the words *hero worship*, a thing that could at a touch or a lingering glance turn into an admiration more personal. Marend's gaze was steady, without any expectation whatsoever. So she had not heard Fenis Senelac and some of the academy senior staff gossiping about what a perfect Marloven queen she'd make, in another five, maybe seven years. After she got some seasoning guarding the southern border from Methden. Her gaze was utterly innocent of that kind of speculation.

David finished, "... social chat, as you said. Look, do a good job at whatever you're assigned as your year of training, and I expect Senrid will be sending you to Methden, and freeing poor Mordan Nauldra so he can come back to the royal city again."

Marend's heart leaped fiercely, then the joy died away. David meant well, but it wasn't him making the decisions. And Senrid still hadn't spoken to her. She thanked David anyway, then he surprised her by saying, "What is your evaluation of the academy?"

She blinked, wishing she hadn't drunk that ale. "What do I think?" she repeated stupidly. "The first year, I didn't think at all. So much to get used to. So many rules. Classes." Being called Methden, and having to ignore it.

"So many invisible rules," she said slowly. "Ones between us, never spoken by the instructors. I guess I always knew that, because we had some invisible rules at Darchelde, when your gang was there, living with mine, but we all knew we had different commanders. Does that make sense?"

"It does."

"There were some who stepped on my heels. Mostly verbal. But sometimes elbows and the like. Until the Ambush class."

"What happened?"

Marend's lip curled. "You remember all MV's lessons. I guess some of the others, the older ones especially…" *Such as Hatch Senelac.* "…were runners during the war. That was dangerous. Not saying it wasn't. But they were to take to the trees or the ground if they saw the enemy. Whereas you know what MV taught us."

"I do," David said, hiding a smile. "And?"

"And so, I knew all the moves when the instructor began. I didn't say anything. Just did them, but I was so used to them, when he put us to spar, I put down all my partners the way MV taught us. The instructor pulled me out, and I didn't quite get him flat, but I tapped two nasty deaths on him." She touched two nerve clusters that MV had taught them. "So I was dismissed that class. But I had to take extra maths, because I was so bad at accounting. I'd thought all that was left to the desk jockey. I guess you have to oversee what the desk jockey is doing, and then there's the applied maths, which I really like. You know, roof joints, walls, sapping. Field logistics. But I meant to say, after I was dismissed Ambush, they, Ha—the ones who stepped on my heels, treated me … differently."

"How?"

"Still the insults and all. But no more elbows. They kept wide of me. But that's me. You asked about the academy. The first year was hard, mostly because of the duels, so we began to have bed checks, and some hard runs in bad weather. Same, the second year. Then … couple of people caught that shit of a commander…"

"I know all about it. Go on."

"Before that there was, oh, I think a sense that you *say* we want peace, and order, but everybody was looking for a fight. Then that happened. Hatch and Blackeye didn't say anything to the king because they really thought they'd be promoted right out of the academy into command. The two who dug up the old laws that outlined that trial and the execution form, I think they expected to jump the promotion list to be royal castle desk jockeys. But instead they got a terrible assignment and demotion."

"Do you see why?"

"I think so. We were talking, and somebody pointed out that what they saw as clever, the king saw as maneuvering behind him."

"It's important to him to be able to talk to the desk jockeys in particular. They are his elites. He shares ideas with them, and welcomes debate. But they used their access to restricted areas without telling him."

"My father said once that he trusted Mordan Nauldra, though he hadn't wanted a desk jockey at first. He said Mordan was like his extra hand, but that meant Mordan did not give or carry out orders that Da didn't know about. But they all thought they were doing a good thing. Is it still breaking the king's trust?"

"Certainly an important aspect."

"I guess that puts them at fault, though a lot of people don't see them at fault."

"I don't know that trying to find fault is a useful way to see this matter," David commented. "If you're going to have a king, then you have to expect that king to want to know what everyone in his command chain is doing."

"That makes sense," Marend said, seeing herself in her father's command tower at Methden. And someone sending off the garrison for some purpose they thought a good one, without telling her. She scowled at her hands. "Yes, I see that. Anyway, Hatch and Blackeye, they didn't get promoted. And they didn't even spend the winter with the rest of us, working on our weakest subjects, and getting to play around with lances and the like. They were sent off to scrape boats. And they came back to do their third year, like the rest of us."

"Why do you think Hatch is drunk right now?"

"The king never spoke to him, even after his wins." Marend looked away. "But he hasn't spoken to me, either." She considered that, decided that she'd talked about herself instead of answering his question, and said, "I really don't know how to evaluate the academy. It just is. I think none of us expected the way things went this year. Like leaving the academy for our part in the eradication project, instead of only for games. I thought it would be boring. But it was interesting, using applied maths for the project. And when we finished our part, laying the foundations," she added with satisfaction, "I wondered who gets to do that at Methden. Mordan will do a good job," she added hastily, in case it sounded like she had expectations. "Anyway, there will be no sign Norsunder was ever there at the North Bridge."

"I agree with your prediction. Meanwhile, before I take myself off, fair's fair. I asked you questions. Have you any for me?"

She looked up, enormous gray eyes startled. Then her lips shaped the word *Retren*.

"Your brother is fine. Right now, I believe, he's having the time of his life working on a very fast ship that is tracking down the last of the pirates that slipped past the Chwahir blockade up north." David rose to go.

Marend nodded, swallowed, then looked up. "Does regret go on forever?"

"Welcome," he said, "to the snake pit.

❧ 18 ❧

Marend was one among several of the seniors leaving the academy still waiting for their exit interview with Senrid when word came down through Assistant Headmaster Marec that the king had urgent affairs, and he himself was passing out their assignments for their year of service.

Marend's immediate thought was that she was still in disgrace, until she saw that she was only one of many. Further, her assignment was assistant desk jockey for South Army. Even Marend figured that it only made sense if her next step would be either South Army (as prestigious a post as North Army) or Methden. She firmly told herself that even if her future was to be Methden's desk jockey, she would be happy, and in any case, even if she was assigned to wand the stables, she would do her best.

She rode south with her bunk mate (sure enough, Seret was assigned as a rider to the light skirmishers at South Army), their spirits high. It was Hatch Senelac and Blackeye Ventdor who got the scutwork assignments, one a night watch sentry on the city walls — not even the royal castle — and Blackeye to West Army, a post everyone hated. But those two left determined to excel at what they knew very well was a silent challenge from the king. They knew that promotion would come if they toughed it out. The army was still hurting too badly to waste anyone. But they were done with trying to run justice on their own, oh, yes.

That king spared them a thought as long as it took to tidy his desk. When he transferred to Tannentaun, in what used to be Vasande Leror (now Sindan-An again), academy affairs fell away.

Ivandred was dying.

Now revered as intensely as he had once been feared, Ivandred had made it two years beyond predictions, partly due to Siamis's unstinting efforts to find a cure, but mostly due to sheer effort of will. Though by now Ivandred's body was so weak it was wearying to wake to another day, he could not die and leave any of his First Lancers alone.

The last one slipped away two nights before the turn of the year, and this morning, a week into the new year 4763, Siamis contacted Senrid on the mental plane, saying only that Ivandred would not last out the evening.

Of all those who worked in the upper reaches of the royal residence in Choreid Dhelerei, fewer than five knew that Senrid had transferred as often as he could to that quiet house rebuilt by Princess Lasva Lirendi of Colend, after she stepped down as Queen of Marloven Hess.

By the end of 4761, ten of the First Lancers were left, in addition to their king and leader; three had chosen to stay with descendants, and died surrounded by family. The other seven, many too young to think of marriage before that infamous ride centuries ago, went with Ivandred to that large, accommodating house, where at first Ivandred wandered from room to room, seeking traces of Lasva. He found them everywhere, in the colors, and the graceful lines, faithfully preserved for four centuries.

Over the next year, he had read through the yellowed scraps stored in a trunk — mostly household accounts — and moved out to the garden she had made.

During the clement seasons, whenever Senrid or Siamis arrived, they often found him in the garden, making meticulously exact renderings of the different plants. The precision of hand to eye that hereto had gone into his martial skills now honed his draughtsmanship, so that he produced increasingly fine drawings.

Then there were the wintry days when he could not rise from the bed, for he, once so hot-blooded, could not withstand the cold. Senrid began reading the Inda record to him, which took all that year and part of the next; sometimes Siamis was there, and the three of them enjoyed discussing long-ago personalities, which led to theories on kingship, and whether war was more weakness than weapon.

When Ivandred asked questions, Senrid wrote them down for Fox if he turned up again. Senrid was thinking of these questions as he transferred to the quiet house, redolent of astringent herbs. That meant Siamis was there. He had learned somewhere about the combining different scents for their soothing effect; the plants that did not grow in that garden, he brought from places all over the world.

Two blond heads turned when Senrid entered, one pale, one golden. Senrid perceived a look in Ivandred's eyes that caused his neck to grip. It wasn't terror. Or anger. Far from it. There was a detachment to Ivandred's gaze. Not indifferent. Liminal.

"You know Askan is gone," Ivandred whispered.

Askan—a very, very distant relation to Hibern, whom Senrid had not seen since the beginning of the war—had been the last of the First Lancers to die.

"I know," Senrid said. He had presided over the Disappearance. As the seven had each wished, there was no public memorial.

"Remember. No parade," Ivandred said, gathering his strength to speak. "No memorial. Let them remember me…" He flicked thin fingers up.

"The return of the banner to the royal city," Senrid said. "I'd want the same. It shall be as you wish."

Ivandred sank back, his expression easing. "I know Lasva better now. Living in this house. Than I ever did when she was alive."

On either side of the bed, Senrid and Siamis bent closer to hear the soft whisper.

"On the other side of death. If I still know myself, I will find her. To see if she is finally happy."

Senrid looked away, then back. He had read the Emras Testament after he finished Fox's Inda memoir, but that he had not shared it with Ivandred, who had spoken little about his own day, when his beloved queen had loved someone else. A subject on which Senrid had nothing to say.

Instead, they had ranged over all the details of their shared ancestor, centuries before Ivandred's own birth, and their speculation had centered around Inda's motivations. He who had been the greatest of all Marloven Harskialdnas—but who had laid that power down with no regrets.

Ivandred's hand twitched on the covers, and he struggled to speak.

Senrid took his hand, and bent close, but this time, though Ivandred's lips tried to shape words, his strength had gone.

His eyes closed. Senrid felt the smallest twitch of the cold hand lying in his, and closed his fingers more firmly around Ivandred's, until that hand slackened, and his breathing stopped.

Siamis touched Ivandred's forehead, and gave his head a slight shake, though Ivandred would never again hear spoken word. Together, he and Senrid straightened Ivandred's hands, and clothes, and the long pale hair. Then Senrid spoke the Words of Disappearance, and looked around the room, his throat aching. The air was still, almost as if Ivandred's spirit hovered, watching. But surely that was mere maudlin emotion.

Time to get one's mind on practical things. "How long, do you think?" Senrid asked.

Siamis's light gaze lifted. There was a slight pause, as if he would say something else, then changed his mind. "No more than two years more, I expect."

Senrid was one of the very few who had guessed—at the outset—that Siamis, and not Norsunder, had been responsible for taking down the world-wide communication system called the scribe desk, a complexity that had grown organically over centuries. Senrid would have done the same. The destruction of the lighters' communication system had been about the only telling blow against Norsunder in its invasion: Imry Llyenthur had counted on taking it, first to follow the enemy's last desperate messages to one another, and then to co-opt it to Norsunder's use.

Ever since Norsunder's destruction, Siamis—in his numerous guises—had been working hard to restore the scribe desk, which both the northern and southern mage guild leaders had gloomily predicted would require at minimum ten years. He only took time to visit Ivandred, and to perform the rare task for Detlev.

"Improvements?" Senrid asked.

"Mostly clearing away redundancies in the magic,"

Siamis said.

Senrid rose, and it was his turn to hesitate. But he had promised. "Clair has asked each of the three times I've contacted her since the war ended to pass along—"

"I know," Siamis said, smiling. "That message has reached me through five or six different sources."

"Was that palace really your home?"

"In the sense that I was born there. My early years were spent there. But we did not regard such places with any sense of ownership. Clair thinks she turfed me out of my home, I expect," Siamis said, heading for the door. "She thinks she owes me something—detritus of the enforced proximity necessitated in the defense against Ilerian. It will pass." He lifted a hand in farewell, and vanished.

There had to be more to it than that. Siamis's haste seemed to underscore the conviction, but Senrid was not one to pry. He hunted up the caretaker he'd appointed to see to Ivandred's comfort. "Tell the servants to cover the furnishings, and tidy the house. Leander might want it back."

He gave a few more orders, picked up the latest roll of Ivandred's drawings, then he transferred back to his study, where he set Ivandred's questions in a drawer, and locked it against the time Fox might return. Then he frowned at the waiting reports, and forced his mind to concentrate.

The drawings … he wasn't sure what to do. Traditionally, the only things affixed to walls were war trophies.

He laid them aside to be considered later.

So passed the rest of winter.

The bitter winter waned, and with it the grief he kept hidden. A new spring brought a fresh crop of academy scrubs. Senrid stepped back deliberately, as Marec moved into his role as Headmaster: all those who had spent their formative years under Keriam had now moved on. Keriam's benevolent shadow would not interfere with Marec's authority.

The time that would have been freed up went to dealing with the west. The largely fictional government of Enneh Rual, which had been created by treaty in order to confine Senrid's grandfather, had pretty much dissolved during the war. The Iascans had gone right back to their preferred style, which was each village governing itself, with a representative sent to a Council of Elders that only met if there was necessity. Otherwise, they expected the Marlovens to patrol the land to the east, and the waters beyond their fishing territories—and otherwise to leave them alone.

Nobody much liked being posted to the western garrisons unless they'd lived there as children and had connections among the Iascans. Such as Marend Ndarga, whose black hair attested to Iascans among the Ndarga forebears. Her diligence at South Army elicited nothing but praise. Senrid would send Marend to Methden as jarlan the next year, now that she was coming of age.

Any thought of Marend never failed to bring her younger brother Retren to mind. Senrid wondered, as usual, where Retren Ndarga was...

...while Retren Ndarga—now coming up on sixteen—stood high on the topgallant mast of the *Lheit*, one arm slung tight around taut rigging as he peered at the four pirates in chase.

"How far?" Puddlenose bawled.

Retren wiped his wet face against his sodden sleeve as a gust of rain drummed sails, wood, rope, and crew. The mast swung another wide parabola, which Retren used to calculate, then he called down, "Five cables, maybe six."

On deck, Puddlenose laughed, rubbing his hands, his long sailor-braided brown queue swinging like a cat's tail. He had been watching the rough coastline of the eastmost of the Delfin Islands approach. Close ... close ... ah, there was Bunghole Bay, and—yes! A waiting ship, poised to pounce.

The moment Puddlenose recognized the *Tzasilia*, rigged fore-and-aft for speed, he shouted to the waiting crew, "Back the mizzen topsail!"

The *Lheit*'s crew had been gathered on deck, either at halyard, helm, or mast, in expectation, in spite of the miserable weather. Those with the most experience had seen in Puddlenose's grin, his pacing from rail to rail, a possible ruse against the *Claw* and *Whiskey Gold*, two vicious marauders they had been chasing all the way up the strait for a couple of months.

In that time, the two pirates had collected a new pair of

followers, who had been lurking in one of the many tiny bays along the strait. Each time the new group of four vanished into a storm, they'd invariably attacked any ship they saw, as the entire coast on both sides was ready and waiting. Puddlenose knew that all four had to be desperate for stores.

The way came off the *Lheit*.

Claw's captain, also watching, saw the fast ship that had shadowed them since the turn of the year slow, as if baiting them. He cursed. "It's luring us," and bellowed, "Wear! Wear!"

Signals flew up the foremast — and *Claw* and *Whiskey Gold*, instead of swooping on the lone *Lheit*, used the wind to slide away, back toward Halia, both crews cursing. They were so close to the Delfin Islands, and supplies, so very close!

The new followers looked from the signals to the humps on the western horizon, and the bolder of the two decided that a fleet of four was too many. They were used to running alone; the second ship, seeing the change of direction, decided that they would also go for the island right before their eyes, and prepared to raid.

The two ships ran for the nearest harbor, which looked temptingly deserted as the Delfs — whose lookouts on the highest hill had been watching — lay in wait, hidden from view from the sea.

"Those two have to be northerners, either that or they're skunked. No southerner would ever take on the Delfs with only two ships full of warriors. And that takes care of those two," Puddlenose said with satisfaction. "Let's make sure *Claw* and *Whiskey Gold* sail straight into the Chwahirs' waiting arms."

The crew worked sail and helm, and the ship gathered speed as it slanted after the two ships heading east. When Puddlenose was satisfied that the targets would sail straight to the waiting Chwahir, he went below and summoned his visitors.

His niece Aurora and Aurora's best friend, Madelon Delieth of Everon, hopped into the cabin. Behind them came Retren Ndarga, just turned sixteen, his wrists protruding from the sleeves of the tunic he'd bought right before New Year's. "It's time for you to shift to Mearsies Heili," Puddlenose said to the ten-year-olds.

Madelon clutched at the medallion that Clair had made

for her, as Aurora scowled. "Is there danger? You said we only have to go if there's danger."

"There's likely to be some danger," Puddlenose said. "We're going to be pinching those two brutes between us and the Chwahir, and we promised half-a-dozen harbors we'd toss the pirates to the mers—those who don't die fighting—and burn those ships to the water line. You are too young for what is bound to be a nasty scene, because they won't go easy. And they know, after what they've done for the past five years, there will be no mercy."

"Oh-h-h-h-h-*kay*," Aurora muttered, and moped out. Not that she wanted to see bloodshed. She most definitely didn't. But it meant their adventure was over. And Madelon would have to return home to Ferdrian. And lessons. Lots and lots of lessons, because the pile of work her mother had sent along was barely half done.

There was no mercy with Tahra, either.

$$\approx 19 \approx$$

Madelon's and Aurora's steps lagged as they left Puddlenose's cabin and dropped belowdeck to fetch their things from the space in the forepeak where Puddlenose's underage crew bunked together.

Aurora's voice floated back, "At least your next birthday will be eleven, and your mother said she'd let you sail with Dtheldevor's old ship. And now you know signal flags, so you can…"

Their high voices faded as Puddlenose gave Retren a friendly smile. "You heard. I can send you to Mearsies Heili, too. But it has to be your choice."

Retren sifted the words for layers of meaning, and as usual, found nothing amiss. Puddlenose was like Jilo in that way: what he said was usually what he felt.

He spoke slowly, picking his words in the Mearsiean language, "I no longer think it cowardice, to not want to kill. Their faces…" He gestured around his head. "Marloven doesn't have the words, so I cannot translate them over."

Puddlenose raised his palm. "I think I have it now. You look at some enemies and you see ambivalence. Or regret. Or confusion. Or a very bad childhood. And you want to fix them. Clair is the same." Especially now, Puddlenose was thinking. "I think you ought to talk to her, and she will be able to send you wherever you want to go next. Whereas I've got this one token, for sending people to Mearsies Heili. I don't know magic." He shrugged. "You've been a terrific crew member. Always welcome back."

When Madelon and Aurora reappeared, each carrying a satchel over her shoulder, Puddlenose said the same to them, then one by one magic seized and thrust them to the

Destination outside the white palace in Mearsies Heili.

"We're ba-a-a-a-ck," Aurora shrilled, Mad on her heels.

They found Clair in the library, with company. Aurora, Madelon, and Retren stopped in the doorway. Then they saw that everyone was familiar, and all three relaxed, as Aurora ran to give Clair and Seshe quick, hard hugs. "It was so-o-o-o fun. Thank you for letting us go."

"Jilo," Retren exclaimed, his usually somber face transforming in a brief, blinding smile.

"Lyren-Sartora," Aurora exclaimed, at the same time Mad sighed and rolled her eyes.

"I know. Here to take me back to prison. Puddlenose musta writ to Tahra-Mama."

"As promised. So I'm here to fetch you. But not right this moment," Lyren-Sartora said briskly. "I barely got rid of transfer reaction. Go get in the last of your playing, if you want."

Madelon needed no second invitation. "Let's go down to the Junky," she whispered, as if being in the underground hideout would give them more time than running around in the palace.

Aurora sent a last, considering glance back, then the two were gone.

Clair said, "How was your journey?"

"We caught up with the pirates we had been chasing..." Retren began to answer, in his serious, painstaking way, then he saw Lyren-Sartora, as if for the first time, and stammered, his voice breaking. Retren had always thought her pretty, but now she was pretty in a way that heated him up all over, and transformed his tongue into a rolled-up sock.

Lyren-Sartora didn't hear a word about pirates, rigging fore and aft for speed and maneuvering, or how tough the Delfin Islanders are. She was considering Retren's reaction. Between their last meeting and this, he had grown at least a head. That, and he was turning into a very handsome lad. If on the skinny side. She'd smiled his way until she saw him blink, his pupils wide—and she sighed inwardly.

Of course it was flattering when boys stuttered to a stop as soon as they laid eyes on her. Or stumbled into a door. But of recent months—she still couldn't define it—the warmth of attraction, which she had begun to enjoy, could in less than a heartbeat turn from potential to intent in those unblinking eyes. Then she felt suffocated, which was worse when she sensed their hurt if she recoiled. She much preferred the trick of smile and glance, the laughing exchange of almost-insults. Banter, that was it. She hated hurting anybody, especially when it happened before she could stop it. She had to learn to dampen down whatever this was.

She let her gaze drift, and her smile flatten to politeness, and noticed at the extremity of her perception that Retren flushed and recollected himself. He remembered what he'd been talking about. Keeping his attention solely on kind, white-haired Clair, he told her how much he'd enjoyed his two years aboard the *Lheit*, and what a terrific captain Puddlenose was, and he was glad the Chwahir Silver Fleet was still there, stationed off the Nob.

While Retren spoke to Clair, Lyren-Sartora said to Jilo, "What did I interrupt? I mean, before the girls arrived back, and interrupted my apology for interrupting?"

Jilo blushed — why? Surely *he* wasn't … oh! He was feeling awkward as he mumbled something about plants not surviving in his attempt at a garden.

"It has to be the soil," Seshe said, rescuing him before Lyren-Sartora could figure out how to. Seshe, out of them all, seemed the least changed in the time since Lyren-Sartora's last visit, except her mellow voice had gotten lower. "I've suggested several plants I thought fairly hardy."

Lyren-Sartora knew that Clair and her girl gang had relinquished the Child Spell, because Tahra had commented approvingly about that. *And once she did, the others followed along, exactly as I predicted,* Tahra had finished. *I feel more confident about sending Madelon there, now that their silly pretense at staying children forever is a thing of the past.*

Clair's calm face still bore hints of sorrow in the corners of her eyes, and in the shape of her mouth. Otherwise she was, at most, a finger's breadth taller, and there was a suggestion of new curves in her flowing tunic-shirt and her loose trousers gathered at the ankle. Lyren-Sartora did not pretend to be wise. She'd made too many mistakes for that. But if that hint of sadness would disappear, Lyren-Sartora could wish the Mearsieans would stay forever the way they'd been. Not her idea of silly at all. However, you don't say such things, unless you want everyone to be uncomfortable.

Jilo explained that as long as he paid the swingeing prices charged at the Nob—and did not try to interfere in their self-rule—those cantankerous, independent-minded people were perfectly willing to permit the Chwahir to use the Nob as their supply base as they continued to patrol that stretch of ocean where the four continents met.

Both conversations ended at the same time. Clair spoke into the pause to ask when Retren had eaten last. Retren's look of extreme hunger caused her to give a quick, soundless laugh. "Let's see what we can find."

Seshe smiled around at them all and followed Clair out, as Retren trailed after them. "Want some help in the galley—kitchen, I mean?"

Lyren-Sartora turned her gaze back to Jilo, who from all reports was doing the work of ten kings. Yet he was here. There was one thing she was sure of. She said in a fast whisper, "Invite Seshe to Chwahirsland."

Jilo blinked at her. "But ... what if she doesn't want to come?"

Lyren-Sartora sighed. "Who keeps offering a thousand different ways to help you?"

"I thought she'd tell me. If she wanted to," Jilo muttered, looking around like a criminal about to be caught raiding the crown jewels.

"You're forgetting you're a king now. How many people invite themselves to a king's place?"

"But I'm—" Jilo flushed even deeper. "I know. I keep forgetting."

Only you. Lyren-Sartora smothered a laugh as Clair, Seshe, and Retren returned, each bearing a tray.

The conversation was general as they ate, but Lyren-Sartora and Jilo both sensed a tension in Retren when the conversation got around to, "Where do you want to go next?"

Lyren-Sartora shifted attention away from Retren by joking about the pile of tutoring lessons awaiting Madelon if she had not—as Tahra suspected—kept up with the studies as she'd promised.

"Aurora will join her," Clair predicted. "Not together. She

also promised to be diligent."

The conversation became general—studies—favorite subjects—hated subjects—how fast time sped by when one was doing something fun, but it crawled when one was stuck with tedium—until Lyren-Sartora asked about improvements in Chwahirsland, as if she'd ever given a second thought to the place before this. She put her question first to Jilo, and then asked Seshe's opinion.

Which left Retren to Clair.

He had not intended to say anything, but somehow their conversation led to the war, as sometimes happened. He found himself telling her about his experiences on the border of Chwahirsland and Erdrael Danara, when he, MV, Mildred, Shontande Lirendi, Jilo and a few others had raided Efael's castle.

"Detlev was so reassuring," Retren admitted. "And I liked being invited to go study on his singing mountain. Yet I could not get past what they did. I'm not saying it wasn't necessary. It was. Those Black Knives were vicious. They lived to be vicious. It was carved in their faces. But when he said to come to the mountain-top, all I've been able to think is, I don't want to become an assassin."

Clair had listened with her eyes closed. "I'm glad you told me," she said finally. "I can assure you that Curtas's House, which is what they call the singing mountain, is not for assassins. The opposite, if anything."

"But it's *them*. There. Right?"

"From what little I've picked up, mostly through Madelon on her visits here, who overhears her elder sister Carl talking to Jessan, the direction of their training is away from assassination. Their intent it to fix what makes assassins."

Retren sighed. "I know I get things wrong. Especially when I was eleven. I once blamed my sister for … for things I know now she couldn't help. She was tricked into doing terrible things, when she was younger than I am now. By using all that we were brought up with. About kill or be seen as a coward. Or, that's how I understood it. And aren't they the same?"

Clair's expression of sympathy did not falter. She said, low-voiced, "All I can tell you is my own experience. Going to that mountaintop saved my life. It wasn't even a building then. Just tents. In winter. Adam and I, mostly, though Detlev came around once or twice, all we did was talk. But the influence of the disirad helps not just calm one's spirit, it enables a … oh, not detachment, but one can bear to talk out what before seemed unbearable. Do I make sense?"

"I think so."

"And so we talked. Sometimes he had me repeat certain truths, simple ones, until I could believe them. Until I could see my life, and what happened, in another way. I can still say those things, when the memory of exulting evil begins to shred my soul again."

Retren's nerves chilled.

"Before I went to that mountain, I was ready to walk into the sea, which I thought was the only thing a polluted person such as myself could do, to prevent the pollution touching the people I love. I think I would have, had Siamis taken me there."

Which was the last time she saw him.

Retren began to protest, "But you were preyed on. I know that much. None of it was your fault."

"I know that. I knew it. Fault was the least of my worries," Clair said. "There are far worse things than pointing fingers and shouting guilt, guilt. I lived every one of those things. The mountaintop saved me. And every time I think I might slip back to that thinking, I know that I can return. And just knowing makes me able to shake it off. It was so *peaceful*."

The conviction in her quiet voice, the lingering imprint of sorrow he sensed in the realm of the spirit, made him uncomfortable, but more profound was his conviction that she spoke the truth.

"I'll try it," he said, at the same time that Lyren Sartora said to Seshe, "Why don't you try it?"

The four looked at one another in a moment of confusion, then Lyren-Sartora laughed, adding, "I mean, testing the soil, and the sunlight there, yourself? Better than putting innocent plants in, just to hear about them failing."

Seshe took in Jilo's shy smile and the tight clasp of his fingers, saw Clair's nod, then said, "I think I'd like that."

When the evening ended, Clair sent Retren Ndarga on to Curtas's House, Jilo and Seshe transferred to Narad, and Lyren-

Sartora escorted a glum Madelon back to the reality of life in Everon.

A month later, spring had even reached the mountain heights. All the students at Curtas's House had been sent on assignments, some near, others quite far. Retren Ndarga, new, and still euphoric about what he'd found, ranged with Jessan Delieth on the other side of the mountain.

Alone, as they very seldom were, David and Adam took out a small boat onto the lake below the house.

At first there was little conversation, as Adam watched fireballs roll down David's arm and fall hissing into the lake water. The sun hung low and golden, the slanting light softening toward dusk.

Adam pulled his hat off and cast it onto the bench below the oarlocks.

David lounged in the bow, his feet resting on the gunwale, and the one arm dangling over so he could trail his fingers in the water. What would have taken concentration from Adam required only idle effort from David to bring puffs of fire into existence and send them rolling into the blue waters.

Adam had let his thoughts drift, like the boat. As often happened, myriad acknowledged and unacknowledged observations coalesced into a moment of clarity. "All our goslings are out testing their honks. I don't fear any of them will end up in a wolf's teeth."

"You're stating the obvious because…"

"Your mood."

"Contemplating," David said, "the speedy progress of a willow growing beside a river. And how people communicate."

"Oh."

"It worked. I've shaken off the world's most absurd crush, on a girl I don't really even know. I suspect it was her aura that got to me, which is almost as superficial of me as everyday lust."

"Ah."

"Which, I strongly suspect, she saw in an instant."

"I'm sure her going away to be a tree for a few years was

not aimed solely at you," Adam said.

"You mean I might be one of an army of languishing would-be suitors? Strangely, I don't find that comforting."

"Then leave her to her seasons, and contemplate the patterns we have before us here. Such as the two who quit, who were brought by Sveneric and me respectively. We were both very sure they were perfect for us. We guessed wrong."

"But they weren't wrong guesses in the sense of malicious intent."

"That is true, and somewhat reassuring. They just wanted different things — one wants to be a healer of the body, and the other got sidetracked into Ancient Sartoran studies. But I'm trying to learn how Detlev discerns them."

"I've given up." David leaned his head back, shutting his eyes. "Especially now that we — that is, I — will be commencing actual dyr studies." He opened his eyes and sat up. "Have you written up what you learned, wearing Nevreath's dyr chain?"

"I still don't have the words," Adam admitted. "So much of what I've translated … hmmm, falls into categories of what language meant then, and means now."

"Are you about to start spewing on the limitations of language?"

"Categories. That, and language as mirror. And language as door."

"And with that door we fall right out again into the air of the indescribable."

"Ineffable."

"When you get kerygmatic, it's time to peel vegetables." As Adam laughed silently, David sighed, sat up, and grabbed the oars. "At least, if I ever get to the other end of that silver chain, I'll know how to spot a good candidate. Let's get at those vegetables, since it's just us making dinner."

20

For so gentle a person, Chantala na Shagal could be insistent.

She had found such good company in Liere on her previous visit—and far more bearable weather—that when 4762 began drawing to a close, she spoke repeatedly of returning to Enaeran, and Liere's calm, soothing company.

Liere was that rare thing, a friend who demanded nothing; Chantala had long sensed the undercurrent of expectation, or even derision in her own court. Even those whose motivations were far more benign seemed unable to keep from pressing noisy parties, or ostentatious gifts, or jokes that everyone else seemed to comprehend, on Chantala.

All it took was once, a sweet-voiced "friend" asking if Chantala could just mention to his majesty this or that thing, and she became wary. Chantala might be cloud-minded most of the time, but her teen years had been spent tending to the needs of Denwy, the considerable province she had inherited from her mother, who had taught her to be wary of gifts and flattery attached to what she had termed invisible ribbons.

Liere never called her "your majesty" in private. She never once tied an invisible ribbon to her kindnesses. And there were so many kindnesses. Liere seemed to know before Chantala even had to frame the words when a room was not warm enough, or it was too noisy. Liere knew before Chantala said anything when she was tired, or did not want to eat, and never tried with jolly or coaxing words to force her to speak when she wished to remain silent.

After Chantala suffered two bad colds in a row, brought

on by the icy, windy weather of early winter in high Nente, Macael gave in, and sent acceptance for the invitation Liere felt obliged to make—having heard all year through Chantala's regular letters how wonderful that visit had been, and how she hoped to have another.

On hearing that the royal pair from Sles Adran was to come again, Liere's mother ended her own visit and returned to Imar. And Liere gave orders for Brydon's guest wing to be scoured and made ready.

Alas, Macael and Chantala's arrival occurred on the heels of a stunning three-day blizzard. The iced-over river was completely hidden under chest-high drifts of snow, requiring the outriders to toil ahead to clear a safe path. At least Shiovhan was looking its best under its fresh blanket, shabby roofs and poor roads alike smooth and white.

But all semblance of peaceful, wintry beauty skidded to a halt when they reached Brydon, to discover that Liere and Andri were not awaiting them on the proclamation balcony. No one was there.

Their own steward, sent ahead, as before, rushed out, sputtering and disclaiming. Macael, concerned for Chantala in the cold coach, said, "Never mind that. Conduct us to the king."

"He is not here, sire."

"Then to the queen."

The steward bowed, silently relinquishing the coming humiliation to the Enaeraneth, and so Macael and Chantala reached the palace to feel cold winds sweeping down the halls. Inside! How could that be?

They soon discovered Liere standing amid the snow-sodden rubble of the state wing. The roof over the high, vaulted ceiling of the ballroom had that morning collapsed under the weight of the heavy load of snow.

Liere saw them, wrung her hands once, then burst out laughing. "We meant to have a more civilized welcome!"

"Are you all right?" Chantala's voice was faint.

"No one was here," Liere was quick to assure her. "The room was empty. Ice cold—impossible to warm—we'd decided to forego using it this year. The guest wing is quite intact, I am glad to report, as its roof was the most recent one repaired." She hopped over the rubble, unable to be graceless even in so ridiculous a circumstance, and held her hands out to Chantala, smiling reassuringly. "No one was hurt, just very surprised. And your rooms are clean and warm. Come! We'll have you comfortable in a trice."

Chantala did not think of asking where Andri was, or the rest of the Enaeraneth court, and Macael—as he explained to her later—did not feel it polite to ask. To which Chantala admitted that even if they had Liere to themselves for a single night, she would be content. She cared nothing for parties.

As it happened, they had the rest of the week before the roads had been cleared enough for the hungry, bedraggled court to arrive. Before then, Liere entertained her royal visitors to the best of her ability.

Chantala was entranced. She relished the quiet every day, and took to a new game that Liere taught her with such passion they had to play it every night. This game involved only pen, paper, and imagination: each player wrote out a famous poem, leaving out key words. Then they asked the other players for random words to put in those spaces. After which they read out the new poem, frequently to hilarious effect.

Liere very quickly learned what sort of words would please Chantala the most, and they played for long hours, Chantala with a singlemindedness much like Trevor Andiran's when he demanded his favorite books and games over and over.

Liere smiled and coped, wondering why Andri had not reached for her on the mental plane. She knew he was alive, but that was all. Something was amiss, and he didn't want to tell her, she strongly suspected. Just like their boy when he was naughty, and tried to hide it.

Before sleeping at night, Liere held imaginary conversations with Andri, beginning with what they told Trevor Andiran when he wailed: "Use your words." Though she was at fault for not using her own words. Andri knew she was adept at farsense. The problem was, she was too adept. She disliked reaching for distant location. Oh, it was always good to sense Lyren-Sartora, glittering like a colorful star, but it was sheer, annoying habit to find her mind drawn west over the mountains, where she knew she would find Senrid. It was past time to shed childhood, child*ish,* habits. Times out of mind she had invaded his dreams when they were unheeding children, sometimes inadvertently, within her own dreams. What if she blundered like that when he was with someone? The thought was painfully humiliating—and never failed to waken her so thoroughly that she would invariably get up, and try to bore herself back to sleep with some necessary but tedious task.

Meanwhile, she had that strange, observant Macael and sweet, dependent Chantala there. At least Macael spent a lot of time in the study with mounds of papers, and Liere suspected he even transferred back to Nente, quietly, when he knew Chantala was napping or reading or being entertained by Liere. That was fine with Liere—not that he was ever rude, or unaccommodating. He was just so very hard to read.

The state wing was firmly closed off until it could be dealt with in spring. What little time Liere had aside from entertaining and overseeing the trickle of state affairs, she spent with Trevor Andiran. He, like most small people, wanted to run and scream and climb and play, rather than attend to lessons. He had to discover for himself he was only rewarded when he finished his task, just as grownups got their grownup awards when they finished theirs.

It seemed that realization was a long way off when he sneaked to the top of the stairs to throw his rock collection down, to watch them bounce—unfortunately, a young maid rushed out with a load of the old crockery Liere and Andri used when alone, to store until the guests were gone. She slipped, took a header, and the stacks of bowls made a loud, satisfying crash.

Trevor Andiran didn't even notice the maid. His screams of delight were solely for the rocks and crockery bits scattering and skidding on the marble. His mirth ended when Liere came out, looked sad, and said, "Rocks go away since they hurt someone."

He began to wail, and Liere could feel Chantala getting anxious, so she motioned to the hovering tutor to bundle the little boy to his room, where he cried himself to sleep, as Liere read Chantala to sleep in her suite. Her own head was aching at the end of that long day, and she was still not certain she'd done the right thing by her son, whose wailing had been solely over his lost rocks.

The following day produced the evidence that the laboring road guild was getting some of the main roads clear; Liere made a mental note to find the time to deal with road-clearing spells, something that many kingdoms sent, or hired, teams of beginning mage students to deal with, as it was tedious more than difficult.

The following day was also clear. One by one, hereto stranded people began to turn up, including nobles coming to Shiovhan for New Year's Week. Then, hard on a trickle of stranded merchants arrived a ragged, exhausted troop of King's Guard, with Andri lying on a stretcher in a cart, his head wrapped in a bandage, and his left arm and leg also wrapped.

He winced as they tenderly lifted him out and began to carry him upstairs. Rolling bloodshot eyes at Liere, he muttered, "Didn't want you worrying over what you couldn't help."

"It's that mine," Gared said, forgetting protocol, as usual, in his genuine upset. "That damned silver mine, it nearly collapsed on him. He was out for a day. The wind was coming in bad, and we thought we heard someone in there. We dug everyone out. Took a day and night, and he was scraped up bad, though nothing broken."

Unconscious for a day, then no doubt headachy from being hit on the skull—no wonder he didn't make contact. She regretted her thoughts about scolding him, as Andri stirred on the stretcher to look up at her. "Travelers. Hiding from the weather."

"Or something like," Gared agreed. "Then the collapse, and in the mess of digging, we lost track of one another, much less anyone else."

Liere stopped in the middle of the staircase, her gold hair swinging in the gleaming candle light, her eyes wide and furious. No one, hovering servants, King's Guard, or royal visitors, remembered having seen her angry, and were unable to look away as she said, "Close that mine. It's been nothing but trouble as long as I've known about it—" She saw Chantala's pale face upturned at the bottom of the stairs, and choked off more words.

Macael stepped forward, his quiet voice like snow on a scorched field. "In Bartal's records, he as much as admitted that. Which is why he let it be taken, while he was securing the valuable land in the south. That silver mine was reported as spent."

"Thank you," Liere called down to him, and ran the rest of the way up the stairs after the stretcher-bearers.

Servants held the doors to the king's suite wide, and others brought firesticks to get a fire going as Liere turned down the bed herself. Andri was laid down gently, his boots pulled off, and covers thrown over him.

"Did we know about that?" Liere looked from Andri to Gared. "The mine being spent, I mean."

"No." Andri threw his arm over his eyes; he had a terrible headache.

"We knew it was getting difficult," Gared admitted. "But we need that mine, he kept saying."

"We'll talk later," Liere promised. "I'd better get the new arrivals settled, and make our excuses to the Adranis."

To her immense relief, as soon as she came downstairs, Macael's chief steward approached, offering apologies, and said that his majesty believed it would be best if they cut their visit short. Thoughtful as always.

Liere was left to see the bedraggled court arrivals settled. Everyone seemed to need to hear the story about the collapsed ballroom, which by now she was thoroughly sick of relating. Then, finally, *finally*, she accompanied Macael and Chantala to their coach and outriders.

She ran up to the balcony to watch them reach the river. They were well and truly on their way.

She fled back to the king's suite to find Andri being tended by the grizzled healer Andri liked, Gared sitting by, and a couple of Andri's old street gang bustling about with bandages, hot water, and listerblossom steep, having stripped Andri and got him cleaned up. He was sound asleep, which was what he needed, the healer whispered.

She backed out, Gared following. His face was unwontedly serious as he said, "I'm no expert in mines, but I was put there once by Adon Marsael. I'm pretty sure it was sabotaged."

"Who? *Why?* Did they know it was spent?"

"Could be anyone. Including Adranis. Of course they

were the first ones blamed. We used to fight over that mine," Gared said.

"So obvious that they'd be idiots to do it," Liere said.

"Right. Andri thinks it was leftover Norsundrians, gone renegade."

"I know what to do," Liere stated. "Let's collapse it. Problem solved. That problem," she amended, thinking of the constant scarcity of funds.

"Not arguing," Gared said. "He won't, either. He went down there thinking someone was stranded. Most of the tunnels knee-deep, or more, in ice water. Mud sloughing from overhead."

"And he just had to be the one to check," Liere said on a sigh. "I know, I know, a good king doesn't ask anyone to do anything he won't do himself." She forbore mentioning that a queen would think of a better way.

That was when the healer said, "He really needs to sleep."

Everyone trooped out. Liere went to Trevor Andiran's room, where he was resisting getting ready for bed. "Come to see Da?" she asked.

Trevor Andiran brightened at once, and they went to the king's suite, where Andri lay. When Trevor Andiran saw the red-spotted bandages, and his father's pale, scraped face, his own face puckered.

Liere took his hand and led him out. "Da is hurt because he fell down, and things fell on him."

Trevor Andiran searched her eyes. She shared a memory of her own pain, when she had fallen down as a child.

"Hurt," he said, his lower lip coming out.

"Hurt is what Finna felt, when she slipped on your rocks. She hurts."

Trevor Andiran remembered the rocks on the stairs, the broken bowls, and the young maid lying amid the crockery, wincing over a twisted knee as other servants picked up the mess. "Rocks hurt Finna," Trevor Andiran said.

"Yes. But rocks don't throw themselves. Do you see why Mama says, no throwing rocks down the stairs?" Liere held her breath, waiting.

Trevor Andiran's eyes filled. "Want rocks."

"Can you play safely with the rocks?"

"Yes."

"If you like to see them bounce, why don't we find a place to bounce them where no one will be hurt?"

"Yes." He brightened a little.

Liere turned him back over to his tutor, somewhat relieved. Empathy was awakening, unlike her eldest brother, who would have scowled and said that Finna should have walked, or stayed out of the way. So very like her father.

C hantala was silent as the royal carriage bumped over the ice-covered river to the outpost and its transfer Destination.

Once they had transferred to Nente and their palace high in the mountains, Macael saw her settled into her room, with two fires going. He waited while her maid tucked her up under a heavy yeath-fur robe.

"Liere and the Enaeraneth. Can't we just give them what they need?" Chantala said presently, as another maid brought in warm spiced milk on a fine silver tray.

Macael took the cup from the tray himself, running his fingers over it to test that it was not too hot or too cold, before handing it to Chantala. He said, "I suspect this is another of the invisible ribbon situations."

Chantala drank the milk down, and he gave the cup to the waiting maid to carry away as she said, "How so?"

"If one government gives another government something, the receiving government can feel as if there is an invisible ribbon tied around them, pulling. In a game, it's fun, as long as the player likes being pulled. But between two governments, the sense of being pulled is seldom perceived as a welcome one, according to what I have read. A sense of obligation. It can be a dangerous thing, and I wouldn't blame Andri for being wary. I would refuse such a thing myself."

Chantala considered this as she burrowed her chin down in the soft yeath, combed off thorny plants high in the mountains above Nente, and woven into these soft, warm blankets. "Do you have a solution?" She yawned, blissfully warm at last, inside and out.

"I believe I've thought of one. When the Elsarions split off to form Enaeran centuries ago, they were able to hold it partly because of military matters, which were funded by the gold mines that my branch of the family holds in Elsarion. When the family ruptured over the throne a couple of generations back, a truce of sorts was worked out when the gold mines were split between the two branches of the family. Andri's branch has been funding the government on half of what it had done previously, in essence. This situation, in addition to far too much civil war, and other poor decisions, have brought them to their present difficulties. If I were to restore all the mines to Andri's branch, it might help. But I have to find a way to do it without creating that sense of obligation."

Chantala reached for his hands, her icy ones pressing his as she looked earnestly into his face. "Do! Do! Oh, I wish gold were to be found in infinite quantities, when needed."

He laughed a little. "Then, I fear, it would lose its worth. Though not its beauty."

"My mother used to say, people cannot eat beauty, or warm themselves with it, when she paid my uncle's taxes. I never quite understood what she meant. But if you can help Liere, so that that roof doesn't fall on her or her little boy, I would be so happy."

Macael's solution was a legal missive sent a month or two later, to inform Andri that his people had been going over the Elsarion archives, and discovered some wording in the truce between the two branches that required either branch to relinquish its claim if it were to move outside the border.

Andri squinted at the heavy, sealed paper—his head still hurt a little late at night—and commented, "I suspect Macael had someone work up new papers, so he could pass off what he doesn't need anymore, and we need desperately."

"And he's doing it in a way that makes it your rightful due, and not a gift," Liere said. "You'll accept, I hope?"

Andri blinked in surprise. "I'd take it if he'd flung it into a pile of horseshit. If I'd ever had any sense of pride, I expect the last ten years would've thumped it out of me. All I feel is relief. And curiosity. Why'd he do that? And why now?" He grinned. "I expect we can attribute this windfall to the ballroom roof. That, and Chantala probably speaking up for your sake. What, you don't agree?"

Her smile had faded.

Andri scrutinized her. "You can't possibly be feeling guilty?"

Her face flooded with color at his incredulous tone. "No! Yes — a little. But the gold mine is not the cause. It's more the, oh, the nature of friendship. I can see Chantala's love reaching through this gift, and I wish I loved her back. I mean, I do like her very much. And I am astonished at the breadth of her knowledge of literature. What could she have accomplished had she not been poisoned? But I will confess this only to you: when I see the Adrani seal on a letter, there is a pulse of dread. And I know I let too many days pass before I write back. Some of that is genuine, in that my day is so filled. And I have to be so very careful what I write about. I bore myself, so I am afraid I bore her. Yet I know she would write every day if she could."

Andri lifted a shoulder. "She hasn't anything else to do. Macael does it all."

"She can't," Liere said on a sigh. "She's said repeatedly how badly she feels, but she cannot control the times when she goes weak, and has to lie down. And she is always cold, poor soul. No, there is no fault in her, and I will forestall the bolstering remark I can see you about to make by saying there's no fault in me either. I just wish … it was a real friendship."

"Every friend is different," he said. "Surely you've learnt that by now? Even with Gared, who I grew up with, there are some subjects I avoid because he doesn't want to hear them."

"Anything to do with kingship," Liere said, smiling wryly. *Or responsibility.* But that was unfair. He took his post as Captain of the King's Guard very seriously. It's just that the duties didn't extend much beyond being on guard at certain times, leaving the rest of his life for roistering. But Gared had never pretended to anything else. "I guess I want something that doesn't exist, the effortless give and take…" She paused, remembering that that had been exactly the nature of her friendship with Senrid.

She shook that off, a physical act, then blinked when Andri said, "You're thinking of Senrid, aren't you?"

"I am. But that was the unthinking friendship of childhood. He obviously doesn't feel that way now."

Andri was about to say, *No, he's crushing on you hard.* He hesitated. Soon after the war ended and he and Liere reunited, he mentioned that Gared was crushing on her—expecting the two of them to go off and do something about it, maybe with a little wine involved. Instead, Liere had looked guilty, and she'd thoughtfully and gently avoided Gared for some time after, until he had taken up with someone else. There were aspects to Liere that Andri didn't understand. And Senrid had been a complete mystery.

One thing he'd learned: what he thought might be a careless remark could be taken completely differently. Look at Thadara, who he knew had been crushing on him. But once, when he'd offered her a fling in thanks for a massive bookkeeping project she'd done, she'd recoiled as if he'd slapped her, and now she was gone altogether. Leaving them missing her expertise badly, though Liere was laboring hard to make up the slack, since numbers just would not stick in his head. And Liere insisted that putting the entire treasury into the hands of an unknown was an invitation to corruption.

No, better to keep his mouth shut until he better understood the nature of their relationship.

All these thoughts streamed through his mind as Liere stared into the distance, unsettled and angry all over again. Senrid had offered the first toast at their wedding, and then she'd never seen him again. Surely he didn't hold a grudge for that stupid argument on the beach? Oh, but the problem had begun much earlier, when she'd told him not to have children. And he had. And lost her to an assassin's knife.

Liere shifted again, as if physical distance could rid her of that horrible sense of grief, guilt, loss. Loss especially. Because Senrid was so good at effectively cutting anything extraneous out of his life. And she had made herself extraneous.

So think about something productive. "Shall we consider what this gold means in the immediate sense?"

Andri laughed. "One thing I know, I can get the King's Guard into uniforms at last. And furbish up the outposts that got destroyed in the fighting. More weapons. We can always use more weapons."

"It seems to me there are already far too many weapons

in this kingdom," Liere muttered.

"The purpose of a kingdom is to keep people safe from attack," Andri said.

"And also to keep people safe, meaning roads, houses. Stores when they cannot afford to get through winter. But we've been having this conversation since I first arrived. At least I can do something about the snow situation, if I shove aside my duties here and take to the road. Or perhaps I could create a token, layer it with spells, so that you could do it with a word as you ride around."

"Happy to do that. Sounds like fun," he said.

"It will be fun for about an hour," she retorted, smiling. "As first year mage students discover. But the effect will be clear roads no matter how terrible a blizzard happens."

"What happens to the snow?"

"It's a tiny transfer spell, so what you see is snow flung to the sides, as if by an invisible shovel, no, it's more like a wind."

"I can hardly wait to see that. Let's get the roof and other repairs done, and the new uniforms," Andri said. "Beginning right here at Brydon. Can't have the place tumbling down around our ears."

"I don't think that the restoration of this mine, or mines, is going to solve all our problems. All I know for certain is, gold is precious because it's a finite quantity that everyone wants." She thumbed her eyebrows. "I'll make time to talk to the bank people about how gold makes a … a treasury foundation, and I'll probably have to talk to the stringers' guild about how they calculate the worth of gold the world over."

Andri hugged her close. "You are so hot when you get that competence of yours going. Heh! I just realized. Here we are, just the two of us, young rover asleep, and no one banging on the door wanting us." He wiggled his brows suggestively.

She was about to say that she was not in the mood, but that thought appalled her. Was she getting old? No, that was absurd. She knew people of sixty, even older, who still got that light in their eyes and the little grin for one another. And it wasn't all that long ago when she couldn't get enough of him.

She flung herself on him, to prove that she was *not* old.

The weeks slid into months. She supervised rebuilding by day, and studying at night. The problem was, once she grasped the fundamentals—that gold wasn't the standard more or less accepted by the world, but *time*, and gold served as its symbol—there were still so many demands for what was definitely a finite source. Plus, the kingdom tokens—the five year credit tokens—would be coming due in less than two years. That meant there must be funds to pay off those tokens to whoever turned them in. Right now, people were even using them in place of money, but she knew if she did not make good on that debt, they would become worthless.

When she was too tired to deal with exchequer matters, she frequently sat by Trevor Andiran's small, slumbering form, repeating the road-clearing spell, over and over, to create tokens with a simple word release, that anyone could use. When Andri tried to remonstrate, she shook her head. "He wants me here while he falls asleep, I want to be here. One thing I know about childrearing is, all too soon they'll reach an age when they don't want a parental snuggle every night."

Andri promised that he could see through his end of that exercise in tedium—no wonder people paid mages—and took the King's Guard on a long exercise. They traded off laying the spells over the main roads, which took him away the latter part of spring, and all summer.

The year vanished fast, as Trevor Andiran's steps stretched from the tippy-toes toddle of a two-year-old to a three-year-old run, and his grasp of vocabulary (and attendant questions) widened.

Andri made one last round at harvest time, hoping that his turning up would keep the nobles from the old days honest in relinquishing their tax share. But this time he offered to take his boy along.

Trevor Andiran was thrilled, loving the horses, riding, and every animal encountered, though birds were his favorites; he was always trying to get them to eat from his hand. In turn, he proved to be enormously popular at Guard outpost and noble homes alike, his happy treble heard in a constant stream of questions. He played with both castle and warrior children; he had not been raised to make any distinction between servant and noble, which boosted his popularity with the former.

While they were gone, Liere oversaw the last of the repairs inside Brydon. She even learned how to reinforce walls and joins with spells, so that the palace would withstand the worst tempest, and then watched with satisfaction as artisans came in to cover bare stone with pilasters and cornices and cartouches, then the painters and gilders added their expertise.

"Next year, chandeliers," she said to her mother as they walked through the new, marble-floored ballroom on a golden, sun-slanting autumnal day. Liere's mother, known as Grandma Elen to her numerous grandchildren, most of whom were now nearly grown, came late each year, around the birthday of Prince Trevor Andiran.

She had decided to revert to her given name when visiting Liere in her capacity as queen of a kingdom, thus she was known as Honor Elenzeh Fer Eider to the Enaeraneth. That first year, when she came to help Liere after the birth, she had been overwhelmed by the size of Brydon, the number of servants, and the different language, in spite of Liere giving her the Universal Language Spell. There was always that tiny lag as idiom caught up with equivalent meaning in the Imaran tongue.

She had also found Andri overwhelming, with diamonds glittering at his ears, and the way he sauntered about, usually with at least a couple of armed guards at his heels, joking and laughing. Very much a king in some ways, but not the ways she expected. She had brought her two best gowns, one for morning and one for evening, which she carefully put through the cleaning frame at the end of each day.

Since then, with each successive visit she became less overwhelmed and more observant. She found royal life at Brydon rather louder and more chaotic than she liked, but everyone was so good-natured. Including, it seemed, Andri's many favorites.

"She presides over them more like a big sister than like a queen," Grandma Elen said later on, when Lyren-Sartora—who had relinquished her job as governess, insisting that Carl at fourteen was too busy with her tutoring in state matters to need one—went to Belann on a family visit. "I can see why that queen from across the river wants to come stay with her every New Year's Week."

Lyren-Sartora put her chin on her hand. Passing sixteen

had brought her to appreciate the family she had hitherto scorned for being boring and judgmental. She now looked back on herself as a snotty, ill-behaved brat. "Chantala from Sles Adran? She's visiting *again?* I'd thought *this* year, at least, I'd be able to visit Liere over New Year's."

"She's coming alone, this time, it seems," Grandma Elen said, as they sat on stools at the prep table, icing pastries for Lyren-Sartora's Uncle Milnat—the only uncle she liked. "Before I left, a letter came. The Adrani king is to make an inspection tour over New Year's Week, but he is sending his queen to stay in Enaeran. It seems an odd way to live, but then royalty." Grandma Elen shrugged, waving her icing knife in a vague circle. "They're different."

Lyren-Sartora snorted. "The king of Sles Adran wasn't born a prince. Though he sure does look like a king, I agree. But Andri? He still looks, and acts, like a street thief, *I* think."

"You don't like him, Granddaughter? He is always kind and welcoming to me. There is nothing said about my being a shopkeeper."

Lyren-Sartora shrugged sharply. "Oh, he's all right. I suppose." In a burst of honesty, "I would like him fine, if it wasn't Liere with him. I hate it, how he leaves all the boring parts of ruling to her, while he runs around with his flirts. He hasn't changed a whit since the days when Adon Marsael chased him everywhere. You know what I think? I think they are sick of each other. Just as I predicted."

Grandma Elen reached for the frosting bowl, and gave the buttercream a thoughtful stir or two. "I don't see them that way," she said slowly. "I know what sick of each other is like. I lived it, though I pretended not to."

Lyren-Sartora regarded her with an arrested expression. "I always wondered. Did someone make you marry Grandpa?"

"No, no, no, of course not. I chose him, though my family was against it. He was tall, and handsome, with that pretty golden hair. Everybody wanted to dance with him at festivals. And he owned his own shop! I realize now that my mother could see his temper in his face, whereas I only saw his looks. And everyone in South End whispered about his grand relations west in the Eid. I had no idea how embittered he was over that..."

Lyren-Sartora stared. She was trying, and failing, to imagine her sour-voiced grandfather as handsome.

"...and my home was so noisy, everyone with hot tempers."

"Like me." Lyren-Sartora grinned.

"You are a little like my sister, but you have the looks of my youngest daughter, your Aunt Marga. You and Milnat's dear Marga both."

Lyren-Sartora accepted that, having learned that her cousin Marga often visited Grandma Elen in her dreams. Unlike Aunt Marga, who had married well, but had shut out the rest of the family and concentrated on her noble relations elsewhere in Imar.

Grandma Elen returned firmly to her subject. "What I want to say is, your grandfather was so orderly, and so handsome. And even though my mother warned me, I didn't listen. I couldn't see that his awkwardness in dancing at festival, which I thought so endearing, meant he hated it, and the day after our wedding he never danced again. All I knew was, I wanted him to myself..." She eyed Lyren-Sartora uncertainly, recognizing the wide-eyed gaze of inexperience. "In any case, I was stubborn. I thought ours was the love story to beat all love stories, and I even adopted into his family, believing myself so grand. And it was good enough, for the first year or so, but that love story didn't last."

Lyren-Sartora vaguely remembered her grandmother being a ghost of herself while her grandfather was alive. The joyless atmosphere of that barren, spotless living area above the store. Where Uncle Lesim had lived, so much like his father that the rest of the family had moved to Belann.

She wanted to claim that Liere had made the same mistake, but she knew it wasn't true. Andri was *nothing* like Grandfather Lesim. He and Liere talked and laughed, and Liere had said she liked being busy. Their little boy was happy, and he clearly adored both of his parents.

Something was missing here, but she couldn't quite define it. Except she was becoming surer by the day that flirting was fun, but crushes were dangerous. She was never going to delude herself with this *falling in love* illusion. Ever, ever, ever.

22

Academy promotions happened at the end of the academy season, late summer. Army and government promotions happened at Convocation, which was the yearly gathering of the jarls and the army commanders. Also, at the bottom of the military hierarchy, the previous year's academy seniors who had completed their year serving somewhere received their first posting.

Marend had been counting the days until Convocation, when she would get her posting. But a day or two before she expected to be dismissed for the ride to the royal city, the commander assigned her to evaluate the storage and calculate what the garrison would need in the coming year.

She dared not remind him of her expected departure. He knew. Everyone knew. Why this, now? The next year's supply requisitions usually went out during Firstmonth, or even Secondmonth. Was there a hidden message in her getting this assignment now?

But no one questioned orders. She clenched her jaw, got her paper, and went to the first storage shed to doublecheck the duty desk's numbers.

She kept at it doggedly, working so late her eyes burned, then after scarce sleep, she rose before dawn, got a lantern, and kept at it. She forced herself to write everything out neatly, double-check her numbers, and then at last, at last, she reported to the commander's office, where she handed over her completed task.

"Good. I need that supply list," he said. "I want to turn mine in early. Better chance of getting what we need, while things are still tight. Oh yes. You've finished out your year, haven't you? You'd better get on the road to the royal city. Looks like weather coming in."

She had been watching the sky for the past two days. She said, trying to keep a tremor from her voice, "What if I arrive late?"

"It happens," was the reassuring answer. "The king knows that. Even if you're a week late, you'll miss the banquet and the exhibitions but your post will be waiting for you."

At least there was that.

Marend already had her gear packed; the quarter-hour sandglass had not yet drained before she was on the road, out of sight of the South Army garrison. Riding hard, and changing horses at the outposts as frequently as she dared, she still missed Convocation Firstday, when the jarls made their vows, and the king made his to them.

And when new jarls were appointed.

But no one said anything to her when she arrived late that night, muddy to the eyebrows. A runner pointed out the temporary lodging shared by the other seniors awaiting postings in a barracks at the very end of the castle guards' area.

Two arrived after she did. "It happens," they were told. "You'll join the rest tomorrow. There's still time to catch a meal in the mess hall."

Marend Ndarga went straight to sleep, skipping a dinner she couldn't eat anyway, as over in the state wing of the castle, the king finished hosting the new appointments. Her insides churned too hard for her to endure the smells of food.

The next morning, New Year's Week Secondday, she pulled on her winter uniform, which had gotten a trifle tight across the shoulders and hips, and short enough at her wrists that her wrist bone stuck out unless she shrugged her arm back up inside. But she'd refused to get a new one made unless she actually had reason for one. Just in case. Though she said nothing to anyone, she knew it would hurt worse if she had a newly made uniform, fitting her now that she'd passed twenty—nearly twenty-one! so *old*—just to be turfed out to some civilian appointment. *Not* a promotion, whatever they'd call it.

It had begun to annoy her, how easily her friends waved

off her worries. "Of course you're going to Methden. You have a perfect record!"

"No, I don't," she'd think, but she never said it. Invariably, memory would relentlessly throw her back to the tower between the residence and the garrison at Methden, raising her hand to give the signal to shoot her brother. Which would have been the start to a bloody career, until some fellow Marloven shot her for being a traitor.

Her worst fear was that she would never deserve what she wanted most.

A runner fetched the former academy seniors to the state end of the royal castle, where they sat on benches around the perimeter of a waiting room. The window stood ajar, letting in the winter air, and though they could see their breath when they talked, Marend was not the only one trying not to sweat into their academy uniform.

They all tried, unsuccessfully, to derive meaning from who was called first. At least the interviews went quickly. Midway through, the runner at the door called in a bored voice, "Marend Ndarga."

It felt like her armpits had sprung two leaks as she crossed the room, aware of silent eyes following her.

The room she was gestured to was huge. It had shelves of old books and rolled maps, with one great one on the wall behind the desk. No one was in the room, so she walked around the desk in order to look up at the map, which depicted Marloven Hess sprawling there in the middle of Halia. Having copied many reports, she recognized the neat printing: Senrid himself had made this map?

A quick step, and here was Senrid. No, the king. Thinking of him as the person who had given her scissors and taught her how to make a string of paper-doll warriors felt uncomfortably … encroaching.

"There you are, Marend," he said briskly. "I had to catch the runner—I forgot a message that I want Temerec to carry north."

She managed to get her dry mouth to stammer, "Tem is going north?"

"He is, along with Rom. Weren't they your bunk mates?"

"Yes." She swallowed. Or tried. "Rom'll be glad."

"He was. Now, to you. A first in strategic planning. And Ambush."

"My first in Ambush was a tie," she put in, then wished she hadn't spoken.

"You finished in the top ten, and no marks against you. Marec gave you the highest praise, especially in applied maths."

She touched fist to her chest, aware that the praise came from the new headmaster, and not from the king himself. But maybe he didn't give out praise when he hadn't been around much to witness classes.

"As you know, the army's death rate was heavy. For a time yet we'll be doubling some posts. Yours is an easy one. No one questions your right to inherit your family's jarlate."

Relief washed through her, so intense it took all her control to keep her eyes from stinging, and her jaw from trembling. She pressed her lips into a flat line, having no idea how her huge gray eyes gleamed with unshed tears, hope and longing illuminating her face.

Senrid's voice got even brisker. "You'll probably be as relieved as I am to be able to dispense with the verbiage and trappings of a formal promotion—those were done yesterday, and I don't really need to hear your oath. Though of course next year, you'll present yourself along with the other jarls and jarlans for Convocation. Though you missed Firstday, you'll leave here as Jarlan of Methden, with all rights and duties appertaining."

He gestured up at the map, drawing her eyes thither. "You'll have a garrison commander shortly, once you've settled in. Mordan Nauldra has promised to see out the winter. Pay attention to what he has to teach you; you'll take his orders when it comes to maneuvering on the border. When he leaves, your garrison commander will remain in contact with South Army garrison, and you will oversee logistics. I know you spent a year there doing the same from that end, so the work should be familiar."

Marend said, "I don't command?" She shut her jaw against a *Why?* Had her mistakes stuck to her after all?

"No—this is a kingdom-wide shift. It'll be the same in the north," Senrid said, and she suppressed a sigh of relief. "In analyzing our defeat, I found that your father had no time to marshal the city while he was running the border defense alongside South Army. He was not the only one. The cities were left wide open, which made our defeat easier. I want you jarls and jarlans to look for ways to train volunteers to down tools, if necessary, and assemble for city defense. And afterward, go back to what matters: making the things we need. You—all the jarls—will be now be dressing civ, unless you are actually running maneuvers. Think of it as a renewal of the old custom of wearing House battle tunics, though no one actually fought in them if they didn't have to. Got that?"

"Oh," she said. "Ah, yes. Sir."

Senrid waved off the honorific, as usual. "I'll come around sometime, probably before the new academy year, to see how things are shaping up. Any questions?"

Questions? She had a thousand of them—a thousand thousand—but her brain had frozen.

Senrid flashed a quick grin. "Go on home, Marend. If questions occur, put 'em to Mordan, or have them sent along to me. I've renewed the com desks." He turned his head. "Call the next one in, Cama."

❧ ❧

The questions were like buzzing gnats as Marend rode home. Home! When she thought about going home—promotion—she soothed herself with a sense of pride. Not happiness. The relief was too near for that, and she still did not know where Retren was, or if he could ever forgive her. Then there were the questions about her new post.

Training the city was an excellent idea, freeing the army to watch the border, especially with that stupid Prince Valta probably soon to inherit Perideth, if his even stupider father died or was deposed. She would be her own desk jockey, it seemed, but she had trained for that, for nearly two years.

When Methden's towers at last hazed the horizon, she looked around, assessing differences. Not too many, mostly repair.

Home. Some of the knots inside eased. Home, home, home.

Her tired horse lifted her muzzle as soon as she caught the

scent of stable on the bitter winter wind. Her plodding walk tightened into a trot. Marend surveyed the towers as she covered the last distance, dirty snow scraped to either side in brown-streaked berms.

The first sign that they were expecting her was the flat hand laid in salute to chest when the stable hands ran out. That flat hand, instead of a finger or two, was the salute for a jarl or jarlan.

She dismounted, and steadied herself against the horse's side before she slung her gear over her shoulder and ventured over the rough, mushy ground toward the entry to the residence side of the castle: the garrison had to wait for her inspection round. She was not a garrison commander, as her father had been. No jarl was, now, apparently.

As she approached the heavy door, memory struck hard: the last day she had walked here, she had been about to—

With an effort, she dismissed that. Retren was *not* dead. And the fault was Imry Llyenthur's, *not* hers. She'd been a stupid brat of fourteen, manipulated by the enemy. Senrid—the king—had said so.

She stalked into the hall, to find it nearly as icy as the outside air. No one was around. Noise drew her, echoing from the stairwell to the bedrooms. When she crossed the flagged hall, she sensed footsteps, and then Steward Halan appeared, looking a little grayer, a little more square, but otherwise the same as she put hand to heart and said, "Jarlan."

"Word was faster than me, Steward Halan?" Marend asked.

The steward smiled a little, holding out her hand to take Marend's mud-splashed gear bag. "We've been expecting your return; Commander Nauldra predicted your arrival around now, based on how long it used to take him to ride back from the royal city after Convocation. But we thought it might be a day or two longer."

"I didn't stay," Marend admitted. Next year she would probably have to remain for the banquets and exhibitions. But by then, she was sure, she'd be used to being a jarlan.

Steward Halan inclined her head. "Your mother is upstairs, supervising the last of the packing. She wanted to have her things squared away for your arrival."

"It's fine," Marend said. "Not like I own any furniture. Everything I've got is in my saddlebag."

With that she vaulted up the steps, noting that it was slightly easier. Her legs were definitely longer, even if no one else could tell.

Marend found her diminutive, blond mother in what Marend used to think of as her mother's lair. Only, the brightly patterned carpets had been rolled up. The tapestries as well, the little enameled boxes, and all the embroidered cloths that had covered every surface. The room looked big and very bare, with only the old trunks and tables, that used to be disguised with those embroidered linens and even silk.

Her mother knelt at an open trunk, as two huge men waited at the side.

The former jarlan glanced up, taking in her difficult elder daughter, now a young woman. Marend was so much a combination of both parents, it was almost painful to see. No, more poignant. It would have been painful if her expression had been the old sullen one of cold resentment, sometimes even hatred.

Marend had grown beautiful, her expression a little bewildered, but mostly overwhelmed. "Mother," she said. "Steward Halan said packing, and I thought that meant moving from one room to another. But there are two carts outside. Are you … going somewhere?"

"Back to my own country. People. Language," Mother said, smiling. "I always said I would. Now that you are here, ready to step into the place you always wanted, I can safely relinquish my half of the duties I never really got used to into capable your hands."

Lesra, Marend's younger sister, sat in the window embrasure, banging the backs of her heels against the stone. She, like Mother, was blonde, but she had grown tall, her legs long and coltish. With an inward sigh, Marend suspected Lesra might be taller than she was.

"Are you jarl now?" Lesra asked, as if they had seen one another yesterday — and that had not been a happy encounter.

"Jarlan," Marend corrected, then remembered that Lesra was a teen now. She'd know that. But she was showing Marend how little she cared. Nevertheless, Marend went on, "Jarlans traditionally guarded the castle as the jarls guarded the perimeter of the jarlate. The titles are evolving as the kingdom evolves, but right now they are equivalent."

Lesra made a snoring noise. And when Marend stopped speaking, Lesra said, "Did the king whack you with a sword, the way they do promotions in barbarian stories?"

"Lesra," Mother admonished, before Marend could speak. "You may apologize, and then remain silent, if you have nothing of worth to say."

Lesra flushed mutinously. "Sorry." And, not quite under her breath, "But it's true."

Marend was remembering that she'd had nothing to say to Lesra except snarling, mostly because of her light hair, which was so like Mother's. But also because Lesra had showed more interest in pretty things than in defending herself against an enemy.

Marend said to her, "There was no ceremony, as there were no witnesses. But I don't think there is any sword-smacking even at Convocation."

"There were no witnesses," Mother repeated as she got to her feet, "because no one questions the succession." She smiled at Marend. "I heard reports on your progress at the king's academy. I was very proud of you."

Marend's throat hurt. She whispered, "Thank you."

Mother dusted her hands, gestured for the men to remove the last trunk, and said, "I believe the meal is waiting. Come. We'll eat together one last time, and if you like, I'll share Retren's latest letter."

"He writes to you?" Marend blurted, as Lesra skipped out.

"When he can. The scribes still don't have the scribe desk restored, and I really dislike troubling the king for private messages, but occasional notes have reached me. Retren is now studying at some new school, which requires knowledge of Ancient Sartoran, of all things."

"Wherever he is, he'll do well," Marend said, and because she was alone with her mother, she said, "You don't have to go. On my account."

Mother smiled a little sadly at Marend, who was now eye to eye with her, her dark curls and gray eyes so like her father's.

"I'm not leaving because of you, Marend. I meant what I said when we saw one another last: I was proud of you for writing out that apologia. It helped me understand you better, for you are so much like your father."

The word "apologia" was said in Mother's home language, which Marend had scorned to learn. Marloven didn't have an equivalent.

"What little I had to do ended with the war," Mother went on. "You know I never really settled here. While I will never regret the time I had with your father — with us as a family — I think I would become a mere appendage here, whereas back in my home town, I have old friends, and my family. And I can earn my living by my embroidery, as I'd always intended, before I met your father." She smiled, though her eyes sheened with tears. "And this is not farewell forever, for we can write to one another, can we not? You might even consider a visit, once things are settled here."

She patted Marend's stiff shoulder, and led the way downstairs to the dining room.

"You sit there," Lesra commanded, pointing at their father's old chair.

By that Marend understood that Lesra's animus against her had pretty much worn itself out. The meal proceeded, if not with mutual pleasure — Marend was too unused to conversation that wasn't military — at least in amity.

By then the wagons had been loaded and tied down, and the foreign coach was hooked up, Mother never having taken to riding except for short excursions. Marend saw them off, for no one knew how long the clear skies would hold, and they wanted to get across the border as soon as they could.

Marend went back inside, alone in that huge wing, to discover that her few things had been put in the huge, nearly empty jarl suite. Her new civilian robe looked lonely, hanging on the clothes tree next to her old academy summer uniform. A trunk had been set across from the bed.

She walked out again, and retreated down to the interview chamber, where a small stack of reports lay awaiting her perusal. With a nearly overwhelming sense of relief, she read these, and then used the rest of the fading day to organize the desk the way she had learned to arrange her inks, seals, pens, papers, finished reports and new reports while at the South Army garrison.

When she couldn't put it off any longer, she retreated to that big, empty bedroom. Something white lay on the battered old trunk that had belonged to her father. Marend approached, seeing the rich gleam of silk in the candlelight. The cloth cover had been edged with embroidery in a design of running horses.

Understanding smote Marend then. She had grown up despising her mother's endless fussing with silk threads, stitchwork, and the rest, as meaningless. But now she began to see how her mother had measured out her life in Marloven Hess with stitchwork, creating these things, which she took pride in. Those cloths were all gone now, just as Marend began to understand them. Except Mother had left this one, made with a popular Marloven theme.

Marend's eyes filled. Her chest ached. She let out one sob, then reminded herself that Mother was not dead, unlike Father. They could write. There might even be a visit, one day.

And Mother had left a little of herself, in this cloth.

Marend bent to touch the soft silk, and to run her fingers over the fine stitches, then she turned to the bed.

The sheets were fresh, the blankets heavy and soft. Someone had stored the sheets in cedar, making a nice scent. The bed had been moved; this room had once housed her parents, but there was nothing of them left in it. She had to think of it as her room, now.

She slept soundly, waking before dawn from habit. She stood in the middle of the barren room to do Sveneric's warmup, walked through the cleaning frame, then went down to the kitchen as she had in the old days.

She'd barely entered the warm room that smelled of fresh bread before Halan appeared and chased her out again. "You are the jarlan now. You ought not to invade others' space, any more than the baker will turn up in your office and begin poring over your papers. If you have orders, summon a runner. Begin as you mean to continue—in the dining room."

"Oh. Uh, sorry."

And so it went. She still felt like the old Marend, the teenager who barely escaped becoming the enemy. It was these others, pointing her to behaviors expected of a jarlan, that made the new post begin to feel real.

Her second day, she went over to the garrison, where Mordan Naudra welcomed her, and led her through on inspection. She followed, conscious that he was in command until the new commander arrived. Whoever that might be.

The best moment was when her old friend Tdor, who had been with her at Darchelde, turned up. She was even taller now, practical as ever, now that she was co-running the family store with her mother.

Tdor looked at Marend's meager belongings, crossed her arms, and said, "I know what to do. Better, whom to go to. You need proper clothes. It won't do you or Methden any good to be seen in the same robe every day, which will get shabby in no time."

"I don't know the first thing about civ clothes," Marend admitted.

Tdor grinned. "I know. But I do. We'll get you tricked out. I know your tastes, nothing fussy. But it has to be well made..."

And so her new life began taking shape, as Marend adjusted to Methden, and Methden adjusted to their new jarlan. She began to believe she was really here, and even to look forward to each new day, instead of bracing for some sort of ambush of the heart.

Really, she thought one morning as she came down to the dining room, to a hot breakfast waiting—all her favorite foods—she could even be ... happy.

If, of course, the new garrison commander turned out to be someone she could work with.

Who would it be?

23

Marend Ndarga worked feverishly that first month, as bitter cold settled over Methden, gray day after gray, icy day. She wanted everything done at once. Morgan Naudra, dragging himself with his crutch to the garrison office, looked as if he'd aged twenty years in the four since the war ended, but he was patient as always.

Not that he had to explain much to Marend. Mostly, it was new orders, for she had run tame in the garrison from her earliest years, and had grown up with a general sense of garrison operations, and vague sense of city matters.

She'd begun with two benefits that she soon appreciated: first, her training at the academy in Mordan Naudra's old role, what was termed desk jockey—a combination of communications chief and quartermaster chief, the actual quartermaster being in charge obtaining, dispensing, and keeping track of the physical supplies. By far the most important of the desk jockey's jobs was communication with the king, going both ways.

The jarl, or jarlan, was now their own desk jockey. This was her expected work, in addition to her supervisory position over the city, which meant constant contact with the guilds. That had been her mother's role, though Mordan Naudra had done most of the work; Marend caught on to the routine in a week. What remained was developing ways to communicate with the city folk, something that would have been far tougher had not she had the aid of her former gang, all having been born and raised in the city before the war removed them to Darchelde, and covert action under the direct orders of the king.

The part of her job she liked best was the expectation that

she would raise and train the city volunteers into a militia.

"A civilian force?" Tdor repeated, rubbing her hands. "What a great idea! We should have done that a million years ago! Of course me and Sindan will be glad to help!" She indicated her brother, whose head as usual was turned slightly so he could see with his one functioning eye.

Several of Marend's former gang would in the pre-war days have been rejected from joining the army. Eyesight problems for Sindan, a bad leg for Rom, and so on. But under the tutelage of MV, they had far excelled most army coverts; Marend now had the experience to know that Rom could have shot against Hamet or even that obnoxious Hatch Senelac and held his own. Maybe even won. And the city — defeated utterly in the first days of the war — now knew it.

Marend thus ended up with an impressive list of volunteers, ranging from ten years old to fifty. There were even a few oldsters who insisted on coming out to join them from time to time. Marend accepted them all, because from her understanding of what the king wanted, it was all these people who would be defending Methden if the garrison was called to reinforce South Army at the border.

Bad as the weather was, Marend's determination, coupled with the enthusiasm of those remaining of her former gang — now respectably employed in various capacities in the city — inspired the nascent force to turn out at the end of the work day for an hour or two of drill, and all day on Restday, following which Marend — on Naudra's advice — hosted a huge picnic.

As a result, Marend was confident that when the king saw fit to send the new garrison commander, Methden would be perceived as ready and waiting for all eventualities. Whoever this person was would not find slackers. She just hoped it wouldn't be one of the abhorrent academy struts like Hamet or Nermand; at least all the bullies of her first couple of years were already posted.

A runner burst into her office late one morning, boots tracking in mud, to report that the outer perimeter scouts had sighted the king's banner and Methden's maroon and sun-yellow vertical stripes. This had to be her new commander, along with replacements for some retiring, and others being transferred along with Mordan Naudra.

Marend allowed herself a single breath of panic, then reminded herself she'd been prepared for weeks. She sent her duty runner to ring the bell for assembly, and so, when the arriving double column was sighted from the castle gate, Marend—resolute in her civilian robe, which was as like her old uniform as she could get while observing the orders—was there to welcome…

Her eyes picked out the tall figure riding at the front, horsetail helmet indicating rank in the cavalry. Below it, an escaped curl of black hair.

Hatch Senelac?

No!

She stared, utterly appalled, as Hatch Senelac stared down at her utterly appalled expression.

He'd had a very rough few years since the day he faced his mother over their burned house in the old village, culminating this past year in the loathed West Army, during which he'd had to earn every promotion, from scut worker to scout captain, and finally to captain of cavalry. The result was, he knew the coast as well as the Iascans. How to attack it. How to defend it.

Now he was here at last, the best qualified captain in the entire army for Methden, at the southwest corner of Marloven Hess. A posting everyone wanted, if they couldn't get North or South Armies. Yet Marend Ndarga, the girl everyone in the academy admired most, was looking at him as if he'd put shit in her shoes.

Then she straightened up, her face the cold blank she had assumed all through the academy when she won contest after contest (or came very near), and saluted. All very proper, but as if they had never met before in their lives.

At least there was protocol to fall back on.

He gave her an ironic grin—how long was she going to play this game?—and saluted back.

"Permit me to conduct you to the garrison. Where Commander Naudra will accompany you in inspection."

She was sticking to protocol. She absolutely was.

All she noticed was the goad of hyper-awareness, Hatch Senelac's sarcastic eye taking in every speck of dust, and every warped board of her beloved Methden. If only she'd known!

Why hadn't anyone warned her? Because shifting people from post to post wasn't a matter for warning, it was an everyday matter. Why would the king give it, or her, a second thought? She didn't want him to, because of course he would think of Retren, almost killed when she was stupid enough to trust that soul-rotted Imry Llyenthur.

She gritted her teeth, bracing for the avalanche of scorn from Hatch Senelac, who had won eight firsts, taking orders from her. But only in certain areas.

At least there was protocol to bolster her, but even that might fail. It was the uncertainty of these new orders.

In as matter-of-fact a voice as she could contrive, she pointed out the tower as his office, though now she regretted that decision. She'd only considered that it was closer to her own office, which would make it easier for runners, especially in winter. But now all she could think of was his proximity to the residence.

She suppressed a grimace as he dismissed his columns to stable their mounts and settle their belongings into the barracks.

She didn't see him again for almost a week, as he got the garrison organized. She had left that the way Naudra had it, not knowing how many reinforcements would be sent, or what the incoming commander would prefer. Also, her scarce funds had all been put into repair of the city walls and streets. She was still negotiating with the guilds about fixing damages to shops and houses; some families had lived doubled up until the repairs could be made. A few were still doubled up.

Hatch sent runners over with minor questions, to which she returned verbal answers as short as she could contrive, after mentally examining each for flaws. At the end of the week, he sent word that they were ready for inspection. That meant she had to go garrison-side, where she was not at the top of the chain of command. They were co-equals.

She grimaced as she put on her best civilian robe. At least there was protocol for inspections. And she knew all the subtle and not-so-subtle insults that imaginative academy seniors had worked into their prep for peer inspections.

She found no insults. The place was as clean and orderly as they could make it.

When the two of them ended up at Hatch's office in the tower, which was scrupulously tidy, he said in a voice devoid of expression, "There are rumors that Imry Llyenthur liked this particular room."

"It was my father's office," she said—and then realized what he was really asking. She fought down a blush, saying, "I'm told it was scoured out after the war ended, and I had it scoured again when I came back. And the furniture changed. Even though he was rarely here, and never slept here." In other words, it had not occurred to her to imply an insult by putting him where the enemy had polluted.

"Ah. Thank you, Jarlan."

"You're welcome, Commander," she said, and walked out, wincing at how awkward that was. Irony in that "Jarlan" or not? She retreated down the stairs as quickly as she could, though his longer legs put him right on her heels.

When they regained the parade court, where everyone was still gathered in the cold air, he said, "Request permission to conduct a field recon."

This was now a foregone conclusion. She had no authority. He was requesting permission as a courtesy. She said nothing, therefore, just tapped her palm to her chest, as he rated the same salute that she did.

Then she turned crisply, and retreated.

They knew the king would be coming on his own inspection tour. That meant not just everything squared away, the garrison well-acquainted with the surrounding land, but there would also be exhibitions. And competitions.

She had that competition firmly in mind as she went over to the city square to conduct her volunteers in their drill.

Tdor and Sindan were there waiting. Tdor met her, widening her eyes. "Who *is* that? Besides being young, and hot as fire."

"Hatch Senelac."

"*That's* Hatch Senelac? You never told me he's so fine, Marend."

Marend snorted.

"What is wrong with your eyes? Or was the academy so

full of heat you didn't notice? Now I'm beginning to wish I'd gone. Except Mother never would have lasted," Tdor finished with genuine regret. "Da's drinking got worse before he fell off the horse and broke his neck."

Marend muttered words of sympathy, knowing better than to say anything about Tdor and Sindan's troublesome, and troubled, father. "All I know is, I mean for us to be really good. Really good. Like, making them look bad if we can, when it comes time for the king's inspection and our games."

Tdor grinned. "So it's like that, eh?"

"Like what? I just want the sneer off his face."

"Oh, Marend, you are so … so *Marend*. Never mind. Good it is. We like good." She turned her head. "Uncle Haldred? You hear that? She wants us good enough to wipe the sneers off our new garrison. Think we can do it?"

All the teens and people their own age shouted, and enthusiasm—which had never flagged—doubled.

The old Marend was back. Not the sullen teenager constantly talking about blood, revenge, and slaughter. The enthusiasm shone in her wide dark-fringed gray eyes, and radiated from her body as she whirled and snapped, her movements just that much tighter after four solid years of Sveneric's warmup, performed scrupulously every day.

She was all the more inspiring because she made no overt effort to inspire. Her gang backed her up, and the fact that no one could beat them caused the more enthusiastic to strive to emulate.

So, as the days sped by, turning into weeks, there were effectively two camps working to perfect their skills for when the king came to inspect. There was some disappointment when Thirdmonth slipped into Fourthmonth, and he didn't appear. Marend and Hatch knew that the academy had assembled by now, and were probably even embarking on their first overnight games. But they also knew that Senrid was visiting all the jarlates. Clearly Methden was not at the top of the list. All the more reason to make themselves into the best, Hatch said to his garrison, to get a resounding shout that sent seabirds squawking and scolding into the air.

Marend, in her office with the windows open to the spring air, heard the shout. She shrugged off her intense curiosity, reminding herself for the thousandth time that that was no longer her concern unless there was an attack. She would just work harder with her militia — and raise the same sort of shout.

But at last, a week before the first of Fifthmonth, as the entire world seemed to be in bloom, word came that the king was planning his visit.

Methden was already clean, swept, and squared, but it could have been knee-deep in filth for the way everyone, garrison and city dweller, went into a frenzy of hauling everything out, cleaning and squaring, then after work, meeting in groups to work on their drills.

Communication between commander and jarlan had been minimal. Marend liked it that way. Less chance of some new version of scornful mockery. Though she was legitimately "Methden" now, she still had too many memories of that title, spoken in his laughing voice, like a flick on the spirit.

For his part, Hatch had given up trying to get her to be human. At first he'd sent over his reports with little comments meant to entertain. These had elicited nothing save the word *Methden* scrawled over her seal.

He'd even tried reporting in person twice — to be kept waiting, and then given a patiently polite look after a formal salute, as if he was taking up valuable time. He gave up. The only solution, he decided, was to show her how excellently he ran his garrison. And that he could do by the excellence of the exhibitions…

Senrid arrived without any fanfare at all. The Destination was in the garrison, so he reported to Hatch, and with Hatch at his shoulder went over to report to Marend. She would have liked to have him alone, in case any of those old questions appeared, but with Hatch right there, she said only, "Would you like to see the city, Senrid-Harvalder?"

"Lead on, Jarlan," he said, callused palm out.

If the city people had not seen their king before, the excitement of Marend's gang made it very clear that the slim blond figure in the black and tan uniform exactly like Hatch's was the king. Senrid was shorter and slighter than Hatch, but Marend was intensely aware of how all faces followed Senrid as he walked about, listening and uttering words of approval here and there.

She had grown used to his company at Darchelde, of course. He was still the same person, and yet not. He made no effort to impress. He radiated kingliness the way the sun effortlessly radiated light. She couldn't stop watching him, hungry for the slightest expression of approval.

The city and garrison tours being over, it was time for the festival meal, which he shared with them, sitting among them rather than at the solitary table they had prepared.

Then came the exhibitions and games. Of course the garrison was going to excel. That was their livelihood. But Senrid cheered along with graying elders and small children as bricklayers and grocers and farmers and wagon drivers competed.

Marend's old gang, of course, led all the scores here, but the rest of the city did respectably. In fact, they did better in one sense: Romarden, perhaps suffering from an over-abundance of enthusiasm, spent immense effort on the spear throwing, and his bad leg collapsed under him. Down he went, which put him out before the team games even began.

Senrid was the first to reach him. Rom, distraught, kept apologizing until Senrid cut in, "Oh, c'mon, Rom, what would MV say if he was here?"

Rom gave an unwilling laugh as his little brother and his cousin helped him to his feet. "He'd … call me a shitbird … say I was sitting on my brains. Oh, Senrid-Harvalder." And on a hissing half-sob, "Oh, I won't be able to do the ride-and-shoot. My team will be down one."

Senrid clapped him on the shoulder. "Never mind that. How about I take your place? If I lose, you can call me a shitbird. Is that fair?"

Rom's answer was not heard, for the circle of family and neighbors shouted, after which the volunteers all cheered, feeling that they had put one in the eye of the garrison, all right.

Senrid had come determined to keep a low profile. He detested parade at any time. And he had his reasons for wanting to remain in the background. However, he'd become fond of the Darchelde gang, who had run some extremely risky tasks for him while they were all still teens. Romarden was one of his favorites. And besides, he always enjoyed a chance to ride an excellent horse in the brisk springtime air, and gallop along shooting at a target.

He also forgot what an impression he would make for someone like Marend, who had been so focused on her studies and skills that the usual trial and error at relationships permitted the academy cadets (strictly outside of academy bounds) had completely bypassed her.

She was already in a heightened state due to the expectations of competition with Hatch Senelac and his garrison. She had begun Senrid's visit noting how extremely flattering to male bodies the otherwise plain, high-collared black-and-tan uniform was. But the sight of him on horseback, his form after years of practice an absolutely perfect line as he drew arrow, then shot, made her entire body ignite in a burst of sunlight and starlight and invisible but tingly flames.

24

H atch still won, but the king was third, cheered by city and garrison before they broke up and began to mill around, talking and laughing as they departed in clumps.

Senrid was left with his new jarlan and commander standing side by side, but not communicating. He didn't have to lower his mental shield. He saw with a glance at Marend's wide, unblinking gaze what had happened, which was exactly what he had striven to avoid for four years. Even worse, he could see that there was little, or no, communication between these two.

"Before I leave," he said, "let's have some strategy talk."

He indicated the garrison side, avoiding the jarlan's castle, which might be perceived as personal space.

"I'm really pleased with what I've seen here. Marend, your volunteers especially. There are a few cities where the enthusiasm had been less inspiring, shall we say. Making me consider some other experiments, like a two-year training camp in each jarlate, run by academy graduates, after which you'd only need to hold refresher drills monthly. But that can wait till I've been around the kingdom, and others' reports come in. It could be that enthusiasm will wane after a year of it, especially in winter cold."

Marend wanted to promise that it wouldn't, but how would she know that? Her tongue had dried out. She responded by a fist to the heart, thump!

"I excuse the enthusiasm of the day, but I heard a lot of warlike talk between the garrison and the city, which gave me a little concern. Even in games, we are not two armed camps with a truce between, right?"

"Yes, Senrid-Harvalder," Hatch said flatly.

Marend mumbled agreement past the boulder in her throat.

Senrid said, "Strategy. Now that we're a few years past the war, and we can evaluate our old and new approaches, it might be worthwhile to examine the map, so to speak. Not a literal map. But our thinking about what war is, and how we Marlovens might rethink defense."

He looked at them expectantly. Hatch said, "Siege weapons."

Senrid opened his hand. "That is certainly an aspect. We'd been brought up with generations of pride in our speed on the plains, and our precision with blade and arrow. We used to have big battering weapons, but they never got used, as our problems got fought out on plains, not in cities, and those things are slow, have to be housed, and maintained. We lost when our cities were attacked. We learned that we need to find ways to defend against such weapons."

The two took that in.

"I'm talking about war in general, not tactical details. What is war? To us?"

"It's defending against enemy invasion," Hatch said confidently.

"That's good. As far as it goes. See if this makes sense to you. War is a human endeavor, a human clash of wills, often fought not only by invaders with different language and looks, but by people like the three of us. At the worst, it's neighbor against neighbor. Brother against sister."

That wiped out Marend's glazed expression. Her eyes narrowed. She was thinking again. Hatch was always thinking. He had come a long way in four years, Senrid was so very relieved to see.

He shifted his gaze to the tower window and over the fields as he said, "Much as we drill to make our muscles behave before our minds catch up, we are not actually machines. What I've really learned from the recent war — and our defeat — is that war is really about changing human behavior. It's a contest of wills, and brains, but the point is often more than taking the other's land and gold, it's about forcing the other side into a behavior that suits you."

"Suits them," Hatch said. "Forcing us to do their fighting and killing. Or turning us into slaves."

"True," Senrid said. "But that's the obvious aspect. What I'm talking about—what takes more thought, and is that much tougher—is figuring out how our long-range archers, our crossbow infantry, and our siege weapons will affect the enemy soldiers' morale. Knowing whether that road we're sabotaging to slow the enemy is the main route the locals, *our* locals, use to get to the market, or how to get our company or wing to go from a rescue mission to killing the enemy. That takes a considerable shift in focus, wouldn't you agree?"

Two fists thumped against two chests.

"We can get too tied to drill and training, because that's the simplest solution, though we know the actual training is far from easy."

Hatch slid a glance at Marend, but she was staring at the king in fascination. She'd clearly forgotten he was even there.

Senrid said to Hatch, "One thing I learned when Stad and I went over the witness reports of our defeat by Norsunder is that most theories on 'what did we do wrong' focus on how to defend against this tactic or that strategy, not on what we did right, once the counterattack did happen. We like to laud Ivandred's First Lancers for the win. It's heartening. And I would never disparage the ballads being sung about them. But it's not actually true. Eighty-one riders, no matter how skilled, did not rout the enemy from this kingdom. They led, but the crucial work was done by the hundreds of your brothers and sisters and uncles and aunts and even parents and grandparents, who rose so that the enemy could not close in behind the First Lancers and swallow them."

"My father told me when I was a scrub that the one who wins is the one who does the unexpected," Hatch mumbled.

"Yes," Senrid said. "I remember he once said that he wanted to read about all of Inda's famous wins in what we'd called the Gand book so that he would avoid trying them. Because everyone else was probably expecting them."

Hatch looked down at his hands; he could hear his father's voice, so clear, telling him the same thing. Which got his attention off Marend, and her cold, still profile.

"You two are as trained as you will probably ever be in

the skills of defense. Now you need to learn how people think. Act. React. You need to learn what gets them to face the enemy, and also learn what their limits are. Marend, this is especially true of your civs, and Hatch here can help with that. In spite of what our ancestors said, flogging people and marking them as cowards is useless most of the time, especially with civilians. All you'll get is outward cooperation, but built on resentment that leads to covert resistance. This overlooks the truth, which is that the most timid person can be a hero if there's sufficient motivation, and likewise the toughest brawler can break and run under circumstances they might not even be aware of beforehand."

Hatch stole a glance Marend's way, but she was looking down at her hands.

"You've been trained in how to assemble reports into action," Senrid said. "But those plans are useless unless you know your command well, in order to give effective orders, right?" He turned to Marend. "You learned this in our war games, that every commander thinks differently. Speaks differently. And when it was your turn to command, you had to find a way to make this group of scrubs understand what seniors would grasp in a heartbeat, right?"

Again, the tandem salutes.

"This is of particular importance to you, because you are putting together companies of people who use their hands to plant, grow, shape, repair, and even make art, like your old friend Ramond, who wasn't so bad once he got some training, yes?"

"It's true," Marend said.

"And yet, when the war was over, where did he go? Not the academy. He's down there in Telyerhas, learning how to paint, as he always wanted. You now have a city full of Ramonds. But you have to train them to kill, if threatened. They are never going to go out conquering. We want them to live out their lives enjoying peace, is that right?"

"Yes, Senrid-Harvalder."

"They are used to being trained, if they belong to one of the guilds. But this is where your training is different, because you're training them to destroy what is made, to take lives rather than build them. It's *never* a moral act. But it might become a necessary one, if, say, you wake up to pirates coming up the river into Methden to take your children to sell in mines overseas. Going back to regular life, once the threat is gone, *that's* the moral act. We want that to be the lauded action. Not a row of dead bodies who will never hear themselves extolled as heroes." He clapped his hands to his knees and rose. "Enough blabbering from me. You have to be tired. You did a superlative job here, the both of you."

He turned away, thinking, if that didn't get those two talking, then he didn't know what would. He transferred back to Choreid Dhelerei.

Leaving Hatch and Marend staring at where he'd been.

Then she whirled around and began to march out, until he said, "According to regs, I should report to you. That I'm going to put in for a transfer."

She had been thinking that in ordinary circs, the garrison and the volunteers should do some summer field runs together, but how would that sound to sarcastic Hatch Senelac?

Then there was his real voice, utterly flat. She whirled back to face him standing stiffly at attention beside his desk, his gaze unblinking. "What?" she said, and after he repeated himself, she flushed, saying, "You don't like Methden?"

"Methden?" he repeated, utterly bewildered.

"If you want a better posting—"

"As if I'd have one for the asking," he retorted, and there was all the sarcasm she had been braced to hear for weeks.

"What is the problem? If you've got some slackers or troublemakers—"

His mouth thinned as if he was about to come back with a heated retort, then his face blanked.

She sighed. "We both know the king won't like it. Better speak plain."

"All right. If spinning it out will get me gone the faster, then here goes. The problem is you."

"Me?" She gawked.

"You've made it clear since the day I arrived that you don't want me here. I can understand it. I made some really bad mistakes. Like the next thing to mutiny, when Blackeye and I hunted down that soulsucker Rianos. But no matter how hard I work I can't go back and undo that—"

"Why would you think I hold that against you?" Marend sighed shortly. "I hate this. Every time I see you, I keep expecting to hear *Methden* again, in that sneering voice. So maybe I didn't finish as high as you did, but—"

"What?" He lost the veneer of military control at last, his dark eyes going wide in indignation, his splendid cheekbones slashes of dull red. "We rode you a *week*. We rode all the newbies, then you whupped the Ambush instructor, and we backed off. Everybody, in the entire academy, knew you were being trained to take over here. Everybody, even Hamet the walking turd. You can't say you didn't notice!"

"All I heard was Methden in that sneering tone."

"Maybe the first time. And I apologize for that. We were being shits, I know. Not the first time I've had to clean up after myself. But not after that first week. Not you. It was a compliment. It was ..." He wanted to say *You were hotter than the summer sun*, but he was wary of anything personal. Anyway, that wasn't it. "Almost the first time I saw you, out in the colt corral, you were doing this sword warmup that nobody knew. It was *so* fine. Then you went on to have a perfect record, honor marks ever damn week, firsts against people twice your height and double your weight."

She shook her head, waving that off, and mumbled, "All I noticed was *Methden*. Said in that tone. When I said my name is Ndarga."

"We all thought you were playing humble," he said.

"After all my mistakes?" she retorted on a ragged laugh. "Every single day I went to sleep examining my behavior, and resolving to be better. To never step out of line. Because it could be my last day, and I loved it so..." Her voice suspended as her throat dried up.

He said, "At least tell me where you got those sword moves. That warmup." His hand moved through the air, one of the combinations he'd tried so hard to recollect and emulate.

"Oh, that. It's Sveneric's warmup. Detlev's, really."

"What?"

"Sveneric taught it to me after one of my many disasters."

"What disasters? No one has *ever* seen you make a mistake! You're perfect..." It was his turn to choke, for he remembered seeing her face when the king was doing the ride-

and-shoot, the ardency in her expressive eyes, her flush, her parted lips. He was not about to admit that he found her perfect. And had, for at least a couple of years.

"I'm used to doing it alone, is all," she said, low. "It helps clear my mind, but it does remind me of all my blunders. But if you want, I'll teach it to you."

Hatch Senelac studied her, then said slowly, "I wish I knew what you meant by that."

"What do you mean?"

"Do you want me here, or not?"

"Why is that up to me? The king wants you here, then that's where you stay. Why, did he tell you something?"

"Yes, but I'll sound like Nermand when he's on the strut."

"Just tell me what he said."

Hatch looked out the window now, his flush spreading to his ears as he repeated in a wooden voice, "Said, 'You're the best the academy has to offer. You now know the entire coast, defense and offense, and you grew up at South Army so you know the border. I'm putting you in the southwest at Methden, where I expect the first trouble.'"

"Trouble from Perideth," she said. "Everybody expects that."

He really looked puzzled now. "But he didn't say as much to you?"

"Oh, I was late to Convocation, as I had a last task at South Army. Commander there likes to get his supply requisitions in early. Which I can understand."

He was going to protest that anyone could have done that task, but waved a hand to go on.

"I arrived at Convocation after Firstday, so I wasn't part of the new appointments parade, and whatever else it is they do. My interview was the next day, with the rest of the senior posts, a quick one because the king had all of us to get through. He mentioned Perideth. Knew I'd understand. Who doesn't?"

Hatch saw the easy conviction in her face, but what he understood was that the king had straight-armed her through as quickly as he could. Maybe even made her purposely late, telling the commander at South Army he wanted one last desk jockey test before she became Jarlan of Methden. And she was completely unaware of his intent. Or rather, of what others assumed might be his intent, though for whatever reason, he was avoiding it. Hatch was quite aware that there were people who thought Marend Ndarga of Methden would be the perfect queen. His own mother numbered among them. But somehow, Marend seemed utterly unaware of it.

And he'd been assuming that, as future queen, she'd scorned him.

"Mistakes," he said slowly. "You keep referring to mistakes. I never saw, or heard, of you making even one."

Marend shut her eyes. She had made a serious error here, almost losing the person the king wanted in the post. All because of her assumptions. Yet again, she was her own worst enemy.

Making a decision, she said, "You drink burners?"

"Whenever I can get 'em," he responded, question still in the lift of his brows; why the reference to bristic-in-coffee, the academy's favorite drink on study and plan nights?

Marend said, "Send for a couple of burners. Before you put in for that transfer, I think maybe it's time for me to tell you *my* mistakes."

✥ **25** ✥

"**I** would love to cover the cost of enlarging your guilds' retirement house," Liere was saying carefully. "But if the crown assumes the entire cost, then the other guilds will be expecting the same, will they not? This while we are also making good on the credit tokens that—"

Trevor Andiran's shrill screech echoed down the halls. That was not a play cry.

Why even make a pretense at dignity, Liere thought, suppressing a rueful laugh. "Excuse me," she said as politely as possible, and felt two pairs of eyes following her as she crossed the room.

After she shut the door, she pelted down the hall, and stopped at the top of the stairs as the noise of mostly male voices echoed through the entry, weapons clanking and boot heels clattering. Liere recognized a mix of the King's Guard and the more plainly dressed border guard, led by their commander, tough old Ban Facobris, who had been their backbone during the resistance to Norsunder.

"Da!" Trevor Andiran yelped, speeding from the other direction.

Andri, in the center of the group, uttered a pained laugh and held out one palm to fend off his son. The other arm was soaked with blood, from below the shoulder down to his hand. "Just a scratch, just a scratch," he said. "Da is fine. See?" Andri turned around, but as that exposed more blood, the effect was to cause the almost-five-year-old to burst into tears.

Liere descended the rest of the way, suppressed the instinct to add her voice to the noise in asking questions no one was ready to answer yet, and took charge, accepting the handoff of the king from Facobris, who stamped out again to return to duty.

Liere sent wounded guards in one direction, oversaw Andri ushered upstairs, and frowned Trevor Andiran to the arms of his tutor—strictly promising he'd see his da as soon as he got a bandage on his hurt.

That happened very soon. When Trevor Andiran saw how small the bandage was, he accepted that it really was just a scratch, and ran off to continue doing his best to avoid the horror that was maths, content that all was right with the world again.

As soon as he was gone, Andri's grin dropped. "We sent Gared around to the garrison."

"How is he?"

"He'll be all right. Two arrows, one here and one here." Andri hit his thigh and his left shoulder. "Looked worse than it was."

"What happened? Was it those dock workers again? We fixed that, ahead of repaving the west-end streets!"

"No. Yes—someone roused them on behalf of river-boaters. A gang of drunken river-boaters busted up someplace on the other side, and the Adranis tossed them into prison. Then they were marched off to work off their time somewhere."

"But we get lists of names when that happens," Liere said. "Both sides of the river, we made it the same sentence for restitution."

"Except these dock rowdies say they don't believe it. They think their brothers or cousins are being marched off to the mines to die. That, and the Riverlands got mixed in. As always."

Andri shook his head, waving off a sore subject—not that he blamed Liere. She hadn't grown up in Enaeran, so she didn't comprehend that trouble was generational. Inevitable. And the Riverlands was nearly always the spark. Which was why he'd wrested funds for the border guard away from what he considered less immediate demands. "Here's what matters." He drew a line from the wound outside of his arm inward, a little over the length of his hand.

"So near the heart." Liere's eyes widened. "Someone tried

to shoot you. *Kill* you."

"Yep. First shot was on me. Not on Facobris, though it was his people who began breaking up the scuffle. Would've nailed me, too, except I know that sound, an arrow slicing the air. Heard it so many times. I turned, fast enough for it to slice my arm."

"Did it come from the Adrani side?"

The guard shook his head, and Andri said, "Nope. Our side." He sighed. "We fought 'em off. Caught a few, and I'll question 'em, but they'll surely turn out to be hirelings. Knowing nothing. I expect the ringleader got away."

"What started it?"

"I don't know. Like I said, probably the Riverland question. It's always been trouble. The latest version seems to be a lot of resentment against us for not making a push to get it back, especially after the war."

"But there were Adranis everywhere!"

"You know that. I know that. Most people able to think know that. But some people insist that, because the Adranis, as Norsunder's allies, lost the war, they ought to have been penalized somehow. Given the damage Bartal had Mandracar do over here. With Adon Marsael's permission, but somehow that never gets remembered."

Liere fought against the instinct to see sinister import now in every complaint—including those two staid, middle-aged guild representatives still no doubt waiting in the interview room.

She said, "I have to finish with the cobblers and the saddlers guilds. I guess we can talk later."

"What's to talk about? We don't know who. Unlikely we'll ever know who. I'll have to be better at sending scouts ahead, is all. Let's not make a lot of noise over it, hmmm?"

She sighed, and left. That would always be his reaction, because he'd spent a lifetime dealing with this sort of behavior. *Resentment against us.* She clenched her fists, glad she had numerous defenses. Magic being first.

Then the ever-present parental fear seized her. If some malevolent person wished to be rid of Andri and her, that meant their son was also in danger. And he had no defenses. Worse, he was reaching the age when the small, safe, circumscribed space of a baby was considered constricting by a child eager to venture into the world. Andri had said once, quite cheerfully, that he and his cousin Bassl had begun sneaking out windows before they turned six. And Trevor Andiran was a lot like his father, right down to the trouble with numbers, and trying tricks to get out of lessons, in favor of battling it out with sticks in the back garden with the other castle children.

She paused outside the interview chamber, considering the two choices she saw: either confining her son constantly or giving him a defense. She knew he'd resent the first choice. Andri might even wave it off. Second choice was something she could accomplish on her own, a transfer spell until he was old enough to defend himself. She could build the transfer spell into an enchantment, so all he would have to do would be to speak a word, make a sign, and he'd be gone. But where?

If the worst happened, and Andri and she were eliminated, who would keep Trevor Andrian safe from threat? Lyren-Sartora really had no home. And she was no fighter. The Mearsieans were safe from Norsundrians, but those were gone. The kingdom was open to everyone else, with absolutely no defenses. Bereth Ferian? Again, Arthur was again no fighter.

Eh, she knew that thinking of them was merely avoidance. Because the first person to mind was Senrid. He might have decided their friendship was over, but surely, if anyone would understand the threat to a child, he would. She wouldn't even have to talk to him, as this would be a backup plan only, a spell to be removed once Andri pronounced Trevor Andiran able to defend himself.

She wavered. It was unfair to Senrid not to even ask. But she shied away from that conversation. *I know your child is dead, but I need to protect mine, and…* Or, even worse, *I would have protected your child, if you'd sent her to me!*

One thing for certain: if Trevor Andiran ever had to use such a spell, it would mean she was already dead. So it wouldn't matter if she hadn't asked first. Cowardly, but comforting. Yes. She'd do it. And no one would have to know. Including Andri, who, she suspected, would come up with a typical male answer like, *I can protect my own son.*

She entered the interview room with determined step,

interrupting a low-voiced rehearsal, one guild representative voicing sympathy, and the other emphasizing the laws between guild and crown. "Keep at it," they'd been told by the old fox who headed the wheelers' guild. "She'll give in if you keep at it."

Liere dropped onto her chair, determined to get this settled as quickly as possible, while the two learned forward, ready with their lines—and another shout echoed down the halls.

But this one was a whoop of hilarity. Once again, Liere excused herself, to discover the amazing sight of one of her staid bookkeeping scribes poking his head into the rooms down the hall.

When he saw her, he shouted with such joy his voice broke like a fifteen-year-old's, "The scribe desk is back!"

"The scribe desk is back!"

One by one, scribes the world over exclaimed with disbelief, joy, wonder, and some with an internal groan, as they knew the real flood was about to begin.

Rulers, nobles, and important people had gone back to the old lockets for communication once the war was over. Then, as expensive golden notecases were cleared of possible tampering, those were again in use. But ordinary citizens who once had been able to go to the local scribes to cheaply send a letter anywhere in the world had lost that method of communication until now.

At Curtas's House, where some of the guests celebrating Sveneric's twentieth birthday had arrived to take a tour, a cheer rang out, the focus on Siamis, newly arrived after years away.

He smiled at Sveneric. "I'd like to say it was a gift for your coming of age, but I suspect you have never in your life used the scribe desk. And I actually laid down the last ward yesterday. It's taken a day and a night for the ward to propagate outward, connecting the various pieces the guilds have been restoring."

They broke into groups, as some wanted to hear about the magic involved, and others how Siamis had managed without anyone knowing.

There were two who didn't participate. Jessan Delieth and

Lyren-Sartora walked out into the garden, which was now well established. Fragrant in every season, full of color around the perimeter, it now supported Curtas's House's fresh produce needs.

Lyren-Sartora tripped along the pathway, finding the atmosphere surprisingly calm. No, more than calm. It was hushed, almost expectant in a way that lifted her mood to just this side of giddiness with every pure breath.

Even though she knew what was coming, she was prepared. She had rehearsed this conversation a thousand times in the last year and a half.

"Why did you leave Carl?" Jessan asked. "She's still upset over your loss. Though she tries to hide it."

"And that," Lyren-Sartora said, "is one of the reasons why I left."

"Lyren," Jessan warned.

Lyren sighed. She'd decided when she passed twenty that she would drop the "Sartora." What had been a banner of independence—a *so there!*—when she was twelve, had begun to sound a little pompous every time she introduced herself to a new person, and then felt obliged to explain it. She'd decided to present herself from now on simply as Lyren, though she would accept Lyren-Sartora from those who had gotten used to it.

"Look," she said to Jessan. "It wasn't good for Carl to have me there all the time, okay?" She still loved that word *okay* that she had picked up from the Mearsieans, but sadly it had never caught on.

"No. Not okay, if that means I don't agree," Jessan said. "She loved having you as a companion. Was it the governess title—"

"You know I don't care a snap for such things," Lyren-Sartora (or Lyren, now) responded.

"She was learning so much from you. She wanted to be like you," Jessan pleaded.

"She wanted to *be* me," Lyren retorted. "And it was diminishing her. And no, don't ask how. She knows how. We talked about it. It's for her to say, or not. She needs to be her own person, is all I'm going to say. You two are sixteen. Neither of you needs a governess."

"She needs to not be lonely," Jessan said, frowning.

"With all those brothers and sisters?"

Jessan sighed. "You know what I mean. But you're going to make me say it? She needs a buffer between her and Tahra-Mama."

"And that's another reason why I had to leave. Tahra was beginning to dislike me. Partly because Carl always came to me first. And hid behind me, expecting me to sway Tahra. I learned a lot about soothing and smiling people out of bad moods, and I wish I hadn't, because I was feeling more false by the day. Scheming. All the worst because it comes easy to me. Also, whenever I left to visit Belann, or anyone, Tahra would interrogate me as soon as I returned, in case I'd been to Laban and was bringing back his contamination."

"Whatever that is."

"She didn't explain. She doesn't have to. She's the queen. I outright lied about my visits to him, and I hated feeling forced to do it. Also. Carl was building up this fascination for him, just because your mother hates him."

Jessan sighed.

"So you see why I can't go back."

"I guess I can."

"If you, or the sibs, have to get away, and you can't make it to Dtheldevor's Island, come to Fortnyal Roth. I'm staying with Laban now, as I have work I seem to be good at."

"I know Tahra-Mama is trying to starve Wnelder Vee out by limiting their trade. It riles me so that I can't talk to her, or Carl, about that. What exactly do you do?"

"You know there's still no ruler in Imar?" Jessan shrugged, which could mean anything, but he wanted to hear her explanation. "Princess Karia, Prince Conrad's sister, did try to come back, but she'd signed away her right to the throne."

"The Imaran nobles are still like kings in their own holdings, despite what a mess Norsunder made of Imar," Jessan observed. How he hated politics!

"Yes. And no one wanted Princess Karia, who merely aspired to reign, without knowing anything about how to get Imar out of the mess the Host left them in, with half the kingdom covered in that weird lake. Anyway, when I used Liere's accent, her Imaran accent, and my connection to her, a queen, and to old Imaran families, it made me more acceptable in the diplomatic end of trade talk than Tahra's people, who just want to shut out Laban and Wnelder Vee. The Imarans, maybe after being stuck with the Host, don't give a snap about Laban. Or Detlev. Who never did anything to them."

Jessan dipped his head in a nod, and she went on, "Laban and I have made trade deals that are good for Imar and Wnelder Vee. Or, were, before Cousin Marga's lake dried up after winter this year. Now that the soil is restored there, everyone suddenly remembers that it was the branch of the Deis that I came from whose land it was. They give me a lot of side-eye now, maybe thinking I want that land. Ha! I can visit almost any palace I could name. Why would I want to go to the trouble of building my own, and with what funds, even if I'd be mad enough to try claiming it over the other Deis? All I own is a trunk of clothes."

Lyren shrugged, breathing deeply as she looked around. "There's a feeling here ... Do you bring people up here to use dyra on them, is that it? And enchant them to fix whatever's wrong with them? Disirad, I remember Siamis called it. Can't you bring Tahra up here and fix her? Isn't that what you're studying?"

Jessan sighed. "You don't fix people by enchanting them. The person has to want to work with us."

"How?"

"That's up to us. We have to find our own way."

"That sounds ... odd. Messy. I thought those Ancient Sartorans had rituals for everything."

"So they did. But life was so very different then. People grew up knowing about dyranarya, and would go to them the way we might go to a healer. I'm still finding my way. There are only two of us besides Detlev who are dyranarya, Adam and Sveneric, though two of the girls are very close. One of those is the youngest of us. Sveneric says that Siamis is also close. I think he's here to finish learning, now that his project is done."

They fell silent as they finished their walk, each busy with their own thoughts. Lyren looked around once more, breathing in that heady atmosphere. She could almost want to study dyranarya and dyra if she could stay. Ha! She suspected she'd get booted out, because she kept wanting to influence people. In a good way. Or what she thought was a good way. Also, she just couldn't be like Sveneric, remaining almost unnoticed in a crowd. Anywhere she went, people tended to notice her, whether she wanted them to or not.

Adam appeared on a balcony, and called, "Meal's ready!"

One by one they shifted down to Detlev's, as the sun began to rim the sea in the west. Finding Siamis in a room with a bank of windows overlooking the terrace with the intertwined pattern worked into the tiles, Lyren said, "I expect you've heard it from others, but—"

Siamis smiled. "Yes, I have. And I will return to Mearsies Heili in good time."

"Why not now? You're done with your big project, yes? Or do you have to go into seclusion when you do dyranarya studies?"

"No, I don't. I'll return when the time is right."

"Why wait?"

He studied her face, comprehending that she wanted a real answer, not just a quick one. "Have you ever read about the way being a prisoner can distort one's emotions toward one's captor or keeper?"

"Not really, but we were talking about Clair. She wasn't a prisoner except a short time at the end."

"But before then, her spirit was under constant siege, and it was I who had to guard her. Ineffectually, too often. While my own experiences were used against her. She has enormous compassion, which can turn to pity, or to a semblance of other emotions. I will not base a friendship on that. I'm giving her time to recover, so that we can meet as equals."

A semblance of other emotions. Lyren nodded slowly, wondering which one he wasn't naming. And would she understand if she knew? She had not endured what he and Clair had shared, and besides, no one had asked her to interfere. Her part had ended with passing on to Siamis Clair's wish that he would return.

She shut up as they joined the company. Over an excellent meal of spiced nuts, mushrooms, and sweet peppers over wild rice, the talk ranged all over the world. Lyren did not think of herself as ignorant—except in this company. Detlev presided, saying very little, which she was used to. She wondered what he had been doing. From the looks of him, he was not idle.

But though the conversation ranged from Sartor to Yaldar, via Arthur's building archive, and Hibern's studies among the mysterious peoples of fog-bound Songre Silde, Lyren found her mind slipping back to Clair, who, as far as she knew, had not stepped outside of Mearsies Heili once since the war had ended five years ago.

When the meal ended, and others went off in various directions, she calculated the time difference, and got Sveneric to transfer her to Mearsies Heili, where it was still late afternoon.

Compared to the days of the war, the white palace seemed deserted, though she heard voices, and glimpsed people here and there.

She headed toward the kitchen, then looked through to the terrace, where she discovered CJ and Aurora sitting side by side on the low rail, sketching a trellis on which wisteria bloomed in spectacular blue-violet hanging blossoms-clusters.

"… and the best thing is, when they drop, we'll have purple snow everywhere," CJ was saying. Then she looked up. "Lyren! Sartora," she added quickly.

"You don't have to say that anymore, if you don't want," Lyren said.

"Okay. What brought you? Are you hungry?"

"I could use dessert."

"Dessert," CJ repeated on a long, lingering note, as if she'd been given a gift. "You've come to the right place. Chocolate pie? Or cookies? Tarts?"

"Any."

CJ hopped up and raced inside. Lyren looked after, unused to seeing CJ around her age, though from the back she wasn't much different, just a bit taller. She still wore a black vest over a white shirt, and a green skirt. Her straight black hair still hung like a curtain to the back of her skirt. Her feet were still bare. But they were longer, still narrow.

She returned bearing a tray, and set it down. Aurora cast aside her chalks, and pounced on the tarts, as CJ offered the pie, and when Lyren selected a cookie she didn't really want, CJ grinned and took the piece of pie.

"I guess your tastes haven't changed," Lyren commented.

CJ's expressive blue eyes flicked up, and her thin, black brows met in a scowl. "Of course not. If I ever get the bad taste to hate chocolate pie, I'll hate myself so much I'll get Clair to turn me into a cactus." She even sounded the same!

"Is it different, letting go the Child Spell after so many years having it?"

"Yes and no," CJ said, shrugging off the subject as if it had already been canvassed much. "It's not as horrible as I'd always thought, when I was down there." Her thumb pointed at the floor tiles.

"Down? In the forest?"

"On Earth. Or down in Hell, take your pick."

"I'm not quite sure what that means."

"This pie is too good to ruin by explaining. Anyway, giving it up wasn't as bad as I dreaded."

"Why did you?" Lyren asked, chin in hand.

"I had to change, because Clair did. And Seshe wanted to. And I didn't want to turn into Mearsieanne," CJ added in a low voice, sneaking glances right and left. "I still hate shoes, and mush, and peas. And I can adventure still. Erenlara of the Venn said that being grown would make some things easier, like talking to Clair when she needed it. I didn't see it until she said it. She was right."

"Mush?" Lyren repeated.

CJ's mouth crimped. "Lovey-dovey stuff. Kissing and *Oh, my de-ear I lovest thee!*" she warbled out of tune.

Aurora promptly sang, also out of tune, *"So do me a favor and abandon meee!"*

CJ leaned over and the two smacked their palms together.

"What'll happen if some of you, um, like mush?"

"Already has," CJ said, jerking a shoulder up again. "Falinneh and Dhana are exactly the same. Maybe because they aren't human. Sherry likes girls. And we think Seshe might be picking ol' Pilo, if you can imagine Jilo kissing anybody but a horse."

"Why a horse?"

"I dunno. Because the mental image is funnier? I can only stomach mush if it's funny," CJ said.

"I think that's a nice picture," Clair said, coming through

the door. "Jilo nuzzling a muzzle."

"True. Kissing kitten and puppy muzzles as well as horses doesn't count as mush," CJ declared, as Aurora looked from one to the other, taking all this in. "Because it's sweet and not sickening."

Clair smiled at Lyren. "Welcome. What brings you here?"

"Just came from Sveneric's twentieth birthday party," Lyren said. "Siamis was there. I passed on your wish that he'd return here, and he said, not yet, or words like it, and when I asked him why, he said…" Lyren watched Clair as she repeated the conversation.

Clair both looked unchanged and also very different. It was all in the expression. There was something ageless in her otherwise unremarkable, square face framed in its long, waving white hair. Lyren could see in the shape of Clair's hazel eyes a hint of sorrow, but her quick smile was merry. She, Lyren thought suddenly, was one of those people who got deep joy from tiny things.

She finished up, "Jessan gave me a tour and a lecture about dyranarya, but I didn't really understand much of it. Jessan said a lot about how life was different in the ancient days, and hoola loola loo, but I think if they were humans, how different could they really be?"

Clair dipped her head. "My own impression is that the ancients had a different relationship to magic, which affected things."

"Like?"

She gave that quick smile. "Come. Let me show you what little I know. Have you ever walked the Purrad?"

Disappointed, Lyren said, "Oh, that maze—excuse me, labyrinth, out back of Atan's palace. Of course. It's very pretty, or was. Maybe it still is, by now. I forgot to look, as my last visit was in winter."

"That is a nice one. Old," Clair said. "But I don't think it goes all the way back to ancient days. Or maybe it does. And maybe the effect can be the same, old or new. I don't know. But what I can show you is the only Purrad that I know is actually from those days. Walk with me."

Lyren did, expecting to tromp out in to the garden. But instead, Clair led her to the spiral stairway leading up into one of the towers. Clair walked in silence, so Lyren remained silent, too. She noticed the golden shafts of the sun slanting through the keyhole windows, lighting the glistening stone of the stairs to molten gold. The pattern of the spiral against the trefoil shape of the window arches pleased her eyes with the harmonic simplicity of design, leading her eye up and up, then over, then down, and then up again.

It felt good to stretch her legs; by the fourth or fifth spire, Lyren began to feel a little giddy, but not out of breath. If anything, her body seemed lighter. The sun shafts glowed ochre, dense with light, striking dust motes to fire, and gradually she became aware of that same stillness she had sensed up at Curtas's House, a peculiar stillness that she could only compare to the stillness of a vast room after a choir ends a song. The fiery dust motes floated in the air as she floated in luminescent gold.

By the time they descended the last spire, she was herself again, walking on solid ground.

Clair faced her. "Do you see?"

"Is it always that way?"

"For me it is. I think the only reason—besides Siamis's generous efforts—I survived the war was because of the Purrad."

"All those stairs! How did I not get tired? What if you're old, or have a bad leg?"

"Did you not notice? You first get the vigor of the climb, then gradually the magic takes over, cutting your mind and spirit free to blend with the disirad. The pattern, oh, gives the expansion a shape, so that you don't lose yourself forever. Toward the end of the war, Ilerian left me so weak I could scarcely move from one side of a room to another," Clair said matter-of-factly. "But I could climb the Purrad five, ten times a day. At the very end, all night, because sleep and waking had blended into a living nightmare. I was pretty much floating, only touching my toe to each step, to anchor me to the world."

Lyren's head buzzed at this reminder that there was a world—worlds—unseen. She did not understand everything. But that was fine.

"That," Clair said, "is magic we don't have now. Maybe we will again, someday. Come! The others are getting ready to attend a play over in the town. They promised us a comedy adventure, which is Aurora's, CJ's, and Falinneh's favorite kind of play. Would you like to join us, and then spend the night?"

Siamis's "semblance of other emotions" would have to go undefined. Lyren sensed a well of experience here that might transcend words, and let it all go.

Part Two

Torrent

4768-4770

A powerful blast of wind drummed Brydon's long windows.

Winter's first bite had come early this year, and so Chantala had arrived early for her annual visit, accompanied as usual by Macael. To spare Chantala the cold ride, they had for the past couple of years transferred to the Destination Liere had made in the great parade ground below the proclamations balcony.

Only this year, Chantala had collapsed on arrival. Instead of returning immediately to Nente, Macael remained, and still sat at Chantala's bedside in the guest wing, where she had been carried. She had not woken since.

All the many palace inhabitants felt oppressed, some by the bitter wintry weather, others by the uneasy whispers about poor Chantala.

Andri, drinking hot spiced wine with citrus scrapings to fight off his inevitable winter cold, busied himself trying to go over year-end reports so that Liere wouldn't have to, but found he couldn't force much sense into them. He hailed with relief anyone who fought through the weather to speak to them.

Their son Trevor Andiran Malcolin raced along the hallways, having been released from the confinement of lessons for the day.

Liere sat in her bedroom, reflecting how the air in the room seemed colder, as if stirred by a frigid breeze. She pulled her shawl closer about her as she gazed out at the merciless swirls of blue-white snow.

The chill was more emotional than physical. Again—as she had done almost constantly over the past few days—she closed her eyes and listened in the realm of the mind. The physical form of her focus lay down one floor, along the length of the guest-wing, in the splendid royal guest chamber with its roaring fire and soft, feather-down bed.

There on the bed, under down quilts, slept a still, thin figure, so slight she scarcely made an impression in the bed. Chantala Shagal Elsarion's mind was sunk deep in memory. Liere willingly spent many wearying hours visiting those memories, and gently shepherding Chantala's drifting, puzzled spirit toward the happiest of them. In this one, a young girl and a tall woman walking in a spring garden, seen from the girl's perspective.

Chantala's gentle, questing spirit was borne along on an ineffable tide, dangerous to the living who must not lose the tenuous connection to the physical realm. Liere broke the connection, and closed her eyes to avoid the vertigo as her reaching mind settled back into the physical world.

There was no avoiding the truth: Chantala was very near death.

Liere's thoughts inadvertently turned to the tall, black-haired man she had sensed sitting vigil beside the bed. With Macael, she dared not try mind-touch, though she knew he had a formidable mental shield. That meant he did not want contact, and he was so … not intimidating—he was far too polite for that—but so enigmatic, that she did not want him sensing her where she was not wanted. Even after, what, nearly ten years?

She'd seen little of him for the past five of those years, and still found him as unaccountable as she found Andri straightforward. Andri's passions lay close to the surface. Macael's were utterly hidden. To the observer—even an acute one—it would seem he had none. Andri seemed to think so, largely because Macael remained not just married to timid, sickly Chantala, but to all appearances monogamous. Liere was not so certain. Though there was no instance of betraying gesture, or tone, or glance, she sensed an intensity she never could define.

Her stream of thought dashed apart when her son bounded into the room.

"Ma!"

"Trevor."

Her darling son still permitted hugs, though at just-turned-eight, he was already growing impatient of them. Grateful for what she always feared might be the last time, she pulled his strong, sturdy little body close and kissed his cheek, sniffing the component fragrances of soap and wood and cloth and horses that did not wholly sum up the blitheness of childhood.

"Can't ride with this curst storm," he said, impatiently shaking himself free. "I struggled through my work, and for what? Went out to the stables. They're *all* restless."

She smiled, guessing that her small son was more restless than the horses and dogs. "It's been a long storm, hasn't it?"

"Eight days," he said gloomily. "For one must count the day it was coming in, 'cause we couldn't do play outside, against its coming."

Liere said, "I'll be glad when it passes."

Trevor's head gave a little twist, expressive partly of humor and partly of impatience. The gesture was so like his father's own way of acknowledging utterances of bland politesse that laughter fluttered behind Liere's ribs. It was the first impulse to smile she'd felt in days.

Trevor jumped from a stool to the bed and up in a somersault through the air before landing lightly, his pale blond hair swinging past his shoulders. "See that?"

"I did indeed."

"Watch this!"

His hand flashed into his tunic and came out with a short dagger. He bounded from table to bed to chair, twice turning flips, making occasional blocks and jabs. He landed at last on one knee, the knife held at an aggressive angle.

It was an exuberant performance, purposelessly unsafe. But this was Andri's son, and she had long ago learned that exhortations to be careful were so much wasted breath. She smiled, and exclaimed her delight at his prowess as inside, she reached — struggling — for that compromise between the terror of what could happen and Andri's unclouded conviction that the boy would survive childhood despite the same reckless games that he'd played at that age.

When Trevor was breathless, he flopped down onto a hassock, and she said, "Where's Da? Still busy with interviews?"

Trevor grinned. Liere delighted in those unconscious little similarities father and son each revealed. She saw Andri in Trevor's gestures, his stance, his breezy moods, and his jaunty walk. Father and son had jokes together—secrets (usually ways to skip studies)—looks and gestures that, were she to ask about them, Andri would instantly explain. But greater was her pleasure in their unconsciousness.

Her question was a test, for only so could she get Trevor to use his Dena Yeresbeth. Contacts were hard for him, as they were for his da. Like fighting a duel under water, Da'd said once, laughing; Andri's Dena Yeresbeth was potentially formidable, but he'd trained it solely for forming a circle during the war, now unnecessary. After the war, he'd gone right back to his old habits. Whereas, Trevor had noticed that his mother's contacts seemed to be as easy as sunlight. Trevor had always assumed that that was just with him. That his mother and father had any kind of communication without him directly involved seemed ... inconceivable.

And so when Ma asked him to check on Da, he didn't think to say, "Can't you?" Instead, feeling a flush of importance, he closed his eyes, shaped an image of his father in his mind, then addressed it: *Da?*

: *Boy?* (came the ready response)

: *Ma wants to know. You still doing an interview?*

: *Nope. Mostly fighting these boring reports, so she won't have to.*

His father's contact was imbued with secret amusement, which delighted Trevor. He opened his eyes. "He's almost done," he said only. Mama prized duty—at least, she always did hers. Always. And didn't laugh when others skated theirs, though she didn't get mad. And when she said, "Invite him to join us for the midday meal," he closed his eyes again: *Join us for lunch?*

: *Lay a place for me.*

Trevor reported this as well.

His mother smiled, then started their brain game.

"Block!"

He shut out his physical senses, and opened his mind again. They played Count, enumerating what they'd noted about their environment in sensory detail. As usual his mother had far more items, but at least he was getting better at it.

The game came rapidly to a close, then she said, "Danger."

And—automatically—he said the weird words she'd taught him when he was five. He knew they were a magic spell, and that (performed with the signs he did after) they would take him somewhere safe. Privately he thought it was stupid. A prince ought to be able to get himself out of any trouble he'd gotten himself into, or how could he ever be a king, who was expected to keep an entire kingdom out of trouble? But he could feel how important it was to his mother to practice this spell, so he always did it.

And when he was done she smiled, and he basked in her smile, for it pushed away, for a short time, that awful feeling that he sensed everywhere else, kind of like an invisible, freezing fog. Thus cheered, he took off to hunt someone up for a game before he'd get to eat. Didn't matter what he did, as long as he did something, because then he didn't have to think about that fog of ice over Brydon, a weirdness that was caused by Aunt Chantala and Uncle Macael.

Liere felt his thoughts veering, but she said nothing as she watched him scamper off in search of playmates. So he too was sensitive to the atmosphere. That meant it was more pervasive, and it was time for her to act.

Bracing herself for the unpleasant decision whether or not to warn Macael that his wife would not recover, she rose and left her chamber, speeding downstairs with noiseless step. Sympathy inclined her to leave him hope as long as possible; duty required that he be told. She knew it was cowardly to hope that his servants would turn her away at the door to the suite. They waved her through, and dark-haired Fan, Macael's quiet, unobtrusive personal servant, opened the inner door for her himself.

Through the open door of the smaller guest bedchamber she saw that Macael still sat on a stool beside the bed, apparently without having moved, a roaring fire giving off heat that was nearly stifling. He was alone, and looked up at Liere's entrance, then tucked away the exquisitely embroidered handkerchief with which he'd been daubing his damp brow.

She crossed to the other side of the bed. The only sounds

were the crackle of the fire, and the rustle of her layers of damask; the aroma from sweetgrass candles placed behind the bed, so the flickering light would not worry Chantala's eyes. It was Chantala's favorite scent.

Liere looked down at Chantala's thin face, so plain and pensive and patient, and an upwelling of pity and compassion constricted her heart. Chantala was beyond feeling cold, but she hesitated before telling Macael he could wave the fire down low. Tears stung her eyes, blurring the gentle face on the pillow.

"The healer visited," Macael said. "My wife has slipped into a coma."

He knew, then. Relieved of a perceived and utterly repellent duty, Liere sank down onto a nearby chair.

"I'm so sorry." She blinked the tears away. "I'm sorry that she had to fall ill here. I know you are hesitant to avail yourself of my magic skills to send her back to Nente." Liere forced herself to glance across the bed at Macael. It had always been difficult to meet the eyes of someone so thoroughly blocked and impassive of demeanor, and now she found it nearly impossible. But she must not be weak and address the bedclothes; even the briefest touch, gaze to gaze, though painful, was at least polite.

Who knew the old magic, which apparently made transfer easier? If only she'd learned it! "I'd be glad to try to summon a friend whose skills far exceed mine."

Macael said, "Thank you, but no. Chantala is content here. As for me ... attribute it to willful ignorance, if you must, but I cannot risk having her slip away in the transfer, whatever kind of magic skills are involved."

Liere met his gaze again and felt curiously adrift; there was no sign, however subtle, of emotion to which to respond. Yet instinct set her heart pounding, and prickled coldly all along the nerves of her inner arms and the back of her neck, an instinct that sensed hidden intensity.

She forced her mind to focus. "The thought was only for your comfort and benefit. Of course you are welcome to stay."

"Thank you." His gaze lowered. The unexpectedly long black eyelashes acted as a shutter.

"Shall I leave?" she asked. "If you'd prefer to be alone with her, I will not be offended."

"She always loved coming here." The meditative voice was not quite an answer, but Liere could be patient. "I really believe she preferred it to Nente, though it has been peaceful these years. Perhaps it is partly due to the weather being comparatively warmer here." He looked up again, at the candle just behind her shoulder, its flame reflecting in his enormous black pupils. "But the main of it was your friendship that drew her. I will never forget your kindness to her over the years. Your willingness to lay aside your regular life and embrace her interests whenever she wished to visit."

Liere thought, he knows it'll be very soon.

Chill harrowed her nerves; his eyes remained as blank as the sky. The feelings he hid had to be sorrow and grief, normal human emotions, and nothing arcane or dangerous, yet her lack of clues summed up her association with Macael. She felt his gaze lift then lower again as she struggled for a reference-point from which to interact with him. Everyone else in her life, from villains to friends, had provided clues for her to react to, but not Macael. Though it had been nearly a decade since they first met, she still really didn't know him.

All this moved swiftly through her mind while she considered her response, and finally she decided that honesty would serve. "Mine has been the pleasure," she said, and once again braced herself to meet his gaze — to find him contemplating the candle.

Macael did not respond, but his gaze flicked to the sleeping face of his wife.

Liere continued, hoping her tone, her words, were balm, and not claws to whatever hidden emotions he suffered. "She reminded me of the importance of stopping to observe the light. To appreciate the subtleties of the changing seasons. Her perceptions transformed nature into art in a way I'd thought only dawnsingers and the morvende capable of seeing. Her poetry was a gift of unsurpassed generosity."

He heard all this without looking up from Chantala. Finally, slowly, he said, "I will not forget your words. Or the happiness you gave her."

Though there was no change in his posture, or in his voice — he was still preternaturally controlled, from the glossy, ordered black locks to the fresh lace glinting white at the wrists of his indigo sleeves—she was suddenly convinced that her presence was painful to him.

She considered various polite words with which to excuse herself, but was daunted by the circumstances, by awe-striking perception of the thinning boundary between the temporal world and that beyond. The intricacies of politesse might be meaningless utterance to one enduring the prospect of a loved one sundering that boundary, or worse, fuss and bother to one whose own standard of courtesy might feel an answer is required.

Right now he might be sick of the sound of her voice, she thought soberly, and so she rose, and keeping her footfalls silent, left the room.

$$2$$

The time was morning. David and Adam sat at a table alone, absorbed in discussing school minutiae, as outside the great windows a solid line of storm clouds slowly ate up the early morning light. It was David's day off, and Adam would take over his chores.

The sudden silence in the room behind them, followed by an immediate and self-conscious resumption of chatter, caused the two to look up.

Detlev had been gone more than present these past few years. The two knew that he had been to Songre Silde, where he had made peace with the powerful mages there. That had taken time, for those mages never rushed things. The result was, with their aid, he had been searching world-gates, and endeavoring to construct a ward strong enough to prevent the recurrence of any entity like Ilerian, the one that had taken human form and created Norsunder.

Despite Detlev's habit of deferring most instruction to David and Adam, they waited expectantly as he brought his coffee to the table in the high-ceilinged, airy refectory where the two sat. He looked essentially unchanged, a man ordinary in appearance, brown of skin and hair, medium height. His age appeared to be somewhere between thirty and forty, but those with Dena Yeresbeth skills on his level habitually healed most physical signs of aging in order to remain healthy; his hair showed a little silver at the temples, a matter of little interest to him.

He nodded a greeting and gestured for them to carry on, as the soft noise of galloping footpads heralded the arrival of long, black Rori, Leander's dog companion. Rori nosed each of them in turn, tail corkscrewing, then ran to the dog door and outside, from which rose the squawking protests of the chickens pecking at withered greens and scraps.

David sent one quick glance at Detlev's oblique gray-green gaze. He saw nothing to alarm him, so he and Adam resumed their discussion, and gradually, as often happened, they forgot about Detlev as the many ongoing not-quite-crises — the decisions and revisions of school life — occupied all conscious thought. But they reached a stopping place after a time, and outside awarenesses flowed back in to claim their attention. Including Detlev's presence.

Adam gathered together the papers on which he'd been making notes, and after a thoughtful glance at Detlev, he beckoned to the remaining students chatting over their dirty dishes. They dunked and stacked the dishes and exited.

Detlev sipped his coffee, and made no move; David, watching Adam depart, realized that some signal too subtle for him had passed between Detlev and his teaching-partner and therefore he was the target. He resigned himself.

Detlev said, "Chantala na Shagal is dying."

"They'll be sorry in Sles Adran," David said, mentally running through what he knew about the kingdom: fairly large, no major magicians, ruled for countless generations by the Shagal family, but as had happened in so many polities during and after the war, it now had a new ruler. In this case, Andri Elsarion of Enaeran's distant cousin. "Though," David added, probing for the motivation behind that blunt statement, "Trevor Macael Elsarion seems to be more popular than she ever would have been, if MV is right."

They both knew that MV was right; that was David's invitation for enlightenment, since he couldn't find any reason why this news ought to occupy his attention.

Instead, Detlev posed a question. "Have you maintained your heirship duties?"

David hadn't been handed a subject-change, but a vector.

"Right," he said with grim irony. "You needn't nag. I'm gone."

Detlev looked amused, but all he said was, "Prepare to stay a day or two."

David sighed. Their students were leaving that day for a research project led by Leander; he should have known better than to look forward to time of his own. Not that visiting Senrid was so arduous a chore. It was why he'd suddenly need to visit him, after months of benign non-communication, that made him wary.

He looked down at himself and sighed again. For a military kingdom, Marlovan Hess could be surprisingly conservative in dress. Wearing an unlaced shirt, loose old training pants, and bare feet would get him the stink-eye reserved for vagrants, a judgment that Senrid probably would not appreciate in his putative heir.

David dug out a good shirt, riding trousers that fit, socks, and forest mocs. Then he calculated the time difference, and spent half an hour arranging his own affairs in case his stay turned out to be protracted. Finally he stood in his room, threw open the window, and looked out at the blue-white snow-crowned mountains, sniffed the pine-scented air, and sensed the disirad beneath the ground on the upper plateau, a never-ending resonance perceived on the non-physical plane. He felt that ineffable sense of regret with which the prospect of leaving imbued everyone who spent time in the proximity of the disirad. Would it always be that way?

He left the room, and the question, in the slide transfer, arriving in Marloven Hess as the bell in the tower on the periphery of the vast royal castle bonged once: an hour before the dawn watch change.

Elsewhere in Senrid's capital city, most citizens wouldn't notice it. Only the seniors at the academy would struggle out of their beds, but David knew he'd find Senrid already dressed and ready, down in the huge private salle below his Residence wing.

David walked along the slate-floored hall, his shoes soundless, and paused in the open doorway of the salle, a room lined down one side with mirrors: the room had, centuries before, been where honor guards and riding captains of jarls gathered at Convocation, back in the days when the regional commanders never traveled except with what amounted to private armies.

The room was lit at four corners by glow-globes so no

shadow was cast, it was bright and clean-swept and the air coming in the open windows high on the walls was cold and brisk. David scanned the half-dozen or so young Marlovens as they arrived, spruce in their black-and-tan uniforms, and found Senrid, dressed as usual in shirt, uniform trousers, and riding boots, talking with his sword master next to one of the mirrors.

Senrid's head turned. He lifted a hand in salute as he smiled slightly, but even that much expression was rare enough to bring the academy teens' attention around.

The two oldest moved well away from the sword master and king. One of the pair whispered to her classmate, "That's the heir." Adding, with a significant glance, "One of Detlev's gang."

A senior curled his lip, eyeing David's lack of uniform. "I thought he was a harvest picker begging for handouts."

"He'll hand you out, all right, if he fights you," the girl—dark curling hair and a very sardonic face—murmured as she shed her jacket and reached for protective gear piled neatly on a side table.

The youngest glowered over at David, who stood before the rack of practice swords, pretending not to hear.

The sword master tapped his weapon significantly on the floor, and the teens sprang to choose weapons and gear, the oldest moving to partner the king.

The youngest covertly watched David select a blade from the rack, and test it. He'd find it excellent, of course. Marloven steel was some of the best in the world. At least he seemed to know how to handle one.

David swung his arm experimentally as he walked to the side of the room where Senrid was just squaring off for his bout.

"Need some practice?" Senrid inquired, as if more than half a year hadn't passed between David's last visit and this one.

David said, "It's just that it's so cold in here."

Senrid's mouth quirked. The youngest whispered to his partner, "He doesn't even have gear on. I hope he gets ribboned."

David watched Senrid salute his partner and take his stance. He knew his cousin was waiting for the purpose of the visit, and David was going to exert himself to convey, as much as he could contrive, the impression that it was impulse. To mention Detlev would be to risk alienating Senrid, not because there was enmity, but any hint of conspiracy — even for his own good, no, especially for his own good — would summarily end what semblance of personal communication existed. David knew that was partly his fault for having tried to force Senrid out of that tight control a few years before.

David's assigned partner was the girl with curly hair. He said, "Who am I fighting?"

"Fuzz — that is, Maddar Senelac," she said, as she saluted. "Sir."

"Just call me David." He smiled encouragingly, and some of her stiffness eased — before she launched to the attack, for she had the honor of the academy to uphold.

As he fought David assessed the others, mentally comparing them to his and Adam's own students.

Aside from the obviously military clothing and bearing, they were much the same. David noted with particular interest the cooperative spirit among them. A change from the early days of the academy under Senrid's kingship, when hard competition and anger were holdovers from the war.

His attention returned to his bout; he matched his partner's skill level with the habit of years of hard work, permitting her two touches after very good offenses, and tapping her gently where her defense was weak.

The sword master, a big, grizzled man, called a halt and resorted the pairs. David now found himself opposite a tall, weedy fellow who stared at him with a mixture of awe and respect that made it very difficult for David not to laugh.

"You'll have to excuse my laziness," he said, trying to put his partner at ease.

The boy shook his head once. "I saw your bout with Senelac. We all did."

Senrid was apparently listening. "Laziness? Limited steel on your mountain retreat, right?" he asked with good-natured sarcasm, his energy and effectiveness not the slightest bit hampered as his partner tried desperately for a hit. "Just abstruse Ancient Sartoran history, magic studies, a contemplative life, and running up and down cliffs with a knapsack full of boulders. Weapons practice only as defense."

Who's been blabbing? David thought with some amusement. MV, of course.

"Boulders only when they have excess vigor," David said, saluting his partner and settling into dueling stance.

All of them grinned. They all knew how to translate it: 'excess vigor' meant quarreling.

Senrid laughed, and his blade rang as he beat back the big boy doing his best to smash past his defense.

The youngest, watching as much as he could, mentally reevaluated. To him, Detlev's gang's standard had been set by a visit from MV, who made it his business to descend on Senrid's academy from time to time, always when he was least expected, and amuse himself with thrashing his way through students and masters. From afar Senrid had noted wryly that MV's brisk and humorously abrasive expertise never failed to have an inspiring effect and he did not interfere with MV's visits or style of tutelage.

The seniors admired David's strength, skill, and especially his pungent and unstinting commentary. He smiled instead of flayed with drawling sarcasm, but he turned out to be as good as MV with a sword, if less bruising on weak guards, and besides, he looked a whole lot like the king, despite being taller and having brown eyes. As the youngest finished roundly defeating his partner, he mentally revised what he'd tell his bunkmates on his return — though of course bragging would not make him a whit more popular than any disparagement.

When they had finished their ending salutes, David's partner gave him a shy grin, and the seniors filed out, some with backward looks. So it was still apparently considered an honor to be chosen to get up at four and march over through bitter cold to the royal palace to get trounced by the king? Interesting.

When the blades were stored, Senrid said, "Breakfast?"

David opened his hand toward the door.

During the practice, David had not just been observing the students, but their monarch as well. As they trod in companyionable silence back upstairs to Senrid's study, he considered what he'd seen.

Senrid seemed much the same as ever: fastidiously neat from the square-cut waving blond hair to the well-made blackweave riding boots, in superlative physical condition, formidably controlled, patient, and utterly walled off from any emotion whatsoever. David still regretted trying to break that wall. Senrid did not seem to resent it. Had he forgotten? No, no chance. It had made him wary, though he appeared to be pleased to see David now.

They reached the study, and both smelled freshly ground and steamed coffee. More evidence of Senrid's unvarying — not to say rigid — schedule.

Senrid sat down, picked up a flattish ceramic cup in both hands, the drinking vessel little changed from those used by both their ancestors hundreds of years ago — and gazed over its rim at David. "Have you decided how your mountain scholars are going to wield their dyra when you're done with 'em?"

They'd do what he was doing now. But that thought stayed locked inside David's skull. "That's entirely up to them."

Senrid leaned back, still holding his cup. "Just as what you and Adam — and MV and Laban — do is entirely up to you?"

"Have you seen evidence of coercion from Detlev?" David retorted.

And Senrid's reply was wry, without sarcasm, "I see in every one of you an individualized version of his point of view."

David grinned. "But we're not him. Among other lacks are four thousand years of experience. Suffice it to say we have no political plans whatsoever, no plots magical or arcane. When Adam's and my students go, with or without a dyr, we wish them well." He lifted his hands. "Today, though, happens to begin my time off. I do get liberty once or twice a year. And you did make me your heir. So I'm entirely at your disposal. Put me to work."

"Very well." Senrid saluted with a casual wave of his hand. "Eat up. I want to be on the move before dawn. There's plenty to do."

And, as always, there was.

Through the long day they worked together, David cheerfully performing whatever tasks Senrid asked, all the while observing Senrid and his conduct as king. Where David was unknown he was unnoticed. Where known he exerted himself to be agreeable.

One place he was known was in the southwestern province called Methden. It was apparent from the surprise in the young Jarlan Marend Ndarga's face that it had been a long while since she'd been favored with a royal interview.

As the visit progressed it became equally clear that Marend, who had grown into a very attractive young woman, had—despite her best intentions after David's well-meaning warnings—fallen in love with the King of Marloven Hess.

Of course that was what it was, David thought with rueful and compassionate humor. She didn't love Senrid. She couldn't know Senrid, for he did not permit anything of himself to be seen beyond the imperviously correct kingly façade. But she was crushing hard on what she did see.

Why is real life so messy? David stood with his back to the window, watching the blond head and the dark curly one bent over the neatly kept ledgers of supplies and reports. One glance at the tall, well-made young commander over by the door made equally clear what Hatch Senelac's feelings were for his jarlan. David studied his bony face, the wry mouth, now tight with the effort to appear detached. He had to be older brother or cousin to the merry young academy student David had fought that morning; an old, old family, loyal for generations to the Montredaun-Ans-even when various monarchs scarcely deserved it.

David, looking at those dark eyes, suspected that Senrid had tried to provide Marend with the perfect companion, and in an orderly universe, Hatch and Marend would have paired off by now.

Of course in another equally orderly universe, Senrid would choose this young woman, who would make the perfect Marloven queen, and they'd live happily ever after, presiding over the annual Marloven war games on the middle plains during the summer—and like as not winning first-ribbons. But it seemed that Senrid was either not capable of loving more than once, or more likely had cut love out of his life entirely, as effectively as one cut a wound gone bad, restitched the skin, and adjusted to living with scars.

David could understand and appreciate Senrid's choosing this visit as an opportunity to meet with Marend, David's presence circumventing any chances of intimacy. Eventually Senrid would have to talk to her. But David avoided bringing up the subject as they prepared to leave. Senrid turned to talk to Hatch, whose dark eyes were now inhumanly blank, his bearing that of the uniformed warrior on the parade ground.

David was glad to leave that mess behind. He saw no resolution that wouldn't be painful for all three of them.

3

Andri Malcolin Elsarion pushed back his plate and watched Liere and Trevor playing one of their mental gymnastics games. The boy didn't even know it was a kind of training. He loved a challenge, and saw this game as fun. Liere had admitted (rather ruefully, Andri thought) that the game, like most of the others of this sort that she used, were not her own, but something one or other of Detlev's gang had taught her daughter. "I never knew how to play when I was small," she'd said. "You can't imagine how much that held me back."

Andri enjoyed watching Liere and Trevor together, noting the ways they were alike. The wide eyes, so pale a brown you may's well call it gold, the quick treble voices, the knitted brows when they considered a problem.

The sudden light-transforming smiles that revealed, like no words ever could, the kind of joy that came from a clean heart.

How he relished his little family. There were times he'd sit, just so, and pretend he was a wandering sword in peacetime who had nothing to do beyond spend days of laziness, just like this. Except were it true, there'd be five yellow-haired rug-crawlers clamoring about, their laughter brightening his surroundings.

It did cause him a pang of regret when he thought of the dreams he'd had of his children's voices echoing through Brydon, the fun they'd have in perfect amity and safety. But there was no perfect safety, and the Elsarions' history was not graced by many examples of amity: most of the troubles had been internecine.

Thus far, at least all threats had come from outside the family; there had been several attempts on Andri's life since the war ended. Which is why the three of them were not alone. There was one of Andri's honor guards leaning in the doorway, arms crossed, smiling at Trevor's antics.

"You're getting mighty quick there, young prince," Haldri commented from his post by the door.

"I am!" Trevor caroled happily. Then, typical for his age, went on to ask questions about his performance, meant to elicit more praise.

Haldri, captain of Andri's guards' day watch, was quite willing to give them; he had two youngsters of his own elsewhere in the city. Liere listened, smiling. Though she had been born to arid order, she had come to accept the free-for-all life of Brydon palace, the servants and guards offering commentary whenever it occurred to them, as everybody went about their routine.

Andri also smiled, but his mind ranged in a different direction. It had been a hard decision, one he and Liere had discussed through nights until sunrise. As the years went by and it became apparent that Cousin Macael, now king of Sles Adran, would not have an heir, Trevor the Peacemaker was how Andri thought of his son. He got along with everyone. The guards loved him even more than did the castle servants. His tutors loved him. The people loved him. Even the local birds flocked to his hand when he whistled, to the unspoken disgust of the gardeners when the birds then turned bandit and raided the gardens for seeds.

There would be no brothers or sisters to fight him; he and Liere had agreed on that between them, and he had sought agreement with his various lovers, who all knew Enaeraneth history and understood.

Andri had never discussed heirship with Macael, who had never introduced it, either. To Andri, talk of official investitures, and treaties, was wasted breath. If someone strong enough to hold the throne ignored 'em, who was going to gainsay? At least Macael had a kingdom of his own. Chantala was the last of the Shagals, as Macael had chosen not to adopt into them. Maybe the breach in the Elsarions would heal with

Trevor.

Andri's frame shook with a sudden onslaught of coughing. He motioned for a passing servant to bring more spiced citrus wine. With cowardly readiness he admitted to himself there was one benefit of this wretched cold: he dared not dance attendance on poor Chantala, lest he make her sicker. Though he was fairly certain she was beyond worry about catching something, he thought with real regret.

The truth was, he'd always suspected Macael's reasons for marrying Chantala were political, though he readily acknowledged that his cousin had done well by her. This belief had only been spoken to a couple of people—MV, and Detlev, on his single visit—and never to Liere, who worked hard to believe the pair were romantically in love. Andri would never disabuse her of this comforting conviction.

"Da," Trevor said. "The cold's lasted over a week. Lake's got to be frozen. Can we skate tomorrow if the snow stops?"

"It'll be gone by tonight," the footman bringing in hot pastry commented as he set down his tray. "My grandmother's knees can always be trusted."

Andri glanced up at Liere: *Chantala?*

: *Tonight. If that late.*

: *Say what to young rover?*

"We'll see," Liere murmured.

Trevor groaned, then his expression altered to question. "If it's on Aunt Chantala's account, you know she likes seeing us skate. She came out to watch us last year, remember?"

"We'll plan tomorrow when it comes," Andri said.

The boy sighed. Shrugged. Smiled at them. "I'm done. May I—"

"Go." Liere reached over and brushed his hair from his eyes.

Trevor gave his head an impatient toss, and bounded out of the room after the footman bearing away the dirty dishes.

Andri signed to Haldri, who looked around once, hand at the hilt of his sword, then effaced himself, to take up his stance directly outside the closed door.

"She's in a coma," Liere said when she and Andri were alone.

Andri grimaced. Poor little sod. Instead of recovering

from that long-ago exposure to poison, Chantala had seemed worse each year when she arrived for longer and longer stays through the coldest weeks of winter. But though she'd stayed longer, she had slept through most days. Once Andri had used mind-touch, and promptly recoiled from the vertigo. No wonder she slept all the time. "Bad?"

"Not for her, right now. I've gotten more adept at drawing her into the dream realm, where she can wander happily about Denwy's gardens in the warm springtime. It just takes concentration. I'm worried about Macael. He hasn't slept. I suspect he hasn't even eaten; I saw Fan hovering around looking worried last time I passed."

"Fan?" Andri inquired. Macael and Chantala always brought so much staff, he'd never been able to distinguish them. Especially as they were all so silent and self-effacing.

"Fan is Macael's personal servant. I met him in the valley that year."

Andri couldn't imagine having a personal servant. What would they do? Mentally he shrugged off the matter as Liere continued, "Macael is so very closed off. I don't know if I should offer to sit with him, or with her so he can rest." She opened her hands. "You seem to understand him better than I. At least he talks to you. Should I ask? Or do it? Or what?"

Andri was taken by another coughing fit, which he did not attempt to control. It gave him time to think.

Two winters before, during one of Chantala's too-brief conscious periods, they had been talking about music, and Chantala brought up the fact that Macael played stringed instruments. *Really well,* Liere had exclaimed. *He seldom plays anymore,* Chantala had said with dreamy regret. *It must have been the war. The last time he played more than one song was when you came to the valley, Liere. Remember that? I know he does. He says he remembers every word of our conversation.*

Neither Liere nor Chantala had seen any significance to that. Andri wasn't certain he did, but it seemed that night got mentioned a lot, for an evening that consisted of nothing more than a meal, jabber suitable for Chantala, and fooling around with musical instruments when they ran out of things to say about the weather and poetry. Something had fixed that night in memory, and he was willing to wager his right arm it wasn't

Chantala's company. But Liere seemed unaware of anything out of the ordinary. Andri was fairly certain whatever it was lay entirely in the vault of Macael's mind.

"Leave them alone," he said finally. "I think if he wants us, he'll come to us."

"All right." And he saw her relief.

"Dutiful Liere," he said, and when she grinned, he bent and kissed her.

The remainder of David's day in Marloven Hess was uneventful.

Late at night David composed himself for long-distance mental contact. He reached for Detlev—

: *Chantala just died. I suggest you stay there.*

: *Why?*

No answer; the contact had ended.

Ha, that was enough to banish sleep.

David kindled a lamp, performed a summons spell he'd prepared when they first commenced the dyranarya school, and his work appeared before him.

Liere was bringing up the fire in their favorite sitting room— one of the few rooms that could be kept warm enough in winter—when she felt a presence in the doorway. She looked up. Macael was there, his pupils huge, his face tight with strain. Her heart rapped against her ribs.

"She's gone," he said.

Liere held out her hands, her first instinctive reaction. Shared grief made all people kin.

Immediately she saw that she had erred, excruciatingly erred. Macael recoiled slightly—no more than a catch of the breath, and the stillness of his person. Then he walked out. It was enough to shock her, for it was the first time that he had ever been rude. Was the prospect of the clasp of her hand truly that repellent? Oh, but of course grief and loss pardons everything.

She was sitting in the same room with Andri when evening fell. They had quietly cancelled all social events. Liere tried to read a favorite book; Andri had given up trying to make sense out of those reports, and played at a card game with Gared and another pair of off-duty guards.

Dorval, on night duty, glanced in to sweep the room with his gaze, backed off, and bowed to someone in the hall. Macael appeared in the doorway, immaculate in dark blue worked with golden embroidery — Elsarion colors — his countenance remote. He addressed Liere, "I beg pardon for my earlier discourtesy."

"It was nothing. Please, Macael," Liere responded, her heart drumming again. She did not offer her hands this time. "Join us, if you like."

He sat where she indicated, at one side of the fire, and stared into its depths. She looked helplessly at that refined profile, the leap of flames reflecting in his enormous pupils, and wondered what to do next.

A movement beyond Macael's shoulder caught her attention. With a meaningful glance in Macael's direction — and a curious, twisted smile that was almost a grimace — Andri jerked his thumb at his chest, and at the door. Gared rolled his eyes, swept up the cards, and departed, the off-duty guards on his heels. Andri jerked his chin at Dorval, who had been standing just inside, and noiselessly they left.

She and Macael were now alone.

Liere waited, hands in her lap, for him to either leave, or speak, or make some other sign to which she could respond.

When he did it was suddenly, in a low murmur. At first disjointed sentences about Chantala, her goodness, her kindness, her infinite capacity for appreciating the beauty in life. And now she was gone, snuffed by the poison of ambition —

The words were spoken so softly she almost didn't hear them. When he broke off there was a painful silence, relieved only by the snapping of the fire.

And then she had a thought. "Her poetry," she said. "How she loved the way you had set it to music! She often spoke of it. Yet I haven't heard you play for years."

"Since the night we all met in the valley." He turned her way, his pupils so huge his eyes looked black. He drew in a long breath — she heard it — and said, "Will it please you if I play again?"

"Very much." She spoke without thinking, for the intensity of that customarily blank gaze reverberated through her, causing her thoughts to flutter senselessly, like moths newly singed by the candle's flame. "If it's not too ... well, I would enjoy it very much. Your musicianship I well remember was so very—" She became aware she was babbling, and shut her mouth.

He bowed, his long hair swinging forward, briefly masking his face.

She busied herself with summoning a servant, who then fetched an old twelve-stringed tiranthe from the music room, left over from the days when Andri's sister Alismira took lessons. It was kept tuned, its tone clear and mellow.

Macael ran his fingers over it, his head still bent, the shining blue-black hair still curtaining his face. A shimmer of sound rose from the tiranthe. A chord, another chord, a progression that ran up through minor keys to major, and back to the plaintive, poignant minor keys again.

And then he played.

He played until the fire burned low, and outside above the clouds the stars wheeled across the sky. He played until his fingernails showed thin strips of crimson—this time she saw it happen—but Liere sat without moving or speaking, because the music reached beyond the beauty of sound to the wordless expression of an isolated soul. At last, at last she believed she had the key: her part was to listen, to provide a living audience that gave his playing a sense of purpose, and her reward was to envision the images the sounds evoked, to connect with emotions so deeply concealed she could only wonder at their infinite complexity.

It was Macael who rose and ordered refreshment some time well past midnight. Liere, dazzled by the continuous pageantry of sound, tried to fight her way back to the here and now, but gave up with an inward shrug. Too many sleepless nights on Chantala's behalf, and gratitude for having stumbled on the right outlet for Macael, kept her still in her chair.

He brought wine to her with his own hands, and then resumed his place by the fire. He drank off his own wine in a sudden gesture, and in a gesture as sudden raised the goblet, his profile turned sharply toward the fire, wrist cocked as though he would smash the goblet in the fire as once he had before, so many years ago.

But this goblet was golden, not crystal, and not his.

He set it gently down. She watched, mildly puzzled, unable to guess at the motivations behind either gesture as he picked up the instrument. Again the miraculous beauty of intricate melody filled the chamber. She could not determine if his remarkable playing was surcease from emotion, or release. She wondered if she would ever see him again. As brilliant cascades of music sparked every nerve, evoking memory, emotion, and image, she knew that she would never forget this night.

And so, her wine finished, she curled up in her chair, her heart full of the best of human compassion and appreciation; she was even less conscious of self than customary, and had no idea what an image she presented, there in the firelight, wide golden eyes and her long sweep of wheat-gold hair burnished brighter than any crown, a smile of surpassing sweetness glowing in all her features. Her hands were posed with unconscious grace, one beneath her chin, and all around her the lustrous folds of her summer sky blue damask over robe made a celestial frame.

Her intention was to watch with Macael as long as he required human company, but somehow the images blended into dream, and slowly — inexorably — faded into the deep sleep of one who has partaken, without her knowledge, of rare herbs.

4

Morning dawned under a leaden sky.

Trevor Andiran opened his eyes to light through the big windows in da's bedroom. He let out a slow sigh of contentment. Always he'd been welcome to crawl into either of his parents' beds if they were alone or with each other and he needed the physical or emotional warmth, the proximity.

He had a vague memory of his father's comforting shape on his right. His father was up and gone at sunrise. Trevor looked over to his left at where he'd unconsciously made space for his mother, but she had not come in at all. That pillow was untouched, and though the heavy, motionless air still smelled comfortingly like his father, his mother's scent was not present.

That was his first hint that something was wrong.

He got up, shoved his feet into his shoes, but loitered at the door. He knew what was waiting in the schoolroom, besides his breakfast: his tutor, and a load of tedious lessons. He knew the rules. Mornings belonged to duty, and afternoons were his, but everything felt so *weird*.

He let himself out onto the icy balcony, ducked below windows, and made his way to the last room, which had a broken window latch that his father had told him about. In that room was a closet with a false door, a secret passage behind, going down to the back larder that always smelled musty from its sacks of food stuff.

He slipped out and snagged one of the kitchen servants. "Have you seen my Ma?"

The maid put a floury hand to her back, for she'd woken well before dawn to get the baking going. "Last I heard, she was asleep in the daybed off her parlor." She added soberly, "The Queen of Sles Adran died last night."

Trevor didn't question why Aunt Chantala's death might cause his mother to sleep somewhere else. The fact of death was enough of a change to make the light look different, to give immediate shape and meaning to the oppressive atmosphere that he sensed over his home.

Ma always said to think everything through before acting. He decided that meant before he had to face lessons. He slipped outside, still wearing last night's clothes, and sneaked through the kitchen garden to the compost in order to avoid well-meaning servants who would insist on his eating, or who would remind him that a prince must always meet his responsibilities. He knew every tree and shrub in the garden. Using those as cover, he retreated to his favorite thinking spot: the thickest and oldest tree in the avenue of yew.

Andri, sensing his distress as he returned from the inner guard salle and a quick warmup, went to find him, ducking past a clump of Macael's own guards, who had years ago been invited to share facilities when they had to stay.

Macael's voice startled Andri as he stepped onto the broad path of the yew walk behind the older, empty Residence wing. None of Andri's guards were in view; Andri figured Haldri and Math had already swept the area, both pretending not to see the boy no doubt shivering high in the tallest tree.

"May I join you?" Macael stood framed in the doorway, his usually ordered hair messy. He wore the same clothes as the previous evening.

"Of course."

Andri hid his regret. Trevor would not talk about what disturbed him before an audience. To him, one person beside either of his parents would constitute an audience. Andri couldn't hear Liere on the mental plane, which meant she was still deeply asleep somewhere in Brydon, so he couldn't try to shuffle Macael off on her, if he was looking for sympathy.

Well, Andri decided, if Macael needed company, they could walk right underneath the oldest tree and leave it to Trevor to determine whether he wanted to be 'discovered'.

They stepped onto the path, walking side by side, Andri aware of the crunch of their heels in the ice and the frost of their breathing, as he ransacked his brain for something to say. Something appropriate, when the man's wife just died, but not that as a subject—

He glanced over, old habit making his assessment fast. Anomalies caught his attention first: he attributed a pang of warning to the startling sight of the impeccable Macael wearing last night's blue and gold, wrinkled as it was, and the dark, thin scab-line under Macael's fingernails, for despite the weather his hands were bare.

Oh. Of course. Strings. Music.

It seemed a safe enough subject to Andri's cartwheeling mind (for the problem of Trevor plus whether or not they were going to stave off interviews for another day in anticipation of a memorial for Chantala did not disappear either) and he said gratefully, "You played music for Liere?"

"Yes," Macael said, so softly it was almost a whisper.

Encouraged, Andri followed the galloping thought so quickly he did not notice until it was too late that the bridge was out. "She'd like that very much. Has mentioned the night in the valley, when you played all night for her and ... and Chantala..." He faltered at naming the newly dead and raced on over the invisible bridge. "Often wished you would play again, regretted that you never..."

It was then that his thoughts spiraled into the air, and fell.

Macael stilled, and in that moment, Andri understood that his half-formed suspicions were correct.

Macael said even more softly than before, "Then you did see it."

Andri winced inwardly, suffused with laughter and regret, and looked up into the yew for his son. Anywhere but at his cousin, whose secret he'd just stupidly bared, and what a damned awkward moment to bare it!

Behind the snow-stippled branches he descried the outline of a small boy. Andri smiled, and Trevor grinned back.

Then his eyes widened with shock.

At that same instant Macael murmured, "Makes this slightly more bearable."

"This—?" Andri's breath stuttered at sudden pain. His mouth filled with hot blood: death, half-expected all his life, had got him at last.

Andri strove against it, because there was so much to do, to amend, to assure. But he couldn't catch his breath, couldn't even look down at the knife in his chest. Macael's face loomed in his vision: his blanched face, black eyes mirroring the excruciating pain.

: *Liere?*

Trevor's wide eyes above. Andri fought to reassure his son, to reach him, but he could not lift his hands, now so numb. His mind fumbled as he stared desperately at those golden eyes, willing with his ebbing strength his boy to get away, to be safe —

The gold faded into darkness.

Above, Trevor Andiran clung tightly to the tree. The swift images had frozen into a weird kind of timelessness. The two tall men, his father's low, husky voice speaking quick words Trevor couldn't hear, then his head lifting, his green eyes full of a kind of rueful laughter that Trevor didn't understand. The change of laughter to surprise, then pain, as he fell down into the snow, crimson splashing brightly against the white, looking up, love, love, love and then his thoughts winged away.

Life stopped. Time stopped.

Then Uncle Macael knelt down, and touched Trevor's father's loose wrist. He raised his head, and his eyes widened with shock.

For a heartbeat Trevor stared down into Macael's taut face. And Trevor saw again how fast his uncle had moved, slipping a knife from his sleeve and ramming it up under his father's ribs in the place on the straw-stuffed dummy Trevor had practiced, over and over again, with his sword master. But this time it had been real.

As Macael began to stand, still watching Trevor, his shocked eyes narrowed with intent. Trevor looked down again at that bloody hilt sticking up from his father's unmoving chest and unbidden came those weird words to Trevor's lips, and his hands made the signs —

And he seemed to fall into nightmare even worse than the one he'd just endured. Only for the space of a breath.

Light returned, and sensation, and he stumbled forward, crying, "Mama!"

He stopped. Stared when he realized that the blond-haired adult before him was not his father, but a man Trevor had never before seen in his life.

5

avid sat at the desk and labored steadily until the pre-dawn watch bell tolled once.

They met outside Senrid's room and walked down to the salle together; if Senrid was surprised to see David still there, he did not show it.

As before, when they were done, hot coffee awaited them, freshly ground and prepared by Senrid's night staff. David accepted a cup with thanks, reflecting on the fact that this servant would be napping at midday, replaced by a steward who would serve until the late hours that Senrid kept. The servants were given more civilized watches than Senrid permitted himself.

David was familiar with this pattern of avoiding dreams: a single watch of sleep a night punctuated by days of no sleep at all, until he was so exhausted one had to sleep nearly round the clock, probably soused, and preferably at a distance. It was the way David's own brother, the wicked Imry, had existed, only without the liquor. It seemed to be a family trait.

The only difference was that Senrid slept in his castle, whereas Imry had never slept well in proximity to others, thanks to his unspeakable early childhood before Detlev found him.

David ignored the marks of tiredness under Senrid's eyes, and reached for a stack of reports from the mountain forge Senrid had mentioned inspecting today, but his hand stopped midway over the desk when he heard Senrid's short intake of breath.

"Magic alarm—" Senrid began.

Then the flash of transport magic deposited directly before Senrid a small boy who choked on a great sob. "Mama!"

He stumbled forward a step, hands reaching, but then the huge golden eyes looked up, met Senrid's hard gray-blue gaze, and the child's expression altered from anguish to terrified confusion.

David strolled forward. Despite the emotions blanching the young face, the bones, the slight build, the long, fine yellow hair, all marked this boy as the son of Andri Elsarion.

And of Liere Fer Eider.

"My mother?" the boy asked in Enaeraneth, and David felt the intense effort he made to get control of himself.

Senrid answered in that language, "She is not here. Did she send you?"

"It was a spell," said the boy, his childish voice thin from the effort he made not to let it waver, though he trembled all over. "She taught me. When I was little. In case of danger. Uncle Macael—" The face spasmed, then his lips whitened from another effort at control. "He killed my father. Maybe he'll kill her. Send me home, please?"

Senrid glanced over his shoulder at David, his eyes narrowed and his mouth tight, but David just shook his head, not masking his own surprise.

Senrid turned his attention to the child. "If your mother taught you that spell," he said in Enaeraneth, "it was to convey you to safety so that she would have freedom of action. The worst thing you could do for her now would be to put yourself back into danger so that you can be used against her."

Senrid paused. The boy breathed in short, compressed gasps, but his brow furrowed; he was comprehending. Thinking. Belatedly, he gave a nod.

"Good. Now tell us what happened."

"They were walking. Yew avenue." The boy's voice rose, and his eyes filled. "Da ... Da. Looked up. Un—he—he ..." The generously curved lips that called Andri to mind compressed again into a white line, then the boy forced out each word: "Uncle Macael stabbed him. Then he saw me. I did the spell. Like I was taught. But my mother—"

"Has been looking after herself for many years."

"So has my da—" The high keen of hysteria, valiantly

suppressed, was back in the boy's voice.

And Senrid said, "She's alive, or I would know."

David's breath trickled out, but he made certain it wasn't heard. The boy accepted the statement with the unquestioning compliance of childhood. He gave a great, shuddering sigh, and clasped his hands tightly behind him.

Senrid looked up in question, and David interpreted the look. He shrugged: over to you.

Senrid turned his attention to the boy. His voice was brisk, his tone kind. "David is going to your country to find your mother if he can. In the meantime, how would you like to stay with boys and girls your own age at the military academy? This kingdom is Marloven Hess. Have you heard of the academy?"

Another deep, shivery breath. A quick nod. "It's the one. Where you train captains."

"Yes. Would you like to stay there for now?"

"Can I ... can I practice fighting while I wait for my mother?"

"Of course."

"Good," the boy said, and David felt him get a grip over his emotions at last, now that he had a goal. "Teach me to fight better. And when I'm old enough, I'll go back and smash Uncle Macael."

"What name shall I use to introduce you to the others?"

"Trev—no. Malcolin," came the steady young voice. "It's my third name. And my father's second name. I don't want Trevor anymore. That's *his* first name. And Andiran belongs to *his* branch of the family, too. From now on I'll be Malcolin."

"Very well, then, Malcolin, let's take a walk to the academy, shall we? And I'll give you knowledge of our language through a magic spell I know."

David watched them leave, and considered where to transfer. Fixing on Liere as a transfer target would be a bad idea if she were imprisoned, which seemed likely if Senrid was correct and she too had not been assassinated. This was a scouting mission; he was not dressed or armed for action. He took from the little boy's radiating thoughts an image of the side court below his nursery, then performed the transfer-slide.

The courtyard was empty, but David sensed terror, tension, anger everywhere, as if it had taken life in the cold, wintry air. He scanned mentally. No sign of Liere on the mental plane, damn it. She was far too skilled at shields. He spotted an uncurtained window, and did another slide to the inside of that room.

From there he made his way rapidly to the mostly-empty wing above the yew path, using images from passing minds, several of which furnished shocked views of Andri lying dead in the snow. When David got to an empty room overlooking that garden, he was in time to see Andri's body being carried away by what seemed to be mostly kitchen help, aided by a couple of footmen, half of them weeping silently, or looking back fearfully at two armed guards.

A tall man in indigo stood by the door: Macael Elsarion. He watched as the pair of guards followed the party with Andri inside. These were dressed in the lavender-gray of Adrani military. Other guards arrived at a run, two with shovels. Under Macael's gaze, they began cleaning the bloody snow off the path; a third appeared, lugging a bucket of hot water, which he poured over the snow. It melted, sinking into the duff below the trees. The bloodstains were gone.

: Detlev, if you foresaw this, why didn't you warn me? No, why didn't you warn Andri?

David hadn't been sure there would be an answer, but Detlev responded immediately: *I did not know if Macael Elsarion would go through with it. And what would have been the result of warning Andri?*

David didn't have to think. It was easy enough to imagine the Enaeraneth going after the Adranis, whose far larger and better equipped army would come right back in force. Even if Andri didn't order his people into war, he wouldn't be able to stop it, because they were halfway there already, something he shrugged and insisted was generational.

: I can take out Elsarion.

: And the reprisals will be even more vicious, as well as the fighting over Macael's throne. And that explained why Detlev wasn't here himself, Davi thought sourly as Macael Elsarion vanished unmolested inside.

A pack of angry, terrified, grief-stricken Enaeraneth moved about in clumps, under the eyes of numerous Adrani guards. So many that David knew that he was seeing the carrying out of a meticulously laid plan.

He backed out of that room, crossed to the other side, and soon found his way to the palace guard barracks—where Adrani guards were in the process of laying out corpses in the blue uniforms of Andri's personal guard. There were no signs of battle; as the guards brought out a last corpse, her head lolled, revealing a slit throat.

When David turned his gaze to the rest, he saw a shadow beneath each's jaw. Looked as if they'd been drugged and killed in their sleep, one by one. He spotted a barn-like building beyond the barracks that had to be their salle. He fixed his gaze on a corner and once again executed a transfer-slide; here he found the evidence of a hard fight, judging by blood splatters and churned up ground. That would be the night watch, probably returning to their rest. As he studied the ground, gaining a sense of the character of the fight—the ambush— some of the Adrani guards who'd laid out the dead from the barracks arrived and began restoring the place to order.

David backed off, unwilling to be marked, though so far he saw no civilian corpses. He retreated to the cover of a garden, and ghosted through it to the front of the palace.

As he moved, he had to slip past the rapidly assembling defense. At key points around the palace perimeter stood armed Sles Adrani heavies, the kingdom's five-pointed crown over twinned lilies on mail coats and helms. Beneath the mail, surcoats of lavender-gray. They were waiting, or patrolling in columns, so far not attacking anyone.

David scaled a tall tree, and peered through its branches down into the city below the long ridge on which the palace was built. Here and there knots of people stood talking, their postures tense, some fingering weapons, but the warriors deploying there appeared not to see them. They stood at exactly the right intersections for command of major streets and watched, perfect formation, weapons ready. Most of the people on the move were making their way toward the royal palace.

David spied an alley below, made the transfer-slide, then slipped into a good-sized crowd, listening to the gossip around him.

"... killed him outright!"

"All the Honor Guard dead. Throats slit. Not even an

honest ..."

"Teldan said it was a duel."

"No such thing," interjected a third voice. "Don't you think our Andri could have taken that soul-sucking, back-stabbing Adrani traitor blindfolded?"

"Of course!" a chorus of voices rose.

"My cousin Erith's brother's in the guard and she's saying the king was stabbed right in the back. The prince too—"

As the talk went on, one question seemed constant, though no one could answer it with anything but speculation: *What will Sartora do?*

David closed his eyes, listening on the mental plane. Still no sign of Liere.

Most people thought as they spoke, without the least shield. The mental plane did not always equate physical distance. The stronger the emotional force, the more proximate the mind, so he walked in a maelstrom of reaction. Along with the constant stream of question ran a common belief: in spite of the anger, the declarations, the fears and speculations, they converged on Brydon expecting to see the great and magical Sartora appear victorious over the treacherous, evil Adrani king.

Another constant, rarely spoken aloud, was the private worries. As David touched one mind after another he recognized that most of the Enaeraneth had reservations about fighting the Adranis. So many of the minds whose fast-moving, emotion-driven thoughts David listened to revealed someone apprehensive for a relative who'd gone over the border to work, or for those who had come here and became close. The kingdoms had apparently been encouraged, by both crowns, to intermingle in order to speed Enaeran's recovery from the years of war.

Not just that. As he was assimilating these thoughts, twice he caught glances between Enaeraneth and individual guards: looks of recognition, of worry, fear, tension. Determination. David did not like sustaining contact while he was moving, as it gave him vertigo, but he caught enough to comprehend that many of the Adranis on guard were related in some way to these Enaeraneth. No bloodlust here. No anticipation of the fun of breaking heads. These had been carefully selected.

This realization was the first hint of the magnitude — and the age — of Trevor-Macael Elsarion's plans. David was too well trained to think it coincidence.

Liere fought her way through a strangely thick sense-shrouding miasma, impelled by a sharp sense of urgency: *Andri? Trevor?*

Mind-call was obviously yet too weak. She heard nothing in the mental realm. Why was it weak? Andri was not good at initiating contacts, but he was very powerful when one reached him in farsense: *Andri? Andri?*

Nothing.

The urgency intensified, enabling her at last to break through the heavy layer of mental haze and fight her way to shallow consciousness.

She opened aching eyes, and found herself staring blurrily up into another pair of eyes. These were sky blue, framed by long dark lashes. With that steady regard came no familiar tendril of mind-touch. She knew those eyes. Her gaze diffused, from long habit, before that unwavering regard.

She turned her head. The room was lit from the east with the wintry pale light of midmorning. She closed her eyes as one by one her other senses awakened.

She lay on the daybed off her sitting room. She was still in her blue damask robe. Her legs were confined by a heavy quilt wrapping them securely, and a weight across her knees. Sound brought from a distance a curious low buzzing roar, like a great crowd, and closer, very close, the light sound of breathing. Smell: stale wine in the air, and faintly, sweat. Not hers. Male, the sharp whiff of adrenaline-laced endeavor.

Sensation: headache. Her body, heavy. Her hands unmoving … from pressure: in specific, a hand on each of her wrists, holding them in a firm grip at either side of her head.

Trevor-Macael Elsarion's hands.

The sensory facts piled like sticks until that last one kindled the fire of danger. And despite the headache, she tried suddenly and with all her strength to free her wrists, to find them pinned immovably to the mattress by a strength vastly superior to her own.

Through the crash of headache she looked up again. Macael stared straight down into her eyes, watching. Waiting.

: Andri?

Nothing.

: Trevor?

Awareness—distance—incoherent, intense emotion, so intense her head crashed again. But at least she knew her son was alive. She blinked at Macael, who knelt at her side, one knee across hers, his hands still gripped tightly on her wrists, so that she could not move, or do magic. Proximity jumped her heartbeat into a frantic gallop. He was, for the first time in all the years she had known him, disheveled. The fine strands of black hair drifting untended across his forehead, the open tunic stippled with drying blood (*whose?*), the unlaced neck of his fine cambric shirt, all of these signs indicated violence. Recent violence.

His eyes. He had not slept at all.

He had stayed awake, then, through how many nights?

Liere remembered Chantala's death, and wondered that she herself could have fallen so soundly into slumber and slept through half a day, when she had never before done that in her entire life.

But she *hadn't* dozed off. She'd sat with Macael as he played through the night one intricate emotion-driven melody after another, until once again—like the first time—his fingers bled. And then ... unconsciousness.

Her tongue moved dryly in her mouth, puckering with an unpleasant, acrid taste. Herbs! An image of Macael offering her wine, and standing there watching her take the first sip, before he'd dashed off his own.

The impossible continued to erode the old, comfortable order she tried to impose on the streaming perceptions, leaving an unjustifiable, distorted world whose air she did not want to breathe, whose sights and sounds she repudiated with all her strength.

But she was held here, by Trevor-Macael Elsarion's strong hands. She could not move—could not perform transfer magic.

: Andri!

Nothing.

No echo, just the great stillness that meant the spirit's tie to the finite world had forever been severed.

: *Trevor?*

: *Ma!* And again the confusing jumble of images that made her head ring.

Instinct overcame personal covenant, and her mind flung a desperate call headlong down the home path, the one she'd had in honor bent her mind from using, from seeing, for years: *Senrid?*

: *He's here, and safe.*

That was all.

The first contact they'd had since the war. Since—

Her thoughts spun away, accelerated by the headache, by the shock that waited to engulf her. She gazed up into Macael's waiting face, and saw the tension there. Tension, and comprehension.

"Two things," he said, as though continuing a conversation. It was the same musical voice, so familiar.

"Andri," she whispered. "He's dead?"

Macael's chin jerked up minutely in corroboration.

"Who? What? Not Norsunder, back?"

"No." The tension was still there in Macael's face, in the steady blue regard. But there was no thought to be read. Only a lifetime of habit could have enabled that. "I killed him," Macael said. "It was fast."

Shock gripped her heart, sinking its claws deep, and she tried once more, using all her training—but he was expecting it. Her wrist bones ground under his fingers.

"I'm sorry," he said, and she snorted in derision. But before she could summon the words to express her sudden flare of rage, he spoke again in that calm flat voice. "First. You will stay here for one year."

"As *soon* as you let go of me—"

"If you leave, it will touch off a civil war of a magnitude Andri's damned family never managed despite all their efforts," he retorted. "And once I win it, I will not stop until I hunt down that boy of yours and kill him. I don't want to kill him. The bargain I'm suggesting is to circumvent that, as well as keep the peace here in Shiovhan."

"He's … not here," she snapped.

"I know. I saw him vanish. But I'll find him."

That silenced her. Dear, darling Trevor—

"You know me little," Macael said, still in that flat voice. "But I trust you will believe what I say."

To her horror Liere's eyes stung with tears. She gritted her teeth as they burned, spilling over the edges of her eyelids and dripping into her ears. Macael waited, his grip on her wrists implacable.

She fought for control, and won at last. "You said first. Your second demand?" she said, when she knew her voice would be steady.

His voice was so flat he sounded dead. In that inhuman lack of tone she believed was the key at last to his emotions: deliberate cruelty.

"Before you leave at year's end you will give me an heir."

6

A whisper ran back through the crowd that the queen was going to come out. She was going to address them. People by tens, then by the hundreds, gathered in the huge parade ground where Andri's ancestors had handed out proclamations and made speeches, and watched parades of military might. They waited patiently, despite the increasing press of angry people, and the painfully cold wintry air.

David waited in the middle of the crowd, his sense of foreboding steadily worsening.

It was just after noon when a flurry of whispers spiraled outward through the throng, sharp as the driving winter wind, and everyone raised their faces toward the proclamation balcony.

The double doors opened and a man and a woman emerged, the woman reed-slender and fair, the man dark, broad of shoulder, dressed immaculately in the blue of a midnight sky, golden kingsblossom worked across the chest of his formal tunic: Elsarion colors. Sometime between David glimpsing him in the yew walk and now, Macael had changed his clothes, though Liere looked rumpled in blue damask, her hair streaming down in uncombed locks.

David looked from Elsarion's utterly blank demeanor to Liere's tense hands gripping her elbows, and held his breath.

Macael did not move, though the harsh cry of anger expelled from countless throats at his appearance was followed by the scrape of blades pulled from scabbards. Then Liere raised a hand. David was close enough to perceives the tremble in her fingers. "Please," she said, and her voice carried. "Go home. Take up your lives."

Another outcry, more like a wail.

Macael still did not move. Liere's hand strayed to the other arm again, gripping, and David saw her chest heave on a scarcely suppressed sob. Then she straightened.

The crowd was now quiet, a frayed and uneasy quiet.

"There is no bringing Andri back," she said, her voice low but carrying, raw with grief. "There is no justice in fresh deaths of innocent people. Do not tear apart everything Andri worked to rebuild. Let living well, and in safety, be your answer to ..." On the last word her voice suspended, and she stood there for an excruciating moment, her uplifted face a rictus as she fought for control, while Macael stood motionless by her side.

Silence from the crowd. Some mutters, surrounded by uneasy, wary glances toward the waiting Adrani warriors. Many faces mirrored Liere's suffering.

"Go home," she cried, her face and voice now high and distraught. "Let history pass judgment. Go in peace. I will bide here — in peace — for the space of one year."

She turned away, head bowed, and groped for the door to the balcony. Macael Elsarion stepped courteously aside for her to pass, and then followed her within, as if he wasn't aware of the firewall of hatred his appearance had kindled, or of the many hands caressing hidden knife hilts right now, and many minds wishing to be the one to take him out with one throw, wishes that were stayed only by Liere's words — and by those bared swords all around the perimeter of the courtyard. But David had no doubt that Elsarion was very aware of them, and took the risk anyway.

David stood poised; from his experience with violence and crowds, if they were going to act, it would be now. He looked past shaking fists and the raised backs of hands and the spitting on the ground, assessing the quick, questioning glances at one another: they were waiting for a leader to make the first move. But there was no leader. Ah, here — over there — a few paces in front — Adranis in civilian clothes, shaking heads, muttering, "Let's go home." A child wailed, the sound carrying over the susurrus of whispers as people looked around. Question — shared grief — fear began to diffuse the bloodlust, and the potential mob disintegrated into knots of angry, wary, saddened and fearful individuals.

Contemplating the scale of the plan, David transferred

back to Marloven Hess.

Senrid was at his desk, but when David appeared, he glanced up, eyes narrow with more suspicion than question.

David addressed the question. "She's there for a year, I'd guess as hostage against the boy's life. Want me to find out more?"

Senrid lifted one shoulder slightly. "Why? Eventually Elsarion will either let her go or she'll figure out what to do about it. The boy is safe enough here. What I want to know is if I've suddenly become another piece on Detlev's game board."

"No," David lied. *You always were. But this game is not of his making.*

And Senrid retorted, "Your so-called hand-through-the-water is horseshit. There are consequences to *every* action."

"Never said there weren't."

"When I act, the consequences point back to me. Bad or good. I have to stand up to them. Your 'hand' is nothing more than sneakery, leaving the consequences of your covert actions to someone else to clean up."

"Whatever you say." David spread his hands. "Unless you have any further commands I should return before Adam quits on me."

Senrid looked amused, aware—they both were—how David had answered without answering. "Assure Detlev that if he has an interest in that boy, he can take him at any time."

"Tell him yourself," David invited.

At Curtas's House, he found Adam standing on a landing painting the white-crown mountains that divided them from Sartor proper. David told him, with as much invective as a considerable education in filthy language could contrive, what had happened. Adam smiled from time to time when David got off an especially crude, unfair, and vivid hit, but refrained from comment until the end.

"Liere losing control," he said. "Interesting."

"You don't think it was grief, but a method of crowd control?" David asked skeptically, watching Adam's gloved hands mixing yet another variation in the twenty shades of blue-white already on his palette. "I don't really know her, but that kind of masterly manipulation doesn't match with my memories of the skinny little Sartora who never remembered to put on shoes even when it was snowing."

"The emotion was real, of that I am very certain. It's just that she made no attempt to control it. At a guess, it was in a sense aimed at Elsarion," Adam said, standing back to eye his work. "She won't hide her grief. Not when it is honest, and moral, reproach." He thought for a time, as chickens scolded and squawked below. "If she has to stay there, it's going to make his life worse than damnation."

David laughed, a gloating crow straight out of their violent past.

Adam looked over, his ordinarily gentle brown eyes sardonic. "You're angry because Detlev foresaw the possibi-lity?"

"Because he sent me to Marloven Hess to teach me a lesson in consequences, and Senrid niffed it. I didn't think I was that clumsy. Or that predictable."

Adam smiled, and painted the side of a mountain as he considered what to say. David knew he ought to have kept up with his visits to Marloven Hess, as he had accepted the heirship — and the implied support of Senrid. There was no use in pointing that out, any more than it would be useful to remind David that they were still very much in training, which meant mistakes like this one were going to happen. David wanted to learn the Long View. This seemed to be shaping into a lesson on how to do it.

Adam said finally, "We are all predictable. As is human pain."

David thought of his brother Imry killing Senrid's four-year-old daughter, at the beginning of a war he'd led just to prove he could. David had exerted his strength to oppose his brother, but he still felt, after all these years, a deep, abiding regret. Did Imry?

No one knew. No one had seen him for years.

Presently David said, "Do you think it was as hard when Detlev watched the circumstances of our lives unfold?"

"Worse."

Trevor Andiran Malcolin Elsarion, now known as simply as Malcolin, didn't mean to talk about himself, but before the day's end he had spilled everything to his new bunkmates.

The famous Marloven academy overawed him at first, giving him something to think about instead of his father's death, and his worry about his mother, and his hatred of Trevor Macael Elsarion. The man who had brought him, he found out directly after his departure, was the king, Senrid Montredaun-An.

Malcolin's parents had never mentioned knowing this king, but Malcolin was used to adults knowing far more people than he got to meet. He'd heard about Marloven Hess from others — travelers, mostly. His sword master. He knew something of its history as well, for the Elsarions and the Montredaun-Ans had been related way back. Marloven Hess was famous for its military skills, and for its academy that trained its leaders. Therefore it made sense that his mother would set up a spell to send him, in case of disaster, directly to the place where he'd get the best training to fight back.

This Senrid-Harvaldar only stayed with him long enough to introduce him to a woman who had some kind of position of command, and then he left. Malcolin expected no more. He'd not been raised with the belief that his rank entitled him to anything that he hadn't earned by his own efforts. *You're the only prince,* his father had said last summer, *but kingship in Enaeran usually has to be won — and held — through good skills with your hands as well as your head.* Adding with a laugh, *I'll depress you with a history of the specifics when you're older.*

Of course a world-famous military mage-king would not have time for a little boy from another land. Instead, the woman gave him a tour, pointing out classrooms and practice fields and stables, ending at a barracks.

And there was a place for him. He was introduced to the three bunkmates closest to his new bed, who, as soon as they were left alone, ascertained in a brisk and blunt give-and-take that he had had some training, though he was the youngest in the barracks, with long hair and a weird accent. Youngest, in fact, in the school, as the usual age was ten. They made it their business to assess that training, right there in the barracks, as soon as the adult had left. Malcolin was no match for any of them at wrestling, but he knocked the sword right out of the hand of the biggest bunkmate, his focus driven by anger and grief. Thus, his new bunkmates' attitude was neutral when he explained who he was — why he had come — and somehow his mouth blathered out what he hadn't meant to tell: that his da had been killed that very day, right before his eyes.

Their neutrality altered to a wary sort of respect as they accompanied him to a meal he couldn't eat, and even extended past lights-out when uneven, gulping breathing could be heard from that top bunk. Enough of them had early memories of adult grief during the war, and felt he had the right to blub.

Malcolin lay with his eyes closed and his lips pressed shut. He did not hear his own harsh breathing, for his mind kept filling with vivid memories. For a long time hot tears trickled down either side of his face. But then, when he didn't think he could bear it any longer, and he knew that the wails he held in were going to come ripping up from his guts, a soft hand touched his brow. Ma was here. Her familiar scent embraced him — a scent that had always meant peace and love and tranquility — and he stumbled out of the barracks into the courtyard, where he wept into Liere's arms.

Liere clung to the slight, shaking figure. Her own tears flowed again, as they had a little while ago. when she'd forced herself to walk into the king's bedroom and saw Andri's belongings, and smelled his scent on the discarded shirt from the night before, which had escaped being put through the cleaning frame due to the upset over Chantala's death.

Her day after she made the balcony speech and Macael left her had begun with puking up that wine, and then collapsing onto her bed as the headache crashed. It was all she could do to hold her mind-shield tight against the roar of emotions surrounding her until she had control again, then send out a tendril to assess the situation, with a vague idea of finding a way to get a knife between Macael's ribs. Except that first white-hot impulse had cooled. Her instinct had never been to react with violence, but to look for consequences, and she knew that if she stalked Macael and succeeded in even wounding him, those Adranis out there would go to war in earnest.

People had knocked at her door, but she ignored them, and eventually they went away. That gave her a clue to her status: she was not a prisoner, then, but a hostage. And it was quiet out there. No killing sprees, though the miasma of fear and anger on the mental-plane roiled up her stomach all over again.

After darkness fell, she forced herself to rise, pass through her cleaning frame, then light a candle. That's when she ventured into Andri's suite, and of course found it empty of life, and wept. After which, though she ached to her bones, she reached in the realm of the spirit for her son.

And when she encountered his overwhelming grief, she transferred.

"Oh, Mama, take me home," Malcolin sobbed into her breast.

She kissed his hot forehead and his moist, swollen eyes, and buried her face in his hair. "I can't, my darling boy," she murmured, her own stinging, aching eyes swollen from a day of grief. "And I can't stay long. I have to go back."

"You can't—"

"I have to," Liere said, her whisper unsteady as she caressed his rigid shoulders. "I made a promise. I have to stay there a year."

"Why?"

"Because ..." She took a deep breath, reached back into her own childhood, and gave him the truth. "If I stay there a year, then Macael won't try to kill you."

"You won't fight him?"

"I can't fight him alone. And I won't raise an army. Too many people would die to no purpose. Not only warriors, but their families. People passing down the wrong street. They control Shiovhan, my darling boy. Try to understand. He planned what he did for a long time. He has trusted people in control in key places."

"A *year*," Malcolin said. It seemed to stretch forever into the future.

Liere lifted from round her neck something dangling on a chain, and set it on his shoulders. "You can call me by thinking of me and touching that," she murmured softly. "If I can come, I will. Do you like this place?" She looked through the moonlit window at the rows of bunks touched palely by moonlight. The atmosphere seemed curiously imbued with Senrid's presence, though she could not have defined how. She knew his uncle had kept him away from the academy as a boy, and they had never spent time there when she had visited so long ago.

"I'll stay," her son muttered. "I can learn here. I told them to call me Malcolin. I *hate* Trevor now."

"Then you shall be Malcolin. In a year we can live together somewhere safe," she said, caressing his face.

Wordlessly she rocked him back and forth, and when he at last made a small movement, it took all her will to back away and let him slip back inside the barracks, where he crawled into his new bunk. She left the little courtyard, as those bunkmates who had wakened at the not-quite-muffled noises lay in silence, some trying to banish their own residual memories of war's grief.

She stood alone in that stone corridor where once she had run to her riding lessons a lifetime ago. For a short time she considered abandoning her promise to that treacherous Trevor Macael Elsarion. But that left his threat against her son. Though Malcolin was safe now, how long would that last, if she reneged on her promise? Macael had just proven that he was very skilled at planning; could she condemn her son to a life of constantly looking over his shoulder? The way Andri had grown up…

Anxiety and horror propelled her through another transfer. She appeared in her room, which was untouched. She staggered to her bed and sank onto it, fists clenched on her knees. She reached by farsense, despite the pounding in her head, and found that her son was already deep in the sleep of exhaustion.

Then she sent a tendril to assess her surroundings more slowly and thoroughly than her earlier scan. She was drawn straight to the intense grief of a cluster of familiar servants in the back courtyard, lit by torches. They had gathered, surrounded by ranks of guards standing at attention, for the Disappearances.

Liere saw through their eyes as Macael said the words, and Chantala's thin form vanished. Then the old, white-haired palace steward came forward, and after a long, straight look at Macael, full of dignity in spite of his trembling chin, said the words over Andri. After that, one by one, various relations, friends, and lovers, said the words over Andri's honor guard, and over those who had tried to fight, and lost.

The onslaught of fresh sorrow intensifying their vivid memories gnawed her heart raw: Gared, lying sprawled in a chair, his throat cut; Haldri on the floor, also throat cut. Servants' hands shaking as they laid Andri out in a peaceful pose that he never had assumed in life, with many quick, wary glances. It seemed they thought to prevent Liere from the sight of him dead, but she saw him through their eyes, his coloring pale, and that bloody wound in the middle of his chest, the color and shape obscenely bringing a rose to mind.

For a heartbeat or two she fiercely resented the Adranis conducting his Disappearance, but the lingering image of that wound, and his face with all the life gone, forced her to accept that nothing would have been "right." It would have hurt just as much, if not more, if she had been there among them. Maybe one of those knocks had even been an invitation—or a summons—to join them. Would she have gone, or refused? It no longer mattered. There was no altering the result.

At least Andri's latest lover seemed to be safe, for no one was mourning, or even thinking, of moody, secretly ambitious Bevara, the Baras of Yuthan's daughter, a patrol captain in the King's Guard. Oh yes, she had requested permission to be sent home for New Year's Week. But the news must be propagating outward, as fast as people could travel in the heavy snow.

Liere pressed her arms against her middle, rocking back and forth in pain as she sent her tendril farther, to discover who yet lived. Most of the servants. So far. Though all the honor guard was dead. A careful planner would see to that, she thought bitterly. For they were all loyal, and would fight to the death. Though from the images caught in grief-stricken minds, it seemed that the day guard had been given some sleep herb—like her—but unlike her, they were killed while senseless.

Only she was left alive, for that cruel bargain.

It was too much to bear.

She blew out the candle, crawled into the cold bed, and lay there, ignoring the headache, thirst. Hunger, far below her consciousness. She wanted to be dead.

7

In Wnelder Vee's capital, Fortnyal Roth, Lyren Fer Eider leaned on the worn rail of the newly renovated palace, which was really more of a rambling, much-added to house with a guildhall that had become a throne room by the addition of a chair on a dais. She was watching Laban and Silvanas train horses as Silvanas leaped onto the backs of this or that wild and frisky young animal. He loved the action and the risk, and laughed aloud as the latest horse tried its best to throw him off. He would make friends with it anon, but first the contest.

Lyren had no interest in horse training, though she'd professed to, as an excuse to be watching. Her interest lay solely in the agreeable spectacle of two extravagantly handsome young men exerting themselves with their customary skill and utterly unconscious grace. They laughed like boys, their old tunics hanging open, sweat and dust imprinted on the brown skin beneath.

Who would have thought! Once, when they were all children, Laban and Silvanas had been the enemy, two of Detlev's pet killers. Detlev. The man she had hated most in all the world. Yet despite that, it was Detlev who'd sent Siamis when she needed a guardian most, and during the war, when Liere's reckless and sudden marriage to Andri once again seemed to divide her off, Lyren had discovered that the former, sarcastic poopsie Laban was in so many ways a kindred spirit.

They'd taken to one another like siblings. Too alike, she had decided, for attraction, despite his romantic good looks and dashing manner. Her first taste of attraction had been a humiliating lesson that she had no desire to repeat.

Look but don't touch, she thought, admiring Silvanas's sweat-soaked black curls whorling on his forehead and neck, his white teeth flashing in his beautifully shaped mouth above the square-cut chin. And especially don't feel.

She propped her chin on her hands. Art, and grace, were *aesthetic* pleasures. Laban had taken this old, weather-worn abandoned barracks of a royal palace and had begun filling it with artisans and art.

And ... she watched him ride bareback once round the courtyard and then swing down, laughing, and land lightly as the young horse tossed its head and pranced, teasing them. Laban loved art, but he didn't *live* art. He moved well. He was handsome, with his winged dark brows and blue eyes as bright as gems. But he did not seek grace. Was there anyone who did?

She shrugged the subject away. For now she was content to live here and finish ordering the decorations to make the palace beautiful again, as it had been two hundred years before. "You've got good taste. And patience. Spend as much as you want. Good for local business," Laban had said. True, all true, but ...

No, she *wasn't* going to think about art or grace or falling in love. A life filled with activity and pleasant company and contentment was much, *much* preferable to the whiplash emotions and inevitable humiliation when one was rejected ...

Suddenly Laban stilled, his gaze diffuse. Mind contact? Something was wrong. Laban and Silvanas dashed inside the morning room below Lyren. She whirled around, running through the half-finished parlor and slipped downstairs to meet them. "What is it?" she asked.

Laban leaned against the carved railing, fingering his hair back into a rough queue. Behind him was Silvanas, his long body tense, dark eyes for once not merry, or teasing, but quite alert as Laban announced, "David's coming."

Lyren sighed. If David came, the others probably wouldn't be far behind. Her own heartbeat accelerated. A poopsie confab? Here? When the poopsies gathered, things *happened*.

Sure enough, the glitter and wild displaced air of magic transfers brought one after another—with one notable exception. Rolfin arrived, quiet, sun-browned and strong as an oak-tree, fresh from shipboard somewhere in the east. Leef, Mac—her first friend back in the Bereth Ferian days—busy now with magic studies. Ferret. Erol, from Chwahirsland. Roy showed up as well, looking much the same as ever, tall, thin, his homely face pensive and observant. The only one besides Adam that Lyren did not see was MV, and no one could ever overlook that knife-lean figure, the yellow-flecked brown eyes that looked as if they were on fire.

MV had to be missing for a reason.

David said, with an apologetic glance Lyren's way (which made her hold her breath), "Some of you might have heard: Andri Elsarion is dead."

Lyren's neck hairs prickled. She had not expected the news would be anything that would touch her. Why didn't Liere contact her? Was *she* dead? Lyren shut her eyes and flung out her mind. She encountered Liere's mind-shield. Lyren knew she was there behind it, which meant at least she was alive. "Who did it?" Her voice came out sounding like a child's.

"His cousin." And David shared with them the images he'd gathered from Andri's son.

For a short space no one spoke. Then Laban said, "None of us really knew Andri but MV."

"And me," Rolfin said, a reminder that he'd been part of the circle fighting Ilerian on the mental plane. "But he and MV were tight."

"I take it this is a general message, hands off? Or you'd be telling us when and where to attack."

David said, "Yes."

"MV?" Silvanas asked in his soft voice, his black eyes narrowed.

"Taken on a field run by Detlev," David said with a sardonic smile. "By force."

"Or else he'd already have ripped Macael Elsarion's throat out." Leefan sounded matter of fact. "Right. Not our affair."

They exchanged some quick talk on other subjects — mostly Detlev, what he'd said, or not said, where he'd been — while Lyren sat quietly and assessed the news. Then, one by one, they vanished by transfer magic, back to their various pursuits.

David remained.

Laban lounged against a table, hands thrust in his pockets.

"That was necessary?" His blue eyes were still angry.

"Quickest method," David said. "We all liked Andri. Detlev knows we'd all like to demonstrate that to Macael Elsarion."

"So why can't we? Killing his cousin in his own home? Macael Elsarion is a total shit." Laban sighed, glaring down at the new wooden inlay flooring, a complicated pattern made in contrasting grains of wood. Lyren was certain he didn't really see it. Then he looked up. "Still no real insight into when Detlev steps in, and when he just watches?"

David said, "You've suffered a sudden lapse of memory?"

Laban grinned at his ironic tone. "I'm not implying it's mere caprice. I lost the comfort of that conviction during the war. But it's no longer Svir and Norsunder as the long goal, so ... what?"

David said, "The most obvious answer is, who would replace Elsarion if we took him out? There would surely be a bloodbath in Nente."

"True," Laban said. "I remember Siamis saying that that court was vicious before Bartal went over to Norsunder."

"This is not to defend Macael Elsarion, merely an observation, but he was the one who pulled the Adrani occupation army back at the end of the war. Though apparently there was a hard internal struggle first. Specifically against the worst of Bartal's inner ring, who had expected to be planting their asses on empty royal thrones all through the east of the continent there, no matter which side won."

Laban grunted. "Didn't know that. Eh. We're well out of it."

David sent a glance Lyren's way, and said nothing, but the mute inquiry invited questions.

Lyren had learned, painfully, that she had fewer secrets than she'd have liked. "Why didn't Liere tell me? And what else should I know?"

"She appears to have made a deal," David said. "Elsarion will keep his hands off the boy if she stays a year."

"A *year?*"

"That's cold." Laban shook his head, lips pursed. "Where's the sprout?"

"Senrid's academy. Any further questions?" David

looked from Lyren to Silvanas to Laban.

No one spoke. He lifted a hand, and transferred.

Silvanas flicked a considering look at Laban and Lyren, then took off without saying anything.

Laban gave Lyren a sympathetic smile. "Don't read anything into Liere's silence beyond grief. Shock as well. That's a fairly sadistic deal, though it makes excellent tactical sense."

Lyren took a deep breath that was, surprisingly, unsteady. "I know. And—well, I don't think I was the only one who underestimated Macael. Not just that he'd do such a thing, but, well, so deliberate. So *wicked*." Again she saw the images that her unknown little half-brother had seen, as shared by David. Not the passion of argument, a duel, an accident, but two men—in some wise cousins—walking, talking, the blond one smiling with a rueful humor that struck Lyren with its familiarity, and then quite suddenly there was the knife, the stab. And Macael kneeling in the snow to watch Andri die.

The thought that Trevor Macael Elsarion had cold-bloodedly planned to murder his cousin—of whom he'd appeared to be fond, and with whom he'd certainly shared bread and wine—take over his kingdom, and force his wife to remain there as hostage against the life of their son, demonstrated the kind of icy thoroughness that she'd always associated with the likes of Detlev.

"He's one of *us*, you know," Laban said.

That *us* didn't mean the poopsies, it meant one of the many descendants of the infamous Dei family. Laban was one in straight line of descent. Lyren was one from the same branch, but different twig.

"I should see it by now, shouldn't I?" she said. "That particular combination of colors or coloring?"

It seemed the Deis had gotten into the Elsarion line, and Macael was a throwback, as were Laban and Lyren. Thinking of Macael as a kind of cousin made Lyren distinctly queasy. Was this how Laban had felt about Les Rhoderan? No, Les had been Laban's actual brother. Macael was a connection a million generations ago. She snorted. That meant he was *not* family, whatever they said.

"We are a handsome gang, even the ones who aren't quite sane, eh?" Laban joked, preening a parody of the mirror-entranced dandy. This uncharacteristic gesture, combined with the grimy clothes and sweaty, tangled hair, made Lyren laugh.

It was an unsteady laugh, and somehow it made her eyes sting, and she was aware of her own fatuousness, feeling badly about Andri Elsarion. She thought back over her childish resistance to his and Liere's romance, all the snide things she'd said about him, and wiped her eyes. "Ought I to go to her?"

"Of all of us except Adam, she's the best at long-distance contacts," Laban said. "Listen for her, but otherwise leave her alone, unless you can mourn Andri sincerely."

Unspoken, but obvious: Liere would know the difference. Lyren's attitude toward Andri had mellowed somewhat over the years, but to pretend that she had ever been close to him — knew him at all — would be an unbearable falsity to Liere.

So here was yet another fence between them. They had never been like mother and daughter. When Liere had returned from Geth, Lyren had hoped they could be like sisters, but Andri had sauntered into their lives, and once again Liere had gone away.

Lyren said, "How about little Trevor? I *can't* think of him as a brother. I'll go get him if you think it right, but I'd feel a real hypocrite. I barely know him. I don't think he'll remember me at all."

Laban said, "Leave him there. He's safe. As you say, you've never been part of his life."

"She could have sent him to me," Lyren said. "She could have sent him to the Mearsieans, or to Rel and Atan, or even to the Fer Eiders. Why Senrid? That's got to be terrible for him! If Liere and Senrid have spoken once in ten years I'll eat that table." Lyren winced. "It would be too trite to hope that this would mean a reconciliation," she finally said.

Laban looked down at the floor for a long time, then he finally shrugged. "Yeah," he said.

As the next few days brought winter all across the south, the news spread. Northwards it was received with mild interest, and then indifference. Enaeran was no major power, and those who had heard of it remembered it mostly for its generations of civil war. That the news spread as far as it did was largely due to Liere's enduring fame as Sartora. Such a famous figure would, people had assumed, retreat to a magic stronghold, and why had she ended up in Enaeran, which no one had ever heard of, anyway?

Friends of Andri, friends of Liere, were affected by the personal cost.

Kingdoms in the south that considered the political ramifications waited to see what Sartor would do.

A day or so after David called the poopsie gathering in Wnelder Vee, Andri's ambassador in Eidervaen requested an interview.

Atan of Sartor chewed her thumb absently, her thoughts running not just east and west, but into memory and speculation about the future as she watched Martande Eldias, the Enaeraneth ex-ambassador — wearing the mourning black of an untimely death — perform his last bow and formally withdraw. She saw the grief that pinched the man's young, handsome face before he vanished through the double doors and sighed inwardly. She understood that Marten had been in some wise a relation of Andri's in addition to his connections in Sles Adran.

She had heard about Andri's death as well as Chantala na Shagal's via private communication from her own ambassador in Nente. By the following day, she'd been informed of Liere Fer Eider's promise to remain a year; she'd had the intervening time to consider how, if at all, to react when Trevor Macael's ambassador inevitably petitioned to present new credentials.

How should she react to an oblique request — demand — that she recognize the beginnings of an empire? Trevor Macael Elsarion, she knew, was no wild-eyed trouble-maker. Every single report from her embassy in Sles Adran had mentioned the excellence of his rule, his skill, and his kindness to his queen, who had been so reclusive as to seem a nonentity. She could so easily have been locked away and forgotten, but Trevor Macael Elsarion had not done that.

And yet he held Liere, an old friend, hostage.

For a year.

The best reaction, Atan reluctantly decided, thinking back again to how worried she was about Liere, was no reaction at all.

No *official* reaction.

A quick glance from Rel's dark eyes. She knew he'd read her expression, and she listened as he fended off two well-born, opinionated court satellites.

He glanced once toward the door, and she knew he wanted to slip out, so she inserted herself once again into the talk, useless speculation about Enaeran, Sles Adran, Trevor Macael Elsarion's famed entertainments, his music school (supposedly sponsored by his queen) to which Atan scarcely heard one word in ten. But her mild, "The Adrani music school is commended by our own Master Janis," served to bring attention back to her.

Simpering slightly, the very young duchas from the east said, "Will the Enaeraneth appeal to us, do you think? If another petition comes to us for protection, we will become even larger an empire than our ancestors'. All except in name."

Atan smiled back, thinking that that name would never be spoken, and the only way that duchas would ever be a princess would be to marry a prince. Atan shut out the idle speculation to wonder why Rel left. He wasn't back; that meant he had an intent.

Gently but inexorably, Atan guided Morning Court to its close. There was no more formal business, and no policy was going to be decided here, despite all the fair-spoken words flying back and forth about how *we should* and *we ought* and self-righteous declarations of, *I thought with the end of the war, violence had ended.*

The great bells outside bonged, and Atan sent a covert hand-signal to her herald, who banged her staff three times on the marble floor.

That was the official dismissal. Atan rose, leading the way out. The courtiers trailed behind, talking. She chose her moment to slide into an unobtrusive alcove, thence to a hidden stair. As she climbed the steps, she reflected how well she and Rel communicated despite their lack of the whatever-it-was that caused Dena Yeresbeth. They hadn't exchanged a word following the wooden little speech from the Enaeraneth ambassador, but they both knew unfinished business when they heard it.

Now, as she sped along the private route to their rooms, she wondered whom Rel had dispatched to investigate, because of course they had to know what had really happened, and more importantly, the results. She arrived at the private entrance to their rooms, untroubled by helpful or prying eyes, and stopped in surprise.

Rel was seated on the edge of their bed pulling on his worn old traveling boots. His court raiment lay neatly folded over the back of a chair. Instead he wore an old shirt, and over it a worn-but-still-sturdy vest, and riding trousers so old they predated the war.

"You?" Atan asked.

"Who better?" Rel countered, grinning. "Got the itch to be moving."

Atan sighed.

"Anyone we send is likely to either be courted or killed by Macael Elsarion. I want to see the country with my own eyes."

"And to rescue Liere?"

"If I can get anywhere near her."

"There's nothing to hold her there now," Atan said, thinking rapidly. "Unless her son is alive and held as a hostage or something equally drastic. She always hated the idea of ruling."

Rel nodded. "Since there's been no word to the contrary, we can assume that she and her boy are alive, and she's either a prisoner, or else she rescued herself. I need to know."

"And if you find out the worst has happened, whatever that might be?"

"Whatever I do won't involve Sartor; I'm not about to start a war. And I'm much more effective on my own."

"Yes," she said reluctantly. "Take the seeing stone, at least?"

"Of course." Rel nodded in the direction of the children's wing. "Stopped by the schoolroom. Made my farewells. Our two incipient itchfeet are angry with me. I'm afraid I'm leaving you to deal with that."

"Their time will come," Atan said, thinking gratefully, *not yet*. It was inevitable that some of their children would inherit Rel's wanderlust. Two of them looked through every window with that same yearning that pulled Rel out into the world to tramp ancient paths. But for now, she did not have to worry about them going.

When he stood up, he held out his arms. She walked into

them. He bent his head and kissed her. She closed her eyes, aware of his warmth, the scent of his skin and hair, the clothes aromatic from the cedar chest they were stored in, with a faint underlying whiff of horse that cleaning frames did not seem to eradicate. She slid her arms around him and locked her fingers together, feeling his strength, hearing his heart thump steadily near her ear. How did Liere feel, to have her beloved ripped from her so suddenly? Atan stood in the circle of Rel's arms as a brief but terrifying pang wrung down her body. It was too easy to imagine the same happening to Rel. This was followed by a correspondingly intense flood of empathy for Liere. Her grip on Rel tightened.

His also tightened, but then she felt the inward tug of her golden notecase. "What do you want to bet whoever this is is writing to me about Liere?"

⁂

It was late at night in Marloven Hess when the news reached Mearsies Heili via Roy.

CJ stamped around, furious on Andri's behalf, for everyone had liked him during the short time he was in Mearsies Heili during the war. They had hosted his wedding!

"I thought we were done with villains when we booted Norsunder out," she snarked. "Is that stenchiferous Macael-cousin a secret Norsundrian?"

"I don't know," Clair said. "I'm trying to think what we might do. If anything."

"Yagh!" CJ held her nose, and whirled around. "Clair, I'm thinking."

"Always a danger sign," Clair said, her face solemn.

CJ picked up a venerable magic tome and pretended to throw it at Clair, who laughed soundlessly. CJ groaned. "I can't stand it. No one will go and see if Sartora is really okay, just because Detsie told 'em not to. Even Lyren! I think it's up to good old CJ to do the deed."

"Why?"

CJ opened her mouth, then closed it.

"You still don't trust Detlev?"

"It's not that," CJ said, waving her hands. "I know Detsie means well, but he always seems to mean well for people in two thousand years, and five thousand miles away." She made a face. "That's the only way I can explain it. It's the only way I *understand* it. But Liere … I still think of her as Sartora, the skinny scaredy-cat who came to see us in Siamis' evil days, and would forget to eat or to put on a coat during winter."

"Good enough," Clair said. "I feel the same way. Go, and spy all you like, as long as good old CJ stays out of Macael Elsarion's clutches. The only thing I'd ask is write to Atan first. If there is any plan to rescue Liere, she would probably know about it."

"Okay," CJ said. "I'll do that right now." She flitted off.

Clair sat where she was, considering the situation. The sound of high voices echoing down the hall of the white palace caused her thoughts to shift from Liere to Liere's little boy. Was anyone thinking of him, alone in a new environment, with one parent dead?

Clair did not want to say anything to anyone about Senrid. She considered from all angles, calculated the time difference, and transferred to Marloven Hess—where she discovered she still had access to his inner Destination.

It was late at night, but she sensed that Senrid was still awake. A runner encountered her almost immediately, blinked at her white hair, and shortly thereafter waved her into Senrid's study.

Senrid rose from his desk, utterly unreadable. "Emergency?" He sounded pleasant and polite, but Clair was suddenly glad that CJ hadn't come along, for she sensed tension in Senrid of a sort that was new, and rather intimidating.

"No," she said. "Talk only."

He indicated a couple of chairs before the fire. She glanced up at his face and read there neither welcome nor aversion. Not even impatience, though she'd obviously interrupted his work.

He looked so different! "Planning a war?" She indicated his map behind his desk.

A glimpse of his old sense of humor narrowed his eyes. "Of course," he said. "Didn't you notice the army on your border?"

"You mean that field of hoptoads?"

He smiled, but the humor faded into a direct gaze. "I take it you're here about the Elsarion boy. He's safe."

"But is he surely grieving. Is there something we can do?"

Senrid sat back. "He'd probably really like Mearsies Heili. That's only a guess. I saw him for mere moments. However, he was sent to me for safety, so I feel obliged to keep him until instructed otherwise."

Clair gave a nod. "Makes sense. Regard us as backup, then?"

"Glad to." That tension seemed to have eased, leaving him more like the Senrid she knew as he said, "It's been a while since we've seen one another. I heard you were in seclusion since your return from Detlev's mountain retreat."

Clair smiled. "I was. CJ calls it marinating. You know that white palace is made of disirad?"

"I learned something about disirad, fighting the Host."

"The disirad in our palace is diminished, but there was enough to, oh, give me the atmosphere I needed to recover from my prolonged dose of Ilerian. I've put in that time doing some studying."

"In?"

"Affinities, mostly."

"Affinities," Senrid repeated. "I think I know what that is, though isn't it largely metaphorical?"

"Now, maybe. Then, things were—"

"—different. The old refrain."

"And true. You remember the books in that underground chamber you stayed in? Roy and Adam have been translating those books. I've been reading some of them. Affinities, I've discovered, are like branches of a tree. There are affinities between objects, between people, between objects and people, between all living things and non-living." And seeing Senrid's polite skepticism, "Take a purely practical view. If you go to a popular tavern somewhere, you might notice that if there is a row of cups on a hook, many will reach unconsciously for a certain one, though they are all more or less alike. Likewise, people will have a certain favorite cup. Won't drink out of another—though the materials are inert, the liquid, whatever that might be, doesn't taste right if drunk from the wrong cup. Then there's the affinity for use, or talent, such as the person who picks up a reed flute, plays a few notes, and then begins a difficult melody that took everyone else years to learn. And of course personal affinities, that which makes people into friends, families, communities."

"I see."

"Then there are symbolic affinities; I'm learning that those are much used in Colend."

"The Colendi are big on symbolism. Sometimes I think they never have any wars because they're too busy decoding each other's fans," Senrid joked.

"Not so bad a thing," Clair said, smiling.

"Not arguing. What do you do with such a study?"

"Generally or personally?"

"Both."

"Generally, the Ancient Sartoran healers could use empathy effectively. I have to learn more, because we don't have these skills now. But you know how, when someone is hurt, you might feel pain on their behalf, but your pain does nothing for them?"

"Yes." His voice was flat.

"It seems that they could ease another's pain. But it's dangerous to do that too much, both for the healer and also the victim. As pain is a physical defense. It's a warning, *Don't touch that fire!* Even though it's pretty."

Senrid opened his hand. "Understood."

"As for personally, I'm ... finding a way to restore the white palace to its original purpose, as a house of healing. Turns out it was layered with magic to enhance the natural affinity of disirad. In fact, I am beginning to wonder if that is what caused Wan-Edhe to want to take it, any way he could."

"That is a disturbing thought," Senrid said. "But then anything about Wan-Edhe was disturbing."

"True! Jilo and I have talked a lot about it. When I can pry him from Chwahirsland." Clair indicated the darkened windows, and the late-night quiet outside. "Wan-Edhe utterly destroyed the, oh, the potential affinities in his homeland, because he couldn't control them. Anyway, magic was so different in Ancient Sartor." As she spoke, she assessed Senrid, and sensed he was waiting politely.

She rose. "Enough of that. If you want to hear more, you know where I am. You can come claim your hoptoads."

She transferred out on his laugh.

$$\sim\!\!\mathcal{S}\!\!\sim 8 \sim\!\!\mathcal{S}\!\!\sim$$

"Neither of them is doing anything," David observed in the tone usually reserved for cursing.

It was late at night. Adam and David had transferred down to Detlev's house, where they interrupted him in the middle of writing.

Adam said apologetically, "I thought maybe it was best to put the questions to you, since I have no answers either."

Detlev opened his hand in silent invitation.

"Senrid is acting as if nothing happened," David said impatiently. "As for Liere, she had the perfect opportunity to open up communication with Senrid again, after sending her boy to him."

"I'm aware," said Detlev.

"What does she do? Sit in a dark room, waiting to die of starvation, if nothing else gets her first. I want to go strangle her. Get her there faster."

"I'm aware," Detlev said again.

"Then that makes three people doing absolutely nothing."

Detlev surveyed them both. "What's the first important rule I gave you when we commenced dyranarya studies?"

David said confidently, "Don't look for logic in emotions, look for patterns."

At the same time, Adam said, "All violence leaves scars. This includes mental and emotional."

They eyed one another. "That one was later," David said.

Adam looked away, which meant he didn't agree, but wasn't going to start an argument.

Detlev said, "You are both right. I said a lot more, but each of you heard what was most important to you at the time."

After this painfully obvious reminder of perceptual

limitations, David sighed out his frustration, and in a far less heated voice, muttered, "I don't understand. I mean, I half-expected Liere to crawl into a hole. That's her usual pattern. But Senrid would bring her out of it fast. He could. He should."

Detlev said, "What did Senrid do with the boy?"

David cast a glance at the ceiling. "Right. Dumped him on the academy as fast as he could."

"More specifically?"

"Minimized as much as he could any risk of emotional engagement."

"Correct. I take partial blame for the stone wall he erected between himself and emotion; Senrid was reluctantly willing, at best, when I began a dyr session with him while you were all cooped up together in Lisdan. My fault is in rushing it."

Neither of the others had known that. But then dyranarya left it to the individuals to speak or not of dyr sessions.

"He was in bad shape," David said.

"It threw him right back to the emotional place he was in after Tdanerend killed his father, when he was five years old. And I knew the war was going to tax us all to the limits of our strength. So I took him apart to commence dyr healing, before events could overtake us. He'd barely begun to open up when Kessler warned us he was about to ward the world. It was the worst possible timing for Senrid, before we could even begin to examine possible anodyne."

"Right," David said, remembering that once Detlev returned to Sartorias-deles, with Ilerian on active hunt, there was no possibility of using the dyr.

"For Senrid, it's reasonable to cut out emotional engagement. He thinks it's effective, because it leaves him productive."

David agreed reluctantly. "And he does get satisfaction out of seeing some success out of the wreckage of Marloven Hess after the war."

"Correct. As for Liere, I intend to do something about that." Detlev tapped his pen on the papers before him. "I promised Hibern two days ago that I would go over her explanation of what we've been calling the Ilerian ward, before handing off a copy to the mages on Geth, and on Five. Make certain that there will be no error when translated into their respective magical languages. While I've been working on it, I've remained aware of Liere, who has, as you say, crawled into a hole. Almost literally."

Adam had been thinking back to the Liere of the early days, so excruciating to be around at times. "It was her defense against her father," he said, remembering the intensity of her memory-distorted dreams—so intense, amplified by her considerable and untrained farsense talent, that he'd had to concentrate on warding them. "To make herself as small as possible, and hide until the storm was over, then blame herself for it having happened, because that the first thing Lesim Fer Eider always did was to use fault and blame as a verbal lash. Those scars run very deep."

David said, question in his voice, "Which she's aware of. I guess I expected she would have worked past that."

"She thought she was working," Detlev said. "But she hasn't touched that deeper scar, which hides so much rage I believe it frightens her. She was not allowed to be angry. She recoils from anger. Except if she deems it justified."

"There's her father's worldview again," Adam murmured.

"Correct. Since the war ended, she, like Senrid, found ways to fill her days with productive endeavor. But it all ended with Macael's knife, propelling her into deep shock. I hoped she would see her way out, but shock is very hard to break. And she is just beginning her real training."

He smiled. The two knew that smile. It had often preceded long, arduous climbs down a mountainside. "Or rather, she is about to. You will excuse me?"

He cast his gaze rapidly over the last of Hibern's text, wrote a few words, dropped his pen, and picked something up. Then transferred.

Several hours later, Liere heard her bedroom door open.

Her room was dark, as it had been for the uncounted days since her return from her son in Marloven Hess. Who dared to enter unbidden?

She wanted to say *Get out* but her voice was a croak. She sent an angry mental query at the intruder, hoping—if it was Macael, of whom she'd otherwise seen or heard no sign—it would hurt. But it was deflected from a shield so perfect there was no hint of identity.

Instead the intruder spoke. "There's a frowst in here that will soon require a pick and shovel."

Detlev?

He snapped his fingers and a tiny mage-light flared. Liere blinked up at Detlev's familiar hazel gaze, now narrowed in cool appraisal. Then he turned away, spotted a lamp, and lit it. The process seemed to absorb his entire attention, during which Liere studied his profile through bleary eyes.

The golden flare of the lamp widened her view, and she saw he was dressed, as usual, in the anonymous brown outerwear and undyed shirt of a traveler.

He set the lamp out of her line of sight so its flame would not worry her aching eyes, then stepped to the window and reached past the heavy curtains. For a moment a sliver of fading afternoon light sent a ray lancing across the room, then came the sound of the casement unlatching and being flung wide. Cold, pure air billowed the curtains, and ruffled across her hot face. She sat up, pulling the blankets around her, and breathed deeply, then gave a shuddering sigh.

She'd managed to close off awareness of the body — it was old habit — while she wandered listlessly through ugly dreamscapes, seeking shadows. Seeking oblivion. Now that she was awake, her physical self assailed her with headache, dry mouth, low fever, and lassitude weighing down her limbs.

"Drink," Detlev said, holding out a flask.

The taste was bracing, reminding her of pine, of the sea on a clear day, of the astringent mountaintop berries that gave the liquid its pinkish color. One sip scoured the nastiness from her mouth, pleasantly puckering the tip and sides of her tongue. Suddenly overwhelmed by hunger and thirst, she drank off all the elixir, and felt the aches sweep away like cobwebs before a brisk broom.

"You'll need to drink plenty of water presently," he warned. "That mixture will parch your tongue into a dry sponge."

"Noted. How did you get in?" she asked.

"Walked across the river," he said, smiling. "There are still tracer wards lying in wait for me here, left from Norsunder's occupation. I can't do any magic within Enaeran's borders."

Meaning that he'd ghosted in on foot past Macael's guards.

"You are not permitted the luxury of self-destruction," Detlev said. There was no anger in his quiet voice, but no pity, either. "You have work to do."

"What work? Andri is gone. The kingdom has been taken by an enemy I'd once believed was a friend. I'm not quite selfish enough to burden my daughter with my grief when she hated my being here in the first place, and has pretty much avoided me since. As is her right as an adult, I accept that. But my son only called to me thrice, so he doesn't need me either."

"That," Detlev said, "is mere self-pity. It was understandable for a time. But no longer. If you do not keep your promise to Trevor Macael Elsarion, what will happen here?"

"War." Her teeth were clenched against the intensity of her emotions. "The people will never believe he didn't kill me as well." She didn't add that that had been her last conscious thought—accompanied by the fierce, angry enjoyment of vengeance—after which she'd slipped into the dreamscapes that had been her refuge when young.

"And?" the remorseless voice prompted, as he glanced around, then pitched her night robe at her, and politely turned his back.

The same anger that had prompted her to withdraw and let Macael suffer blame for her death prompted her now to deny Detlev an answer and to demand what right he had to nag. Except she knew he never nagged, never said the obvious except as a connective to underlying, perhaps unperceived, truths.

She yanked the robe around herself and slid out of the bed, saying, "History repeats itself. But isn't that going to happen anyway? If I die, at least *he* takes the blame. The popularity of 'Sartora' would finally be of use, wouldn't it?" Her sarcastic expression tightened to a wince. "And how many innocent people would die? No. It's wrong, very wrong."

Detlev made a brief, negating gesture. "You can stop it."

"No, I can't." She said heard the whiny petulance of her own voice, but did not care. Right now it was all she could do to keep from passing out from lightheadedness.

"You can," he replied. "Do you really want to loose a

massacre?"

The anger formed into an arrow of intent. "As you did in Everon?"

It was a nasty shot, but if the arrow struck him there was no visible sign. "Duplicating my errors gives yours validity?" he answered without heat.

"No," she said, shuddering, as she sank into her desk chair. "No." All the anger leached out of her, leaving only the pain. "I apologize. You tried to balance impossible threats. I don't have any—" But she knew that wasn't true. Lyren had rejected her authority when she was four years old, but Liere did have her son. "My life is rudderless now," she stated, hating how weak she sounded.

"You made me a promise once."

She rubbed her eyes. "I did?"

"You chose your tower," Detlev said. "It's time to leave it. You might consider continuing your education."

"Education." Her thoughts flickered like the sun through wind-tossed tree leaves, leaving mind—memory—dappled with light and shadow, and then she had it: the day they stood on that high plateau above the disirad while Marga lay surrounded by flowers, and Detlev told Liere about his plan for a future dyranarya school. She had yearned to number among them—then remembered she had a new, more exciting path, hand in hand with Andri. And she had totally forgotten that mountain. "The disirad plateau."

"You've never come back to the see what we built there," he commented. "Did the plateau have so unpleasant an effect?"

Memory of that day seemed centuries past, on another world. "No," she said finally. "The opposite. But the disirad. It does have a strong effect, if not what you'd call unpleasant. I don't think I could bear that now."

"You have a year."

"I don't think I can bear that either." Her mouth crumpled. "Do you know exactly what I promised Macael? People here know only that I will stay a year. But. There's something else. Andri's *murderer*." The tightness in her throat squeezed her chest, and a sob wrenched her body, choked into control after one spasm.

And Detlev said, dispassionately, "I know. Adam and I

have both heard you in the dream realm, which is why I am here."

She breathed in. Out. Control.

Detlev leaned over to snuff the lamp flame with his fingers. "There's a pattern here that you have failed to comprehend."

A sarcastic rejoinder sparked in her mind, to dwindle and die away. Sarcasm was utterly wasted on Detlev. She said, "Are you going to tell me?"

"No," he replied, his voice mild. "If I tell you, you'll see it merely as a weapon. If you perceive it on your own, I believe you will find the wherewithal to start Enaeran, and Sles Adran, on the road to peace. Wouldn't you like to leave here with that kind of accomplishment behind you?"

She wiped stinging eyes. "You make it sound as if I can take over and rule. The obstacle—and the real subject—was Macael."

"Yes," Detlev said.

"Pattern? You said a pattern. You can't mean the generational warfare? I assure you, that one I grasp. Andri even talked about it, with resignation and regret."

"And yet he did nothing about it."

"He couldn't, he said. He tried to see a way, but that pattern seems to be part of Enaeraneth life. All we could do is raise Trevor An—our son to be able to handle it."

Detlev said, "There is another pattern."

"What are you saying? Detlev, be clear. For once. You seem to imply that I can break the old pattern by seeing another pattern? What has that to do with Macael, outside of the fact that he cold-bloodedly betrayed Andri, murdering him and taking his kingdom?"

"There is something else. I use 'pattern' in this instance as a neutral term."

"Neutral—"

"Think," he cut in. "Of the ways he could have done it. This way you will not have to carry forever, as he will, the memory of Andri's dying."

"He and my son," Liere murmured. "Trevor was there, too."

"I don't believe that was by design."

Liere sighed. "No. No one but us knew about Malcolin's yew tree hideaway." She gave a brief reassessment to the circumstances of Andri's death, though it hurt to do so, and she acknowledged that it could have been more cruelly arranged. Prudence dictated that Liere be rendered unable to act, because of her magic, and mental contact abilities, but she could have been secured by violence. And she could have been forced to witness Andri's death, the better to underscore the transfer of power.

I will never forget your kindness.

Mental—emotional—vertigo pulled at her fragile sense of balance, and she looked up. "The signal was Chantala's death. The signal for the takeover."

"It seems so."

"He must have known she was dying when he brought her. And used that. And while she lay there at the brink of death, he must have been secretly moving people into place. People he'd been slipping over the border, for days. Maybe even weeks. And he sat there playing that tiranthe—which I will smash to splinters—and gloating over his plans, to be put forth as soon as she was gone."

Detlev hesitated, then said, "I don't believe he was gloating."

"You believe he was upset about Chantala? Andri never believed Macael loved her. I'm beginning to believe he was right."

"You won't know until you ask."

She recoiled from the idea, and muttered, "Even if I could ask Macael such a question, I no longer would believe his answer."

"That's up to you. My point is, you won't be able to take effective action until you scout the territory, then make your plan. The time to begin is now." He told her the necessary spells to break the wards against him, and when she had performed them, he vanished.

She rang the bell. Her own maid did not come, instead a small, square-built, gray-haired woman whom she recognized as one of Chantala's servants.

"Oh, I am so glad to see you awake," the poor woman said, in a strong Adrani accent, her hands clasped together tightly. Then she closed her lips, but Liere heard the next thought, as clear as speech: *What would he have done if you died in there?*

'He' was Macael, of course; with his face came a flurry of images that Liere sorted with the ease of long habit, the most important being Macael's order, *You will wait on Liere Fer Eider. Whatever she requires, you are to provide.* And the woman waiting outside her chamber day after day, replaced only by her daughter at nights, so she could sleep.

"I apologize for my silence," Liere said, ashamed. "Where is Nandra? Vikiras?"

"I was to tell you that they have been given a year's wages, and sent away from the city." The woman hesitated, her eyes dark and anxious in the gray wintry light. "My name is Melthanir Ghan." And Liere heard her thought run on: *The Dear One used to called me Thani, ought I to tell her that?* With the thought came a vivid image of Chantala's pale, pensive countenance.

Liere had taught her servants to shield their thoughts, for their own protection; she could not say anything now, for she'd learned that a measure of trust must be earned before she could broach so intimate a subject. "I am very sorry about Queen Chantala."

Melthanir's face tightened, and her eyes glittered in the cold light from the window. She bowed her head to hide the unshed tears, and whispered conventional words of gratitude.

Liere worked to shut out her sorrow. She asked, "May I have something to eat?"

"At once. At once." Melthanir Ghan turned, her skirt swaying with her quick retreat, expressive of someone relieved to flee a fraught situation not of her making.

What to do next? Leave her room, but first, she needed the kind of armor that had nothing to do with steel, beginning with mourning clothes.

Once she'd eaten, stepped through the cleaning frame, and changed, she transferred to Bereth Ferian, where she knew Lyren got her clothes made. She ordered some fine linen made up into the most severe mourning possible. Not the white that honors the life that has passed, gently and naturally at its proper time, but the black of the untimely demise, of a loved one ripped from the world by murder. The proprietor, seeing Liere's face, asked no questions, but promised to put her order first.

It took two days for the clothes to be done. Liere used that time to drink water, to eat well, and to—slowly—resume the exercises she had learned on Geth, and had performed nearly every morning until the day Chantala died. Though her emotions were still raw, she fought the instinct to hibernate with soul cut from the physical realm, her old defense. Detlev was right. It didn't *fix* anything.

When she returned with the new mourning, Liere ventured on her first foray, noting other changes. Brydon was still Brydon, but her own floor of the royal wing was cleared of the old things, including Andri's suite. Room after room she passed, glancing in each open door to see old, impersonal furnishings: heavy carved tables, chairs, storage chests and glassed-in display cases, beautiful rugs and tapestries, woven in once-popular patterns or in symbols celebrating ancient treaties, all of them old, and no sign of habitation.

She passed her son's rooms, and saw that they, too, were changed, a splendid rug in the center of his old schoolroom, one of the rare, precious rugs from Bermund, a riot of intertwined shapes of birds and flowers. Around the room a series of lyre-backed chairs from earlier centuries. There was no sign of little-boy battered furniture, toys, clothes. Books.

Even the scent of the air had changed; Andri usually succumbed to illness in the winters, and so he'd like the palace shut up and as warm as it could be made. Now windows were open to let in clean, cold air, smelling faintly of cedar from the grove on the palace grounds. No guards in sight.

Liere considered the unspoken message that she'd been given: hers and Andri's suites were no longer those of the rulers, but there was no overt offense conveyed, for guards had not been posted around her. That would be one kind of message. Nor had the servants' hall been shifted to surround her. That would have been another.

Liere proceeded down the lengthy halls toward the center of the palace, and her first engagement in her battle. Its weapons were all new, the strategy unclear, the tactics to be carried out in words, movement, dress, silences.

She had promised certain things, and if she couldn't get them rescinded she knew she must keep those promises in order to safeguard her son's life. Promises? Armistice — agreements. For there was no doubt in mind or heart that she was at war, a personal sort of war, with the man who had with premeditated calculation betrayed her, Andri, and the kingdom.

She turned a corner and glimpsed the huge floor-to-ceiling mirror that had always been there, reflecting the lights across the landing. She paused a heartbeat, long enough to consider her own reflection. Her hair was braided into a simple coronet, her outer robe of heavy black cotton-linen fitted with flawless smoothness from neck to wrists to waist, the skirt slit up the sides for riding. Black shirt and loose trousers beneath. No adornment.

She reached the outer chambers of the government rooms, which had changed little as yet. There was her first sight of guards, wearing lavender-gray, with golden twined lilies on the breast. Their faces unfamiliar. The guards' eyes flicked in her direction, but neither of them moved; a young page rounding the opposite corner, again unfamiliar, stepped to the wall, bowing gracefully as she passed. These were the manners of Adrani servants.

She passed through the doors into the reception chamber, and across the thick rug of blue and gold and white, to the private chamber within. Macael had made it into a library-workroom. Both carved doors stood open. She paused.

Her first glimpse of Macael was a shock, because he too was dressed in black. Oh. Of course. He had lost his wife to lingering effects of poison mere hours before Liere had lost her husband to Macael's knife. He was entitled to mourning black, but it did not please Liere that she and Andri's murderer thus appeared a matched pair, implying the harmony of a shared grief.

He stood in greeting, his face as blank as always. There was no sound beyond the snap of the fire in the fireplace; the air was still, the scent an indistinct astringency from the burning candle on the desk.

"Good morning," Macael said.

There was nothing good about this morning, so she did not speak.

He made a slight gesture to the two scribes working adjacent to the desk. They rose, assembled their papers, bowed to both Macael and Liere, and retreated. Liere did not recognize either of them. The younger, a girl maybe sixteen, sent one covert glance Liere's way, her expression troubled, then she dropped her gaze as she followed her companion out the door.

Liere moved to the window. This room had once been the private receiving salon for ambassadors. Its aspect was pleasing, the view a fountain surrounded by roses, and beyond, young cedars obscuring the windows opposite. It being winter, the roses were barren stems, the fountain still.

It seemed that Macael was not using any of Andri's rooms, private or public. Liere wondered if all traces of Andri had been replaced by tasteful furnishings inherited from a long line of warring Elsarions. She wondered if any of Macael's own rooms looked out onto the yew walk.

And decided the question would serve as an opening strike.

"Shall I send for refreshments?" he asked.

"No," she replied. No need to inform him—yet—that she would never again share sup or sip with him. She turned around to face him, her hands clasped tightly behind her back. "Do any of your rooms look out on the yew walk?"

"Yes," he said. "My bedroom."

It was completely unexpected. Though maybe she ought to have foreseen it; did he know that that wing was the old royal residence? She said, "A gesture of dispassion? Or is it gloating?"

He was much better than she at the blank face and voice. It would have seemed that he had no reaction at all, except for the shift of light along the edge of the discreet gold belt buckle at his waist, which indicated some alteration in his breathing. "A gesture," he said, "of expedience."

Twice he'd deflected her, and she still saw no opening. What she desired, if she could contrive it, was a reaction commensurate with her own pain.

And so she attacked for the third time, striking directly at the matters that lay between them. "I do not sense the Birth

Spell on my own," she said. "The other possibility requires that we join hands." She let her distaste for the prospect of his touch flatten her voice, though intensely aware of his proximity. "I believe that is figurative; a touch will do."

"Whenever you are ready." He was still standing behind the desk. She could only see one hand, the fingers resting near the feather of the pen he'd laid down. The leaping fire reflected, cobalt blue, in the square-cut stone of his signet.

She reached down to brush her fingertips over the back of his hand, scarcely enough to feel the warmth: already she knew no Spell would come.

She snatched her fingers away, though he hadn't moved, and burst out, "Why did you murder Andri?" She added on a bitter note, "He was so proud of your friendship."

"I liked Andri," Macael said slowly. "I valued him. As a man."

"But that just makes your treachery all the worse."

"He was a bad king!" For the first time in all the years she had known Macael, some of his suppressed passion escaped. "Not merely mediocre. A mediocre king at least leaves his kingdom more or less as it was, or maybe a little worse. That was not going to happen. I could see it. He was a terrible king."

She crossed her arms, head to one side. "If he was so rotten, you could have enlightened him with your wisdom?"

"I tried!" Macael caught himself, and lowered his voice. "I tried. He wouldn't listen. Maybe he couldn't. I tried in a general way when we were all together. You might remember I made one or two suggestions, to which he invariably laughed, then insisted that this was not the time for serious matters, that our visits were social—diplomatic. And he'd look Chantala's way. I tried repeatedly when we were alone, just the two of us, and he'd still laugh and say that my questions or suggestions were fine for Adranis, but I didn't understand Enaeran. Or, if I tried to press, he'd make a joke about my wanting both kingdoms."

"He was not wrong about that, was he?"

"I didn't at first," Macael retorted, without heat. "I wanted to take it from Adon Marsael, but … ah, I can't prove any of that to you. Instead, look back. Can't you see how detrimental it was for Andri to keep riding around, flinging tax money out in largesse for big banquets and the like? It pleased locals at the time, but did nothing to address the serious matters, while you were here, coping with the bleeding exchequer, and being cheated by very practiced thieves in guild chief positions."

Liere flushed. "Not recently."

"You learned fast," Macael said. "Admirably. But there still remain trunks of tax gold in the vault of the Road Guild Chief's home, for a single example. While she speaks so confidingly to you each New Year's Oath Day about children and raising puppies, and promises repairs that never happen. But you were not trained at all to deal with these matters —"

"Neither was Andri," she interjected quickly.

"And he did not want to learn." Macael raised his hand, the Elsarion blue stone flashing on his hand. "I'm not referring to his inability to parse numbers. I understand this is why you took treasury matters over. I mean his comfortable assumption that we would be at war over the Riverlands sooner than later. Among other decisions that betrayed an inability to think past the moment."

It was unanswerable. But that did not make murder just.

She took a deep breath, and hated showing that much reaction. "Release me," she whispered, "from that promise."

Again that change of light along the edge of the gold buckle. No need to be vulgarly blunt. However he felt about it—impossible to discern—he took her meaning.

"No," he said.

She walked out.

Next morning she woke to the sudden thunder of many horse hooves echoing along the buildings from the southwest side of the palace. Her inner eye painted him riding at the front of that column.

She knew—somehow, since there had been no mental contact in any way that she recognized—that he was gone, and she was alone in the great palace, except for servants and the quiet, self-effacing guards.

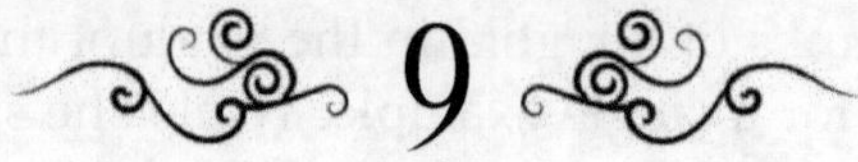

"W e *what*?"

The time: same day. The place: the city of Methden, at the southwest corner of Marloven Hess.

The question was asked in a tone midway between whisper and groan, by the youngest of the four candidates the Jarlan of Methden was bringing to Choraed Dhelerei to test for enrollment in the academy, at the end of Convocation, New Year's Week.

The second youngest, a weedy boy of fourteen, glanced furtively around, but the Jarlan was talking to Commander Senelac at the head of their cavalcade.

Under cover of that earnest, low-voiced conversation, he repeated, "We're to get up before dawn and drill each day on the road."

"On whose orders?" the youngest, a fair-haired eleven-year-old, demanded, his voice sounding strangled with his effort to hide his dismay. He glared at the tall, straight back of Commander Senelac; everyone knew how tough he was, demanding far more of Methden's guard than any other city guard in the kingdom. Methden's garrison was run like South Army. He had to be to blame.

"Hers," was the answer.

Four pairs of eyes shifted to the equally straight back of Jarlan Marend Ndarga, whose small, slight body was neatly set off by a coat military in cut, though not in color. Her short black curls jounced beneath her winter cap at each step of her mount; as they watched, she gestured quite suddenly, and the Captain opened a hand in agreement to whatever she was saying, his long, lean, tough face outlined in profile against the peachy stone of the old portion of the castle.

"But we *won* the competition at home. Why sweat *now*? We'll be doing that soon enough when we get tested," the youngest muttered.

The jarlan turned her head to look back at her candidates, her expression, always vivid, altering from some adult complexity that none of the four young people understood to a chin-lifted pride. She lifted a gloved hand, pointing at that peachy stone, most of it covered by drifts of snow, gray stone blocks above it forming the more modern wall. The gray had been fitted carefully to the ruin of the older, mellow stone, so careful the line between sandy and gray wavered, the signs of former ruin a badge of honor. "Do you know what that old stone once was?" she asked in her high, clear voice.

All four slapped a finger to their chests. Indeed they knew; part of the ferocious competition for these academy spots was learning Methden's history.

"Lendred?"

The oldest boy swallowed, his throat knuckle bobbing. He knew the answer, but before Jarlan-Marend's intense gaze he was afraid the truth had somehow changed. "The old Marthdaun castle," he said, his voice squeaking on the last syllable.

"That's almost right," she said. "We do call it the old Marthdaun wall, but what is the exact truth?"

The second oldest was Corand Hrarth, the only girl candidate this year, unlike last, when it had been four girls, two of them cousins. Only the cousins had been accepted.

Corand said, "It was the old Marth-Davan castle, back in the Iascan days. By the time the name shortened to Marthdaun, the castle had already been destroyed and they'd built the one the Ndargas live in now."

Marend smiled at Corand. "Exactly." And she went on to ask about the battles appertaining, which the boys all knew with the effortless ease of years of songs, stories, and study.

As they readily spoke, Marend Ndarga glanced back at the old wall, the sand-colored stone warm in the light of the new-rising sun. It slowly passed behind, the last wall of her beloved city, as they clopped onto the thick, fortified bridge spanning the river.

How Marend loved her home! It cost a pang to leave it, but not too strong a pang, for she was leaving it for the capital, her second love.

An inside voice whispered, *Third love*, and there was the king's face before her inner eye: his gray-blue eyes watchful, remote, the fine mouth hard at the corners. The habit of command so effortless it was part of his physical being: a king.

She shut away the image, embarrassed, even though it was solely in her own mind. She wouldn't think about the king before Hatch Senelac's quick, ironic gaze. "We'll be the best," she said. "At the testing games. Methden always gets candidates in. So we will drill along the road."

Her four charges saluted again, mittened fingers to hearts. No surprise or resentment in those faces. Excellent. Good candidates all.

Marend turned her gaze to the road, but her mind slipped ahead, winging to the capital. Where would he place them? When would she see him?

Hatch watched his jarlan, the wry humor in his eyes and mouth deepening to sardonic awareness. Marend had gone blind again. Was she already dreaming about her meeting with the king? Probably. Every time they rode northeast she either looked blank like this, or else she winced in pain. Those pained expressions were rarer, but he'd finally figured out, after several years of watching, that they came when Marend was reminded of her younger brother Retren.

The third expression she habitually wore was the downcast pensive one of the home trip, which would result in commands to be better next time, to excel. She was, he knew, determined to fashion herself and her people into the perfection that would impress a warrior king. This was a teen's crush, on an image. She didn't see that she could become the best commander in the world, that Methden could outfight even the legendary First Lancers, but it was not going to match her with this king.

She was going to have to ride it out herself, just as Hatch had to ride out his own misconceptions until he understood that Senrid was not the kind of king to find justice in torturing a bloody-handed felon to death — the sort of justice that all those youngsters gathered to watch would remember. Maybe even might have tried to imitate, had not the king made his condemnation very clear.

Overhead a white-feathered raptor wheeled, screeched, then dove rapidly away behind one of the snow-dusted hills to the west, as three weeks' ride away, in the royal city, the academy was breaking up until spring.

"Bye, Malcolin! See ya next year!"

With a happy wave and a clatter of iron-capped heels, the last of Malcolin's bunkmates disappeared out the barracks door.

Malcolin watched them go. It seemed he'd just gotten used to things in the few days he'd been here, and now they were all leaving. They were all going home for New Year's Week, all except Kerdevan, whose family had been killed in the war just after he was born. He lived now with Stefan.

Malcolin sat on his bunk, his fingers moving to his chest. He didn't unbutton his tunic or shirt. It was enough to feel Ma's chain through the cloth. Reassurance steadied him. If he needed his ma, she would come.

After New Year's Week, how many months more did Mama have to pay to save his life? Then he could see her every day again. He'd *never* again see his father in this world, in this life. His fingers crushed the chain through the fabric of his tunic, and for a time he burned with hatred against Uncle Macael.

When the hate cooled, and he could breathe again without feeling he was going to blub, it left him empty, aware of the silent room around him. He'd had something to do every day, from dawn until lights out, and then he'd been surrounded by the comforting sounds of his bunkmates' breathing. Three times, he'd called his mother, and she'd come right away, just as she'd promised. But he'd been determined to get control, to not disturb her, to learn to bear what must be borne because it wouldn't change; his mother had wept as hard as he had, and it made him feel very bad.

It took all his courage not to call her after that.

He looked up through the window at the bleak gray light outside. Snow was coming again. Was it snowing in Enaeran? There was this long time stretching ahead, as cold and gray as the sky, now that everyone had gone home. He'd listened to their plans and thought that he'd be staying here, and he wouldn't mind, because he liked it here. He liked the people, and he didn't mind the uniform, which was really just riding clothes. They didn't make him cut his hair — there were others at the academy with long hair — all foreigners, like him.

He endured the lessons, but no one seemed to mind that he was terrible at numbers. They thought it was because he was eight. He loved the outside activities. He even liked the plain wooden furnishings, and the smells of wood and horse that reminded him of the palace guards' garrison at home, where he had practiced since he was four.

But now the place was empty. He realized he only liked it when people were around, and there was a busy schedule. When would their radlav get back? She'd know what he could do to pass the time.

Heels rapped the stones in the courtyard outside their barracks, a light, quick step that was unfamiliar. The steps stopped at his door, and he looked up, surprised to see the king there, not as tall as his da had been, but imposing enough in his uniform; light hair like his da, but worn short.

Senrid looked back at the small, hunched figure on the bunk, the fine hands curled into fists, one of whose knuckles Malcolin rubbed absently against his front teeth. Until this boy's appearance, Senrid hadn't thought of Liere from one year to the next, except to consciously wish her well, the reward for winning the long inward battle begun the night Crystal Ingrid was killed. He did not like any reminders of that battle, but that was not Malcolin's fault. "How are you doing here?"

"Fine, Senrid-Harvaldar." Malcolin scrambled to his feet, and performed a quick salute.

"Relax," Senrid said. "I'm Senrid when we're alone; the saluting is a Marloven custom. This is your liberty time, and I am here to ask you what you want to do."

"What are the choices?"

"You can stay here, and I'll assign one of the instructors to remain with you, or you can bunk with the castle guard, along with the seniors who will be demonstrating at our New Year's Convocation. Or you can go to visit the Senelacs at East Army outpost. You've been riding with Master of Horse Senelac, right? She and her brothers live in Sindan-An, where there are youngsters your age, lively and friendly; they'll be coming to the academy in a year or two."

For the first time since that terrible day, a little bubble of anticipation rose in Malcolin's chest. "It sounds good," he said cautiously. "But would my mother be able to find me if I needed her?" His hand closed over the chain again.

The king glanced out the window for a long breath or two, then turned back. "She's been here, then?"

"Three times," Malcolin responded. "That first night, and two others. But I haven't called her since." He hesitated, then decided not to mention the nightmares. Bear it, he told himself. You have to learn to bear it.

The king said, "I see. To answer your question, she would easily be able to find you. If not by whatever it is that she gave you, then from me, if she were to ask."

Malcolin sighed happily. "Thank you, yes, I'd like very much to go."

"And so you shall," the king said, and transferred him.

And an hour later, he was told he had an outland visitor.

WNELDER VEE

Lyren was alone. Several days had passed since the shocking news about Andri—and she still heard nothing from Liere. Of course.

Laban had gone off to resolve a bitter dispute between a sheep herder and a farm whose vegetation apparently proved irresistible to the neighboring sheep, involving who was to pay the cost of a soon-to-be-erected stone wall. Neither had a guild to intervene for them, the stonemasons wanted to be paid first, and the few remaining noble holdings in Wnelder Vee had no influence in this particular region: kingship in Wnelder Vee was more of a cross between a tax collector of coin and kind, and a roving mediator.

Lyren could go early to Eidervaen's royal palace, though New Year's Week was still a few weeks off, but she refused to visit Sartor in this mood. Now that it was too late, she regretted all her various excuses for not visiting Liere's little family in

Enaeran.

In retrospect, her snit about how tiresome it was to make a family visit when she didn't feel like family with them seemed horribly petty. Is that why Liere didn't reach for her, or think of her to send that little boy to her?

She decided to go to someone sympathetic to talk it out, and transferred to Mearsies Heili, where she found Clair, Sherry, Dhana, and Falinneh at breakfast. Clair said, "What's wrong, Lyren? You seem unhappy."

Lyren's expressive winged brows puckered her forehead. "Oh, no real problem. More of a question, and Tahra is not one to go to for advice about anything but numbers. I wondered if I ought to look out for the little half-brother. Hard to remember that he *is* a brother."

"Then think of yourself as an aunt," Clair suggested. "Your family is not one of those in which your place in the order of birth is your title for life. You can change the terms."

Lyren's lips parted.

"We do," Sherry said, her big blue eyes earnest.

"Yes!" Falinneh smacked her chest, which was covered by a scarlet top embroidered with butterflies and bees. "With each other. You *know* us, a ready-made family. Can't fix the past, but you can fix things now."

Lyren smiled suddenly, her cheeks dimpling. "Fix the past. Yes. You won't mind if I bring my brother-nephew-cousin here for a visit? I know the wise and omnipotent Detlev said hands off, but he's not in charge of *me*. And I'm Trevor's family, am I right?"

"You are always welcome, the more the merrier," Clair assured her.

Clair did the transfer magic to Marloven Hess for Lyren.

Lyren was not kept waiting long. In fact, she would have quite happily been put off longer so she could nose around Senrid's castle. As she followed a runner through the halls, she thought rather sadly of the days when she raced about freely. She'd noted on her arrival that transfer wards still did not prevent her from coming straight to his castle, but she felt that this was now a privilege she ought not to transgress. How many were on that pass-free list? David, of course, as heir. Herself. Probably Leander Tlennen-Hess, and Jilo of the

Chwahir. Was Detlev?

Was Liere?

I don't dare even ask, she thought as the polite young runner ushered her into Senrid's familiar study. Once, when she was small, anyone who'd wanted had access to this room. Adulthood had brought boundaries—caused, Lyren strongly suspected, by emotional burdens she was now able to sense, like sensing dawn just beyond the rim of the world though the sky is still dark. But she still couldn't see them. In fact, there seemed to be so much pain involved she didn't *want* to comprehend.

"Hallo, Senrid," she said, making an effort to sound cheery. "I know we haven't talked for a few years, but unless you want it, we can skip the polite chatter. I can tell you're busy. Look, though Liere hasn't seen fit to contact me I do know what happened to Andri, and that Trevor Andiran is here. I thought if you didn't want charge of my half-brother over the coming New Year's Week, I ought to do the sisterly thing and fetch him away."

"A laudable gesture," Senrid replied. "But you're too late. I sent him to Sindan-An this morning. The Senelacs claimed him. He's going by Malcolin now, as it happens."

"Do they have boys his age?"

"A pack of them, between Jardan, Janred, and a couple of Senelac cousins."

Lyren did a quick mental calculation, and grinned. "A lot of marriages right after the war?"

"They saw it as the back of the hand to Norsunder, the idea to repopulate Marloven Hess as fast as possible," Senrid said, smiling back.

"Playing with a pack of eight-year-olds will be a lot more fun than anything I could have thought of," Lyren admitted. And because Senrid's attention was still on her, and because if anyone was adopted family, it was he, she said quickly, "Do you know why Liere didn't send him to me?"

"She didn't send him anywhere." Senrid's voice, never expressive of emotions, was even devoid of sarcasm. "It seems to have been an old spell she set up years ago, in case of trouble. They must have agreed on my kingdom as a likely destination. You have to remember that the Elsarions and the Montredaun-

Ans were related some generations back."

Lyren took a deep breath. "I see. Laban thought it was something of the sort. But ... no message. Nothing. Silence. I found out because David came to tell us that Detlev decreed no one was to interfere."

Senrid said, "I'm not aware of what's going on in Enaeran, but you know Liere's adept at taking care of herself. And her silence probably means that she's sufficiently unhappy to want to protect you from the burden of her emotions."

"Well," Lyren said. "That's her usual pattern, isn't it? To hug unhappiness to herself lest it burden anyone else, especially her frivolous, superficial excuse for a daughter, and so she closes everyone out?" Lyren turned to the fire. "And besides, I'm a stranger to that little boy. I didn't even know he'd changed his name."

Then, because she'd broken her own resolve and had managed to get upset anyway, she used her token to transfer back to Wnelder Vee, where Laban, who had just returned, took one considering look and said, "Come on, Gloom-Face. Let's go for a ride."

$$\sim 10 \sim$$

The following days passed swiftly at Curtas's House, but not so swiftly that David didn't find himself pausing in the middle of various tasks, ruminating on the Enaeraneth situation.

Obviously Detlev had foreseen the bloody change of king, but then that probably could have been predicted by anyone who knew Enaeraneth history. With a certain amount of self-mockery, David reflected that, after all, the Elsarions were related to the Montredaun-Ans, so what could be more natural?

One cold, gray afternoon, he stood at the window staring westward over blue-white peaks while his language development class tracked variations in Name Day rituals.

"I think it just strengthened the family bonds in Chwahirsland when Wan-Edhe Sonscarna forbade Name Day celebrations," Tadric retorted.

Everyone's eyes flicked David's way; belatedly he realized it, recovered the conversation, and said pleasantly, "You 'think'? By tomorrow you will have on my desk a written proof."

Tadric sat back, hiding his grin. He was a tall, weedy youth from a dye-maker family in Bermund, observant as were they all, but seldom content to just observe. David caught a flick of a look between Tadric and Kassaea—she'd come from the vintners of Tevyask on Toar—obviously a wager made and won. And with it, most likely, a charitable offer of help.

"Kassaea," David added, "will have on my desk a report on the same subject, but from Siamis's library, covering northern Toar's Name Day rituals, and how they vary."

She rolled her eyes. Tadric looked stuffed; any other offers of aid had just been circumvented.

"Now," David said. "We'll take a look at the Landises' adoption traditions ..."

The class lumbered to its end, and he watched his five students file soberly out, waiting until they reached the hallway to begin the fierce whispers. Then he ran downstairs, to find Adam waiting in the kitchen. "Go," Adam said. "You're a stick in the beehive."

David raised the back of his hand, and in case that wasn't rude enough, struck it with the other.

Adam's fine brows quirked. "No, Jessan, he's not angry with you. No, Mata, David's not angry with you. No, Retren, it's nothing you've done. And just today Sveneric drifted by and asked if things had taken a turn for the worse in Enaeran."

"You are subtly hinting that I ought to go to Enaeran?" David asked, coming down mockingly on the word *subtly*. "Not Marloven Hess? To which I would retort that you ought to remember how much success I had the last time I tried to meddle in Senrid's private life. That's one of the reasons I've stayed away as long as I have. Senrid would not welcome my intervention any more now. When Detlev so unaccountably sent me there before Macael Elsarion took Enaeran, I had to sidestep fast to avoid the impression that we were involved. And failed."

"Then do not go there," Adam said, serene, and certain. "I did say Enaeran."

"I can't go to Enaeran. Whatever you and Sveneric might think, Detlev made it clear we were to keep our mitts strictly off Elsarion."

"Off Trevor Macael Elsarion, yes. I believe your quest is different."

"You can't mean Liere? I don't even know her."

"You will, after you speak with her," Adam said.

David warded off Adam's words with a swipe of his hand. "I think you'd be far better than I with this one."

Adam was silent a time, as snow drifted softly outside, a continually moving tapestry of white lace against the blue-white mountain peaks, and the silvery gray sky beyond. David also stared. Glowered. But without seeing it, until it occurred to him that this might very well be *his* dyranarya test. And it was the perfect test in the sense that he had emotional ties, complicated as they were, with Senrid and Marloven Hess. It was relatively easy to separate oneself from circumstance when the problem to be solved meant nothing in one's own life. But when it concerned self? David had been struggling to keep a clear eye from the very beginning: one of Detlev's other early lessons was to remind oneself constantly that you cannot live people's lives for them. In spite of impatience, irritation, and a desire to give Senrid a clip at the back of his head, if only to get an emotional reaction, and an equal desire to—

Oh, yeah. It was the perfect test. Damn it all.

He uttered a sharp sigh. "I'm off. Turn my group out for a run, if they claim to have finished their research projects early. They obviously have too much free time."

Adam smiled, opening his hands. "So it will be done."

David ran back to his room to change from his sloppy teaching clothes to the sturdy and anonymous brown tunic-jacket and riding trousers and boots of the average traveler, a habit he'd consciously acquired from Detlev, then fixed in mind the isolated garden he'd discovered on his scouting prowl, among the trees on the ridge overlooking Shiovhan, Enaeran's capital.

He did his transfer slide. Then looked around as the pure blue-gold morning light revealed Shiovhan's shabby streets. He sniffed the smells of cooking food, horse, wood, and stone blended into a familiar scent he could hardly define. Every city has its characteristic scent, sometimes easy to identify, sometimes a complexity that could only be called by the city's name. Everyone knew the Eidervaen scent, which had at its base very old stone. Here, tradespeople went about their daily tasks, the worn stones of the street clear of snow. Evidence of Liere's hard work as Enaeran's mage as well as its queen. David also smelled snow on the way.

So far, Macael Elsarion's plan was a success: despite losing their popular king so recently, the Enaeraneth appeared to be at peace.

He reached mentally for Liere—and to his surprise, niffed her location. She was in one of the four rose gardens David had spotted previously. He transferred to the barren garden, where Liere sat on the carved marble rim of a fountain, staring down into the frozen water.

She looked up, and when she recognized David, alarm zipped through her nerves. Merely old habit. She knew he was no threat, but why was he *here*? She would wait until he spoke; politeness, right now, was beyond her.

He gave her a quick appraisal, aware she was doing the same. Had he changed as much as she had? He knew he'd never remember to look into a mirror to assess. The only feature he recognized from the old days was her great, wide-set golden eyes with their perceptive, direct gaze. The severe black robe, which was fitted expertly to her slight, straight-spined body, was a stunning contrast, though he strongly suspected she had no idea of its effect. There was too marked an absence of self-consciousness in her countenance, her posture, and a total absence of the decorative touches people put to their clothing when they wish to draw attention. Her golden hair was tied back plainly with a black ribbon.

Liere, he thought ruefully, as he tried to assimilate almost a decade of change, was probably as little interested in the mirror as he himself was.

All this passed through his mind as her brows furrowed. Then her shoulders tightened, and she spoke first after all. "Bad news from outside?"

"None that I know," he hastened to reassure her. "And Detlev told us not to interfere here. But Adam seemed to think you might need company."

"Adam." Liere's brows lifted in surprise, then she remembered the Adam of their childhood and her smile was brief, and sweet. The effect was all the more breathtaking because she was unaware of it. "Detlev interfered," she said, the color fading from her cheeks.

"Did he?" David asked.

Her voice was so low, it was nearly inaudible. "He forced me out of a funk."

David looked an inquiry.

"My son only called me thrice. When he did not need me anymore, I felt ... unneeded."

David glanced briefly at the three floors of handsome windows staring blindly on four sides, and wondered who might be behind them, watching.

Give 'em something to watch.

He dropped down beside her. "Detlev is not one to allow for mere personal tragedy."

She smiled at the joking irony in his tone, but her golden eyes were still pensive. Yet she had not sent him away.

Test. He considered what to say next. He really didn't know Liere. His first experience of her had been in the bad old days, when she was a humorless stick of a ten-year-old clinging to the Child Spell, sometimes timorously priggish about hating Detlev's Evil Boys, and at other times astonishingly farseeing, by unsettling turns.

Senrid had taught her a sense of humor, that much David remembered. And then, around the time he and the boys left Norsunder, she vanished. The next time he saw her she'd appeared to be somewhere around sixteen, obsessed with Andri. It had disgusted him at the time — but then he'd been at the same threshold, with the usual intolerance of that emotional age.

Their next encounter, she had helped him recall Marga to the world, with an effortlessness that he never could have compassed, not without years of training. But she'd had no real training. She just did it.

Liere flicked him a puzzled glance, wondering why he'd come. Of course Detlev had sent him, despite his words to the contrary. Detlev was still watching out for her. Yet he wouldn't tell her what weapon lay to hand.

"Does Elsarion spy on you?" David asked suddenly, waving a hand at the windows.

"I don't think so. I think he's away, in fact. There was supposed to be a shared exercise, the Adrani border guard and ours. I have no idea if they are still doing it."

Macael had indeed been gone for several days. No one had said anything, but she had sensed his absence. She knew that he did not walk the long halls, did not work or sleep or sup in any of the rooms, and the occasional scraps of rehearsing musicians from the far wing were unheard by his ears.

She said, "He's as shielded as Detlev."

"I noticed." But not impossible to read; David remembered what MV had told him so casually a few years ago. *If that is true*, David thought with a brief spurt of compassion, *exactly how hard does it hit Elsarion to look at Liere, and feel her hatred?*

"What do you do with yourself?" he asked. "Has he shown his customary finesse with establishing hostage ground rules?"

"I seem to have perfect freedom," she said. The last word carried a fair load of irony, without the leavening of humor. "Within the demands of the promises I made."

"Promises? Stay a year. And?"

Her breath hissed, her fingers tightly interlaced in her lap. She looked at him, and then away. So Detlev had not told him, then. She did not know whether to be relieved that he hadn't blabbed, or resentful that he hadn't made this conversation easier.

David saw her face leach of all color, except two hard red spots high on her cheeks, the red of shame. "Give him an heir."

"Damn."

She smiled slightly, and the angry red deepened.

"Did you tell Detlev?"

"No. But he and Adam apparently plucked it from my dreams." She drew in another breath, a painful one from the sound, and then spoke to her lap in a quick rush of words. "Do you think. Detlev comprehends what it means?" She glanced at David again, her pupils wide and black, her mouth long and thin. Then again away.

David thought of Senrid on the other side of the mountains, drinking himself unconscious on the anniversaries of his daughter's birth and her death, and then shut that away. Liere was too damned sensitive.

He said, "I can't tell you that. His personal life—if there is one these days—remains a mystery. Adam might know something to the purpose. Want me to send him over?"

"No, that's all right. Don't disturb Adam on my account."

David sensed not just a pitfall but a precipice looming just beyond the scope of his vision. Somehow this situation had turned into one requiring the Long View. It was definitely a test. And so far, he was flapping around like a fish who thought it a fine idea to leap up onto a rock to command a view of the world.

"Look, Liere. I'm here, a ready and willing ear. But for Detlev's explanation of what he does or does not understand, you really have to ask him."

"I hoped ..." Her fingers gripped more tightly in her lap. "It would be slightly less unbearable to talk about something so ... intimate ... with someone my age."

Now, that he understood. "Atan? Hibern?"

Liere's face had paled, her forehead tense. "I have agreed to something ... iniquitous. Neither of them has ever stepped beyond the boundaries of moral behavior. I would not blame them if I saw their disgust at my agreement to Macael's choice in their eyes. Which would not help me at all. I can judge myself well enough."

David heard the self-loathing in her low voice. "I know what it is to cross moral lines for a greater good, though for us it was always the use of force."

"But what here is the greater good?" She looked up at last, and he saw the gleam of tears along her lower lids. Tears of not just anger but shame.

Though he knew he had failed miserably, more important was the pain in her face. "Saving your son, for one?"

"But how do I know he'll keep that promise? He killed Andri! Who was his friend! All our talk was of peace!"

David put up his hands between them. "I'm not about to get into a discussion of what Macael said or didn't say in conversations I never heard. You might think back to recollect exactly what he did say. Because from here, it sounds as if he's pretty careful with his words."

"I can't even face him right now," she said miserably. "It's too humiliating. The Birth Spell didn't come."

"Ah. Hm. For a shitty situation such as this one, yeah, I encourage you to talk it out. We're always there at Curtas's House, but if you're not sure about us, there's always Detlev." David knew he was abysmally failing here, but her tangle of emotions was the priority. He gave her a little smile. "I think he passed the threshold of being shocked a long, long time ago."

11

U nder the sheep-backed ceiling of gray clouds, riders streamed in orderly swells, row on row, like the long rolling breakers on the sea. They charged between two neat columns of foot warriors equipped with shield, spears, blunted swords. Archers behind and on the wings.

To either side of Trevor Macael Elsarion the breath of waiting horses and riders puffed, the animals untroubled by any hint of wind, though a few of the spectators tried not to shiver. Presently Macael heard behind him a mutter that no doubt he was not supposed to hear: "Damn my eyes, he's brought it off."

The voice was low, old, husky; he identified the speaker by that flat west-country accent: old Ban Facobris, former Commander of the Enaeraneth border guards. He was probably speaking to his aide, a tough young woman from the northern mountains above Elsarion.

Macael watched the Enaeraneth warriors in blue ride to meet the Adranis in lavender-gray: feint, shields clashing, mounts churning up mud. The clatter of dud arrows on shields. A knot formed over by the river bend—but before he could raise the field glass they dispersed, streaming away, away, and there was no telltale red on the brown-mashed snow, no lumps of fallen warriors.

The scheduled winter exercise was happening, though one of the two kings was no longer there to witness. First, days of drill, Adranis and Enaeraneth side by side—the Enaeraneth outnumbered by a factor of three—then together in a wargame on this, the last day.

The foot warriors came together, worked more or less in unison through the drill they'd been commanded to perform, and then, at the sound of a horn, turned and regrouped. The riders also regrouped, orienting north-south, one side to attack the bridge that jutted up like a fingernail on the horizon, the other to hold it.

That completed the second of the three exercises planned for the day. To the naked eye they all looked the same: silent, obedient, trained. A sweep of the field glass revealed tension, determination, deliberate holding back, and no friendly banter between the Enaeraneth and the Adranis. Here and there some in Enaeraneth sky blue clumped for what had to be quick asides, followed by sidewise looks, and then hasty dispersal to designated places, as behind them young squires and stable-hands ran to pick up the blunted arrows lying scattered over the muddy churned-up snow. So far, three quickly aborted plots. There appeared to be one to go…

Every warrior on the field was aware that someone could, and might, try to start something, but so far, no one had seen an opening to start it.

So far.

Macael turned his attention away from the swarms of riders called to new formations by horn and flag, and waited to hear what Ban Facobris would say next to his aide.

Facobris had decided that what he had to say next, Elsarion would hear from his own lips, man to man. The chuff of hooves in snow neared, and there was Facobris's scarred face and weather-reddened nose, his lined eyes squinting under iron-gray brows. "May I speak."

Macael opened his gloved hand.

"What happens now? You want trouble, or no? If one o' them young hotheads of Andri's loses his sword in someone's back, or shoots a real arrow, and not one of the duds, then what?" A nod toward the riders forming up for the bridge defense exercise.

"What do you think should happen?" Elsarion asked.

Facobris fingered an ear, causing his helm to rock. He finally shook his head. "I don't see how what I think makes a whit o' difference. Especially as what I expect keeps turning up shards."

His reference to the old card game caused a brief quirk of humor at the corners of Macael's mouth. He returned no answer, obviously waiting for Facobris to go on.

Curse it. I came forward, the old man thought with bitter inward laughter. And I keep expecting to end up a dead man, so why not speak my piece and get on with it?

"The day you killed the king," he said, his guts griping on the word *king*, "I woke up in my outpost with an Adrani sword point at my neck. In the next room over, young Basrel, one of my captains, was lying in his own blood. No reason given why I lived and he died. By noon I found out that the king was dead, the queen a prisoner and about to be killed, the prince was gone, presumed dead, and dead was every one of our king's own guard. Killed while you did for the king the only place he ever went alone, the yew walk." Facobris's voice had sharpened into accusation; his throat hurt. He stopped, and waited.

Macael did not speak immediately, and the two sat on their horses in silence for a short time, midway along a hilly ridge shaped like an arm curved protectively around the river bend.

Macael saw the stubborn set of Facobris's lips, and knew that the man would not speak again until Macael made some reaction to his outburst. He said, "Andri was not alone. His boy was there." And, "I had not known about that."

Facobris said, bitterly, "Would it have made a difference?"

"No." The voice was calm, but certain, cold as the wind fingering those barren beech trees in the distance.

"What was supposed to happen to the young prince?"

"He was supposed to eat his morning oatmeal, as usual, and wake up on his way to an estate I inherited from my grandmother."

Facobris said, "Do you know where he is?"

"I believe so." Macael lifted his glass to his eyes, swept left and right, then waved his hand, and his own command silently urged their horses forward.

Reserves, cavalry, one of whom broke away and approached, saying only, "The bridge?" He was dressed exactly like the others, but he had to be Macael's personal guard, the ones you almost never saw, Facobris thought, looking away.

The contrast made it too easy to remember Andri's

laughing, easy-going but hard-trained guard, dressed in sky blue and edged with crimson and gold, uniforms designed to intimidate. Cheap trouble-avoidance, Andri had said once.

Macael's quiet voice broke the memory. "We will observe from the other side."

A nod, and the rider kneed his horse into a gallop. The command group also started forward, but at a sedate pace. Facobris followed. Strange, he thought bleakly, how unlike Andri's style of command was Trevor Macael's—and yet how like in some ways. And why is Bevara Yuthan out of riding order? She should never have been promoted, but Andri was always generous with his favorites … Did Andri ever see how ambitious she was? More ambition than skill. Ah, it didn't matter now, Facobris thought heavily. Andri was gone, and few wanted to follow the volatile baras's daughter, even though most wanted the Adrani king dead.

On the next hill, hidden in a clump of old gnarly apple trees as foot warriors and horses circled the snowy plain around them, Bevara Yuthan muttered to her two companions, "He's going that way. It's the bridge next."

Her companions, one old, his jaw working, one young cousin pale with determination, turned toward the bridge.

"You sure you want to try?" Cousin Vos spoke. "Not enough of us, I'm thinking."

Bevara glowered. "They're all cowards. We'll show them."

She tested her bow, nicked her chin down, then they rode single file down from the trees, to join in behind a company of Andri's King's Guard.

Bevara glanced back once, but her stinging eyes only made out a row of silhouettes, the tallest at the center. Sitting so still.

He'll be stiller yet, she vowed.

Macael held his horse in a loose rein until Facobris caught up. And then he said, as if there had been no interruption, "Who died and who did not might have appeared arbitrary, but it wasn't. Those loyal to Andri as a person had to die with him, or the bloodshed never would have stopped."

Facobris had to agree it was true, considering Andri's

guard, the roistering, swaggering group admired by just about everyone. They had been hand-picked by Andri, not only for their martial skills, which had been formidable, but they were all people he liked being around, who shared his humor, his tastes in drink and game. He'd said at the outset that if they had to live with him, and he with them, why not pick those who'd as soon spend time with each other.

And they all died by the knives of those they'd accepted as visitors and fellow-guards. For the day guard: herbs in their hot cider, then a swift knife. One of them Facobris's nephew, Haldri. No honorable duel, no words spoken. Just the sleep of herbs turning into death. For the night guard coming in tired after their watch: ambush, each to a target.

Facobris tightened his gut, eyeing the muddy road ahead, and the two armies — lavender-gray and sky blue mixed on both sides — spread in a dark line under the lowering sky. Facobris knew young Haldri would never have stopped trying to kill Macael the regicide, no matter how many got between his blade and the object of his vengeance.

Macael went on, "Captain Basrel was loyal to Andri, and not to Enaeran. Your first loyalty is to the kingdom. Therefore you lived."

How did you know that? Of course he'd know. He'd had ten years to find out everything he wanted about everybody. Facobris sighed, then became aware he'd done so. But a quick glance at the Adrani king showed no change of expression.

"On New Year's Day I will require your oath," the imperturbable voice went on.

"To you?"

"To Enaeran Adrani."

Facobris recognized the name from before the split into two kingdoms. He shook his head slowly, fighting against memory, emotion, question. He had initiated this talk. He had to accept the answer, or die. He could not live a lie.

Around them the guard raced, inner perimeter, outer, the Adrani Household Guard in two wings. They crossed the road to the little bridge over the frozen stream, where the two armies were drawing up for the next exercise, and passed north to circle around. Macael turned his head, watching to the west; once he raised his glass, then he lowered it.

And Facobris said, "What happens to the prince?"

Macael glanced back. Once again that brief hint of humor, not quite a smile, shadowed the corners of his mouth. "Nothing, at present. I trust that that will continue, if certain conditions are met."

Facobris sighed. "What conditions?"

"You will know by the end of the year." Macael lifted his head and glanced westward.

Facobris hesitated, wondering if he should ask what they were, but what did it matter? In any case Macael raised his hand and the horns sounded. As snow began to drift down from the sky the masses of two armies moved again, orderly, obedient on the surface. Watchful.

And from a vantage near the bridge, Bevara Yuthan watched the Adrani murderer and his followers ride north, and she exchanged glances with her two fellows. They'd missed their chance at the bridge, for the murderer had only observed. Three chances gone by, then.

Leaving just one more.

From the top of the hill the two mixed armies, one side with red armbands and the other with green, could see Shiovhan lying in the distance, rooftops interleaved white squares.

One last wargame, the attack on the city: when the horn blew the signal, loud enough to echo back from the long line of hills behind them, a thousand pairs of feet stamped forward, a thousand horses surged into motion, and three thousand hearts thumped. Green army was attacking, red defending.

Death, sang the mind of Bevara Yuthan. *Death, death, death.*

Her cousin urged his horse up next to Bevara's. "You sure?" he asked, sending a quick look back under sandy brows, and fingering his bow. "You sure?"

"He has to die," Bevara said flatly.

"But he hasn't done anything we thought. Not one killing this whole week, not one. Not even a flogging."

"Did that bring the king back to life?" Bevara sent an ugly look over her shoulder, her pale hair fingered in the wind under her helm. Bevara saw misgiving in her cousin's perplexed wince, and added, goading, "You turned tail like the rest of those rabbits, Vos?"

Vosri saw their third conspirator, old Kaevan—the former Yuthan Guard Chief—riding hard, head bent over his horse's mane. Kaevan had no doubts, but then Kaevan, too, was avenging someone he'd loved, Bevara's father.

Was that it, then, Vos asked himself as they raced with the general melee toward the Adrani lines that were to defend the city. Everything backwards, mixed Enaeraneth and Adrani foot and horse, but still a visible division between those in blue and those in lavender-gray. Of course, all was blunted weapons, but still ...

Mud and ice smacked his face, kicked up from Bevara's horse in front. He gasped, bent lower, and shook his head. His helm, so familiar a weight for eight years, rattled on his sweaty head. Fingers in gloves, toes in boots, nose, all were cold, but his body was drenched in sweat because they were riding for death, and for what? Because the bonds of love required revenge? Was that supposed to be right? And what if the "love" had only gone one way? He'd known Andri since they were teens, and Andri had been frank about how it didn't seem to be in him to *fall in love,* whatever that meant.

"Sorry about the mud," Bevara said, her voice barely carrying over the thunder of hooves mushing the ground. She looked back, and he could see the white of frozen tears on her eyelashes.

"Brace up." Her throat burned. "Think of the prince on the throne." She hated herself for that piece of hypocrisy. Too late, too late, too late, and Macael Elsarion was going to die for it.

Vos felt words shape the insides of his numb lips: *Putting the prince on the throne won't bring back the king either.*

But he didn't say them, and Kaevan began the last ride, breaking them from their wing and into the next. Bevara shut everything out except the urge to kill. She kicked her horse in the sides, jolting the animal into a gallop. And all around them, from their own people, looks shot across, back, ahead—angry looks, apprehensive, grim, questioning.

Vos's insides trembled. They couldn't possibly get away with it, of course. The question was, whether or not they could get near enough the Adrani king to kill him before they were brought down.

Vos stood in his saddle to survey the field. There were the

flags, marking the command group. The king rode bare-headed, that much they knew. He seemed to ride alone, ahead of an ordinary company. No personal guard.

Vos heard his own wing commander, five days ago: *The exercises start tomorrow, just as our king and the Adrani king had planned. Every one of you needs to think about what your oath meant. If you swore to Enaeran, is civil war, with a possible king at the age of eight, the best thing for this kingdom? If it's to Andri, do you want to throw your life after his, especially as the queen surrendered in order to keep it for you? What would Andri say to that?*

In the distance, the clatter of wooden swords.

"Vos," Bevara snapped, and his head turned. "Now."

Kaevan rode point, weaving steadily north. There was Adrani king, riding between two wings, a wide space around him so that he could see. A scattering of Adrani horse before, behind, and Facobris, the border guards' former commander, back a ways.

Vos lowered his reins, flexed his left knee, and his mount obediently followed. Vos bent lower, trying to keep his head down, avoiding any of the glances from familiar eyes. No one spoke, but he sensed their alarm, their question: everyone was angry. Because they were afraid.

"Back to your riding!" Vos heard the shout, and he obediently began to veer southwards, but he also slowed, and three ridings shot by, none of them looking back; once again he veered north, catching sight as he did of Kaevan and Bevara nearly in place, nearly —

And the formation around the king changed suddenly, with no horn, no sign that Vos could see. The world filled with kicked up snow, flying hooves, and then shouts. He glimpsed Bevara standing in the saddle with her bow drawn, a real arrow nocked, and he obediently reached for his sword, clapping knees to his horse's sides so he could ride to protect her long enough for her to get off more than one shot. Then he saw Kaevan fall sideways from his frightening, kicking horse, hands outflung, four arrows in his back.

Fire! Pain!

Vos was on fire, what, where? He couldn't breathe, lungs cold. His neck burned like ice. He opened his eyes. Faces. Flame in his side, cold melted snow down his neck. "Urr?" he said, his mouth dry and numb. Nothing seemed to work, including his brain.

"Yes, he's alive," someone said. "Arrow between the ribs." A hesitation, then, "He'll bleed to death soon if we don't treat it."

"Then wrap it up," came a quiet voice.

Hands lifted Vos, and there followed a very painful interlude, ended by lister-laced kinthus, held to his lips by efficient if untender hands. Pain dwindled to a faint warmth in his side, and in the back of his skull a faint scream, permitting him to hear what was going on inside this gray canvas tent.

His ears caught Bevara's voice, reedy with pain and despair and anger. "Yes," she keened. "Yes, yes, yes! Everyone was in the plan, everyone! We all want you dead, you murdering traitor."

Vos forced his head to turn. He couldn't see Bevara, but he heard the tremble of tears in her voice, the helpless rage. Yet there was no reaction at all to be seen in the tall figure in the long black cape standing over her.

Vos closed his eyes. His wits had returned, with the knowledge that they had failed. And now they would suffer the consequences. There remained only the manner of death, up against a wall and fast, or slow and nasty in some stone dungeon somewhere.

Noises surrounded him, then the shift of cloth, the sound of boots chuffing on icy snow. Bevara's words had given away to high angry sobs of rage, then those too faded to whistling breathing. Vos realized he lay on a folding camp bed, under something heavy. Absurd, to be under a blanket?

"You are?"

The voice, so quiet, compelled his eyes to open, and he looked up. Startling, how much this man looked like the king, and yet so unlike.

Vos worked his mouth, then whispered, "Vosri Yuthan."

"What," said the Adrani king, "and why?"

No more than that, but Vos knew what he meant. Everyone knew what he meant. Vos lifted aching eyes to a few other faces, one above a regular foot warrior's uniform, others above stable hands' gear. He knew now what he, Kaevan, and Bevara had missed before: that there was a personal guard, but they didn't mark themselves off with their own uniform, they wore the same blue as Andri's honor guard. Elsarion blue. Only these had twined lilies on the chest, and their blue was a denser color, like the sky at twilight.

Behind them, looking old and tired, stood Commander Facobris.

Regret seized Vosri, so sharp, so acrid it was worse than the arrow striking him because his body could go numb, but his mind had no defense against reaction. Images flitted through his mind, moon-lit moths, to wink out again: the smell of his lover's hair, the first sip of new cider. Laughter in the barracks, a fast horse between his legs. Pleasures all to be taken away, snuffed out. Honor required no less.

Vos said, with gritty determination and some despair, "What m' cousin said. Stand with it."

The king said, with perceptible irony, "Your cousin said what would best get her killed, not necessarily the truth."

"Where's she?"

A glance in the other direction, somber, serious, not at all casual. Or indifferent.

"Still alive?" Vos whispered.

"Unconscious."

Vos let out his breath in a long sigh, and shut his eyes. He'd tried to talk to Bevara, but she was so very certain that Andri was tired of Sartora the foreigner. He just needed a little push to set her aside. Vos had been unpersuasive, she'd been— determined. Was it weak to see the endless possibility of life, to want to see tomorrow's dawn? What was strong anymore? He was too tired to think, he just knew she'd turned herself into a weapon of vengeance.

And it hadn't worked.

"Kill me now."

"The killing has to stop somewhere," that even voice retorted. "Why not with you?"

Vos opened his eyes.

"Does your definition of honor really require you to throw away your life for someone else's cause?"

Vos tried to move, but his ribs sent white lightning through him, and he fell back. He gasped, sweat stinging his eyes, and he blinked, blinked, he had to see. To hear, but that rushing in his ears made voices sound so far away.

The shadowy figure with the long black hair gestured, and someone put a hand to the back of Vosri's head, and a ceramic cup clinked against his clenched teeth. Hot liquid splashed in his mouth. He gasped, and some of the pain receded.

He remembered where he was, and what had happened. "I can't fight for you," he gasped.

"No," came the quiet voice. Steady blue eyes regarded him. "You can for the kingdom. A united kingdom once again, benefitting everyone, the way it was in the past. Not yet, perhaps. One day?"

Vos flipped his fingers. "This life. All I know." He realized after he said it that he was negotiating. That he did indeed want to live, oh so much, that Bevara was wrong: life did have meaning, even could under this new king. Even if she wouldn't become the new queen.

"Fighting is not all you know. You know horses. You know how to see to their gear. You can tend them for a year or so, while you think about the decisions you made recently, for you did not lead, did you? You chose to follow. Even if you did not wholly agree."

Vos said nothing. This king seemed to know already what was in his thoughts.

"My suggestion is this: follow orders for a year, and work in the stables. Then we shall talk again. Can you live with that?"

Vos worked his lips, but they were too numb for speech. He pawed his chest in an attempt at salute.

"Then that is agreed."

He heard the Adrani king's steps withdraw before he slipped under the influence of the herbs he'd drunk, the soft sound of snow patting the tent roof, which smothered the quick, efficient end to Bevara's life.

A fter fruitlessly chasing thoughts around in her own head, Liere Fer Eider rose that next morning, dressed, and sat down to her breakfast, which she took in the window seat of her bedroom so she could look out at the sky.

Though she asked no questions of Thani, she was aware, just as she'd sensed Macael's departure the day of their single interview, that he was expected to return, perhaps even that day. And so, because she was held by only her own sense of honor, she must carry out her quest now, and return before he did.

She transferred. Detlev's house looked exactly the same. The air smelled the same, too, despite the cold, a distinctive combination of pine and the sea.

Liere crossed the terrace and entered the main room with all the windows. The diffuse lighting caused by up-reaching curves and lines that made the most of the sun's yearly arcs brought back her memory of her first visit, after he left Norsunder, and how her old fears had warred with her astonishment at clean-lined Old Sartoran architecture, when she had unconsciously expected a grim fortress. In a mood of challenge she'd come to ask for Detlev's help—as if daring him to prove himself useful—and she'd ended up going to Geth to repair her ignorance.

Here she was again.

She sniffed the air that wafted along the halls, stirred by distantly heard fountains; it was warmer here, still smelling of mountain pine and ocean. No human scents at all.

She wondered how long he had considered where to place his house. Was it colossal arrogance that had motivated him to plan out every detail while he was at Norsunder's beck and call, or the hope that keeps one sane? On her first visit she'd noticed only that this place complemented the environment in a natural way, but now she recognized the style of her far-off ancestors. It all fit together, no boring spaces, no unnecessary lines. It reminded her strongly of a simpler version of the white palace in Mearsies Heili, though she couldn't define how. It had something to do with the way light and line integrated to lead the eye.

She headed for the study at the east end of the upper floor. Her heartbeat drummed. Not in fear of violence from Detlev. That had been purged many years and experiences ago. Fear, however, of what he might say.

The door was open to an empty room. Oh.

She ran back downstairs, to find him in the kitchen, a half-eaten hunk of bread stuffed with greens and cheese in one hand, and a bottle in the other. From the smell perfuming the room in spite of the open windows, it was white wine. He was in the act of pouring some into a soup tureen on the stove.

Hazel eyes met hers in a brief assessment, then he said, "Come and taste this soup, will you?" He bit into his sandwich.

Liere found a spoon, dipped it into the simmering golden brown mixture, blew on it, then tasted cautiously. "Pepper-fish soup!" Somehow the homely task eased her inner turmoil. Even awakened her sense of the ridiculous, if briefly.

"It seemed flat. Either more pepper, or wine, I thought," Detlev said. "Anyway it's not nearly as good as Siamis makes it."

"The wine flavor is a little strong."

"I just added it. Should cook down by dinnertime." He hefted the sandwich. "Bread? Steep?" A brief smile. "Wine?"

"Am I so obvious, then?" And not all her practice at control could prevent her from blushing hotly as she dropped onto a stool by the prep table.

The sandwich waved in a gesture of negation. "I know the situation."

"I think you've hinted fairly strongly that you know more about it than I do," she said, relieved now that he'd gone directly to it.

"Somewhat," he said as he sat on the other side of the prep table.

"But you won't tell me what I don't know because I might see it as a weapon."

"Correct."

"Have you any idea how humiliating this subject is?" The words, once begun, were impossible to stop. "How loathsome I shall find the experience, and thence myself, if I keep that promise? I *need* a weapon. Have you lost all sense of ... of human feeling, and can't see how that's the only way I can ... fight a battle I can't seem to avoid?"

He took the time to finish another bite. "What I see," he said finally, "if you set aside your entirely justifiable reaction, is the potential for another generation of war. Only longer, and more widespread."

Her breath shuddered behind her ribs. She no longer tried to conceal her emotions. "Oh, but isn't that a given? What do *you* think Trevor will do, probably before he turns eighteen?"

"I think there's a good chance he'll be up there on the mountain above us, studying with Adam. Or reefing sail on a ship. Or world-hopping. Or raising parrots. He loves birds and animals, doesn't he?"

Liere covered her face with her hands.

"I know you sent him to Senrid because it seemed the safest place to send him. I also know that Senrid farmed him out promptly to his academy. Have you studied what they learn there?"

"War skills," she said. "I remember that well enough."

"What you remember from all those years ago was Senrid dealing with two generations of training for offense. He could not change at once. He told you that, I believe."

Liere nodded. "He did, but that was a long time ago. When we were so young and thought we understood the world. Since then—well, I didn't know what to think."

"And you never asked."

Liere managed to get control of her breathing. "I can't ask Senrid," she said quickly. "You don't know—well, at a crucial juncture we parted badly. I, well—"

"You haven't spoken to Senrid since your marriage. That's been fairly obvious."

"You think me wrong?"

"It doesn't matter what I think. Neither of you is going to

rip apart half the world as a result of your lack of communication, though each of you is capable of it."

As Senrid's cousin Imry Llyenthur did. But *he* seemed to have had no problems with communication.

Liere's stomach churned. She shrugged off those memories of David's noxious brother. "Back to Macael. And weapons. You won't tell me what I need to know. Then why don't you say whatever it is you want to say?"

"I don't want to say anything," Detlev retorted in an even voice. His sandwich gone, he pulled a cloth from a shelf, dipped it in the rinsing bucket, and began to wipe down the prep table as he said, "You came to me. Anger," he added, "is more bearable than humiliation, but it's still not going to afford you clear sight."

"Clear sight!" Frustration seethed through Liere. "Easy for you to say. Have you *ever* lost the far vision? Found yourself in an untenable—" She thought back over his history—what she knew of it—and the exasperation died away. The trap surrounding Siamis when he was a boy. And then that mysterious stuff about Ilerian.

She got up, and faced the open window. The cold wind felt good on her hot cheeks. "Your past includes worse things. Much worse. I know. I think those choices would have killed me. But they didn't include such, ugh, *personal* trespass."

"No," he said.

"Implying that at other times you did face the same kind of choice?"

"If I thought anything I've done would serve as enlightenment," he said, "I'd provide date, place, and as much detail as you could stomach. But I don't think that's to the purpose."

"It's very much to the purpose."

"Why?" He smiled. "Will the evidence of physical trespass or emotional or moral ambivalence on my part exonerate whatever decision you make with regards to Macael Elsarion?"

Physical trespass. She saw again Macael's face, the unreadable, dense blue eyes. She heard his voice, *Before you leave you will give me an heir.* And, more recently, his refusal to give back her promise.

She clasped her arms tightly against her body. "But I have to know if you really understand the cost of what you are asking of me."

"I am not asking anything of you," Detlev replied. "I am merely offering an insight afforded by accumulated experience in hopes you will be able to avoid living through some of the same kind of experience."

She took a deep breath. "Insight. Yet you won't spell it all out. Only half."

"Yes." He smiled faintly. "Because the half that you must learn to spell is going to gain you insight, I believe, that you would not learn otherwise. It's important. But equally important is that you find it for yourself, at the right time, the right place, and in the right frame of mind. Right now your grief is too new, and your anger too strong."

"All right. So what is it you think I ought to do, until I learn to spell?"

"Get your heir, as soon as possible. Imprint as much of yourself on the child as you can before you leave."

"And ...?"

"Didn't you once want to know how to use a dyr effectively?"

"I did. When I was ten. And had nothing else to do," she muttered, knowing she just sounded sulky, but she was too upset to care.

He said, "Remember, right now only the Enaeraneth people's faith in you preserves the truce."

"So my actions ..." Her chest heaved. She couldn't finish.

"Do not," he said, "mistake moral superiority for integrity."

She looked away, wondering how anyone could feel both numb and sick at the same time, or was she the only one with that talent. "I hope I'll comprehend that eventually." She turned from the window and started toward the door. She couldn't utter meaningless words of thanks, though she knew she'd probably be grateful someday. If he was right. And wasn't Detlev always right?

"Liere."

She turned.

The light was directly behind him now, making him a silhouette. Not that it mattered, since no one ever read his expression anyway.

He said as he dipped the cloth in the rinse water, "For what it's worth, I too know what it is to find the right person at the wrong time."

Taken completely by surprise, she paused there in the doorway, but he said nothing more as he finished cleaning the table. "Anything else?" he asked, in that easy, even voice as he wrung out the rag and hung it up to dry. "I have to admit I have an errand I ought to see to."

"Nothing else," she said, and walked out into the hallway. Now a thank-you was impossible. Even a good-bye was inadequate. Was that the first-ever Detlev personal revelation? Despite all the terrible emotions still roiling about inside her, the briefest butterfly-touch of humor fluttered in the region of her heart.

Brief, already gone. She stopped on the landing, and leaned her forehead against the cold glass of a window. She could smell the snow-laden fir trees outside, looking bluish white and still, before her breath clouded the glass into gray opaqueness.

She closed her eyes, unable to guess why he said that now, after so how many years of silence? It made no difference, really, when his wrong time had happened, whether four thousand years ago, or forty. It had nothing to do with what she faced.

Or maybe it did.

The urge to comprehend how the world could change so swiftly gripped her. Nearly ten years a queen, looked up to by all as a mage, as a dedicated ruler, the peace maker, unassailable in her devotion to duty and good acts: she had lived a good life, a meaningful life, built carefully, and her reward had been contentment, comfort, shared laughter, respect. And the truth was, it had never been enough.

Oh, Andri.

Tears burned. They felt hypocritical, because if no one else knew the truth, she did: though he had not changed, or done anything amiss, her lust for him—she recognized now that it had only been lust, no different than that felt by any other teen of sixteen—had not lasted much past Trevor's birth. But there had remained friendship and affection and shared cares for the kingdom, and of course their shared love of their son.

She pushed away from the window and trod down the stairs, using her sleeve to wipe her eyes. Talking to Detlev made her feel stupid. She needed someone to decode his words, to explain in ways she could comprehend.

Who?

There was Atan, of course, but … But. Why the but? Was she being unfair to Atan? She couldn't imagine the queen of Sartor repudiating her, or scorning her. Atan just didn't do such things. Liere knew that her misgivings were not caused by anything easy, such as the lack of shared Dena Yeresbeth. She and Atan had communicated well enough without …

Do not mistake moral superiority for integrity.

Liere grimaced, then put her hands up to rub her tense forehead. The truth. The truth was that she had always enjoyed the moral high ground. Not just enjoyed. She'd *needed* it. It had become essential, ever since —

"Say it," she whispered.

Ever since that day on the beach when Senrid had told her, in words sharper than knives, what a fool she was, and why.

Who was it who said he understood moral trespass?

David.

Liere transferred fast, too fast to argue further with herself.

It was the second transfer in a relatively short time, and it left her head pinging with reaction. Her first thought, when she could think again, was the realization that there was no ward keeping her from the mysterious school on the mountain.

Though she'd never been back after her single visit during the war, even before transfer reaction completely dissipated she recognized the liminal, resonant atmosphere, and braced for the instant magnification of her grief.

Intellectually she knew the disirad did not work that way, that an increase in perceptions — sensitivity — would not automatically select one emotion and distort it into artificial intensity, as had the warped dyra years ago. Yet she could be flayed by memory, and not just the fresh ones, but old memory of past error, like the morning she stood on the beach and shouted at Senrid, whose words had cut so deeply —

Again she thrust away that memory, and forced herself to look around. Like Detlev's house, this building was long, deceptively simple in design, set into the hillside in such a way as to invite the winter sun and deflect it in the summer, affording a spectacular view of the distant sea in one direction, and the ranks of snow-topped mountains in the other.

Chilled—for it was far colder up here than below—she spotted the archway leading inside, and almost collided with a pair of bundled-up teens heading outside, a sled tucked under each one's right arm. They looked at her with muted surprise.

Polite nothings—stated reasons—she couldn't speak any of it. She said, in Sartoran, "Is David here?"

One of the teens, so bundled Liere couldn't determine gender, pointed with a mittened hand back up toward a stairway. The child answered also in Sartoran, but with a heavy west Toaran accent, "Top. Down to the end."

The other studied her for a long moment. She felt that appraisal, and turned her head to meet a pair of watchful, wary gray eyes, then she sensed the teen extinguishing the mental scan, quick as a snuffed flame.

She nodded her thanks, the two passed by, and Liere walked father inside the building, breathing easier when the air warmed into the scent of fresh-baked cinnamon buns. Voices echoed from various chambers. The atmosphere was distinctive, somehow both cerebral and physical; she identified the sounds of converse mixed with those of some sort of slow, dance-like drill.

The sounds gradually faded behind her as she passed swiftly up the stairs. The very top floor was empty, she was relieved to find, and so she walked to the end, and again her heart pounded.

The door stood open. She stepped within.

The room was empty. She looked around the neat, plain space, which was dominated by a huge pair of windows, one looking northwest, one northeast. Furnishings were a desk, two chairs, a bed, a storage chest. Interesting, that David would permit access so readily.

She looked at his things. She knew nothing about him, really. It did seem clear from the sparseness of this room that he had learned from Detlev not to make of a place an inner citadel—a home. She thought of her own lack of a home for so long, and how she had considered that an insurmountable detriment.

Enaeran was no longer her home. Probably had never really been. She had made Andri's life her home, with all her concentration and energy. Is that Detlev's secret, that he and his group carry their home here? she wondered, touching her aching head. Is life easier when your nature anchors you to a place, or harder?

The thoughts, images, memories — emotions — were coming faster now. This truly was a place of power, and she wondered if she'd ever be ready for it. To escape her thoughts, she left David's room and wandered back down the hall, examining the strange stone that the Old Sartorans had known how to draw up from under the ground for building. One would think that white stone in winter would be repellent, but afternoon light streaming in the windows was the pure, clear air of high mountains, shading with breathtaking subtlety through the entire spectrum, and how exactly did Detlev achieve that? Was it the way the windows were set, or was it somehow the white stone that refracted it?

She paused on the landing. Most buildings, shorn of decoration, would be ugly. Heavy. The stone oppressive. Castles were built for protection. The walls here were entirely bare of decoration, but did not need such arts; every window looked out at natural splendor. The sweeping lines were decoration in themselves.

It was so peaceful here, so *safe*. She had twice been invited. She knew that those invitations were quite rare. Should she just ... never go back? Who was to stop her? The idea of Macael chasing her into Detlev's territory gave her an angry spurt of pleasurable anticipation.

Her thoughts winged straight to her son, far away in Marloven Hess. Macael might send as many assassins as he liked, but Liere knew that Senrid would never permit them past his border. But what if Malcolin left? She had been asked to remain a year. If she broke that, she suspected that Malcolin would be in danger his entire life.

She started down the stairs, a sudden physical movement, an attempt to separate herself from her selfish desire to escape the promise she had made, leaving her son to be shadowed by the consequences.

She looked around Detlev's school. People, mostly young, with a couple of exceptions (that was definitely a gray head on the stairway) moved about. Laughter echoed down a wide, airy corridor. In the distance, faintly, a child's voice rose in song.

Music.

The visceral reminder of Macael bent over the tiranthe until his nails bled struck her an inward blow.

She shook off the reaction. A couple of running figures appeared round a corner, nearly knocked into her, and veered with deft speed. When they halted, she stared in surprise at Jessan Delieth and Detlev's son, Sveneric. Jessan reminded her very much of Glenn Delieth, except without the manner of one who is aware at all times of rank, as if it had been armor, that had characterized his uncle.

She turned her gaze to Sveneric. Gray-green eyes stared straight into hers with the kind of reflective assessment so characteristic of his father it was unsettling. Like meeting Detlev again—like meeting Detlev in the past. Only Detlev never could have been so beautiful.

That's what Sveneric was, beautiful. Not just in feature, but it was his expression, the combination of austerity and sweetness she'd seen when he was small, now combined with a wisdom found so rarely in a young face. Though she'd always expected him to be something out of the ordinary even among an extraordinary group, ever since she met the eight-year-old runaway from Norsunder who would have been justified in temper tantrums or whining, or glowering threats, or bravado, but who instead had embraced every unexpected moment of beauty and of humor with the gratitude of the parched soul who has found at last the river.

"Liere," Sveneric said, smiling a welcome. "Did you come for a visit, then?" And on the mental plane: *Adam. David. Liere is here.*

"I—I had begun a discussion with David," she murmured, looking away through the window. "But I used to know Adam, when he visited Arthur in Bereth Ferian—" She realized she was babbling, and shut her mouth so fast her teeth clicked.

Sveneric breathed in. Out. *Ah,* came Adam's inward voice.

Sveneric said, "You will find them both in the salle. We were about to join them. You won't be interrupting anything."

Jessan pointed as Sveneric spoke, and Liere looked over the landing to the room from which voices echoed up. She descended the stairs to the ground floor, where she found a big salle banked with high windows on one side, and a huge wall mirror on the other, a scattering of people of various ages standing around the perimeter.

Adam's back was turned, but she recognized in his slender form and cloud of curling brown hair a grown version of the artist boy she'd found so friendly, years ago. MV looked the same but older: black clad, strong, lean, and tough. Thoroughly villainous, if you missed the sardonic quirks to his strange light eyes, or the wry humor at the corners of his long, thin mouth.

David was barefoot, wearing old baggy riding trousers and an outsize shirt, loose-laced, with no sash; it hid his contours as they led some sort of warmup form, moving with such slow deliberation it was very like a dance. David pivoted on one foot, a hand tracing unhurriedly through the air. The shape of his eye sockets, cheekbones, and the angle of his square jaw, were familiar. So familiar. Montredaun-An familiar. Her heart squeezed in her chest.

The room had gone silent by this time. Students unfamiliar with the sight of the famous Sartora, however familiar they were with her name, were transfixed by the sight of the thin, elegant form with long golden hair and a robe of unrelieved black, framed there in the doorway. Liere was more adept than most at the mental shield but she was not used to the effect of disirad. She was also unused to those training to use it. Liere thought she blocked away her unhappiness, but the subtle signs in her posture, her coloring, and wreathing her presence in the mental realm effectively leached every impulse to laughter from the entire room.

Adam shut his eyes, his face lifting skyward, though his hands kept up the slow rhythm. Skilled they all were, MV and David the strongest, but only Adam could perform this drill with his eyes closed—and that only here on the mountaintop, where his own bond with the disirad was so powerful he seemed at times to exist in two planes at once, one finite, one the infinite. Here, for such things, sight was a mere distraction. Effortlessly he balanced on the upper part of one foot, back leg extended high. At normal speed this would be a hop and a kick, but at slow speed it required perfect balance, and all around him, students waggled and windmilled, except for one young woman whose poise indicated the discipline of dance training, and a short girl on the verge of teens, muscular and sleek as a seal.

MV toppled forward, and turned it into a somersault in the air. Liere saw him send one fiery-eyed glance in her direction, then he sauntered away, motioning to two of the wide-eyed students to come out and take a turn with a more mundane drill.

Adam watched, and somehow he was invisible, not through magic, but through some arcane method only known to him, as if he drew time and space around him to flow on past.

But David knew he was watching. And so was Detlev, through him, down on the mountain. This moment, the imminent conversation, was that important, and though his skills did not nearly match those of Detlev or Adam, it was apparently he who must make the endeavor.

David beckoned to Liere, and led the way out.

❧ 13 ❧

"**I**s MV mad at me?" Liere asked David as soon as they were alone.

David snorted. "Forbidden to talk to you."

"If he wants to rip Macael's head off," Liere stated with forced calm, "I'll happily stand by and watch him do it."

David gave her a curious grimace that she could not interpret, and once again she realized she did not know him at all. The urge to turn around and leave again was almost irresistible.

He saw her poised to go, suppressed the cowardly impulse to let her, and said, "My room is this way."

Need, rather than want, forced her around. He could feel the effort she made, for she still had not yet realized how insubstantial was her mental shield in this place as she followed him back up the stairs. When they reached his room, he said, "What's on your mind?"

He dropped into one of the two chairs before the open window. Liere sat in the other, and breathed deeply of the cold, clean air, and the complexity of scents that somehow hinted of summer's promise, though the year had not quite ended, and winter still gripped the southern half of the world. The disirad's resonance heightened the senses, rendering the air so pure it was almost painful to breathe. No, not pain, or at least, not physical pain. The anguish was emotional, antithesis to the high, skylit joy one feels as the last note of a beloved song fades into silence.

David reached into the battered trunk that had followed him across three worlds, and removed a wooden flute. He sat, his eyes closed, blowing softly across the instrument as his fingers played the same five notes over and over, a minor chord, much like the distant call of a bird: the beginning of a very, very old plains song, a lullaby.

It gave him something to do with his hands. Her gaze was drawn to how his long fingers handled the flute with such ease. She wondered if he might have made it himself. She hadn't even known he played. How much, she thought desolately, does one ever know of anyone else, outside of matters that concern the self? She, who prided herself on her insight, had never seen any hint of Macael Elsarion's true nature —

"How long have you played?" she asked, and blushed at the unsteadiness of her voice.

"Since I was little. I've never managed to get much past beginner, so I seldom play in public."

She thought about his early days under the inimical eye of Norsunder, and questions streamed through her mind, to vanish forever. She would not ask; those days were long over.

"I just came from Detlev's," she said. "As you so advised."

"I take it you were not satisfied with what you heard?"

She made an attempt at a smile, the crookedness of her mouth an answer on its own. "If I could understand some of what I heard, I could tell you whether or not it was satisfactory. I, well, I feel *stupid*."

"You won't be the first," he commented. "Over time one learns to decipher the, ah, gnomic utterances. If I'm to try, you'll have to tell it all to me."

She blanched. But go on she did, not stopping until she'd repeated the entire conversation. David listened all the way through without interrupting. When she finished, he said, "Now, what do you need from me? Glosses? Or corroborative evidence?" His lips quirked at the corners, and she tried an answering smile.

"What kind can you offer?"

"Nothing about that last bit." He twirled the flute in a circle. "Surprise to me, too, though I don't think it will be to Adam."

"You and the others wasted as much time as we did on fruitless Detlev speculations?"

"It's an innocent enough diversion."

She sat up straight, her voice acerb. "He must find us vastly amusing. Or does he think it a reward to drop the occasional 'gnomic' nugget?"

"I believe he sees it as not wasting words." David lifted a shoulder. "As for the rest. If he even knows how much we speculate I don't think he cares. He believes his own life, his personal life, is largely irrelevant. Except when this or that event can illustrate a point, or show how a mistake will spin itself out if he sees someone committing a similar one." He ran his thumb idly along the flute, then added, "You gain a different view on privacy when you've been denied it for centuries by Ilerian."

"Yet Detlev successfully kept his master plan intact... Oh. Of course. So he had to have permitted Ilerian to trample through all the rest of mind and memory."

"Right. That's why we thought of ourselves as Norsundrians up until the break."

Liere thought that over, her imagination veering away from what had to have been the uttermost horror in personal trespass. For the masters of Norsunder pleasure had been the purest when shredding that which makes the I, and then consuming the spirit. "Well," she said.

David seemed to find this reaction sufficient. And because he did—because he really seemed unshockable—she edged closer to the question that bothered her most. Closer, but not there. She said, "I guess when one considers centuries of that kind of violation, my trouble with Macael's demand must seem merely fussy."

David leaned back in his chair and put his bare feet on the windowsill, where powerful magic warded the cold, yet permitted the free movement of air. "Proportion and degree. You know that." His brown eyes met hers, calm and direct. "Or you wouldn't have come here."

"Implying I'm weak?"

"Implying only that this is your first experience with ... we'll call it moral ambiguity. And Detlev takes it, and you, seriously enough to allude to his own past. It's encouragement to gain perspective."

"But I don't need perspective. I want a way out. I don't know why Macael would make such a cruel demand, when I never did anything cruel to him, and I tried so hard to make life easier for his wife."

"I'm sure he knows that."

"He did say so, but then he turns around with that impossible…" Her voice suspended, tears sheening her eyes as she looked away.

David said, "From the purely political perspective, it was a masterstroke, because you are so admired in Enaeran. He knows it. A year buys him time to make some necessary, and even overdue changes. And you probably know people are less inclined to throw it all away when life has finally gotten better. He just has to get through this year."

She looked at the window, her shoulders tight, reminding David that compliments still made her anxious. "I could see some of that. Perhaps. Stay a year as a hostage. But the heir part…"

: *If she flinches from a mild reference to her popularity, how's she going to handle a description of how Macael probably sees her?*

: *'Probably.' We don't know enough about him,* Adam reminded David.

Who said to Liere, "I'm afraid that's a question only Macael can answer."

Liere knew that very well. It was time to ask the real question, or go. She swallowed, nerved herself, and was pleased when her voice came out even and unemotional. "Why do you think Detlev said that about Senrid?"

And there it was: the reason he, and only he, had to be the one to hold this conversation. David thought of his cousin sitting there in his castle on the other side of the continent, walled off from the rest of the world. From emotion.

Tread carefully, David. "That's something I've been considering. Underestimation is one thing that does make Detlev impatient."

"Underestimation ... I hadn't thought of that. I was afraid he was twitting me on my scruples for the lack of communication since—"

"Since—" David prompted.

Liere felt heat in her neck and cheeks, and willed it away. "Since Senrid and I had a nasty … discussion." She avoided the word *argument*. "During the war." Her eyes narrowed slightly, and he realized his lack of surprise was an answer.

Still, he hesitated, considering what to say. Her jaw twitched as she clenched her teeth, and he saw her hands grip tightly in the folds of her robe. He could feel the effort she made to brace herself. "You knew."

David looked out the window, then back, one side of his mouth lifting wryly. "Not exactly. But you two had been comrades for so long, and then that silence, I had come to the tentative conclusion that there had been a parting, and that it must have been ..." He hesitated.

"Go ahead. I'd love to hear how you'll put it."

His amusement was more pronounced for a heartbeat. "I was going to say 'somewhat brisk'." Then he looked serious. "The habit of understatement isn't meant dismissively, you know."

"I know that. Now." She sighed. "I think it always annoy-ed me before because it implied an ability to distance oneself from the currents of emotion, which I never was capable of." She gripped her hands in the folds of her black velvet skirt. "That argument with Senrid was awful. I think the worst event of my life."

"Senrid does have a tongue," David said appreciatively.

"The most horrible part of it is that everything he said was right, and everything I said, I believed was right, but it was wrong."

It took courage to admit that, he acknowledged. A good beginning.

Liere saw David's gaze go abstract for a long moment, and she wondered sickly what Senrid had said about her since then. Oh, it had been so much easier to think of him frozen in time, unmoving, uncommunicative, for ten years —

David turned his gaze out the window at the high plateau as he sorted through the emotions Liere sent so powerfully, without being aware. If he tried, he could probably hear her thoughts, but he resisted; he did not want even as much as he was getting. Bracing against her considerable strengths was tough enough.

: *Adam!*

: *Steady on.*

David looked up. "You do know what Senrid's been doing during those ten years?"

Her eyelids lifted in surprise. "Protecting his borders and making his army into something that can never be defeated again? We hear *that* much carried by traders."

"Mmm, that's a part."

"A part? What else would he do? If he's taken up art, or collecting kittens, I will fall off this chair in shock. Lyren says he lives in uniform."

"Is derogation a guilt palliative?" David retorted unheat-edly.

"Who is derogating whom? My last comment was only to imply that Senrid seems to live much the same as he did, which is entirely appropriate for a king whose primary interests, and talents, are military matters."

"Military matters." David did not hide his surprise. "You did diminish him. Interesting."

"How can you see any of my words as diminishing, or derogation—"

"The uniform," David cut in, "is a retreat from social expectations. It's also a gesture of control, part of having every day planned down to the moment—just what you've expect of a king with *organizational* talent. Do you know what he's been doing the last few years, or did you assume he rides around leading his cavalry in order to impress the populace, like his uncle had so loved to do?"

Liere sighed. "Of course I didn't. I expressed myself bad-ly."

"Or did asking one of your mutual friends how he was doing, and what, even your own daughter, trespass against your fine sense of honor?"

"I knew he was alive." The words were so low they were almost a whisper, and his irritation doused like a snuffed candle: he was failing yet again. A dyranarya doesn't let exasperation become a bludgeon.

"I'll tell you what he's doing," David said, easy again. "He's slowly, by degrees, waking up the economy not just in Marloven Hess, but through trade with all of Halia, while training his army to aid in reparations and rebuilding, and other uses of tools besides weapons. Visegn was shocked into severe depression for a long time, due to my brother's and especially Efael's tenancies, and the Iascans have been coping with the problem of Efael's leftover fleet, which predictably turned pirate." David saw a spasm of disgust tighten Liere's features at the mention of Imry — something he had become accustomed to.

But all she said was, "Enneh Rual?"

"The fiction of Enneh Rual dissolved. The Iascans under Senrid have complete local autonomy. His people are busy rousting those pirates while the Iascans get overseas trade without having to pay those stiff tariffs of the past. They couldn't avoid them before, as their government had no strength, but now that they are known to be under the Marloven wing again, Toar's eastern harbors have backed off from forcing traders to pay for home reparations. Though the Marlovens still pride themselves on their readiness for defense. But it is defense, and unfortunately it is a prospective need. That idiot in Perideth is becoming more troublesome ... Eh, I've gone on long enough. You get the idea."

Liere might once have comprehended little, but the matters of taxes and tariffs were familiar now. Though those did not command her attention. Instead she looked back in memory at the short, skinny boy who had been embarrassed when humid weather made his hair curl, and who'd loved games. Who'd loved his daughter —

"Did he marry?" There. It was out.

"I'm tempted," David said, "to tell you to ask him yourself. But you could find out easily enough: No."

She got up. "I'm wasting your time."

"No, you're not. You're running away."

She glared down into his face, her emotions a tidal wave of hurt and confusion — and affront. "I did not come here to discuss Senrid."

He stayed where he was, leaning back in the chair, his hands laced behind his head, his gaze steady. "Yes, you did," he said, and saw a tangled and difficult path opening before him. If she had to use anger as a motivator, better to point her in the right direction. "You came here for exactly that reason. But you probably told yourself you came to the morally stained remainder of Detlev's gang in order to vilify Macael Elsarion and, incidentally, get from our evil selves a reason to renege on your promise, thus neatly shifting the blame for the inevitable civil war."

She gritted her teeth. "I do not consider myself your moral

superior."

"You don't? Excellent! You should be grateful! Who else
in the past ten years has scaled your pinnacle of virtuousness
to force you to think about the real consequences of your
actions, Liere? Andri," he added, smiling, a sardonic smile that
for the third time struck her with the inescapable truth of his
Montredaun-An ancestry, "had too much compassion."

She transferred out, directly to Brydon.

As David had intuited, it was anger that enabled her to
seek Macael out, finding him in his private study, dressed for
riding — he had just returned from overseeing the exercise with
both armies, and was writing out orders.

He rose courteously. She faced him across the length of
the room, ignoring his scribes and servants.

He gestured. The scribes and servants filed out.

When they were alone, she said, "Let's get it done." And
walked out.

L iere suppressed the impulse to slam the door behind her. The door was just being a door. It was time to put her frustration and turmoil to work on something besides gnawing her fingers raw.

As she passed down the long length of Brydon, she noticed the beginning of preparations for New Year's Week: tubs of indoor plants being brought from the conservatories, the guest wing being heated and aired, dishes and counter-panes and pillows trundling in by the cartloads. Under that noise, music, the faint, sweet melodic rise and fall of children's voices running up and down the scales in vocal exercises preparatory to rehearsal.

She retreated to her own quiet, empty wing, leaving the voices and activity behind, as if she left time behind. There she prowled around her bedchamber in circles as the white-hot fire of her anger cooled to embers.

Not virtue. Virtuousness. That connoted someone who made a virtue of virtue: another term, even less palatable, was self-righteous. Moral superiority was right in there as well, the pinnacle from which her father had poisoned all confidence and self-respect from her early life. Was she turning into her father unaware?

She *really* needed to think about that: patterns. Not just current, but those from early childhood —

A quiet double knock on her door: it was an unfamiliar knock, and automatically she reached mentally for the mind behind the door, to find herself as effectively blocked as the wood here blocked her sight.

She opened the door to find Macael standing there.

She slipped out, closing the door almost on her heels; she

would not receive him in her bedchamber.

Yet.

The outer parlor was empty. He retreated two or three steps, moving near the window, the bleak afternoon light outlining his profile, and his shuttered eyes.

"I have to see to the herbs first," she said, coldly, and once again came that whisper, *Pinnacle of virtuousness.* It irritated her with its sting of truth. "It takes a couple of weeks." Implying that she would not permit him nearer until conception was possible.

Macael made a slight gesture toward the window, a gesture so quick it was difficult to interpret, but it seemed almost as if he recoiled. "You left before I could speak to you on another subject. I have come to request you to make an appearance on New Year's Firstday," he said, not to her, but to the thin-fingered cedars outside. His head turned, and he looked at her at last. "And any of the rest of the week that you can spare. There are many who need convincing that you still live, and there will be those with questions specifically for you."

Many who need convincing? Did that mean people were fighting back? Liere was not certain how to feel—except her foremost emotion was regret. Was this how struggles for power escalated into bloodshed of the innocent?

She said, "Our custom was to address serious issues on Oath Day. Debt Day was for the people among themselves, and we gave over to revels Thirdday on, with general interviews early. My presence is not necessary for revels," she stated firmly.

"I hoped you would preside; beginning with Secondday, I will be in Nente. I expect to return by Fourthday."

"Who will I see? Anyone I know from Andri's court?" Her words came out high, quick with the irritation she would no longer hide. "Or are they all dead, their holdings handed off as prizes for your assassins and spies?"

Macael said, "Andri's inner circle are confined to their estates for a year. I refer to the remainder of Enaeran's court, as well as the guild chiefs."

At least Andri's "inner circle" was mostly still alive—if Macael could be believed. She drew in a deep breath. Political masterstroke … prevent a massacre … Right. She'd lost sight of the terrain once again, as Senrid would put it.

She would not pretend gratitude, but she could at least cooperate, and do her part to preserve the tenuous peace. To stand by and permit uprisings in her name to uphold her honor was no honor at all. "I will be there," she said.

He bowed courteously, monarch to monarch, and left. She withdrew to her bedchamber, and when the younger of her two maids appeared, Liere gave a new order.

A day later, Jauni Ghan, daughter of Melthanir, clutched her basket close and stood on the old castle walkway, roofed and glassed in during the time of her great-great-great-grand-mother, and waited.

Zing! The snow on the streets, which had reached a finger's depth, vanished upward in a quick flash of white powder, leaving two or three small children, bundled into spheres, jumping about laughing. In the other direction a horse laid its ears back and whickered, the sound lost but the steam from its nostrils clear in the cold, cold air.

Jauni loved watching magic happen, but today, only the once, then she hurried on, exulting, though it was terribly cold, so cold the snow had squeaked dryly underfoot when she left her rooms to cross into the residence wing. She laughed inside because she possessed the greatest secret in the whole king-dom. She! The youngest in the upstairs staff, and an Adrani, and wouldn't it just drop the jaws of those older women, who seemed to think everyone under thirty was scarcely fit to fold a handkerchief?

She pressed her basket tighter against her side and hurried her steps, ducking through the discreet door at the back of the residence wing and up the narrow stairs. Where the toffs would have to traverse the long hall and then up that great central stairway, then toil back down the hall again, the Brydon servants had their own unadorned but highly useful shortcuts.

At the top of the stairs was one of the many little rooms in which the Enaeraneth servants used to foregather in the old days. Now, with only one inhabitant in the entire wing, there were just the five of them—four of them here gathered—in this one, comfortable little room: Jauni, and the three Enaeraneth house staff who oversaw the wing.

"Good morning, Jauni," said Bandral, who was steward for the wing. "Did the snow keep you?"

Jauni bobbed her head politely. "Good morning, Chief Bandral. I apologize for my lateness, but I was given a task by Queen Liere, and Fan dismissed me to see to it at once."

To the staff, even the Enaeraneth servants, Fan was as important as Him.

"Of course that would explain it. You are always punctual," Bandral said, striving for the politeness that the two staffs struggled to maintain. She bustled to the pot over the little warming flame.

Hot chocolate for everyone, of course. Relations had been very, very polite, but strained, ever since The Death — however that was defined. *We think of the death of our Dear One, and they their king*, Thani had said to her daughter. *We all must be careful to respect the others' grief if we're to get on.*

The Enaeraneth women were talking about the trouble of drying laundry when there was no sun. Jauni listened with part of her attention as she sipped the creamy chocolate. It warmed her, it tasted good, but the warmth and taste remained subjacent to the glowing cinder of anticipation right under her throat.

The urge to blurt her news was almost overwhelming, but she could not say anything until her mother was there, so she lifted her cup and thrust her upper lip into the cream.

The door opened then, and Thani entered, her breath whooshing. She hated cold.

"Come, Thani," Bandral said, holding out a cup. "Take a sip."

"My thanks." Thani gripped the cup in her fingers first, as the others resumed their conversation.

When at last Thani opened her eyes and drank, she looked across at her daughter, and Jauni watched her mother's expression change from habitual worry to question. Jauni wondered what her expression must be like. But even that didn't dampen her delight. Since her mother wasn't fooled by what Jauni had thought was a properly blank face, she let the grin come.

" ... and our queen will be coming out to attend Court, we were glad enough to hear," Bandral said. "But the arrival of court means extra laundry, and not a sunny day for weeks. At least our queen gives no trouble. She will probably even avoid the revels. Though those will probably not be anything as merry as when the king was alive."

The former king, Thani's lips moved, and Jauni thought it as well. Thani—mindful of that truce—said, "It will bode well for the two kingdoms, won't it, to see them together?"

"I just wonder what it means," murmured Talcra, the oldest of them all. She was the nicest of the Enaeraneth, a tall, thin woman with a genius for repairing tapestry work, no matter how old or delicate. Needed, Thani had observed, as everything in Brydon was older than her grandmother. "A queen of one kingdom, and the king ..." *Conqueror.* "...of the other."

Everyone turned to Talcra, a sign of their respect, though she said nothing more. She seldom spoke even that much.

Jauni tried not to preen as she said, "I think I can answer that."

All four pairs of eyes swung her way.

She knew that this was her moment. She was the most important person in the kingdom today, that's right, the *most* important, and she didn't meant to let it slip by without any notice.

"What do you mean?" Thani asked her daughter, mistrusting that tilted chin, and the lilting smile of triumph on her lips. Emotions such as these had no place in this city any more, or so it had seemed these past long, anxious weeks.

Jauni looked from one face to the next. Averted gaze and tight shoulders from Chief Bandral. Distrust from her own mother. Worry on the worn, unhappy face of poor Artisan Talcra, who after all had seen how many violent government changes in the past fifty years?

"Queen Liere," she said quickly, softly, to Talcra. "She sent me to fetch gerda root." And she lifted the cloth cover to her basket, displaying the wrapped packages inside.

Thani gasped. "Queen Liere? But her king is..."

Talcra bowed her head so they could only see her braided gray hair.

Bandral sat down with a thump. Her sister exclaimed, "What? When? *Who?* She can't lie with a ghost, surely? Ah, well, I suppose she could, but would a ghost be able to *do* anything?"

Jauni cast an anxious eye toward her mother. "I confess I don't want night duty, if there really are ghosts. Would her king be able to attack us?"

"Stop, daughter," Thani said, glaring her down. "Remember your manners, or you may go down and scrub cook pots. We maintain our dignity up here, and ghosts are not dignified. Ghosts, tchah! Ridiculous. Perhaps she had a lover, and the king is letting him up to visit her? He's been very generous so far, as always."

Bandral crossed her arms, recognizing that the comment about being ridiculous had been aimed at her sister. Who was often ridiculous, but no one outside the family ought to be pointing it out. "Ridiculous," she returned, laying crisp emphasis on the word. "Our Queen Sartora had no lovers, except our king."

Everyone considered that. And then, one by one, they looked at one another owl-eyed as the alternative occurred to them. But no one quite knew what to say.

Bandral got up again, and walked to the window. "I never told anyone what I saw the night everything changed."

Everything changed. Not *The night your king knifed ours.* They all had at least tacitly agreed on a truce, or the palace work would be unbearable.

Bandral spoke softly. "The very last night. Your king sat in the parlor playing for our queen, and when she slept, at dawn, it was he who carried her to the parlor daybed." Her voice sank. "And—and before he went out. To the yew walk. He ..."

They each reacted characteristically at the reminder of what had happened there. "He stood there a long time, and then covered her very carefully with a quilt, as careful as if she'd been a newborn. He'd left the door open and I was standing behind, waiting for Queen Liere's orders. He never knew I was there, because I saw that and I went away, quick as I could. Not knowing what—what—" She closed her lips, hard.

"What *does* it mean?" her sister asked in a whisper, and turned to Thani. "Does your king have lovers?"

"No," Thani said slowly. "At least, none that I know

about, though he might have done anything when he was away. If so, it was very discreet. To our knowledge he was devoted solely to the Dear One. Who…"

"Who slept alone," Bandral said briskly. "We knew that from the winters she spent here. That bed was not big enough for the two of them, and we had to launder two sets of sheets when he stayed here with her."

Thani pursed her lips. "I think… I think it's Him. And Queen Liere." At the shocked looks in Bandral and her sister's eyes, she couldn't hide her affront. "Our king is quite handsome. Any number of both men and women in court, including the highest ranks, have tried to lure him. To no avail."

Bandral stroked her chin with her thumb. "When Princess Alismira was a girl, I was her chambermaid. I heard a lot of her lessons, being as I was right there when she had to read aloud. There was one, about a prince in Sartor. Who got away, when the family was fighting each other, then, ah, you see he was the only one left, so they hauled him back and he had to …" She stopped there, avoiding the Adranis' eyes as she finished hastily, "The invader was twenty years older, but their child was a Landis. And became the next ruler."

"But your king *killed* our king," Bandral's sister whispered, her eyes huge.

Talcra lifted her apron to her face, bowed her head, and wept.

15

usic echoed up stairways. Voices, wind, bells, strings. Liere knew that Macael Elsarion had turned part of that huge, rambling palace in Nente into a music school, but it seemed that school—or part of it—had moved to Brydon, at least for New Year's Week.

The morning she identified the scent of gerda herb mixed into her favorite blend of Sartoran summer steep, she stared at the eggshell-thin porcelain cup before her, edged with gold and painted with delicate blue queensblossom. She had to suppress the impulse to throw the drink out the window into the snow, summon hot water, and drink the herb plain. As if the bitter taste would somehow exonerate her in this, the first deliberate step on the path she had to follow.

Jauni, hovering in the background as she dusted a gleaming side table and twitched curtains that were already perfectly straight, kept sending curious looks her way.

Liere gritted her teeth. It seemed the wrong time altogether to bring up the subject of mind-shields, but Jauni's tangle of emotion-charged thoughts battered her, a sky-shadow of screaming crows. Liere braced herself to say something when shards of Jauni's recent thoughts and memories snagged her attention. A Sartoran prince? Coerced to mate with…

Liere knew little about Sartor's long history, and there was no use in frightening Jauni with questions. Those surface-thought shards had made it clear enough that that was the extent of her knowledge.

It was time to rectify her own ignorance.

Liere swallowed down the fast-cooling steep, scarcely tasting it. As soon as Jauni took away the dishes, Liere transferred to Bereth Ferian, where she found Arthur, Roy, and—"Clair?"

"Liere," Clair said, her smile of welcome brightening her entire countenance.

"I … thought you were in seclusion. In Mearsies Heili," Liere exclaimed.

"I was, until recently," Clair said.

Liere exchanged greetings with Arthur and Roy, who were sitting side by side in the new archive chamber, stacks of yellowed papers with faded ink before them. Clair had new paper before her. It seemed she was making notes.

"Liere," Roy began.

"Don't ask," she said, palm out. "Not yet. Maybe never."

Roy lifted a single brow, an expression rare for him, and odd on his long, homely face. "I was going to inquire if you wanted some reading material while you are stuck in your durance vile."

"Sorry! Sorry, sorry." Liere put her palms together. "I beg pardon for my rudeness. My life is … rude, these days. And, yes. I came for something to read. But I can leave and come back if I'm interrupting. Which I see I am." She became aware she was babbling: her dilemma was not the world's dilemma, and their pursuits were as vital as hers. If not more so.

But Roy said, "What is it you need?"

"Where can I find a quick summary of the history of a Prince Sandios?"

"I can tell you that," Roy said, sitting back and flexing his fingers as he spoke. "Rest my fingers a bit."

"Please. I'd be grateful."

"That was a bad time for Sartor. The Landises of that era stood out only for their mediocrity, holding the throne through inertia and brute force alternately. Resulted in the nobles living like monarchs within their borders, when they weren't fighting each other or throwing their weight behind this or that prince or princess."

"Sounds like Imar in the past half-century."

"Not far off. Sandios Landis was the youngest of four, and grew up mostly hiding from his royal siblings, who were fighting each other and their parents. The parents played them off against each other. When Sandios reached eighteen and was given his own home, he ran."

"I know this story!" Arthur shoved his pen behind his ear, adding a streak of ink to those already there. A northerner born and bred, he had not grown up with Sartor at the center of cultural history. "Sartor was nearly insolvent when the Lim invaded it, that much I remember, because Lim vocabulary entered the language afterward."

"Lim?" Liere asked.

Roy said, "They were sea-going people, descendants of the Venn—large and blond. Married strictly among themselves, the way the Venn did for centuries. They settled in the extreme south of the Sartoran continent, where it's very cold and dark in winter."

"Mirror to the Venn homeland up here in the north," Arthur commented.

"Anyway, after their chief died, Skadi-Erai of the Lim tangled with her elder brother at their breseng—their chief election—lost, and was exiled. She was a teen. She went north to Sartor and worked as guard in a noble house. Spent years learning. Watching. Returned when her brother got himself killed in a brawl, and consolidated the Lim by promising gold and land. Her plan was to infiltrate Sartor once the royal family had finished one another off, putting people in key places, so that when she later invaded, all they had to do was take out the various leaders, each more corrupt than the last. They held Sartor without too much difficulty."

Arthur nodded. "I know this part. She refused to become a Landis, as she felt that the Lim were superior—"

"Who'd blame them?" Roy commented. "Ah, at that time. No reflection on Atan."

"—but she'd learned enough to know how important tradition was."

"More inertia," Roy interjected, clearly in a fey mood. "The secret weapon of bad kings."

"Is this helping?" Arthur cast Roy a look, then said to Liere, "She added Erai to her name as a compromise." The linguistics were always more interesting to Arthur than the politics.

Roy returned to seriousness. "Meanwhile, she'd sent her two nieces to hunt down Sandios and bring him back. He was the last Landis. By this time, Skadi-Erai was nearing the end of her childbearing years, but she prevailed on Sandios to mate with her, a trade, his life for a genuine Landis heir, as a way to legitimize her takeover. The resulting child was the required genuine Landis, frog eyes and all," Roy said. "You'll find that term in the records."

"What happened to Skadi-Erai, after this coerced production of an heir?"

"Nothing. Who can do anything against a successful conqueror? Also, there were many, including on the Sartoran side, who shrugged and said that she had at least preserved the Landis name—tradition—ancient days, hoola loo. She held Sartor until she died, and Frog-Eyes took over after. Things actually began to improve, mostly because the worst nobles had been replaced by Lim, who brought in Venn ways with their bresengs and swapping out chiefs below the royal level every ten years. That was the beginning of the council system."

Arthur raised an inky hand. "But. Her name dropped completely out of use. And laws got passed to prevent that kind of thing happening again."

"I see," Liere said. "What happened to Sandios?"

"I don't remember much more about him," Roy admitted. "I believe he was locked up in a palace somewhere and married off to one of the nieces who had hauled him back. She was at least closer to his age, unlike Skadi-Erai, who was mid-forties to his twenty."

"And the Lim retained their rule? I was never aware of that."

"That's because they blended in, as more and more of them moved north, abandoning their buildings and adopting Sartoran ways. By the end of Frog-Face's long reign, they were more Sartoran than the Sartorans. Their old settlements were eventually taken over and expanded by Norsunder, until it became the Norsunder Base we knew and loathed."

Did this story lie behind Macael's plot? Patterns, Detlev had said. How could she use *that* as a weapon? "I definitely need to read Sartoran history."

"Go ahead and borrow ours," Arthur offered. "The mage school has their own set."

Liere thanked them, and went off in the direction Arthur had pointed. She found the Sartoran history, approved by

Twelve Towers, in old, beautifully bound volumes that took up an entire wall. And this was the abridged version! She needed a ladder to reach the first volume, which she pulled down and set aside. But then she decided to look for the Prince Sandios incident.

It took a few tries through random volumes—tracking mentions of the Lim—but she found it, and discovered that Roy's summary was accurate. Her eyes snagged on a single direct quotation from Prince Sandios, his promise before the recording herald: *I will agree to lend Skadi of the Lim my body for the length of time required to achieve one heir.*

Lend his body. *Lend* his body. Was that what Detlev meant by perspective changing?

Liere slowly slid the book back into its place, then looked up as the door opened. "We haven't seen one another for so long," Clair said with a warm smile.

She no longer appeared to be a young teen. She had grown a little taller, the bones of her face having emerged, so she looked a lot more like Puddlenose. But her eyes were so different, her steady gaze like … Adam's. Siamis's. Detlev's, a little. When she smiled, Liere could feel the warmth of friendship as well as see it in her countenance. Clair had moved to the other side of that deep, fathomless, rushing river of unimaginable experience, the worst excesses of human endeavor, but it had not drowned her.

"I'm in the same situation as Prince Sandios," Liere said.

"I was just about to go home." Clair held out a hand in invitation. "Come with me?"

"Please," Liere said, bracing for another long transfer, but Clair touched her arm, and the room flickered away, depositing them painlessly before another library wall. The air smelled different. Familiar. They were in the white palace on the mountain in Mearsies Heili.

Liere turned to Clair in surprise. "You know that old magic transfer! Isn't it dangerous?"

"They call it the slide. I only use it to very firm Destinations," Clair admitted. "Siamis taught me, once he realized how much it was in his memories."

His memories. Liere shivered; there was that fathomless river again. She said, "The quotation that I just found came from Prince Sandios directly: he agreed to lend his body to the conqueror."

"What is that suggesting to you?" Clair asked, as if they were continuing a recent conversation.

"Several things. For me, right now, it implies removing oneself from the center of events. It's an idea both Detlev and David tried in their own ways to get me to discover. I think I'm beginning to see it: blaming myself for everything still keeps *me* at the center of events, so to speak, but in a dreary, even self-destructive way."

Clair nodded soberly, remembering the anxious Liere of the early days, who tried so hard to remove herself from attention that she managed to lock every gaze onto her. "Aren't you at the center of events?"

"I see it as more of a very tenuous balance. My answer to Macael's offer—demand—would have been an instant and unequivocal NO!, had not I been threatened with my son's life, as well as the prospect of more civil war. If I carry out what I agreed to, Malcolin will be left alone. And the truce, maybe peace, might hold."

"That's a very hard choice. But in no way your fault."

"Oh, I've managed to see myself at fault. David called my … preoccupation virtuousness. Instead of virtue."

"That's the way they talk to each other, I discovered," Clair said.

"Which I appreciate, actually." Liere gave a brief summation of their conversation. "Once I got over the irritation. It implies, oh, a kind of comradeship, as though we're all making mistakes. Not just me. But when he first spoke, it irritated me, because it made me begin to see how close I came to repeating my father's … no, it's more than that. How like him I am by nature. Which might be why Lyren and I never understood one another. She's so much like my mother."

Clair said, "But not completely."

"True. We are not our parents. But there are inherited patterns in personality, outlook, and behavior, yes? Whether inherited in the sense of a pair of twins separated at birth, who both around the same age scratch their head or tug their ear in the same way, though they have never met? As opposed to inherited traits one has been seeing, or experiencing, and copying, all one's life."

Clair acknowledged that with a sober nod.

"I'm seeing this pattern in me. I don't want it, but it's there. I need to fix it. And I do plan to repair my relationship with Lyren, once I get my life in order." *And with Senrid, too.* "Back to inheriting my father's nature, and my conviction that I deserve whatever bad things that happen," Liere said quickly.

"Did he grow up that way?" Clair asked.

"I don't know. His family had rejected us. Or so we were told. In retrospect, I don't know the truth of it." Liere thumbed her temples. "I was so ignorant when I ran away!"

"You were ten."

"True. An *odd* ten. No one quite knew what to do with me, Dena Yeresbeth being so new. After I broke Siamis's enchantment—and I know now how very flimsy it was, meant to buy him and Detlev time—I let myself get shuffled off to Bereth Ferian, because Arthur offered, he was grieving for his tutor, and there was plenty of space. But that Queen in Bereth Ferian nonsense, and 'Sartora,' oh, I know it was well meant. And I realize it cheered people to think me a hero as Norsunder moved closer to their attack. But for me it was terrible. I knew I was a fraud. Ignorant."

"Again, you were ten."

"Oh, even then I knew my ignorance wasn't my fault. Learning outside of shopkeeping actively stimulated Father's wrath: his children need only learn barter and bookkeeping. Anything else was getting 'above our place.'"

Clair winced.

"It was my total inability to be that hero that rankled, because it was my personal failure, do you see?"

"I think I do." Clair's gaze remained steady, her posture a listening one, as if she had nothing whatever to do in the world but be here, giving Liere all her time and attention. That, plus the quiet, subliminal hum of the atmosphere bolstered Liere.

"I tried to banish my ignorance, but I went about it completely wrong, beginning with trying to force myself to memorize the incredibly long list of Sartoran kings and queens. It made sense for heralds, because, I learned later, locating records was so much faster if you knew where a name fit in the warrens of archive chambers in and under Eidervaen's rambling palace. But the heralds also learned at least a gist of context. After grinding the list of monarchs into memory as far as the Connar who married Alian Dei in 3355, I began to comprehend that without context, such a list was absolutely useless."

"Except to impress people with," Clair said with a grin.

"More like bore them with. And nobody could do anything about my cheerless and futile toil because they were afraid of me, and my mind-reading, even though I tried so hard to shut out all those thoughts blasting at me. Nobody except Senrid. He was the only one who could kick me out of those moods."

"I remember," Clair said.

"Lilith tried to make time for me, but I clung so hard to my ignorance — believing that I deserved my misery — and she was trying to guard the fifth world, as well as protect us and Geth. Geth! It wasn't until I got there that I made the astounding discovery that learning history was not meant to be a drudgery of memorizing tables and lists, as learning maths for ledger work had been in my gloomy, anxious home."

"Tell me more about Geth."

Liere said, "History was *stories*, such as the ones Senrid told me while we went out riding, or while we built cities with his wooden blocks. He'd begun by telling stories to his cousin Ndand, the only companion his uncle allowed him to have, so he knew exactly what a ten-year-old would like. The best part was the discussion after. The way we'd talk about those stories was the way my Geth classes talked, a free exchange that was exciting and fun and full of ideas."

Liere rubbed her forehead, which seemed to pang every day about this time. "Enough of that. Back to virtuousness. This morning, I caught myself thinking in the old pattern. I was going to make myself drink the gerda herb plain, knowing it would gag me. But I realized that forcing myself to drink the herb bitter would be like forcing myself to memorize that list of kings and queens, though I loathed memorization. It was like cutting off my hair with a knife whenever I overheard someone saying it was as pretty as cornsilk, because, oh, you probably remember how tedious I was."

"I remember you chopping your hair off."

"Well, all these things are part of that pattern learnt before I turned ten. I see it now. Before I overheard Jauni's thoughts about this mysterious prince, I was struggling with my unexamined conviction that because I once was Macael's friend—even had found him attractive, or at least compelling, in his distant, unreadable way—I was the one crossing moral lines."

Clair blinked. "But you were the one threatened."

"Exactly. It's *he* who crossed the moral line the moment he uttered the words. It is *he* who is coercing *me*, but I don't have to be a miserable victim. I can make my own conditions, and it's not wrong to not be as wretched as possible. Does that make *any* sense?"

"Ah," said Clair. "Is this related to the difference between doing evil and being evil?"

"That's a part," Liere said, breathing deeply as she glanced around. "I never really considered it. Well, I couldn't, because I was also ignorant about disirad. But this place has the same effect as the disirad plateau, doesn't it? Intensifying everything in the realm of the spirit, but affording a sense of distance, if one needs it."

Clair rocked back and forth on her chair, a whole-body nod. "It does, it does, it does. It took a long time, but the presence of the disirad in this place helped to clear all Ilerian's poison from the realm of the spirit for me. And so, I want to learn how to do that for other people. But talking about that can wait, because your dilemma is immediate."

"I still don't know what Detlev meant about weapons. But he could be wrong. He himself admits that he's been wrong many times. My thinking now is this: to save my son's life—to try to prevent more civil war—I'll lend Macael my body to get his heir. But the wrong is his. The wrong is *wholly* his. Not mine, even if, in itself, it turns out not to be a terrible experience."

Clair recoiled, then apologized.

"What is it?" Liere asked. "If I've trespassed—"

Clair raised a hand. "Siamis's memories. They do sometimes obtrude. I'm learning how to protect myself from them. But meanwhile, permit me to earnestly assure you that making it a terrible experience would not, in *any* way, make it right. This goes back to our beginnings as humans in this world.

Macael Elsarion is taking a step, as Skadi-Erai did, back toward that path."

"I see that, yes," Liere said. "I'd forgotten about that."

"Skadi's name dropped out of history," Clair said grimly. "And new laws were passed. This deal of yours, have you told people?"

"I haven't. I can't see a way to without risking people fighting on my behalf. Which I don't want, even if Malcolin's life wasn't in the balance! But now that I think about it, Jauni's thought means the servants are talking. So, it's going to get out. Even if I say nothing, some might put it together."

Clair rocked again, harder. "Yes, yes, yes. Though you'll find that many won't care, or will find it makes political sense. But there will be consequences. The Sartoran Mage Guild for one, surely."

"The Mage Guild?" Liere repeated on a flat note.

Clair comprehended what was unsaid. "They have done some stupid things. And have had those catch them up hard. For example, their treatment of Hibern, before she came back having single-handedly dismantled Norsunder Beyond entirely on her own. Oh, you ought to hear Erai-Yanya on that subject!"

"I didn't know Hibern was back from Songre Silde," Liere admitted. "I was furious at the way they treated her early in the war, when she and I were defending Eidervaen. Despite how hard Atan tried to get them to accept her. What happened?"

Clair's grin flashed. "Lilith asked Hibern to report the Songre Silde accord to the Sartoran mages. Hibern said that when she got to Eidervaen, at first they stood like a bunch of statues at such a distance from her that she wondered if she should go around the corner and do a quick sniff test, in case she'd trod in something and began to stink. But then it hit her this was what *respect* looked like. I think it was closer to awe. Anyway, flawed as they are, when they hear about this matter, and you can be sure it will get to them, it will not bode well for swift mage help at reasonable cost to Macael Elsarion. It strikes all the way back to our beginnings with magic, and the earliest mages eradicating sexual coercion."

"As I said, I never thought of that," Liere admitted.

"No," Clair said softly, sober again. "It's good that you

didn't. It's excellent, because it hasn't been a problem for millennia, though it clearly comes up once in a while. Such as in Macael's threat. Skadi-Erai's, long ago. Oh-ho, Atan will have something to say as well. I pity the Adrani ambassador! Anyway, the debate about whether such things are part of our human nature or not belongs to another time. But that brings up another question: what if you do get a child?"

"In truth, I haven't put much thought there. Though if it happens, of course that is the next dilemma. If he thinks a child will keep me around to continue hostaging for Enaeraneth good behavior, he will get a surprise. But also, if he thinks I'll dump her and run, he's in for another surprise."

"Her?" Clair asked.

Liere blushed. "Maybe because of Lyren, I tend to think of prospective children as girls. Malcolin was quite a surprise!"

"Did you sense him before birth?"

"Of course I did. But I tried not to, except to send calm and peaceful and loving thoughts. And of course there is no awareness of gender in infants before birth, so Malcolin was just a forming sentience, who jumped around inside when he—or I—heard bird calls, and the like." Liere's reminiscent smile faded. "I might have to leave her with Macael—that is still a question—but I will be in contact. Macael has no idea how adept I am at that, because he's been inside that mental shield of his. But I can tell you, the first sign of unhappiness caused by him or whoever he puts as caretaker, and I will carry her away, and proclaim why to any who hear me. And he'll get his heir back only when she turns eighteen, or twenty, or even thirty, and has been educated far away from his bloody-handed ways. But all that is so very hypothetical. So much depends on who she is, and how he acts, and of course, I still must be careful with my own bitter herb thoughts reaching her before she's born. Oh, if only we had training in Dena Yeresbeth and pregnancy!"

"Actually, we do," Clair said.

"What?"

"We have all those records Detlev had kept hidden. Roy, Arthur, Adam, Yanli, Erai-Yanya, Lilith, and Hibern, are busy translating them. Along with others at Curtas's House. Lilith can't always be around. She still looks out for the fifth world, and I believe Siamis has been on Geth, though I haven't heard from him directly since he left me on the plateau after the war."

Liere said, "Did you have a falling out?"

"Not in the least. I finally figured out that he was giving me the time to heal, to not exist in his shadow, as I had during the war. He couldn't even tell me that, or I'd have insisted I was fine, but neither of us would have been sure I wasn't being a dependent rather than a friend. Yanli agrees with me. My Aunt Murial as well."

"I see. And I agree, for what little that is worth."

Clair smiled quickly. "Thank you. As for those records, sometimes the work slows until Detlev or Lilith can explain the more figurative language, and the missing assumptions that everyone knew then. But we're uncovering life under the ancients, little by little. That includes the use of the dyr, and the study of the affinities, which is my particular interest. Your situation comes under the heading of the affinity of parent with child. There's an entire book just on that. Maybe more than one. Though we only have the first page of that book done. There is so much to do! It's like ... like scrubbing a mossy, smoke-blackened wall to discover golden inlay beneath, in beautiful patterns."

Learning—translating—paradigm—the longing to be a part of that seized Liere. "Detlev twice invited me to go to their school to learn about the dyr. Now I see why. It's exactly what I love best," Liere breathed. "Oh, I want to go right now."

It was then that she recollected herself, and the time.

And the dilemma that had brought her.

Her smile flattened to determination. "Thank you for listening to me, Clair. I'll be back for more talk, and not just about my woes. I want to hear more about your plans for this palace, but first I must straighten out my life."

Clair barely had time to tell her she'd be welcome before Liere vanished.

Back in Brydon, she saw that she had been gone through most of morning. It was time to keep the promise to be seen. She looked outside. The weather had finally cleared after weeks of snow, sleet, and rain. She dressed warmly and went out.

That day, few recognized her, with her knit hat hiding hair

and ears, the rest of her bundled into her coat with a cloak over that to ward the icy wind. Those few who knew her immediately cast their widened gazes toward the patrolling Adranis, then kept their distance. Most bowed, with such deliberation it had to be a gesture of significance. She bowed back, a conscious decision to remind them that the fiction of her being a queen would end with the next year.

When her fingers, toes, and nose began to numb despite her consciously raising her inner warmth, she returned. It was mid-afternoon, and the inevitable result of bringing up her core temperature had left her actually hungry for once. The day servant brought a hot meal. She sat down to it, opened Arthur's book on Sartoran origins, and began to read.

16

Each morning Liere drank gerda mixed with Sartoran steep, which cut the taste to a not-unpleasing astringency that brought back the days before her pregnancy with Malcolin. How happy she and Andri had been! How much Liere had wanted another child, and another, to recreate the happy sort of family life she had only seen in other people!

Each cloudless morning, she ventured into the city. Gradually, people emerged to speak to her. At first general inquiries, but before too long she was drawn into conversations—confessions—unburdenings.

She chose her words carefully, always offering sympathy first, for those in genuine grief. For those from whom she sensed a seeking for an excuse to target Adranis, she spoke words of peace. Sometimes the result was sharp disappointment, even a glare of accusation. Those hurt. But mostly, acceptance, from grudging to relieved.

She knew that these conversations got repeated. She tried to be simple and clear, to minimize distortion of her words. By the dawn of New Year's Firstday, she saw fewer of those who wanted to fight; they were no longer counting on her to figurehead their potential retaliations.

When Liere was announced by the Herald at court on New Year's Firstday Enaeraneth nobles stiffened, covertly glancing at one another for clues. They still felt like hostages in their own country. Which in fact they were.

The Adrani nobles Macael had invited to attend Oath Day looked over at that slender figure in the black robe, two among them thrown back in memory to the wintry night during the war when this beautiful young queen arrived alone to attend Macael and Chantala's wedding, the candelabra overhead making a crown of her golden hair and glimmering over her blue silk gown.

It had been Halli Elardian, a mid-ranking Adrani noble, who had come forward to greet her. Now it was the king himself, who walked all the way to the door, and courteously offered his arm. Liere looked ethereal in her unrelieved black, her simply braided hair shining in the brilliant candlelight. Her fingers rested in the air above the king's arm as they paced side by side by side to the chair that served as a throne, where he insisted with a soft word that she seat herself, and he stood at her right, next to a gold-inlaid table bearing a seal, paper, pens, and a stack of bound ledgers.

Liere was grieved, but not surprised, to see downcast faces and averted eyes from the Enaeraneth gathered there. Do you feel like a traitor not to have died? she thought, wishing she could speak. Has life become so distorted, then? But it wasn't life that distorted, it was power, and its proximity.

She shifted her attention to Halli Elardian's friendly, encouraging smile beneath her shocked eyes: Beautiful Liere was, but also wan and far too thin, especially contrasted with their last meeting at the king's wedding.

Liere was a little relieved to see one of Chantala's few actual friends. It was enough to steady her: she was there to listen, and to make peace. She saw that they were in the small ballroom, the largest antechamber off the throne room, newly fitted up, the walls freshly replastered and painted with stylized lilies of green and blue and yellow-gold. The furnishings were ornate, gilt, with blue cushions, and potted plants stood in elegant groupings, green fronds arcing grace-fully. Firesticks burned steadily in the fireplaces at either end of the room.

Macael was hearing the petitions that landholders could make before speaking the oaths that would bind them for the year. To break it was treason, the penalty not just death, but confiscation of property. It was the Enaeraneth who spoke, some trying to hide fear, and humiliation, as they tried to fumble their way to an accord with the enemy.

The young Baras of Pausand stood before Macael, making a perfect formal bow, her hands hidden in her long sleeves as she said, "Before I can speak the oath you ask of us, I wish to present a petition."

Macael said, "Please."

She sent a look at Liere, perplexed, unhappy, muted anguish in the tension under her eyes. What to expect? Andri would have waved a casual hand, encouraging her by saying, come, have a glass of wine. Talk it over in comfort.

The baras shifted her gaze back to Macael standing there beside the throne, and lifted her chin. "I can house and feed the warriors you have s-placed on my holding. Just." Her voice had risen, but again she stopped, her throat working. She was a young woman, the sister of one of Andri's friends before the war. Young, and dedicated to managing a difficult land, there in the southern corner of Enaeran on the border of Danith, directly above the treaty-kingdom of Ghend.

Macael waited. They all waited, and Liere found her own hands gripping tightly in her lap as she willed strength to the baras.

Who straightened her shoulders. "I can house them, as required. But the guilds in both my towns say that they cannot compass the added expense of your, your *guard*, and the abolition of the import taxes."

Macael replied, "I do not recall the exact figures, but your guild taxes of last year indicate an ability, if not a willingness, to comply."

"Last year," she said, "was a very good year." Her voice rang with suppressed emotion, and a stir through the court caused her to redden.

"It's true," Liere said softly, to shift attention to herself and permit the baras time to recover. "The years after the war were especially hard, there in the south. The import taxes helped the recovery. Meanwhile, there is no comfortable margin in case of bad years coming back."

Macael glanced through a ledger on the side table. "Thank you. I will look more deeply into the guild records."

More whispers, and a stiffening from one or two of the guild chiefs as Macael turned to the baras. "There will be no difference in prices between this side of the two rivers and the eastern side," Macael said, and though he did not raise his voice, or sharpen it, they all felt the finality of royal fiat. "But as I explained before, I did not intend the guard to be established there permanently. Their orders are to refrain from interfering with trade, or the conduct of your affairs. They are there to see that the roads are clear in that region. The Road Guild will furnish the wherewithal." His soft voice was uninflected, but his glance toward the Road Guild Chief caused that woman to shift slightly in her chair, her invincible smile that Liere had believed so friendly and confiding now looking rather forced. Her mind-shield was as tight as ever.

"You will keep the prices as required, but I will grant quartering vouchers to the commander, for use in your towns, for two years," Macael continued. "Which the Road Guild will honor." Behind him, one of his well-trained, well-groomed scribes wrote it all down, quill flickering rapidly over the ledger. "We will review the situation then, and if there is no more need for the guard, the matter will resolve itself."

In other words, if there was no trouble, there would be no guard. And though she retained a mind-shield, it was clear that the embezzling Road Guild chief was beginning to understand how much trouble she was in, as the baras saw that she had gotten as much compromise as she was going to. She bowed again, and then in a voice so controlled it sounded dead, she spoke the oath of support and obedience. And then bowed again, and withdrew to her chair, to hold hands tightly with a balding man in plum silk.

It was now an elderly duchas's turn, a duchas old during Adon Marsael's days, suave, experienced, dry. He spoke his oath with a sort of weariness that indicated he put little trust in any human pledge.

Liere made herself listen to his words, and those of the people who came after, some angry, some grieved, one or two fearfully obsequious. None were comfortable, unlike the merry Oath Days of Andri's reign.

A few questions came her way, as Macael had promised. After her years compounding with the exchequer, she knew the kingdom well enough to suggest areas of compromise where none might have suggested itself before. But these were suggestions, underscoring that her tenancy as royal treasurer of Enaeran had ended. She caught herself feeling disjointed, though the sight of the stiff, apprehensive Road Guild Chief right in front was a reminder that Liere's judgments had not been irrefutable.

Macael listened, permitting no other talk if Liere spoke. At the last, when it was over and Liere rose to withdraw, the people bowed to her, some with deliberate meaning and others with formal honor, under Macael's inscrutable gaze.

She was still a queen, then, however anomalous; it was the way Trevor-Macael Elsarion willed it. Her people obeyed with evidence of relief, and his with care.

MARLOVEN HESS

Marend Ndarga stood with the other jarls and jarlans in the great throne room in Choreid Dhelerei's royal castle.

The time was noon, and as the bells rang out, the voices in the throne room spoke their oaths in cadence, reaffirming their vows to protect and defend the kingdom. Marend reveled in it all: the huge, vaulted room, the voices echoing up into the far reaches, the ancient banners hung high up on the walls: the black and gold screaming eagle, flag of the Marlovens, hanging high over the throne.

She gloried in the sight of the throne, symbol of power. And she gloried, with trembling passion, in the sight of the king on that throne. She spoke those ancient land-vows with the heartfelt conviction of a marriage vow as she kept her gaze on him, garnishing for later memory every detail of his black and tan uniform, flattering a faultless body, his light curling hair worn short, his subtly changeable eyes now the color of smoke against a winter sky, keen as they met the gazes of every one of his liege people. His head turned, and she felt his attention nearing, nearing, then he met her eyes and heat flashed through her, almost blinding her until she remembered to breathe again. She dared a look—just to discover that his gaze had already moved on.

In the past, rulers had forced the Jarls to speak one at a time, some of them even to kneel, to abase themselves here at Convocation, a reminder of who was at the top of the chain of command. Senrid-Harvaldar did none of that.

And yet he looked so very kingly as the roomful of people finished the oaths on a shout and struck their fists against their chests, a satisfying thud in unison, one kingdom, one will: *Marloven Hess is our homeland.*

Marend wished, again, that the jarls and jarlans wore uniform as they had in the past—that is, during the years that Marloven Hess had had a uniform. She had discovered, while delving through history, that that had not always been the case: in the far, far past, before the Ndargas came to command at Methden, jarls and jarlans wore House colors in battle gear, considered barbaric now but which she secretly thought splendid.

Secondday was the candidate trials; she paid scant heed to the goings-on with guilds and the like in the state wing, and she was not privy to the outgoing seniors' new assignments. Of primary importance to her was the academy and her own candidates' performances.

Thirdday meant senior exhibitions by those academy seniors going off to their year of service—or, in the case of foreigners, home.

Below, the riders raced back and forth across the magic-swept parade ground, some dancing from saddle to ground and back again, others throwing spears through tiny rings, all at magnificently controlled gallops. From the comments of the crowd, most eyes were drawn to a pair of foreigners, especially the dark, exuberantly handsome one. The foreigners were dressed like the rest of the seniors, but their long hair gave them away.

"Savona … Remalna … where is that? Some flyspeck of a kingdom somewhere … king's allies…" Marend half-listened as she covertly swept the stands for the king himself. She had no interest in fly-speck kingdoms half the world away. Or in larger ones, for that matter.

Hatch Senelac dropped down beside her. "Did you want me to compete in the captains' games tomorrow?"

She was surprised. "There is a question?"

"You declined your spot in the lists."

She'd hoped he hadn't seen that. To the others she'd said she did not feel well, after the long journey, but she could never lie to Hatch Senelac, curse him. Not even in their academy days, when she'd competed so desperately against him.

Her face heated. "Danna from the coast is here," she

admitted, in a low voice, though no one in the stands paid them the least heed. Most attention was on the horses cantering in the far corral to warm up, and on the seniors setting up for archery demonstrations.

Senelac thought of the splendid Danna Taraca, the young Jarlan of Eveneth. He gave Marend his old academy smile. "If you can't be the best you won't compete, eh?"

She flushed, just as she had when a girl. "It's not my personal honor at stake, it's Methden's."

"There's no dishonor in losing against someone that good. I can't guarantee I'll win, since David the Heir showed up this morning, and word is, he will also compete tomorrow. Good I am, but you and I both know he's better." No need to remind them of their early academy days, right after the war, when some of them had made the mistake of trying to lynch David for reasons that at this remove were no longer even clear.

What Hatch Senelac did remember, with acute clarity, was David's apologetic attitude when he dislocated Hatch's shoulder before he whirled around and dealt with the rest of the gang. Alone. No weapons, even, and Hatch knew at least two of the would-be lynch mob had been carrying knives.

He shook his head, smiled, then asked, "Do you want me to resign from the list?"

Marend refused to think about David, just as she avoided talking to him. The sight of those acute brown eyes reminded her too much of past mistakes—of the pain of Retren's long silence. Her fault. Her fault.

"There is no will or want here," Marend said, more tartly than she meant. "You know we are equals. We acquitted ourselves well with our student candidates. Corand and Lendred are in, as we'd hoped. The rest of the week is just games."

"Just games," he said, and laughed, but he said nothing more as he turned one of those splendid shoulders and sauntered away, raising a hand in greeting to the Captain of the City Guard, one of their old academy mates.

He vanished into the crowd, and Marend, feeling unaccountably irritated, realized she had no interest whatever in those seniors performing so well down there. Ordinarily she would be watching for new refinements in sword technique, except she knew that Hatch would do the same.

She scanned the stands. The king was still not in sight. Tdor had said sympathetically the night before Marend and Hatch left for Convocation, *Ask, Marend. Ask the king straight out if there's a chance for you, and if he says no, then ride on.*

Maren passed down through old stone archways that had heard the echo of Marloven voices for centuries, then unexpectedly encountered Daltan, even more gray-haired.

During the war Daltan had been a mere cobbler, her shop serving as the headquarters for the Resistance. When Marend first arrived at the academy, Senrid had had her stay with Daltan. They'd spent some time trading stories—though Marend had never told her about Imry Llyenthur.

Daltan, stout and imperturbable, looked up. "And a welcome to you, Marend," she said. "Enjoying the Games?"

"As always," Marend said. "But it's getting colder by the moment, and I'll see more sword battles tomorrow, when the captains compete."

Daltan studied the vivid little creature before her, the straight black brows, the changeable gray eyes. Daltan had not admitted to Marend what she knew about her near betrayal of the kingdom, and the close call with Retren.

Marend had been not quite fifteen, twisted by someone far beyond her wit and strength, and she'd worked hard, none harder, to overcome her own sense of dishonor. She had not after all betrayed the kingdom, the king himself had taken up her cause, and had seen her brother Retren safely out of the kingdom to a new life.

The problem was, about the time Marend learned how to be a human being, she also discovered love. Daltan had watched it happen, knowing that both Marend and the king were far too prickly for anyone to give the slightest hint of the obvious. The king had given Marend Hatch Senelac as her commander, the best, and incidentally the handsomest, of all the career warriors; Marend took no more notice of him than she would a new horse. Less. To the rueful disgust of many young women.

And so Daltan said, with care, "Oh, news? Not much. No change, really. Another year, another harvest, another crop of pups to be trained." She smiled.

Marend breathed freely, not realizing until then that she'd been tense. Daltan didn't babble about things that didn't matter, and she always knew just what to report.

So the king was not courting, or that would have been news. And no one was courting him—but then no one would mention favorites, who had nothing to do with leading a kingdom. Or had that come a little too quick, a little too ready?

Marend sent a troubled glance at Daltan, who then went on in the smoothest way to describe how her son had just promoted in the nascent navy, and how exciting life was there when the occasional pirate tried forays from Land's Bridge northwards.

To which Marend only listened with a part of her attention. No, she'd said what she had because there really was no other news. The king was safe, he worked, there was no one worthy of the Marloven crown. It was Marend's goal to be worthy. But the king had to *see* her first. How could he, when he worked day and night?

She was smiling when she took her leave of Daltan.

But Daltan only shook her head, and returned to her work. She had five bets going that there would never be a queen, bets she hoped she would lose; she was fond of Senrid, but she just didn't see that things would ever change.

$$\sim\!\!\text{\textbf{17}}\!\!\sim$$

"The most common speculation," Rel said to Atan about ten days after he and CJ began their journey into Enaeran, "is, 'What is Sartora going to do?'"

He sat on his bedroll under a cloudy sky, hunkered under his thick coat and cloak, while CJ lay asleep in their tent on the other side of the campfire. He didn't care much for this seeing-stone magic. It made him dizzy if he used it while walking. He sat cross-legged with the thing in both hands, staring directly down into it at Atan's face. She did much the same.

"I take it the hostage year is universally known?"

"Seems to be. She has to stay a year to protect the peace, that's how most put it, though many added with side-glances that it's to protect the prince's life," Rel said. "Their boy is as popular as Andri was. Local youngsters all seem to know the name of his favorite horse, and that he'd trained birds to eat off his palm, and that he had been good with a sword and bow for his age. As for Liere, the consensus seems to be that for a foreigner, she's wonderful—especially given her 'real' identity as Sartora. There's a lot of pride in the fact that the world-famous Sartora chose their king to marry, and their kingdom to settle in."

Atan sighed. "What are the attitudes toward the cousin?"

"Admired by Adranis. Had been liked in Enaeran, leaving mixed emotions. Betrayal, hatred. That's the easy way to sum up what I've been hearing."

"And CJ?"

Rel grinned. "Traveling with CJ is just like old times. Minus the pie fights. She's decided that Macael Elsarion is a villain, so she gives every improvement a death glare, and mumbles a lot about doom."

'Sounds like she's there for your entertainment, and little else," Atan commented wryly.

"You'd be wrong. She volunteered to try the jail test."

"Got herself arrested, to see what underlies their way of governing?"

"Exactly. Collared for theft. Violence seems to get a different handling, but she was not willing to test that, nor I."

"Please don't," Atan said, heartfelt. "And you can thank her, for me, for shielding you, if you had to use yourselves for such an experiment. I've heard of too many situations in which big men, tall men, attract bullies simply because of their size. And prison-keeping too often is a popular job for bullies."

"A serious answer! Here I was hoping that you would warn me that Sartor's prestige would be shaken if it got about that the mighty King Rel was behind bars."

"I'd love to see who would foster the rumor, and in what words," Atan said grimly.

"Ah, we already know. Our irritants are at least predictable," Rel replied with his usual deadpan humor. "Unlike Macael Elsarion, cousin, popular king, and assassin. In any case, my Lisdan disguise serves me well. Too late to grow the beard, but I put gray in my hair, and use the walking stick. No one gives me any trouble. CJ has her medallion, so if there's any danger, she promised Clair to transfer out. She says there are no wards here at all. You'll know what that means better than I."

"And?"

"The result was what CJ calls the Aunt Naggy treatment. You can either sit in durance for a specified time, or you can work your sentence off for the cost of the labor and materials, pretty much what we have. There's no pay, just as we do in Sartor, as it's restitution, but if they like you and you like them, you might get a job, and the business gets some sort of tax voucher from the local guildhall for taking you on."

"A little different from our system, but same idea. Why is that naggy?"

"Because the sentence came with a long lecture about vagrants turning into thieves, and thieves into troublemakers, especially when there was a sign right across the street stating that laborers were wanted. And there are plenty of apprenticeships to be had, hoola loo. CJ claimed the lecture was far worse than the work. There are apparently also follow-ups, but as she used a false name and origin, they will not be benefitting from her opinions about their nagging. Also, it didn't take long to get herself arrested, which she terms the Big Brother treatment."

"Big Brother?"

"One of her homeworld terms, meaning there is a high condition of alertness. And the wherewithal to carry it out. Judging by the number of armed and uniformed Adranis I see, his army must be huge."

"We already knew that," Atan said. "It was large enough to occupy the entire eastern end of the continent during the war. That large an army from one kingdom must be crushingly expensive to maintain. Of course, we know that Bartal looted voraciously. But that plunder would be gone by now."

Rel said slowly, "And we never heard of Macael Elsarion disbanding huge numbers."

"He'd be insane to turn masses of highly trained warriors onto the streets all at once," Atan said. "Suddenly I am very interested in exactly what he's done there since the war. We've heard about improvements, peace, and popularity, but what does that translate out to?"

Rel gave her a grim smile. "We seem to be thinking along the same lines. I don't want to make any accusations, at this point, but I cannot help remembering Detlev's casual suggestion that we form a fleet to cruise the Sartoran Sea in order to watch for trouble."

Atan's brows rose. "I thought that meant pirates. Do you think Detlev foresaw an Adrani attempt to expand into an empire?"

"Again, I don't want to say anything without proof. Yet."

Atan paused, and her face distorted as she leaned into the scry stone closer, so that Rel was gazing right up her nose. "There's something else, isn't there? I can hear it in your voice."

The impulse to grin vanished like a puff of vapor. "Mentions of Macael's dead wife are rare. It's as if she's almost forgotten. CJ had never even heard of her. I find it sad."

Atan nodded. "Do they speculate on whether he killed her as well?"

"No one in Enaeran seems to care. From what little we've overheard from Adrani guards, the few mentions paint a picture of a very weak young woman who was sickly and largely incapable of governing. From no one, not even Elsarion's outspoken enemies, have I heard any speculation about Chantala na Shagal's death. Even though she died in Enaeran, and he apparently had half an army in position—but that had been under the prospect of winter maneuvers, run by both border guards."

Atan said, "An exercise run in Enaeran."

"Correct. Joint maneuvers. With Andri's full cooperation. He was reported to have been looking forward to the fun. Until the morning Andri was killed, and his people crawled out of their tents to find themselves at sword-point. Or in the case of some of the captains, never crawled out at all."

Atan pursed her lips. "Planned down to the last detail."

"As you say."

"You are finished, then?"

"CJ wants to stay through the rest of New Year's Week, as there's been a lot of free food and music and the like. It remains only to see Liere and Elsarion in person, if we can. Barring a bad storm we should reach Shiovhan tomorrow."

It was late on Thirdday when they reached Shiovhan. They were able to secure a corner of an attic room in an inn. They shared this attic with a large family accompanying a grandparent who was required to bring a regional report to a guild.

They were in time to forage among the last of the offerings in a local square. They carried their pickings up and ate in the attic, talking in Mearsiean, while the family's children played a fast game of Cards'n'Shards and the adults gossiped.

"The worst thing," CJ admitted, "is that even I can tell there are a few people who just want someone to lead them in rising against that slob of a Trevor Macael. And I don't mean just here. I've heard it all along, since we crossed the border. Especially in jail, before the naggers dispersed us to work off our sentences. But they all talk about revenge, and Banan—I mean, Andri being knifed in the back, and not anything else, like bad taxes, or mean laws, or nasty governors."

Rel set aside his empty plate. "In justice, I must point out that many of these same people either don't know about—or shrug off—the fact that Andri's branch of the Elsarions took the throne from Macael's branch through violence, a couple generations ago. And there was more violence when Andri's father was deposed."

"So no one is right," CJ muttered, the light of the fire reflecting in her eyes as she glared. "I hate that. I hate it."

From their very first encounter years ago, Rel had learned that CJ craved seeing justice done. She preferred villains to be utterly evil, and friends to be utterly in the right, and that action would cleanly resolve conflicts for the side of good. To give her credit, Rel knew that she strove mightily to be a good person, though she had apparently come from a background in which violence against children was common.

Nothing they saw here so far divided neatly into good and bad categories.

CJ was still sighing over that the next morning, as they slung their travel gear over their shoulders and trudged up the zigzagging road to the royal palace visible on a ridge above the city. "I know that look you're giving me. I am very aware that my opinion is mostly grudge. I'm not sure I like the way this creepy cousin wants to know what everybody is doing in this kingdom. Not all the people like it either, from what I can tell. He can *say* he's trying to circumvent riots and stuff, buuuuut I dunnooooo...." Her voice descended to a drawl of doom.

"All the more reason to end our scouting mission by taking a look for ourselves at how he handles things, don't you think?"

They had heard from several directions that noon was when the royal palace doors opened to anyone, for the remainder of New Year's Week. From the stream of people trudging between the piles of snow, it seemed that others had the same idea.

They joined a crowd in the courtyard outside the palace entrance. CJ bounced on her tiptoes, scanning the others. Rel looked around, noting alert guards. No weapons drawn, but no one was asleep on the job.

The doors opened as the distant tower carillon rang, and the crowd began to shuffle inside. Rel watched both guards at either side of the door sort him visually from the others, scan him for weapons, note the walking stick, then wave him through.

CJ pressed forward, cast one impatient glance Rel's way, then with a faint shrug disappeared in the crowd. Rel interpreted the glance successfully: she couldn't see much beyond heads and shoulders, and she was there to check on the ruler and hostage, so she'd squeeze her way forward in order to do that.

As usual Rel was taller than everyone around him. From the back, he was able to watch as the herald came forward and announced, "King Trevor-Macael and Queen Liere." No *their Majesties the King and Queen*. Nothing that coupled them. Custom or compromise?

They walked in side by side, both dressed in black, both strikingly handsome. They did not touch, not even their garments, as they sat in the two chairs on a dais.

The petitioners came forward then, apparently selected by the soft-footed, ubiquitous heralds in Elsarion blue. Only two armed guards were in sight, though that didn't mean there wasn't a host of others in some alcove off one of the archways beyond the throne area, as well as salted through the crowd. Elsarion himself appeared to be unarmed. Interesting. Had there been any assassination attempts? All appeared orderly, civilized.

Liere remained silent for the first interview or two. Trevor Macael Elsarion spoke briefly, and without raising his voice. As yet Rel couldn't hear him. The third petitioner caused him to turn his head and address Liere. He waited for her response, then made a slight gesture indicating agreement. To the fourth, only she spoke. Was that to CJ? No, Liere's manner was not even remotely familiar.

And so it went for a time. Rel remained at the back, content to shuffle forward slowly and watch the while.

Midway through the audience, CJ suddenly reappeared at Rel's elbow.

"Speak to her?" he murmured in Mearsiean. The quiet whispers of conversation around them served to afford them privacy.

"No. This is gunna sound weird, but I don't think I'm going to," CJ added, grimacing fiercely. "I never understood

Sartora much when she was a kid, but now, it's double that. Except she looks like she's made of ice." Another scowl. "Also, I came thinking we'd find her wrapped in clanking chains, and that I'd get to use my lockpicking tools." She patted her travel gear. "If we found her in the clink. But it looks to me like the chains might be … invisible? I don't get it. There's *something* stinky going on, my smidgen of DY is just enough to smell it, but I don't think talking to 'em is going to make anything clearer. I think I'll just go home, if you'll promise to have Atan zap a message to us if you find out anything we should know."

"I'll do that," he promised.

"Okay. See ya." She flapped a hand, and walked out of the audience hall. He assumed she'd find a secluded spot and transfer home from there.

He edged forward another small step, glad he'd promised to report on 'need to know' rather than 'interesting'. He found the scene before them very interesting, but not in ways he'd discuss with CJ, or Clair—or indeed most anyone save Atan and a rare few.

When Liere spotted him, she tensed subtly, and Rel mentally congratulated CJ on managing to stay unseen. It was clear that Liere didn't expect to see familiar faces from her past—nor did she particularly want to. But she beckoned to him. He hitched his travel gear and folded tent over his other shoulder and stepped forward.

Macael Elsarion finished speaking to an elderly woman, who bowed and was escorted away. Rel was now near the front of the crowd. They all made space, obedient to Liere's gesture, and Rel walked up to the dais.

Liere said, "Rel? What are you doing here?"

Elsarion's blue gaze narrowed. "Welcome, King Rel." There was no haughty disbelief at Rel's scruffy travel gear, no affront at a lack of warning for this visit that was clearly not a state visit. Macael's only reaction was the fast gaze-to-gaze appraisal of possible intent that you expected of the experienced leader.

"Thank you," Rel said, and to Liere, "I don't need a private audience. Atan wished to know how you were. Old time's sake."

Macael Elsarion rose politely. Rel discovered that Elsarion

was nearly his own height. Though they'd met before, that was on his own ground. Now he was in Macael's territory. A lifetime of habit caused Rel to evaluate Macael's potential as an adversary. He did not need to look for callused palms. The muscle-contours beneath that silk, and his stance revealed years of weapons training. Yet there was nothing in Macael Elsarion's manner to indicate that this wasn't simply another diplomatic encounter. "Please, join us in here?" He made a sign to a steward, who bade the crowd to wait.

Remembering Andri's careless egalitarianism, briefly encountered during the war, Rel decided as he followed the two mourning-clad figures into an adjacent chamber that Macael seemed to have inherited both family branches' worth of invincible politesse.

"Welcome," Elsarion said again, when it became apparent that Liere was not going to speak first. "Would you like food or drink?"

"Nothing, thanks," Rel said, setting his travel pack down at his feet.

"Was there a problem with the recall of the former ambassador?" Macael asked. Less politely: *Are you here to make trouble from the outside?*

"None," Rel said. And: *No, I'm not.*

Because he had no quarrel with Elsarion, and because Liere very clearly didn't want him there, he turned to her and said, "May I take a message back to Atan?"

Liere's hands were tense among the folds of her skirt. "Just my thanks for her concern, and my greetings."

Macael looked from one to the other, nodded courteously to Rel, and went out.

Liere watched him go.

When the door had closed softly behind him, Liere said, "Rel, I am as well as can be expected. I don't want to be here, but circumstances require it. A true act of friendship would be to tell Atan that I'll see her when I'm finished here."

"Fair enough," Rel said, bending to retrieve his gear. "If you change your mind, you know where we are. I'll transfer from here, then." He showed her the transfer token Atan had given him. When she nodded, he vanished.

When the transfer malaise had worn off, he went up the

back way and changed into what he privately thought of as his king costume. Once the clothes were on he didn't mind them, for everything was chosen with comfort a priority, but his preference was still for his old travel togs, and it was with a real feeling of regret that he passed them through the cleaning frame and then laid them in their cedar chest.

This was one point on which he and Atan differed, and he rather enjoyed it. The exigencies of their respective childhoods had required them both to wear others' castoff clothing. Rel didn't mind, and had never minded. Atan loathed old clothes — would give up a favorite gown when she saw it looking worn. This evidence of vanity in someone who otherwise never troubled herself about her looks delighted him.

He was still smiling when he found her. They did not immediately talk of his visit, for there were the children to greet, and then there was Sartoran business to catch up on, and finally there was supper as a family. After, their children ran off, and they followed more slowly, and sat on the balcony in the residence wing overlooking the big room that had been adapted to a winter playroom. They sipped warm spiced wine and watched their three play an elaborate game of hide and seek. Rel noted lazily that the rules kept changing. Who among them would want to do some traveling? Two talked about it. He wondered if he ought to go with them if it ever became a serious wish, or if he ought to let them have their adventures on their own.

"What are you thinking about?" Atan asked.

"Our youngsters." He told her his thoughts.

She looked down, her fingers playing with her wineglass. "What's the right thing? I confess it's hard for me to decide because I never could understand wanting to wander."

"You had a homeland to worry about."

She lifted a shoulder slightly. "So did Julian. So did you."

"I never felt any kinship with any one land. Maybe it was the way I was raised."

"I think it's born into you, like writing with right hand or left. All three of our children make up games about distant lands."

"Doesn't mean they'll all want to go."

"If we can just keep the peace ..." She shook her head, then said, "Never mind that now. Tell me about Liere. Clair wrote a short time before you returned to say that CJ was back in Mearsies Heili, and that she was disturbed enough by what she saw that she left before you. I did not inquire further; I assumed you'd tell me about it."

"I stayed long enough to speak to Liere, to be told that she is handling the situation on her own."

"Something's happened," Atan said with conviction. "Something she doesn't like."

"Such as?"

"Tell me everything you saw."

He described his observations in detail, including the suppressed intensity with which Elsarion regarded the widow of the cousin he'd assassinated.

Atan listened silently all the way through, her glare at the fire surprisingly a lot like CJ's. "I don't really know what to think. Too many conjectures running through my mind, with no way to support them. But one thing is certain: she wants to handle it on her own. Also: Trevor Macael Elsarion might not realize just how much trouble he's brought on himself, should she choose to unleash it. Because she is still the girl who climbed onto a horse made of lightning and rescued the world."

❧ **18** ❧

Liere had read up to the 4100s when she reached the thirteenth day. Everyone knew that conception was less likely to happen until a woman had been ingesting the herb for at least a couple of weeks.

Before Thani left for the night, Liere said, "Thank you," as she always did. Then she said firmly. "Will you pass on to Fan that tomorrow will mark the two weeks?"

Thani bowed, not hiding a little smile of anticipation, for she was a romantic. Liere turned away, to hide her own irritation with Thani's well-meant but utterly misplaced idealism. Thani was not cruel or unfeeling, but to her, Andri was less a person than a bad king they were well rid of. But she'd never known him. Only knew of him. Liere could not fix that now.

It was late. She closed her eyes and reached for Malcolin, who as usual was not shielded. It was early evening in Marloven Hess. She sensed him in the middle of a game, and withdrew quietly before he sensed her. He was happy, kept busy by Fenis Senelac's family.

Liere then sent a tendril to Lyren, whose moods were the quintessence of summer thunder: she was dancing, apparently at a local wedding. Again, Liere withdrew before she was sensed: she needed to solve her dilemmas before facing Lyren. Right now it would hurt too much to catch even a whiff of *See? I told you so.*

The next day, she worked through her exercises, then walked to a new neighborhood until sleety rain drove her back inside. She warded off the Adrani servants' offers of hot baths, hot drinks, and fine clothes laid away in summer herbs and warmed over the fire; she thanked everyone, aware that the Adranis in her immediate vicinity were in a mood of expectation. They liked their king. They saw nothing wrong with him matching up with Liere.

Liere remained polite but aloof. It was easy enough to keep them at a polite distance, but much harder not to let herself get close to the Enaeraneth servants, with whom her sympathies lay. That day, they all seemed to find duties elsewhere; they had guessed at the bargain she'd had to make. But she would not acknowledge their sympathy, lest she find herself the figurehead of the very sort of revolt she was here to prevent.

She read as the sun continued its inexorable slide across the sky. At the end of the day, she was surprised when both Jauni and her mother approached her, after a more thorough than usual scouring and dusting and changing of all the linens. "Shall we make an herb bath?" Thani asked. "We have some very precious herbs, whose scent —"

"Not necessary, thank you," Liere said.

"You don't want your hair brushed out, or dressed?" Jauni asked, a little wistfully.

"It's not necessary. My braid is tidy enough for the night. Go enjoy your evening. I need nothing more."

The two exchanged glances, bowed, and left. Liere put her clothes through the cleaning frame and hung them on the clothes tree for the morrow, then pulled on her wrapper. She'd learned to sleep nude except on field exercises while she was in Geth. She loved the sensory delight of clean, sun-dried sheets against her flesh, and hated the binding of sleepwear on joints.

She might as well continue that now.

But as she stood in the bedchamber doorway, looking at the bed, she examined her emotions, aware that there were plenty of people for whom her situation would scarcely be worth a shrug. Andri, as it happened, would have been one. Even Dena Yeresbeth changed his opinion little about the intimacy of sex — though for Liere, it could intensify the sensory perception. Sex, for her, had never been casual.

She'd agreed to lend Macael her body to get his heir, but he would get nothing else of her. And maybe that was all he wanted? She didn't know what he thought of her. Did not care. She was not going to give more than necessary.

There was one candle lit in her outer room, and one in the

bedroom.

She could hear her own breathing.

Outside the midnight bell rang once. The castle guard made their rounds, everywhere else quiet. She had never, during all these years, sensed any hint of Macael Elsarion on the mental plane, yet she knew that he was near.

She wiped her palms down her sides, and huffed out her breath. All right, the time had come. At the sound of that quiet double-rap on the outer door, she said, "Enter," her voice flat.

He opened the door.

He was dressed in somber black with hints of white at neck and wrists, and the subtle gleam of silver at his waist. His gaze was grave, a hint of question; they were here together by his will, but he possessed enough grace to permit her the ordering of events.

She would not thank him for it. "Come within." She picked up the candle, and led the way into the bedroom. "Do you want the light?"

"Your choice," he replied, standing very near, but without making any move to touch her.

She made no answer, but walked to the far side of the bed, the candle flame flickering in her eyes, and lighting her hair to gold. She faced him straight on, eyes meeting eyes. "Did you kill Chantala?"

As she intended, the question stunned him enough that his shield thinned. Briefly. Less than a heartbeat, then it was back, strong as ever. But in that moment, she sensed the genuine shock — even horror — that her question induced.

Good.

Then he said, in the flat voice she had begun to recognize as a signifier that he was disturbed, "She was my childhood friend. And my responsibility. I tried to make her life as easy as I could."

"I saw that. But it's not answering my question."

"I did not kill her, but neither could it be called a natural death, because of the poison I had not known she had ingested until it was too late. As soon as the war ended, I called in the best healers I could find. They said different things — it is impossible to see inside a living body, as you know — but they all agreed that she would not live to see thirty. With care, they said, she might make it to twenty-five. I made it a priority to provide that care."

Liere knew that Chantala had reached twenty-eight. "So you brought her here to die, while you launched your plot," she said.

"She wanted to be here."

Liere knew that was true; it seemed that Macael's plot, then, had been shaped around her prospective death.

That changed nothing.

She set the candle down and snuffed it, and snuffed the other as well, so the room was dark, save for the soft blue square of moonlight painting half the bed, and half the rug beside it.

Moving into that square, she lifted a hand, undid the wrapper, and let it drop to the floor. "Here it is," she said, and struck her fist against her breastbone. "Sartora's body on loan." Her voice cracked on the name she hated. "Let's get this done."

She climbed into the bed, which was clean, and cold, and smooth. Each movement was deliberate, the opposite of invitation as she stretched out, and closed her eyes. Her body shifted when a weight joined her on the mattress, and she heard the sounds, so like the sounds made by a once living man: the thunk of shoes, one, two. The whisper of cloth being removed.

His first touch made her jump, and he lifted his hand, but then it was back, tentative, question implied, and implied in her lack of response was tacit permission, though no participation. She turned her face away with a jerk, lest he dare to try to kiss her.

He did not. His hand was warm, and smelled of sage-soap as he stroked the tightness from her forehead; somewhere he had learned the art of massage, and knew the exact muscles that began to pang first. She didn't want to, but she found it soothing, and the slight headache that seemed never to go away actually eased. She resented him for it, but then thought bitter herbs, and deep down a flutter of laughter steadied her. Patiently, he eased the tension from the sides of her jaw, then the back of her neck, one hand holding her head steady and sure, the other continuing those careful presses along the muscles until they smoothed into ribbon.

He moved to her shoulders, and the knotted muscles

beside her neck, until they, too, smoothed to ribbon. She hung onto her determination not to respond, but the physical tension altered subtly to a kind of tingle. The rest of her flesh, with its own direct needs, prickled with expectation, and when, at last, his hand drifted down, her physical self was ready.

The body's needs are simple, and unhidden, but the mind is more complex. Not for her the lies the mind can tell, pressing another's face over the reality of living, breathing flesh. She knew she lay with Macael Elsarion, and she sensed his intensifying desire. And she knew, presently, that he had the control, and the skill, to leash that desire long enough to kindle her physical response.

But she would give him nothing other than what was required. And so she sent her mind away, not into the world but above it in the world of waking dreams, roaming through remembered forestland, far from human beings and their expectations. Their passions.

She drifted alongside a river, sheltered by great cedar trees, and gazed down into the water to see, wavering, the pleached branches from overhead. She dove for the cold, the dark, but was caught by a warm summer wind, fragrant, caressing, soft, softer than a whisper. The warmth of the sun traced over her skin, splashing in the water, flinders of fire.

Around her the shadows swayed, leaves dipped in gold, drifting, one by one, against the lightening star-scattered sky. She turned, as turn she must, into the sun's lancing beams now running bright through every vein. Caught by the fire she stilled as the sun torched the trees, struck the river into molten gold, and fire-touched the stars.

When she became aware that her flesh was cold, she opened her eyes, and found herself alone.

MARLOVEN HESS

David walked through Senrid's castle, which was filled with at least a hundred people inside and out, and these were just the night watch. Yet, now, on the heels of New Year's Week, it seemed empty.

When he reached the third story, he began to consider the

idea that he wasn't just missing Senrid—easy enough to do in this huge warren of a castle, even when you know someone's schedule—but that Senrid was gone.

Steward: "I saw him this morning, but not since."

Study runner on night duty: "No, he hasn't been in his rooms this evening."

Watch captain: "No. Haven't seen him. Orders haven't changed."

The watch captain ended on an interrogative note, and David found himself promising to let the man know if there was any reason to think those orders might change. Idle questions could still turn in a heartbeat to alert, even ten years after the war began.

He reined hard on exasperation. It had been impulse to come here for the last couple of days of New Year's Week, late enough to avoid the ticklish matter of oaths, but early enough to see Senrid interacting with the people who carried out his will. To listen, to silently offer companionship, which was all his cousin would permit. This was the third day—the first of the new year—and they had exchanged maybe fifty words all told. It was time to get back to his own life, except where was Senrid?

He sped down a back way and into the Residence hall, in case there were any guests lingering, with whom Senrid felt obliged to spend time, and he almost ran down Marend Ndarga.

"David," she exclaimed. Her eyes were wide, anxious. "Have you seen the king?"

He forced himself to be cheerful. "Did you have an appointment with him that he appears to have missed?"

"No." She sighed. "Do you think he'll be back soon?"

"If he had to go south to Perideth, or on some diplomatic mission, he might be gone for a week," David said, quite kindly.

"Except they would know, wouldn't they?" She waved a hand. "His people, I mean."

"Well, then, might he not have his own concerns? Even a king is entitled to privacy at times."

Moments trickled by, measured out in heartbeats. Her eyes shifted between his, back and forth, as she tried to read him, and he only smiled, trying to convey sympathy while she struggled jealously against her own ghosts. He felt her win. Barely.

"Hatch is ready to go. We should ride out before the weather changes," she said, with a heroic try for detachment.

When she was gone, David sat down on a hassock, and considered. Why would Senrid leave? That would give a clue to where, since he had left no word with anyone. He once had had the habit of going off alone to mourn his daughter on various anniversaries, but it was nowhere near the time Crystal Ingrid had been murdered by Imry's hand. That had been in late summer. Her birthday had been in Ninthmonth.

Cursing under his breath, David fetched his coat and then transferred to their old underground hideout, where at one time Senrid had retreated to drink himself insensible. The hideout was cold and empty, the air thick with dust, obviously undisturbed for at least a year.

David stood there, a cold mage light burning in the air before him. He was missing something. The sense that he ought to know it kept him there in the freezing, dusty air as he mentally reviewed the week. Everything had gone well. Marend, poor little soul, had invented an excuse to stay, but Senrid had simply avoided her, as usual.

Marend — ah.

Liere.

Liere, and —

Oh, yes, that had to be it. But how would Senrid know? David reviewed people who might have blabbed. Busybodies who might dare to — no, wrong pathway. Many knew about her year's hostage stay, but no one, he would swear, about her other promise, outside of Detlev, Adam, Roy, and (according to Roy) Clair of the Mearsieans. Clair was as closed-mouthed as his own group.

Oh, but again he was thinking wrong. After years with Adam, he ought to remember that to certain people with extremely powerful sensitivity, little matters like physical distance ceased to have much meaning. Especially that inner ring who had trained so hard in order to ward Ilerian on the mental plane.

What had Senrid said that day, when Trevor Malcolin first

appeared? "She's alive, or I would know."

That was it. Without the least wish, Senrid was hearing Elsarion and Liere on the mental plane.

There was one other place he might be. David transferred to the other end of the mage-blasted forest of Darchelde, once one of the finest castles in the kingdom—where one could almost believe that Marlovens had their own form of art.

And there was the family castle, for several centuries a ruin. David saw no lights anywhere, just a confusing jumble of shadows, darker than the darkness of the sky, except where the ceiling had been breached, permitting starlight through. He made out the jagged remains of the great doors that had once protected his ancestors' citadel, and he walked in, sniffing mold, moss, and the cold stirrings of the air that soughs off stone. He heard the steady drip of water somewhere high above. Grim, but the blast of dark magic had nearly dissipated since David's initial visit early in the war, when he experimented with a very minor bit of the old magic, and set the dark magic enchantment to slowly unravel. Norsunder never noticed.

The effect was noticeable now.

The doors gave straight onto the Great Hall. David took a few cautious steps inside, and paused. Instinct had become conviction. If Senrid was anywhere, this would be the place.

And, after all, the huge chamber was not empty. Against the far wall, a high stone structure covered with moss, starlight limned blond hair.

"Who's there." Senrid's voice was short, a warning.

David focused, snapped his fingers, and summoned the old magic. Above them, in ancient sconces cold for nearly four centuries, fire sparked into being, revealing Senrid standing at the wall, one hand raised, palm flat against the stone.

"It is I," David said. "I came to find out whether you want me to stay in Choreid Dhelerei longer, or not." David made a little business of looking around the huge hall. "The infamous ancestral home!" He peered back at the tremendous double doors, high enough and wide enough to admit a coach-and-six, iron-reinforced and studded. Or had been, once, until they were blasted open by a tremendous force, and left standing ajar.

Get him talking. And Senrid echoed the thought, within the pain-bound fortress of his skull. I can talk, if he talks. Natter about the inconsequentials of the past.

He turned his back on the east, though he knew the gesture was futile; the fire he could not avoid sensing was on another plane entirely.

David turned his face upward, studying the vaulted ceiling. "Damn, this really is *old*. Much older than I initially thought."

"This room is all that's left of the Iascan days. The rest of the castle has been rebuilt two or three times, once to enlarge, once because it was destroyed in fighting. There's one corner of the residence wing that is supposed to be fairly civilized, though a century or two overdue for a cleaning."

"I wonder if Imry ever poked his nose in."

As usual, there was no response to the intrusion of Imry's name, not even here in the long-ago ruined citadel of their shared ancestors.

David tried to imagine what Inda had looked like, sitting up there on the wall, talking to a much younger Fox, and failed. "Hard to believe Inda left no records at all."

"Fox told us — Ivandred and me — that Inda hated writing. It wasn't that he couldn't do it. He was very well educated, before he got sent away from the academy. It had something to do with the method of communication, and Evred Montrei-Vayir riding him constantly. Of course, Fox was the first to admit that was his own bias. He enjoyed, he said, a robust and recreational hatred of Evred Montrei-Vayir."

David laughed. "That sounds like Fox."

"Something of Inda did survive, via the strangest path. One of his lovers was a Venn, whose story lay in a Venn archive. Erenlara of the Venn sent a copy through Sveneric not long ago. But then you probably knew about that," Senrid observed wryly.

David avoided the subject of what he knew or didn't know. "Oh, when you consider it, we have relatives all over the world. And so does everyone else." David bent to study the carving, sadly crumbled, of the raptor-claw legs of a great slate table set before the enormous empty fireplace. Then he hitched his hip over the corner, heedless of thick dust, which, disturbed, swirled lazily in the still, cold air. "Part of the reason why I think that the word 'family' is little more than a state of mind. But do go on. Tell me more. Does this Venn view of Inda present a villain completely contrary to legend? A cringing coward, cruel, his one world-renowned deed, the clearing of the strait, a mere accident?"

Senrid waved an impatient hand. "You can read the record yourself. It's easy, once you get past the archaic language. Forgotten now is that he seems to have refused to conquer a bigger empire than we held at the time."

"Didn't Fox say something of the sort?"

"He did, but Inda's laying down command seems to have struck deeper with the Venn. Especially given that he was regarded as the world's greatest military leader, defeating even the renowned Durasnir, but then he gave it all up, went home to teach at the academy, and after years of that, to ride his land and gossip with farmers and artisans."

"The Venn do like their hierarchies."

"If Erenlara is to be believed, they distribute authority more evenly across their tree, as they call it. Which is why their system has been relatively stable for centuries. Though it is still a pushcart."

"Pushcart?" David prompted.

Senrid turned his way. "You really don't know this? I'm surprised the omniscient Detlev regards the Venn as outside his interest."

"Enlighten me," David said.

"According to all sources, Jeje sa Jeje, the pirate fighter, loathed kings."

"We all know that. The plays about her still come out, especially in Colend, whenever people are miffed with their ruler."

"But the Venn recorded different quotes from Fox's. She apparently gleefully reported to our Venn witness that Inda regarded governing as a cart with wheels, carrying everyone. But carts have to be pushed by someone, like kings. And eventually the weight bows their backs and breaks their bones."

"Sounds more like a discussion of power, and what an excess of it does when it lies in a single individual. If this cart driver was covered in horse dung, I might believe the quotation was from Jeje."

Senrid gazed up at the fantastic interweavings of webs far overhead, pale gray in the torchlight light. He lifted his hand toward the blackened stone behind what was probably once a throne, on the wall adjacent to the great fireplace. Time and nature had made their depredations here, but even they could not hide the extreme violence that had smashed this hall, and the walls outside that once had protected the way in—even the hill the castle had once stood on, overlooking Montredaun-An ancestral lands.

Then Senrid turned away, his heels ringing on the stone once, twice, thrice, a slow rhythm evocative of the war drums that once had echoed, year on year, century on century, in this hall.

"Go home," Senrid said.

David hesitated, wondering if he should insist on staying, pretending more ignorance of a history that Detlev had long ago helped him to learn, if only to provide a semblance of companionship. What would Adam do?

And as usual thinking about Adam brought his instant awareness: *It's over. Come home.*

"All right. Be back in spring," David said, flipping a hand in salute, and he performed the transfer.

The sun was not far from rising when David reached his room. There he found Adam waiting. The rest of the building was quiet, everyone still asleep.

Adam had clearly not been to bed yet, but except for marks under his eyes, he seemed neither tired nor fog-minded.

David stood in the window, breathed in the pure air, and looked out at the softly falling snow, deep blue against a deeper blue. The disirad sang its eternal chord, below hearing, above sensation, pure as the air, and more peaceful.

He tipped his chin in the direction of Marloven Hess. "If he can hear Liere and Macael, and that's pretty bad, it's also nothing new, right? He has to have been used to ten years of that when she was with Andri. Or does jealousy never get accustomed?"

Adam shook his head. "You are wrong." He stopped, his gaze going diffuse. David stayed at the window, enjoying the fact that all he had to do was stand there, and not fight against onslaughts from powerful but ill-trained minds, until Adam said, "How much do you want to hear?"

Surprised, David dropped into his easy chair. "Since I'm involved, I may as well get it all."

"I only niffed Senrid for an instant, when he first became aware of them. Elsarion's farsense is akin to Andri's, but his emotions are far more deeply engaged. His mind-shield is maintained strictly by ongoing, and I do mean ongoing, effort of will. But there are times when even the strongest shield, if untrained, cannot be maintained."

"And sex would be one."

"Yes."

David pursed his lips. "All right. But that's Elsarion. Where's Senrid in all that?"

"Back at home. Ten years ago he sensed Andri and Liere at such moments, but briefly, no more than the reflection of moonlight off water. He soon figured out what it was, and blocked it easily enough. Macael Elsarion, focused on Liere, is more like the sun appearing suddenly in the night sky, a high-summer, desert sun, and it took Senrid utterly by surprise."

"And he can't block it."

"Not when Liere is involved."

David grimaced. "He's going to hate that. Probably sees it as the last betrayal."

"Not at all, not at all," Adam said, suddenly in motion, walking back and forth in the little room. Rare, for him, was the energy he shed, almost as overwhelming in its own way as that reflected sun-power from the Adrani king. "David, you must stop seeing what you expect to see. Liere and Senrid, with that kind of bond, there is no jealousy, none of the misapprehensions of more ephemeral connections. Senrid is defenseless against her lack of joy."

David grimaced. Looked up. "So what we've got here is a case of Adamas Dei's comet?"

"Seems to be," Adam said.

"Ah, shit."

The second time was easier, in the sense of the expected being simpler than the unknown.

Again, as soon as Macael walked in, Liere threw a question at him: "How many times did you try to kill Andri?"

Again, he answered. "Three."

"Three? I don't believe it. I distinctly remember seven attempts, and there were probably more that he didn't tell me about in order not to worry me."

"I tried thrice," Macael stated. "The first one was after he sank most of your year's revenue in mounting his followers to make a cavalry, then ran to that damned spent silver mine to try to wrest the shortfall from it."

"You and Chantala were *here* then," Liere said slowly.

"Yes. My thought was to offer my aid when the news arrived of his death. And through that aid, gradually put people in place to reunite the kingdoms. Then I saw the effect when they brought him in, battered and scraped, and I regretted that method. It was sloppy. Also a terrible way to die. There was no assurance it would be quick and relatively painless."

"Painless!"

"Everyone dies," Macael said, still in that flat voice. "Kings *should* die when their decisions will result in misery from border to border."

"A little exaggerated?" she shot back. "And insulting. I worked hard to prevent misery from border to border — not just I," she amended quickly. "Andri worked hard as well."

"Listen to yourself, Liere. *You* worked hard. And you were failing, partly because you were trying to learn a lifetime's study while events outraced you, but mostly because Andri could not amend his view of Enaeran as an enormous wargame playground. To be at his best, he needed another Adon Marsael to lead his followers against. Within five to ten years that was going to be me. Over the Riverlands." While she tried to find the words to refute that, he said, "You don't believe me, that's as you will. You asked a question. I am answering."

"Go on, then, finish your answer."

"Thank you. I determined that if I had to remove him, it must be fast. I decided to test matters with the goldmine. Perhaps he'd take the time to learn if I bought him the time. But he did not learn. The second attempt was after I discovered he'd given away half the gold that should have paid off Enaeran's treasury debt, a debt I could see would strain both sides of the rivers. My chief archer missed—insisted Andi heard it coming. After that, I decided, if it must be done, I had to be the one to do it. It had to be fast and clean. It took me two years to learn how, and to bring myself to it. All others," Macael said, "were your Enaeraneth brawlers."

After that there was silence between them.

The third night, she attacked from a different direction. "You claimed you had to nerve yourself to kill Andri. Killing seems to have gotten easier for you."

And again he answered, his gaze steady, as if seeing the skepticism she never troubled to hide was his own bitter herb: "To what do you refer?"

"The one I refer to happened during that combined exercise before the new year. I'm told the only deaths were Enaeraneth, and none accidental. Including Bevara Yuthan, who was barely twenty when you had her throat cut. Or did you do it yourself?"

Macael said, "She attempted to assassinate me. Poor planning and worse leadership. Her ambition far outstripped her skills. Did you know that you were her target previous to me?"

Liere dismissed that with a wave of her hand. "She was not the first to try to seduce Andri into a crown and throne. Most of them just wanted an easy life, and they knew he was always generous when parting. She was more ambitious in wanting to reign over court."

"A court," Macael said, "that had already begun to fill with more and more of Andri's favorites, drinking and carousing with him, and flattering him into thinking he was the most genial king Enaeran ever had."

Liere flinched inwardly, knowing that there was an element of truth there. But not the whole truth. "You seem to assume," she retorted, "that I would be standing by witlessly? I always talked the favorites out of unreal expectations, usually by inviting them to help with the ledgers. In any case, it is useless to surmise about Bevara Yuthan, because she's not here to learn to be better, is she."

The fourth night, once more she varied the direction of her question: "When we first met, we toasted the future, and you smashed your cup in the fireplace. Considering where we stand now, it was a threat?"

"I did not see it as a threat. It's an old custom, when making certain types of vows, to ensure that the cup would never again be used for frivolous purposes."

"You couldn't just wash it?" And when he didn't answer that, "What kind of vow, if it was not a threat?"

Tiredness, and the shock of the question, had thinned his shield, and her little sea crab antennae were waving, but all she got was the flash of an image: her own face in a borrowed gown of blue. The image of herself was such a shock she shielded right then.

That fifth morning, she woke to thunder, and the hiss of rain. By the time she got to the window, it had turned to snow again. She retreated to her bed, thumbing her eye sockets as she became aware that she had left several days slip by before checking on Lyren and Malcolin.

Malcolin was so easy to reach, involved with small boy concerns. Like his father that way, he seemed to have landed on his feet. It helped that he really liked the Senelac children he was with. Liere's mind streamed with images of mostly black-haired urchins with names like Stinker and Big Toe and Butter. Butter! There was surely a story in that, and she wanted to hear it, once she was free.

She was always more careful with Lyren, who might find these mental touches intrusive. Usually Liere checked at night, when everyone was safely asleep. Liere had been navigating the world of dreams since she was small, tethered by her contacts.

She sent the smallest tendril, then stilled with shock: Lyren was weeping, the loud, passionate tear-and-snot-filled weeping that had so terrified Liere when Lyren was small. There was still that impulse to listen for Father Fer Eider's tread, for tears and whining had never failed to bring down withering sarcasm along with consequences: *Lyren?*

: Why do you hate me?

Liere didn't think. She transferred, using Lyren as a Destination, then staggered from the jolt of reaction. She found herself in a beautiful bedroom overlooking the vapor-shrouded old growth forest of northwestern Wnelder Vee. Fine furnishings completed the room, which Liere scarcely saw.

Mother and daughter stared at each other. Lyren flushed with dramatic coloring, tears ribboned on her cheeks. She was dressed simply in dusky pink and silver, ornamented with lace edging at sleeves and neck. The effect was both graceful and stylish. Fascination? Charisma? Whatever it was she had been born with it, but only now was it flowering to full strength.

Lyren stared, appalled, finding her far too thin, her cheekbones too sharp, her forehead tight with strain. "You didn't tell me," she said, her voice trembling. "You didn't tell me."

Liere dropped her head, her long golden braid slipping past one shoulder, wisps escaping. "I was afraid I'd hear 'I told you so.'"

Lyren wiped her eyes on her pink sleeves. "I haven't said that kind of thing since I was *twelve*," she exclaimed, her voice rising.

Liere said, "I know. I ought to have known. I think … I'm beginning to think I see my own worst traits painted over other people, so that I don't have to own up to them. Because it's very much in *me* to say 'I told you so.'"

This straightforward admission utterly disarmed Lyren, whose kindling temper vanished. She offered a tremulous smile. "That sounds like Grandpa."

"You remember?"

"How could I not? I once counted up the times he said to Grandma Elen, *I told you so, that brat will never…* He insulted you more than he did me."

"Lyren, I'm sorry. About the silence, about my stupid assumptions."

Lyren threw herself into Liere's arms. Liere, startled, staggered back, and they both sank onto a pretty couch set before the window. "I'm sorry," Liere said again, brushing back a tear-damp curling tendril off of Lyren's cheek. "I'm sorriest that my stupidity caused you to cry."

Lyren shook her head, and let Liere go. How skinny she

was! And the black was startling. Liere had never worn black. "It wasn't you. Oh, it started out—something else—and then everything that bothers me piled in. You know me, a big storm, then whish! It's gone."

That was true, but Liere was not ready to be forgiven so easily. "I'm trying to be more aware. This is not accusation. Far from it, as I've no right to. But why did you not contact me... no, even that sound accusatory." Liere's eyes stung. "Please forgive me."

"Of course you're forgiven!" Lyren studied her. Liere's eyes seemed larger, shadowed beneath. It was very clear that she had undergone an awful time—as usual, taking it in silence. As though she deserved it. "Is that a real question, about contacting you? Liere, nobody in the *world* has a better mental shield than you. Excepting Detlev, but everybody knows he's not actually human."

Lyren's careless tone, half-laughter, underscored how her childhood grudge was now pretty much recreational. "I wrote to you. Five times, three of those three days in a row. Those letters probably sounded snotty, and actually I'm glad about what Atan told me, that golden notecases, if they get too full without being opened, the letters exceed the boundary of the spell and vanish into the between. She said she wrote to you, and I know Hibern did as well. Arthur, too. You didn't answer anybody, but Rel and CJ saw you at New Year's, so we knew you were still there."

"CJ? I saw Rel, but not her."

"She was there, and you should have heard the insults she piled onto that Macael Elsarion. She also said you looked really scary, sitting there next to that scary king. But Adam said to leave you alone until you were ready, and Clair said so, too." Lyren looked away. "It was that knowing that you'd talked to Clair that made me feel sorry for myself. Just a little. Because she's no relation."

"I'm sorry," Liere said again, ready to repeat it as many times as needed.

But Lyren was no grudge-holder—except her recreational one against Detlev. She hugged Liere again, her hair soft. She smelled of subtle perfumes. "Why did you close me out when *he* killed Andri?" Her voice was young again, muffled by

Liere's sleeve.

"I didn't. I closed myself in," Liere said.

"That's what Laban thought. And Clair said."

"They are right. I froze into a soggy ball of anger and self-pity, the more because I had a difficulty that I agreed to."

"I can see whatever it is has worn you down," Lyren commented, frowning in question.

"Ah, old and bad habits. I'm working on them."

Lyren looked even more uncertain at that, and then said, "Malcolin—you know he changed his name? He's happy in Marloven Hess."

Liere smiled. "You've checked on him."

"Yes." Lyren flung her hair back, then got up and whirled around the room. "What happened with that ice fortress of an Adrani king? I'm surprised you haven't killed him yet."

"I considered it, but I could not, for the same reason I agreed to his bargain." And at Lyren's startled look, Liere said, "The situation with Macael is difficult. To keep the peace, I agreed to remain there a year, and I do my best to talk to the Enaeraneth, to try to keep a semblance of peace."

"I gathered that much."

"There is another requirement. I have to give Macael Elsarion an heir, and in turn he promises not to hunt down and kill Malcolin."

Lyren recoiled, then tried to hide her reaction. No wonder Liere looked wan! "You? Why you?"

"Because I'm the queen of Enaeran. He maintains it's my popularity that keeps the Enaeraneth from throwing themselves on Adrani steel. I think it's more that they outnumber us, and also half of Shiovhan seems to be related in some way to the Adranis."

Lyren listened to all that, her expressive brows knit. There still seemed to be something vital missing, to demand such a thing. "And then you can leave?" she asked.

"As soon as the year is up."

"And after?"

"I'm working on that. Between now and then I might take up Detlev's invitation to visit the plateau school to repair my ignorance."

"You could learn and recover while you stayed with me

at Laban's," Lyren said, indirectly testing. "And you wouldn't have to worry about the etiquette of the perfect guest with him and Silvanas."

Liere shook her head. "If Tahra knew I stayed with Laban, there might be unpleasant repercussions."

"Tahra." Lyren sighed. "Yes, I ought to have remembered that. I lived with her shadows for so long. But I hate to see you stay away on account of her pet hates."

"Is Wnelder Vee really a home for you?"

"For now," Lyren said. "Laban's so much like me that I'm quite comfortable. I don't feel silly and frivolous for liking the things I like. He likes them, too. And I even have work to do, making the Troiad family's old barracks of a palace livable again, for when the rangers and the guilds and elders come for their meetings. But I—well, I don't think it's permanent."

"Rootless, that's us," Liere said, looking away.

"But we're learning, aren't we?" Lyren blinked, her coin-gold eyes earnest. "I *don't* feel as frivolous as I was at sixteen. And you say you're going to Curtas's House? I like it up there, but I can't see myself learning the dyr. It's ... I think I'd want to influence people too much. Sveneric told me you're not supposed to. Or, maybe ignorance never sees itself, or sees itself in other guises?"

Liere patted the couch. "What do you mean?"

"Here's an example. Tell me if I'm wrong. I often am. *So often.*"

"That makes two of us," Liere murmured under her breath, as Lyren dropped down beside her. "I was trying to track what happened to you, all those years ago. To try to understand you. And us, but mostly you. Anyway, I thought it might be a good idea to find Devon, who I know you haven't seen for years and years and years. And she's right there in Imar. It's a school for noble children."

Liere's expression shuttered. "She still has it, then?"

"Yes. It's even more successful, since the war ended. This woman greeted me with a little smile. A smirk, though I expect she thought she was polite and correct. I didn't tell her you and I are related. She gave me a little speech, *Our Teacher Devon is quite famous around here, you know. You've heard of Sartora, the Girl Who Saved the World? Well, the only reason she survived to tell the tale was entirely due to Teacher Devon. Sartora was so fog-bound in the head that it was our Teacher Devon who had to take care of her, and even watch out for danger, young as she was!* And I asked, *Does Teacher Devon tell this story?* And she tee hee heed at me, and said, *Oh, yes. She sometimes will tell the children stories about Sartora as a reward for being good.* I said my thanks and left. There was a lot about good birth and the behavior expected of birth, and the like. But I could tell they use your name to get students. I had to get out of there."

"And now you know why I never visited her," Liere said. "It became apparent not long after I moved to Bereth Ferian that she needed me to be this other person I did not recognize. I could see that if I entered her life, I'd either have to lie, and become the fog-head who couldn't survive without Devon, or else I could correct the misunderstandings, and make everyone uncomfortable. I thought it better to let our visits lapse."

"I won't go back. As for your deal." Lyren ran her hands up her arms to her shoulders. "That means a new sister. I always wanted a sister."

"Or a brother."

"Or a brother. Will I ever get to see this brother or sister?"

"I'm sure that can happen."

"But it will be strange."

"I am making plans for all eventualities."

Lyren sighed. "Your situation puts my silly one into perspective."

"Want to talk about it?"

One rounded shoulder jerked up. "It really is silly. There's this Knight, you know, from the Everoneth Knights of Dei. On the border patrol. I thought Ferold pretty decent—looking the other way rather than shooting us, as Tahra ordered. Most of them do, though Laban has his rangers try not to be seen. Anyway he's very handsome. Popular with all the girls. And boys, too. I thought a flirtation would be harmless, and I even told him, just a flirtation, but I guess he thought that meant a dalliance, and over New Year's Week, he had made all these plans to surprise me, and I said no, flirting is just flirting, a kiss or two at most, and *he* said I was selfish and playing with him, and Laban said my romances are my affair, but could I *not* add to his trouble with Tahra? Which I thought quite unfair."

"So it is."

"He doesn't mean it. And I know it. We both have flash tempers. But that coming after Ferold's rant, and his friends giving me the ice-eye, Laban says was I really blind to Ferold being serious, like changing their schedule so he always had the route through here, and his fixed regard, and how he never paid anyone else any attention, and *I* said, how was I supposed to notice their schedules, and if *I* wasn't giving Ferold a fixed regard, how was I supposed to see *his*, and *Laban* said, if I was going to flirt, I ought to be watching out for such things, shouldn't I?" Lyren sighed. "He apologized right after — Laban, I mean. That was right before you came. But I really hate arguments, especially when they come at me by surprise. And I was feeling that the world hated me."

"That I had abandoned you," Liere said, her throat hurting. "I'm so sorry."

"It wasn't you, really it wasn't. And you never rant and storm," Lyren said. "I hate being ranted at. I can't help it when I rant, but mine doesn't mean anything. When it's over, it's over."

"At least you don't smolder," Liere said.

"Thank you. I mean, for coming. And explaining everything. I feel *so* much better. And I think I'll go visit Darian Selenna for a good long while, so Ferold and his sniffy friends won't see my horrible self at all. Darian keeps inviting us, now that he's king and can't go junketing about as much, although being king in Sarendan is even easier than it is for Laban, because Ian kept all Peitar's delegations. But he does have to oversee them. Anyway, I haven't gone. I keep waiting until Dirk gets back from wherever Detlev sent him, but as usual, he didn't see fit to tell us where or when."

There was a little more to the same effect, and then Liere felt obliged to return — but she promised to get out her golden notecase, and to not shield off the world.

Lyren beamed. "I'm so glad you came." She hugged Liere yet again, and Liere transferred back to her quiet room in Brydon, bringing with her a trace of Lyren's pleasing lavender and bergamot scent.

The bell rang — the snow had lifted — time to go into the city.

20

Liere strode out into the city, taking with her a renewed determination to contact Senrid. She walked to the western section, inspecting the new building there where had existed ramshackle houses converted from the barns when this area had been a gathering place for sheep shearing.

She saw no familiar faces. The wind was so cold and wet that everyone who had to be out hunched into their clothes. No one spoke to her. So though she walked diligently, she was very much alone with her dilemma, mentally writing what she suspected would be the equivalent of five, six, eight, ten pages, but it was never enough. Trying to figure out what to say and how to say it added another invisible chain to yank her in different directions.

She returned no closer to a decision on how to write to Senrid. It had to be writing. That was the only thing she was certain of. This deal with Macael—bringing a child into the world, when Senrid was surely still mourning his—no, she was *not* going to risk a face to face encounter, and even less would she risk a mental contact. Lyren had commented on how bad she looked, but Senrid would see straight into her heart. She was afraid that this prospective heir and the memory of Crystal Ingrid would hurt him too much, and seeing him in pain would rip her emotions even further. Especially knowing she had to come right back and face Macael's dense blue gaze.

Each day ended with no solution except to wait until she wasn't trying to handle ... what to call it? Storm was the easy and trite word, but Brydon palace these days was quiet. Orderly. No roofs falling in. The only sounds were the exquisite rise and fall of voices and blended instruments of wind and string from the music school. Occasionally, when she opened the windows to a sunny day, she caught the laughing chatter of the young musicians on a break, and once she spotted them having a mock battle between snow forts in the far garden, where once her son had played. She resisted the temptation to go among them. Get to know them. There must be no ties when she left.

The thunder was internal. At least she was very good at shutting out Macael during the nighttime encounters. The other yanks on her emotions were harder to endure: the encounter with Lyren and her own cumulative misjudgments; the careful conversations with Enaeraneth that she would review over and over, especially the ones from which she parted with bitter thoughts following her. Disappointed thoughts. She was *Sartora*. Why didn't she rise up and slaughter the enemy with all her mighty magic?

"Do you really want to see not just the willing fighters dying, but all those caught in the vicinity?" she repeated over and over. "Don't you remember what it was like when the Norsundrians were here?" There was also King Alored's guard before that, but faces closed off at the suggestion of Enaeraneth fighting one another. The *us against them* now was Enaeraneth against Adrani. There were always a few who remembered the violence, and backed off, but too often it was the young whose faces remained stubborn, and she would return in weary defeat.

One thing was clear from her conversation with Lyren: her own judgment was not to be trusted. That left guilt, and doubt, and blame. So she wrote pages of imaginary letters, and consigned them to imaginary flames, yet again.

To avoid the pang starting in her head, she chose at random a book from the shelves in the alcove next to her bedchamber. Andri's books, collected when he was small, had shifted back and forth from the castle where his father had kept him prisoned in luxury to Brydon for his sporadic visits, before he was disinherited altogether and tossed out to live or die. At the front of this book about the horses of Nelkereth a boyish scrawl of some urgency to Gared Inmael, son of the Elsarion Master of Horse. Andri's boyhood friend.

Liere looked up from the message whose urgency had sped down the river of time into eternity's sea. She thought with a mixture of longing and regret of Gared, who was gone; it was probably better so. Liere suspected that of everyone in Andri's life, Gared had loved him the longest, and the fiercest. Then she thought of Marten, and Thadara, and Bassl, and Andri's other close friends, who were at least alive, if confined to their family's land, or dispersed altogether.

The bell rang — it was already late. Macael would be here soon.

Liere shut the dusty book, probably unread since Andri's early days, and returned it to the shelf to think out another question to strike at Macael's "ice fortress."

He appeared most nights. When his circumstances required him to be otherwhere, he sent a message, a courtesy for which she thanked the messenger, but returned no words for Macael.

She came up with more questions, her weapons in this strange duel. Sometimes she scarcely listened to the answers, for example, when she asked whether he'd personally killed Bartal na Shagal. She had no interest in Bartal, or how he departed the world. The question was intended to imply that Macael had very bloody hands for a man with the "nature of a seneschal."

There was an unexpected result of these encounters: he could not stay shielded altogether. She only became aware when she no longer felt the need to withdraw into herself. She was able to wall him off from any of her thoughts or reactions, resulting in her discovery that when he was undone, his memories broke past the shield, vividly intense, sometimes mercilessly lurid, and not a one was the sort of memory one might expect under the circumstances: in the first, Macael must have been Malcolin's age, and yet as he studied a group of laughing women being drawn along on elegant sledges, he was not certain which of them was his mother; in another, Macael stood before a handsome older man whose slack-lidded expression conveyed nothing but boredom as Macael was reciting. Cutting abruptly across his voice, the older man said to someone above Macael's head, *His Sartoran is adequate, but his accent in Colendi betrays the shop: find a better tutor;* and, heartbreakingly, a young, round-faced Chantala flinging her ribbon-tied hair back as she chattered about the verse play she was writing. She couldn't have been older than eleven or twelve.

Patterns, patterns, patterns. He answered Liere's questions, no matter how rude, with thorough, one might even say confessional answers. And his memory images leaked in a cascade of shards from a broken mirror, winking in and out of a brief shaft of light, faster than a heartbeat. When her own face flickered by, as happened often, it jolted her, and she'd withdraw.

Another long bout of terrible weather kept her from her perambulations through the city. She continued to read Sartoran history, which sometimes reached out into the world. Marloven Hess appeared and vanished from those pages, sometimes distorted, sparking again and again the old impulse to talk to Senrid.

She wanted so badly to sit on the floor in his sunny study, with the cadenced shouts of the academy students drifting in the open windows, and build cities with blocks as they speculated about how and why streets were laid out in squares and circles. Except that they were no longer children. There was no going back to the ease of the old days. She remembered the grief in Senrid's face, glimpsed after her arrival at Rel's hideout in Lisdan, following the fall of Eidervaen. But she had been too dazzled by Andri at the time—the one good thing she could hold onto while the world fell apart around them.

And he was a good thing. It's just that Liere had tried so fiercely to force him into a "forever" good thing when Andri himself admitted he didn't believe in forever.

The rawness of unresolved relationships pulled her in so many directions as she struggled against the impulse to turn it all against herself. Especially when she knew that her breach with Senrid was her fault. Her fault. Her fault. She must consider how to approach the biggest apology of her life. But not while she was (of necessity) sleeping with the enemy.

Secondmonth trudged onward, bringing ranks of storms from over the mountaintops, to pass on east to Sles Adran, and thence to Colend and beyond. The skies stayed as bleak as her mood, the color of a dirty wool blanket at the height of noon, and starless dark at night. Everywhere snow, ice, the constant drip, drip, of a partial thaw, just enough to churn up mud, and then the hard freeze again.

But even hard freezes melt.

Toward the end of the month, Macael Elsarion sat by the fire in his private study, working his way through a stack of naval reports. There had been no interviews for days. Though the streets of the city obligingly cleared of snow in the mornings, responding to magic, the rest of the country that Andri had never gotten to was lost under drifts and drifts of snow. He had even sent his scribes home to their families when a report came of three bad storms on the way over the Ghildraith mountains, back to back. When he had to travel, he endured the wrench of transfer, now that he had Destinations in all places of import. He paid for boxes of transfer tokens.

There was no one but him to be surprised when the door unlatched, and Liere Fer Eider walked in for the first time since the end of the previous year, dressed as always in black, her hair smoothed away from her beautiful face, her eyes blank as golden coins.

"It is done," she said. "There will be a child in late autumn."

He rose. The sudden smile that illuminated his face took her entirely aback. Her retreat was immediate, and so fast that, though he crossed the room in half a dozen steps, by the time he opened the door to look out, she was gone.

He stepped into the hallway. Empty, the clean marble floors softly gleaming in the light of glowglobes, and duty pages standing at their posts. It was as if she had never come, that he had dreamed that moment, except for the scent of the herbs her clothes were stored in, lingering on the wintry air.

When he ventured to her side of the palace, vital questions proliferating at every step, he discovered that her suite was locked.

"It's done," she said at the same moment, facing David, who was in the middle of slicing turnips, potatoes, and yams.

She had transferred straight to Curtas's House on the plateau, knowing that in a sense it was a retreat. But wasn't she learning how not to force herself to stay in painful situations just because she deserved the pain?

That heady sense of the disirad's hum washed through

her, like a cool dip in a forest pool after a long, hot, thirsty hike. This time she'd expected it, and shielded enough so that she could concentrate.

David paused, knife in the air. "What's done?"

She shut her eyes, evaluating the subtle physical signs yet again. "I'm pregnant. I've kept my promise. Well, part of it."

"Ah." David flipped the knife into the air and caught it, a useless gesture that seemed to absorb all his attention, then he said reflectively, "I've never been a parent, but I feel fairly confident in predicting that you're just beginning."

"I'm done with Macael Elsarion in my bed."

"That part is certainly true."

It was definitely true, but the triumph of acknowledgment barely lasted a heartbeat. As David rightly said, she was not done with Macael. Would never be done with Macael. The angry exultation following her abrupt declaration to Macael and the snap of the door on his expression of joy was fading, leaving her mostly tired. At least she recognized this lassitude. With Malcolin, those first few weeks, she'd slept and slept and it never seemed to be enough.

She said, "I promised myself, once I achieved this part of my bargain with Macael, I would do two things. One of those is to start learning about the dyr. If I still can."

"Any time you are ready."

"I'd like to begin now. But I cannot move here. That is, I would love nothing better. But part of my bargain is being visible to the Enaeraneth. It's a little over three months since Andri was murdered and their kingdom taken over. Or, reunited, as the Adranis say," she added sourly.

"Staying here is not a requirement," David said—fairly certain her second, unspoken thing was Senrid. *Let her introduce his name first*, Adam had warned him. *She knows what you think.* "If you were a twelve-year-old burgeoning with talent and little discipline, I'd return a different answer. But you know how to study. And you know how to lend a hand, right? Your first official task as a new member of Curtas's House is to get the spots out of these veg. We've got a full house expecting supper tonight, most of them returning from a long field trip. They will be ravenous."

He tossed her an apron. She tied it on swiftly, and got to

work. She hadn't had to cook since she was on Geth, but her mother had trained her well, and her hands remembered the tasks. She proved to be faster than David, so they re-divided the jobs, she de-spotting, chopping, and slicing the root vegetables. David handled dunking the slices in a mixture of crushed onion and garlic. The flat sheets over the fire gleamed with pressed olive oil, heat wavering until he began tossing the slices on to sizzle to crispness. The air filled with delicious aromas, and Liere discovered that she was hungry, for the first time in months.

"What do you want to study?" he asked, once they got a rhythm going.

"I—don't know? Ancient history, maybe? I've yet to even see a true dyr. I don't consider the distorted one I carried long ago. How many masters have you? I gather Detlev must be your primary teacher?"

"You'd gather wrong, though you'd be entirely justified in thinking so." David grinned. "Pile 'em in that bowl—I need to crush more garlic. When Adam and I finished the building, we, or I, waited for Detlev to produce some robed Wise One stashed beyond time somehow, who would orate on the hidden mysteries, or at least dictate volumes of wisdom while we wrote madly. But it turned out we'd been learning the basics along with the evil window dressing, and in Ancient Sartor, it was common for people to teach one another. That's pretty much what we do."

"Our first year, one of our most well-liked classes was taught by a twelve-year-old, in embroidery," Adam said, entering from behind. "Here, let me flip those. You're burning them, and I'm so starved I am ready to gnaw these dishes."

"I'm done with my part," Liere said presently, indicating the empty baskets the vegetables had been in. She sensed a jumble of minds approaching. She found that shielding against them took effort, and she was fighting lassitude. "I'm not all that hungry," she lied, "so if you'll point out what I ought to start reading, I'd better return."

"Go ahead, I'll finish up here. You made prep go much faster," David said.

Adam said to Liere, "I'll walk you to the library while the others change and ready themselves for supper." He swiped a handful of crisped slices and popped one in his mouth as he exited.

Liere followed him. He said with a whimsical smile, "It turns out that embroidery is very meditative. Like drawing."

"Is learning to embroider a skill meant to foster discipline?"

"I guess it could be for some, but most tried it because dyranarya have to earn a living somehow, if they decide to take their dyr on the road. Hlareas was our first to get her dyr, right around the time she turned seventeen."

"Really! Twelve to seventeen, five years. It's that easy?" That was the amount of time she'd spent in Geth, and after her return, Detlev had said that his training would begin when theirs ended. Was she that backward? Probably.

"Easy? Don't know how to answer that. In a sense, she'd been practicing all her life. But also, her focus is mostly the everyday problems that are inevitable in real life. Many times a person merely needs another person to listen. Surprising, how important it can be to feel one is heard. Seen."

"That can also be horrible," Liere said, remembering her Sartora days. "When people are listening to your every word, but that's expectation. You're talking about something different, yes? I'm probably on the wrong path here, but it seems to me that people like to matter to someone else."

"I like that way of saying it. Hlareas is very good at being a sympathetic listener, and guiding a conversation so that the speaker might the sooner find their path among the oh, call it the rocks and precipices of regular life."

Liere nodded. She was not so wrong, then.

"To learn to guide deeply broken people requires more experience, and more … mmm, focus. I keep wanting to slip into Ancient Sartoran here, for terms we just don't have yet, because Dena Yeresbeth is so new. This might take longer. A few years. Decades. The important thing to remember is, learning goes on all the time, and everyone has something to teach. That happens everywhere, all the time. Here, we make it a focus."

"I can't imagine what I would teach, save to be an example of what not to do," Liere retorted, and raised a hand. "That was actually an attempt at humor, but I probably sound more like…" *Father*. "… my bitter herb self than my *See, Liere does know how to make a joke* self. Clair helped me to identify the bitter herb self, which is a habit hard to break. Has Clair been learning up here? She is really good at being a listener. Another who has done it all her life."

"She has, though she mostly studies in tandem with us. She has the disirad influence of the white palace, which was one of the houses of healing in the old days. But I'll let her tell you what she's been discovering."

"She said a little about that, and I intend to learn more. As for now, I will read anything you assign me. But Clair told me about a book on parent and child. She said only one page had been translated."

"Ah." Adam turned, his gaze distant, considering. "Yes. She is quite right. I wouldn't give that one to a beginner … but. Yes. A good place for you to start."

"I am a beginner."

"In a sense. In other senses, you've also been practicing all your life. We'll find what needs training and what doesn't, soon enough. I find that fun, actually. The kind of challenge I like most."

They'd entered a large, quiet room. Adam waved the glowglobes to light, and turned a slow circle as he regarded the shelves on every wall, full of scrolls as well as books. Then he muttered under his breath, went to a shelf and brought back a scroll.

She opened it, and when she laid eyes on the neat vertical lettering, all her old frustration at trying to force herself to learn Ancient Sartoran flooded back. "Maybe I ought to begin with something simple," she said uneasily.

"You know by now that translation is not like carving stone," Adam said. "It's more fluid. And yes, while it's so easy to make an error without realizing it, we learn by comparing notes. For example, one of the regularly used texts, from centuries ago, translates this word right here as *teacher* or *master*. The Scribe Guild insisted on it. The various mage guilds also. But Detlev told us that those distinctions were not a matter of hierarchy in the same way they are now. We've begun using *elder*, but it requires a gloss, as the root of the noun is *much-lived*, which connoted *wise*. Unless we speak the old language, with its ancient connotations, we don't have quite the right word, because their culture was so different."

"I see! I think. What you're saying is, don't be afraid to be wrong." Unspoken: she was certainly well-practiced at that.

"We're often wrong. But it does get easier." Adam grinned. "Copy out a page or two's worth. I'll lend you the lexicon we're developing."

"No additions to the Universal Language Spell, then?"

Adam gave his head a slow shake. "Not until we truly understand the terms. There is a reason Detlev kept removing additions the guild scribes and mages made."

Adam brought her materials, then went off to get his supper; he was out of sight when his effortless contact reached her: *I'm here if you have questions.*

As soon as she finished copying out two pages, she picked up the lexicon, and transferred back to Brydon, while back in Curtas's House, the dining room was noisy with all the chatter.

Adam drifted around to David's side.

David said, "Between one visit and the next, she figured out how to shield up here."

"I noticed," Adam murmured.

"She hopped out with that remark about the dyr. Distorted, she called it."

Adam's eyes narrowed. "What exactly did she say?"

David shared the conversation, then said, "That's the one Detlev masked, isn't it, so Efael wouldn't be able to use it to rip into minds?"

"It was."

"I'd completely forgotten. We were pups then, and Siamis's charade was little more than village mummery, but she really did use that thing, choked off as it was, and then woke up Senrid's Dena Yeresbeth, as if she'd been guiding all along. What was she, ten?"

Adam's chortle was soft, nearly inaudible. "Why do you think Detlev's been waiting for her?"

T he next morning dawned bright. Liere threw wide her windows, and though cold air blew in, she smelled a hint of green things.

Spring was nigh.

Theoretically, anyway. By the time she had eaten breakfast and dressed, clouds had rolled in to dump an unwanted load of mushy snow on defenseless Shiovhan.

Very well, no walking out.

It was time to keep her promise.

After weeks of worrying over the question, she had finally decided to begin with simple. Nothing personal. Stick to practical, the obvious subject being her son, thrust on Senrid without warning. She knew Malcolin was content, even happy when he was busiest, but how did Senrid feel?

She wrote on a fresh slip of paper: *How is Malcolin doing? Ought I to remove him?*

Her heart beat a rapid tattoo as she folded the message, put it in the notecase, and tapped out Senrid's sigil.

On the other side of the mountains, Senrid sat with a circle of experts in shipbuilding. After nearly ten years, Marloven Hess would once again have a navy; the old treaty barring the Marlovens from the coast had dissolved, useless even before the war. Even the king of Perideth did not dare complain—much. Fox had been sending back pirate ships captured since the war ended, many of which were slowly being rebuilt. But creating a navy was expensive, a slow process.

In the middle of a discussion hammering out the costs of refitting Tarual Harbor, the experts were surprised to see the sharp-eyed king glance up, blink, and stare into the distance as though his wits had strayed.

Then he blinked again. "Yes. The rope walk. Previously, the best ropewalk was in Perideth—once Fera-Vayir, effectively out of reach now..."

They returned to their discussion, which rambled on, circling back as such things do. While two merchants argued about who made the best sailcloth, Senrid slipped his golden notecase from his pocket: that had been his old sigil, abandoned at the start of the war. It had to be Liere. And yes. It was her handwriting, still the tidy, clear lettering of a ledger-keeper, only very small: *How is Malcolin doing? Ought I to remove him?*

He considered those few words, written in tiny, tentative letters. The handwriting was adult, but the brevity was very much the old Liere, braced for the expected rebuff. Ten years could make many changes, though he did not believe her essential nature had altered. Under cover of a third guild chief entering the brangle, he wrote: *Fenis Senelac has him until spring. He's happy in a pack of Senelac pups. Take him only if you need to.*

Then he hesitated. Liere could easily know all those things by contacting Malcolin. He knew she regularly contacted her boy—

"Senrid-Harvalder?"

Senrid pocketed case and paper.

Liere sat in her room on the east side of the mountains, losing the battle against wondering if he'd seen her note yet, and what he thought. What if, what if, what if, until she was interrupted by Jauni, who brought a message from Macael that he wished to consult her at her earliest convenience.

The present slammed her right back in her cage.

Liere suppressed a comment, thanked her, and went into the other room. She was not going to be summoned. Macael could wait on her "convenience." She was well aware that this response was petty and mean-spirited, very much like her father, but she was the wronged one here. Little reminders to Macael were justifiable.

Her gaze fell on her desk, and the papers there. The Ancient Sartoran scroll!

She sat down and began slowly puzzling out the text, with frequent references to the lexicon—after which she'd begin a sentence all over. She'd forgotten that so much of Ancient

Sartoran writing was in the form of dialogues.

> The new parent came to the elder. There is a child within. What is the most important gift I must give to my child?
>
> The second parent answered, surely it is love. A family does not commence without love. It does not survive without love.
>
> Love is important, the elder agreed.
>
> The first parent asked, is not happiness as important as love? Love arises freely out of happiness. Happiness arises out of love.
>
> All these things are true, the elder said, but you are forgetting joy. Let happiness be as a rainbow, for of all the emotions it is one of the most fleeting. Therefore let love be the wellspring. Joy is the sunlight. The rainbow lingers longest where love and joy meet.

Joy.

Inadvertently, Liere's mind flashed back to the previous day, and that utterly unfamiliar expression on Macael's face before she slammed the door. That had been joy.

Liere drew a breath, shut her eyes, and thought: *Not so wise, were they, Adam? Because I know for a fact that joy can be angry. I've seen angry joy.*

She was startled when Adam answered, as easily as if he stood in the next room: *Just about any emotion can be poisoned by anger. These learning scrolls were meant to provoke discussion. I should probably warn you that thinking my name brings me if I am awake. And sometimes in sleep, too, O Dreamwalker.*

She laughed a little, recognizing a gentle challenge, but thought: *Poisoned?*

Adam was gone before she could protest that angry joy could be justified. Which meant it was *not* poison. For instance, when the word came that Adon Marsael was definitely dead — they had seen his corpse — people had shouted for joy. Althora had done a dance around his recumbent form. He had killed her family. She was joined by many. And yet, Liere thought as she rubbed her fingers absently over her flat belly, Adon

Marsael had once been someone's beloved child, a new life full of promise and hope and joy. So, for that matter, had Macael—

And here was the forcible reminder of those images of his parents, the mother he didn't recognize, and the father who so very clearly regarded him as a thing to be polished properly for his own plans. Every child *should* be a matter of promise and hope and joy.

And here again was her angry exultation in slamming the door on Macael's joy. But she was *right*. Wasn't she? Except that his joy was not an expression of another successful assassination. It was at the prospect of a birth that had not happened yet. Was she being her father here, wishing to deny him any right to rejoice at what in *any*one else would raise a smile?

Further, would she take away his joy if she could?

Then came the unsettling thought: is this how tyrants are made?

She rolled her eyes. Who was falling into the "It's all my fault!" trap yet *again?* Except … No, there was no except. He had contrived the creation of this baby, by threatening the life of her son. And there would be consequences, oh yes there would, especially if he assumed she'd hand off the baby and let Macael turn the child into a replica of himself.

Very well then, time to have that talk he wanted so much.

She cast a glance down herself to make certain she was tidy, and then left her suite. Did someone run ahead? She loathed the thought that someone was on the watch, and yet she'd prized the conspiracy among the Brydon servants when Andri was alive, watching over him when he began fighting the symptoms of his yearly cold so that they could get hot liquid into him as often as possible, and remind him to dress warmly…

Remembering this good-natured conspiracy tightened her throat. She fought back the sting in her eyes, and here was the surge of righteous anger, so insidiously prompt that she halted on the landing, pausing to pick at imaginary lint on her sleeve. Who am I becoming?

It was a disturbing thought. She almost turned back, then saw the door open on the other side of the shining marble floor, and Fan emerged. Whether by accident or calculated no longer mattered: he'd seen her. She brushed off the sleeve and crossed the landing, reminding herself the sooner she held this interview, the sooner it was over.

Fan bowed and effaced himself.

She passed by him, and he shut the door, leaving her alone with Macael, who was as usual behind the desk. "Would you like anything to drink? Eat?" he asked.

"I'm fine," she said, still mulishly reluctant to thank him, though now that, too, seemed petty. Avoid poison, she reminded herself, and so she said, "In fewer days than I'd like to think, the thought of food or drink will be … unpleasant, if previous experience is anything to go by."

"I see. Is there anything that can be done for that? I wanted to ask, what can we do, or bring, to assure your well-being?"

"Eventually I'll probably want sliced ginger steeped in spring water. But I can arrange that. I trust that phase will not persist long."

"I also wanted to ask if we ought to arrange for a carriage, either open or covered, for when you wish to go into the city for an airing."

And surround me with spies? Eh, the spies were no doubt already there, and in any case, she framed every single conversation for possible overhearing. She was not going to lend herself to whoever wanted to raise trouble on either side. "Not necessary," she said. "I need to walk, the farther the better. But spring is coming. The weather will very soon draw me out of doors."

And then she decided that the prospect of her child's future meant talking to Macael, instead of shutting him out. "Do you intend to hand this heir off to a tutor and governess and an army of servant-guards?"

"You and Andri did not follow Elsarion tradition," Macael observed.

"Am I about to hear critique of our son's raising, based on the quarter of an hour, cumulative, you spent in his company? Or did you learn by suborning his servants?"

"The sort of upbringing to which you referred previously was customary in some circles, in my admittedly limited experience. It was true for me. I had very carefully selected tutors and caregivers…" He hesitated, his gaze shifting to the desk, then up again, as he changed the subject. "Your son seemed not only happy, but his relationship with the two of you appeared to my eyes as sincere as it was strong. I thought these were not emotions often to be found at that age."

Liere was struck by some of those inadvertently gained shards of memory: Macael at Malcolin's age, not certain which courtly woman was his mother; the father cutting across his recital to comment on his accent as if he was not present in the room. Liere bit back the impulse to utter a sarcastic rejoinder, and said, "Our keeping our son around us as much as we could was a mutual decision. Andri hated his own upbringing."

"My preference would be to dispense with the old ways as well."

"You mean to raise him yourself?"

Another slight nod, and another of those oblique glances, then he said, "Do you have an alternate suggestion?"

Here it was. Her primary concern now was a human life, someone completely innocent of their method of entering the world, but who nevertheless would be forever a part of both her and Macael. Someone moreover who probably would rule two kingdoms.

She said, "There is a text from ancient days that claims the most important emotions are love, joy, and happiness. If these are present, then talent—-ambition—the inspiration to be a good human being, arise naturally."

"I would like to see this text," he said.

She was surprised, and unsettled, by the spurt of angry instinct to keep it to herself. "I will bring it to you as soon as I finish translating it," she promised.

He made a few more offers, to which she returned a pleasant, polite, but decided Not Necessary. She had not sat down, and once he seemed to run out of things to say, and requested her to be sure to send for anything she might need, she took that as her exit cue and left.

It was a beginning, she decided as she sped back to her suite, where she checked the golden notecase: no answer. Disappointment was a sharp blow. I deserve no less, she reminded herself. No, don't get sullen. Think of joy, think of joy. But telling oneself to be joyful was just as successful as exhorting oneself to be happy.

She sat down at the desk and bent over the ancient text

once more.

There it was again, *Joy*. The most important gift to the new life. She slid her eyes past it, and worked assiduously through a second dialogue, that appeared to be similar to that first, the focus on happiness and love in everyday life. The elder reminded the prospective parents to look for those things in the little matters of the day, and they would surely be found.

Liere sat upright, rubbing the sides of her neck as she considered the truth of it. Her father served here as a perfect example of the opposite. She remembered hers and her siblings' dread at the sound of his step on the stairs. In retrospect, it was clear that Father used to tromp through his day looking for things to be angry at — even two-year-old Lyren had noticed!

That brought another uneasy question: what had Father's early life had been life, to make him so bitter?

There was no answering that, so she returned to her work, which was satisfying, as meaning slowly emerged, individual words building into phrases, and phrases ordering into sentences.

When she finished that first page, she discovered that the sun had vanished. No wonder she was tired! She agreed when Thani offered dinner, and as soon as the maid went away, her eyes strayed toward the drawer where she had put her golden notecase.

She closed her eyes and reached for Malcolin, though it was early in the west. Sure enough, he was busy whispering something to Big Toe. An image of a round urchin face with a gap-toothed grin crowned by a thatch of straw-colored hair appeared. It seemed they were supposed to be at lessons.

Liere withdrew gently, suppressing the urge to issue a stern warning to pay attention. Whoever was conducting the lesson could be trusted to see to that; she comforted herself with the fact that he was busy, having fun. Like his father, he seemed to have landed on his feet.

She sent a contact Lyren: *How are you?*

: *I'm in Sarendan. If nothing else, I'm getting an interesting view of how different governing runs here, especially compared to Sartor. How are you?*

: *The hypothetical is now real. The spark of a new life is here.*

: Have you kicked the evil king out of your bed?
: Consider him royally kicked.

Lyren ended the contact on a burst of mirth, and wishes for good sleep.

Liere fell into bed, and sank into slumber within two breaths.

Her dreams had always been at least partly lucid; she had come to suspect that it was due to her awareness floating free, tying her to reality through the people she cared about, and those she feared. She had become a vast undersea creature. Up on the surface floated a bark, bright with a star of hidden life. She floated around and around it until the dream began to metamorphose to an alien landscape, as on the western side of the mountains, the bell rang the watch change.

Senrid sat in his study, looking out toward the ruddy embers of the vanishing sun. He was aware of mild hunger; they all were. No one starved, but ever since the war, the end of winter emptied larders, including in the castle. Senrid refused to eat anything different from what the kitchen help ate. In fact, they probably did best of anyone, as scraps were their rightful gleanings. But spring veg and berries would come soon.

What would Liere think, were she to come back to this kingdom? It was no longer a wreck, but the shadow of war still lay here and there, discernible in countless ways. Such as the uneven click-step echoing from below, as one of the academy instructors passed from the tunnel into the academy. What would Liere think if she were to walk into the academy to see that not a one of the instructors had survived without bearing evidence of war's brutality?

He watched Hauth's head before it disappeared into the warren of rebuilt corridors, as Hauth hobbled toward the barracks where he stayed with the few winter holdovers. Hauth, who had spent three nights hiding under a roof amid bird splatters with several arrows in that leg, unable to make a sound as the Norsundrians swarmed in search, back again every day after Hauth had taken out a particularly venal spy.

Senrid thought of the academy about to assemble over the next weeks, and the now-become-traditional trading off of old uniforms to those who had grown over winter. What had been practicality was now a mode: no one had new clothes. Even though most jarl families could now afford them, their progeny adamantly refused to look "toff" in newly made clothes. The shabby old uniforms that revealed evidence of having been worn by heroes—such as embroidered initials in collars—were far more prized than stylish embroidery and fine cloth in another country.

Senrid tried to picture Liere walking among his scruffy seniors, but his tired mind only brought up that first glimpse of her the day the war began in earnest, the pure curve from cheek to chin, the hints of different curves in the folds of her summer robe, and her ruffled fall of golden hair to her hips. Not at all the nail-bitten, scrawny ball of misery he'd known, and yet that girl had looked at him out of those same golden eyes.

All day he'd considered what else to write back, as if this would be their last exchange. But it would not be, unless she chose to end it. Whatever she wrote he would answer, again and again. That was just the way it was.

So don't overthink it. Steadying himself with that counsel—equal parts resignation and humor—he scribbled below the previous note, folded it, and sent it.

Then he went to hear the day's reports, as on her side of the mountain, Liere felt the inward tick of the golden notecase and struggled out of bed, the first signs of unsettled stomach a reminder of this further step on her path.

She snapped a glowglobe to light, and grabbed the golden notecase from the bedside table.

There was Senrid's familiar handwriting, tidy and clear for mapmaking:

> Fenis Senelac has him until spring. He's happy in a pack of Senelac pups. Take him only if you need to.

Then, in a more angular hand, as if he wrote more quickly:

> But you know that. I suspect your query was nothing more than a scouting foray. My first thought was to assure you that you've only to say the word and I will come over the pass with an army, but I know that if you wanted to make Enaeran into a battlefield you'd be leading your

own army. I expect your solution will be a better one.

Malcolin said you have a year. If my part is to wait, wait I will.

✦ **22** ✦

Liere reread the note five or six times. Then her mind exploded with questions, leaving her head as empty as a blown egg.

Sense returned, bringing with it the conviction that here was the Senrid she knew, as steadfast as the stars in the sky, notwithstanding the false Senrids her anger and fear had fashioned in his place. Those few words made it clear that he had faith in her, even if she wasn't sure she had it in herself. And that he would wait. How much did he understand of what her year entailed? No, she did not have to agonize over that. He said he'd wait.

Her hands trembled as she slipped the golden notecase back in its trunk. He'd promised to wait.

She slid the little paper under her pillow as she crawled into the now-cold bed, and fell asleep with her fingers curled around it.

The Jarlan Marend Ndarga accompanied her small group of youngsters returning to the academy for another season. The youngsters had been told by their elders that it was an honor to be escorted by the jarlan herself, and they acknowledged it—outwardly—but among themselves the prospect had raised a sigh. It meant that their strict, exacting jarlan would be watching them, maybe even drilling them, whereas if they'd been sent with someone's uncle, or a low-ranking guard who'd been stuck with the duty, it might have become a fun journey.

Much to their surprise, there was no drill. But that was because the jarlan rode as hard as the horses could handle, as if they were late instead of very early. So early there was still snow on the shady sides of hills and trees.

Lonely ruminations through the long nights alone in her tent kept bringing Marend back to the past. Was it possible that Senrid did, after all, harbor a distaste for her because of her brief, nearly-lethal alliance with Imry Llyenthur?

Some people did not overlook past mistakes, she knew, for her brother Retren had never come home. Nor had he communicated. She knew he was alive only from second and third-hand reports, gleaned by her efforts, not his, for he never sent word through others.

The truth might hurt worse than these surmises, but Marend was no coward, and the time had come to stop hinting, hoping, conniving: she had to know. Her grocer friend Tdor had encouraged her. "Go find out. You'd make a great queen. But if it's not to be, get over it and ride on."

Hatch Senelac had said nothing when she turned Methden over to him. But there had been a look of awareness in those observant black eyes of his. He'd been leading the morning drills, early as it was, leftover academy habit. She waited until he was done, and then he joined her just as he was, in shirt, trousers, and boots, in his little office.

"You are riding out?" he asked.

"Taking the academy youths to Choreid Dhelerei," she said, looking away from the little hollow between his collarbones in the open neck of his shirt. "I have directed my scribes and the guild counsel to come to you if there are emergencies."

Senelac dropped his sword in the rack behind his desk, then turned to face her. "Did the king summon you?"

"No."

"I see."

Nothing more, and his face was inscrutable, but her cheeks warmed as she walked briskly back to the castle, where she found her gear strapped to her favorite cross-country mount, the academy teens chattering, their breath clouding in the air.

Spring began to show more signs as they crossed the kingdom to the royal city, until they rode into Choreid Dhelerei, the weak spring sun sinking beyond the horizon.

Marend took her charges to the academy, where they brightened considerably to discover that they were not the first arrivals. She led their string of horses to the academy stables, where they would be trained alongside the other animals, until the return trip to Methden in winter.

Then, alone, she rode slowly into the royal city, approving of everything she saw. It was clean, no sign of war damage, except in paler stonework. The dominant smells of cabbage and onion emanated from doorways as citizens settled down to what was probably a fairly lean supper, but that was true in Methden, too. It would be a fine thing to reign as queen here. For *that*, she could bear to leave Methden.

Lights glowed in the high windows of the royal castle, ruddy-gold and welcoming. The cold air was fast turning bitter. She clucked to her tired horse, who had already picked up speed at the smell of the huge castle stable.

In a short time—as soon as she gave her name—a runner took her along the fine halls to the state wing. There she was shown into an interview room, where she was invited to refresh herself while the king was made aware of her presence. The runner paused to snap the firesticks to flame and then departed. She bent to warm her hands, wondering if Senrid had made these firesticks himself, the way he had in those precious Darchelde days.

She discarded her cloak, but gave no other thought to her appearance than a spurt of resentment that she could not live in uniform all the time. Her proudest days had been those spent at the academy, where she had earned her position. And respect. She stood before the new fire and stared down into the flames, recalling all her dreams. Either they were about to be made real, or they would end. She could no longer bear the wait.

Someone knocked and brought in a tray of fresh coffee, a couple of small rye biscuits, and a cup of preserved apricot slices. She sat down and made quick work of the food. Then she wrapped cold fingers around the warm mug.

She was still breathing the aromatic steam from the coffee with another knock came, and the king himself appeared. She gulped a scalding sip, then almost choked, tears stinging her eyes as she set the mug down.

"Good evening, Marend," the king said, his air one of question, and muted surprise.

She opened her hand, trying to evaluate her mixed reaction. She was gratified at his prompt response, but she was also disappointed that this interview did not take place in his private rooms.

"Problem in Methden?" he asked.

"No," she said, having recovered her voice. She rose, gripping suddenly sweaty hands behind her back. "Personal only."

"Yes?" He sat down in the chair opposite hers, and indicated that she should sit down again, but she remained where she was.

"Are you still angry with me for betraying Retren, and Methden, when Imry Llyenthur promised to give me command?"

"No," the king said, and if he was surprised, he did not show it. "I never did harbor any anger about that. How could I, with my past?"

Marend said, "Then if you are not angry with me, why do you not come alone to Methden on inspection? It's always with David. Why don't you invite me to come here, except at Convocation?"

Senrid had been thinking that it had been two days since Liere's first communication in ten years. She had not responded to his answer, but all his instincts insisted the best gift he could give her was more time. He forced his attention to Marend's searching gray gaze; he had done his best to avoid the interview she seemed bent on having anyway. He was aware of two things: there would probably never be a convenient time, and that it might be best to get it over with now. "I thought we had a good working relationship," he said, miming surprise.

"Working relationship," Marend repeated, feeling the effects of her long journey, the whipsaw hopes and fears she'd been unable to control, now panging behind her temples. "Please, Van, speak plainly. Is another kind of relationship possible? I want it to be."

The nickname he'd used during the war slipped out, made from his middle name, Indevan. It was common all over the kingdom, but Marend liked to think of him as Van—for she liked to remember those days when very few knew who he was. When she and her gang constituted an inner ring in the resistance.

The king made no sign that he'd noticed.

"Are you certain you want me to speak plainly?" he asked in a kind voice. And with faint, rueful humor, "You won't like it, I'm afraid."

"I don't like the way things are now," she said.

"Marend," the king said. "You're a bright, courageous, honest person, one who comes instantly to mind when I contemplate my best choices for governing in Marloven Hess."

She made a quick, flat-handed gesture of negation.

He said, "Hear me out. You've worked hard. You've made Methden one of the strongest and fastest recovering of all the jarlates. You know it's true, and I do as well, and I am praising you for that work now, as perhaps I should have before."

"Why," she said huskily, "do I just keep hearing 'however' in your voice?"

Senrid opened his palm. "If you want to hear what I have to say, permit me to say it."

"Go on." Her throat tightened. "Your pardon."

"And I beg your pardon, for not, oh, holding this conversation, which obviously should have been held, long ago. Blame my own cowardice."

She grimaced. "Never that."

Senrid gave her a wintry sort of smile. "Courage in the field comes easily to most of us, because we've been trained to it all our lives. In personal relations — it doesn't. But I will try. You are smart, strong, a good governor. We've established that. You're also one of the first to mind when I think of personal attractions. Unfortunately the heart seldom makes rational choices."

"Then there is someone else."

"Yes."

Her headache throbbed, but she was proud of her straight back and dry eyes. "Is she worthy?" Her voice was thin, but steady.

"Eminently. If she decides to choose elsewhere, David is my heir."

"She might choose *elsewhere*?" Marend demanded. "Does she *know* you?"

"None better," he said. "There is no one who knows me better."

Marend shook her head in disbelief, and he added, his voice still kind but his gaze steady, "You must forgive me, but your own perceptions of who I am are distorted by the title."

Just as Tdor had said, and Hatch had hinted. Marend's eyes stayed dry, but the old humiliation, and the hurt pride were fierce. But then she recognized her foremost emotion as just that: hurt pride.

The king said nothing, giving her time to think. She had chosen this interview, and therefore must abide by what transpired. She bent her head, her mind working furiously. Pride. Thwarted longing for ... yes, she had envisioned his arms around her, but those images had never been as strong, as alluring as the one with her standing next to him in the throne room at Convocation.

He was right. She did want to marry a king. Did she want the man? She forced herself to look up at his face, and she tried to see him as just that—a man. He was attractive, but so were a lot of men. Like her own commander. In fact, she discovered, she really did not know nearly as much about Senrid's tastes, his likes and dislikes, his little private stories, his jokes, even his abilities in the field, as she knew about Hatch Senelac's.

So ... was it not real love, but only a semblance, under which she had been laboring?

"Thank you for being honest," she said, her guts sick, her mind numb. "I don't need the praise."

"Shall I have the runner bunk you over garrison-side?" he asked. "You've got some old friends there."

"Please."

Tdor was right, she thought the next morning, as she set out riding in a light rain. And Marend had agreed: ask him, and if turned down, get on with what was otherwise a good life, the life she had chosen.

As she began the ride home, she imagined conversations going differently, but invariably stalled out not long after "Yes." Whereas when she imagined what she was going to say to Tdor, or even to Hatch, somehow she could hear the likely response.

Maybe she would even tell Hatch what a fool she'd been. Why not? There was nothing to hide. She had no pride left. And everything in the world, from past to future hopes, she'd examined and argued and sometimes laughed over with Hatch Senelac — everything except this one thing.

When Liere finished the second page, she took her translation to Curtas's House, where she hoped it was late enough not to be interrupting classes — however classes were conducted up there.

She and David and Adam went over the page, after which Adam gave her a stack of papers. "I copied out the scroll," he said. "The scrolls themselves we feel should be moved about as little as possible."

"I would have done that," she exclaimed. "You did not have to go to that labor."

"Oh, I enjoyed it. I'm adept enough in the language to have followed everything, so it was no tedious chore. I even added a few words to the lexicon, after consulting Detlev. He thinks the actual written translation is a terrific first project for you."

"I told Macael I would share the translation with him," she admitted.

"Excellent idea," Adam said.

Liere heard voices in the background. Adam turned his head as if listening. "Then I'll get going," she said, gathering the stack.

Over the next few days at Brydon, the translation went quicker; she had always been good at languages. When she finished the section of prebirth and infant care, she kept her promise, sending the pages with Jauni, with a verbal message to let her know if anything needed explaining.

Jauni was back so soon that Macael had to have set aside whatever else he was doing to read those pages.

Very well, then, if he wanted to learn how to take care of an infant, she would oblige. In that mood, she crossed Brydon to what she'd begun to think of as his side. Though (she reminded herself) she didn't actually have a side. Even her suite was now his.

They met in another room, with what appeared to be a different set of books, and for the first time, Liere wondered if he was going to shift his capital from Nente, which had belonged to the Shagals for centuries, to Shiovhan, which the Elsarions had set up as their capital. But she was not going to ask. A year only, then she would be gone.

The pages she had written lay before him. He still wore black, though two months of traditional respect had passed. She herself had decided she would resume colors the day she shook the dust of conquered Enaeran from her feet. She had no idea what was going on in his mind, but here was another subject she refused to show any interest in.

He thanked her for making time for him, and then, skipping entirely over those first few pages about joy, happiness, and love, put questions about the practicalities of infant care. "I'll need time to make sure everything is in place," he said.

From the subject of infant care, which they canvassed at first with awkward politeness, they progressed to how fast babies grow. He asked questions about crawling, speaking, and walking, which she answered as completely and neutrally as she could.

"Lyren," he said finally. "Where did you get that name?"

"At the time, I was living in the public eye. I needed a first name that did not belong to any of my many acquaintances, lest someone be hurt. So she was named for a friend I met when taken through a world-gate, and all my Sartorias-deles and Geth friends' names were piled after. Lyren used to say that she didn't have a name so much as a callover. Of course, that is how she began. She has adapted her name a time or two since. As young people sometimes do when defining who they wish to be in the world."

He gave a slight nod. "I came to hate the sound of Trevor. Which never failed to precede admonishment." He added, "I notice your son has also dropped it. But I suppose that is to avoid sharing a name with me."

Her eyes narrowed, alarm burning her nerves.

Before she could demand how he knew that, he said, "You yourself have referred to Malcolin, which was easy enough to guess replaced Trevor Andiran. Liere, so far you've kept your promise. Your son will take no harm of me unless he comes over the border with a pack of mercenaries."

"I'll see to it," she retorted, "that he finds a better life than becoming a conqueror." That came out rather poisonous. She shrugged internally; this poison dart was deserved. "If you don't have any more questions, I'll get back to translating that text."

He rose and bowed.

Macael departed for Nente early the next day.

Left in peace, Liere divided her time between working on the translation, walking out into the city, and sleeping. So much sleeping.

Most nights, Liere contacted Malcolin and Lyren before she slept. Lyren kept up a humorous commentary, mentally rehearsed during her days to be as entertaining as possible, as she toured Sarendan with Sveneric, observing Peitar's dream being carried out by his son.

Malcolin's days were simpler: he was back at Senrid's academy, any ideas of governments or kings as distant as the moon. Of vital importance was his ability to draw a bow and hit a target, and his worst conflict was the dreaded maths. He still missed his father, but the ache wasn't as bad. Especially when he thought of things he'd tell his father. Ma had said, you never knew if ghosts were around, and if they heard you. Malcolin was absolutely certain that if Da was a ghost, of course he'd be watching over Malcolin, so sometimes he thought things to him—practicing his contacts, as Ma would say. He imagined his father laughing, and admiring Stinker Senelac, just as he did, for his amazing ability to fart on command.

Liere's dreams were extraordinarily vivid, even before Adam turned up in them. The first time, she was again an undersea creature, the size of a ship, with long, streaming tentacles. What was that about? When another such creature swam alongside her, conveying a wordless invitation to follow, she knew it for Adam and with practiced ease remained in the dream.

At first Adam led her on a hide and seek game. He sank down a layer, vanishing. An expert since childhood at navigating the dream realm, Liere followed, enjoying the surge of the current, and the rippling grace of her tentacles training behind her. It was fun to propel upward, break into the air, and fall with a mighty splash.

Then they grew wings, and soared up to chase among the

clouds. The games were easy, changing rapidly. They did not last long, releasing her into the sort of sleep she needed.

She was close to finishing the next segment of the scroll, which addressed the joy of learning language. The dialogues reached into what early words meant, and how important they were, and how children learned not only through intentional teaching, but they listened avidly to everything. Including interactions between others, sensing currents they could not express. But they learned them just the same.

That whole section felt as if it had been written specifically for her.

She had been working so hard that her hands had begun to cramp, which meant she was falling into bad habits again. The next day, unless the weather poured, she was going to walk as long as she could.

She woke to a world full of drips. Icicles rapidly melted, the early sun of spring lighting drops to crystal. Everything trickled as snow melted from rooftops and trees. The fragrance of wet bark, and soil thawing, and little green shoots, filled Liere with promise. She was smiling when she moved down the zigzagging path into the city, and on impulse turned toward the dock.

Not three blocks away, she spotted one of Andri's former followers, a scrawny girl—now a slim young woman—with short, flyaway hair and a long, narrow face marked with the shadows of what would be worry lines sooner than later. Fronsa's gaze was wary rather than friendly.

Liere reached a tendril, to encounter a shield. Fronsa would be the type to remember a mind-shield. Liere had tried hard to make friends, but Fronsa's jealous preoccupation with Andri had kept Andri's female friends at a distance. Liere remembered hearing that Fronsa had moved in with one of the dock bosses, and she'd been glad that Fronsa had grown out of that teen fixation.

Fronsa clearly recognized her, but turned away, moving slowly, as if uncertain whether or not she wished to speak to Liere. Surprised—curious—Liere followed. They'd stepped into a narrow alley near the warehouses between the two main docks when a rustle of footsteps closed in on either side, and Liere found herself cut off.

She could transfer out, of course. Nevertheless, her heart beat fast as Fronsa addressed her. "You really did go over to the traitor?"

"I did not," Liere said. "I promised to stay a year. I will be gone as soon as that year ends." Forestalling the inevitable next question about whether or not she was sleeping with him. She would explain that that was part of her bargain only if she had to.

That conversation no doubt was inevitably, but apparently not today. She'd spoken so firmly that those circling her stared, some looking at one another. Most, she saw, clutched various types of tools that could be used as weapons — one of Macael's laws forbade anyone but his guards to possess swords.

"Inside." That was a new voice, a man's.

Fronsa swept a very ironic curtsy, her mouth tight with resentment.

"I'm sorry," Liere murmured as she passed by Fronsa.

Fronsa startled. "What for? Scared?" she added.

"Not really. I'm ... sorry you still seem to be angry with me."

"Too late for that," Fronsa retorted, and crossed a cramped room filled with what smelled like beer barrels, to stand beside a bulky young man gripping a club in one fist.

Liere's attention shifted from him to the dark-haired young man wearing stable brown. She almost didn't recognize Vosri Yuthan out of his uniform--he had been with Andri in the old days, and had been one of the first to join the King's Guard. Now apparently, judging by his clothes, a stable hand.

"Vos," she said. "I am very sorry about Bevara."

Vos blinked, his gaze shifting. "It was either him or her. Turned out to be her." He cleared his throat, and then said quickly, as if he'd practiced, "You've been walking around, telling people to give up. Surrender. Accept the traitor. We really liked you," he added, raising his voice as the brute with the club made a motion toward Liere. "You were loyal to Andri, and you did good things for us. But then you just let the traitor have Shiovhan, without a *try*."

"I'm trying to save lives," Liere said.

Vos raised his voice. "This is how it's going to be. Either

you agree to lead us against the traitor. We'll help you take him out," he added. "We have several volunteers willing to give up their lives if you can get them close enough to strike."

"And then?" Liere asked.

"And then you rule us. Like before."

"With what?"

"What do you mean, with what? Like before," Vos said. "We get rid of him, and his purples go home."

"Do you really think they'd go home?" Liere asked. "But that's a side matter. Let's backtrack. You said either. That promises a choice."

Fronsa spoke up, her arms crossed tightly, her voice shrill. "Or we kill you, kill him, and rule ourselves. That's what *I* want to do. Little Trevor Andiran is too young to be a king. We can't have Andri back, so I say, let's get rid of kings altogether. We can rule ourselves."

"Ah," Liere said. "How?"

"What do you mean, how?" Vos asked.

"Don't let her talk us out of it," Fronsa snapped. "She wants to be queen."

"I do not want to be queen, Fronsa," Liere said, keeping her voice even. "I accepted it because Andri wanted it, but I won't try to justify my past decisions. Andri is gone, or he'd tell you that himself. Instead, let's talk about ruling yourselves. How? I hope you don't mean to go back to the chaos before Adon Marsael rose the first time. You do remember how bad it was when gangs roamed around beating each other, and the occasional passers-by? If you don't have a plan in place, and agreement from everyone, isn't that going to happen again? Think how many houses burned and people accidentally caught in the violence ended up dead. Especially you who have small children."

A few side glances revealed uneasiness.

Liere went on. "There are a couple of forms of self-rule that I know of. The Fhlerian one wouldn't work here, because only those who were in the army at least ten years can vote."

"That would leave you king, Vos," someone muttered, amid a couple chuckles. "One vote, for yourself."

"I'd do it, if there was no one else," Vos said, but his shifting gaze did not hide from Liere how tenuous was his grasp of this conspiracy: he was not their leader, though they might have pushed him forward, probably because he was the nephew of a baras. He was not *a* leader.

"We'll not talk about how there is no treasury any longer, so there would be no way to pay a new guard, once you were able to fight off the Adranis, unless you began looting your fellow-Enaeraneth," Liere said. "And wouldn't that make you popular. Let's talk about governments. There's another form, which I know several trade cities have, and at least one country: that is guild councils. You have to belong to a guild, but then your guild chooses someone to represent the guild's wishes at the greater council. How many here belong to guilds?"

From the shuffling feet, and the looks, fewer than half.

"There is also the Sarendan kingship," she said, rapidly reviewing what Lyren had been telling her. "Sarendan's government is a monarchy pretty much only in name. There is a king because people expect a king. But this type of kingship was predicated by Peitar Selenna on the belief that, given the chance to govern themselves, people would take up the responsibility where the king relinquished it."

Vos's expression eased. "That sounds like what we want here. If we get rid of the Adranis, we govern ourselves."

Liere said, "It's a fine idea. The problem is in maintaining it."

The big man with the club grated, "What's so new about that? Every government has to be maintained. What else are those purples now doing, in spite of their new blue? They are Adrani purples through and through."

"Yeah." "That's right!" "Can't fool us."

Liere waited until the comments died down. "Yes. And no. We're talking about governing. Those guards, whether in blue or purple, enforce the laws. They don't make them. How would you govern yourselves, should the Adranis cooperatively disappear?"

"Which they won't," Vos muttered.

"True. Which is another reason I walk the streets nearly every day. Because I don't want to see blood in the gutters ever again," Liere said. "Peitar Selenna's style of government distributes power as far down as he could reach, to individuals. But because his system expects civic virtue, fair-mindedness, and impartiality, it is the easier to corrupt. Peitar's government demands far more moral responsibility from the people than rulers do of their subjects."

This unexpected attack caused a lot of confused faces. Moral responsibility?

She went on quickly, "Subjects of a monarch granted power for specific jobs—a captain of a patrol, a tax collector, a judge—do right, or wrong, because they know that the crown has law and force behind it. But in Peitar's style of government, the subjects—who are still earning their daily bread as laborers or artisans—must be moved from within," touching heart and head, "to curb greed and avarice for the public good, as there is no guard watching the people. The people truly do have to see to it that their community can sleep easy at night, and conduct fair trade by day."

"That's like us, when Andri and Gared looked out for westside," Fronsa said. "That's what we'd do. Like that. Like they did."

"But it worked because Gared and Bassl helped Andri run us, right? They couldn't patrol the streets and work. We had to steal to eat, I remember that well." Vos said. "Also had to threaten old Bangiar, who cheated everyone, and those snitches up on Street of Crows. Think the likes of them would trade fair, if there's no guard? We have to have a guard."

Fronsa reddened, but before she could retort, Liere spoke quickly. "Monarchs can look away from greater degrees of self-interest, for they have the power to yank the chain if the underling fails to carry out at least some of the expected work. But Peitar's net of mutual trust and effort tears into tatters if one cheats, then the next cheats because their neighbor is cheating, and so on. Especially when there is no real recourse."

Vos turned to her. "What are you telling us to do? Let the traitor live, that much I'm getting."

"I'm not telling you to do anything. I was once Macael Elsarion's friend, but no longer. If he dropped dead today my eyes would be quite dry. However, if he does die, who will that huge army answer to? It won't be anyone from Enaeran, that's for certain. It might be someone as bad as Bartal, or nearly."

That caused more shuffling and angry looks.

"I don't think Enaeran can take back the kingdom. We

were not strong enough to withstand the Adranis before Macael Elsarion moved in. I will say that he did it without great slaughter. That seems to be his style. The laws seem fair enough—on Oath Day he repeated that prices would remain the same both sides of the river. Life is not getting worse. That's why I say, wait. Don't throw yourselves on Adrani steel just to get the old ways back, because there is no getting Andri back, or the way we lived when he was alive."

More shifting; she sensed intent diffusing.

"What can you do? My thought is, if you want to rule yourselves, start practicing locally. Right here, dockside. With the people you know. Neighbors. Kin. Shopkeepers, and traders. Try ruling yourselves so well that the Adranis don't have to come around on patrol. I'm sure they'd rather be nearer their own homes anyway. Teach your children how to look out for each other, to trust and be trustworthy. Live well. That's always the best choice, to live well. If it works, more people will want to join you, won't they?"

Vos said, "Are you going to lead us?"

"I can't. I'm no longer a queen, and I'll be gone at the end of the year, remember? You don't need a queen anyway. You start with each other. Agree on what's fair, and stick to it. Fairness spreads on its own. Doesn't need a club." She waved at the brawny young man's weapon, and started toward the door.

Fronsa stepped as if to block her, appealing to the others, "Weren't we going to take her hostage?"

"For what?" Vos said bitterly.

Liere said, "You can't take me hostage. Remember, I have magic." So saying, she fixed on a Destination between two stacks of barrels and shifted across the space, startling the group. Several raised their weapons, then lowered them, looking back and forth in question.

Fronsa's voice rose, shrill and nearly teary. "You have that magic and you can't use it on the traitor?"

"Magic doesn't really work for fighting. And even if it did, what would happen, besides more lives lost?" Liere gripped her elbows, pressing her forearms over her stomach, which was rumbling uneasily. "I *hate* what happened. But it seems to me that life has not worsened, except for the mourning of those who resisted, like Bevara Yuthan. What value in making more people dead? Please. Whatever you do, really consider what comes next. And whether life is going to get better for the people you care for, before you act."

She then walked out, and this time no one stopped her.

As always as she trudged back up the zigzag to the palace, she went over the conversation mentally, wincing at the parts she could have put better, and wondering if her agreement with Macael had really been a betrayal after all.

That night, she shared her conversation with Lyren, whose response was: *Only you would worry about saving lives as a betrayal. What good would a riot outside that proclamation window have done, except making a lot of work for people scrubbing up the blood? I wish I'd been there! I'd give them something to think about, taking you hostage when you are ALREADY a hostage! It sounds to me as if you did as well as you could, without having time to think out your words.* Lyren's indignation on her behalf left Liere smiling wearily when she fell into bed.

As spring ripened, her dreams took her to an imaginary woodland, where again Adam joined her. And again they played a game, chasing each other from tree to tree while avoiding squirrels and crows. Liere began to understand that these games related to what she had always thought of as walls and filters in the mental realm. Perhaps Adam meant these to be lessons, but most of the tricks and traps were familiar. She found these games mentally exhilarating.

During the following days when she walked out, no one approached her. Most of those who recognized her continued to bow politely, which was somewhat of a relief. There were a few long looks, but no one cursed her, or made threatening moves. More importantly, she did not hear the rush of guards being called away to put down a rising. You might hate me, but you are alive to do it, she thought as she paused on the zigzag to peer down at the dockside area beside the river at high water.

She got more of a sense of accomplishment at her desk as the translation sped up, dialogues exploring the delight of different ways to teach infants to develop mind and muscle.

At night, her dreams continued to build more complicated games, until one night she woke abruptly, feeling as if she had labored hard instead of resting. And yet the games elated her, and most mornings she woke refreshed, especially as her inward parts settled down, helped no doubt by the appearance of the first tender carrots and steamed and seasoned cabbages of the season, with cherries later in the day. Now relishing her morning meals instead of choking them down, she returned to translation with renewed vigor.

When she had a sizable pile of pages, she transferred again at night. She found David at his own translation, his duties at the school finished for the day.

"A lot of this about the joy and importance of ritual seems no longer applicable, except of course the reminders about kindness and observance and so forth," she said. "In particular these long dialogues about the nature of the Four Cities. Every second word was new. I was thinking of skipping all that rather than copy it out fine for Macael."

"Detlev told us that memorization was believed to be mind-strengthening, as repetitious movement was muscle-building," David said. "The rhymes for toddlers and three-year-olds to memorize were also supposed to train their speaking muscles as well. The rest of the book probably will offer alternatives, but these are generalities."

"True. However, I wonder how much use any of this will be for Macael," Liere remarked. "He certainly made no mention of the first dialogues in the pages I gave him. I mean the ones about joy and so forth. He probably skipped straight to the practical stuff about infant care."

"Are you thinking of giving up on the recopying?" David asked. "I'm hearing an assumption that these wise words are only for those parents you deem good and deserving."

"I've been sharing them with Macael, as I told him I would. Though our first discussion didn't go well." She described the conversation. "It's difficult to see past my resentment for being forced into this decision."

"It's a difficult one," David admitted. "I wonder if he understands how difficult, given what little we know of his background. Why do you think he went to so much trouble to get this heir?"

Liere thought of Macael's sudden burst of joy before she slammed the door in his face. And shrugged it off. "He needs an heir? He clearly couldn't get one with poor Chantala, or on his own. Since he didn't get one from any of the women in his court, I'm assuming he wanted it to be half Enaeraneth and half Adrani. Or close," she amended. "As I'm not really Enaeraneth. And I happened to be the most convenient vessel to hand, even handily supplied with a son he could threaten in order to get said heir."

"That's a lot of unprovable assumptions already, so let's leave aside his reasons for choosing you," David said. "What have you learned about him as a prospective parent? Beginning, perhaps, with his upbringing?"

"Arid," Liere stated. "What little I've discerned. I did not want to get even that much, but what I can tell you is that his upbringing was utterly arid. He was not quite sure who his mother was when he was Malcolin's age. As for his father…" She shivered.

"No ready examples of joy, happiness, or love, would you say? It seems to me that you might translate every scrap here, no matter how obscure. That is a lot of what I hope is empty void you need to be filling if he's to become the kind of parent you want for this child."

"You *hope* is empty—" She paused, eyes narrowing. "Right. I hadn't considered that. How, if he knows little of happiness, joy, or love, then other emotions have that space. That is an argument for my taking this baby away from him sooner than later."

He waved a hand, the chair creaking. "The rudiments might be there. How did he react when you told him that the baby exists? Satisfaction? Triumph? Gloating?"

Liere thought back carefully. Much as it might bolster the rightness of her resentment, she had not seen the upper-lip smirk of gloating satisfaction, or the chin-lift of triumph below a calculating gaze. She had slammed the door on the widened eyes and the parted lips of joy. "None of those. It was joy."

David shrugged. "Seems to me that that joy might be something to work with." While sending a thought to Adam: *Do I tell her the truth about him?*

For a heartbeat there it was again, Malcolin's memory of his father's death, mercilessly vivid: the quick exchange between the cousins, Andri's falter, Macael's *Then that makes this slightly more bearable…* Malcolin had not understood the words, which were likely already sinking down in his memory. His attention had fixed on the knife. But he had brought the whole experience fresh to Senrid, where David had caught it all.

Adam's thought was quick: *We don't know the truth.*

: Sure we do. Andri saw it, and Macael saw that he saw it, that that encounter in the valley hit Macael with a thunderstrike. Obsession, lust, love, whatever you want to call it. Macael was angry that Andri saw it. Jealousy? Which gave him the strength to do the deed.

: *From what little we know of Macael, I don't think it was jealousy. None of his behaviors that we know of match with jealousy. I think his first thought was that surely Andri would use it against him.*

Liere looked up in question. "Is Adam listening through you?"

"Yep." David blinked. "He says, carry on."

Liere nodded soberly. "I really do have to adjust my thinking about Macael from conqueror and threat to my son to parent. Potential parent. Meanwhile: recopy all the pages, whether or not he reads them."

She transferred away, and David went downstairs to make a round before calling it a night.

He was surprised to find Detlev in the alcove off the kitchen, the summery smell of steep in the air. Adam gestured with a fresh cup.

David waved that off. "Something I ought to know about?"

Detlev said, "I think you ought to try Liere with the dyr."

David plunked down on the window seat and stretched out his legs. "Isn't that rushing things?"

Detlev drank off the steep as Adam said, "She's been burning through the preliminary guides. I've made them into games, to lessen how many stressors she's dealing with."

Detlev said, "She's known them for years. She could refine that knowledge, and shift it from instinct to consciousness, but that will come."

"I haven't approached the specifics for using the dyr," Adam said.

"And I'm still practicing them," David put in. "I can't teach her those. She's too fast."

"Yes." Detlev set down his cup. "Siamis and I made sure she learned the dyr guides when we were all on Geth that summer. She integrated them like..." He snapped his fingers. "Without knowing what they were. I think she instinctively figured out the basics when she carried the dummy dyr I'd made for Efael."

David whistled. "Withdrawing my objection. Though other things being what they are, it still might be bustling her along. Any reason why?"

Adam and Detlev both stilled, and David knew there was something in the air. But neither of them was sure of it, so they were mum.

David said to Adam, "Right. Since I don't have a dyr yet, I'm officially turning her over to you for the duration."

"For now," Detlev countered, and vanished.

As all of Brydon was opened to the warm spring air for a thorough cleaning of what had already been spotless, Liere plunged back into translation, making the discovery that the text had a structure after all. The initial dialogues had encompassed the importance of joy, love, and happiness. Then the lessons had devolved to the joys of nonverbal support before birth, infant care, teaching.

Now the dialogues went back to nonverbal support, but the focus had shifted to the importance of love.

> The elder said, first we must understand what love is.
>
> It makes no demands, but rejoices in the beloved's ultimate good, said the first parent.
>
> If it is used to demand, to command, and to admonish, it is not love, said the second parent.
>
> You are both right, the elder agreed. If love is not given freely, it is not love. Love is as quiet and steady as breath, and as sudden and loud as a tempest. The first delights us as the child slumbers in peace, the second strives for the child's survival. Both are equally vital…

The dialogues continued to define the entire range of loves, stressing the family bond. The first of this new set claimed that love was the adhesive binding families together.

That caused Liere to look up from her work and out into the garden, where the roses had begun to sprout dark red nubs as she considered her own family. Her mother had definitely been the adhesive holding them together. It had been a helpless kind of love. Much like Liere's love for Lyren, in those early days when she had no control over Lyren's exuberance: from the time Lyren was two to her fourth birthday, Liere's memories were mostly chasing Lyren and never quite catching her. It was always someone else who did. Senrid. CJ and the Mearsiean girls. Atan. Rel. Lyren had adored Rel. Arthur—sometimes. And finally Siamis.

She looked back again at her own childhood memories. How did Father fit into these lessons? He was never *evil*. He obeyed the laws and rules, by his own lights. Did he love his children? He probably would have said so—especially of Liere's eldest brother, who had been most like Father. But that had really been more pride than love. Had he experienced the tenderness of love? He must have, with Mother—or was that merely passion, a very strong emotion, but as ephemeral as happiness?

This caused Liere's mind to stray to her own situation, and the memory shards so reluctantly and even unwillingly witnessed from Macael. There had been no sign of love in any of them. Ambition, yes. Intent. Competition. Not a vestige of love.

Liere thought of David's "empty space." Could Macael possibly love this baby? "I'm going to have to steal you away," she whispered to the growing mound of her belly.

❧ ❧

Macael had yet to return when Adam contacted her: *If you are ready to try the dyr, can you come to Curtas's House? We'll walk up to the plateau.*

Liere remembered the dyr she'd carried for so long—she and Senrid, when they first met. She had subsequently found out it had been hobbled by magic, but she did remember a vestige of the plateau's heady sense.

It seemed that Adam had the time for her now, rather than when she chose. His was the difficult schedule; she was alone within the boundary of her agreement, the pages for Macael stacking up. She even found herself adding little margin notes to some, mindful of what David had said about experience.

That meant a daylight visit, possibly with the other dyr students around. It was not until that moment she became conscious that she had been avoiding them, not for any reason other than far too many tugs in different directions.

She assembled her papers in case Adam wanted to see them, wrapped herself in her cloak (for it was raining hard outside) and braced for the transfer.

He was waiting off the Destination area. "You can leave those here," he said, nodding at the papers. "No one will move them."

Here the sun shone, bright and warm, the snow on the peaks in the distance considerably diminished. She could hear a rushing waterfall on the far side of the plateau, below the steep drop as they walked up the gently curving stone stairway to the upper level. Liere remembered picking her way over broken stones undisturbed for four millennia when Detlev and David first brought her here, during the war. Norsundrian violence had vanished from this place. She wondered if that was true everywhere else as she followed Adam.

From this upper level, she could appreciate the angle of Curtas's House tucked against the landscape. Beyond the house, the white blossoms of a line of pear trees formed a lovely frame for the enormous garden. Around her, starliss and loethe bloomed, a scattering of bright yellow, gold, and deep blue. Far in a corner, kingsblossom lilies stood tall and elegant, a reminder of Macael.

Liere turned her back, though the usual spurt of anger at reminders had muted below the peaceful resonance that she felt more than heard as a hum: the sounds were water, wind, and birds chirping as they foraged for seeds.

The broken stone of the plateau had all been repurposed in the building of Curtas's House. The only construction on the plateau was a gazebo, open on all sides, the twelve-sided roof angled to a point. Inside the gazebo, a round stone table, with stone benches.

They crossed to it, Liere snuffing in the fresh air that smelled of wild pine, and a drifting sweetness of magnolia from somewhere below the cliff. The hum resonated in her bones, making her want to skip and laugh. How beautiful it was here! Though she appreciated the house, she was glad that the plateau was left to nature, save for this one small stone building.

"The dyra are here," Adam said, dropping onto a bench. "Choose whichever one you like. You can always trade, or if the one you choose suits you, but you want a different form, we can teach you how to shape disirad."

"I thought dyra were coins," Liere said.

Adam grinned. "That was the most cumbersome shape. Detlev chose it deliberately when the Host demanded his for their use. Round shapes easily get lost, roll away, fall out of pockets — as you probably remember."

"I do. I take it the lore about the round shape being traditional was concocted for Norsunder's benefit?"

"It was. Though it wasn't outright lies. There were a few dyranarya who actually preferred the round shape, Detlev said. It had to do with how they fit into the palm. Many people who came for guidance found that shape comforting. The dyranarya would then change it back to a more convenient shape."

Liere peered into the shallow dish. There was the silvery white glisten of pure disirad, worked into chains of various sizes and types of link. Several rings also lay there, as well as a couple of coins, one more of a convex shape than the other.

She hesitated, and Adam said gently, "Don't be afraid. There is no wrong here. If it's overwhelming, just shield and put it down. David still isn't ready for the dyr. He prefers to work with his own strengths. And he's not alone. This is merely an experiment."

"All right."

"Go ahead. Pick one. The rings can be resized for any finger."

Liere ran her fingers above the choices without touching them. She liked the rings, but she had never worn one, and was wary of attracting attention to it. She suspected that a ring not worn was easier to misplace than a coin.

She chose a chain worked in a pleasing braided pattern.

"Try wearing it."

She picked it up, and poured the chain from one hand to her other palm. It felt light, and cool, spilling like ... dry water: silken, cool, shapeless, but not wet.

She slipped it over her head and pivoted on her toes to gaze out over the hazy slopes. The hum had intensified to another sense altogether, indescribable except akin to stepping out of a small, still room into a vast wind atop a mountain even higher than this, one on which sight went on forever and ever.

She closed her eyes. And gasped. The mental realm was as familiar as her own hands, or so she'd thought. But never like this. It was as if all her life she had seen the stars through a veil of vapor, so only the strongest gleamed. The dyr ripped the veil away, revealing thousands—no, far more than that, millions—of colored lights winking, streaming, coruscating. She reached, soaring above, sensing the whisper of minds amid a dizzying cataract of sensations and emotions.

Instinctively she narrowed her focus, reaching for Lyren—and there she was, scintillating in a sensory array. Laughter reached Liere, who withdrew, and reached farther, to snag on an unusual rippling coloration. Liere's focus sharpened to recognition: *Marga?*

: Liere! I'm trying to be human again!

Liere caught the image of a willow tree, and smiled in amazement. That was Marga, all right! She ventured farther. It was a test, like running as fast as she could, as she reached for any familiar awareness, and there, almost at the edge of her mental grasp: *Siamis?*

Dim, but there: *Liere?* Steady as moonlight, surprised and amused.

A touch on her arm, and Liere's mind crashed back into her physical self. She staggered, and abruptly sat down on the bench.

Adam said, "Was that … did you hear Siamis?"

"Only my name. He was very indistinct, though."

"Liere, he's not in this world. He's at Songre Silde. *I* can't hear that far. Not without great preparation."

"I'm … a little dizzy. I think."

Adam chuckled, a breathless sound. "Right. I'd expect so. You're going to need a lot of practice up here. It seems you are able to endure the resonance without getting lost. But it does take getting used to. I advise you to wait on contacting other worlds until you've, oh, had the dyr a week?"

Her head panged, and sight swerved and jerked, swerved and jerked: vertigo. She could only nod, and then breathe. All her senses were alert, the tiny sounds of insect wings clicking. Whirring. Adam's breathing. Her own breath, in and out, her heartbeat. She could even hear the tiniest, faintest rhythm— was that the infant's heartbeat?

Liere closed her eyes, glad she was sitting down.

"All right. Here's what you do. Go back to Enaeran, and

practice with the dyr. Don't overdo anything. Get used to wearing it, and shielding. Focus on a specific thing. For example, contacting Malcolin or Lyren should be easier now, as if you called to them in the next room."

"Like you," Liere managed. She exerted her inner control, and banished the vertigo. But her head still panged.

"Is that what my contacts seem like? Yours probably will as well. But right now practice shielding. Later, when you're more comfortable, we can experiment with what the dyr can do for you. Farsense, I'm guessing, leads the list." He laughed again, and led the way down to Curtas's House, where Liere fetched her papers, and transferred back.

The dyr was an unfamiliar weight around her neck. She put her fingers to it and looked around her quiet room, expecting a muting. But there was none. All her senses clamored: the smell of beeswax polish; the cedar of her clothes tree. Taste: a lingering of the sweet-sour cherries she had eaten earlier, and below that the astringence of her steep. Sound: the high, crystalline voices of children in song, clear above the rush of the rain. Touch: the slide of her familiar linen robe over her arms, her legs, as she moved; the firmness of the mound at her waist; the warmth of the dyr lying against her skin. Sight, the muted gray of ran and cloud outside, but behind them the strengthened sun of spring; her feet in their ten-year-old slippers, molded to the contours of her toes.

And within, ready to suppress all those, the powerful, soaring sense of the world around her, all the living things. Her awareness spread to the roses, and sensed the rising of the sap toward the strengthening sun. She turned toward the wing where children sang, and brushed the surface of their thoughts, so busy. Thani, a floor away, scolding a yawning footman. Liere shut out their emotions, for this was intrusion. As she thought that, she was aware of Fan in the other wing, Macael's trusted … what was he, now? Once, a personal servant. But it seemed that Fan had charge of Brydon. Liere wondered if Fan and Macael had grown up together. Had that bond been love? It would be an uneven one, master and servant. Or, that's how it might look to the outside. Between them?

From there her thoughts shifted to Macael. Immediately her mind winged to him, and though he was shielded, she got a sense of him far away, toward the southeast of Sles Adran. Not in Enaeran at all.

She pulled her focus back to her translation work, mostly to test the dyr. She was not certain she could endure the heightened sensitivity, and yet it was also exhilarating. Her focus snapped to the work, and the words she had written the day previous.

… and the elder cautioned, how can a weaver be expected to spin glass? Or a glazier to weave satin? If there is no love from day to day between those in the family, can you expect them to know how to share love with the newcomer?

Liere had been yawning as she translated that, grateful that she only had to look up the terms for satin weave, and glazing. The whole had seemed so obvious it was not worth writing down, except that she had promised to do so.

But now, her mind reached not between locations, but between memories: Macael's, the earlier text, and again she considered whether or not there had been love in Macael's life.

Words that had seemed superficially obvious the night before took on significance as those memories cascaded, mercilessly clear. Was he capable of showing a child love? Kindness, yes: Chantala was proof of that. But love? So seemingly simple, so vital. It was completely missing from the parts of his childhood that she had seen.

What about now? Had he loved Chantala? He'd said at least once that she was his responsibility. Had he mourned her? There was no knowing, because within a day after her death, he had taken control of Enaeran. That argued against broken, isolated grief.

Maybe he was incapable of love? Or of the type of love the elder went on about so painstakingly. Who was it recently who talked about … And here again was Lyren, leaning against Liere as she spoke in a teary voice about a young Knight named Ferold, and his "fixed regard." *…Laban says was I really blind to Ferold being serious, like changing their schedule so he always had the route through here, and his fixed regard, and how he never paid anyone else any attention…*

And here again was that memory image of her own face, as seen by Macael, that wintry day. Because the dyr diffused emotional reaction — or maybe that was her own shielding — the pulse of revulsion faded quickly. Was it possible that Macael had made a … a love object of *her?*

She walked around in circles, rejecting the idea. But then there was Andri laughing at her when he told her one night that Gared had had the worst crush on her — right under her nose — and she hadn't even noticed. The first ever not to. "Did you really not see it?" Andri had asked.

Liere had not. Gared was firmly in "Andri's most trusted friend" category of relationships. It never occurred to her that Gared's wandering eye might light on her. Even though Andri and Gared had shared lovers since they were teens.

She turned again, looking at the fine furnishings, and beyond them to the wing of musicians, and then back again, recollecting the succession of fine dishes with the very earliest garden produce. And ended with the very distinct memory of Macael, who Chantala had said had laid aside his tiranthe for all the years between, having played through two nights, until his fingers bled.

She sank down onto the bed, thinking: I've found Detlev's weapon. It is I.

$$\sim 24 \sim$$

T wo days later, David woke up to Adam's summons: Detlev's house.

David niffed Adam's mood, and a change in atmosphere. Energy, query, acid humor—

The combination was familiar, but not in Detlev's house. "Can't be."

He realized he was speaking to a wall, pulled on his clothes, and transferred. Voices echoed along the usually quiet corridors. Siamis's among them. Returned from Songre Silde already?

David headed toward the voices, and paused when he saw Adam in the doorway of the big windowed parlor off the terrace, his light brown eyes—usually so mild and austere—narrowed in wary question.

"Imry's come back," Adam said.

Come *back?*

David rounded the corner, and there was Imry, lounging against a wall, apparently unchanged from the last time they'd seen one another. Yeah, Imry had indeed heard that "come back," but other than a sardonic quirk to the corners of his mouth he showed no other reaction.

"You're still alive?" David said, pitching his voice to express astonishment and dismay.

MV appeared then—alone, without Mildred. The two had been apart for a few years there, then suddenly they were together again, tighter than before. But of course any questions to MV about their relationship got a snarl as a response, or at most, a comment about how Mildred had taken to living in Tsauderei's cottage and reading her way through his magic books, now that Mondros had finished cataloguing them.

MV being alone whiffed of intent.

Imry's laugh was quick, inward. He shrugged. "What you see is what you get." It was an answer to David's rhetorical question, but addressed to the room.

"Have you been off world?" Silvanas asked.

Except for Detlev, Siamis, Adam, and MV, the rest began throwing questions at Imry, striving against one another to be heard. For the first time since the old den days, they were together. Those who were still alive, anyway.

Imry spoke twice, and both of those were single word deflections.

"But I don't think you've been *here* before, have you?" Silvanas asked, hands on hips, indicating Detlev's house with a jerk of his chin.

"On the contrary," Imry said. "Ilerian did a thorough inspection shortly after they were penned on the world. Insisted I come along."

"Of course. They'd need someone to man the broom," Rolfin said.

Several of them laughed, and Silvanas turned a wicked grin on Detlev. "You knew, I suppose?"

Detlev lifted a hand. "Why not? There are no locks on the doors."

MV only leaned against a table, his countenance so still that David's nerves flashed with warning. MV and Imry were across the room from one another. Imry — even while exchanging cracks with Silvanas and Laban — was braced for action.

Adam stood near the window, looking out, his eyes half shut. David drifted to his side, and asked in an undertone, "Did you know this was going to happen?"

"By 'this' you mean Imry's appearance among us?" Adam turned his head. "I niffed him around the dyranarya academy. Told Detlev."

Ten years ago Imry had started a world-wide war just to prove that Detlev had no claim, influence, or even communication with him. Yet here he was.

Yeah. About that war.

It was apparent from his slight smile that he was aware of the lightning-fast glances between the others selecting MV as judge, jury, and executioner.

David flicked a glance toward Detlev, wondering what he'd do, but he was talking to Siamis as though he noticed nothing. David moved away from Adam, who appeared to be absorbed in gazing out the window at the faint gleam of sunlight on the distant sea, and thought indignantly, are they expecting *me* to do something?

It happened so suddenly he missed the spark.

Physically they were an even match. Maybe MV was a trifle the taller, but not by much, and they both were built lean and strong. At first the fight caused sarcastic raillery and mendacious encouragements from the onlookers, which the two shut out with the ease of long practice. But when a block and lightning-fast flat-handed blow from MV sent Imry staggering back, Laban and Silvanas had to dive out of the way. They looked from the spray of blood on the floor to Imry's bleeding face.

That changed the atmosphere, and charged it.

They were all trained to fight without causing damage when they so willed. It was second nature to strike with speed and precision and to judge the force required mastery of control. They'd learned to take damage (and to minimize it) for they'd grown up in a violent environment, and when they dealt it out it was deliberate. Accidental damage had earned the dealer the general scorn reserved for the clumsiness of the dropped sword or missed target.

It was a surprise that first blood went to MV.

Fast looks went Detlev's way. He remained seated in the deep chair, Siamis leaning his arm on the high chair back, both mere spectators.

Crash! MV landed on a fine table, which smashed. Wood shards ripped across his back and neck.

More blood smeared across Detlev's fine floor, probably for the first time, for the house had seen no violence during Imry's war. The Norsundrians in command, after their single inspection, hadn't bothered with the place. They'd known Detlev too well to think they'd find anything of import there, or that its destruction would in any way discommode him. David was surprised they'd bothered to come even that once.

The two fought desperately for a hold. David watched the

character of the fight, and knew what it was MV wanted: not to rip Imry apart, but to get him down. And Imry had to know it, and was fighting to deny him the option.

Suddenly — an exchange almost too fast to follow — MV got a hold on Imry's arm, and Imry used all his own weight to break free. He misjudged MV's grip a trifle, MV did not give, so Imry's elbow gave with a loud crack. Imry stiffened, then — in less time than a blink — his foot arced up behind him in a fast, perfectly placed, deadly hook-kick, straight to the ribs. The same ones broken in the fight at Efael's castle in Chwahirsland.

MV's face blanched, but somehow he kept enough control to sweep Imry's ankle. Off-balance, Imry went down hard. MV dropped on him, one knee across the good arm, the other on Imry's ribs.

They were motionless for a suspended breath, Imry on the floor, MV kneeling on him, gazes locked. Whatever passed between them from mind to mind was shielded, for the room and the mental plane were silent, except for the sounds of pain-harshened breathing. And then the physical plane won out, as it always will while the soul is still tied to the flesh; MV fell to the side in a dead faint.

Imry rolled free and rose to one knee, good hand gripping his fractured elbow.

Detlev came forward. "Can you take care of it?" he asked Imry, indicating the elbow before stooping to touch MV's ribs to assess the damage.

"Yes." Imry's mouth was twisted. "But I'll puke."

Detlev turned a thumb toward Imry's elbow. "I told you there's training for that."

"Why d'you think I'm here?" Imry said derisively, then closed his eyes.

David watched him gather the remains of his strength, then lift away his hand. He felt the inner tug of the old magic: buildup, release! A blue spark, and the shattered bones aligned, but Imry was not able to reknit them; the flesh was still angry and dark. His face paled. Nausea was outrun by shock; he slid to the floor in an anticlimactic faint.

Several turned to Detlev in question.

Siamis rolled his eyes, and gestured to Leef and Ferret. Together they hefted MV and carried him off, where they would clean off the blood, wrap his badly bruised ribs, and stick him in bed. Rolfin and David were already lugging Imry out.

Roy sighed, and fetched supplies to clean up the blood.

Laban said to Detlev, "They could have killed each other."

"True."

"MV backed off because of what happened at Efael's castle? But Imry could've kicked his ribs in."

"True."

"Why didn't he?"

"Why did he do any of the things he did after he saved MV's life? I suspect it's all the same answer. Maybe he will give it to us." Detlev turned to Adam. "He won't talk to me yet. Do your best."

"Me?" Adam repeated, appalled. "The only consistent behavior I ever saw in him was despising me, from the day we first met."

"You, too." Detlev nodded to David, reappearing just then.

Siamis said to Adam, "He's here to learn. You knew that."

"I suspected as much when I niffed him on the mountain," Adam replied. "Once long ago, and then again just the other day. But I know nothing of that level of healing."

Siamis smiled. "There is a scroll for that. I'm not quite there yet, either. Imry has the talent, but has been fighting it his entire life."

Detlev said to Adam and David, "You've had several years to practice. Now you come to real purpose."

For Liere, it seemed that the entire world had broken into pieces the way ice cracks and fragments. Only the fragments expanded, turned, and then fit back together, bonded by emotion and memory, into a new pattern whose immensity stunned her.

She lay back and let her mind dart from image to image, emotion to emotion.

Fixed gaze … weapon … *how can a weaver be expected to spin glass?*

Is this how tyrants are made?

And her mind kept coming back to that memory of her own face. Perhaps this was merely the dyr making connections where none were. She pulled the dyr off, deciding to test and reevaluate everything.

She dropped the dyr on her desk, bracing against the expected crush of sensory change. But nothing happened—at first. The extraordinary sensitivity remained sharp, then gradually began to dissipate as her physical self resumed the primary focus. Though it was still early, she pulled the blankets over her and burrowed down, listening to the rain until she fell asleep.

She woke at sunset, willed away a slight headache, and welcomed the supper that Jauni brought to her. She felt much better after eating, enough so that she decided to return to her translating, leaving the dyr lying in a silvery puddle on the desk.

Except there was that paragraph still.

At first it had seemed so facile until she considered it through dyr eyes. Even without the dyr, it retained its potency. In fact, rereading it again without the dyr, she was aware of a pulse of urgency, as if she had erred and must fix the error before something worse occurred. She recognized her habitual pattern of worry and self-blame curling like smoke through her mind, and fought it back: this situation was not of her making. But the conviction grew that it was hers to mend if she could. How? And perhaps more important, why?

Macael was the one who had wronged her. She imagined saying to him, "I don't think you got much love growing up, did you? By any chance, was forcing me into this situation by threatening my son's life your method of courtship?"

Merely the juxtaposition of the words *courtship* and *Macael* was enough to bring the anger back. Oh! With this awareness, she could wield his own weapons, using them against him in a kind of justice: music?

Beauty?

The dyr opened her eyes to the hidden world, and she imagined herself flying like a shadow over it, sensing and smiting those who did evil. The image was so entrancing she smiled, rocking back and forth as she relished the image of descending on perpetrators....

Of what? What specifically? Murderers came to mind first. What constituted murder? She knew that. What would she do to them? She'd use her dyr skills to dispense justice as she saw it. It would be *easy*. So easy.

So *insidious!* Revulsion surged, sharper than the morning sickness of winter. Justice was so very volatile a subject. How would she know she was right? Her father had always been sure he was right.

She shivered. There was something especially pernicious in using good and beautiful things with evil or even selfish intent, at a cost to others.

She picked up the dyr, running it between her fingers, and sighed out the anger as she banished the emotion-driven sick dream. She had answered her own idle question: it didn't take much thought to understand that this was indeed one way tyrants were made. Including those who set out to use their skills and wits to do good, and then gradually forced others to tread the same path because, after all, she meant well. Who defined the good?

She set the dyr down again, grappling with the awareness that she was entirely capable of sailing out like some figure of vengeance. There was that much of her father in her, she had to acknowledge. She would need to question everything, beginning with identifying whether an action was right for her, or for the world.

So passed another day of rain, and a restless night.

The following morning dawned clear. She dressed for walking, headed for the door, then returned to fetch the dyr. She did not believe the servants would disturb it, but the fewer questions the better.

As she walked out, she slipped the chain over her head. And once again perceived the gradual sharpening of sensory observation, and the vast reach into the realm of the mind. But she knew how to shield against the battery of emotions and others' sensory jumbles.

The walk felt good. Nothing terrible happened. She still had no solution, but at least there was time. As long as Macael was away, doing whatever he was doing, she need not decide how to approach him.

When she returned to her suite, Jauni and Thani were both

there, mother and daughter's smiles alike in their happy anticipation. "The king is back," Jauni said.

David kept himself busy with school matters while he tried to get used to the idea that Imry was actually here. At Detlev's house.

On the third morning—well aware of his wish that Imry would have decamped between then and now—he transferred down, and found his brother alone in the breakfast room, drinking what smelled like cold, stale coffee. Outside low clouds rolled in from the west, changing the light to a fretful blue.

"I didn't know about that," he observed, pointing at the wrapped arm slung close to Imry's chest. "I mean about aligning bone fragments. Did you know? I mean, when you were on Five with us?"

Imry lifted a shoulder.

MV said from behind, "If you're going to nose around, at least you can fetch a chair."

David turned. MV leaned in the doorway, ribs still wrapped in Ferret's neat bandage, his shirt hanging open. Imry kicked a chair out. David caught it before it could tumble, and righted it with silent reproach.

MV sat down somewhat abruptly, right where it was. David knew what sort of pain MV was feeling; very seldom in a violent life had he suffered bruised or broken ribs, but most of those times, the two before him had been the cause.

Not all.

"I suppose you two clowns want to be served?" he asked.

Both Imry and MV flipped up the backs of their hands. David went to the kitchen, rummaged around, discovered half a loaf of yesterday's bread, and in the cool-cupboard some fruit from up north and half a bowl of olives. Below those, he spied a big wheel of cheese and a few eggs from the bucket brought down a few days before. Nearby was a small portion of the cream someone had brought for coffee, in a little ceramic jug.

He snapped up a fire, and crushed olives onto a flat pan rather like those his ancestors had used out on the plains for centuries. He beat together a couple of eggs with the rest of the cream, sliced the stale bread and soaked it in the mixture, then cast the pieces onto the sizzling pan to fry.

While the bread browned, the edges good and crispy, he scouted out a pat of butter, some good blueberry jam that Siamis had probably bought in Colend, judging by the handwriting on the top of the lid, and sliced up some peaches and apples. When the bread was done he scrambled the rest of the eggs in the remains of the olive pressings and crumbled cheese over them. Then he divided the food into three portions, and carried it all into the other room, where he found the other two moving silver about on the table.

"Eat," he said, dumping plates down in front of each, sending their markers skittering. "What battle are you refighting?" Thump! "Or planning a new one?"

MV sat back.

Imry glanced up, sardonic as always, and with his usual indifference, he said, "Ivandred. Against Ralanor Veleth."

David met MV's glance, and then everyone picked up forks and began to eat.

Later that day, Adam collapsed on the western balcony outside his room at the dyranarya academy and let out his breath in a long sigh. The sun was still above the horizon, striking a jewel-lit path on the distant sea, and glowing with fiery splashes of color below the clouds. It would be a sunset of surpassing beauty. He hated to miss one. Sunsets like these were his reward for very long unceasing days of labor.

He leaned back and let the extravagant wash of colors bathe his spirit. No urge to paint, no impulse to move stirred him. He was content to sit and look and listen to the whisper of the pines beyond his window.

The sun was half gone, its color the glow of embers, when he became aware of someone approaching. He had long ago grown accustomed to the acute awareness of all living things that the presence of the disirad gave him. No query by mind-touch, but he knew it was Imry before he heard the footsteps on the stair beyond the open door of his room.

When the steps reached the door to the balcony, he said, "Someone show you around?" The sun's rim had vanished. Adam closed his eyes, the better to enjoy the after-image.

Imry said, "I thought that was your lookout."

"No," Adam said, his eyes still closed. "Usually the first year people like to show newcomers around."

Imry didn't answer, and the pause had stretched to a silence before he said, "Siamis mentioned some mysterious old scroll."

"Yes," Adam said. "And you can start translating it, if you want to try one-handed. Or you can accustom yourself to the disirad first, so the concepts don't keep sliding out of your mind. There's a lot—a *lot*—we are relearning."

He sensed Imry evaluating his words, with the singular clarity he'd cultivated since coming to the mountain. So very intense, yet effortless. Adam didn't need to look to know that Imry had refused to wear a sling, merely a bandage to keep those bone fragments in place. As boys, Imry had maintained he never felt pain. It had seemed important to him. Adam knew now that this was not true—no surprise, he was no different than any other human. There was very little that remained hidden from Adam, here on the mountain. Even Detlev was less opaque.

Presently he realized another silence had spun away time. David, used to how he'd fade from the here-and-now, would nick him by mind contact when it was necessary to concentrate. Adam was surprised that Imry waited it out, until he said at last, "The lack of schedule is not an avoidance tactic?"

Adam said, "Does it matter?"

"No." There was no anger, just considerable amusement, but behind that, wariness.

Adam opened his eyes and sat up. Imry leaned against the balcony with his back to the glory beyond, wearing a loose shirt that hid the bandage. Yep. No sling.

Adam said, "It is true that neither of us had any respect for the other in the past. But if you are willing to listen, I will show you what I can. You should probably know that the process will be slower if you lie to me."

A pause, this time Imry's, then he said with an increase in the amusement, "I take it that's supposed to mean that your powers of penetration are formidable?"

"Up here," Adam agreed. "At least until now no one has been able to lie to me up here. Down there—" He shrugged, then grinned. "If you see that as a challenge, well, we can take the time."

Imry also shrugged. "This is your turf, not mine."

Adam said, "Is it vertigo, or headache?"

Another pause, then Imry said, "Both."

"On your previous visit as well?"

Imry laughed, his surprise a quick zing.

Adam said, "You've been up here twice while I've been here. The first, you spent a little time on the plateau, the second, a few days ago, you scouted the house. No, no one else saw you. No one knew you were here, for you took care to come when David was elsewhere."

Imry gave a derisive shrug. "What else? Or can you think my thoughts for me so I needn't put myself to the effort?"

Adam said, as if he hadn't spoken, "Have you experienced the headache and vertigo each time?"

"Yes."

"Vertigo passes. The headache will only vanish if you cease trying to block the disirad."

The implication was clear enough: no one blocks the disirad.

"I did try to not block it. Made me dizzier."

"That should pass. You had the right instinct. Go spend time on the plateau above. A night, ten nights. However long it takes. We have tents. No one will disturb you."

Imry was still a vortex of simmering nerves. That would probably never change. Adam looked around, realized his fingers had gone numb, and he flexed them, consciously adjusting his inner temperature.

Imry had been only wearing a shirt and trousers—and an open-necked summer shirt at that, rolled to the elbows. He probably hadn't even noticed the cold, just as when they were small.

Amused at the vagaries of life, Adam rose and went inside.

25

Outwardly, nothing changed. But as Liere alternated between her walks—longer each time—and her translations, she accustomed herself to the dyr, which she'd begun to think of as a portable version of the plateau that one could carry everywhere. But the effect was so profound that she discovered she could lose herself in ramifying perceptions, and thereby be oblivious to the passage of time.

From the reactions of the servants—carefully shut out except for what she observed through ordinary sight and hearing—she discovered that they were startled, then a little worried, when it took her a few turns of the small glass to answer a question like, "Are you warm enough?"

She tried to be a little less unmindful of the waking world. On those long walks up through the tangle of old garden being slowly tamed by Macael's army of gardeners, she could fling her mind open and follow the stream of thoughts without interruption.

The first realization she grappled with: there was no going back.

She could remove the dyr, and her awareness of the mental realm would dilute, giving way to her physical reactions and surface thoughts. But she would always know that the vast dyr-revealed world was still there, as if a pair of new eyes had opened between her physical self and the realm of the spirit. She must learn to integrate the two. It was going to take time.

Macael arrived back at the head of a sizeable force. His errand—one of them—had been military, then. She sensed his presence, but sent no messages, and as she came and went on her walks, she was aware of an increase of traffic going to and fro. She did not attempt to sit in at court, though she suspected he would permit it. But that was the problem. It would be by his sufferance, just as all eyes had shifted to him after she spoke during New Year's Week, and he corroborated her words. She was no longer a queen, except by courtesy, an unexpected (and unwelcome) reminder of her "Queen in Bereth Ferian" days.

The servants continued to offer her fine clothing and expensive accoutrements, but she turned them down. Her two black robes had been made to expand at the sides. They would see her out the year. Her mind remained on her dilemma: as each day ended, she returned to the inescapable fact that she needed to talk to Macael. There was a pile of pages to give to him. She must do what she could for the child, who now fluttered about within her: each movement brought from her a sweet rush of joy: You are there, my child. I love you. But sending silent messages of love to the unborn was not enough. There were two parents. And he expected to be raising this child.

If she honored the agreement.

Until she strode the paths of the ridge above the city, looking down on rain-washed rooftops, she had been considering various plans for taking the child away from him. What she would say to explain her breach of their agreement to him. To the world. But with the dyr expanding her consciousness to the myriad possible consequences, and drawing her awareness back again and again to what she knew of his own upbringing, she struggled against a sense that adding wrong to wrong was not just, but only increased wrongness.

Then came an evening when Thani brought her dinner, and with it a message from Macael: "He would like to know if you have any more for him to read. At your convenience."

This was it. No more hiding.

Liere looked from Thani's wide, questioning eyes to the growing stack of papers on the table, and said, "Tomorrow, whenever he is ready."

Thani's quick smile was hidden by her bow, but Liere sensed Thani's intense flash of relief at being able to carry back a message that she would not be sorry to repeat.

Liere began prowling her room, which was suddenly too small, too cramped. Even walking the outskirts of the city had not afforded her the space she needed. She had to go to the plateau to think out her campaign.

She gave in to impulse, fixed that stone gazebo as a Destination, and transferred to it. When she recovered, she spied an angular shape across the field of peonies, wild orchids, and other wildflowers glowing in moonlight: a tent. Liere was glad that her shield was tight. She did not want to disturb whoever was in it, nor have them disturb her.

She lifted her gaze away from the cliff to the distant mountains, thence to the stars. And shut her eyes, open to the immensity of the other realm and its millions of shimmering lights.

She stood poised between worlds, intensely, almost painfully aware of her heightened awareness. But it was the pain of poignancy: she did not try to argue with herself, but let the memory images cascade, falling like raindrops in a vast pool, connections and possible consequences ringing out. Intersecting, creating wider and wider ripples.

She could sense Macael back in Shiovhan, across the width of the Sartoran Sea. She did not dive closer, though she suspected that she could if she desired, and remain undetected. It was enough to recognize his solitary spirit, knowing as she did how it had been shaped by these old, emotion-remote memories.

How many children in the world today wept in the darkness, loveless and alone, whether lying in a byre or between soft sheets in some palace? A twitch of effort — like shutting out the ducks and only seeing the squirrels in Adam's dreamscape — and she saw them.

These were real children, their distress immediate. She could feel the sobs. The weight of their desolation crushed her heart, bringing her to her knees in the thick, dew-drenched grass. The urge to find them, to take them away to warm and loving arms, seized her. But how could she carrom from here to there, snatching strange children away —

Was this what Detlev saw when he looked out at the world? How could he bear it?

She slid her hands over her eyes, and instinct brought down her mind-shield. She shivered uncontrollably, though the air was balmy, until sense returned, soft as snow on a burnt field. If she saw them, the other dyranarya would. There were also good people in the world who knew nothing of dyra, who might know some among the children, and be making an effort to extricate them. Relying on these unknowns to act was not the perfect solution, but until there was more training, and awareness, there was not a better. *You are not forgotten*, she whispered in mind to all of them, as far as she could reach. She had no idea if her message could be heard, or if it remained confined to her own skull.

She turned her gaze toward the lower level. There was Curtas's House, a few windows still gold-lit, though here it was very late, not far from dawn. This, after all, was the purpose of the dyranarya, to find those who needed healing. She was learning how: she would only get better at it if she kept working, once she was free, and she would seek, and find, the troubled, the angry, stumbling down a thorn-strewn path.

She lifted the shield again, flexed that inward filter, and calmed herself with the contented glow of slumbering young souls. A far greater number.

There was still so much to learn! Beginning with translating the rest of that scroll, which was beginning to set aside generalities for specifics. Though the words were written millennia ago, humans were humans. And she had an important task before her, to clear a path of safety and love for this child within, and thence for a kingdom.

That meant renewing her campaign with Macael, beginning with figuring out how the absence of love shaped — shadowed — the young. She could not know how many nights Trevor Macael Elsarion had cried alone in the dark when he was small. She doubted she could get him to trust her enough to find out. It was reasonable. The day he threatened her son was the day her trust of *him* had ended. But she could, and — she vowed — she would, find a way to mitigate his shadow so that it would not shadow this new life.

She rose, brushed the grass from her knees, and transferred back to Brydon. Ignoring the damp grass stains on her robe, she dropped into her chair and worked on the translation late into the night, until her tired eyes blurred the letters.

The next day she was ready, the dyr worn under the high neck of her robe, her neatly recopied pages in hand, when a footman arrived to invite her to join the king.

With her heightened awareness she saw for the first time how subtly he braced for their encounter. And yet he still asked.

She nodded in acceptance of his "Good morning," determined to tread carefully. Macael's shield was that of a very private person. She already knew he was wary of words. Perhaps that privacy had been a method of survival. She had resolved to no longer throw those lances of spite that had seemed so necessary when he visited her bedchamber.

"I see you've accumulated quite a bit more of your text," he said.

Before, she would have laid it down and walked out again. Today, she held out the papers. He hesitated, then reached to take them. Their hands did not touch, but the gesture must have meant something to him, for she caught his quick hitch of breath, and his pupils widened, one of those very subtle signs that few in the world could completely control.

"If you wish to glance through," she said, "I am here to answer questions."

He looked up, searching her gaze, then said, "May I take the day to read them? I have to admit that a hasty glance, while keeping you standing, will probably result in my comprehending one word in twenty."

"I can come back," she said.

"I would appreciate it."

She dipped her chin in a slight nod, then said, "Do you want to set a time? Or send someone? I'm generally at my desk nights."

The tension above his eyebrows imperceptibly eased, his quick glance one of question, but all he said was, "Please."

After her walk, Liere worked on translation through the remainder of the day. Whenever she took a break to shake out her hand, she rehearsed words in her mind about the importance of infant love, then mentally ripped the words up. Everything speech she planned sounded like platitude, if not arrant maunder.

In any case, Macael asked no questions about the dialogues on joy, love, or happiness. His questions were about some of the practicalities, and then he said, "This one about the rhymes to be memorized. What little I recollect of memorization was the tedium. Is it really necessary?"

"I wondered, too. The rhymes in Ancient Sartoran were comprised of words thought to develop the speaking muscles. I'd translated the sense of them but whether or not such words would train the speaking muscles effectively is a question to put to a header. The lesson is useful in that the little songs are more effective when practiced with clapping games and dance games. It's so much easier to learn words by rote if there are movements to go with them. And children of two and three and four love repetition as well as movement. That much comes out of my own experience. My son liked certain books and stories, wanting repeats until I was tired of the sight of them. But I could see his intense pleasure in knowing what was coming next."

"I have a vague recollection of the comfort of constant re-reads, until they were removed and I was expected to advance my learning. You mentioned that you are translating Ancient Sartoran texts. Whence did these come?"

Liere had decided not to disclose anything about dyr training. "There was an entire cache of ancient scrolls, revealed once the war ended. The scribes and libraries interested in ancient texts are involved in translation."

"Bereth Ferian," Macael said. "I remember reading about the great archive there. And that's where you lived before coming to Enaeran, correct?"

"With time out for magic studies," she said.

"That brings me to another question. The snow-clearing spells in Shiovhan are better than those in Nente. But they are far from complete. I received numerous complaints during the worst of winter about trade stalled."

Liere thought sadly, *We did, too, last year and the two years previous.* "The spells have to be repeated over and over. Far more tedious than childhood rhymes," she said. "I was never able to get away to perform it, and our volunteers would work for a week or two, then take up some other task."

"I see. If you will teach, or prepare, whatever is necessary, I will dispatch trustworthy people to carry on the work over summer and autumn."

"I'll prepare the wands," Liere said. "It will be far easier than trying to teach magic to those unfamiliar with its disciplines."

"Thank you."

On another night, they discussed early reading, and texts with illustrations versus those without—thus requiring imagination. Liere spoke about visualization being easy for some and difficult for others; Macael listened with close attention, and finally said, "I've never been around babies, except when they are held or in a bed, covered in fine, embroidered clothes. Their noises and wrigglings seem random. Horses are easier to understand."

"My suggestion is, make the time to visit an orphanage. Babies might be harder to find, I'm relieved to say, this many years after the war. But orphans do exist. And, don't find one here, not where you're known. You'll just get a lot of bowing and they will whisk the noisy babies away, except for the perfectly groomed ones quietly asleep."

"Thank you: I will see to it."

These discussions took place several days apart, during which she translated more rapidly by the day, trading off with layering spells on the road wands. When she and Macael met, she handed off the new pages, and he asked questions, invariably about practical concerns, skipping over the lessons on emotional fundamentals as if they were so much airy rhetoric.

The days sped by, spring ripening into summer, which brought, at Macael's command, a selection of fresh fruits every day, as well as the pick of the garden produce. The promised road clearers were sent off.

Time was shortening. She looked back at winter, and her angry belief the year would never end. But now she sensed the compression of time. Her work was just beginning, but this pattern of meeting and answering general questions was getting her no closer to seeing a way to break past that wall of early experience.

It was time for her to ask the questions.

CURTAS'S HOUSE

Imry Llyenthur spent the rest of the month in a tent on the plateau, then one day reappeared with the tent wrapped up, and his gear bag slung from it. He was using his elbow minimally.

He ignored the stares of the dyranarya students as he entered the refectory, and said, "Where do I put this gear?"

David rose. "I'll deal with it."

Imry dumped the gear on the floor.

"Want something to eat?"

"Later." Imry walked out, and David found him next roaming the library.

He was not a popular addition to the community of Curtas's House

The most outspoken resistance to his presence came from the younger students, most of whom had been unheeding babes during the war. They'd grown hearing stories about desperate times, and they knew the names of the chief enemies.

Outspoken did not mean direct confrontation. No one said anything to David's infamous brother unless it was unavoidable. But little knots of talkers occasionally met on seldom-used landings, or out in the garden while weeding or harvesting, breaking apart and going their separate ways if anyone older appeared on the horizon.

The reactions to Imry were not undiluted hatred. Retren Ndarga, who was trying to sort his own very mixed emotions, sensed some of the same mixture in others. Interest, curiosity, doubt, fear, even pity, all were there to be detected, like hazy traces in the blooming fragrances of late spring, for anyone to niff them.

Retren suspected he was the only one who felt residual shame and humiliation. For years he'd endured the nightmares resulting from Imry's unspoken judgment when he selected Marend to command a special group — and her first order had been to oversee Retren's execution.

He knew now that the putative command had been nothing more than the bait in a trap. But for too long that had translated in his mind as simply being unworthy. He'd recognized, finally, that day on the border of Chwahirsland, that what was truly at fault had been the value system with which he'd been raised, after which he'd felt a vague, residual feeling of foolishness at how long he'd suffered needlessly.

Recognizing *that* had enabled him to laugh at himself, and

go on.

He'd thought the bad old days behind him, until he saw the person who'd served as catalyst. He didn't want to relive old stuff any more than he wanted to go back to Marloven Hess. Hearing Imry's familiar voice so unexpectedly brought back the past. Retren slid out to think all this over. When he had found his balance within, he sought people again, to find out why so unlikely a figure would be at Curtas's House at all.

"To learn from Adam," was the unexpected reply from Jessan Delieth.

"Why? A wager? Detlev do something to him?"

"I wish someone would do something to him. Like a knife in the back," Jessan Delieth said with a warlike not-quite-grin, and moved on to his next class.

The days passed in much the usual pattern. Twice, thunderstorms closed them in. Imry Llyenthur was little in evidence. At first Retren assumed his presence had been some sort of fluke on either David's part or his brother's. Either that or some incomprehensible piece of Detlev-gang business, for they still appeared and disappeared—most particularly MV—for reasons that no one ever explained, but Retren was certain had far-reaching consequences.

But then Ret would see Imry again. It was Adam who mostly dealt with him. The older dyranarya largely ignored Imry, except for Sveneric. Retren would have expected enmity, at least from David's brother, but instead he saw them twice sharing a midnight meal, and both times they were laughing.

A first-year student named Terith finally spoke up, when they took a break to sail on the lake below the house.

"Why do we have that villain among us?"

Retren turned with interest to see what Adam would say, now that the bad bold brother was not in earshot. The canoe rocked: others were turning as well.

Adam went on with his explanations about the balance of small vessels on water.

Again the girl spoke, more directly. "Adam, you said we are free to question. I want to know why you're teaching the villain who sent an army to smash up my country, and caused thousands untold deaths."

Adam shipped his oars, and smiled down the length of

the canoe at the little group. "Have I been such a poor guide?"

"What?" Terith asked, looking puzzled.

"I must be," Adam said his face and voice mild, "to have conveyed the impression that dyranarya are only called upon to guide only those we like."

Terith looked away. "It doesn't seem just," she said finally.

"Would you kill him?" Adam leaned on the gunwale.

Terith looked at the others for support, and saw them considering the question. Retren thought, *Yes.* But he knew he would not volunteer to do it.

"At least it would ensure he wouldn't do it again," she mumbled.

Adam said, "Do you really think he's here, enduring migraines, in order to learn to conduct better wars?"

Silence fell, and presently they rowed back.

Nothing more was said about Imry, at least in Ret's hearing, during the remainder of the field run. After they left the relative warmth of the slow Colendi river and returned to the bitter cold of the mountains, he noted that his classmates were uncharacteristically sober. He wondered if someone would leave over this issue; no one did, but he sensed their reassessments of what they were learning, and why. Of what they might be called upon to do.

Retren found that the most interesting, for it indicated that others might suffer as much self-evaluation as he did.

He mentioned as much when he and David talked alone.

Retren enjoyed these talks. He knew it was by design, and not by chance, that David and Adam found time for one-on-one conversations fairly frequently, though there was no set schedule. No set place, with one seated behind a desk and the other standing before it. Neither David nor Adam showed any taste for the customary outward forms of authority. Perhaps that underscored their innate authority, Retren sometimes thought, for when they decided circumstances required them to exert it, the effect was unequivocal.

Thunder kept him awake most of the night. He finally rose a little before dawn and went down with a book tucked under his arm to study in the breakfast room. There, the warmth and welcome smells banished the somber mood of the bleak blue light, as rain poured in a cataract.

Retren was not alone long. Two or three others came down, each with some work. The last one was David, and when Retren happened to look up, and happened to catch David's gaze, he found himself no longer alone.

Retren looked around just in case. Then, "I listened to what Adam said. And I thought about it. But I still want to know, why is Imry Llyenthur here? I mean, why doesn't he stay down at Detlev's house?"

"His presence does appear to be a catalyst for reevaluation. What conclusions have you come to?"

"That many of us had assumed that dyranarya would go out into the world and guide good people to be better. But that's only part of it, isn't it? Those are the people who would need us least." The old worries emerged, and he said slowly, "It might have been better for Marend and me to have had a dyranarya come when things were at their worst. Except we wouldn't have listened. We thought we were heroes."

"Opposing Norsunder did make you heroes," David commented. "I take it you've come to some personal conclusions as well?"

"I think I finally truly believe I don't need to feel guilty over the past."

David opened his hand in agreement. "And you've seen that any kind of a person can come to us for help."

Retren chewed his lip as he considered that: Imry had come to *them*. Right.

Then David surprised him. "So, will you go home and give poor Marend some closure at last?"

"What?"

"Your sister will never truly forgive herself for her mistakes until you go back and see her."

Retren flinched back. "I thought she was happy being jarlan. Busy. That I'd be forgotten. Just as I've tried to forget Methden by putting it all behind me."

David flattened his hand and struck it away in the Marloven gesture of negation. "She's had a few residual setbacks as well, but underlying it all is remorse — grief, even — over the past. Not Imry. You."

Ret sighed. "I guess it was easier to think ... well, hope,

that she'd forgotten."

"I take it you haven't really forgiven her?" David's voice was neutral.

"Not that. I don't think so, anyway. A reluctance to go back ..." Retren considered it further. "It's fear, really," he said. "How my father would have lectured about cowardice were I to admit the word out loud! Marlovens don't show fear. Don't know fear!" He gave a laugh, then rubbed his tired eyes. "But fear it is. When I examine my reluctance to go home, I fear that in returning to Methden, and to Marend, I would somehow slide into all the old patterns of thought and behavior. It's easy to identify habits of childhood, but so much more difficult to change them. And if Marend despised me for running off, and not helping Marloven Hess during the war, I think I would go back to feeling as if I was a coward."

David said, "Were you to return, Marend would treat you like a king. Better, because with more caution and care. She misses you terribly. She measures every single decision and action against what she thinks you might say."

Retren shook his head in disbelief. "How is that?"

"Because she knows that when my brother meddled with your family she was chosen for her moral weakness and you were ignored for your moral strength."

Retren drew in a deep breath. "Why didn't you tell me that before?"

"Because I wanted to be sure you'd come to the same conclusions on your own. I didn't know how, or when, I'd find out. It wasn't until Imry showed up and I watched the reactions of our little band of brethren that I saw what I had hoped I would see."

"I did reach the same conclusions, though 'moral' was never a word in our childhood vocabulary. I still have trouble comprehending it, really."

"A residue of your early training," David said, palm up. "Something we all face from time to time. But keep thinking on it. We all do that."

Relief surged through Retren, followed by a sudden, almost overwhelming urge to curl up and sleep.

David picked up his coffee and gestured. "Get your rest. You'll study better after."

❦ **26** ❦

When Liere considered her earlier encounters with Macael, though she had thrown questions at him to unsettle him, perhaps even to drive him away, he had always answered. So thoroughly, in fact, she began to wonder if these answers—from someone who was so very sparse with his words—were less informational than confessional.

She decided to try again, modulating her tone to the neutrality she was using to go over the text on infants learning what "No!" means—and how using Dena Yeresbeth to keep them from making errors was one of those things that came under Liere's own mental heading of trying to live the child's life for them.

When she said things like, "Using Dena Yeresbeth to direct a child away from an error takes agency away from them, even in that little bit. Small children fall down a lot, but it doesn't hurt. They must be allowed to make the small errors that teach them how to navigate in the world," Macael listened, but he never quite brought himself to admit to his own Dena Yeresbeth. She sensed that it was far too early to press. In considering the times he did talk, those always seemed to be about the past.

She'd try the past.

"You said last year," she began one evening, as crickets stridulated outside the open windows, "that Chantala was a victim of ambition."

"True." Macael paused in adding the latest papers to his neat stack. The subject had been the necessity for small children to be able to invent their own games, for, the elder said, *Children listen to everything. And in mimicking everyday life during their play, they rehearse for real life. The wise parent listens for repeated patterns; if these are angry, or truculent, or morose, what is the child hearing when not playing?*

"Bartal's," Liere stated. The memory of Macael's torrent of words so soon after Chantala's death, choked off suddenly after that one observation, had come back to her again and again during the long spring walks of uninterrupted thought.

Macael said, "And mine."

Shock lanced through her. She said, "You told me that Bartal had caused an agent to poison Duchas Chantal, and through her, by accident, Chantala. And you said you did not kill her."

"Yes," Macael said. And, in the same mild voice, "It was done by Bartal's agent, but it was I who removed the poisoner."

Liere's heartbeat accelerated. "I guess I ought to have figured that out."

"How? Shall I explain?" There it was, that remote, confessional tone.

Liere said, "If you will."

Macael said, "Bartal arranged the poison, threatened by Duchas Chantal's ambition. I believe Bartal knew she was maneuvering behind him. She planned to take Enaeran after she deposed him. She often referred to the great Mathias of Colend, and his bloodless victories. I took in her ideas in governing, and ruling with as little bloodshed as possible. They seemed enlightened to me. As they were, compared to Bartal's corruption and tyranny. But subsequently I discovered that though her enlightened ideas had been adapted from the Colendi, she despised the Colendi methods of social compromise."

"What I have seen here in Enaeran since winter is not what I understand of Colendi compromise."

"I know," Macael said. "I found gang rule entrenched here, where the crown did not or could not reach. It will take time to undo that."

The first was sadly true. The second might only be platitude. Liere shifted away from Enaeran. "Chantala adored her mother. Andri and I both heard countless little stories from her about their happy days at their palace in Denwy. How loyal the people were to Duchas Chantal, how popular she was. How well-managed Denwy was, how prosperous despite Bartal's heavy taxes in order to build and support his enormous army."

"The Duchas of Denwy," Macael said in that remote voice,

"raised Chantala to be a cipher, permitting no one else any influence on her at all. A less malleable child might have become a master dissembler just to survive. Chantala never had an opinion of her own—even the most trivial—that was not either squashed or twisted to the duchas's own use, except for the poetry, which she was permitted to have because it looked and sounded well in court, and because it did not interfere with Duchas Chantal's plans. When I found out about the poison, I waited, because to my young eyes, Chantala's diminishment from the eager, musical, chatty friend of my boyhood happened because of illness. I saw Duchas Chantal smilingly correcting her daughter's every utterance, almost her every breath. In company, they never shared their plates, so I had no idea that Chantala was eating the poison as well—sharing the same plate—in fact, she was Duchas Chantal's poison taster. "

Liere recoiled. "That's horrible."

"Poison was not unknown in Bartal's court. Most of his inner circle refused to eat anything from any kitchen but their own—or at the huge banquets, because there was safety in numbers. Anyone who dropped dead at Bartal's table would spark an uproar. Kitchen staff was chosen as carefully as treaty marriage partners. More."

"How did you find out she was being poisoned?"

"Fan revealed it."

"What is his story? Did he grow up with you?"

"No. I never had any servant longer than a year or two. My father wanted my loyalties staying with the Elsarion line. Fan was one of many comely, smart boys Bartal kept around him. If they were too smart, they had a tendency to vanish. Fan got in trouble when he witnessed Mandracar cheating in a personal duel, and made the mistake of calling it out, without knowing Bartal was behind it. Bartal sent him with an ostensible message to the dungeon, but Fan had observed no one ever returned from there, so he ran. He'd come with royal messages to Duchas Chantal (as his cover for spying), and I'd exerted myself to be friendly, as he was my age. He came to the duchas's wing looking for a safe place and I hid him. He told me what he had seen while under Bartal's orders, and I came to trust him."

Macael paused there. He passed his hand over his brow,

and continued. "I kept quiet about the poison because I wanted Duchas Chantal to die, for I had come to see that she was more dangerous than Bartal. Neither of us knew about the shared plates until the duchas died, and Chantala could not eat without her mother telling her what to try first. She was quite ill by then, and we understood at once what had happened. I vowed then that I would care for Chantala to the end of her days."

An invisible fist squeezed Liere's heart. "Their close bond sounded loving through Chantala's dreamy stories. Had the duchas a purpose?"

"Of course. Chantala was raised as bait for me, for Andri, for Bartal's enemies. Events in Enaeran developed too fast for Chantal to secure Adon Marsael or Andri as possible bridegrooms. The duchas planned for her daughter to marry at least one of us. The spouse would die in a duel or by brigands whenever convenient, and Chantala would be married to the next victim, until her mother was strong enough to secure the throne."

Liere shook her head. "Chantala used to talk about how they governed Denwy. Compassion and peace seemed to be the watchwords."

Macael said, "Duchas Chantal did do well by Denwy, though much of it was window decoration. Also, by an old law Denwy was tax exempt, and everything that was collected for the Wicked Bartal actually went to fund Chantal Shagal's plans. The irony is, after her mother's death, with my aid from the background, Chantala carried out the reforms in the places her mother had ignored because no one would know about them and so she would gain no credit. Chantala cared nothing for credit. She thought she was upholding her mother's wishes, and paid Bartal's supposed taxes from the family fortune. The result was universal admiration from the people of Denwy."

That much Andri had testified to.

"It was in carrying out Chantala's wishes that I learned the most about governing, for she was steadily less capable, though she tried her best. As a result, Bartal was given his 'tax' money, but he watched helplessly as the real wealth dwindled, and so he concocted his plan to marry Chantala to Mandracar the moment she turned eighteen. It was then that Andri rescued her, and told me where he had left her. At her request I made certain that her improvements at Denwy continued to be carried out. They were used to my giving orders by then. This was around the time that Bartal was effectively replaced by the Norsundrian commander from Sarendan, Kinarde, who had orders to hold the kingdom, and not interfere until the Host of Lords broke through to regain access to Norsunder."

"And while all this was going on, you met Andri," Liere said, shivering despite the warmth of the fire. Now, at last, all the strange facts and memories fitted together. She had no doubt that Macael told the truth. At least, as he saw it. Still, she said, "Have you proof of the mother's duplicity?"

"Sheaves of it," he replied, apparently undisturbed by the imputation that he might be lying. "Including the arrangement of the assassination of both my parents. Who didn't get to her first."

"They were both killed?"

"Yes. By carefully arranged accident. Early on, I believed the image of the beleaguered heroine Duchas Chantal crafted, for she courted me assiduously after Alored rebuffed her attempts at a treaty betrothal with Andri. But certain ... discrepancies ... caused me to investigate more closely, and the first proof was an intercepted letter to Adon Marsael."

"I take it you had a staff by then?"

"Yes. Fan knew the smartest and best of Bartal's cadre of messenger-spies. He brought them over one by one, after Bartal let the Norsundrians in. The letter was intercepted by Fan's cousin; she had grown up in Enaeran, before she was brought back to Nente and put to work as a maid to spy on the Edris family, who were too powerful for Bartal to attack directly. I was nominally Chantala's betrothed by then. She thought so, but the duchas was disturbingly vague about the treaty as well as the year we were to marry, when usually those things were negotiated precisely and signed quickly. At the end of this letter, Duchas Chantal promised, if Adon Marsael agreed to marry Chantala on her eighteenth birthday, she would arrange my death in such a way that he could not be implicated and he could then inherit both Elsarion branches' holdings. By then of course Andri was living on the streets of Shiovhan as an outlaw."

Shock chilled Liere's nerves. She realized how very young not just Andri but Macael had been when they found themselves involved in death-dealing high politics.

"Subsequent investigation and interception turned up similar communications with various Adrani nobles, with Bartal's removal from the throne as her stated goal. Which is why," Macael said evenly, "when I found out she was being poisoned, I did nothing about it."

Liere winced. If only Andri had known all these things, what might have happened? He would still be alive, for he would not have underestimated Macael. *I am by nature more of a seneschal then a war chieftain*, Macael had once said; it seemed another lifetime altogether. The strange thing was, it also appeared to be true. But, like so many of the things Macael had said, it had carried hidden meanings.

Liere said, "Was it difficult to suborn someone to remove the poisoner?"

"No," Macael said with his usual calm. "I killed him myself."

CURTAS'S HOUSE

Adam snuffed out his candle and sat at the window to wait for his eyes to adjust. The quarter moon was a cool silver-blue, partially hidden among ghost-lit clouds. Stars, brilliant as gems in the summer sky, glittered here and there.

A beautiful night, a quiet night, after a series of thunderstorms. Summer, late to arrive, had burst upon them. It was likely to remain dry for a while. All he could hear was the chirr of insects, and the occasional beat of wings as silent night birds foraged the wealth of seeds shaken down by the storm.

Adam sat back, enjoying the hush. His day's tasks were done. Perhaps tomorrow there would be a sunset. Now the world lay below his window, full of flowers and greenery.

He closed his eyes, and effortlessly dropped into the waiting pool of lights eternally gleaming on the mental plane. Fast — faster than a shooting star — he dove through the dreams of his charges.

There was little that Adam could not do — tracelessly — up

there on the mountain. But that did not mean he would do it, for he was still finite, and would pay the cost of trespass in human terms. He was also patient, and was beginning to comprehend when to act, and when to wait.

He waited on Imry Llyenthur now.

Detlev had said once, when they were all impatient of constraint, that their apprenticeship would end when they discovered how and when to set, and keep, boundaries. Imry's interpretation of those words had been his break with the group. Now he was back ... in a sense. Prowling restlessly around the borders of the community, watching, wary. He'd been that way when he was four years old.

Where was he now? Ah. The library at Detlev's house.

Siamis had, over the passing centuries, patiently collected what interested him, keeping it all off-world against the day — if ever — their plans were complete. He'd brought that library to Detlev's house after Norsunder's defeat. I want to live long enough to build such a library, Adam thought. It would take at least several lifetimes to satisfy his curiosity.

David drifted into his room. "Imry's down at Detlev's, in the library again. Know what he's reading?"

"He hasn't told me, but from the laughter I'd say he's reading about himself."

Not surprising that he would choose to read about the war that he had initiated. Many were the records, and varied, but all shared one characteristic: unstinting opprobrium for the enemy. Adam and David knew that Imry would be highly entertained by the unflattering depictions of himself, but he'd be interested in intelligent assessments of his performance, both in winning and in losing.

Adam saw it as a first, tentative, movement toward being able to perceive others as individuals and not game-pieces. Imry's world, he'd realized long ago, had been comprised of self, Detlev, enemies, and tools.

David's thoughts ran parallel. "He's still having disirad headaches?"

Adam nodded. "He's fighting it still."

"But he keeps going back up there. I'm beginning to wonder if that's simply his old, rotten habit of trying to prove that he's made out of stone. Mere pain is for the weak." David rolled his eyes.

Adam hmmmed below his breath, then said, "He knows that there can be no lessons in healing until he can become a human being."

David grinned. "I wish I'd been there when Siamis told him he has to do healer studies before he can tackle whatever text they found under the lake."

"He cursed," Adam said, as if surprised David would even wonder. "Predictable to the language—".

"Shit-for-brains being the most-used."

"—but he keeps coming back."

They fell silent as a distant owl hooted, soft and low. Its mate hooted back from the peach trees.

David tapped his fingers absently on the lintel as he leaned against it. "I'm beginning to suspect he began his 'comeback' during the war. Do you really think, as Laban does, that it's as simplistic as his interest in Marga Fer Eider?"

Adam made a negating movement. "It was you," he stated firmly. "I'm sure of it. I believe it was when he had you in his tower, after Charis-Merian stabbed you. And you hinted at everything he missed when he left us. Meanwhile, you were the result of all the things Detlev had tried to teach him when we were small."

"Slid right off him. I remember that much."

"I think he finally could hear some of it. I don't want to overstate."

Later the next day, MV and Mildred turned up, as always without anyone expecting them.

At once MV chivvied Imry into co-supervising a weaponry practice session. David and Adam knew how foolish (and how futile) it was to deny knowledge, and though the exercises most often done at Curtas's House were hiking, rowing, chase games, and slow martial arts forms meant to tone bodies, they didn't forbid anyone who wanted to learn martial arts defense. That, they knew quite well, was a sure way to heighten interest.

Adam sometimes contemplated how, despite all the changes, young people were attracted to, and by, effective mastery of deadly weapons. David had shrugged it off, saying,

"We never expected to change the world overnight."

No, but Adam thought deeply about how to change it over longer time. If he had a purpose in life, that was it, or close to it.

Perhaps that time would come.

MV and Imry running a practice session together seemed to function as a magnet to even the most pacific students. They all crowded in, though not a few were there hoping to see MV throw Imry on his ass a few times. The two kept the room in a continuous fizz of half-dizzy hilarity as they traded mock-blows and insults; it was Mildred who did the most actual teaching, with her usual superlative skill, until the participants were stiff and sore.

Adam observed from the sidelines, maintaining his usual neutral affect. If Imry followed his old pattern, he might amuse himself by an endeavor to charm the distrustful students, then play divide-and-conquer. If so, Adam resolved not to interfere. His work would have to withstand such tests sometimes.

David also held himself aloof, neither participating nor censuring.

Later that day, though, Imry went right back to his reading, as if nothing had happened. MV and Mildred vanished again.

That evening, Adam was surprised when Imry appeared just after supper. "Well? What shall I do?" He lifted his hands. "Teach me."

Adam said, "You're still getting headaches."

Imry retorted, "Start with how not to."

Having been prepared against just this invitation, Adam smiled and said, "Find me."

He'd decided that a teaching relationship after years of distrust and dislike would have to begin in the metaphor best suited to the learner. So Adam made of the first lesson a challenge, a game.

The playing field was the weird, unchartable mental realm, where Adam was utterly at home. From the overlapping realities he eschewed dreamscapes where others might be — for that put them at risk — and the disirad's own essence. Instead the metaphor was in his own lucid dreams, the level just above memory.

Risk was involved, for Imry could choose to be destructive merely because it was habit. Adam, in looking back, had recognized that the instinctive ability Imry'd demonstrated in knowing how to hurt the most, or what to say to gain the greatest effect, had been the sign of the warped healer's talent.

But he trusted his own strength. And so they chased through Adam's dreamscapes, phantom Adams flitting hither and thither. Adam hid himself away from the track he wanted Imry to take, but the track was there, carefully laid, for Adam now was a master at manipulating dreams.

The game did not last long.

When it was done, Imry said impatiently, "What did you get out of that, besides the back of the hand to me in territory I don't know?"

"The intent is for you to get to know it," Adam said. *And to learn that you are part of the human community, something that was slapped and beaten out of you before your fifth year.* But that, he kept to himself.

$$27$$

Midsummer passed, a very subdued festival day in Enaeran. There was a single Night Fair that Liere was aware of, at Five Points at the upper end of the city. That was for the citizens; the younger generations whooped it up as best they could, while their elders made a good try, but in spite of the smiles and hoisted glasses, they were aware of the Adrani patrol columns neatly turned out, weapons sheathed. These did not interfere, even in horseplay such as fountain water fights and a few drunken brawls that were more noise than threat. No duels, as no one could carry swords in the streets anymore. There were not a few among the silent celebrants who were just as happy to see young people required to find jobs rather than loiter around looking for trouble, which had been the life Andri had loved.

Macael did not host court in Shiovhan, with so many Enaeraneth nobles confined to their estates. Others were still stung over having been summoned for Oath Day. But—Liere sensed, through scraps of emotion-charged conversation drifting on the still summer air—they appeared to be more or less resigned. If there were secret conspiracies, Liere was not aware of them. Her reign had effectively ended with the spread of the belief that Sartora was not going to rescue the kingdom and smite the Adranis into dust.

Weeks of blazing sun passed, the weather Liere had first experienced when she arrived in dusty, dilapidated Shiovhan. She could not avoid noticing that the roads had improved, and not just in the wealthier neighborhoods. The tumble-down hovels of the west, where once Andri's gang had imposed a semblance of order, were completely gone, replaced by rows of tidy houses with shops at all intersections, and fruit trees in the center where there were no fountains. Either fruit or aromatic trees in all the former dueling squares as well, their roots reaching down to the vast underground river that had been the reason the city was built long ago. The sounds of repair still echoed down stone corridors, roofers bringing cartloads of tiles in hopes of finishing before winter.

By now Liere's daily walk was shortening to a determined waddle. The dry air had crisped the grass when a great storm rumbled over the mountains, bringing relief for a night, the gutters running with dust. Harvest time had begun, the air increasingly sultry as hot weather vegetables and fruits were brought in, and over the weeks that followed, the haying, grains, flax, and cotton.

Liere continued to meet with Macael when he was not elsewhere. She came armed with pages and questions; he discussed the practicalities of the first, and answered the second. He was very guarded behind those complete answers explaining, in detail, everything he did, but seldom what he thought, and never what he felt.

By the time the days began shortening, and her walks were confined to rambles through the gardens, all she knew about him was that he discovered early that he enjoyed the complexities of governing: the seneschal. All that ledger work that used to fret Liere's dreams with images of chasing rainbows and mirages, never to be caught, was to him vital with interest.

He knew how to rule; he learned how to reign by doing. And she now knew enough about the matter to see that he was good at both—if you accepted his style, which included the sudden removal of obstacles. Such as Andri Malcolin Elsarion, cousin at a removed degree.

She tried not to waste time considering Macael as king. Her business was with him as a man, specifically as a father. Kings, good or bad, did not necessarily make good parents. Her inclination leaned in the other direction, mostly because of the time involved in ruling, which argued for children left to others to raise. Andri's style of kingship might be in question, but he had been a loving father.

Was she right to separate king and man so neatly, when after all they were bound in the same person? For in an orthogonal slash through all her considerations ran the fact that there was a cost to power. Her father, a shopkeeper, had been tyrannical within the confines of their small shop with the living quarters over it. The quiet, diffident Macael of ten years ago, who had been troubled by Andri's ability to scythe his way through brigands and Norsundrians, was now merely quiet. Diffidence was the wrong word for a man who could kill another man and then threaten his wife into joining him to have a child.

It wasn't until a breathless night, as she sat by her window remaking her under-dress so that she would not have to wear an over-robe at all, that she became aware of Thani and Jauni fussing around more than usual.

It was fussing. What else could you call dusting the already gleaming surfaces, and twitching the perfectly smooth sheet on the bed, the blankets having long been stored away between sachets of cloves and thyme?

Liere had finished a contact with Lyren — back in Wnelder Vee again — when she became aware that the Ghan mother and daughter were still there, one making a surreptitious motion toward her daughter as she fluffed the curtains unnecessarily, while the other shook her head, and restacked the dishes left from Liere's dinner.

Liere turned from the round-eyed daughter to the mother, saying, "Have you a question for me?"

Thani took a step toward her, then hastened back.

"Please ask," Liere said. "I beg pardon if I have in any way conveyed the impression your questions are not welcome." She softened her voice, truly remorseful at the idea that she could be perceived as intimidating.

Thani saw the sincerity in her face, and heard it in her voice. She said quickly, "It's not my question, the truth of it is. I ..."

Jauni made shooing motions toward her mother, and mouthed something that made Thani screw up her face in her attempt to interpret it. Then she sighed, and finished, "It's just that Fan says, the king doesn't — hasn't felt — is Enaeraneth custom so different, that he is not permitted to feel the kicking?"

Liere stared, overwhelmed by the bittersweet pain of memory, how Andri had adored running a hand over her belly to feel those baby ripples and bumps. When the baby hiccoughed, as had happened more often before he was born, Andri had laughed out loud, and Liere had been convinced the infant within heard his father's voice.

"I … never thought of that," Liere admitted, the memories vanishing before intensely conflicted emotions at the idea. "I will see to it," she promised. "When next the king has time for one of our meetings."

Thani's face bloomed into a smile, and she bowed her way out, her daughter on her heels.

Macael made time the very next day. She took her latest pair of pages of translation, which went into detail about encouraging elder siblings to begin caring for younger; as she'd crossed to Macael's wing, she was aware of her wish that the babe would sleep within. But no, as she bent to hand off the papers, a surge and a bump against her hip bone made it clear that Child Within was awake and swimming vigorously.

She said, "There is quite a bit of movement today. Would you like to feel it?"

As soft-spoken as wind through the cedars, and as cool as the moon on the water, Macael stepped up beside her. His breath stirred the top of her head. She suppressed the flare of attraction; no longer did it anger her, or (beneath the anger) spark guilt. She acknowledged it, knowing she would not act on it.

He laid his hand over the top of her belly. As if aware of this new presence, the infant fluttered again, and Macael's face lifted, his eyes closed, his smile transcendent. For no more than a heartbeat. Then his expression shuttered to its habitual dispassion, though his fingers lingered before he stepped away.

"Sometimes the infant sleeps, and nothing is to be felt," she said briskly. "But if it moves, you are welcome to feel it. The elders insist in the text that the child senses your emotions through touch."

He seemed to have nothing to say, so she left, trundling back down the marble halls to her suite, where she could throw off her robe in an effort to cool down.

Thereafter, every time she met with him, he would ask if the baby was moving. Just as when they met in her bed, it got easier after the first time, and she knew that it was her own conflicted feelings that formed the barrier. He always asked, in sharp contrast to Andri, who had sneaked up on her as one who knew he was welcome—as he had been. Macael did not take this intimacy for granted, which—she realized—underscored her lack of success in discussing emotions. And Dena Yeresbeth. Macael had learned not to take that risk.

And yet he never avoided her.

The rains held off until a few days before Harvest Day. Two spectacular thunderstorms in a row brought cool weather at last, in time for the feasts, dancing, and fun—again in Enaeran somewhat subdued.

Liere, racing to finish the book, had plunged into the third part, the dialogues that addressed the ephemera of happiness.

She dipped the pen, scrawling, *The elder agreed with the first parent, saying that happiness seldom comes to those who begin a statement with If Only. There is far more promise of happiness in acting in benevolence n—*

She reached to dip the pen again, then stilled as her lower belly gave a slow, but definite squeeze.

"Thani," she said, keeping her voice calm. "I believe it is time to summon the midwife."

Thani ran to the door, skidded to a halt on the smooth, shining floor, and whirled around, her hands bunched in her apron. "Is it coming now?"

Liere tried not to laugh. "Not now. With my son it was a few days. But …" She gasped at another, more intense pang. "Imminent."

❧ ❧

David loathed that back-of-the-mind nagging sense of having forgotten something. He mentally considered every one of his students, including Imry. All busy and accounted for. Even Liere, living apart—

Liere? Wasn't she about due for childbirth now?

From there his mind winged to Senrid—who was not at all a part of that, for which he was thankful—but then to the date.

"Damn!" he shouted, so sudden and so loud that halfway down the hall a glass crashed to the floor, and in the other direction, someone else let out an outraged squawk.

He transferred straight to Senrid's castle. Where of course he did not find Senrid in residence. He'd always gone off somewhere alone on the anniversary of his daughter's birthday.

From there he transferred to the Darchelde hideout, but that was empty, too. He remembered where he'd found Senrid during winter, and shifted himself to the Montredaun-An castle in the middle of the forest—to discover it full of people. Marloven Hess being quite a distance to the west of Curtas's House, it was late morning here.

David walked in, staring in amazement. The great doors had been removed from their massive, twisted hinges, and lay on trestles in the newly-cleared courtyard, being worked on.

Inside, the tap and chip of chisels and stone-making tools raised a maddening almost-rhythm. In the middle of it all stood Senrid, watching workers on a scaffold swarming about a balcony high on one wall in the main hall.

He turned his head when David appeared. "Ahah," David said, noting Senrid's clear eyes. Of course, it was still early if he was bent on drinking himself once again into insensibility. "What's going on?"

"Fox," Senrid said. "He hasn't said anything, but I suspect he's going to be retiring sooner than later."

"He has to be in his eighties," David observed. "Even a geez in good condition probably wants to do something else besides board pirates in the middle of thunderstorms."

"Precisely. His latest communications are about how Barend Montrei-Vayir went about running our navy in those days. He thinks we couldn't do better than to organize along those lines. The fact that he wants to oversee it suggests to me he's ready to hand off the cruising for pirates to the likes of Heraford and Puddlenose."

David knew that Fox had been cruising in company with the Mearsieans, as well as a couple of independents crewed mostly by Chwahir who had escaped from Wan-Edhe's rule. The idea that Fox Montredavan-An would organize the new Marloven navy appealed quite strongly—and from Senrid's faint smile, it seemed he felt the same way.

David glanced around at the work, then at Senrid, who stood in the posture he adopted when hiding tension:

seemingly at ease, but his hands clasped tightly behind him.

"This is a very expensive project," David observed.

"Not as bad as you'd think. The materials are all here. The wood was even sound, the Wood Guild inspector said. The wood preservation spells had been thorough. Was that to Detlev's credit?" A wry glance.

"Maybe. But if so, I never heard about it."

Senrid grunted. "In any case, the worst of it was the cleaning. Did you know how large spiderwebs can get over centuries? Fox, I learned, tough as iron and ready to charge enemies fifty years younger, does not like spiders. Especially ones as big as his head."

David said, heartfelt, "I'd as soon leave the spiders to their part of the world and I'll stick to mine. Too many eyes, and way too many legs. Though they probably laugh at us for our lack."

"Laughing or not, I don't want them in Fox's house," Senrid said. "Most of them did scuttle off into the woods when their webs were disturbed, and light let in."

He went on about how South Army volunteers carried out the labor, five weeks of work for a week of paid liberty. It was a popular job, and as it happened, a pair of twin sisters from a very old stonemason family out of Eveneth had offered to take charge of the rebuilding. "They called it a dream project," Senrid said.

"It'll make their reputations for life." David squinted around.

He attributed Senrid's tension to the anniversary, and remained where he was, listening to Senrid's plans for refurbishing part of the castle and leaving the rest to Fox to organize as he wished—after which Senrid took David completely by surprise by suggesting they return to Choreid Dhelerei by magic for the evening meal.

David stayed late, then finally returned, knowing that if Senrid wanted to go off somewhere and drink alone, there was no stopping him. Was it or was it not a good sign that he hadn't yet begun?

He mentioned that to Adam before going off to bed (dawn was bluing the east on the mountain), to get a very Detlevish, "We shall see."

David let out an exasperated sigh. "What do you mean?"

Adam grinned. "Senrid has lifted his inner shield. He's listening again."

Two days later, Liere woke mid-morning to the stir of the warm shape nestled in the curve of her arm. A flash of contact: sweet, innocent need. She complied, and the newborn baby dropped into contented sleep.

Liere stayed awake, listening to the well-trained rise and fall of voices. Children's voices, singing an old, beautiful round. Echo, antiphony, blend ... *Point. Counterpoint. Compromise.*

Windows had stood open all through the previous two days of childbirth labor, enabling music to echo up from dawn to dusk. The change of state had been so quiet—so very like Queen Liere—that at first no one knew anything was happening, until a page spotted the midwife striding up the back stairs, followed by maids with cloths and hot water, after which she told her favorite among the footmen, who took the news to the kitchen. From there it spread fast.

But the queen's door remained locked, until the midwife strode out again halfway through the previous night, the maids once again at her heels, with a heavy laundry basket between them.

"Boy or girl?" a venturesome page asked, her voice shrill. Then she withered as the midwife stamped past, ignoring her thoroughly.

Inside, Liere sat in the newly made bed, clean and exhausted, but floating on a cloud of bliss. She did not need the dyr to cloud this heady sense; it lay on the desk where she had thrown it when the first cramp came.

The room, and her self, had been restored to order, the babe lying in her arms, before she thought to find out if it was a boy or a girl. She'd looked up at the midwife, who—knowing the ways of mothers—said shortly, "Boy." She was gone soon after, for she highly disapproved of the stories that had been whispered around about how this child had come about. Not that she blamed mother or child.

Liere woke this morning to discover that the midwife was gone, leaving behind a crushingly expensive bill for the king to pay, which would indeed be promptly paid, with a sizable honorarium atop it.

Unaware of this byplay, Liere lay back, content just to look at the wonder of that sleeping face. Another boy! She had been so certain it was a girl. She seemed to be following her mother's pattern, except in the Fer Eider family, the two girls had come after the row of boys.

Five had always seemed the perfect number of children, Liere was thinking sleepily, stirring a pang of sorrow for the family she and Andri had wanted, and had not had. Now, with things as they were, she found she was glad that she only had one half-orphaned son, and not a raft of them. Would Macael have spared—

No. She would not let her mind rile itself with something that had not happened. She already knew the underlying prompt: the trust she had lost forever after she woke up on the daybed, his eyes staring down into hers.

She turned her gaze to the infant, wondering if he would love music. He gave a little sigh, and tenderness poured its molten silver through her veins. She kissed his soft little head with its silken brush of black hair, and breathed in his baby scent. He subsided into sleep.

With long-practiced skill, she folded those emotions away so that no trace reached the young life in her arms. Then she turned her mind to the baby's father. And she knew that he was just as aware of her.

After a time, the baby squirmed and began to fret.

She shifted again, made him comfortable, and looked down into the tiny face with its miniature Elsarion brows, the eyes that clear-stream color midway between blue and brown that indicated yet again there'd be another gold-eyed child in the world.

Presently Jauni tiptoed in, carrying a tray. Her gaze strayed to the baby, and the corners of her mouth tucked in as she set the tray down on the bed. Was she also a mother, or did she wish to become one? Her round, kindly face canted, her lips curved in the distinctive smile that newborns evoked in those with the capability to love young creatures of whatever kind, all around the world.

Liere suppressed the urge to talk, to share, to bind herself emotionally to any person in Brydon. Time for the next step.

"Could you tell the king we are ready if he wishes to meet his son?"

"Yes, Queen Liere."

Liere thanked her, and Jauni slipped out of the queen's bedchamber.

The little crowd of waiting servants saw from the surprise in her face, the parted lips with a hint of happy curve, that at last, at last, there had been orders.

Nobody spoke as she shut the door soundlessly, and then she clasped her hands and said, "I bear a message to the king."

Thani wiped her eyes. "May I take the news to him?"

Jauni's brows contracted. As soon as Liere had spoken the words the women had been waiting for, Jauni had envisioned herself running through the palace, object of interest to all.

But they all knew how much it would mean to Thani.

How much it would mean to the king.

Even Jauni, who seldom saw the king, and had never tried to comprehend him, had felt the quiet months of summer as a strange sort of timelessness, like a dream, even though the season had been hot and dry, then hot and sultry, and the harvest one spectacular day after another till the rains came. But there had been no masquerades or picnics or parties. Only the rise and fall of music measuring the journey of the sun across the sky each day. They all knew the music was for the Enaeraneth queen, who asked for nothing, and who spent her days either writing or taking solitary walks in the garden. When she did not meet with the king.

Back in her room, Liere tucked into the breakfast she'd been brought. A chambermaid appeared just as she finished, and bore away the tray, leaving Liere and the baby to themselves.

She was soon wrapped in a fine dressing gown. Her bed faced the circle of windows that looked out into the rose garden beyond the courtyard. The wind was cool, and brilliant leaves drifted from the rustling trees. She looked out at the hypnotic patterns made by the undulating branches and knew she was, at last, ready to face him.

A sudden stillness in the suite was her only warning of his arrival. The maids did not come in. Just Macael alone. She smoothed the blanket around the sleeping baby and then held him out.

Macael took the small bundle with slow care. Holding the baby in both hands, he looked down into the sleeping face. His thoughts were impossible to discern. Liere could not even see his eyes, shuttered as they were by his long black lashes.

After a time he spoke. "Have you given him a name?"

She hesitated, then said, "I did not consider. I didn't expect to be consulted on such a question, and I have terrible trouble with names. I'm always afraid someone will feel slighted, which is why I let Andri pick our son's names. And I told you about Lyren."

"If you change your mind, please let me know."

He kissed the baby, handed him back, and went out.

Liere fed the infant once again, and when Thani appeared, elbowing back the other maids to take the infant to change him, Liere closed her eyes and reached for Lyren: *He's here.*

: He? The baby? He? I was so sure it would be a girl!

: I was as well. He has your coloring, and Elsarion bones.

: Laban says that Macael is a Dei. I refuse to think of him as any vestige of family! How are you?

: Fine. Sore. It was much easier now that I know what to expect. It seemed slow through the day and a half previous, then things went very fast. I'll be sore for a few days, then fine.

: Right now I can't imagine ever needing the details. But who knows what the future will bring. Right now I'm glad you're done.

: Not quite. I want this baby to thoroughly know me, and I still need to reach a better understanding with Macael.

: Ugh. It's so odd to think I have a brother I might never meet.

: Don't think never. We probably will not see him when he is small, but once he is able to get about on his own, who knows?

There was a little more back and forth, then Lyren gave up trying to joke Liere into decamping.

: I have to tell Malcolin now.

~ 28 ~

As the pale disc of the sun rose behind thin streamers of cloud ribboned across the sky, the academy rode out to their last game of the year, Senrid—having transferred to catch up with them—rode at the front, and Malcolin at the back with the youngsters known as the puppy pit, the cold autumn wind buffeting their faces. Now that the king had joined them, the academy trotted in a strictly maintained double column, pennants attached to lances at the front snapping and streaming in the wind, their tight, wide-skirted cold weather coats and high boots making them resemble their ancestors riding out of one of the big tapestries back in Choreid Dhelerei's royal castle.

Frost glittered on dry grass tufts, and on south-facing rocks, so Senrid had decreed that they would wear their winter coats. The seniors had obeyed with nearly as much delight as the order to pack for their last field run. Senrid, looking back at them, wondered if the pride in those coats was inherited, or learned, or some typical Marloven combination of both.

Senrid had transferred from the royal city to the column during the night; they had, according to orders, turned down one of the market roads, instead of one of the straight-cut, unmarked military roads that had been laid down over the ancient courier paths.

After riding past square after square of wheat, oats, rye, they stopped at a village half a day's ride inland from Toraca's coast, and the headman came out to the sturdy gates, striking fist to chest in salute. It was clear they'd been spotted as soon as they appeared on the horizon.

"It's our turn, then, eh?" he asked Senrid.

"I know it's harvest time." Senrid indicated the fields. "But my thought is, an attack won't wait. Your choice, though. We can ride on to the market town."

"No." The headman was tall, gray-haired, scarred. He'd probably fought in the recent war, and had survived Senrid's uncle's savage rule decades before. "We should be ready any time. That's what a militia is for, is it not?"

Senrid raised his hand. The column wheeled and trotted down the road. The old man trudged back inside his gates, and Senrid said to the seniors, "Remember, you're pirates. You landed on the coast, and now you want to take this village." He then opened his hand toward the two seniors who were pirate captain and first mate of this expedition.

Senrid sat astride his mount, who lowered her head and lipped at the sparse grasses still growing this late in the year as he surveyed the excited pirates; he spotted Malcolin Elsarion in the cluster of youngsters at the back. The king was now officially invisible. He ran his thumb along his horse's bony neck as the pirate captain and his first mate studied the terrain: flat, a stream winding its way out of the east, marked by clumps of wild willow, cottonwood, and ash with the occasional birch etched white against the endless sky. The squares of crops, each marked off with weather-worn stones, some of those dating back well before Ivandred's time.

"We're pirates," said the eighteen-year-old senior to his riding captains. "Pirates would set fire to the crops to draw out the villagers."

"Yeah," agreed the first mate. "And cut them up before looting the village..."

The seniors conferred in mumbles, then, studiously ignoring Senrid, the pirate captain said to his doughty crew, "We'll attack from the west. It's already afternoon, so let's wait for sundown. I want torches affixed to the lances ..."

At the back of the column, Malcolin grinned in expectation at his bunkmates. They couldn't hear anything — and anyway, their part would inevitably be at the back of any sortie — but if they were eager and sharp, some among them would get to run messages and scout.

The pirates gradually forgot the king as they stashed their gear at the side of the road, distributed their wooden weapons, then formed up for the attack.

The moon rode high in the sky when the campaign ended. Smoke billowed up from outside the town hall into the night sky, and red beat reflections in the windows from other fires as the village bell tolled the all clear.

The pirate captain cast his ash sword onto a table, then worked his sore arm; some of those farmers had put up a tough fight.

"Well, that's that." He turned to the others in the small room, which was lit by a single candle on a table. In one instant they changed from an enemy search party into very tired teens—and younger. "You, scout away and help release the prisoners." And to Malcolin, "You go tell the dead they can wake up now, in case no one has thought of that already." To Fnor, one of Malcolin's mates, "And you get over and help bring the horses back in."

The three ran out, clattering down the stairs. The former pirate captain saluted as Senrid mounted the steps. The woman of the house appeared in the doorway a moment later, smiling wryly. "You scared my children right well, you," she said. "They won't come out of the attic."

Senrid smiled. "We'll get ourselves out of your way."

The academy and villagers alike assembled in the single cobbled street, talking while some rubbed tired necks and backs. They faded back as Senrid emerged from the house, looking unsettlingly like one of his ancestors in his long gray coat tight to the sashed waist, flaring to the tops of his high blackweave boots. Only his hair was different, too short for their wild-riding ancestors, whose long horsetails had stream-ed in the prairie winds.

The head man and head woman approached him as he gave swift orders for the students to join the locals in putting out the fires (most of which were so small as to be largely symbolic; only one barn fire had gotten out of control) and they retired into the head man's small house to confer.

Soon they sat around the low table on cushions, hot wine being served out in wide cups.

Senrid saluted the town leaders, drank, then said, "Good, brisk defense at first."

"Not good enough," the old man growled.

"That's why they are here, Favid," the woman said. She turned to Senrid. "We fell apart once the fires got going."

Senrid said, "The goal is to hold out long enough for reinforcements—which means getting someone out first thing. How long before you remembered to send messengers?" Senrid went on to describe both strengths and weaknesses of the village defense. By the time they finished, a child came running in to report that the big fire was extinguished. "The roof is half gone," she added, her eyes round.

"Won't be for long," the head woman said comfortably. "We'll lay tiles, this time."

"We've found that a healthy competition gets the work done fast and well," Senrid said. "We'll be ready at dawn."

"Then let us supply the breakfast. All the households agreed to contribute. It'll be a merry feast before we get to work."

Senrid tipped his head back as he surveyed the town hall. The two village elders observed his face, outlined against the lights in a shop. Despite his evident tiredness, the king seemed relaxed, far more then he'd been when sneaking in and out during the war.

While the elders shared a meal with their king, the academy, well-practiced, set up camp as the day's cooks prepared their meal.

Malcolin had devoured his rice-and-cabbage balls and two rye rolls when he got that open-the-door-in-the-mind feeling that meant a contact from his mother. He was glad, now, that she'd made him practice that stuff when he was little because all he had to do was make sure he was sitting squarely and shut his eyes. He knew one other puppy in the pit with Dena Yeresbeth, but any kind of contact seemed to make her dizzy.

: *Malcolin?*

: *Mama?*

: *You have a brother, who will stay here in Shiovhan, which means you are now safe. Macael Elsarion promised he will not come after you, unless you lead an army over the border.*

Anger zipped through Malcolin. Some. Not like winter, when hearing the Evil Assassin's name made him want to throw up, or smash things: *He killed Da! And you think he's to be trusted?*

  : I think he will keep his word.

  : But he's evil! Da wasn't evil, and he killed him. Stabbed him to death, and they weren't even mad at each other. I saw it!

  : Oh, my darling boy, all I know is that it would be evil adding to evil to go and kill him, and set the Enaeraneth fighting one another for ever and ever. It has to stop sometime. I've tried hard to make it stop now.

Malcolin was going to think to his mother that his da had wanted it to stop, except he paused, remembering the wry warnings his da had given him. He became aware for the first time of what he'd known all along — that his da had wanted it to stop, but hadn't believed it would.

How many times had Da said that his job was to teach him how to be strong enough to hold Enaeran? He'd overseen his sword lessons himself. And Malcolin had been better with steel than these Marlovens two and three years older than he, the first day he came. What was that except preparation for expected war?

  : Are you still enjoying being there?

  : I like it here, but I want to see you.

  : I am nearly finished with what I promised to do. You will see me soon.

He sighed as her warm, embracing gold and rose and flame-bright love enveloped him, and then the inner door closed. Noise returned suddenly, a buzz of voices amid the clatter of camp dishes. Malcolin oriented himself, then looked up to find his tentmates staring at him.

Esrid Kolar's face was puzzled and curious. Lnor, Malcolin's barracks-mate, looked worried. "I tried to reach you," she said, tapping her head. "Couldn't. But I got the feeling you were feeling something bad." She winced. "That sounds stupid. You know what I mean?"

Malcolin sighed. "It's all right. I got a contact, that was all." He didn't know Esrid or these tentmates well enough to tell them more than that. Only Lnor knew everything, but the rest of their bunkmates were in other tents.

"You all right?" Esrid asked, his dark eyes now just concerned. He was four years older, and their riding captain. Malcolin hated the idea of pestering so exalted a figure with his problems. Malcolin—still the youngest in the academy, to his disgust—wanted to yell, I'm almost nine! I'm not a baby! Except he'd learned that yelling was babyish. "I'm fine. Thanks."

Lnor waited until Esrid went back to the upper school tents, then said, "I don't want to be a noser, but the feelings I got were pretty bad. Though maybe that was just me getting dizzy." She smiled tentatively. He saw that she was trying it to see if he'd smile back. Contacts always left him sensitive to others' feelings, though he didn't try to be a noser, as she'd said. At least Lnor understood about Dena Yeresbeth, because she had it, though hers was different from his.

"If you're gonna barf, don't do it on my grub."

"No. I'll save it for your shoes," she retorted. "Sure you'll all right?"

"Yep."

She turned back to her food and soon the seniors came around insisting that they sleep now, because they'd be up early for repair work.

Lying in his bedroll much later, Malcolin couldn't sleep. He wondered if he was still a prince, now that this brother that he'd never get to play with had replaced him in Enaeran. No. Being a prince had gone away when he changed his name that first day.

What had being a prince ever meant, besides being the son of his parents? It had meant living in a castle, but so had his best playmates, who were the sons and daughters of servants and stable hands. It had meant riding first in parades. That had been fun. He'd loved everyone waving and cheering. Did those same people now cheer The Evil Assassin? Or did he have the festival parades?

Malcolin shrugged the question away, and considered whether he liked not being a prince. His mother had always said that true merit was not conferred at birth, but earned. Well, that was true here as well. Esrid was an orphan, raised by some stingy relatives as a stable boy until someone else discovered him and brought him to the academy. And he was first in his year. Earned worth.

Malcolin ran his fingers over his eye-ridges. Every time he looked in the mirror he could see his father in his own face. He was still an Elsarion. He would never not be his father's son. But Prince Trevor Andiran was dead, killed by the same knife that had stabbed through his father's heart. He didn't even want to go back to Enaeran, which would be different without Ma and Da there. Instead, there was this new brother, who had the Evil Assassin as a da. He was glad that boy wouldn't have Ma, though he knew it was mean.

Malcolin was still struggling with these conflicted emotions when a soft step outside the tent caught his attention. He wasn't alarmed. It had to be a senior on patrol. Sounds of even breathing from the others in the tent indicated he was the only one awake. Then the tent flat opened

The tall, dark-clad figure was a black silhouette against the nightscape, the angle of shoulder and upper body a man in uniform. A silhouetted arm beckoned to him.

Surprised, Malcolin slid out, landed silently on bare feet, and followed the figure into the chilly air. Malcolin curled his toes against the cold stones of the field. Then a light gleamed into being, and Malcolin stared up in silent amazement at the king.

No one could read his expression, or his surface thoughts. Certainly Malcolin couldn't. He waited mutely, wondering if he'd done something wrong.

"Some of your mates were concerned about you," the king said in a quiet voice.

Malcolin couldn't suppress a hot flush of embarrassment. Esrid Kolar had reported on him! And Lnor too? His insides buzzed with even more conflicting feelings—gratification that they cared, but annoyance that they'd blab. Mostly embarrassment.

"I'm all right." Because it would never occur to him to hide anything from the king, who seemed to know everything, he said, "My mother got a baby, a brother, to take my place, so the Adranis won't kill me. She said that means her treaty is almost done, and she can be free."

"This is good, is it not?"

"Oh, yes," Malcolin said. "Except we no longer have any home. And I'm no longer—" He stopped, afraid 'no longer a prince' would be misconstrued.

"No longer yoked to heirship, am I right?" the king asked.

There was no scorn or anger in his voice. It sounded like he understood.

"Some people have been saying that I can do whatever I want now," Malcolin said. "I even said it. But if the Evil Assassin is bad, who is going to get rid of him?"

"Do you consider Enaeran your responsibility? You don't think the people have any responsibility?"

Malcolin curled his toes more tightly, his mind winging through memories and more recent discussions. "Everyone has responsibility for his own actions. Every adult says that. But that doesn't mean giving orders. I always thought giving orders meant being a commander, you know, leading the guard. Making people do what you want. The people don't have that."

"They do if enough of them rise."

Malcolin said, "I've learned in history class that the civs — farmers, people like that—mostly don't fight because it's their land that the fighting gets done on, not unless life is so bad it doesn't matter. But Ma told me there's no fighting in Enaeran, so the people must have what they want. But I thought every-one'd been happy with my da! I don't know what to do."

"You do not have to decide now. But you ought to get some shuteye. If you perform poorly tomorrow, people will fuss over you. As for the other matters, remember, you do not have to decide your future actions today. Or tomorrow, or even next year. Sounds like your mother did what she did so you won't have to worry about those things."

"Right," Malcolin said with a sigh of relief. "Right."

BRYDON PALACE - SHIOVHAN

The awkwardness of those first few days would have been heartrending, had Liere felt she had heart whole enough to rend.

So different were they from the early days with Andri after Malcolin's birth! Then their only trouble had been learning to manage with an infant, for Liere's experience with Lyren had been limited by all her willing helpers. Andri had had no experience at all. Their shared delight had made all the small troubles and adjustments exciting and wonderful and endlessly fascinating.

Now she had the expertise with the infant. All the awkwardness was in learning to communicate with Macael.

They never discussed the future.

At the end of the first week, when she had settled on two wetnurses, one for night and one for day, he asked her, polite as always, if he could take the baby for the morning.

What was she going to say, no? She handed the infant over without speaking, holding tight until Macael was gone, and only then did she realize she stood in the middle of the room, her arms wrapped around herself, rocking back and forth as she battled that inward pain.

He brought the infant back a couple hours later, fretting but not screaming. The baby was merely hungry and wet.

The next day Macael was back, and asked with an echo of his old diffidence, "Would you like to join us? You could bring your work, or read, or even sleep if you wish."

She gripped herself against the urge to say yes, if only to be with the infant longer. "You have to get used to being with him without me," she said, her brow puckered, having no idea how much her sadness hurt him.

"Yes," he said, in the usual flat tone.

This time he kept the babe a bit longer.

That established a pattern. Macael arrived early in the morning and returned on some days mid-afternoon, some days at sunset or even later, depending upon the demands on his own time. From a distance Liere monitored the infant, whose feedings were divided between two wet nurses, both experienced women whose profession was tending to children brought into the world by the Birth Spell. They both were kind, and overflowing with ready affection. Liere had meant to give up nursing at the outset, but she couldn't quite bring herself to it. Not yet. The baby would always know her on the mental plane, but she wanted to create some sensory memories — for them both.

By the second week a maid would bring Macael warmed milk in a tule-woven pouch with a water-rose bulb fitted over the opening. Apparently there was a spell so the wetnurses could transfer milk to this pouch, which gave Macael the opportunity to feed the baby himself.

The baby did not like this peculiar method of feeding at first, but Macael persevered, his hands patient, his face unreadable as always, and after a day or so the baby accepted all three forms of feeding, though when Macael brought him back at night, the infant always sank against Liere with a contented sigh, making little nestling movements to mold himself against her body, filling her with equal parts bliss and pain.

As soon as Macael was gone, she curled up in a comfortable chair with her little son, covered him with kisses as she breathed in his own sweet baby fragrance, which was now overlaid with his father's more complex scent. It, like her monitoring, conveyed an unsettling sense of intimacy.

And so the days passed, each a little shorter, a little colder. When the baby was not with her, Liere worked in her rooms, trying to finish translating the text.

> … happiness is also glance through a crack in the curtain in time to see a white horse take wing, explained the elder. The glimpse might not last but a moment, but the memory will sustain you for years. First, however, you must remember to look up, and out, or you will not catch those instants of wonder.

Liere's eyes stung. Everything about happiness threatened to gouge her spirit, but she was getting much better at warding the old anger, and consciously appreciating the moments with the baby. She looked up at the window as music surrounded her, softly rising and falling, sung by sweet childish voices.

From time to time she mentally checked on the baby when he was with Macael, to find him content. Mostly asleep. Once, she caught him watching the play of light on the crystal drops of the chandelier in the room where Macael worked. Macael had found a way to anchor his papers so that he could use one hand to write and the other to hold the baby. The baby was there, safe and warm and content, in the crook of Macael's arm.

The next day, Liere bent to pick up the infant, and carried him to the window, where she stood looking out at the rose bushes, now being trimmed down by the gardeners after two seasons of riotous blooms perfuming the air. The cluster of cypresses was readying for winter, feathery leaves drifting down, over the stone wall.

The babe made a soft noise, and she drew in a sharp breath, but hid her emotions away. Just as the physical self will bypass mere mental boundaries, so too can instinct. On her first glimpse of him after he was born she fell in love just as hard as she had with her previous two. His face, his smell, the sound of his breathing hollowed her behind the ribs, her mind giddy with adoration.

The bells rang, and her senses heightened; the babe had fallen asleep in her arms when she heard Macael's quiet step outside.

She turned. It seemed to no longer matter that he entered her bedroom. But then it had gradually ceased to be hers. Now it was just a room to sleep in. Her sense of a place here at Brydon was slipping into memory along with Andri.

"May I?" He held out his arms.

Liere stepped up and laid the babe in them.

"His name will be Iliosi Mathias. Iliosi Yenlath was Chantala's favorite poet, and Mathias is a traditional name all through the eastern half of the continent. Names that begin with M are traditional for second names in my family." Macael looked at the babe's sleeping face, and then up at Liere. "His Name Day will take place in a month," he added. And when she only nodded, he went on in the same tone, "How do you know when he is cold, or too warm? Read his thoughts? Your text only says to be aware, which is less helpful than it might have been four thousand years before."

"Being aware merely means to dress him as you'd dress, paying attention to how you feel. If you're warm, cover him lightly, and if you're cold make him snug. Bear in mind he won't be moving to warm up for some time, and it will take much longer to learn the inner control to ward cold." She considered the second question, which was so strange coming from a man who in all the years she'd known him had never even acknowledged the existence of Dena Yeresbeth. "You can read his instinct, of course, but I agree with the elders that it is a mistake. He won't try to communicate if you are doing it for him."

"When do I start talking to him?"

"Now. He will very soon begin making sounds back. Let others talk to him, too, and he can babble back at them while he learns how to form words. Andri once said the silence with which he was surrounded by command of his father, who apparently didn't want him learning servants' country accent, drove him to find friends in the stable, the kitchen, and the streets."

"I was given that same silence," Macael murmured.

One of his rare personal admissions. Or, semi-personal. She said, quite firmly, "No one wants to grow up isolated on the mental plane. And those who do learn to adapt — in one way or another."

There was no reaction. Of course. There never was.

He left soon after.

Liere spent the rest of the day working rapidly. She could not have said why. The scribe desk would easily send pages after she left, as they would not cease contact with shared parenthood, but she wanted the text finished before she left. She knew she had not yet breached the wall that instinct maintained was there, and she hoped that this ancient collection of wisdom might succeed where she was failing.

When she rested her hand, she maintained a delicate rapport with Iliosi Mathias. He was going to inherit her gift with farsense, that much she was certain of, so she worked to demonstrate contact and identify as much as is possible with a newborn. If he wanted to find her (even if only in dreams) she wanted to make certain he could.

Macael brought the baby back late.

His voice, always so polite, had deepened in tone, carrying conviction. "I'd like to keep him for the night," he said.

"He will waken several times," Liere warned.

"I have to get accustomed some time." Macael smiled a little. "May I sit down? I wish to describe some observations I made."

Liere indicated that they go into the parlor, where they sat in armchairs on either side of the fire. Iliosi Mathias made rooting motions with his mouth. Liere threw her wrap partway around herself, and beneath its cover let him nurse. He cozied up, boneless with contentment. Liere's unconscious tenderness, the baby's equally unconscious, trusting repose, the transcendent picture they made together, there in the glow of the fire, Macael watched with unblinking intensity.

Finally she looked up. "You said you had observations to make?"

"Yes." And for a time they discussed, untiringly, the minute changes Iliosi Mathias had made that day: the little mouth movements — was this the beginnings of speech? — the flailings of a tiny fist learning to grasp, the way the baby had watched the drift of branches outside the window, all were thoroughly canvassed in the manner of parents and guardians for untold years.

Gradually these evenings lasted longer, Liere working at her desk, except if the baby fretted. Macael brought his own work, but he often laid pen and report aside to observe the two of them, the small family he had wanted, and worked so hard to bring about. That he knew he was going to lose, in part.

The elder said, Choose the path of peace, with every step, even if you are shunned. Choose peace, with all your wit and power, and pain—chaos— ruin are likeliest to depart like the thunder, making way for the warmth of balance and harmony. It is the balance of harmony that opens the spirit to joy and happiness.

29

There came at last an evening when Macael brought Iliosi Mathias back to Liere and said, "Tomorrow is his Name Day Celebration."

"Ought I to be there?" Liere asked, painstakingly neutral.

"Please. After it, though it has not quite been a year, if you wish to go, I'll consider the conditions of our agreement met." His voice was husky.

Her first instinct was anguish at the prospect of separation from Iliosi Mathias. And she sensed that Macael saw it; the baby made a fretful noise—she had tightened her grip on him.

"I know," she said with care, "that he could make the change now, and it would be fairly peaceful. But ..." She looked down at the dear, innocent little face, and was nearly overwhelmed by the wrench of grief. "I thought I was better prepared."

He seemed to struggle inwardly, his gaze sliding away, then it snapped back. "Nothing to apologize for," he replied, his voice still husky. "Do you object to his carrying your name in addition to Iliosi Mathias? It's common for royal children to have several names."

"Fer Eider? No, I'd be pleased."

"Then it's agreed," he said, and withdrew.

She settled into rapport, bathing Iliosi Mathias's small awareness in love. He knew her, and would soon be able to reach her. But we are physical beings, she thought wistfully, and the arms holding him would be others'. She hoped those loving arms would give him all the affection he needed. Her love must reach him from the realm of the spirit.

The next day, the bells rang out, and festival noise caused by largesse of coins and booths of feast goodies carried through the great doors in the throne room as Liere stood opposite

Macael, still wearing her again-remade black mourning, with the draped and decorated cradle between them. But the tension between them had altered.

The profusion of late flowers, and even hoarded blossoms brought from conservatories, filled the room with their scent. This mute testimony to Mathias' status among the servants bolstered her hope that he would be surrounded by love and care.

Many Adrani courtiers were there, at the front of the crowd. Liere's gaze searched among the smiling faces, finding a few Enaeraneth nobles she had not seen for a year or more.

Once, during a lull after an old duchas from the remote southwest corner had made his stately way down the aisle, Liere was aware of some subtle reaction from Macael. "What is it?" she asked.

"Him." A nod toward the white-haired duchas. "I remember him from Andri's Name Day."

"You were there?" Liere asked in surprise, recalling the violent rift between the two branches of the family.

"Under armed guard," Macael said with a small smile. "For that one day we were indeed at Brydon."

And she caught a memory from him. Distorted, from the perspective of a toddler who had already learned to be watchful. The perimeter of the fabulously decorated room glittering with the drawn steel of the king's honor guard. Bared steel for an infant's Name Day! The center of attention was not the baby, but a big, bluff yellow-haired man with a hearty grin showing too many teeth. And providing an unpleasant counterpoint to the determined scraping of the stringed instruments in the gallery overhead, the angry squalling of the two-week-old Andri Malcolin Elsarion.

The memory lasted only heartbeats, then it shuttered, and there before them stood several high-ranking nobles from Sles Adran to speak personal congratulations amid garlands of flattery.

Liere let the words flow by as she looked into each face. The surface reactions were complex. After a time she realized that some of what she saw was question. She remembered that these people had known Chantala, and one or two had even valued her, bringing to this occasion a sense of Chantala's gentle spirit. Liere acknowledged their words with a bow and a real smile, contemplating the fact that she had been wrong. Macael had once had the care of a child. It was too easy to forget the long years of watchful, patient guardianship of Chantala na Shagal. It could so easily have been otherwise, for who would have defended Chantala if Macael—once he had secured the wealth and power Chantala had been heir to—had banished her to Denwy under guard, and had never bothered with her again?

Her inner thoughts dissolved, like sun on snowflakes, when she found herself face-to-face with a small deputation of women.

Determination tightened the countenances before her, making angles of waiting postures. Liere looked at the women—all shopkeepers or artisans from the city, with two barases among them—as she voiced a polite greeting.

Lantra Parlion, with whom Liere had a special wartime connection, glanced to her right and left. It was clear she had waited until Macael was busy with someone else before she spoke. "We're glad to see you well again, Queen Liere." Once again a glance. Macael was still engaged in conversation with two of the senior guild masters. Though by now Liere suspected he was aware of everything going on.

"We have you to thank for that, we know," Lantra said, her gaze unwinking.

Liere fought against a vortex of conflicting emotions, and forced herself to say, "In spite of his beginning, do not underestimate Macael's intentions. He wants peace. What happened could have been so much worse."

"We know," Lantra said again, and gazed at the other women. She gathered consensus from their nods and the tightened lips. "All of us here. Every one of us a mother. We know what you did for the sake of peace, and we know the cost." A toss of her head in Macael's direction. "It was wrong of him, as wrong as taking Andri's life. But that is not this little innocent's fault."

Liere tried to find something to say, and couldn't.

"We wish you would stay to rule and guide us. But we understand why you cannot. And we wish you well even more," Lantra said, her voice trembling.

They all bowed low, a wordless expression of respect, then they withdrew without speaking to Macael.

Liere's throat hurt. Her eyes stung. It took time to regain her composure, and to accept the murmured polite words of the Adrani nobles eager to be seen flattering her, in order to curry favor with Macael.

At last she was able to take the newly-named Prince Iliosi Mathias Fer Eider Elsarion, and withdraw to her rooms, where almost immediately, a page entered, bowed, and said that she had a caller.

Liere was going to deny whoever it was, but sent a tendril, and smiled. "Let him in, please, and bring refreshments." And, a few moments later, "Marten!" Liere exclaimed with the first real flair of pleasure she'd felt in company for a long time.

Martande Eldias walked into her parlor, a slim, dark-haired, handsome man with a warm smile. He held out his hands and Liere took them.

"You're free, I take it?" she said. "I know you were recalled as ambassador."

"And confined to the family estate in Sles Adran. But Macael Elsarion released Andri's inner circle this week," Marten said, adding wryly, "except Bassl. He's still at home. He took Andri's death especially hard, I'm afraid."

Liere nodded. "I received a letter from Pavri last winter. He said Bassl was so angry he tore apart several rooms in their castle."

"Barehanded," Marten said. "And he's rebuilding every wall and stick of furniture he destroyed. He says when he finishes maybe he can be trusted to leave."

"Macael has withdrawn his warriors from everyone's estates, then?"

Marten opened his hands. "We're all free." He added with mild dryness, "So I am back in Enaeran, and, like the others, free to move about. As long as we don't take up arms. And I dare swear he's suborned someone in each of our households to ensure that his wishes are carried out."

Liere sighed, relieved that what remained of Andri's old gang was going to be permitted to live after all.

"You came to visit?"

"I was invited for an interview."

His pronunciation made it clear that he'd seen the invitation (no doubt expressed with exquisite politeness) as a summons.

"But I promised myself, for the sake of the old days, to see you once again before you left."

Liere poured out tea, feeling an inexplicable sadness. Of all Andri's old gang she had always liked Marten the most. She was not surprised that he—even kept at a distance as he'd been—had assumed that she would leave. He'd been, always, the most insightful of Andri's circle.

"Do you know what it was that Macael wanted?" she asked. "Surely he's not sending you back to Sartor as ambassador?"

"He is not. The Adrani ambassador remains in Eidervaen, now representing Enaeran-Adrani. I just came from my interview," Marten said. "Macael Elsarion was very cordial and pleasant. When I asked after you, it was he who gave me the directions to your rooms." He sipped his steeped leaf, then set the cup down. "He requested of me a year as an adviser, after which I'd be posted to Colend as ambassador."

"Adviser?"

"He used the term 'voice of conscience'. I don't exactly comprehend his meaning. I found him fairly oblique before he assassinated Andri, and impossible to understand now." He looked troubled. "Evidence of guilt?"

"Assuredly," Liere said. "Though don't misunderstand. Were we to go back a year, I suspect he'd do it again."

Marten was silent for a time, looking down into his cup with a forlorn expression. Liere had long suspected that Marten was in love with Andri, not an occasional flare, like Bassl, but steadfast, silent, true. And unacknowledged because Andri never saw it.

"Did you give Macael an answer?" Liere asked when Marten looked up again.

"No. My inclination is to go home and bury myself in my history project. But I suspect I owe it to Andri to serve, even if I end up being killed for voicing what my conscience dictates. And so, when the time comes to give an answer, I will probably comply."

"I don't think he would have you killed," Liere said.

"Organize a revolt, a counter-revolution, and he won't hesitate. But I suspect you can safely say whatever you want and you won't see much reaction."

Marten shook his head slowly. "I'd really believed that the bad days were behind us," he said.

Liere agreed, her eyes stinging for the thousand-thousandth time. But she was aware that the grief had lessened to a deep regret.

They talked a little longer. When he left, Liere wondered how Macael would react to a year of Marten Eldias's remorse—for his consent—and sorrow, so easily read in his beautiful, honest brown gaze.

EIDERVAEN - SARTOR

Atan Landis customarily read reports very early in the morning while Rel was down in the practice yard working with the palace guard. When he returned, she was usually done, and she'd pass on news to him over their breakfast, which was always private, them and the children.

Their three younglings usually gobbled as fast as they could and then ran off to tutoring or training, after which she and Rel could discuss whatever concerns they had before going out as king and queen.

When she saw the name on the third report down, she set aside the others to read it immediately. She'd debated early in the year over the appropriateness of setting a spy in an ally's kingdom—the Adrani king and queen had visited Eidervaen early after the war, and the Adrani navy had joined the pirate patrol ranging over the Sartoran Sea. Rel had since mentioned that they were excellent sailors, participating in all maneuvers, and ready to rescue ships in distress, right down to the smallest fisher.

But then came word about the Adranis taking Enaeran. And after Rel's return from Enaeran midway through New Year's Week, his report about Liere so disturbed Atan that she finally dispatched a trusted individual there, to live peaceably as an artisan in Shiovhan, forwarding news whenever she heard something that she felt Atan ought to know. Three months ago the news that Liere was seen walking about pregnant—far later than would have been possible for Andri to be the father—had seemed uncharacteristic.

Rel came back at last, and Atan did not wait for breakfast, but followed him into their bedroom while he walked through the cleaning frame and changed from his practice clothes into what he jokingly called his king costume.

"Selveris reports that Liere had a child," she said, her eyebrows a formidable line across her face. "And there was a royal Name Day."

Rel said, "Oh?"

Atan scowled even more. "Bells ringing, handouts, a festival day declared for the birth of an heir, by no less a person than *Queen Liere Fer Eider.*"

Rel distinctly remembered the way Macael Elsarion had looked at Liere before leaving Rel to speak alone with her. But she had not given Macael the same sort of look.

Atan's tone could have cut glass. "Rel, this has to be a Prince Sandios situation."

"Who is?"

Atan told him bluntly.

It was Rel's turn to scowl. "If that's true, it's damnable."

"Oh, I will find out if it's true," Atan said grimly. "No wonder Liere didn't want to talk to you. I wonder what the— oh, of course, of course. Macael Elsarion holds Andri's boy, or threatens him, and that rat's got her by the heart."

Rel had wondered from time to time what was going on between those two. He never would have guessed that. "Liere," he said with regret.

Atan scowled. "I want to say the worst possible person to get caught in a trap like that, except it's terrible for anybody!"

Rel agreed. "Knowing her, she'll be feeling guilty about having a baby with Andri's assassin, guilty about having to leave the baby, and probably the most guilty having failed to take a knife to Cousin Macael." He added with a brief grin, "Though that would've been a tougher hill to ride than most people think—"

"Oh, that's irrelevant," Atan muttered, impatient.

Rel snorted a laugh. "Contrary. If she'd muffed a stab attempt, he could have clapped her into a cell and hostaged her life against any comers. No wrong decisions."

"Except *she* didn't make the wrong decision if she really did have her son's life threatened. Oh, I'll investigate before I badger her about it. So far all we know is that Macael Elsarion had a son by Liere Fer Eider, former Enaeraneth queen, and he's celebrating all over the place. If what I think is true," she said, rubbing her hands slowly, "it's our turn to see that Macael Elsarion regrets that decision for the rest of his life."

Rel looked at her askance. "I hope you haven't decided to go to war. May I remind you we don't have an army?"

"I don't need an army. Oh ho, let's see, we might begin with a fashion for resurrecting old plays. Historical plays. There is at least one about Prince Sandios that's thunderingly non-subtle, and our friend the Adrani ambassador—excuse me, the Enaeran-Adrani ambassador—will be honored with a seat in the royal gallery." Her huge, protuberant eyes glittered with malice, and her grin was quite piratical. "For other private social affairs, that ambassador is going to find his invitational status slipping to third circle, and we will not accept any invitations to whatever events he hosts."

Rel snorted. "Will that be enough?"

"Oh, my dear, that's only the beginning. There needs to be a cost that the entire diplomatic world talks about, so that *no* one will be tempted to try that again. I'll begin with the Mage Guild, who will be prepared when he next needs a mage to renew necessary spells."

"They won't refuse him?" Rel asked. "Seems to me it would be the people who'd feel that, if water goes unpurified, and roofs cave in, and the like."

"No, no, it's exactly as you say. But every. Single. Task. That requires magic is going to come with questions about how the magic will be used, to ascertain that there is no coercion even remotely in the plans. Because the Mage Guild will want to be assured that the king will not, in any further action, betray the *fundamental agreement* with the indigenous beings when we humans were *first given magic*." She smacked a table on every emphasized word.

"Everything? Even purification spells?"

"Everything. If that Macael Elsarion doesn't like it, he can find ways around it, though few mages outside either the northern or our southern mage guild will offer their services. Or, might at triple the cost."

"He could always learn magic on his own," Rel said. "In his free time."

"So says someone who never put in the years of grinding work it takes to master magic. My guess is, free time is not in great quantities for a king who appears to oversee everything. No quarrel with him that way—so far..."

⁓⊙⟋ ⟍⊙⁓

Atan went off to write a series of letters to mages and rulers all over the world, while in Brydon, Liere prepared for her departure.

Mostly this meant careful disposition of Iliosi Mathias' furnishings and belongings that she'd accumulated in her suite. The greater part of Liere's own things had been given away during winter, except for a very few keepsakes, and those she shifted to her old room in Bereth Ferian, still empty. When she departed at last, she would leave nothing behind.

Nothing except a child.

As the hours passed, the inward pressure intensified until, when she stopped for something warm to drink, she sensed that the ambient changes were physical more than emotional. A glance outside showed a steel gray sky, and the still air of impending storm.

Midafternoon, the wind rose, escalating with terrifying speed into a blizzard of heroic magnitude. The palace seemed empty as Liere followed the new nanny down to Macael's wing in order to inspect Iliosi Mathias' room. Business had been suspended, the day servants sent home early.

Iliosi Mathias' room, which was a small one directly adjacent to Macael's bedroom, was exactly as she would have wished it. Colors, pictures, two windows, all just as she'd desired, a frame for all the little furnishings.

The nanny disappeared to oversee the stowing of Iliosi Mathias' clothing herself. Liere was left alone in the silent suite. Outside the windows, nothing but swirling white. Inside, still air, a steady fire, everything in readiness, even to the familiar text sitting on a side table.

Liere crossed to that table and leafed through a few pages.

She discovered additions written in an unfamiliar hand in all the margins, and even between lines she had inscribed so carefully.

The only page still bare of comments was the last page, handed off the evening before.

> ...happiness can be shared, but it cannot be taken, the elder said. When it arrives in the midst of sorrow, it can seem miraculous. To answer your last question, yes, there is happiness in the child's smallest achievement, should you be willing to see the joy in every effort, but I believe your greatest happiness arises in seeing the sudden burst of happiness in the child at the sight of you...

She turned away and touched the cradle, fighting the onslaught of anguish: she was now a visitor in her son's chamber. Even a trespasser. She would not walk about this room, seeing the light alter, and the seasons, as each day Iliosi Mathias grew and changed in endlessly fascinating ways. She would not hear his first laugh, or his first word. Would he hold up his arms to her if she visited in future, or would he regard her as a stranger?

A hot tear splashed onto the edge of the cradle. She dashed her sleeve over her eyes, and with the other hand scrubbed the tears off the cradle frame with a handful of her robe. Her chest ached with the effort it took not to wail.

Then she hugged her arms tightly against her, struggling for control. Looking down at the empty crib made it worse. She slid her hands up her arms to her face, and tried to steady her breathing. She would see that baby once more, and she must not burden him with her emotions.

She was not shielded, so the shock of pain that accompanied the glimpse of herself as seen from behind was equally shocking and equally painful.

Reaction ricocheted through her, most of it wordless: the sight of her own bowed shoulders, tense arms, hidden face. The anguish that Macael felt, coming so suddenly on her here, in his suite.

His emotions shuttered away faster than hers did, but not before she spun around, her hands dropping. There was no hiding red eyes or a blotchy face, but neither could he call back his own reaction. They both could pretend that nothing had happened, as they had during all their previous personal encounters, rare as they had been, but that had been when there was time.

They had run out of time.

"Where will you go?" he asked, with a fair semblance of his old mask.

"I wrote out two copies of the parent and child scroll, I think I told you," she said. "This one is yours. The other I will take to the archive. After that, I have a friendship to mend."

"You need not go, Liere," he said, and when she looked up, not in the angry repudiation that had caused him so much torment, but with fresh tears, he added in a rush of words, "You can have anything you ask. Anything. I'd thought to give you a throne, but I know now that you care nothing for such things. Though I would value your wisdom and compassion more than I can say. But if you cannot bear the idea, there is my grandmother's estate, or if that is too small, there is Denwy. The palace there is beautiful, far more beautiful than this pile here. You can be as isolated as you wish, with an army of scribes for your work. Or I can bring the music school to you, or performers. You have only to say."

"My going is what we agreed to," she said, wavering in that moment as she looked at Iliosi Mathias in his arms.

"I agreed because you wanted to go," Macael said. "I agreed because I thought a year would be enough time to win even a vestige of the love I feel for you."

"Love," she repeated, thoroughly taken aback. Desire, she'd acknowledged. Detlev's weapon.

"Love," Macael said, more firmly. "Those pages there are filled with advice about the healing properties of love. Every day, almost every breath, I have tried to find a way past the hatred that I know I earned when I killed Andri. I kept thinking, you are not a hateful person. Love is your natural element. I saw it in the patient way you listened to Chantala, even when she was so lost she repeated herself endlessly. In your voice when Andri's rabble of servants imposed on you. In your smile at your son, and at Andri, while he cavorted with younger and younger women —"

"Please leave Andri out of this," she said, a pulse of the anger back.

Macael recoiled as if she'd hit him; his shield was gone, baring his thoughts—his carefully guarded emotions—to her, as he said in a tumble of words, "I loved you ever since I first saw you in the cottage behind the Harieses. It was not just your face and form, though I was entranced, nor was it the silver shimmer around you, which I had never seen before around anyone, not even Chantala, whose shadow had been blue, ever paler. Everyone else's shadow was dull red, or storm gray, or streaked or mud-colored…"

Liere gazed at him, stunned. He saw auras?

"…you were kind to Chantala, without forethought, as if that was the only way to be. And she, though living more by day in a cloud, could see your sincerity. Do you know how rare it is to meet someone both beautiful and kind?"

"Everyone is beautiful when they are kind," Liere said.

He could see that she believed that, too, that she considered herself like any other woman, when there was no one like her in the world. There was kindness in her eyes now, but nothing more.

"I tried to court you in every way possible," he said, heartache—a familiar companion—nearly unbearable in its sharpness. "I thought life without joy was the human condition, and I accepted it. Because I know that taking joy is not possible. And giving it, I learned, is difficult…"

His voice suspended, and she tried to find speech, for her dyr-enhanced skills had flashed through his anguish to other memories of anguish, some of them shockingly recent, but the strongest was the affirmation that yes, he had wept himself to sleep when very young. One of his earliest memories was a distorted voice, *Shut the door. As well he learns self-discipline sooner than later*, as thunder shook the walls.

His childhood anguish kindled hers. "But you did give people joy. Music was your solace, your safety, but it gave those who could hear its excellence great joy. I know it did for Chantala," she said. "And it gave me great joy the night we first met. As for the second—" She drew a deep breath.

"Don't say it." Macael looked away, then moved to the cradle and gently laid the infant down. "Don't say it. The first time was the joy of discovery. I did not feel joy the second time. There was no joy in anticipation, worsened with Chantala gone. But I tried to give joy to you — and atonement, if you will — for what I was going to do."

He saw her stiffen. He said, "I will always see Andri's dying look. It was betrayal. It still harrows me."

"But," Liere said, "you did it."

"I weighed the alternatives," he began.

She kept her voice neutral as she cut in, "Except the one in which you explained to me the way you are explaining now, so that I could… But I don't want to get into an argument about what Andri might or might not have done in future. I've heard that Adranis approve of what you did. To them Andri was not a father and a friend, a complicated man who lived and breathed and loved life, he was merely a bad king, and we all know how to get rid of bad kings. I will only talk about my own experience, which was to wake up with a man I'd thought a friend holding my son's life over my head to force me into the situation we are in now."

"I never would have hurt you," Macael said, pleading. "Never. I tried to make you as comfortable as I could. I—"

"But you did hurt me," she said gently.

"I did not want to kill Andri's boy. I'd planned to keep him at my old holding — the same one I could give you — where he could ride and play in the lake. I even brought in parrots, because Andri had mentioned his boy had pet birds."

"Never caged birds," Liere said. "He couldn't bear birds to be caged… No, I won't draw comparisons. I know that you exerted yourself to make my stay as comfortable as you could. You required your servants to bow, and address me by my former title. You even had me sit in on Oath Day, and supported my recommendations, though I saw how gazes shifted to you to corroborate. I also know that when we did come together, you made it good for me, even though I did not cooperate."

"You saw that?"

"Of course I did. I know that it all could have been so much worse. But that was not a courtship, which implies the courted one is free to choose. Although I agreed to be in that bed, it was not because I chose to be, it was to save my son's life. There is a vital difference, and the fact that you did not see that is a disturbing revelation about the world you grew up in."

She drew a shaky breath. "There is also something else to consider. Right now, word is spreading through the kingdom that you and I made a child, and while I appreciate your effort to accord me the respect of my old title, and your determination to emphasize peace in the restoration of the once-mighty Enaeran Adrani, there are still many in Enaeran who are going to doubt everything I said and did, regarding me as a traitor."

His quick frown preceded words, but she raised a hand. "I don't want you to defend me. I don't think you could. You hold the power now, so no doubt if confronted they would bow and smile, but the stern appearance of law will not assuage the hatred in their hearts. Mmmm… I almost would prefer that to those who will know what really happened, and grieve. Especially parents," she added, remembering the empathetic pain in Lantra Parlion's face. "Do you understand how terrible it would be if someone threatened to kill this baby unless you mated with someone for their political gain?"

Macael's brow contracted. "But it's not the same."

"It is exactly the same. Back to your own Adranis, who might see what happened here as a masterstroke of political expedience. Got an heir everyone will acknowledge! Saved lives! But that story will be told, and maybe in the future some duchas's son, or daughter, will find a chance to make a similar threat to round out the borders of their holdings. I take it you were not inspired by Prince Sandios?"

"Who? The name sounds Sartoran."

She told him in as few words as possible, then added, "Even if you didn't know that history, it just occurred to me that the Sartorans will. I think … I feel certain that there will be repercussions."

He looked up, his face distraught. His pain was real, spiked by remorse as he saw, for the first time, how his actions appeared outside of the citadel he had built to protect himself.

"Stay, Liere," Macael whispered. "Show me how to make it right."

Neither breathed. Distressed as she was, she was aware of what such a request, sounding so simple, cost him.

Her lips shaped the words, though she had no voice: "I

can't."

A year ago she could have said, *You destroyed my life here. You destroyed my life.*

The second part was not true. The first one was. But he knew it, knew it as well as she. The ringing shock that had ricocheted back from him, like a knife to the psyche, would have served as a potent reminder had she forgotten just how intense, how inescapable was his awareness.

Instead, she thought back to Detlev's warning. Indeed she held a powerful weapon, which, if wielded, would cause Macael's years worth of pain—additional pain. Too much of that warps anyone, no matter how well-intentioned, and the kingdom would pay the price.

There was no purpose to more accusations, or declarations, or even anger. That last emotion (and pride) had kept her silent for months, but both those were gone now, leaving her the freedom of plain speaking.

"I can't stay," she said, and though her voice trembled and her nose ran and her eyes blurred with tears, she no longer cared. She dashed her wrist over her eyes and sniffed. "Because you cannot make things right. It is too late for that. But you can make things better. I've been fighting my own shades all this time. It's not easy. I can tell you that it gets easier when I talk to someone who is a little farther down the road of peace and humanity than I am. It's easier when I realize that becoming the person I want to be begins with each little decision, the goal to choose better. To do better."

Iliosi Mathias made a little noise then, and both parents broke off to look down into the cradle. The infant gazed up at them, his eyes the color of a stream. Liere's chest heaved on a sob. "I didn't think it would hurt so much. May I ask something of you ..."

He swallowed, and she felt the impact of his inner voice, an echo of hers: *choose better.* "Yes."

She picked up the baby and buried her face in his soft clothes. The sound of Iliosi Mathias's heartbeat, so quick and fragile, brought fresh agony, but she could not drown in it because there came a tendril of question, and under it a vague sense of apprehension.

The ancient instinct to shield and protect furnished Liere

with the strength to wall off her own emotions and send comforting thoughts to her little son as she held him close, rocking from foot to foot, a steady, gentle sway, her awareness acute through all senses: the golden-lit room, the soft, warm bundle in his blanket, the sweet scent of baby, the muted sounds of wind-lashed snow and, closer, the breathing of three people.

Her work with the baby must now commence in the realm of the spirit. It remained only for her to leave.

She laid Iliosi Mathias in his cradle, pressed last kisses on his eyelids, his brow, and on his tiny fingers, then she straightened up and her gaze met that of the baby's father.

She could raise her hands and make the transfer in that moment, for her part of the bargain had truly been fulfilled. But she had spent these last days striving to impart good memories to her little son, both for his sake and for hers. She knew the clarity and intensity of Dena Yeresbeth-enhanced memory, and she had contemplated its effect on one's actions, motivations, reactions.

She had also brought herself to contemplate, finally, what it meant when one found in someone else's memory a mirror, leaving her staring at herself as she'd looked that evening in the northern valley hideaway. With the image had come Macael's emotions, mercilessly sharp. Liere had also seen the memories behind it, glimpsing a life lived without love, someone who had never in life known tenderness.

It had made subsequent events clear: how he did not love and never could have loved Chantala, how his emotions regarding her had been a conscious effort to compromise between ambition and his own sense of honor, and the nascent kindness in someone who had never known it himself. How he could murder a cousin he liked and respected for what he'd believed the greater good, resolving to make it quick and painless.

He could talk about what he'd done, with a dispassionate acknowledgement of intent that was almost unnerving, but, until today, he seemed to be incapable of saying anything about what he felt. The same instinct that had prompted him in early life to wall off his mind so thoroughly that no one (except, apparently, Detlev) ever knew he had Dena Yeresbeth had caused a terrible isolation of the spirit that made communication about normal human emotion beyond him.

Not that he didn't feel. He'd been relieved at Chantala's death. He'd regretted the necessity of Andri's death. But every action that caused Liere pain compounded his own personal nightmare.

It did not remove his culpability. It did not assuage her grief. What the knowledge did was transcend anger and render the desire for vengeance meaningless.

Liere stroked Iliosi Mathias's cheek one last time, then held out her hand. "I ask you to give him music, with the same joy, and love, you gave it to me."

Moving as one ensorcelled, Macael came around the cradle and laid his hand in hers.

She kissed him, with all the tenderness she had in her. And then she let him go.

✦ 30 ✦

W hen Liere recovered from the transfer, her instinct was to keep moving. Keep busy. Stay ahead of the wrench of separation. As the transfer reaction faded, she glanced around the Destination area, her goal to find David so she could hand off the rest of the text. It seemed, at first glance, that she'd found him, for there was a familiar cast to the long body and blond head lounging in a window embrasure, reading.

"David?"

The blond head lifted, the propped foot swung down to join its mate, and Liere found herself looking up into not-quite-David's face: the eyes were bright green instead of brown, the hair sun-bleached on top and light brown beneath, the bones more extravagantly drawn, his flyaway hair drifting down to his shoulder-blades instead of being squared off collar-length at the back. She blinked — tired, emotionally spent — and recognized Imry Llyenthur, of all people. It was a very unexpected and unpleasant jolt.

Her unsuppressed reaction sparked a derisive grin.

"Obviously I won't do," he said, sketching a mock gesture of greeting.

Liere was too emotionally exhausted to fence with him. "Is David here?"

Instead of reacting with the usual shock or resentment that never failed to amuse him, she walked past him with - indifference. As if he was irrelevant. The only times he'd seen that disinterest had been when he went undercover. Never when he was recognized.

Intrigued, he looked after her just as David appeared from the hallway.

"There you are," Liere said, trying to smile. "I'm here to hand off my translation. I'd be glad to go over it whenever there is time. Or ought I to take it directly to Detlev? I had a question for him anyhow."

"I think he's still asleep," David said.

"Two hours past sunset?" Liere asked, looking around.

"He was in another time region," David began.

"And I'm no longer asleep," Detlev said from behind, having just mounted the stairs. His face was ruddy, and his hair damp.

"A bath?" David asked. "In this weather?"

"The last swim in the stream," Detlev said. "Before it gets too cold."

"It's too cold for me already." David made a warding motion. "You and MV are half fish."

"Come down to the house," Detlev said to Liere, and to David a lift of his chin. "Remind me to teach you the slide," he added to Liere, touching her on the shoulder before shifting her painlessly to his house below. David appeared half a step behind them.

They were in the main room with all the windows looking out on the terrace with the Purrad pattern. Liere drew in a breath, consciously steadying her voice, as she said, "Here's the text." And as Detlev took it, she added, "You were entirely correct to call Macael's feelings for me a weapon. I worked hard not to use it. I don't know if I did any good, but I don't think I made things worse. And I could have. So easily."

Detlev glanced rapidly through a few pages, nodding approval, then set the text aside. "How are you feeling?"

"How can you bear it?" she burst out, her voice thinning. "The world, I mean — the disirad, it is pitiless in showing *every-thing*. How can you not be rushing everywhere to rescue, and mend, and..."

"Because that doesn't work," he said. "You achieved what I hoped you might, and in an astonishingly short time."

From anyone else that would be an observation, but from Detlev it was the highest compliment. She blinked, surprised at how much that steadied her.

He added, "I know your habit is to throw yourself into work whenever you are uncertain, but you have earned time to yourself. Several times over."

She shut her eyes, immediately thinking of Iliosi Mathias, then gave her head a shake. "Say I've done that. What would be next?"

Neither Detlev nor David were surprised at that question. Detlev said, "The next level of learning, for you, is what I term the catalyst."

"What? I don't understand."

"You are the most recent catalyst, and we can talk later about how important you were. Crucial. One of the hardest parts of learning to spot catalysts is the awareness that you cannot be everywhere, living others' lives for them. This is, I believe, the most difficult of the many branches of dyr studies—this and what Imry may or may not learn."

'*He's* learning? He's *learning?*" Liere repeated in disbelief. "What?"

"Healing," David said, with a chortle.

"Healing? The world's leading assassin?" She immediately thought of little Crystal Ingrid.

"Not leading," Detlev said, unsmiling. "There were far worse. Though he certainly did his share."

David hitched a hip on the edge of a table. "My brother will tell you himself, he was raised to be an assassin before he could even read. You can imagine—or maybe you can't—how savage that sort of training had to be. He was proud of that even after Detlev bought us off our shit of a father. It mattered to Imry, because that meant he'd survived. To oversimplify, he had to terrorize or be terrorized. When he initiated the war, he enjoyed the fear and loathing he sparked. I think he got tired of it fast. It's so easy to make people fear you—you give them pain. He was never invested in their pain, unlike, say, Efael. He relished a challenge, from someone of equal wit and strength."

"I see," Liere said, still trying unsuccessfully to equate healing with someone who would stab a four-year-old to death. That had certainly been no challenge.

David grinned. "It was salutary for him just now, when you arrived. You didn't give him the back of the hand. You barely gave him a glance, as if anything he could say or do mattered less than spit." He chortled again. "I'm glad I saw that."

"I see," Liere said again, her mind leaping from Crystal Ingrid to children to Iliosi Mathias, newly abandoned. Though she had already pulse-checked him twice, because the two were looking at her, she said, "A moment. I need to listen for my little one. For my own peace of mind."

"It's only been, what, less than half an hour? You don't think Macael would have done him in already?" David teased, brows rising. But she didn't smile back, and he grimaced slightly. "Too early?"

Detlev shot him a *Shut up while you're ahead* glance, and said aloud, "Entirely natural. Don't think I didn't scan frequently when I had to leave Sveneric with you lot. Especially the first time."

"Conceding," David said, palms up. He wondered if he would ever be ready for the emotional ferocity of parenthood.

Liere shut her stinging eyes, and reached: Iliosi Mathias was asleep. No alarm. She let herself linger for several breaths, before withdrawing; in Brydon's quiet palace, Macael blinked, torn from his attempt to bury himself in reports, as a shaft of sunlight lingered, bathing the infant in warmth. This one was longer than the first two, and he laid aside his pen, contemplating how little Liere trusted him.

The only answer, he concluded, was to become trustworthy. Even if he never saw her again. And as the infant let out a wail, he got up at once to pick him up.

Detlev withdrew undetected, and turned back to Liere, aware of her unsteady grip on her emotions. For her, he suspected, distraction would be a relief. "The other word in Sartoran for catalyst is fulcrum. You'll learn the Ancient Sartoran terms presently, when you better comprehend their connotations. Right now, I suggest you take time to accustom yourself to a new category: the parent who must adopt a child out through necessity. Whatever that might be."

As he'd hoped, this unexpected mention of others in the same emotional group arrested her attention, underscoring that she was not alone. But ... "Adopt!" she repeated. "I didn't really adopt Iliosi Mathias out. I left him."

"I use the word in the looser sense, the adoption that makes an extended family possible. Or did you decide that you will cut Macael Elsarion completely out of your life?"

Her lips parted. "I thought so at first, when I was seeing everything through the filter of anger. Leave forever. But my instinct now is to wait until Macael has established a rhythm to his life. And won't expect me to join it. Then perhaps I can go visit, and talk, and do what I can. And he might even permit me to take our son elsewhere for visits."

"That," said Detlev with approval warm in his voice, "is the essence of the extended family. It might prove to balance the opprobrium that will be coming Macael's way as word spreads of the choice he coerced you into."

Liere was aware of a pulse of gratification, then thought, don't gloat. It won't help. Balance. Balance. Balance.

"Who is cooking up at Curtas's House?" Detlev said plaintively. "Not the boys, I hope?"

"I told them one more experiment, and they will serve as stab dummies for the next week," David said. "And I'd invite MV to do the teaching. The gustatory atrocity we're talking about was an attempt to use up a lot of leftover cabbage," David said to Liere.

"In *cake*," Detlev said. "Why not get one of fifty Chwahir recipes for fermenting the cabbage? It stores in jugs all winter."

"Because Jessan wanted cake, but they had two baskets of cabbage. And that mess was so disgusting that Hanold's husband Zand ran an invade-and-occupy of the kitchen while you were up north. It was backed by everybody else. Except Retren and Jessan."

Detlev said to Liere, "We are talking about a renowned Colendi chef."

David put in, "Zand came up here to be Hanold's eyes when he needs. Otherwise, he's in there creating masterpieces just for fun."

"Yes," Detlev said. "While I stand here, very aware that I haven't had anything to eat since yesterday, on the other side of the world." He turned to Liere. "This is my suggestion. Use or discard as you will. Bide up at Curtas's House for a day or two, while you listen for your son as much as you need to. Whatever you decide to do next, you will do better without feeling tethered in two directions. And when you are ready, we can talk a little more about catalysts."

"Who else is learning about catalysts?" Liere asked. "Are

you teaching a class?"

Detlev said, "Just you and Adam. Siamis, of course. Hibern is coming at it from another angle, through magic. Did you know that Lilith has chosen to pass guardianship to her?"

"I didn't."

"There's plenty of time to catch up," Detlev said easily, and turned his head, as if he could see all the way to Curtas's House up on the distant mountain. "I think I'm going to storm the kitchen myself, in case Jessan is in there experimenting again. If Zand is still wielding the skillet, I want the first plate." He vanished.

Liere turned to David. "Aren't you doing the catalyst study?"

David said, "Trying. But I'm a few steps behind you in some ways, and in others more of a generalist. Not quite sure where I'll land. Want something to eat?"

She knew she should, and she was curious about Colendi food, about which she had heard off and on for years.

It turned out to be beautifully arranged on the plate, tasting of complex flavors. It was also made to be eaten in small bites, with the elegant, long-handled, tiny-pronged utensils, something between eating sticks and forks. The food was tasty enough, but plain food was equally tasty.

She was thinking of that as she contacted Lyren later that night, to tell her she had left Brydon, and she was there on the mountain, eating Colendi food: *Have you ever tried it?*

Lyren had been learning how people would often talk of inconsequentials before they could get to the hard stuff. If they even got there. She wondered if this was a little like Marlovens scouting an area before doing military things. She would go along with whatever Liere talked about. She could sense Liere's powerful emotional turmoil beneath the easy surface, very like when the moon eclipsed the sun: *I've had what I've been told is Colendi food, but I haven't actually been there to stay. I've been through Colend, I think. I certainly have seen Colendi styles, so pretty. Lots of silk. The food, whether truly Colendi or not, was wonderful.*

They had a few more exchanges about silk, and style (which Lyren knew Liere had scant interest in) and then here it came: *Lyren, I'm trying not to grieve too much. I'm letting myself check a thousand times in hopes that I'll be able to stop obsessing. All is as well as I'd dared not hope. But it hurts.*

Lyren had been listening for what Liere intended to do next, but curbed her impatience: *It seems odd that all three of your children are scattered, but on the other hand, we have managed to have our own kind of family, haven't we? The older I get, the gladder I am I had Siamis when I needed him, before I turned into Dtheldevor, or even worse. Laban says, when Malcolin and little Iliosi Mathias are older, they'll likely want to get together. He says, look at Imry and David — who were not close when they were small, not at all.*

: An extended family is what Detlev called it, Liere responded, and at the end of this conversation felt immeasurably better.

She remained distantly curious about Imry's presence, but her own concerns kept her from engaging with the others, except in politeness over breakfast after a sleepless night, during which Liere had to use the Waste Spell to get rid of milk twice. But she knew from Malcolin, who had lost interest in nursing as soon as he figured out how to tackle the same foods his da ate, that that would dry up soon.

Her air of absence — the friendly smile in the beautiful face — and the hint of sadness that they all sensed created interest in the other students, of which Liere remained unaware. Except once, when Retren Ndarga, who was usually very quiet, muttered at the end of breakfast, "How long will we get stuck weeding? It's not as if we *deliberately* set out to ruin that cake!"

Liere's head turned.

Jessan said, "Cheer up. Hanold says he smells snow on the way."

Everyone was getting up. Liere studied Retren, who appeared to be about twenty or so, black-haired and sun-brown, like the Iascans along the Marloven coast. His accent was Marloven.

When he found her next to him, she said softly, "May I ask where you are from?"

"Marloven Hess," he said readily.

"Oh? Where?"

"You know Marloven Hess?" Retren asked in surprise. "Methden. South coast."

"I know where it is, but I was never there," Liere admitted — in Marloven. It felt unexpectedly good to speak it again.

Retren brightened, hearing his home language. "I've been away a long time, but I'm about ready to return. Probably for New Year's Week."

Liere smiled, he smiled back, and when she went away toward the library, Candra, who was a few years older than Retren, came up to him. "She talked to you?"

"Just to ask where I'm from. Why shouldn't she?"

"No reason." Candra waved a hand. "It's just that she's interesting. She's scarcely been up here, never in disirad classes, but she already wears a dyr. Can't you feel it?" And at Retren's assent, Candra added, "Nerien says she's like a beacon, if you see the mental realm in lights. And some of the others think Detlev came back just to teach her."

Retren whistled, and when Jessan approached and elbowed him in the side, he went to fetch gardening gloves.

Since all of them had gotten used to ignoring Imry Llyenthur, they paid him little attention as he listened to this byplay, then drifted after Liere as she headed for the library.

She'd caught his interest; she was the same, and yet not the same, as the teenage Liere he'd captured and used as bait to trap Senrid during the war, before she was sprung by Andri Malcolin Elsarion. He'd wondered what either of them saw in her, other than a pretty face; up here near the resonance that tried constantly to shred his awareness, her affect was profoundly different, a banked fire somewhat like Adam's.

He rounded a table, and when she looked up, he said, "When did you grow a spine?"

She blinked, her thoughts clearly far away, then said, "Spine. A metaphor for what? Courage? Anger, perhaps?" She glanced at the cold green eyes shaped so much like Senrid's and David's. "I'm afraid I don't understand it enough to answer your question."

Her reply was, if anything, patient. Exactly the same way Adam spoke to him. As if he was no threat, merely a lamb wandered from the fold. He found that annoying and intriguing both.

She went on in a musing tone, "Anger is a measure for what, in your estimation. Skill? Threat?"

"Are you trying to maintain it is not a motivator?"

"It is certainly a motivator, for certain kinds of action," she said.

"Certain," he mimicked, and of course had to try to provoke her. "A motivator only for those of us steeped in villainy? What an insightful piece of condescension! Andri, of course, was motivated by the best of human interest when he ran the streets of Shiovhan during the early fifties, taking out Adon Marsael's favorites just for sport."

Her brows rose. "You saw him at it, I gather?"

"No." His lips twisted. "You don't believe me? Do you really believe it was his drawing room manners that caught the interest of Yeres and Efael?"

She said, "I know a great deal about his early life. It was violent, yes, but I can promise you he was not motivated by anger. Or by pettiness, or spite."

"That one misses the mark," he retorted.

"You murdered," she retorted right back, "a four-year-old girl. Convince me that wasn't spite."

He lifted his shoulders. "Call it what you want. When I was four, I made my first kill. It was the only time I ever got rewarded." He said it flatly, with that sardonic curve to his mouth that was so characteristic of the Montredaun-Ans.

He watched as he spoke, but instead of flaring to anger, or an emotion he knew how to deal with, she studied him, then said, "Are you getting headaches from the disirad?"

It surprised him enough to answer, "Yes." Then, back to provocation, "How long did *you* endure it before vaulting to mastery? Want to brag a little?"

"I'm still learning," she said. "I don't get headaches, but a different sort of pain unless I..." She wove her fingers together as she sought a suitable word. "Filter. Apparently there are terms for all these things in the old language. I really want to learn their context."

He had no answer to that, and anyway Adam was here. "Liere, Detlev is looking for you."

Since Detlev could locate her without any effort, she took that as a polite request, and left a conversation she had not wanted.

"She integrated within an hour. Probably less," Adam said, leaning against the wall, his gaze steady. "Faster than I, faster than Siamis, faster than any of us. But in a sense she'd trained all her life."

"Boring." Imry decamped.

Liere found Detlev in his study. She repeated her part of the conversation to him, then said, "I let my temper slip when I flung Crystal Ingrid at him, but then I saw that indulging it shut off any possibility of communication."

Detlev dipped his chin. "It's difficult," he acknowledged. "But you don't need to engage with him unless you want to. He's someone else's challenge."

Liere said, "I want to know more about catalysts. Though just thinking about it makes me feel as if I'm clinging to a fence by my fingernails as I try to peek into another, greater, and more dangerous world."

"Well said! There is no need to climb that fence now. I should probably apologize for pushing you as hard as I did this past year."

"No, no, no." Her palms came up. "The pushing was internal, my choice. I could have ignored you and David both. I certainly did in the past." She smiled ruefully. "I was the one who grabbed hold, because I needed a project, a goal, that lay outside my quandary with Macael. So very much. I think I would have drowned in my own emotional whirlpool if you hadn't offered one."

"Perhaps. Though you are still recovering from the emotional cost of your quandary."

Her eyes narrowed. "It's mostly the physical separation from Iliosi Mathias. Babies are so very tactile. Yet he does know me." She brushed her fingers over her forehead. "And so far, it's very peaceful. He's almost never out of someone's arms, mostly Macael's. Iliosi misses me, a little. Only a little." Her lips trembled. "But he's doing exactly what he should be doing, looking to others. I'll be all right. If I don't brood. So." A deep breath. "Tell me more about catalysts. I was one, you said."

"This is a subject to approach over time," Detlev replied. "A catalyst is someone who may or may not be at the center of events, who might be able to change a situation. Who may only be the lesser of a range of bad choices. In Enaeran, the catalyst turned out to be you, which was a benefit to everyone that some may see some day."

"Isn't it too early to claim success?" she asked.

"Absolutely. But there are certain signs. Patterns of possibility, you might say. Things could have gone in a different direction."

Liere said, "Macael going east instead of west like Mathias the Magnificent, to straighten out those little kingdoms like Halarialgre and Fal for their own good?" She shuddered. "Halarialgre I know very little about, but Fal I recognize. The dueling squares is a custom borrowed from them, is it not? Sending his army in there would be a horrible sort of war, wouldn't it?"

"It would. He'd win because he has the numbers, and the wealth, but it would be at such a cost. And there'd be nothing to stop him from pushing east all the way to the Colendi border."

"Did you see that coming? What he did to me?"

"I did not. Seeing likely patterns is not reading the future. If there is such a thing. We are all making decisions all the time, including you and me sitting in this room talking. What we choose to talk about will ring changes on tomorrow's decisions."

"Oh, yes, I see."

"It so happened you ended up in a place where you could instigate change. And become aware in doing so. It seldom falls out so neatly. Catalysts are usually not aware. They might not be willing, or prepared, to make change. And it is difficult to spot them. I've made errors. So many. In your lifetime, Kessler Sonscarna was one."

Liere let out a long breath. "I don't think I'm capable of meddling with the affairs of kingdoms. I'd rather rescue children who have lives like Macael's when he was a baby. And like Imry Llyenthur's! Though isn't he past rescue? I keep coming back to his killing Senrid's little daughter."

Detlev said, "This is the terrible side of catalyst and pattern observation. Do you want to hear more?"

She braced herself. "The context is the war, is it not? Norsunder was coming anyway. Imry Llyenthur was not the cause, he was one of their tools, or minions, yes?"

"That's it exactly. When I discovered he was leading the invasion, before events began to outrun me, as happens in so vast a war, I could probably have taken him out, except that would have left either Aldon or Efael running the invasion. The brutality would have been exponentially higher."

"Why did they pick him, then? I thought the Host liked brutality?"

"As bait for me," Detlev said. "And they didn't trust Efael, who was actually the leading assassin. Though a terrible commander. Back to the death of Senrid's daughter, which I still regret not having seen as a possibility."

Liere flinched inside. Oh yes, she understood that. So well.

Detlev said, "As I learned later, Imry really thought he was doing the right thing as well as the expedient thing. He had to break Senrid's hold on the army. Though Senrid was going to lose — Norsunder had the advantage in numbers — Imry was using far too many resources and too much time to get there. They had believed my little fiction about Senrid being a loud, foolish lackwit like his uncle, and they'd expected to overrun the Marlovens within ten days at the most."

Liere remembered her confidence that Marloven Hess would throw Norsunder back. But she'd been so very ignorant about war.

"I missed how closely Efael was stepping on Imry's heels that week. Efael was the first to think of Senrid's daughter, because that was always his fallback, to attack the weak and defenseless. Imry acted because he knew what Efael would have done to her. He so placed the knife that Senrid was able to be with her at the end. In Imry's mind, that was a boon."

"That ... that is *horrible*. For them both," she added. "All three," she amended in an undervoice. "For Senrid especially." And in a lower voice, one of sorrow, "I wish I'd been there. To help. I was useless in Eidervaen. If I could have taken her away..."

"I wondered how long before you would begin to blame yourself?" And when Liere reddened, catching herself in her old pattern, Detlev went on, "The chances are good the child would not have gone with you. You were a stranger. The other alternative — if Senrid had tried to force her to go with Leander and Kyale — would have brought Efael on the hunt. He got vindictive when denied a target. He would have discovered Rel's safehouse in Lisdan, and you can guess the rest. It's one of those situations that both Siamis and I might have caught, but missed, because there were far too many like it happening all the time. And we were on the run as well."

Her lips thinned in a line as she nodded: he could see that she was beginning to comprehend the Long View. And its occasional heartbreaks. But that discussion must come later.

"As I said, Imry is not your challenge. His catalyst might be someone altogether different. Time will tell. Your task now is not to plunge yourself into more studies until you are truly ready. You earned time for yourself, if anyone in this world has."

She knew that, of course, but the newness of clearing sight still required confirmation, it seemed. She could accept that; she had decided that it ought to be a crime to cling to misery, especially for no reason than old habit. She took immense pleasure in sloughing those old, smelly, thorn-strewn habits, leaving her free and light as air, and in that freedom and clarity, she was the more intensely aware of the home beacon.

Senrid was there, waiting. He had always been there. It was she who had wandered away, and then pushed herself farther into the shadowy tanglewoods because she had wandered. No more.

Liere's smile was sudden, and sun-bright. "I *am* going to do something for myself. I need a day or two more, to be sure about Iliosi Matthias."

"Excellent," Detlev said, aware of the drift of her thoughts —and she knew he was aware and approved, and she rejoiced. "Excellent."

And though she sensed that he was ready to get back to whatever he'd been doing, "One more question?" she asked.

"Certainly."

"The dyr." She said patted the chain below her collarbones. "It's so very different from the one I carried when I was ten. This one is so very much, oh, more woven into the world than that coin-shaped one was."

Detlev laughed a little. "That one was deliberately hobbled by me; Norsunder expected me to have a dyr, so I prepared that one, and another that they could then force me to disclose, underscoring my surrender. I was able to use those two hobbled dyra to shape events, and incidentally to protect a couple of my chosen catalysts. I think … yes, I believe it would be a good idea to hand off the true Emras Testament to you."

"The true one?"

"The Sartoran mage guild suppressed a great deal of the one in the archives, for reasons they thought good at the time. And Emras suppressed more in the record she handed them. She wrote more completely in one that remained hidden for centuries. Siamis made a copy for his library here; this might be a very good time for you to read that, and for more reasons than to see the false dyr's place in history."

""I'll go find that now. Thank you," she said.

"Come in if you have questions," he called after her as she rushed out.

In spite of Jessan's wishes for bad weather, the storm that had battered Enaeran the day Liere left was still a hazy line on the northwestern horizon, leaving a still, warm day perfect for outdoor reading. Liere sat on a stone bench adjacent to the stair leading up to the disirad plateau, surrounded by aromatic pink and purple and yellow starliss. She was deep in Emras's experiences with the dyr—the scribe-mage must have had at least a little Dena Yeresbeth, Liere was thinking—when once again she was interrupted.

"What I'd wondered," Imry said as if continuing a conversation as he sauntered up and dropped uninvited on the bench, "was if it was insight or foresight that inspired you to step back and leave Andri Elsarion's crown to Macael Elsarion."

"You," she said, "are wrong in every possible degree."

"I liked Andri," Imry said when she did not explain, as he lounged back on his elbows. "We didn't actually spend much time in one another's company, the one time I did manage to pinch him, but not from lack of interest. I had Efael hovering over my shoulder, drooling to get his fangs back into his old victim, and he couldn't wait until we'd finished our conversation."

Liere was aware of a brief flare of humor. Andri had actually used almost the same words in describing Imry Llyenthur the one time he was Imry's prisoner, *I only saw him for a moment or two, but those were entertaining enough. Too bad that rat's-ass*

Efael couldn't wait to resume the old fun and games.

Imry went on, "His ruling style was much like his personal style: careless, haphazard, good-natured. Your Macael saw that the time, the economy, and the diminished population, were ripe for change, and he's got the vision to break the pattern of generational civil war that you decried so much. Andri did not see a way to break it," he added.

"No," she said. "He didn't."

Imry's assessment of Enaeran was a reminder that he had organized a world-wide conflagration that probably have succeeded had he not been betrayed by his putative allies, and a magical binding spell that had prevented his occupation force from crossing from Norsunder. Ethical considerations aside, she had been on the periphery of international politics long enough to acknowledge the scale of information-mastery required of so large a command.

She said, "Why did you do it?"

As soon as she saw his derisive smile, she knew the question had been the wrong one to ask. Or she was the wrong one to ask the right question.

"War," he said, "is the sport of kings."

If he was expecting a reaction, he was disappointed. Liere's big golden eyes merely rounded in a reflective expression a lot like Adam's as she murmured, "A violent action is still a reaction."

"It's an action if you change the situation," he countered.

"Destruction," interjected a new voice, "is not change. It's an end."

"Marga!" Liere cried joyfully as Marga ran down the stairs from the disirad plateau.

"I thought it might be fun to come back for a visit when I sensed you here," Marga said, throwing her arms around Liere in a warm hug.

Until that moment, Liere had not known how much she needed a hug. She sighed and for a moment or two relaxed against Marga a lot like Iliosi Mathias's boneless curl against her, then she straightened up, feeling oddly refreshed. "What was it *like* being a tree?" She tucked the book under her arm as she began walking toward the house, forgetting Imry.

Who looked after aunt and niece, their mind-shields nonexistent, their awarenesses so intense they minded him a little of old dreams of rents in that sky beyond the sky, and the wild glory he'd glimpsed. And so distrusted.

Then Marga glanced back at him, her smile wry, her eyes crinkled in fun. She threw a thought to him: *Find me when you have something more interesting to talk about than the sport of kings.* Aloud, she said, "Words are almost useless when talking about tree existence. The pace of life is so very different..."

Liere woke a few days later knowing that it was time.

Adam was at first afraid he'd made a very great error when, on impulse, he asked Liere Fer Eider to help with a training session on grappling, focusing on the muscle-contraction skills she'd learned on Geth. He seldom acted on impulse, especially he was alone in charge of the school while David went with Detlev elsewhere, but when these impulses came he had learned to trust them.

He wondered if instinct had finally betrayed him when they entered the practice salle ahead of the expected class, and Liere glanced around, and then stopped before the sword rack. Adam felt the impact of memory on her, the pricking of a sword point breaking through dreams in a duel that was partly play, partly test, and mostly flirtation. Andri's face, grinning.

Grief's ache crashed through them both, thunder after the lightning-flash of memory. Adam held himself still lest he betray any sign of the inadvertent sharing, and then, practiced by now, he let the images and emotions all drain away.

Liere had as well, though the images remained. The anger and pain of grief had diminished to a lingering and poignant tenderness. She knew that if she'd met Andri for the first time now, they might have become friends, for he'd liked anyone who met him halfway, but she would have recognized the flare of attraction as simply that, and no more; part of the fascination had been youth, everything about relationships so new. It was the height of summer, and they were surrounded by other young people. Dear Andri! They had made one another happy for a time, and when that faded, it had left genuine friendship. That, she decided, was how she would remember him.

She touched one of the worn, battered hilts, and then

turned away.

"I'd better stretch," she said, sitting down on the floor.

Adam busied himself with rolling out the practice mats while Liere worked through a set of exercises that looked so habitual she could perform them with her thoughts worlds away in space and time. She had muscle tone despite her thinness. He suspected that she'd spent a portion of each day during her year's isolation doing just such warmups. Always alone, always without human contact.

That would come, he trusted.

The newest group of students ran in, chattering and laughing, a couple of them finding the waiting mats an invitation for a room-length series of handsprings. Adam turned the class over to Liere with a gesture, and retired to the other side of the room to watch.

:You didn't ask me to teach, but to help.

He met her reproachful thought with an encouraging platitude: *Teaching IS helping.*

A golden-eyed glance promised later discussion, then she walked out onto the mat, a thin, fraily-built figure in baggy kneepants and an outsize tunic. From across the room she still looked like a teenager, for her face was still roundish, the curves emphasized by the two long braids wrapped around her head.

Then she stirred, and the illusion dropped. No child moved with the economic elegance that was so characteristic of her.

She was a patient teacher, using humor and encouragement when they had trouble mastering the Geth dance-warmup. Very different from MV's style. Liere modeled mistakes herself, making the students laugh.

At the end, Liere's color was up, her smile less pensive, than it had been. Adam noted this alteration, and decided he'd be more active in promoting her interactions with the others. But she forestalled his plans by saying, "The time has come for me to move on, I believe."

She paused to wipe her forehead, and he said, "Is Imry driving you away?"

She gave her head a dismissive shake. "Not the least." She looked up toward the window. "I've worked hard this year, and I will keep working. I kept my bargain. I left behind as much peace as I could contrive, and I waited for six months to go where my heart draws me, for reasons that protected others. I am ready to do something for myself."

"Fair enough," Adam said.

The corners of Liere's mouth deepened as she turned her head and met his eyes. "Besides, I expect you'll welcome a respite from my ghosts."

Adam drew a breath. "It's inadvertent," he said, for once truly nonplussed.

"I know. You can't help hearing, any more than I can help sending. I am beginning—barely—to comprehend the disirad world, and the concept of catalysts. I have so much more to learn."

"Will you stay in contact with Macael Elsarion?"

"If he contacts me, I will listen. I think it would be wrong to have given him a glimpse of what conscience and compassion can do when we help each other, then shun him back into his isolation." She glanced away, and he knew she was thinking of her last, impulsive gesture to Macael Elsarion before she left. "It was easy enough to sense your presence when I forgot to shield, and Macael was unable to."

"An act of grace," he said, giving voice to a thought he'd assumed would never be spoken.

She took a steadying breath in her turn. "Some would not see it so."

"But 'some' will never know," Adam said, now on surer ground. He considered the life-changing reverberations resulting from Macael's first encounter with tenderness. "Though they might, in time, feel the benefits."

"The widening ripples of consequence?" Liere asked, her thin, arched brows quirked. "You really think I will have made any difference? Ah, don't answer that. I can hope for no harm and little beyond, for it wouldn't be appropriate. That part of my life is done. It's done."

"Then let me wish you well," Adam said, opening his hands.

❧ ❧

And so I am back again, Liere thought as she walked down the main street of Choreid Dhelerei a short time later. She remembered — so very vividly — walking this way all those years ago. Unbeknownst to her the war had begun that day. She knew what she wanted. What she needed. And she'd contrive it if she could.

Winter traffic trundled by. Marloven Hess had apparently suffered under the same massive early winter storm that was now howling around Curtas's House. Old snow lay piled everywhere, already turning to brown mush.

The city was busy for all that, busy and prosperous-looking. Liere walked along, anonymous in the plain winter clothing she'd chosen, another blond head among a mostly fair-haired people.

The gates to the castle stood open. She slipped in, trusting in her old abilities to move without exciting notice, for this time she did not want to signal a series of "Sartora's coming!" fanfaronades.

Inside, she needed a little more care, but with patience and quiet steps she arrived on the landing not far from Senrid's old study, and there, balked by a couple of waiting servants, she slipped into the deep-set window slit, and resorted to Dena Yeresbeth. It took only a moment to touch those minds. Puzzled, one worried, they conversed quietly. The king, it seemed, was missing after all, and had not thought to tell any of his stewards where he was going. They dispersed to other tasks.

Pain zapped through Liere. Warning? Rejection?

Stop asking yourself questions you can't answer, she scolded herself. The only thing she was sure of was that he knew she was coming.

When the servants moved on, she entered his empty study. Without touching anything, she walked carefully around the desk, looking for clues. There were none. The familiar plain, neat handwriting glossed lists and reports. There was nothing even remotely personal.

She looked at the row of unshuttered windows and then turned her back to them to survey the room more slowly, her senses open to the low early winter sunlight slanting in, a mild milky gleam striking highlights on a few stirred dust motes; the scents of paper and books overlying the faint traces of aromatic wood, and horse; a stillness as empty as the space around her.

Nothing to touch but inanimate objects that had been touched, and retouched, by his hands. Yet she sensed no proximity.

She turned back. The row of tall windows seemed damning.

He had indicated he would wait, but what did that really mean? It was too easy now to recall the terrible things she had said all those years ago, the last time they were alone together. His parting promise that he would never again interfere in her life. And he had kept his word.

Walking to the nearest window, she looked down on a winter-white parade ground and to the academy beyond, where her son was now busy at his work. He did not know she was here, yet, for she had promised herself to see Senrid first.

Resting her forehead against the cool glass, she let her mind range over the past. So many mistakes, made with the best of intentions. So well-intended, in fact, that some of the villains she'd faced had taken on the role of instructor. My own worst enemy was myself, she thought wryly. And Senrid had known it, trying in his own way to counter it.

How much they'd shared, all those years ago! The desperately needed bond of friendship had gone both ways, and had continued to go both ways until they both — in the headlong search for strength and insight and wisdom — had relinquished childhood and had fallen, unprepared, into the emotional maelstrom of adolescence.

Who had taken the wrong path away from the bond of childhood? She had. When she saw Andri, and clung tight to her illusions. And yet, would she have been the companion Senrid needed after the double devastation of losing his kingdom and his daughter, the daughter Liere did not know? Ah, here she was yet again, asking herself questions she could not answer, rather than *acting*.

She looked around a third time, still seeing the present overlaid with the past. For nothing in this room had been changed since ... since ...

Suddenly she knew where he was, and even why he was there. Here in his citadel he was surrounded by the symbols of his power; at that secret place Leander had made when he was an outlawed prince in his youth, Senrid could just be Senrid the person, and not a king.

And so she did the transfer spell, picturing the curved little wooden bridge spanning the broad stream that meandered through Sindan Wood outside of Crestel.

She appeared at the foot of the bridge, and breathed in the cold, pine-scented air. Pine and dark-oak and ash and cedar grew as brethren in this forest. All the trees wore a frosty sprinkling of white. Pure white blanketed the loam, and the stream ran quietly under a thin coating of ice.

It was a beautiful, quiet spot, undisturbed by humans. Overlooked by one.

Liere's gaze snapped to the figure leaning on the rail, contemplating the icy stream. Again, for a moment memory overlaid the sight: a small figure, light-haired, round-faced, standing with hard-learned patience and straight-shouldered wariness, listening to Leander talk about beauty.

A blink, and the child was grown, though the light hair, and the patience, and the wariness, had not changed.

Did he know she was there?

She knew it with visceral certainty.

After all these years, it was up to her to cross the bridge.

She stepped up, her shoes crunching through the dusting of snow on the old wood.

Senrid stayed still until she stopped next to him, within arm's reach. Then he turned his head.

The physical impact of that gray-blue gaze was sudden, intense: frost poured through her chest, ramifying out, swift as lightning, through all the rest of her nerves, from fingers to heels to the top of her skull. She watched the corresponding impact in Senrid, visible only in the widening of his pupils, but discernible as the birth of a new sun in the realm of the spirit.

"You were right," she said. Her throat had gone dry, and she trembled, not from the cold, but from the firepower of his proximity. "It took me a few years to see it. But you were right. Though I did love Andri, in my way, I was more in love with the idea of being in love."

He spoke at last. "And so?"

And so they had reached a nexus. She had not permitted herself to think past this moment. Had he?

"I can't wish to undo the past ten years," she said, "not from my perspective. If I could undo your share, then I would."

She braced herself, though her jaw ached and her hands trembled. "I've come to the belated realization that Andri knew all along. Even after the fire cooled to embers, he was generous enough to cherish our friendship, and our shared parenthood. I will always be grateful to his memory for that."

Senrid smiled faintly. This was no surprise to him.

Her temples throbbed; the winter air around them was not cold enough. Not all her hard-won control could keep her calm and serene, for she had come to repair a friendship, but what she found was entirely different, wilder and deeper, for here at last was not just the intense awareness of his nearness, but the inner bond, so long denied, of mind, of heart.

The unity of three.

"And so," she said unsteadily, "I'm here. Foolish, emotionally backward — you know my faults as well as I once knew yours. What I do know is that I love you, have always loved you ever since we ran from Siamis together, long before I understood what love was. I think I loved you so much it frightened me, and then there was the deep conviction that I was unworthy of love. If I could go somewhere and spend ten more years to make up for it, I would, except what would be the use? All I know now is that I won't find real happiness without you there beside me."

His mouth thinned, and all the color bleached from his fine-boned face, leaving his eyes dark, his pupils enormous with emotion.

How long had it been since he'd even permitted himself to feel emotion? The wall was gone now, and all the pain and passion, old grief, older hope, all of it smashed down like a tidal wave.

She brought up no defense. Instead, all her own barriers were gone. Self nearly obliterated in the tide, and when at last it emerged, his grief had become hers, and hers his; together they mourned Andri and Crystal Ingrid, and shared the pain of separation from little Iliosi Mathias, and all the losses of people and hopes and laughter they'd endured apart, and alone.

Shared grief cauterized pain, leaving at last the bright fire of need. When she returned to physical awareness, it was to warmth, and touch: she was in his arms at last, and when their lips met, the first taste was of tears, but then that was gone, too.

When they broke apart, both breathing in gasps, she heard ragged laughter. Hers? His? Her ears pounded with the pulse of her own blood, and she could no longer trust them. Not that it mattered.

The long journey was over. She was home.

⛬ AFTERWARD ⛬

"**W**hat?" Daltan was aghast. "The Little Girl? What was her name …?"

"Liere," Fenis Senelac said, smiling.

"But…" Daltan exclaimed in dismay, picturing that scrawny, nail-bitten little mite, afraid of her own shadow. "I'm happy for him, I guess. I mean, you know how much I've wanted him to find someone, though he could not do better than Marend Ndarga."

"Oh no, leave Marend out. She might have done in the old days, but Senrid is making Marloven Hess into something new, and Liere is the one he wants to do it with. Besides. This is important to me! Hatch has had his eye on Marend since they were throwing each other around in the academy. And she seems to be eyeing him right back, these days."

Daltan struck her hand away impatiently. "But can the Little Girl possibly be a gunvaer?"

"It's been years since she was 'little,'" Fenis reminded Daltan. "And they were such good friends when he had been friendless so long."

Daltan thumbed her chin, looking back in memory. "I thought she was merely a replacement for his cousin Ndand."

Fenis said, "It did look that way, but I got to know her when I taught her to ride. She and the king chattered constantly, the way he never did with his cousin. Anyway, he seems sure. He wants Liere. We had better get used to her name. Liere-Gunvaer. It actually sounds good."

"Marend-Gunvaer sounded better," Daltan mumbled — but she was accepting the inevitable.

Fenis laughed, then said, "You didn't see his face when he told us. I almost didn't recognize him. He has an unexpectedly sweet smile."

Daltan was utterly loyal, and admired Senrid as an excellent king and a superlative commander. But try as she might, she could not imagine Senrid-Harvalder and sweet smile together. "Where is he now?"

"Went back to that house where they let poor Ivandred-Harvald of the First Lancers live out his last days. Where she's doing some recovering, and they prepare to tell little Malcolin together. You do realize that she was that queen, the one who sent her little boy here while she singlehandedly kept Enaeran and the Adranis from turning the Sartoran Sea red from mutual slaughter?"

"Oh-h-h-h," Daltan exclaimed, rubbing hands gnarled from decades of work. "*That* queen, Sartora! Why didn't you *say* so?"

While the two gossiped, Senrid finished going through everything on his desk, then went up to the Harskialdna tower, where the academy headmaster Marec had his office.

The sense that Keriam was present hit him stronger than ever as Senrid mounted the last steps. He still had no idea if that was real or his imagination, but he no longer cared. Heady with happiness, he had time for nothing except getting back to Liere as quickly as he could. Though they had talked through two days and two nights, there was so much more to say. There would always be so much more to say.

Marec looked up, then blinked when he saw Senrid's face. His eyes widened, but all he said was, "Senrid-Harvalder?"

"That storm earlier in the week convinced me winter's going to strike early and hard. Let's let the academy go home for New Year's now. I want to get them in the habit of going home early anyway. They all have things they can be working on there."

Marec pressed his fist to his chest. "I don't think you'll get any argument. The extras to the garrison, as usual, I take it?"

"I'll see to Malcolin Elsarion myself. Otherwise, yes."

Marec gestured to the runner waiting in the alcove, busy studying a map, and Senrid left.

When he transferred back to the house in Tannentaun, he walked into the room Liere seemed to prefer, which had also

been Ivandred's favorite room while he could still walk. It looked out over the garden, with its last lingering chrysanthemums,
dahlias, lilies, and loethe. A row of cedars rustled slowly beyond.

As he approached the door, he sensed someone with her:
Lyren.

Liere turned, and there was her quick, sunbeam smile,
startlingly like the grin that brightened Lyren's face.

"Senrid!" Lyren exclaimed. "Liere said you'd probably be
gone until nightfall. I was trying to talk her into taking me to
get dinner somewhere really good. It's cold *everywhere!*"

"I have a hot meal coming," Senrid said. "I can add to it."

Lyren's eyes widened. "You have one of those hot meal
transfer spells with an inn? Those are expensive!"

"I set it up for Ivandred. But I never cancelled it. I thought
this house might be a good place for whoever needs rest and
recovery, or just a quiet place no one knows about."

Lyren tipped her head, watching as Senrid trod over and
sat next to Liere, who promptly scooted closer so they sat shoulder to shoulder. Though seeing the two like that gave her
intense pleasure, she was aware of a thrill of, oh, what do you
even call it? Laban would probably say it was self-pity. She
certainly wasn't going to mention it to anyone, but she
wondered if there would ever be anyone for her. Like this, so
obviously not just happy but *complete*.

"Not necessary," she said as blithely as she could. "Liere
and I had a good chat while you were off kinging in Choreid
Dhelerei. Just make sure you remember to let me know when
the wedding is. New Year's Week? Can't be soon enough for
me!"

Liere held out her arms, and Lyren bent to swiftly hug her
as Liere murmured, "Too soon, I think. We have to tell
Malcolin, and let him get used to the idea. It was not quite a
year ago he lost his da. I think we ought to wait until he's
ready."

"Understood. Just don't forget me!"

"Never," Senrid said wryly, and Lyren used her transfer
token to transfer back to Wnelder Vee.

Liere's eyes closed in a way Senrid had begun to recognize, and he waited until she opened them and turned his way.

"The servants are already calling him Yossi when Macael is not there."

"Iliosi Mathias. Seven syllables. It's a lot for a tiny pup," Senrid said. "Is he looking for you?"

"I … don't think so. He knows my touch by contact now." Her expression was pensive, but she did not say more about the infant.

Time to shift the subject. "Was it I who brought out the sad eyes in Lyren just now?" Senrid asked, lacing his fingers through hers.

"Not at all." She brightened. "I think it's being twenty-five and romantic, but unfortunately, though we are opposites in so many ways, it turns out we're alike in one: it seems she is not one for light-hearted dalliance. Though unlike me, she can flirt endlessly."

Senrid said, "Her temperament is pretty volatile, but beneath all the drama she has a loyal heart. She'll find her way." And when Liere agreed, "The academy will release tomorrow. The outlying jarlates' escorts are no doubt already on their way, so it might be a few days for them to arrive, but the rest of the academy will be clearing off over the week. My question is, do we bring Malcolin here, or up to the castle? Let him pick a room?"

"Let's bring him here. It will be neutral ground," Liere said.

"Done." Senrid glanced at the side table. "I take it you didn't get much farther with Fox's memoir?"

"Not with Lyren here," she admitted.

"Good. I find I like reading it together…"

They took turns reading aloud over dinner, pausing when Senrid reached for the map to explain a maneuver, or offered an anecdote that Fox had supplied during the time he was in Marloven Hess. When sleety rain began drumming the windows as it stripped the last lingering flowers, they went up to bed, and continued trading the text back and forth.

Before she slept, Liere smiled in the darkness, listening to the rain as she reveled in the exquisite felicity of lying in Senrid's arms: love with him, she had discovered, reached past the mere needs of the body, their pleasure echoing back and forth as they soared into the realm of shared bliss.

But it was not enough.

As usual, Senrid was up long before dawn, at which time Liere, instead of kindling a fire, stayed warm in bed and read on in Fox's memoir until she heard voices: Senrid's familiar timbre, the other her son's treble.

She rose, dashed through the cleaning frame, and threw on her old practice clothes, reminding herself as she ran barefoot downstairs to get new things. The mourning clothes could be laid to rest.

She was a little worried about how it would go, but Senrid wasn't. He'd gotten to know Malcolin a little, though he'd initially avoided that. Fenis Senelac, with whom Malcolin had lived with over winter, agreed that Malcolin was as good-hearted as he was venturesome. Like Andri. But there was much of Liere in his honest gaze, beginning even at not-quite-nine to become discerning. Senrid left it to Liere to guide the conversation.

She took Malcolin's hand, and then reached to take Senrid's. Keep it simple, she reminded herself. "Malcolin, you like it here in Marloven Hess, is that true?"

"Yeah," he exclaimed, then his forehead puckered in question. When adults asked obvious questions, it meant something was coming.

Liere said, "I want to make our home here. I want to marry Senrid. We will have a family of three. Though he and I will become husband and wife, he will not try to replace your da, whose memory we will all treasure."

Malcolin frowned at the toes of his boots. Then he looked up at Senrid. "I didn't know you knew my da."

"We fought in the war together. We were also together in the Darchelde hideout. You've probably heard a little about that."

Malcolin nodded solemnly, trying to figure out why it felt that something was about to be taken away from him. Though nothing was. Except his da, and his home, but that had happened last year, because of the Evil Assassin. Before, Ma had been happy. It looked like she was happy now. People you loved were supposed to be happy...

Her hand stroked the curve of his cheek. "You don't have

to say anything now. But we will be moving to the royal castle pretty soon, for Senrid has work to get back to, and I need to discover how I can help."

Malcolin considered that, then said, "Do I get my own room?"

"You can pick any room you want over in the residence wing. The throne room is already taken," Senrid said.

Malcolin's grin flickered a little at that, then he said, "Do I get to stay there when spring comes? I hate it, I'll *still* be the youngest in the puppy pit!"

"That won't last long," Senrid said, laughing.

Malcolin cheered considerably when he found out that they were not very far from East Army garrison, where the Senelacs lived. He ran off to explore the house and garden as Senrid and Liere discussed dinner, then did the spell to order it.

"He might want to spend a few days at the castle, and if there aren't enough children his age to play with," Liere said, "he'll probably want to go back to Big Toe and Stinker and the others."

Senrid accepted that, but looked an inquiry, as he sensed she was leading up to something. "And?"

"And you and I will have a winter to become us now, instead of us then with ten years of memories."

Still with that air of question, he said, "I thought we were pretty well caught up. I don't need details."

"I mean dyr work," she said, taking his hands.

He left his fingers in hers, but she sensed his inner recoil. Then he looked down with a slight grimace. "I really don't think that's necessary." He added quickly, "No objections to dyra mysteries in general. I understand it's important to you. And it sounds like it'll be good for someone, when needed. I don't." And when she tipped her head slightly, he added in a rush, "Detlev corralled me before we left Lisdan. I didn't tell anyone, but he seemed to think I needed that dyr. This happened right before Kessler closed the world. It was like being flayed." He hit his forehead. "Here."

"Ah," Liere said. "He was worried about you. The timing was not the best, and you got interrupted, probably at the worst moment. It won't be like that for us."

"No need," Senrid said, and for the first time, his gaze shifted. Then back. "I'll admit my outlook was pretty bad there for a time, but I got control soon enough."

"Senrid, two things."

His gaze shifted back to her eyes, though he could feel her endless love, vast as the sea. She said, "First, we have been doing dyr work, for two days."

"What?" And then he remembered that dish of gleaming silver in the underwater cave—and he knew she was wearing a chain around her neck. That was her dyr?

"And second," she said even more gently, "I know you had tight control. Hard as steel. And it was killing you. Because people are not made of steel."

"Liere..."

"I'm not being dramatic like my daughter." Liere smiled a little, but her eyes stayed steady, and serious. "It really was killing you, by degrees," she said. "I could feel it. I could hear it. It's taken me two days to be sure, because I'm still learning, and I keep having to fight my own habits of self-blame. Because I do feel responsible in part. Only in part. I never intended to hurt you, and I was so tangled in my own nightmare that—no. Enough of me. You had such steely control that I suspect you would have surprised yourself as well as Marloven Hess if you fell off your horse dead in ten years. Maybe fifteen."

His mouth pressed in a grim line.

"That's the cost of that kind of control. Emotions don't go away. When you use that kind of control, you squeeze them down into your heart, so tight that the heart actually breaks. Oh, I'm sure the healers would explain it another way, but I could sense it. And I want to have you for another fifty years. More. Until our great-grandchildren boot us out for boring them with stories of *when we were young*."

He gave that a flicker of a smile, but he fell so silent Liere could hear Malcolin yelping in delight at a swam of kittens he'd discovered playing out by the garden's back fence.

Then Senrid said, "But it doesn't hurt. Your dyr."

She dipped her head in a tiny nod. "That's because you were giving me yourself willingly, and we began healing a little at a time. In Lisdan, your mind was fighting Detlev at the same time you ... yes, thank you," she murmured as he remembered the incident—and shared it. "You were wary. Beginning to listen. The dyr actually helps to put a, oh, a bit of a distance between self and the storm of emotions. We will be the healing of each other, as I learn. It'll be exactly like these last couple of days. Only better."

"I trust you," he said.

Spring rains had washed Choreid Dhelerei clean when David arrived. He wandered in from the city gates, looking appreciatively at the decorations everywhere. Where had people found flowers? Green things were barely making their reappearance on the plains.

Then he saw that many of the flowered vines twining up poles and draped over signs were not recently plucked from the soil. People had made most of them, from paper, from cloth, from every material at hand. Silent testimony to the popularity of their king's wedding. David knew that Senrid would never have thought to have ordered his city to be decorated, and Liere would not have presumed.

Crowds had already staked out places along the route of the progress from the royal castle.

David raised his hands and transferred.

The academy was half-empty; the wedding had been timed with the beginning of the new academy season, so that jarls and jarlans escorting academy youngsters would not have to make two trips. David did a fast mental scan, and discovered that the academy seniors had been coopted for crowd control. The younger ones (Malcolin included) were busy at their studies.

A familiar voice echoed down a stone archway: Marend Ndarga. David faded into a convenient nook in time to see three figures strolling along one of the corridors. One tall and broad-shouldered, one very familiar, not as tall and quite slender: Retren Ndarga. The tiny third one being Marend, wearing a blue robe over peach—an actual robe, rather than a garment cut to look like a uniform. All three curly dark heads turned this way and that as Marend and her garrison commander, Hatch Senelac, traded off telling Retren hilarious anecdotes as they pointed out the buildings and various practice courts.

Ret was relaxed and smiling. His week clearly had gone well, as David had expected it would. Marend radiated happiness.

That job is done, David thought, and slipped unseen through the mostly silent school until the great bell clanged changeover. The doors to the classrooms burst open before a stream of academy youngsters released to enjoy the festivities.

With practiced skill David winnowed out Malcolin Elsarion from the rest of his group. The boy, still in his uniform, grinned in recognition. Now nine, he looked like a weed, Andri's bones already emerging from the child-round face.

A quick scan revealed the steadying, and not surprising, happiness Malcolin felt.

But still David asked. "Looking forward to this wedding?"

"I get my own horse," Malcolin said. "Pure Nelkereth-bred. Ceremony's gonna be boring, except for the swords. That's the best part. I get to be in it. I saw the food. We'll get our own table."

"Lots of rehearsals?"

"Four," Malcolin said, rolling his eyes. "But Ma is really good at tossing the swords."

"And you?"

"I already was a prince," he said, one shoulder jerking upward. "They said I could use my title from Enaeran, if I wanted, but what's it worth to anyone? Nothing. Little Yossi has my old place, and by the time Mama and Senrid get their own princes, or princesses, I'll be on my own."

"Feel all right about your mother marrying Senrid?" he asked in a mild voice, leaving Malcolin the option of a noncommittal answer.

But Malcolin had hit the age that values earned status, and by now he seemed to have soaked up enough of Detlev's past to regard David not just as another unaccountably well-meaning and intrusive adult, but as an Icon. Use it or lose it, Detlev had said once.

"At first I wasn't sure," Malcolin said as they climbed slowly up to one of the walls. The quickness of his words indicated that this articulation of old thoughts was a first. "It happened all of a sudden!" He clapped his hands. "No warning."

"Not outwardly," David ventured.

Malcolin ducked his head. "Oh, Mama explained how she'd been his friend since she was my age, but I know there's something missing." He wrinkled his upper lip. "I suppose it has to do with romance. Yecch."

David grinned. "Give it a few years."

Malcolin shrugged dismissively, used to that sort of response from older people. Then his expression altered to seriousness. "I don't know what romance *means*, really, except what I saw when she and I and da were a family. I thought, when you marry, it goes forever."

"Humans don't last forever," David said. "But they do deserve happiness while they are here."

Malcolin sighed, toeing the wall. "Yeah. So she said — they both said, when they told me they wanted to get married. But they also said they wouldn't until I gave the word."

They sat down on the wall, and Malcolin kicked his heels against the stone as he looked down into the academy paradeground. "I like the king, no mistake about that. That's how I thought of Senrid, as the king."

A quick look. David opened his hand.

The words came faster now. "He took me out for a ride, just us. Said I could stay, my whole life if I wanted, and welcome, but he wouldn't try to be my da. It was straight out. Honest. I knew he meant what he said. I liked that, because I knew right off where I fit in, with him, since the day I came, and he didn't change when Ma came. You see? He said when they have babies, we can be adopted brothers and sisters. The others, they told me Senrid never had any family, that is, his parents were killed early, and — " Malcolin hesitated, giving David an uncomfortable glance.

"And he didn't know about Imry and me for a very long time," David said.

"Well, I was thinking more that your brother murdered his little girl."

"One of the first acts of the war," David said. "It was only one of the ways that Norsunder stuck its knife into this particular family."

Malcolin grimaced. "Is it weird? I feel weird, with a little half-brother back ho—back in Enaeran, who I might never see. I cannot cross the border, though it used to be home. Now they'd kill me, not for anything I did, but because I was once a prince. I don't want to be a prince if people want to kill you for it!"

"You have time to get used to it all," David said. "You can even stay your age if you want, until you accustom yourself to a new life."

"That's what Lyren said, when she came to see me. A sister! But she's more like an aunt. We talked about homes and the like. She said she made a temporary one with King Laban Dei in Wnelder Vee, and when you don't have inherited responsibility, you have the freedom to change your mind, and go where you like. Do what you like." He made a face. "She said I can come stay with her if I don't want to be here. She said they have lots of horses to wrangle."

"Fallbacks are always excellent."

"But you asked about *them*. Lyren and I went to the window, and we looked out when we saw them. Laughing. Laughing! I hadn't seen Ma laugh for so long, and as for him, the others said he *never* laughed."

"It has been a long time," David said.

"And they are always talking. When they stop they look at each other, like they're still gabbing here." He tapped his head. "And so, well, all of a sudden I knew my da would like seeing her happy. And, it might sound stupid, but I thought he'd also like him."

"They respected one another's skills during the war," David said.

"That's what Senrid said." Malcolin sighed, and tugged at his high collar. "I take it you won't be an heir any more, either, if they get some princes and princesses?"

"Never wanted to be," David said. "This is a fine kingdom, but I don't want to be yoked to any thrones."

Malcolin flipped his palm up in agreement, a Marloven gesture.

The bell rang once—a summons—and they parted.

David continued his cycle through the palace grounds, and then the palace itself. The atmosphere was charged with expectation. He walked silently through, taking care to go unnoticed as he passed along halls busy with liveried retainers from all the regional governors, and envoys from northern and southern Halia—Perideth notably absent. David was satisfied with the surface thoughts of all he encountered.

His last private interview was with Senrid.

The four windows were wide open, and the faint sounds of stringed and brass instruments drifted on the brisk spring air, an arresting melody that combined the typical Marloven galloping rhythm with melodies from elsewhere: this had to be music written by Senrid's cousin Ndand, who he knew had turned up abruptly, offering to bring music as a gift.

David sauntered into Senrid's study. Senrid looked up from his desk. "There you are."

David was still trying to assimilate the changes in Senrid's face. Not that they were overt. He didn't grin like a maniac, or chortle. He seemed somehow very much younger, with the old tension smoothed from his countenance. "I've been spying about all day."

"And?"

"You're prepared for war, of course."

Senrid snorted a laugh.

"Did you see Liere?"

"I last glimpsed her catching up with Hibern, but that was a while ago." David would not admit to how closely he'd monitored them all afternoon, moving counterpoint to Liere and Senrid, who were like twin suns in the midst of a constellation of orbiting satellites. They were seldom far from one another. Even now, David sensed Liere nearby, along with Lyren of the golden aura, and Marga Fer Eider, who in the realm of the spirit shone, as always, the brightest star in the sky.

David said, "I'm here to officially relinquish my heirship pending appearance of one of your own, and to ask you what you expect of me in the future."

"Default heir." Senrid sat back in his chair, hands loose on the desk, the habitual tension gone from his fingers. David knew that Liere had been working with him, and the evidence was here. Senrid looked ten years younger. "I take nothing for granted anymore," Senrid said. "If Liere and I vanish tomorrow, I hope you'll take the kingdom. No one else could hold it."

"I will exert myself to make sure there are no secret assass-ins in your future. What else?"

"The family connection is still there, though you mislike the name," Senrid said with a slightly quizzical smile.

David laughed silently. "Here's the strange thing. With the possibility of heirship removed, I find my objections to the name no longer exist. Explain that if you can."

"I can't," Senrid said. "Welcome to the family, David Montredaun-An. Come, when you can. Do what you've done. I know Liere wants to send Malcolin to you if he shows any interest in what you teach."

David opened his hand in acknowledgement. "No need to wish you happiness: you have it."

"I have it," Senrid said, and smiled, a smile of such joy David experienced a brief but vivid image of an ancestor they both shared, many centuries ago, and David thought of his sword, left in his room in Curtas's House. But Detlev had not given him leave to share that memory, so he said nothing, just gave a casual salute and left Senrid to his chores, for even on his wedding day, Senrid's stewardship was unceasing.

Senrid left his study and walked down the hall to the room where once his parents had slept, warm and loving. After all the work he and Liere had been doing, combing their past history in order to heal the hidden knots, he had begun to suspect that buried memory of his parents' love had given him a shape for what love could be, though he consciously recoll-ected so little of them. But the hurt of separation had caused him to leave this room empty until now.

It felt right for them to fill it.

The light slanted in, golden with tones of silver-blue of early spring. It limned handsome furnishings, both old and new, the design harkening back to the Marloven past: smooth, asymmetrical lines in table and chair legs curved like the legs of running beasts, and the upsweep of arms and chairbacks evoked the wings of raptors. On the walls, Ivandred's draw-ings. They fit perfectly.

"Surprise me," Liere had said, and he caught her inward thought, *Let there be grace.*

Was there grace? How does one define grace, outside of

that inward sense of gratitude and joy, the emotions one never thought to have.

A single knock at the door. It was a bit too early to gather for the wedding ritual. Senrid listened on the mental plane, but heard nothing.

Habit caused the impulse to take up a weapon before he moved to the door, but when he saw Detlev, he cast the knife onto one of the tables, his emotion one of surprise, and wariness.

Detlev entered—with Fox, Senrid's ancestor from eight centuries ago.

Detlev smiled as Fox carried a flat box, the wood old and dark, carved with running horses, and displayed it to Senrid.

Fox said, "Though it wasn't mine, it seems someone took it out of time." He jerked a bony shoulder in Detlev's direction, then moved to the table under the windows, placed between two great wing-backed chairs. He set the box down with deliberate care, and Senrid knew that here was not a mere object of monetary value, but something far more precious.

Senrid opened the hinged box, then lifted out and unfolded a long linen shirt, somewhat yellowed with age, its voluminous sleeves, cuffs, and both front and back embroidered with objects whose color had faded to subtle grays and greens, pale blue and gold, and a rose that might once have been red. The first impression was of a jumble, and Senrid's brows drew together; he had never liked embroidery particularly, and this was not all that good, he could see now, as his gaze traveled from a lopsided ship in a very old style to flying owls and other birds, running horses, clumsy sea-waves below clumsy boats, and here and there an odd, very old-fashioned semblance of the old Marloven fox banner.

Senrid's first reaction was suspicion, for the stitchery was uneven, and the fabric looked dull. He realized this shirt was old. From the look of those ships, all fore-and-aft rigged, the way ships had been, what, six hundred years ago? More. And weren't some of those birds and animals from old Iascan House banners?

Very old.

He drew a deep breath. "What is this?" His nerves fired— then chilled when Detlev said, "This is the wedding shirt worn by your ancestor, Indevan Algara-Vayir. Made, as they were in those days, by his wife, the estimable Tdor Marth-Davan, who was the first to admit that she was no hand at sewing."

"But it shows so much work."

"She worked on it steadily over months, when Inda rode off to battle. The Andahi Pass battle, in fact."

Senrid gazed down in amazement.

"Ivandred wore it to his wedding as well. He even mentioned it to me, when I visited him in Lasva's garden. We both thought you might like to wear it, should you marry," Detlev said.

"Make that three of us," Fox put in.

Senrid drew in a deep, unsteady breath. "Why?" He flushed a little, then said, "I'm nothing like him."

Detlev's brief smile creased his eyes. "Inda—the man who laid down the sword—would have approved of you, of what you have been doing. What you have achieved. And what you faced to get here, he would have understood."

Senrid reached down and tentatively touched the heavy linen shirt. Silk would have rotted ages ago. He looked up. "Will it withstand a day's wear?"

"Oh yes. It's good linen. Ivandred wore it without mishap, after which I stored it beyond time."

Senrid laid his hand on the cloth, thinking of Ivandred, his ancestor, so briefly known, and farther back Inda, once a living, breathing man, wearing this shirt. Every day, from now on, would be a gift.

Senrid let out his breath. "I'd be honored."

Detlev turned to go. "Liere is on her way upstairs."

"I want to see those swords spark," Fox said with a hoarse cackle, and limped after Detlev, thin, white-haired now, but still vital.

When Liere found Senrid, he was alone, standing at the table, looking down at the shirt, covered by the clumsy symbols of long-ago ancestors. She looked into his eyes where the sheen of tears still stood, and slid her arm around him.

He leaned into her as they talked with all the freedom of old. But now, just as she'd said, everything was better.

About the Author

Sherwood Smith writes fantasy, science fiction, and historical fiction. Her full bibliography can be found on her website at https://www.sherwoodsmith.net.

About Book View Cafe

Book View Café is an author-owned cooperative of professional writers, publishing in a variety of genres including fantasy, science fiction, romance, mystery, and more.

Its authors include New York Times and USA Today bestsellers as well as winners and nominees of many prestigious awards such as the Agatha Award, Hugo Award, Lambda Literary Award, Locus Award, Nebula Award, RITA Award, Philip K. Dick Award, World Fantasy Award, and many others.

Since its debut in 2008, Book View Café has gained a reputation for producing high quality books in both print and electronic form. BVC's e-books are DRM-free and distributed around the world.

Book View Café's monthly newsletter includes new releases, specials, author news, and event announcements. To sign up, visit https://www.bookviewcafe.com/bookstore/newsletter/